# Bounty Inc.

## Adam Holcombe

BOUNTY INK PRESS

**Also by Adam Holcombe**

**Chronicles of Gam Gam**

A Necromancer Called Gam Gam
The Wishing Stone
The Knitting Club (Coming 2026)

**Bounty Inc.**

Bounty Inc.

# BOUNTY INC.

## ADAM HOLCOMBE

BOUNTY INK PRESS

bountyink.com

*For Vivian.*
*My latest and favoritest obsession.*
*Happy First Birthday!*

# BOUNTY INC.

**WYN KELDA**

**SAGE VALEN**

**BESARI TAL-MAR**

**CEE**

**ZETTA NINTH FOROX**

**SHELLESH**

**ACHTREK-SIX HIVE**

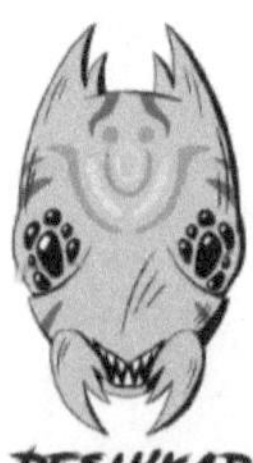

**PESH'KAR SELK**

Three days after his twentieth birthday, Wyn Kelda buried his father in front of a crowd of six thousand employees. On his deathbed, Iolas had told his son two things. First, that attendance at the funeral was required of all employees. Second, that he should terminate all contracts with the disgusting non-humans and never make such a mistake again. Wyn knew the official cause of death had been an alien pathogen that had jumped from a client, mutated, and ruined his father's immune system before doctors had a chance to do anything—but this was not what had made him speciesist. Iolas Kelda had just always been that way.

There were whispers of assassination. Rumors that Iolas had been murdered for his company's practices. Practices like producing specialized pieces for equipment to create demand, then raising prices and therefore raising profits. Iolas Industries absorbed other companies and corrupted their trades, seeking only to further its own coffers. Iolas had been a businessman at heart, however small that one organ of his may have been.

Wyn knew, too, that some wondered how the son would match up. Trained beneath one of humanity's greatest corporate leaders, his education had been tailored for the role. But he had always been timid at public gatherings, peaceable by nature, lacking his father's decisiveness and occasional cruelty. A business valued at well over sixty billion Raiyrium credits had fallen into a young man's lap, a business that was a central pillar to Terrask's economy. Millions of jobs, billions of raikers. The world held its breath as it waited to see what would happen. Some were more patient than others.

"I'm so sorry for your loss, Mr. Kelda." Sasha Sterra spoke in a sickly sweet voice that unnerved Wyn. The simpering executive was tall, her height accentuated by a long black dress that was quite revealing up top and down the back. She had long black hair and the face of a twenty-year-old woman despite being in her fifties. Money could do wonders for looks.

For Wyn, his wealth had only been a prison, walling him off from friends, from a normal education. It had kept him away from the public and fed him exactly what his father had wanted to feed him. But it had also provided Wyn with a comfortable life that made it hard to complain. At least to anyone else who could hear past the raikers. Always fed, always comfortable, and he always had access to the data network for all the entertainment or information he needed. As long as his tutoring progressed well. How could he possibly be unhappy?

"Thank you, Sasha," Wyn said. The day was bright, a stark contrast to how he was supposed to feel. The sun shone down into the large courtyard outside of Iolas Industries. Colorful flowers filled the gardens to either side of the many seats. A holographic image of his father, digitally slimmed and looking a little more muscular than he ever had in life, was displayed over his casket. Beyond, a beautiful fountain painted a tiny rainbow among an array of sculptures. Terrask's wealthiest came to pay their respects at the wake, and Wyn grew tired of each and every one of them. Not that he would ever admit to such. No, he would smile and accept their expression of sorrow, knowing deep down that their biggest worry would be what Wyn was going to do next. They needn't worry too much; Wyn already had a plan.

"I can't imagine how hard his death weighs on you," she added, placing a cold hand to his shoulder. Cold enough to feel through his jacket. Were her hands made of ice? Wyn held back a shiver. "I'm sure you haven't been sleeping well. I have some makeup for those bags under your eyes."

Well, she was partially right. "No worries, Sasha, I'll be getting my rest soon enough. There was a lot to take care of before my father's funeral."

Wyn could almost see the executive's brain churning, a small fire of panic at the back of her eyes. "I thought Charmout arranged all the funeral plans."

"He did, which was a great help to me."

"Then what occupied you so?" When Wyn did not respond immediately, she added, "If there is anything you need assistance with in this time of transition, please let me know."

"Your assistance is appreciated, Sasha, but entirely unnecessary. But I do promise to put your name in for recognition and willingness to help the company succeed."

Sasha blinked. "Put my name in?" She scrutinized him. Gone was the caring facade. A chill colder than her hand permeated the air between them.

Wyn gestured over his Vico, and a virtual interface flared to life across the back of his forearm. Various icons popped up, overflowing with notifications, his father's associates, friends, and sycophants reaching out to send condolences personally. He had responded to the first twenty before it had become overwhelming, and now there was just a constant red number increasing with each new message. The time and date blinked to one side, as did one of the icons, a newly created communications ID only one other person knew about. The message he'd been waiting for had arrived. "Actually, there is something you could do for me, if you don't mind."

That simpering look returned to Sasha's face, followed by a bright, big smile and a voice so sweet it was acidic. "Of course, Mr. Kelda. Anything you need."

"As of twelve minutes ago, Iolas Industries was sold. New ownership will begin tomorrow. During the transition, please have your department continue as usual until new orders are issued. Would you be able to pass this along to the others? There are still a few things I need to wrap up personally."

As Wyn spoke, Sasha's face twisted and contorted. First to shock, then to open anger. "You *sold* the company?"

Wyn held her gaze, even if it turned his insides to jelly. "Um, yeah."

"*Why?*"

Wyn hadn't expected a happy response, which is why he hadn't made the executives of his father's company aware. But her outright anger was unanticipated. He would have expected them to want him out of the way. Except now there was a mysterious person hovering over their heads, wasn't there? And the person they expected to bully into submission had bailed. Wyn felt the blood rush from his face as he realized the reaction he had instigated.

"I'm not made for this business, Sasha," he justified, aware of the nervous edge to his voice. "You wouldn't have liked me as the president."

"Who did you sell it to?"

"Gianna."

"*Gianna*? The person who owns ninety thousand sandwich shops across Terrask and the outlying colonies?"

"They're up to a hundred thousand now." Wyn flicked across the virtual display on his wrist and sent a packet of information to Sasha as he went through it. "The business plan is solid, and they want their child to have something to do. As long as they stick to it, all should be like my father never left. I have a clause that reverts company ownership to the executives if certain criteria aren't met, but there are loopholes in it. I didn't have a lot of time to set up the contract. Either way, I think it should turn out fine. The new president will be lazy and easy to boss around."

"You're a fucking disgrace."

Wyn jumped at the acid in her voice. He looked into her hateful gaze and shuddered. He tried to talk, but his mouth failed to form any words, the moisture evaporating away. Instead he croaked, and she jabbed a finger at his chest.

"Your father raised you for this role. He spent so many resources on your education, on your *life*! Instilling you with the knowledge to succeed him. And as soon as he's in the grave, you throw it all aside. You spit on his name, and you run away from your responsibilities."

"His money was a prison. It—"

"I don't fucking care about your petty problems, you little shit!" Her face actually reddened more with each word. Other mourners turned toward them, and Wyn wanted to shrink away into nothing. He saw Charmout step forward, then think better of it.

"This is my fucking career we're talking about. I worked my ass off to get to where I am, and I'm about to lose all of it because you want to run off and live off your inheritance in ease!"

"I'm sure Gianna will like you," Wyn suggested. "My father liked you. You're very good at what you do."

"Shut up!" Sasha began pacing back and forth, hands running through her perfect hair, nano-hair spray instantly correcting the mess she made. "There has to be a way to veto. We can overturn the sale. If you want to leave, you'll sell it to us."

"Um, the veto period has passed."

"When was it?"

"During the funeral preparations today."

She froze, rage burning in her eyes. "You planned all of this. To have the sale when we were busy so we couldn't veto."

"Yeah."

"Tell me something, Wyn. What will you be doing with your father's hard-earned money while our lives are being turned upside down?"

Wyn smiled now. Perhaps he could cool her anger if she understood he wasn't squandering it. "I'll be starting my own business venture. One that fits my desires, and who I want to be, a little better."

"And what kind of business fits a pathetic worm like you?"

Wyn swallowed, ignoring the jab. "I'm leaving Terrask for the Raiyrium Confederation, and I'll be starting the galaxy's first bounty hunting service. A single company that can handle bounties, distribute them, and be a key piece to assisting the Raiyrium Peacekeepers. Right now, every bounty hunter is working solo unless they team up, but it's their choice, right? So this will help bring organization to the chaos. It can allow for teams to more easily be formed and, most importantly, trusted. They'll be able to take on more difficult bounties, making the galaxy a safer place." Wyn took a moment to catch his breath after the excitement filled him. Sasha had guessed at his lack of sleep, but she couldn't have known how he'd lain in bed late into the night thinking of all he'd do, planning every last detail. He could barely sleep, barely hold in his contentment.

"It'll be called Bounty Inc."

Sasha stared at him in open bewilderment, mouth agape, eyes wide. All anger had fled her, replaced by confusion. She stayed like this for several silent moments, then said, "Are you fucking stupid?"

The question hung in the air while it slowly weaseled its way into Wyn's brain. His smile faded, and he blinked. "I don't think so."

"*Why bounty hunting?*"

"Because bounty hunters are cool."


If Sage had one belief at that moment, it was a simple one: anyone who thought bounty hunting was cool was also an idiot. It was a job for fools, people with too much money and a death wish, or the insane. Luckily for Sage, she was a part of that last crowd, though maybe one too many smacks to the head was righting her. For the first time in her life, she contemplated retirement.

She did this job because she was damn good at it, but fifty-eight was the sort of age at which one shouldn't be jumping headlong into fistfights and firefights. Especially while wearing a stiff silicone mask with no proper ventilation. Her face was hot and moist from her breath, and she was nearly ready to abandon her plan and hope for the best. Maybe it'd be her death, and she'd be saved from a dull retirement.

She scratched at the mask uselessly and let out a little growl. Two other human guards looked at her, then looked away. They had spent much of the time ignoring her, which was fine to her. She hated making friends with the deceased-to-be.

She glanced around the barren office again. It had every look of a typical workplace: each desk embedded with interfaces, a little table to one side for some recreational holographic game, a break room with drink and snack machines.

Sage leaned against a pillar near the entrance, and besides the pair with her, five more security guards wandered the first floor, plasma rifles held at the ready. Roshran was expecting trouble. Which was fair; that *was* why she was here.

The door to the stairwell slammed open, and a squat blue form waddled into the room in a huff. He was no more than four feet tall, his entire torso encased in a spherical shell that made general movement look like extreme athletics. Torshk they were called, unfortunate creatures, though Sage supposed they could always withdraw into their shells and hide whenever there was danger. Maybe there was some use in that. She knew better than most how effective a protective shell could be.

Then again, what stopped someone from just firing down the neck hole?

"Bring the vehicle around." He barked the orders from a toothless mouth that jutted out below two tiny eyes that always appeared to be squinting as if everything was just out of view. A guard ran off quickly to do his bidding. "We need to get off Chrysanax immediately. The Rose informed me the bounty already went live."

The patrollers ran over to surround their boss. Sage watched this all happen, busying herself with idle fantasies of what it would be like to push the torshk on his back. Would his limbs flail uselessly, or did they have a way to get back up? She couldn't imagine a species that would evolve to this point and still have such a fatal flaw. But she had seen a lot of strange creatures in her life. She *needed* to know.

Roshran shuffled toward the entrance as the other guard near Sage stood at the ready. He was squawking out orders to the others when he paused at Sage's pillar. Then he gawked at her.

"Is that a party store vrolak mask?" he asked, his incredulity sending his squeaking voice to an even higher pitch. Sage jerked free from her fantasies and stared down at the little blue torshk.

"Huh?" She hadn't really expected to have to answer that question and had nothing prepared. This is what she got for planning things last minute.

"Take that off, you idiot!" Roshran yelled.

Sage didn't move. The plan had veered wildly off course. She had to try and correct it. "No," she said.

The torshk waved at two of his guards, who stepped over and tore the mask from her head. She could not correct the course, but thank the empyreans! Sweet relief! Cold, fresh air hit her face, and she took a deep breath, a smile raising her lips unwittingly.

Her disguise dangled in the guard's hand, the lifeless eyes off-center in the stiff orange silicone, the jaw jutting out and open as if in a constant roar. It was so poorly made, Sage wondered if it had been designed off a child's drawing or if the model had been severely beaten right before the mold was taken.

"Who are you?" Roshran asked, his wrinkly face scrunching even more than usual. She felt like a book being read by an old person unwilling to admit they needed glasses.

"Zetta," Sage answered immediately. She had that answer prepared.

This caught Roshran by surprise. Then he looked at the mask again. His tiny eyes widened, and his hands shook. Perhaps angry?

"*Were you trying to trick me into thinking you're actually a vrolak?*" His voice ratcheted up again.

Definitely angry.

"I was told torshk have bad eyesight," Sage admitted. Apparently it wasn't as bad as she had been led to believe.

"*Bad eyesight?*" he squawked.

Sage clenched her eyes shut. If he didn't stop talking like that, she was liable to tear her own ears off.

"My kind may not be known for our eyesight, but I know a mask when I see one! Not to mention you'd be the shortest vrolak in the galaxy."

"Hey!" Sage pointed a finger at him, and a half dozen guns rose to point at her. She ignored them. "I'm taller than most of the children. I've seen one shorter than you."

"*Are your arms and hands painted orange?*"

"Listen, you little ball, I'm going to need you to quit squeaking so much, or you're going to give me a headache!"

"If you don't answer my questions, I'll make sure you get that headache," Roshran growled. "Why are you here?"

"Oh, I work here. I'm a guard. Like these idiots."

Roshran gestured to one of the guards at Sage's side, and the man drove his fist into her midsection. She heard the bones snap from impact, then the man fell to the ground screaming in pain and cradling his limp wrist.

"Ouch, that looks painful," Sage said.

The torshk gangster stared down at his guard in surprise, then shook himself out of it. "Enough of this. I don't have time. Just kill her, and let's go. Sovereign will be disappointed if we're caught. You four take care of it." He waved at four guards, ignoring the crippled one still writhing in pain, then turned to waddle away with the last of his retinue.

"Four?" Sage called after him. "Aren't you underestimating a vro-lak?"

A man replaced Limpwrist and shoved her against the pillar while his buddy to the other side held her steady. They pinned her arms and shoulders tight, and a third guard, a human woman, walked up to her. The fourth guard stood back, rifle at the ready.

Sage smirked as the woman pulled a pistol from her holster. "This is usually a second or third date. Don't you want dinner first?"

She slammed the barrel of the gun to Sage's forehead and hissed, "Shut up."

Sage felt a heat rise in her. Oh yeah, there was more to bounty hunting than just the money. She felt the rush seize her, that insanity that took hold of her in these life-or-death situations. It was a special kind of thrill chasing, and it was one she excelled at. "Straight to foreplay then."

The woman rolled her eyes, and then she tensed, about to pull the trigger.

"Wait!"

Shockingly, she waited. So Sage continued. "This can all go down one of two ways. I'll let you all decide."

"We're not letting you go," the guard said.

"Wouldn't dream of it, doll. I only mean weapons or fists." She glanced at the fourth guard, which turned out to be a tesing—akin to a bald, sparkly human—and then at the other guards in turn without moving her head. "Throw your weapons to the side, and we can fight this out with fists. None of you have to die." She looked again at the woman. "But if you use weapons, then I'll have to kill you."

"I think I'll risk it," the woman said, then she pulled the trigger.

The pistol exploded in her hand, and Sage saw spots floating in front of her. *Shit,* she thought, *should have closed my eyes.* But she couldn't let a little vision impairment hamper her.

She pulled her arms free from a pair of shocked and distracted guards, a cloud of sediment following her movements and filling the air. She turned to the first guard and coated her fist in a thick, hard shell of the carapace secreted from her skin. A splash of blood and a loud crack, and the man fell still. She circled around the pillar just as the tesing began firing.

The woman had dropped to the ground, cowering and yelling (between her and Limpwrist, it was quite the chorus), which left the second guard to pin her. He circled around the other side of the pillar, pistol drawn and raised. She grabbed the barrel with her left hand, a thick coating of carapace on her thumb to block the shot he fired. She still felt the heat of the shot, but her organic armor held.

She kicked his foot out, and when he dropped, she slammed his head into the pillar with her still-coated right hand. The body dropped, and if he wasn't dead, he would likely be so soon enough. She waited as the tesing fired to either side of the pillar indiscriminately. And then she waited longer, wondering how many rounds he'd waste.

Her answer came soon enough with a pause, finally, in the shooting. She had to take this carefully, or they'd go through the whole thing again.

"Hey," Sage called. "Offer still stands. Drop your gun, and we'll fist fight this out. You get to live, unlike your two friends here."

"You think I'd drop my rifle to fight a Thresha-infused?"

She slowly stuck her two hands out and wiggled them, the carapace coming off in a fine dust. "No Thresha talents. I promise."

There was a long pause, then the tesing dropped the gun. "Fine," he said.

Sage smirked and stepped out from behind the pillar. She half expected to be shot then and there, but this tesing was trusting. Or confident. He tossed his rifle to the side and stretched his arms and rolled his shoulders.

He strode up to her, a smile on his face, stretching his arms out. "I'll warn you, however, that I am advanced in tesing martial arts. No common thug will be able to beat me."

Sage scoffed as she settled into a defensive stance. Obviously, he wasn't aware of who she was. Her skill in hand-to-hand combat was second to none, even without her talent. This *common bodyguard* was about to learn a—

The jab smacked her in the face, slipping around her guard and knocking all thoughts from her head. She jerked back, coughing as blood ran from her nose.

"Motherfucker!" She ducked as another jab nearly hit her again, then swung back. He jumped inside her reach, grabbed her arm, and spun with her attack. The world twisted as she flipped around, then slammed into the ground, pink mist spraying from her mouth as the wind blasted from her chest. Then he was on top of her, fists raining at her head.

She hid behind her arms, avoiding the worst of his punches while bucking her hips to no avail. He was a damn good top.

Fuck it. She dropped her guard, taking a fist to the head as she grabbed at his arms. The tesing tried to twist free, but she got a strong enough grip, pulled down, and brought her forehead up to slam into his face.

He yelled as she tried to blink away his blood. He leaned back, but she brought him in again, slamming her forehead into his mouth a second time. She heard the bone crack as she felt shards slice into her. Fuck, that hurt. When was the last time she'd done that without her carapace armor?

Dazed by her own attack, she lost her grip, and he scrambled off her. Sage rose to her feet, wiping blood from her face. They paired off again, defensive postures raised. His nose and mouth were a ruin, and she smiled. He spit a bloody tooth out and glared, his anger pulsing in her skull as was the way of his people. Well, that wasn't going to distract her if that's what he anticipated. This wasn't her first go with a tesing.

They charged at the same time, fists flying. Unfortunately, most of Sage's missed while all his hit. Fuck it. Fuck this. She was done getting her ass kicked!

He ducked her swing and came in with a fist to her ribs. They hit reinforced carapace instead, wrist snapping and knuckles cracking. He screamed, and she grabbed his shoulder, coated her fist in stone, and slammed it into his face. The tesing crumpled to the ground after one strike.

Her stony coating fell away as dust, sprinkling from hand and shirt. She spit a wad of blood at the tesing's face. Honestly, this was his fault for believing she'd fight fair once she started losing. "How's that for a common thug, asshole?"

Now for the torshk. She brushed herself off, sediment dust puffing out around her, and made for the exit as the woman coughed and glared at her.

"You're a fucking liar," she growled. "You promised no Thresha talents."

Sage walked back to the woman and crouched before her. "Yeah, but I never said I play fair. At least I left him alive." She looked over the woman once more. She had pulled herself away from the main battle, leaning up against the wall and cradling her mangled hand in her lap. Sage sighed and set a hand on her shoulder. "It never would have worked out between us, sadly."

"What?"

"I just got out of a long relationship, nearly eight months. But I just can't seem to get her out of my thoughts. The sex. The violence. The more sex." She sighed. "You almost had me. Gun to my head was quite the turn-on." Sage mimed the gun to her head. "Unfortunately, you're not my type."

"What? You don't like *honorable* people?"

"Honorable? You work for a glorified drug dealer." Sage grabbed the mangled hand and lifted it, and the woman yelled out in pain. "You're a pansy. This wouldn't have stopped me from fighting. Abyssal hell! You could cut my fucking arm off, and I'd strangle you with the other one. Giving up after a few broken fingers is pretty pathetic."

Sage dropped the hand and walked away but stopped near the sniffling Limpwrist. "You're better than him at least." Sage shook her head and grabbed the tesing's discarded rifle. Then she stepped outside.

A long walkway led out to the street, where smoke rose from the ruins of several vehicles thanks to a bit of earlier sabotage. Which meant they were on foot. If they were getting off planet, that meant a port. The main port into the city would be straight ahead, an hour's walk or more for a healthy person. For a ball with legs, she'd easily catch up.

She started along the path to the street when movement caught her eye. Two humans and a ball with legs ran across the grass to a large building in the distance (rather, waddled, in the case of one of them). She raised an eyebrow.

A private hangar.

She had almost lost her quarry. She set off after them, shouldering the rifle. She took aim and fired. One round after another. The guards fired back but in panic while dropping to the ground. Plasma bolts flew wide around Sage while every single one of hers hit its mark. Even with the inferior Koestock Dicklick, or whatever this model of rifle was called. Within moments, all that remained were corpses. And that ball with two legs waddling as fast as he could. She could smell the fear wafting from him. Or maybe that was the rifle melting in her hands due to being made from garbage.

"Hey!" Sage shouted. "Come back!"

"No!" Roshran gasped.

"Come on! I just want to talk."

With a sigh, Sage jogged up to the shelled man before he had even made it halfway to the nearby hangar, then kicked him over. He fell to the side, and with one booted foot, Sage rolled him onto his back, then stepped away.

His limbs flailed as he rocked back and forth, but whenever he got close to righting himself, she'd use a boot to roll him onto his back again.

"You look ridiculous," she said with a smile.

"This is your fault!"

Sage sighed. It was true. She was picking on a pathetic creature. When had she become a bully? She was getting too old, and the bounties were all the same. The money was supposed to give her freedom, but it felt only like a trap, holding her to the same life because she didn't know how to change it.

"Right. Well, I should probably tell you that there's a bounty on your head and I'm here to collect it."

"A bounty hunter?" Roshran stilled his flailing, letting his arms hang limp to either side. "I can pay you more than the bounty if you let me go."

"Wouldn't be much of a bounty hunter if I let my bounties go."

"It's that, or you *will* die. Sovereign will not suffer this slight against him. Let me go, and he never has to know."

"Sovereign? That your king?" Sage almost waited for an answer but instead kicked the torshk in the head to quiet him. "Doesn't matter, actually. Haven't you heard? Democracy is way better."

Sage exhaled slowly over the weeping drug lord, something inside of her cracking just a bit. Was this all that remained for the rest of her life? She needed something stupid to do. Too bad Zetta wasn't around anymore.

# PART 1
# BOUNTY INC.

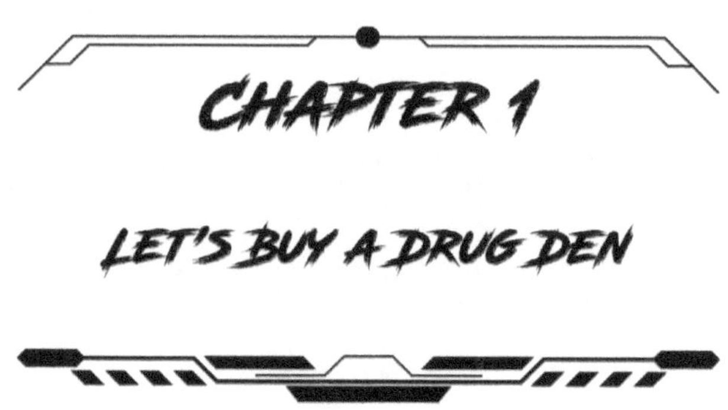

# CHAPTER 1

## LET'S BUY A DRUG DEN

"**I** know you seemed set on this location, but I took the liberty to provide some alternative options."

Wyn's real estate agent was a tesing named Hesheh. Tesings looked human, but a quick (and discreet) search on his Vico told Wyn they were closer to reptiles. And they came in a huge variety of skin colors. Or scale colors, he supposed, their scales being so imperceptible as to look like skin. Hesheh's shimmered a light blue, her eyes a shade slightly darker and sparkling like two extravagant gems, split only by the slit pupil. She did not appear to have hair of any kind, and her facial features all seemed slightly smaller than they should be, though Wyn wasn't sure if that was a feature of her face or common to all tesings. She adjusted the strap of a very revealing dress. However, given the lack of...um...*mammary glands*...maybe it wasn't as revealing for tesings as it would be for humans.

Wyn blushed and looked out the window of the cab flying over the city, the *only* city on Chrysanax. Which happened to be built into the many layers of a pit, an endless ocean of light delving deeper and deeper until Wyn was sure it had gone straight through the core of the moon. Pathways crisscrossed the central gap, filled with pedestrians walking between destinations. Hoppers, like the one they currently rode in, weaved between those walkways, flying between levels or, rarely, leaving for one of the few outlying locations. A location like the one Wyn was headed for.

Hesheh continued talking. "I'm not sure if you were aware when choosing this location, but some unsavory events occurred on the grounds several days ago, and its previous ownership has come under speculation."

Wyn adjusted the screen on his window, zooming in on a few of the buildings on the upper levels. There were restaurants, clubs, and stores of all kinds. A legal aid market, an Imberlii Arms Station right next to an Imberlii Adult Store. Wyn coughed and skipped to the next set of buildings. The small moon held a bustling economy so similar and yet so different from Terrask. Down there, dozens of other species intermingled. He glanced at Hesheh, who had paused in her conversation, her fingers tapping nervously against the holopad she carried.

"Some kind of drug dealer, right?" Wyn asked, remembering the news story.

"To put it plainly, yes."

"And that's why it's cheap?"

"Yes. For good reason."

Wyn shrugged. "I don't see it. Something bad happened there, but it's an office building all the same. Why would that matter?"

Hesheh rubbed her cheek, a nervous gesture as she contemplated. "How aware of Chrysanax law are you?"

Wyn blinked. "I skimmed it."

"Chrysanax is a central travel point for hundreds of systems. We have more travel gates than anywhere else, and all are used around the clock. A lot of goods travel through here, and the Raiyrium Confederation fines heavily for missed contraband. Chrysanax makes up for that by having extremely strict drug rules. If found in possession of a small amount of illegal substances, one could face multiple years of prison."

"So, you're telling me not to do drugs?" Wyn flashed her a smile. "Don't have to worry about that. My father drilled that one into me already."

"No, I'm saying, don't *possess* drugs. Don't have drugs on your property. Even if they aren't your drugs and they were there before you purchased the property."

Wyn's face fell as his mind whirred through it. "Surely the policing force here would have searched the building?"

"They have, but that doesn't mean they found everything."

Wyn looked away, out to the sky and a massive gas planet that dominated the horizon. Colors swirled on the surface of Jel, mimicking Wyn's thoughts. He'd found the perfect building, but it might be loaded with drugs. Could one of the other options work? He'd have to remap his specifications, something he had already spent the last few days nailing down to every perfection for this specific building. Not only that, but prices would increase dramatically. He had the money, but he needed to make sure he'd have the money until he was making money. No business plan succeeded when hemorrhaging funds.

Perhaps if he saw it in person, he'd have a clear answer. "Thank you for the alternative options. Please add them to our itinerary. I would still like to see this one in person first, however."

"Understood, Mr. Kelda."

A wave of anxiety radiated through Wyn, and he nearly changed his mind. He opened his mouth to voice his concern when Hesheh spoke first.

"My apologies!" She lifted one hand to hide her eyes from view.

"Apologies? For what?"

"I did not mean to project my emotions like that." She lowered her hand a tad and peered over it. "I am normally much more professional than this."

"That anxiety was you?"

She nodded quickly.

"You can do that?"

She paused. "I don't think I've ever had to explain this before." She dropped her hand as she continued. "Tesings project their emotions onto each other all the time. It is an added form of communication, like body language for other species. It is considered deceitful to hide emotions, and with the exiled of my kind being unable to share them, it is shameful to have any comparison to them. However, other species are typically unnerved by it, so when conversing with others, we tend to suppress them."

"Why are you anxious?"

Hesheh paused for a long moment and looked out the window in thought. "I do not wish the purchase to reflect poorly on the company or myself. If you buy the building, then get arrested, you could blame us for having not told you about the possibility."

"Oh, is that all?" Wyn smiled, and Hesheh shot him a surprised look. "I'd be happy to sign a disclaimer saying I was aware of that possibility before purchase. If I go with that building."

Hesheh blinked and her shoulders fell as if the tension had been lifted. "That would be a wise idea. Though I still do not recommend the building."

"I understand. I'm hoping I'll see something there to persuade me away from the building."

Hesheh smiled. "A wonderful idea, Mr. Kelda."

It was, in fact, a terrible idea. After a short tour, Wyn saw what Bounty Inc. could be, and there was no turning down the building after that. The isolated location allowed for easy expansion, the nearby private hangar could be negotiated with to provide a nearby dock for hunters' ships, the price was dirt cheap for the type of building he went for. Not just that, but everything he saw for the future of Bounty Inc., he had designed based on this building. The bones of it, anyway. After that, how could he look at any other building like it had a chance? No, this one was perfect. He knew his own mind well enough to understand that opinion would not change. Which meant he needed to figure out what to do with any hidden drugs, not even factoring in that he needed to find them first.

Hesheh led Wyn down from the third story and back to the entrance. One of the pillars that lined the entry was blackened by plasma bolts, and there appeared to be splotches of blood on the floor and one wall. Even that had failed to dissuade Wyn, since he'd have it all torn out anyway.

Fuck. He was really going to buy the building.

Outside, a square of green grass surrounded the building, bisected only by a walkway that led to a rural road far from the bustling pit city. Beyond the grass, the ground became rust-colored dirt, growing a collection of strange brown shrubs. The only other building nearby was the private hangar, for which Wyn had already thought of uses, if the owner was willing.

Hesheh continued walking toward the parked shuttle, already talking about the next location. Wyn stopped outside the door and turned to face the building. He saw the future of Bounty Inc. in its bones, if not its face. There was no other option.

"I'll take it," Wyn said.

Hesheh stopped and turned. "What?"

"I want this one."

"But what about the drug problem?"

"I'll do a thorough search tonight to make sure nothing's left behind." He turned to face her, wearing a smile he couldn't tear from his face if he tried. "Don't worry, Hesheh. I'll take care of it."

"I'm still making you sign that disclaimer." She stared stoically for a long moment before slipping into a smile. "As long as you're happy with the choice, I am too. Now, what bank will you be going through?"

"No bank. I'll pay direct."

"Direct?" Hesheh's eyes widened. "But it's eight hundred and sixty thousand raikers."

"And where do I send that?"

Wyn did not sleep that night. Between searching the entire building—under every desk, behind every wall hanging, within every closet, and everywhere else he could think of—and tweaking the building's new design over and over, the sun rose before he thought to lay his head down. And with the sun came the first scheduled visitor.

The thrum of the Boz-kai Construction vehicle sounded through the window of the top floor office Wyn currently stood in the center of. Furniture had been shoved to the sides, and a projector orb hovered above him, projecting a holographic image of Wyn's redesign. With a gesture from his Vico, he deactivated the orb, and it descended into his waiting palm. Then he ran down the steps. The offices he passed were a disaster now, upturned, ransacked, and thoroughly searched; office supplies, desks, and chairs were strewn about the rooms as if a natural disaster had hit the building. Wyn blushed at the thought of the construction representative seeing the mess and wondered how easy it'd be to blame the previous owner.

Wyn reached the celuein doors, painted to look wooden, just as the contractor did and opened them to welcome the visitor.

"Helloooo…" The word started enthusiastically enough, then clung to the last syllable longer than intended, the extension of which drew the greeting to a complete halt.

"Hello," a mechanical voice responded. "You are Mr. Kelda?"

Wyn stared at the contractor, who stood more than a head taller than he did. The height was not what distracted him, nor was it the black box tied around the contractor's neck from which their voice came. No, it was probably all the feathers and the particularly sharp, curved beak. Recognition flared within Wyn. The contractor was a falvian, a bird-like species that had evolved past the need for wings. Though their upper limbs still resembled them, they couldn't be used for flight. Instead, they bent like arms, and the feathers at their tips moved like large, flat fingers. Incapable of speaking Galactic Common, the black box translated their thoughts into words. A sash hung across the contractor's chest, from which several tools dangled out of pockets and loops. Beyond that and the Vico, they wore nothing else, showcasing the beautiful spread of green, blue, and yellow feathers across their body. Their eyes were small orange beads ringed by tiny white feathers, and they watched Wyn, waiting for an answer.

"You are Mr. Kelda?" the falvian repeated.

Wyn shook himself from his stupor, trying to hide the blush that formed. "Yes, yes, I am."

"My name is Devours-Sun-Berries-With-Joy. I am here for my appointment. You have scheduled two days of service from Boz-kai."

Wyn had scheduled that as promptly as he had the appointment with Hesheh, two of the three things he had planned from a small planet several systems away. But being preoccupied was no excuse for being startled by the sight of a falvian. He was somewhere new, surrounded by more species than he'd ever known existed. He mentally reprimanded himself for the reaction.

"Yes, welcome Devours—um, berries..."

"Devours-Sun-Berries-With-Joy," Devours-Sun-Berries-With-Joy said. "But you can just call me Devours if it's easier."

"Welcome, Devours." Wyn stepped aside, letting the falvian enter before activating the door control to shut it. "I figured we could go room by room to discuss the design and modify it as needed. I have a projection orb, which will be able to give you an idea of what I was going for."

Devours studied the entrance hall carefully as they spoke. "I had anticipated the designs would be finished. Was that not the agreement made for beginning work?"

"I have an initial plan, and I do not expect it needs to be changed overly much."

The falvian gestured at their Vico, and two small disks floated up from their back. The disks unfurled, scanners and tools popping out from their bodies. Then they zipped along through the building. "Would you be able to send me the designs?"

"Sure." Wyn sent them with a few flicks of his fingers and watched as Devours pulled up a replica of his designs, a holographic image floating above their wrist. After a few gestures, small red spots began appearing, a dozen or so by the time it stopped pinging. The disks returned, settling into their location on the contractor's back.

"It seems your design should work remarkably well. I do not feel there is any need to discuss it room by room." They gestured, and a readout appeared next to the red-spotted designs. "There are a few minor problems. I will send you the list, and you will have to make corrections, but I should be able to begin immediately."

"Begin? I thought this was a design meeting. The person I talked to only scheduled out two days. Will we have to schedule more time?"

Devours glanced at the designs again. "No. Nothing more than was discussed has been added. We should be able to move forward and complete the project within the two days."

Wyn glanced out the open door at the shuttle Devours had arrived in. It couldn't be large enough to hold more than a couple people, assuming it held no supplies. "Where's your crew?"

"I am my crew." Devours stepped outside, swiping away the design plans. Another quick gesture sent dozens of black drones of various sizes spilling from the rear of the shuttle. "To meet your designs, it will be better to tear down everything but the skeletal structure. From there, we can reuse what materials are still good and purchase the rest of the materials to build out the design. When a room is scrapped by my drones, you should be able to step into that space and adjust your designs more precisely to update the issues. Any questions?"

Wyn rubbed at his head, feeling somewhat sheepish, and asked, "Do you have a hammer that could be used to take a first swing to celebrate?"

"No."

"Oh. So the drones will just take care of everything?"

"Yes. A hammer would damage the material. They will be able to precisely remove everything so it's reusable."

"Oh."

"Is there anything you need removed from the building before we begin?" Devours asked.

"I have a bag I'll need to grab quickly."

"Understood. Then I'll have the drones begin when you've exited."

"Great!" Wyn turned away from the door, then paused and turned back. "Um, I do have one more question."

"Yes?"

"I'm not sure if you're aware, but the previous owner here was a, um..."

"Criminal, yes. It made the news."

"Yes, well, there might still be illicit goods on the property that are *not* mine. If you find any, please don't report me."

The contractor considered for several moments, then said, "For a ten percent bonus, I shall collect any contraband found."

"Are you also able to dispose of it?"

"No, but I will pretend it doesn't exist. Disposal will be up to you."

"Understandable. I'll take you up on that offer, thanks."

The falvian cooed, then returned to the drones hovering outside the building. With quick feather fingers, they started sending instructions to the groups, readying them to tear the building down. Wyn returned inside to collect his things.

As he stepped outside, the drones swarmed the building, and the air filled with the ruckus of saws and energy beams as well as copious clouds of dust. Devours studied his drones from outside, occasionally checking readouts on his Vico to monitor the progress within.

"I'm going into the city to purchase something," Wyn said. "I'll be back in a couple hours. If you need anything in that time, feel free to reach out."

Devours cooed in response, which Wyn took as an affirmative. He called up a taxi service through his Vico and waited for his ride. His first two appointments had gone well. Now he just needed the third to succeed. He just hoped someone had responded. He'd had so much on his plate he hadn't had time to check the *slightly* abnormal bounty request. There was every possibility the job sounded too odd and had been ignored.

When Wyn returned several hours later, he had made two major purchases. One was a simple hopper, convertible so he could feel the wind in his hair, hover height of around three thousand feet so he wasn't restricted to the ground streets, and colored magenta because it was the only one on hand. The other was a Yokandai Legal Bot Type N-3644, a robot designed entirely around handling legalese for companies. It had encrypted access to nearly endless databanks of laws, court battles, lawsuits, and more, both local and galactic. It was expensive, but worth every raiker if it eased his understanding of company requirements. On the ride back, the bot had written up and filed every form necessary for Bounty Inc. to be legally recognized as a company, even with its complexities in pioneering a new type of business. Though, mercenary groups had been close enough to provide a solid foundation.

Wyn parked his new vehicle near Devours's and stepped out, looking in awe at the decimated building. Just about everything had been stripped from it, and a pile to one side of the building held materials neatly stacked and prepared for reuse. To the other side, another pile had formed, this one messy and prepared for refuse. Only the building's skeleton remained. The egg-shaped legal bot, or L-Bot, hovered nearby, a single glowing eye at its front.

"I will need to refile some forms if this is the structure you wish to operate from," it said.

"It's under construction," Wyn said, hoping the bot didn't already refile.

Devours waved Wyn over. "Tear-down is complete," they said. "We were just about to begin utilizing the materials to rebuild the shell."

"That was quick."

"I did not lie when I said it would be done in two days."

"I didn't mean to imply you did. It's just something else when seeing it done."

"I'll need the corrections sent over by tomorrow to wrap up everything."

"Right, I was about to do that."

Devours cooed and then stepped to the side and started sending orders to the drones through their Vico. Wyn entered the framing of his building and stared around at the emptiness. It certainly would make the projector orb's job easier.

He pulled up the first problem: part of a wall jutted incorrectly into what would be the lounge. He made his way to that side of the building and threw the orb in the air. The room came to life around him. The largest in Bounty Inc., it was meant to allow for camaraderie, conversation, and general relaxation. Couches and chairs spread out in a large area, angled toward the wall where a large display would be placed. A palmball table was set to the back of the room, and to one side, a secondary room was added on, featuring a small kitchen and fridge. He searched out the flagged points and began fixing the issues one by one.

Drones buzzed around, adding ceilings and walls, floors and pillars. Slowly, the barren frame regained composure, transforming into a building once again. Or a partial one, anyway. When Devours found him and told him they'd be leaving for the day, there were still many holes.

"Thank you for all your work, Devours."

Devours cooed. "I have sent the expected invoice, with new material calculated in. We had to trash much of what was here due to lack of quality." He gestured to the large garbage pile outside.

"Sounds good. I'll send the payment over tonight."

Devours cooed, then with a wave of their hand, the drones returned to the shuttle, and so did the falvian. Then Wyn was alone.

He sighed and returned to the issues he needed to solve. Then, given the lack of roof, he'd have to find somewhere to sleep.

Wyn walked through the ruins of his building and found a strange stack of tightly wrapped packages. They were clear, allowing Wyn to see the brown powder within. Even still, it took a moment for him to understand what he was looking at.

"Oh fuck! The drugs!" He'd never seen anything like them before. His father had made sure of that. He glanced around frantically for a sack that he could at least hide them in. Anything so they weren't out in the open.

"Fancy place you have here." Wyn whirled and found a new guest standing in a hole in the wall. She stood a head taller than Wyn, muscular arms and body defying the age that showed in the wrinkles on her face. Black hair speckled with gray fell back across her shoulders, and her dark tan skin accentuated a pink starburst scar on her jaw.

She wore a simple, tight vest, leaving her arms bare. Which allowed Wyn to notice the bits of orange paint splattered along the bulging muscles. "I'd recommend walls though. Still, it looks better than it did when I was here the other day."

Wyn stepped in front of the packages, hoping she wouldn't identify them. "Who are you?"

She raised an eyebrow and tilted her head to the side. "Are those drugs?"

# CHAPTER 2

## SAGE VALEN, READY TO RETIRE

Sage Valen, as he would soon learn her name to be, was the single scariest individual Wyn had seen up to that point in his life. She radiated a calm ferocity, as if embodying a storm. At any moment, she could be the wind and the lightning and the thunder, or she could be the eye. A predator, relaxing right up until she decided to kill with no regard. It made Wyn contemplate if *he* was the prey. Especially after she spotted the drugs behind him.

Wyn shook his head. "Nope, no drugs here."

She smirked.

"Who are you?" Wyn asked, his voice rising in pitch more than he'd like.

"Sage Valen. I'm responding to your stupid little bounty." She pulled the bounty on her Vico as she spoke. "Not that it's actually a bounty. Seems more like a job request."

Wyn's eyes widened, and the fear washed away. "Bounty? I didn't get notified of an acceptance!"

"Wyn Kedla, right?"

"Um, Kelda actually."

Sage glanced at the bounty, then looked up at him. "I think you spelled your name wrong."

Wyn's cheeks burned, then he coughed. "Right. As you said, it's actually a job request, not a bounty."

Sage crossed her arms and crooked a brow at him. "Why would you file a job request as a bounty?"

"Well, it's kind of a part time job, and I specifically needed someone with bounty hunting experience—"

"And what's this bit about looking for a *human*?" Sage's eyes narrowed, and Wyn began to sweat. "You're not a speciesist, are you? I don't really get along well with human supremacists."

"Oh no! I didn't mean it that way. I'm not trying to be speciesist at all. I can explain!"

"Go on."

"Well, it's two jobs actually, and you can accept only one of the two if you wish. Basically, it's not all or nothing. The first job is that I'm looking for someone to train me as a bounty hunter. I'm afraid if I try it myself, I'm likely to get killed quickly. Which is why I requested a human. I figured a human would be able to recommend a fitting diet and training regimen better than another species would. I swear I didn't mean anything by it!"

"Fine, fine. You're not scum. Yet. Just go on."

Wyn wiped at his brow, still nervous, though Sage seemed more relaxed. "I would pay weekly until a point at which one of us deems I have graduated the training or either of us decides to end it for other reasons."

"That might be a pretty long job," Sage said, looking Wyn up and down. He blushed and mumbled some nonsensical words that she ignored. "And the second one?"

"I need a partner who knows the industry and understands bounty hunting in a way I don't. It wouldn't be a paid job. Instead, you'd be offered stakes in the company. It shouldn't take you much time unless you want to participate. Most of the work is done upfront when I'd be paying for training, assuming you take that job. But the idea is a low-risk investment that could result in you receiving payments for the rest of your life, whether you participate in the company any further or not. Depending on how successful it is, of course."

"What company?"

"Bounty Inc., the galaxy's first company of bounty hunters. We'll be able to field requests no individual..." Wyn trailed off as Sage started laughing hysterically. He watched as the laughter at last died out, and she wiped a tear from her eyes. "I'm guessing you don't approve."

"It's stupid."

"Why?"

"Bounty hunters don't work well together."

Wyn shook his head and brought up his Vico, beginning a search through the data he'd formulated weeks ago. "I've seen several cases of bounties being collected by multiple persons, so it's definitely been done before. Just—"

"Listen, I don't care about your research," Sage interrupted. "I never said it doesn't happen. It can happen, once or twice, then egos and greed get in the way. Partnerships are broken apart, and grudges are formed. People are abandoned in the Viridian Wastes to die. It doesn't work. Bounty hunting isn't typically a job for those who want to work together."

"What would convince a bounty hunter to join a company like this? What would convince you?"

Sage contemplated the question, stretching the fingers on one hand as she thought. "You'd need to offer an incentive so staying on board is better than burning bridges. Especially since it's assumed you'd need to take a cut of the bounty."

"What about access to equipment?"

"Vehicles?"

"I can make it happen."

"What about weapons?"

"Definitely. If you have any suggestions, I'd be happy to hear them out."

Sage raised an eyebrow. "I might have one," she said. "Cutting out costs for bounty hunting would be a start. Even if you take a cut of the bounty, it'd be easier and cheaper to go after bounties."

"I've also started on some software that could make tracking the bounties easier."

"That might help make them stay, but it wouldn't get them to join." Sage sighed. "Either way, it's a start, I guess."

"So you'll join?"

Sage huffed, looking deeply in thought. "How much are you paying for the training?"

"Eight hundred raikers a week."

Sage's eyes twinkled at that, and she smiled. "Just how much money do you have, kid?"

"Um, I don't see why that's important. But I sold off my father's corporations for several billion raikers. Plus free sandwiches for life at any Gianna's."

Something flashed across Sage's face, a conclusion determined, a decision made. "You've caught me at a good time. I was about ready to retire. But kicking your ass into shape could be fun, and sitting on my ass while you pay me sounds even better. I'll do it, but I want a guarantee that if this company is shit, I can leave whenever I want."

"Of course. I can add a termination clause for you. You'll have the option to leave at any time with no fees."

"This could be a perfect little vacation." Sage smirked, and Wyn felt a shudder down his spine. He suspected that her "vacation" was going to be more enjoyable than his next few months. "Let's get something hammered out. That your legal bot out front, just hovering around?"

"Oh, L-Bot." Wyn scratched at his head. "I forgot about it. Yeah, it's mine."

Sage took a step to exit the building, not towards the door, but rather towards the large hole in the wall by which she'd entered. Wyn stopped her, then glanced nervously behind himself.

"You don't happen to know how to get rid of drugs, do you?"

Sage's face broke out in a frightening smile. "What kind?"

"You have a gym?" Sage took a slow bite of food, which had been a slab of meat, with gravy, vegetables, and some bulb-shaped bread, but was now cut up and mixed together into a slop. Her bloodshot eyes looked through Wyn as he took a nervous spoonful of his soup, as if he were merely a window.

"Yeah." Being built even as they spoke. Devours had returned in the morning and talked over the minor changes Wyn had made to the designs. Everything was approved, and the invoice was paid. Then Devours had told him he wasn't needed any further. The job would be done by nightfall. So, Wyn had decided to reach out to Sage to begin early planning. She had replied several hours later, suggesting breakfast.

"How big?"

Wyn brought up the specifications and projected them over the meals at the table, primarily focusing on a cross-section of the gym. She studied it and nodded with approval, which sent an unexpected rush of joy through Wyn.

"That will work for your training." Then she pointed to a room to the side. "What's that?"

"Oh, these are the locker rooms that can lead to either the gym or the armory." Wyn shifted the display, pulling out to show a top-down view of the first floor as he pointed out the rooms.

"Armory?"

"And over here is attached a shooting range for weapons practice. The room is insulated so it should be able to contain most weapon fire."

Sage raised an eyebrow, impressed at the design. "And this?"

"Oh, that's just a palmball table in the lounge."

"Of course it is."

"What? Bounty hunters don't like palmball?"

Ignoring him, Sage took a large bite of her food, chewed, and swallowed quickly, then sat a little straighter. "All right, your training will have four different phases. Cardio and strength training, diet, sparring, and weapons training."

"Sparring? Don't bounty hunters just shoot people?"

"They do until their weapon is knocked free or they're caught off guard. Don't let a crippling weakness develop, or it'll get you killed."

"Understood!" A virtual note popped into existence over Wyn's Vico, and his finger glided through the commands to enter the information. Sage rolled her eyes but continued.

"For cardio and strength training, we'll begin with a jog around the gym for an hour, plus—"

"*An hour?*" Wyn dropped his hand away from his notes, eyes wide in terror. He didn't think he had ever run for more than five continuous minutes.

"If you want to be a bounty hunter, you'll train like one, or you'll give up. Your choice."

He nodded. "An hour."

"Then we'll do some basic strength training. I'll be able to customize your workout better once I see what you're capable of. For now, that will get us started."

Wyn nodded, his mouth dry. This was starting to sound troublesome.

"Diet is easy as long as you can handle bland."

"Sure. Why would bland be difficult?"

Sage blankly stared at Wyn as she took another bite. "Remember that in a month. I'll send you the nutrition packets to order. Mix 'em with water into a kind of porridge; eat it three times a day. You should be getting everything you need."

"Sounds easy enough."

"As will weapons training. We'll just stick you in the shooting range and run you through the basics. Then practice until your fingers bleed. Sparring will be difficult. It works best if we have someone closer to your ability, but we can at least get you started on learning some hand-to-hand."

"Perfect. I'll set that up to start next week."

"Your building's being finished today, right?"

"Yeah, by nightfall. I'm excited to see it finished!"

"Great. Start tomorrow."

"*Tomorrow?*"

"Stop echoing everything I say that displeases you. There is no reason to push off your training another day. Tomorrow."

"I just thought it might interfere with any last-minute setup for the business."

"What else needs doing?"

"Finalizing contracts, strategy for getting people to join up, weapons and equipment procurement, just to start."

"I can get you a list of people and equipment."

Wyn deflated a bit. That had been the part he was looking forward to. "What if we both try getting people and interview them to pick the best?"

"Sure, whatever." Sage ate the last of her meal and pushed the plate to the side. "Do you know many bounty hunters, or were you just going to ask some people off the street?"

"Well, I don't know any personally, but I was going to put out a job request that people could sign up for. I already have one drafted for hiring an assistant."

"So you *are* just going to ask people off the street."

"Well, they would have to fulfill the requirements."

"Yeah, you're going to get some strange people."

"We might find someone useful though."

"Uh huh."

Wyn sighed and let it drop. She couldn't stop him from trying his route. "Either way, I think we shouldn't just indiscriminately invite people. We should interview each option and only bring on those we both agree on."

"Are you going to finish that?" Sage pointed to Wyn's bowl of soup. He pushed it forward without comment, and she upended the bowl into her mouth and downed it in one go.

"I'm worried the terminology of the contract will scare off prospective hunters. They may not trust the equipment and weapons incentive and only see the cut we need to take."

"Don't take a cut then."

"I need to take a cut, or the whole business model would be ruined."

"Special first year deal. Give them back the cut you take if they stay on for a whole year. As long as they make it through the year, they don't lose anything by trying."

"That's a brilliant idea!" Wyn scribbled down the idea so he wouldn't forget it.

"In addition to shared equipment, I'll send you a list for personal equipment, though that could be modified once we see your talents. If you have any." Sage stood up from the table and gave a low, roiling belch. "Now, if you don't mind, I either have to shit or vomit. Maybe both."

Wyn had received the message early: Bounty Inc. was completed. Now Wyn walked through the building with L-Bot trailing behind, the sun casting long shadows through the building as it set. The doors opened to a gorgeous entrance hall with pillars leading to a large desk. A door to the right led to the lounge, with furniture ready for use. Wyn walked through the mini kitchen and made a quick note to purchase a wide variety of snacks.

He went through the hallway which connected to the locker rooms and the communications room. The gym was a large rectangular room, with an area that remained padded for sparring practice. It gave him anxiety the moment he stepped into it, dreading the next morning's workout already.

The armory was barren. Several of Sage's items had been ordered, but they would take a few days to arrive. There wasn't even any shelving or racks since Wyn didn't know what he needed. The shooting range had been integrated with projectors and an interface that could help speed training. It could mimic actual firefights without the danger.

Satisfied with the first floor, he moved up to the second and found it just as thrilling. It consisted of a larger kitchen and cafeteria, a couple meeting rooms, and several dormitory rooms in case anyone wanted to stay the night. Wyn had doubled the size of one of the rooms for Sage, but the rest were still large enough to comfortably live in for an extended period. But Wyn was most excited about the third floor, which was entirely his. Half office, half apartment, with a single, short hallway bisecting the two. He began with the office.

"What do you think, L-Bot?" Wyn smiled as he looked around the room. The walls were glass that could tint if he needed privacy. A communications hub had been installed, and the large desk had an integrated Vico system so Wyn could work with much more space.

"About what, sir?"

Wyn blinked, not realizing what L-Bot was asking, until he remembered the question. "Oh, about the office. What do you think of it?"

"It looks like a decently optimal setup for office work."

There was no one to blame but himself for expecting more than the bland reply. Why he had asked L-Bot anything not legal-related was beyond him. Maybe he was just getting lonely.

The apartment was designed much like his rooms back home on Terrask. A combined lounge and kitchen for himself, a wall display for news or games, and, most importantly, a door which led to his own private bathroom. Another door led to his bedroom, which held a large bed, dressers, and a closet. It felt very homey, and he was happy to drop onto the bed.

"My dream is becoming reality, L-Bot. I never believed I'd have the chance. Who would have thought it just took my dad dying to make it happen?" Wyn's stomach clenched at the words, and guilt warred within him. He shouldn't find happiness at his father's death. Yet Iolas had been a cruel, cold man in life. He had forced Wyn down a chosen path and scolded him if he tried deviating from it. His death had bought Wyn's freedom, had erased his prison. So it was complicated. Grief and happiness roiled together to produce an uncomfortable stomachache. He focused on the worst parts of Iolas to help him push forward.

L-Bot didn't notice Wyn's distress. "I have found many cases of inheritances being used to start businesses, and eighty-four percent of them had strong legal foundations that could not be challenged. I do believe your case falls within that. You have done a remarkable job handling your inheritance without a legal bot."

"Thanks, L-Bot." Wyn sighed and decided to keep his thoughts private from now on, then smiled, reminding himself he deserved this. That smile didn't leave him until about five minutes into his run the next morning.

"It's been forty-two minutes," Sage barked. "Get back up."

Wyn tried to push himself up on trembling arms, but his legs were jelly and his lungs were gasping for air. He had pushed himself too hard too early and had nothing left for the end. He collapsed again to the ground, too tired to respond.

"Get back up." Sage nudged him with a boot, not quite a kick, but it didn't matter since Wyn couldn't feel it anyway.

Wyn groaned in response and shut his eyes. He knew what would come next, what always came next whenever he failed his father's commands. She'd yell at him until he did it correctly. Failure wasn't an option. But at that moment, he wasn't sure he could handle the verbal assault. He was too drained and exhausted and too embarrassed at how quickly he'd hit his limit.

But then Sage crouched down, and her voice was unnaturally soft when she said, "Hey, Wyn, look at me."

Wyn pried his eyes open one lid at a time, his body still heaving with each inhale.

"Training is about learning our limits," she said. "We train to find them, and yes, we want to exceed them, but understanding our limits is the most important aspect of being a bounty hunter. If you rush into a bounty and push yourself too hard, you'll end up dead. If you chase someone and find yourself in a position you're not prepared to handle, you're dead. Is this all you can handle?"

Wyn looked away, ashamed, but still he nodded. He couldn't go any farther if he tried. Everything was numb, and he wasn't sure he could even stand again.

"Then you know your limits, and you have a goal for tomorrow. Forty-two minutes." Sage smiled and patted him on the back. "We have a long way to go, but I get paid by the week, so take your time. Rushing will only lead to injury and setbacks. No weight training until you can make it through the whole hour. Rest there until you're ready, then let's get some breakfast."

Wyn looked at Sage's retreating back and closed his eyes on the tears that formed. It was stupid. All she had told him was to try harder next time. Yet her way had struck a chord that he hadn't felt in a very long time. Sage wanted to lead him to success. She didn't just want him to be already successful.

Wyn pulled himself to unsteady legs and wobbled over to Sage *after* he made sure his eyes were dry. "I'm ready to try that sludge."

Sage glanced up from reading something on her Vico and raised an eyebrow. "I'm not sure you are, but we'll see."

Every step was torture for his tired legs, but they walked to the second-floor cafeteria together, and he found a nutrition packet. Sage had already eaten, so she sat at a table, still looking at her Vico. Wyn mixed the packet with water, shoved it in the reheater, and a few seconds later pulled out steaming hot sludge. Thankfully, as Sage had promised, it smelled and tasted like nothing. If he closed his eyes, then surely he could eat this nutritional goop without issue.

"You need to cut down this list," Sage said as Wyn sat down at the table across from her, grateful to be off his legs.

"What, why?" Wyn said around a mouthful of paste.

"I'm not sitting through twenty-five interviews of these nobodies. How'd you even get so many? You just posted this yesterday."

Wyn shrugged, slightly taken aback by Sage's lack of enthusiasm. He had been ecstatic to learn so many people were interested in joining up and had thought Sage would feel the same. "They must like the idea."

"Or they're leeches trying to make some easy money by teaming up." She shut down the Vico display with a grunt. "We need experienced hunters who can bring something to the company. Bringing aboard anyone useless will just slow us down."

"We'll be able to find that out through the interviews."

"Sure, but cut out the obviously useless ones first. I have five experienced hunters who have agreed to listen to our requests. More isn't better here, and juggling a bunch of nobodies will be time-consuming and interfere with company growth. I found five people. Now *you* will choose five people from the list."

"*Five*? That's barely anyone! What if we miss someone who could be really impactful?"

Sage glared at him. "I doubt that. Your list is ass. Half these people have only one bounty under their belt. Remove them, and you're already that much closer."

"Fine," Wyn grumbled. "I'll narrow it down to five."

Wyn finished his sludge, barely noticing as he ate it, and Sage ran him through several basic forms and strikes for hand-to-hand combat. Wyn was relieved there was no actual sparring. He worried he'd throw up his food if that was the case. When weapons training came around, Wyn's legs had lowered their screaming protests to more of a groaning disinterest at existence. His mood was at an all-time high when Sage handed over a pistol for him to try shooting. The first time he ever laid hands on a weapon.

"Charge pack goes in the rear," Sage said, pointing to a slot in the back, then sliding a glowing vial into it and locking it shut. "One capsule can produce a hundred or so shots depending on the efficiency of the weapon. Always go Imberlii. Their readouts are the most accurate, and their consumption is as well. You'll get more shots per capsule than any other weapon on the market."

Sage twisted the pistol in Wyn's hands and indicated a slider at the bottom. "Press here, and this can slide. This direction uses more energy, this way less, and in the middle is standard. How much energy you use will affect the drain on the capsule as well as how strong the shot is. Want to knock someone on their ass but not kill them, slide it lower. Need to take out a haushedin or vrolak, switch it to full power. For now, we'll keep energy at the lowest. More practice shots, with no chance of killing yourself."

"Do all guns have a slider? That could be really useful for training on different weapons."

"Everything Imberlii does, and some of the other companies prioritize it. The cheap shit never has sliders. Most of the stuff I sent you for requisition should."

"Speaking of requisitions, you listed a slag cannon?"

"Yes."

"Why?"

"Because they're cool. I've always wanted to get one but couldn't justify the cost."

"So you're having me buy it?"

"You're rich."

Wyn sighed. For the next hour, he practiced firing several of Sage's weapons, including the pistol, a rifle, and even a scattergun, as the training program projected stationary targets for him to hit. He seemed slightly better with the pistol as that was the only one with which he almost hit the bullseye. Though, he wasn't sure if that counted since it happened when he accidentally dropped the gun while trying to set it down. Sage was unimpressed.

The day sped on: training, planning, sludge, repeat. The routine made the hours slip through his fingers like water, and a part of him grew anxious at the speed at which things piled up versus how quickly he could tackle them. That night, his priority was trimming candidates. From twenty-five to five.

He did as Sage had suggested, cutting out any who had only one bounty to their name, and ended up with fifteen. Still far too many. But for the life of him, Wyn couldn't figure out how to choose from that list.

The swirling greens and blues and yellows of Jel filled the sky outside Wyn's office window, leaving just a rim of night sky at the edges in which he could see sparkling stars. He stared out at the strange sight that never failed to mystify him. Terrask's skies held only the small silver orbs of its three moons, the stars almost entirely blotted out by light pollution. He sighed.

"L-Bot?"

"Yes, Mr. Kelda?" L-Bot hovered in the corner, in constant communication with the internal network for the building, filling, filing, and refiling countless forms.

"I have fifteen candidates for the company, and I have to narrow it down to five. How do I decide who to pick?"

"Any with current legal issues in any Raiyrium Confederation system would require several extra forms and legal loopholes. It is my recommendation to avoid such individuals."

"That was already a requirement to even apply." Wyn rubbed his palms into his eyes. Everything ached from his workout, and all he wanted to do was sleep.

"Then I am not sure, Mr. Kelda." The legal bot whirred, then spoke again. "In most cases of hiring, the company took aspects required for the job and compared or ranked them. It is the most common method to avoid species bias in hiring."

Wyn's hands dropped. "Ranking?" He spun in his chair and the virtual interface flared to life. Within moments he was coding a quick calculator together, the flash of an idea still bright in his mind. "So what's valuable for bounty hunters?" he mumbled to himself.

"I am not sure, Mr. Kelda," L-Bot answered. "That would be a better question to ask Ms. Valen."

"Well, bounties for sure," Wyn muttered. "Not just how many bounties you complete, but how much they're worth. Someone who does two large bounties is more valuable than someone doing ten really small bounties. So the biggest rate would be bounty value, but also efficiency in time. I'll also have to take into account shared bounties and how they are split. The values will need tweaking and maybe some more factors brought in, but this should give some value." He hit execute, and the program took in the data from the applications and spit out a ranked list. "I'll call them Bounty Points."

Wyn smiled at the readout. He'd need to adjust the algorithm to take into account past careers, such as for the Peacekeeper candidate. But, with this, he could find his best five, then invite those for an interview.

Wyn stumbled from his office in the early morning, having fallen asleep at his desk while modifying his Bounty Points calculator late into the night. His eyelids stuck with every blink, and a deep weariness had settled into his bones. Wyn wasn't entirely sure how he was even moving. So when he nearly stumbled into Sage outside the door, it took him a few moments to realize who it was.

"Oh, hi," he said.

"Good. You're up. Get changed, and get ready. Let's see if you can last longer than forty-two minutes this time."

"Right," Wyn mumbled, then stepped around Sage to open the door to his apartment. He paused and turned. "When did you get here?"

"I've been here all night. I moved into the room you gave me."

"You were here the entire time and never said anything? We could have grabbed food together or something."

"Why?"

Wyn blinked, his mouth opening and closing but failing to answer the question.

"I'm your trainer," she said. "And sure, a partner in this company. But that doesn't mean we're best buds or anything. I see you all day. I can enjoy the nights to myself."

Wyn's mouth closed, and a pang of something ran through him. Discomfort. She was correct. They were just partners. Why had he expected anything more? He shook his head and brushed it off. He wouldn't let it distract him. "Fair point. I'll be down in the gym in five minutes."

Sage nodded and walked away. Before she got too far, Wyn called out after her. "Almost forgot. I made my picks for interviews and had L-Bot schedule everything. Everyone should be able to make it in three days, so that's when we'll have the interviews."

"Great. You picked your five then?"

"Seven, actually."

"Wyn!"

"Couldn't decide between two, then a really good candidate came in at the last minute today. He checked all the boxes."

Sage started storming back so Wyn ducked into the apartment and slammed the door shut with a button.

"Wyn!" she called, hitting the door with her fists.

"Five minutes!" Wyn scampered away to change.

# CHAPTER 3

## TWELVE INTERVIEWS

Wyn collapsed into a chair at the long table, with a glass of something cold and full of sugar in one hand. His legs ached from running, his hands were sore from shooting, and a sharp pain jolted through his neck from sleeping on a desk. He wondered if this constant pain would eventually feel normal or if there would be a day he would stop hurting. That morning, he had reached the full hour for the first time, but he was so weak they still hadn't added any form of strength training. Wyn didn't mind. He worried about being able to lift a mere glass to his mouth once that part would hit.

Sage sat down next to him, holding a glass of something far stronger than his own drink based on the pungent smell. Wyn raised an eyebrow, and she glared at him.

"I told you five."

"I didn't want to miss out on any good options! It's only two more interviews."

"And this will help me get through twelve fucking interviews. We should have just picked my people and called it good."

"You don't have to be here, you know."

"I'm not letting you choose without me. We'd end up with a whole host of freaks."

Wyn smiled. He had threatened that if she wasn't a part of the interviews, she wouldn't get to pick the candidates. Despite her grumbling, Sage wouldn't let that happen. And so they sat, early in the morning, in one of the meeting rooms on the second floor, waiting for their first candidate.

"Who's first?" Sage growled.

Wyn pulled up the list of candidates on his Vico. "Looks like a vrolak named Zetta."

"Fuck."

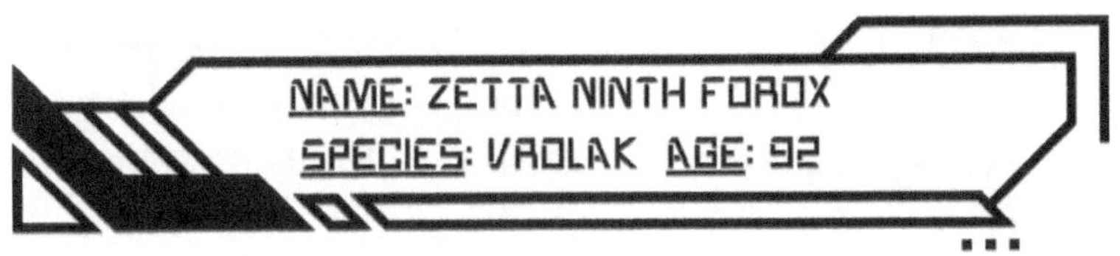


"Fuck? What do you mean 'fuck'? I thought you handpicked her?"

"Yeah, she's good. It's just, I didn't think I'd have to deal with her first thing—"

The door slid open, and a spinning, whirring L-Bot flew into the room, belting out requests for calm. A hulking, lizard-like creature squeezed through the doorway, snarling. Nearly twice Wyn's height and five times his weight, the vrolak was all orange-scaled muscle, including a thick, heavy tail that smacked the ground as the claws on her feet scraped the floor. She slammed two taloned hands down on the table and leaned forward, growling as saliva dripped from a protruding snout filled with razor-sharp teeth. Angry red eyes flashed as she stared down Sage. Wyn had jumped from his seat and backed away, a primal terror awake in him from which all his aches fled.

L-Bot quietly snuck out of the room, closing the door behind it, and Wyn wished he could have followed.

"How fucking dare you?" the lizard roared.

Sage stared down the monstrous woman without moving an inch, except for the eyebrow that raised just a hair. "Me? You're the one who left me stranded. If anything, I should be the one mad at you."

"You knew the rules. Thirteen missions and we never see each other again. You tried to stay longer to make our partnership something it wasn't. You're lucky stranding was all I fucking did."

"You stranded me in the Viridian Wastes! A death sentence to most people."

"I wouldn't fuck anyone weak enough to die that easily." Zetta's eyes flicked over to Wyn, who crossed his arms and tried to act nonchalant. "Oh, hey."

"Hey." Wyn lifted a hand, awkwardly waving.

"Why are you here if you're so upset to see me?" Sage asked, pulling the vrolak's attention back to her.

"Right," Zetta said, leaning back from the table, her head nearly scraping the ceiling as she dug into the pockets of her outfit, a loose robe that appeared to be made of stretchy material. She pulled a scatter gun from one of the large pockets and set it on the table. "Found this under my bed aboard *Slaughter*. Thought I'd return it since I was in the area."

"You accepted an interview just to return my weapon?" Sage asked, eyes narrowing.

"Sure. Why else would I be here? Sure as void ain't interested in joining your little bounty band."

Sage shrugged. "Maybe you just came to return the gun. Or maybe that's just an excuse because you're too afraid to admit you missed me."

"I'm not afraid of anything," Zetta snarled, once more leaning forward, her claws digging divots into the brand-new table. Wyn's mouth opened and closed, battling the desire to request that the giant lizard woman not make scratch marks against the desire to continue living.

Sage rose from her seat so fast the chair slammed against the back wall, then she mimicked Zetta's pose, staring the larger woman down. "If you're not afraid, then just fucking admit it. Quit hiding behind excuses like a coward."

"A coward? *I'm* a coward? You want the truth, Sage? Here's the fucking truth. I had to dump you on that rock because if I didn't, I would never be able to. Being with you, I enjoyed that. And that's dangerous. I had a tingle in my chest where it didn't belong. The only thing that should have been tingling was my crotch. Partnerships never last in this business. You would betray me if the incentives were good enough, just as I would you. Then it'd be even worse!" Zetta's tail whipped around, smacking one of the askew chairs across the room as she huffed in exasperation. "And then you reached out, and I should have said no, because now I'm here wondering how I'm going to say no to this terrible business plan you sent. Partnerships don't last, Sage!"

"Well, good news, Zetta, because the contracts here highly motivate *not* fucking anyone over. They don't even force you to work together. You just bounty hunt like normal, but you get your bounties from us. Not to mention I have a stake in the business that motivates me to have it succeed. I am in far more of a vulnerable position than you." Wyn noticed she conveniently left out the easy exit clauses in her own contracts. "We never have to work together if you don't want to, but if you join up, we can see each other and I can make your whole body tingle. Best of both worlds."

"This shit is going to end with someone dead."

"Any hunt can end with someone dead. At least in this case it will be fun before it ends." There was a long moment of silence as the two women stared at each other. Then Sage smirked. "He's buying a company slag cannon."

"Now, that's still—" Wyn started, but Zetta's snarl suddenly shifted to awe, then a grin more terrifying than the snarl.

"I'll never die, but you have a point that you might. And others." Wyn didn't care for the way Zetta eyed him at just that moment. Then her gaze slid back to Sage. "And the fucking wasn't half bad."

"Don't you lie to me, Zetta. The fucking was fantastic."

"Most importantly, the slag cannon." She licked her lips.

"Wait," Wyn said as everything clicked. "You two dated?"

Both women stared at Wyn, and he felt himself melting into a puddle beneath their gazes.

"Who is this fragile thing?" Zetta asked.

"Wyn Kelda, the man who decided to try this stupid endeavor. I'm also training him to be a bounty hunter."

"Ain't he a little thick to be a bounty hunter?"

"Hey!" Wyn braved the single word but had nothing to back it up.

"I'll whip him into shape soon enough."

Zetta sniffed the air in the direction of Wyn, then smiled again. "Fuck it, I'm in."

"Shouldn't we ask her any questions?" Wyn asked. "We've barely talked about the situation, and we're both supposed to agree on every candidate we bring on."

Sage glanced at Zetta and back at Wyn. "Are you going to tell her no?"

Zetta licked her lips. "I don't eat human often, but I do enjoy the taste every now and then."

"You enjoyed the taste nearly every night from what I remember," Sage said, sitting back in her chair.

"Hey," Zetta pouted, and Wyn's eyes widened at the scariest face the vrolak had made yet. "No saying shit like that while I'm trying to be intimidating."

"Don't intimidate my little garnack. He hasn't had the training to stand up to it yet." She looked at Wyn and said, "Zetta's one of the best hunters I know and is tireless on the job. Not to mention it's a lot of fun when she bulks up and goes wild. She is the perfect candidate if she's willing. Don't miss this chance."

"Bulks up?" Wyn asked, barely registering his body at this point.

"Yeah," Zetta said, leaning back. "That's what I call it when I expand my muscles and get bigger. Bulk up." She glanced at Sage. "You said it's not stupid, didn't you?"

"You get *bigger*?"

Both women looked at Wyn like he was the crazy one.

"You know nothing outside of humans, do you?" Sage asked.

"I grew up on an isolated human supremacist colony. They didn't exactly teach alien anatomy."

"Whoa," Zetta growled. "We're not aliens. We're just different species. The galaxy belongs to everyone."

"He's an idiot," Sage explained, like that explained anything. Wyn glared, which was hard to pull off when he was still nervous about Zetta. "Listen, Wyn. I don't know all the details, but I'll explain it to you later."

"Well, if we're already deciding on it, shouldn't I know now?"

Sage sighed. "Fine. Zetta here has a parasite inside her head. It's a symbiotic relationship, where the parasite stimulates and feeds off chemicals in the brain, and in return, they react to neural receptors and provide a type of fast-acting, temporary steroid into the system. Vrolaks with these parasites can pull on them to enhance their strength, making them several times stronger and, as a result, bigger."

"I call mine Geble." Zetta smirked, sharp teeth poking out.

"Not all vrolaks get them," Sage continued. "Some of the stupid ones think it's more pure to not have them. But they can't bulk up, as Zetta calls it. Downside is, if Zetta's is removed or killed, she can't survive because her brain will be overproducing the chemicals the parasite feeds on. These would flood her system and overwhelm her organs, shutting down her entire system within an hour or two."

"They'd have to get through my skull first," Zetta growled. "Which is unlikely. That, or I'd have to be stupid enough to overwhelm Geble enough that he croaks."

"It takes a lot of skill," Sage added, "to control the bulking up. Too much and they can start tearing skin and causing permanent damage. Including killing the parasite. Too little and what's the point. Zetta is a genius at pulling just the right amount, maximizing her use of the parasite. She could claw her way through a pure celuein wall or punch a tesing into a puddle of goo."

"I've honed it with years of killing."

Wyn stared at the two, mouth open, gaze darting back and forth. He closed it, moistened his tongue, then tried speaking. "I thought you said you didn't know much?" He directed the question at Sage, whom he was more comfortable looking at.

"Well, I said I don't know all the details."

"What details don't you know?"

Sage looked at Zetta, then back at Wyn. Then shrugged. "I'm not actually sure how they get the parasite in their heads. I never asked that."

"Through the nose," Zetta said. "Feels like the worst sinus infection of your life, but fuck if it ain't worth it."

Wyn's mouth moved, but his voice had no more energy. Overwhelmed, he slumped in his seat and gave up. Guess they were getting the homicidal lizard woman on the team.

"If he gets this riled up by me..." Zetta smiled. "I'd love to see him around Mecillis."

"Stick around, and you will be able to," Sage said. "She agreed to an interview."

Zetta barked out a laugh that shook the room. "Good fucking luck getting that freak to join. I'm surprised she even said yes to the interview."

Sage shrugged. "It's a long shot, but she'd be invaluable."

"Ain't nothing Mecillis can do that busting in the front door ain't just the better option." Zetta waved a large claw as if to swipe the conversation away. "Oh well. I'll see you tomorrow."

"There's sleeping quarters on this floor," Sage said. "My room's the biggest one down that way." She pointed.

Zetta grumbled a reply and walked out the door, L-Bot in hot pursuit to lead her out of the building and bring the next candidate up.

"What the fuck?" Wyn gasped as if he'd held his breath the whole time. "I thought she was going to kill you."

"Nah." Sage gulped down her drink. "I had hoped to have more liquor in my system before seeing her, but that went better than expected."

"Are you two going to…"

Sage stared at Wyn and his unfinished sentence, waiting for him to voice what she knew he was going to say.

"…um, cavort?" Wyn finished weakly.

"Cavort?"

"Date? Be together? Intimately?"

"Why are you prying into my sex life, Wyn? That's fucked up."

"That's not what I mean! We just didn't talk about dating among hunters. Could it lead to problems? Should it be discouraged?"

Sage smirked. "Chill out, we're all adults. And it's not like anyone is stuck inside the building but you and me." She shrugged after another mouthful of drink. "Who knows, maybe you'll meet someone of your own here. Or multiple someones if you're into that sort of thing."

Wyn's cheeks burned so hard, his vision seemed to tunnel, and his ears clogged with the beat of his heart. "Let's just move on!" he shouted louder than intended.

"Who's next?"

Wyn sat and pulled up the Vico. "His name is Cee. He's a human with cybernetic modifications."

"I fucking hate cybernetic modifications," Sage growled.

Wyn almost asked why, but L-Bot's return cut the question short.

Sage sat frozen, eyes narrowed, mouth agape, brow furrowed. She leaned slightly back in the chair, a loose grip on her drink.

Wyn sat frozen, eyes wide, mouth tight, eyebrows stretching up to his scalp. Rigid in his chair, his sugary drink forgotten on the table.

Cee sat still, eyes flicking between Sage and Wyn (at least, Wyn thought they might be, as they were just two glowing blue spots), mouth a straight line (also glowing, and Wyn thought the straightness might not be optional), brow a flat sheet of metal. Its hands folded in its lap. "It" because Wyn didn't know what else it could be. It had registered itself as a human with heavy cybernetic modifications, but Wyn had trouble finding what was human.

"Hello," Cee said, likely not for the first time, but at least this time it knocked Wyn out of his stupor. The thin blue light of its mouth pulsed in time with its words.

"Hello," Wyn started, stopped, continued, forgot where he was, then settled on another "Hello."

"What the fuck are you?" Sage asked.

"Sage!" Wyn hissed, but Cee didn't seem to react. Not that Wyn would have been able to tell.

"I am Cee, a human cyborg."

Wyn ran a thumb along his palm in a circle over and over again. "It says in your application that you have many cybernetic enhancements." He tried not to stare at the thing across from him and failed. "Can you tell us about them?"

"To explain all of them would take a lot of time, not to mention some may be hazardous to my security if I were to describe them in detail. But I would be happy to share a broad scope of my adjustments. These include a mesh overlay that acts as armor, several hidden weapons throughout my body, sensors and scanners that can detect everything across the color and sound spectrums and plenty of other things, such as chemical compounds. I have a wireless communications system so I can act without a Vico and interact with almost any network with a mere thought. If wireless is not available, I have alternate methods to connect to systems physically. My strength compares to that of a much larger species, such as the vrolak I passed downstairs. My endurance is endless. Pain sensors have been modified to produce a diagnostic but not cause distraction, which allows me to fight through injuries that others would succumb to long before. Most of my organic parts have been replaced to produce the ultimate performance."

"Is there any part of you that's not replaced?" Sage asked.

"Yes," Cee said, then lifted its left hand. Wyn had found his drink and had started to take a sip as it came into view. Attached to the pinky finger was what looked like a dehydrated strip of meat. No, that was a human finger, embalmed to avoid decomposition. Wyn choked on his drink and began coughing viciously as it spewed out in front of him and ran down his chin and out his nose. Sage and Cee ignored him.

"That's it?" she asked, eyebrow raised in what was now a familiar reaction to a light surprise.

"Correct. To become optimal, I needed to replace everything I could. To be considered human, I needed a part of my body to remain. Thus, the finger."

"You said you have wireless communications installed. What's to stop someone from using that as a point to hack into you?"

"I monitor all my systems and have countermeasures that outstrip every security system I've encountered. It was created like an immune system, able to respond to invasion, and with my sentience able to guide it, I can root out hack attempts in less than a second. Then usually I can trace it to its source and counter hack that. It would take a brilliant mind to find a way to penetrate my security."

"That's what they all say, but I'd want to see some kind of proof of your—" The lights flickered, then shut down. Wyn's Vico raised alarms as he finally finished clearing his lungs, then the building's systems rebooted, though now with the wall display activated.

Cee waved to them from the display and spoke. "This was not a very challenging system to hack, but I hope the speed at which I did it shows you some level of my abilities."

The Cee in front of them continued the conversation. "If brought on, I would be happy to upgrade your security system so it's almost defensible against me."

Wyn cleared his throat and wiped at his raw eyes. "Can you make it so it's defensible against you?"

"Without a mind to constantly monitor, that would be impossible. Given the governmental restrictions on artificial intelligences, the best I could do is almost defensible against me."

"You seem to be doing well as a bounty hunter," Sage said. "You've been doing it for three years and have collected nearly eighteen million raikers through bounties. Why is it you want to join Bounty Inc.?"

"The idea of a conglomeration of hunters intrigues me, and I feel I have skills that can help it succeed. The least of which is the upgrade to security." The Cee on the display waved. "I'm willing to assist in improving areas of software and hardware as well in my free time, as those are things I do for enjoyment anyway."

"We didn't budget for software development," Wyn said.

"That is fine. I can work for free. Money is not really important. My personal upkeep is quite minimal."

"Right," Sage said. "Well, thank you for your time. We'll be reaching out within the day to let you know what we decide, but it is a very promising application."

"Thank you, Ms. Valen. I pride myself in my abilities." The cyborg rose, then bowed slightly to them before exiting the room.

"That was definitely an artificial intelligence, right?" Wyn asked.

"There's no way it wasn't." Sage's face was filled with a grin that worried Wyn.

"That's illegal."

"Only if it gets caught."

"We're not bringing that thing on."

"Think on it, Wyn. Would you rather have a supremely intelligent A.I. assisting you where you can watch it or let it roam free?"

Wyn returned to rubbing his palm with a thumb. "Why does it want to be here?"

"You heard it! It's interested." Sage smirked and turned to him. "And I'm interested to learn why it's here as well. Besides," she continued, "this will probably be the only good candidate from your list."

"I doubt that. This next person seems like a great candidate. New to bounty hunting, but he's been a Peacekeeper for years. That experience will be invaluable."

"What's his name?"

A portly, middle-aged man with a bushy mustache only rivaled by his bushier eyebrows stepped into the room with a big smile.

"And I thought *you'd* take work to get in shape," Sage whispered.

"Not everyone who's fat is out of shape," Wyn hissed, then smiled back to Jefferson. "Welcome. I'm Wyn Kelda, and this is Sage Valen."

"Wowza, yeah, nice to meet you," Jefferson said as he patted his thighs. "Those are quite a lot of steps, eh?"

"I don't think he's one of those," Sage whispered again.

Wyn ignored her and shook the man's hand. "You get used to them," Wyn said, his hand slightly wetter than it had been moments before. He discreetly wiped it dry as he sat. Up close, Wyn now noticed the flushed face and the quicker breaths and wondered how a successful Peacekeeper and Bounty Hunter could get winded so easily. "It says here you became a hunter six months ago, and in that time you completed three bounties, including the rather high-profile capture of a terrorist. Would you be able to speak on that one?"

"Oh sure, yeah. That was my first hunt." Jefferson's eyes sparkled as if he were about to cry, then he sighed. "I remember it like it was only a few months ago."

"It was," Sage said as she rested her head on one hand, clearly bored. Wyn shot her a glare, which she ignored. Jefferson seemed unbothered.

"I was still a Peacekeeper at the time, and the terrorist—his name was Bonger—wanted to turn himself in. Well, he called up some people who got in touch with the Peacekeeper offices and they decided on me, being that I was the most expendable in case of anything going wrong. My wife was mighty mad about that, but them Peacekeepers are nothing if not straightforward. I would be compensated by filing it as my own bounty. I signed up for my bounty license, and turning him in was the most exciting time I've had."

"Did something happen?" Wyn asked. "Anyone interfere with turning him in that you had to protect him?"

"Oh lordy no, it was as smooth as can be. I picked him up, drove him to the Peacekeeper offices, and got my bounty. But that first bounty awakened something in me. A thrill for adventure. I invested that money and a lot of my personal stash into buying myself equipment. I quit my job and started hunting for a living."

Sage stared daggers through Wyn, and he could understand the threats they implied well enough. He averted his eyes, focusing on their guest and blocking out Sage's frustrations. The man was a Peacekeeper; he had to have some decent experience somewhere. "What about these other two bounties? How'd they go for you?"

"Oh yes, well, there was the first one after I quit my job. I had to track down a thief who was stealin' all the paintbrushes along this river, right? So I set a trap, just put a paintbrush out, and I watched. For twelve hours, I was tucked away, hiding, when this waterfowl comes and picks it up. Turns out, the thief was a bird the whole time, building out a nest from the bristles. We told the people to not leave their paint brushes out, and there wasn't another problem."

Wyn swallowed hard as Sage finally turned away and took a deep swig of her drink. "And the last?" Wyn was afraid to ask but did it anyway.

"A dine and dasher. That one was mostly an accident. Ran right into me as I was getting lunch. We went tumblin', and I broke her ankle when I fell on it. Helped me, though, cuz she was quite quick before the broken ankle."

"Okay. Shifting gears a bit. You were a Peacekeeper. Did you want to talk about your time with Raiyrium's galactic policing force?" Wyn felt desperation creeping into his voice.

"Oh, sure! For twenty-five years I worked as a 'keeper. Every district in the confederation is required to have an office, and I headed up the one on Mruck."

"You led your own division of Peacekeepers?" Relief washed through Wyn at the possibility they had finally found something viable in his history.

"Oh, well, sorta. I was the only one in that office. Mruck is a small outlying colony of a few hundred people. The R.C. didn't think it too necessary to divert a lot of resources to it."

"That's still a lot of people for one man to protect. What were your days like?"

"Well, most days I would get up and get food at a local diner. Then I'd go for patrol, a quick walk around the block. After that it was just monitoring messages and takin' on requests. This one time, Phyllis came in saying someone was stealing her panties. Turned out, it was just her husband throwing the holey ones away. Turned into a big fight until she found out he bought her all new ones. I left before she started tryin' 'em on."

Wyn stared at the man, speechless. Even Sage looked a little flabbergasted, though she fought through it to ask a question, as if urging a shuttle wreck to crash a little harder. "You mentioned a wife. This kinda work can be hard on a love life. What does she think of it?"

"Oh, she's no bother." Jefferson waved his hand as if to brush the question away. "Not since she left me for the new Mruck 'keeper anyway."

"Thank you, Jefferson." Sage nodded. "We'll be in contact with you about your future with Bounty Inc. in the next day. Good luck with your endeavors in the meantime."

"Oh, gotcha." He stood from his chair, then stumbled as his jacket caught on the arms. In an attempt to free himself, he knocked over his chair and an adjacent one, then came up red-faced once more. "It was a pleasure to meet you both. I look forward to hearing back." He stuck a hand out for Sage, who just held up her own to indicate she would not be grabbing the hand. With another "Oh, right," he shifted his hand to Wyn, who, still rather flummoxed, took it and shook it. It came away even wetter than the first time.

"Thanks! Good day! Bye!" Jefferson said as he backed out of the room.

"If he made one of your top picks, who in the void is still on the list?" Sage growled after he had left.

"I thought his Peacekeeper experience would be a lot more relevant."

"He's just going through a midlife crisis. We can put him down as an absolute no."

"But he just seemed so happy to join us." Sage's eyes widened with danger, danger for Wyn in particular. "Okay, okay, he'll go into the no pile."

"I hope for your sake your next five options are better, or I'm liable to kill you."

"Well." Wyn swallowed and saw a certain kind of hateful truth in those eyes. Fuck. He hoped they were better too. "These are going pretty quick! And we have one of yours next."

"Who?"

"Someone named Mecillis."

"Fuck."

"Fuck?" Wyn sat straighter in his chair. "How many of your people are you going to be upset to—" Wyn's throat froze. His skin chilled and itched, as if maggots were crawling just beneath. His lungs seized, unable to inflate. The edges of his vision blackened as sweat ran down his spine. His heartbeat thundered in his ears, drowning out everything else in the world until it was only that one constant beat.

Sage leaned over and patted Wyn on the knee. "Sit this one out. You'll feel better soon."

Mecillis stepped into the room, and dread followed her like snick-ts on shit. Wyn almost blacked out at the mere sight of her, though he didn't know why. She was taller than Sage, with longer limbs that had an extra joint. Her fingers stretched out like the legs of a spider, six on each hand. Her skin was bleach-white and smooth, and embedded into her bald, angular skull were six black eyes like pits. Two had been set into her skull in a typical human location, but a set of two smaller eyes were stacked just outside of the main pair, broadening her range of vision. The design made her appear as if she were a walking skeleton, if not for the white tongue that slipped out from her mouth and licked sharp, blackened teeth.

"—terrible idea," Mecillis said. Conversation had been ongoing, floating around Wyn but never really entering his focus. He shook, his skin pale, his head filled with stuffing. Everything came to Wyn as muffled noise, all meaning behind it lost.

A hand grabbed his, warm and firm, squeezing the life back into his fingers. He gripped it as hard as he could, a lifeline pulling him back into the room. Slowly, he brought his breathing under control, and with that, he could understand the conversation again. He noticed then that the hand was Sage's, discreetly under the table, and though it made sense to be the only hand that would grab his, it still threw him off.

"We could use your talents to help the company succeed," Sage said. "There's almost no risk on your part. Working as a team is optional."

"I don't work well with others." Mecillis's voice was sing-song, completely contrasting her looks. Or maybe fitting them perfectly, Wyn couldn't really figure it out. "I usually end up killing the people I work with."

"You haven't killed me."

"Yet." Mecillis smirked, flashing her black teeth. Wyn's eyes fell away, trying to let his mind pretend she didn't exist.

"If you're not interested, why did you even show up?"

"I'm hurt, Sage." Mecillis held her hands up to her flat chest, and Wyn realized the drapings he had taken for clothing were actually loose folds of skin. "Maybe I just wanted to see you again." Wyn felt her eyes shift to him, though their movement was imperceptible. "Or maybe I just wanted to meet your new partner. I liked Zetta more. This one is...*weak*." Mecillis leaned forward, a hand sliding across the table, reaching for him. "He won't even look at me."

Wyn pushed himself back from the table, away from the grasping hand. She laughed, a melodic chiming. Then the hand stopped moving. Sage stood, pistol in hand aimed at Mecillis's head. The nairwid smiled. "Do you think that will work?"

"It will make your day unpleasant enough," Sage said.

Mecillis laughed but pulled back her hand, standing straight again. Sage's pistol followed the movement of her head. "Wyn Kelda," Mecillis said, the name rolling around like bile in her mouth. "I shall remember you. I do hope we meet again."

"You're wasting my time," Sage growled. "Leave, or I'll see just how small of a piece you can regrow from."

Mecillis placed a hand gently on Sage's wrist as she smiled. "Do you think you'd live long enough to discover that, Sage?" Then she leaned forward and ran her alabaster tongue along the barrel of Sage's pistol. The gun sizzled and melted at her touch, melding the tip closed and effectively rendering it useless. "Do you think you'd be able to stop me from destroying this building and everyone in it?"

"Killing a nairwid has always been on my bucket list," Sage said, not moving the pistol or flinching from Mecillis's touch.

"I would love to see how well you fare, Sage Valen. But that day is not today. I'm afraid I'd have to be paid a lot of money to kill you."

She released her touch from Sage's wrist and turned toward the exit. "Farewell, Sage. Nice to meet you, Wyn Kelda."

Then she was gone.

The moment the door closed, Wyn grabbed the nearest trash bin and hurled his guts into it. The strange, goo-like nutrition meal looked far too similar coming out of him as it did going in. He heaved until nothing came out, then dry heaved several times more for good measure.

"What a bitch." Sage rubbed a hand through her hair and sighed, tossing the destroyed gun to one side.

Wyn coughed, his throat stripped raw from the acid. His voice came out hoarse. "What was that?"

Sage chuckled, *actually chuckled*. "Sorry about that." She looked down at him, pity flooding her eyes. "She likes to see how bad she can make my day, and you got caught in the crossfire. You did well though, no tears!"

As though waiting upon the very word for the right to begin, tears streamed down his cheeks. "*What?*"

"Do you know what a nairwid is?"

Wyn shook his head.

"Nearly indestructible shapeshifters. They can modulate tissue, muscle, skin, bone, anything. Pretty sure no one outside of other nairwids knows what their original form looks like. They might not even have one. Mecillis is old and cruel, which is an unpleasant combination for someone who can change their body at will. She messes with producing a pheromone that causes intense fear in humans whenever I'm around just to fuck with me. She does the same to other species. It constantly gives her an advantage in conversations."

Wyn shook as he sat on the floor in front of a trash can filled with vomit, though at least the effects of the pheromones seemed to be wearing off. He could think straight, see straight, and mostly his mind only recoiled at how it *had* felt, not how he was feeling right then. "That's fucked up. Why would you ask her to be part of the company?"

"Do you know how useful a shapeshifter would be for bounties? It's like a cheat code."

"It doesn't seem worth it." Wyn wiped at his face and took careful breaths, trying to bring his body functions back to a semblance of normal.

"Do you need a moment?" Sage asked. "I can handle the next interview on my own if needed."

"No, I'm fine." He positioned himself back in his chair and hit a button on the trash can. It rumbled, reducing the innards to atomic waste and removing any lingering bad smells. "Who's next?"

"Caws-At-Second-Dawn," Sage said. "Some falvian on your list."

Wyn glanced at her. "You just wanted this interview on your own so you could end it right away."

Sage shrugged. "Hey, your list is fifty-fifty so far. I'm actually interested to see what comes in next."

The door slid open, and a falvian stepped inside.

Where Devours had reminded Wyn of spring, Caws-At-Second-Dawn reminded him of winter, with cool shades of blue and white. One eye, a diamond, sparkled as though lit from within. The other, cybernetic, glowed a bright blue from deep within a forest of circuitry. The implant wrapped around his head to the base of his skull. More cybernetic implants ran along his armwings and one taloned foot was replaced. Where Cee's cybernetics had erased any humanity, if any had even existed, Caws's seemed to enhance his falvian body, turning it into a weapon that could react with a single thought.

Wyn was awed. And he almost said so, until Sage spoke first.

"Thanks for coming. We'll be in contact shortly."

"What?" Caws asked.

"What?" Wyn echoed.

"I said thanks for coming. Goodbye."

Caws flicked his gaze between the two, the voice box speaking his thoughts aloud. "I thought I was coming for an interview."

"Yeah, the interview is over," Sage said, flicking open her Vico and ignoring the falvian.

"Sage, what are you doing?" Wyn asked. Consternation boiled within him. "He just arrived. We haven't even asked any questions."

Sage sighed. "If you want me to put it plainly, he's a no. We just interviewed someone who could hack into his cybernetics in less than a second and turn him into a writhing mess. He's a liability."

"Excuse me?" Caws glared at Sage, his feathers shaking. "I am not a liability. I have plenty of experience as a bounty hunter and have never been hacked."

"Just because you haven't doesn't mean you won't. Good luck in your future endeavors, Caws-At-Second-Dawn."

The falvian looked as if he were about to speak. Instead, he angrily cawed, then turned and stormed from the room.

"I thought his cybernetics were cool," Wyn said, watching Caws leave, still confused.

"That's because you're an idiot. I've seen the coolest cybernetically-enhanced soldiers drop to one uncool person with a Vico. Absolutely no cybernetics."

"What about Cee?"

"That thing doesn't count. It's not cybernetically enhanced, it's just...*it*."

"Well, we have time before the next interview. Want anything to drink?"

Sage shook her empty glass, then shrugged. "Nah, I might take a nap. Who's next?"

"Achtrek-Six Hive? What kind of name is that? It sounds like something you would name a contingent."

"Fuck," Sage said, setting her glass down hard. Wyn's eyes flew open, and he whirled on her. Then she burst out laughing and patted him on the shoulder. "Relax, I'm kidding. Achtrek is great."

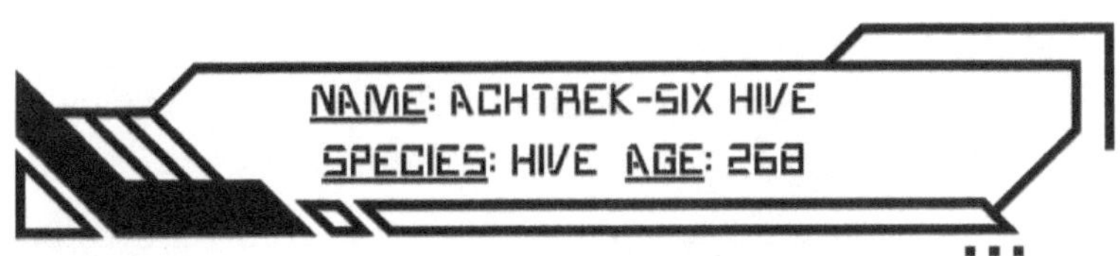


Whatever Wyn had suspected of something called Achtrek-Six Hive, he had not expected the completely normal human being who walked into the room. Shut off from the galaxy as he had been on Terrask, he supposed there were plenty of other human colonies, but he didn't know what to make of a human referring to itself as a hive when listing species. Maybe it was a group of humans with a hive mind? He wondered what it would be like to constantly share his mind with others. If that was how it worked, surely the chaos would be unbearable.

Achtrek was of average height, no taller than Wyn, and had brown hair and brown eyes. He wore normal dress clothing appropriate for an interview. No armor, no weapons. He could be applying to any number of jobs. Wyn could shut his eyes and imagine any generic human, and a picturesque version of Achtrek would form in his mind. He had expected one of Sage's friends to be weirder based on previous examples.

Something flittered on Achtrek's shirt, and Wyn's eyes were pulled to it, but whatever it was had disappeared. He blinked and rubbed at his eyes. He was tired, and his brain was still playing tricks on him from whatever Mecillis had done. Thankfully Sage had taken up most of the talking this time around, giving a quick rundown of the ideas behind Bounty Inc.

"It is a concept we resonate well with," Achtrek said, a faint hum to his voice. "It would be good to see you and Zetta again as well. With little downside, we think this would be a great opportunity to try something new."

We? Maybe it was a hive mind thing. Something moved on Achtrek's shoulder, and again Wyn's gaze shot to it, expecting to see an insect but once again finding nothing. It had probably entered the building with all the people coming and going. Hopefully it didn't bother Achtrek too much. He'd have to find a way to swat it or something.

"You're more optimistic than I am," Sage said with a shrug.

"As it doesn't seem to interfere with bringing money back to the Mother, we would be grateful to join."

Wyn's brow furrowed. How strange. Whenever Achtrek spoke, it was like watching a poorly dubbed movie. The lips didn't quite fit the words. It was subtle, but Wyn started noticing the more he watched for the errant bug.

"Welcome aboard, Achtrek," Sage said. "We'll be in contact shortly with more information."

Wyn stood and put out a hand to shake. "It was a pleasure to—"

His mouth filled with glue. As Achtrek gripped his hand, a part of the hand had broken off and crawled across Wyn's wrist before reattaching to the body elsewhere. The hand vibrated and shifted beneath his palm as it realigned itself, looking once again like a normal human hand. He looked up at Achtrek's face, and it had dissolved into dozens of small beetles all shifting together in a large mass. When they calmed, their shells shifted color until the face of Achtrek returned. And Wyn understood. The strangeness of the man's face had been its lack of depth. Sure, the nose poked out, but everything seemed smoother, and the mouth didn't seem to be a hole, but rather that part of the face just turned black.

Achtrek extracted his—their—hand from a frozen Wyn and said farewell. Wyn was slow to return to his body, his sheltered mind overflowing with too much newness. Everything was so different from what he knew and what he was used to.

"You know, I thought being referred to as a hive would have given a bit more clue," Sage said. "But no, you really didn't know until the end, did you?"

"He—they—bugs?"

"Yes, Achtrek is a hive mind of beetles working together. Their Mother is their planet, with trillions of them. They can branch off and act as self-sustaining units, but their minds link back up if they get close enough. Not as effective as a nairwid for disguises, but they still do well."

Wyn absently rubbed his hand against his pants. "Who's next? Is it one of mine?" Wyn hoped it was. Those ones had been less troubling.

Sage checked and grinned. Not a good sign. "Nope, one of mine. Ah, it'll be good to see Shellesh again."

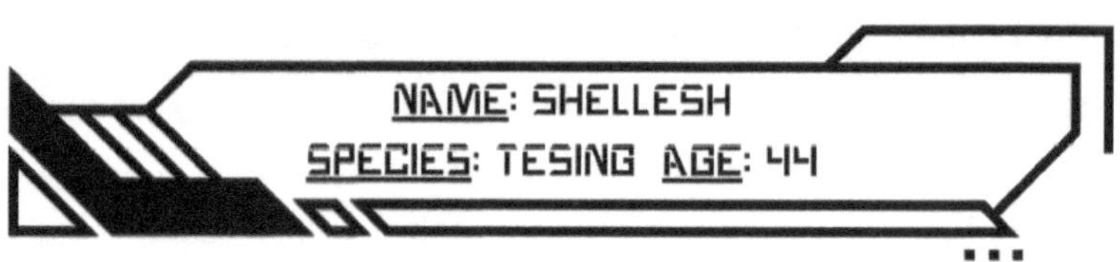


Shellesh sat slumped forward in his seat, resting his head on his hands. His eyes were half-lidded, his disinterest clear as if he was too busy brooding or too exhausted to care. However, Wyn's eyes slid past his expression and posture and instead focused on his exposed skin. Every tesing he had seen up to that point (which, to be fair, had not been very many despite how populous a species they were in the galaxy) had skin of bright colors. Reds, blues, greens, and purples. The color didn't matter, but they sparkled as if their skin was made of gems. Shellesh was dull by comparison. His scales were a mixture of white and gray that sucked in the light and lazily spilled it back out. There was no sparkle, no luster. His eyes seemed to lack the characteristic shimmer as well, a muted gray color that reminded Wyn more of a wilted flower petal than a sparkling crystal. He had a strange white pattern around his eyes that Wyn hadn't noticed others having either.

"Are you sure you want me here?" Shellesh asked, even his voice sounding devoid of emotion, the words grinding against each other like gravel.

"I already told you, Shell," Sage said. "You're a perfect fit for the team. There's a spot on it if you want it."

Wyn had given up trying to tell Sage she couldn't just give the spots to the people she asked. He was now just resigned that everyone on her list would get in with or without his input.

"And you?" Shellesh asked, his flat, gray eyes gliding to Wyn, who was glancing out the window. He blinked and straightened up, taking a moment to register the question.

"Yeah, I'm fine with you here." He glanced at Sage, but her expression gave nothing away. Then he smirked and added, "Not like I could stop Sage from inviting whomever she wants."

"You're learning," Sage said, a corner of her mouth rising a hair.

"No," Shellesh said, not loud or angry, but so sudden it pulled all of Wyn's attention back to the strangely-colored tesing. "I refuse that answer. She hasn't explained, has she?"

Now Wyn was very lost. He tried to connect that question with anything else that had been said and looked to Sage, who seemed to be glaring at Shellesh. "What?"

"Some of Shellesh's people don't much care for him. Some loud mouths might try to cause trouble, but it will be all bluster and no force."

"Some?" Shellesh's lazy gaze sharpened into a glare.

"It doesn't matter, Shell. Your people suck ass," Sage said. "Anyways, Wyn here just joined the galactic ecosystem like two weeks ago. He's not going to understand the delicate political nature of your situation well enough, so he'd take my advice. And my advice is that we're far better with you on this team than without."

"What?" Wyn asked again. He was quickly losing all traction on this conversation.

"Is this true?" Shellesh asked Wyn. "You hold her advice that highly?"

Wyn looked between the two. Sage glared at him, and Shellesh maintained that same blank stare. "Sage isn't wrong. I grew up in an isolated human colony. Contact with other species was severely limited to the point that I hadn't met a non-human species until I left. My father never even let me meet any of his few alien clients either. I hired Sage to be my voice of reason in all things related to bounty hunting, but I think that extends to knowledge of the R.C. as well. If she's that sincere about your position on the team, I would take her advice wholeheartedly."

"It would be my honor to represent your company as a hunter. I shall request an addendum to my contract that allows you to release me from it at any point you deem necessary."

"I don't think we'll need that," Wyn said.

"I will request it anyway. A safeguard, whether it gets used or not, is still helpful."

"I understand." Wyn did not understand anything. "Welcome aboard!"

Shellesh thanked them, then slipped from the room. Sage relaxed back in her seat, sipping from a freshly filled drink.

"What was that all about?" Wyn asked.

"Don't worry about it. Just Shellesh being Shellesh."

"Yeah, but his people don't like him? Why?"

"Something with his history. I don't like to pry. He's great though. Let's just move on to the next person, and we can talk about it more later."

"Right. Next is Carac. He's a tesing bounty hunter as well, tons of experience, and—"

"Wait, a tesing?"

"Yeah, why?"

The door slid open and a very angry tesing stormed in.

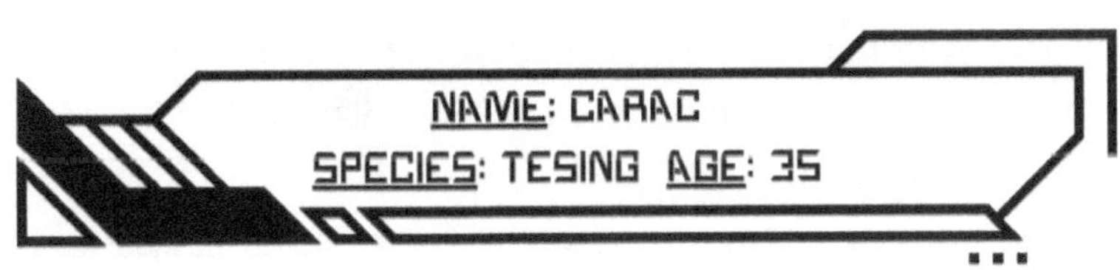


Wyn jumped in his seat, and Sage clutched a pistol (a new, unmelted one) but didn't draw it. A tesing, scales sparkling golden yellow like the sun, strode into the room.

"Why is there a dirty exile here?" he shouted, slamming a hand down on the table.

"You're Carac?" Wyn asked.

"You'll want to watch your fucking mouth before I seal it shut with a plasma bolt," Sage said, her voice deadly calm. Wyn shivered from the pure malice radiating off her at that moment. The pistol was drawn but kept low under the table, out of sight.

"I will speak about my people how I like," Carac, for that was who Wyn presumed this man to be, growled back. "Now, are you hiring that exile?"

"Yes," Sage said, returning the deep golden stare with unmatched intensity.

"Then you can throw away my application. I refuse to work with garbage like that."

Sage was out of her chair in a flash, pistol raised to his head. Carac's hand flew to his side, then Sage fired. The bolt skimmed the tesing's cheek, and he froze, hand halfway to his own weapon.

"I told you to watch your fucking mouth."

"Wait!" Wyn jumped to his feet, gaze flicking between the two. "Let's just talk this out, okay? I would rather not have anyone end up dead in my building before I even start my business." Wyn forced a chuckle, an attempt to make the situation lighter than it was. It absolutely did not work.

Carac glanced at him. "Then I don't recommend hiring exile trash if you don't want bodies." He looked back to Sage and ran a finger along his chin. "Harborer." He spit the word out like an insult, then turned and left the room. Thankfully, Sage didn't shoot him for either his words or his gestures.

When the tesing was gone, Sage dropped back into her chair, pistol holstered, and sipped from her glass as if nothing had happened.

"What the fuck?" Wyn asked, every nerve in his body vibrating intensely.

"Told you already, most tesings suck ass. He just proved my point."

"What is an exile?"

"Oh, yeah. So, Shellesh is an exile, and that's why his people don't like him."

"What does it mean? Why is he exiled?"

"You know how some species have a death penalty for severe crimes?"

"Yeah." Wyn's gut roiled at where this conversation was going.

"Tesings don't because they're all high and mighty. Instead, they just exile their worst criminals. They put them through some chemical sterilization treatment that bleeds the color from their skin and makes them infertile so they can't spread their evil on to the next generation. Pretty fucked up, to be honest. I'd rather someone just kill me than put me through that shit."

Wyn felt bile at the back of his throat. "We just hired a branded criminal who committed horrific crimes?"

Sage waggled a finger at Wyn. "Now that's just stereotyping! He's only considered a criminal by his people, and as we've discussed, his people suck ass."

"What were his crimes?"

"Don't know, I never asked. Seems pretty private, right? Feels rude to make him relive that traumatic experience."

Wyn threw his hands up, anxiety coursing through him, sending him pacing up and down the table. "Sage, he could be a mass murderer for all we know. What if his mere presence destroys the reputation of this company?"

"Oh, I doubt that his crime is murder," Sage said. "As long as I've known him, he's never killed a single person. I've seen him almost die because he refused to kill. You might have trouble getting tesing contracts, but that's whatever. Plenty of other species in the galaxy."

"Tesings are one of the most populous and widespread species *in* the galaxy."

"Yeah, but I've found only the heart of their government is really into all that anti-exile business. The outlying colonies or the ones living in mixed-species environments usually aren't prone to that religious indoctrination. Which is how you know that exile business is total shit."

Wyn stopped and rubbed his hands across his face, panic and fury beginning an all-out war within his chest.

"Relax, Wyn," Sage said. "Besides, Shellesh is giving you a way to get rid of him if there's any trouble, remember?"

Wyn took a deep breath. She was right. Shellesh's clause gave him an out. And Carac had been pretty rude. Maybe Shellesh was the right call. If Sage thought so, he had to be. Right?

"Let's just focus on who's next," Sage said.

Wyn sat down and pulled up the list, trying to pull his brain away from Shellesh and the problems of the future. "A woman named Chandriss."

Chandriss glided into the room, flowing with the ease of water down a stream. She wore an easy smile set beneath a pair of radiant purple eyes. Long red hair cascaded down her back like lava from a volcano. Her lipstick matched, striking against her pale skin, and it drew Wyn's eyes.

Sage took one look and scoffed, perhaps assuming she was yet another failed pick. But Wyn took many looks and disagreed. A silence stretched until Sage kicked him. He jerked in his seat, coughed into a hand, and repositioned himself, pulling his eyes elsewhere.

Then pulling them away from there as well.

"Looks like you have an extensive background in bounty hunting," Wyn said as he fiddled with his Vico, bringing up her application. "Would you be able to tell us a bit about your last bounty or one that stood out to you?"

"Oh, I would love to," she said, her voice like sickly sweet music to Wyn's ears. She leaned forward on the table, resting her head against one hand and sighing. "This one was about a thief. I don't really remember his name, I'm very bad with those, but he was some small-time crook until a burglary went bad and an old man ended up dead. Nothing you don't hear a hundred times over in this business, but he ended up with a bounty. Must have been a rich old man too, because it was a pretty decent bounty.

"The thing with small-time crooks is they haven't learned to ditch their lives yet. I was given an identity through the bounty, and from there I was able to track down his family. My contact told me he still visited his mother and grandmother regularly. If anyone knew where he was hiding, they would."

"Clever use of research," Sage admitted.

"My thoughts exactly, and even better, his grandmother had moved in with his mother, so everyone was gathered together." She smiled prettily at Sage's nod. "So I started with the grandmother."

"Questioning her?" Wyn asked.

"Oh no, I tortured her. Never start with questions, then they know what you want. Wait until they're begging you, willing to give you anything, before you ask questions."

"What?" Wyn and Sage asked simultaneously.

Chandriss chuckled. "I had her screaming in moments, the mother bawling as she watched."

"You tortured an old lady?" Sage asked, a dangerous growl in her throat.

"And her daughter, yes." Chandriss nodded with enthusiasm, still smiling. "It didn't last long, unfortunately. He was hiding in the house and couldn't take those screams." She sighed. "It was music to my ears."

Sage's hands lowered, and Wyn suspected she was reaching for her pistol. Wyn couldn't blame her. He wished he had a gun too. And that he could shoot it straight. His stomach roiled within him, and he wanted nothing more than to be away from the psychotic woman, but he was also terrified to say the wrong thing.

"I killed him when he showed up. Sure, a death merits a penalty on the payout, but it's so much cleaner than keeping them alive. Plus, I didn't want him to tell the bounty office that I tortured his family. I mean, that's why I wore the mask, obviously." She chuckled as if she were telling a joke, then brushed a strand of hair from her face. She looked out the window with fondness as she continued talking. "After that, I just brought the body to the bounty office, and they paid out."

"Thank you, Chandriss," Sage said. "We will be in touch within the next day if we decide to move forward with your application."

"Wonderful!" She reached out her hands and grabbed Wyn's before he could jerk it away. "Thank you sooo much." Wyn wondered if he would have vomited in that moment if he hadn't emptied his stomach not long ago. Instead, he nodded.

She rose from the chairs, waved to them, then turned to walk out of the room. Once the door shut, Sage turned to Wyn, her face dark with fury.

"I *told* you your open invitation would lead to some freaks. You were supposed to filter the list. Instead, we end up with someone going through a midlife crisis and this psycho bitch."

"How was I supposed to know she tortured people and delighted in killing? She didn't exactly put that down in her application."

"That's what a fucking background check is for."

"Clearly, that wouldn't have caught anything if she's getting away with it." Short, shallow, insufficient breaths pulsed through Wyn. He ran a hand through his sweat-soaked hair. "Fuck! Is she going to retaliate if we say no?"

"She'll probably retaliate if she gets the chance," Sage said, rising from her seat. "I alerted Chrysanax security and sent them a recording of the conversation. They're going to arrest her on her way out."

"What the fuck? You couldn't have them arrest her elsewhere? She's obviously going to attach it to us."

"Probably, but I couldn't risk her getting away. Want to watch?"

"Yes."

A minute later, Sage and Wyn stood by the window down the hall that faced out the front of the building and watched as two Peacekeepers dragged Chandriss between them to a vehicle. She kicked and screamed but failed to break free. Wyn's stomach still felt sick, but his mood improved when she was tossed into the back of the shuttle and taken away.

"Please tell me the next is one of mine," Sage said. "I don't know if I can handle another one of yours."

"You think that's bad? I can't handle *either* of ours." He sighed and pulled up the list on his Vico. Then he sighed again, closing his eyes. "It's one of mine."

"Fuck."

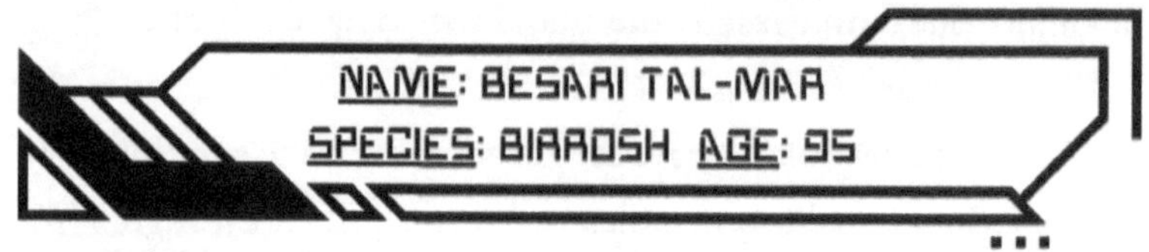


Wyn had hoped more than anything that Besari Tal-Mar would be someone normal. Someone that would not strike the nerves of his anxiety. Someone without surprises and capable of an easy conversation, even if she wasn't a good fit for Bounty Inc.

The birrosh woman sat across from them in a fully-sealed atmospheric combat suit, her face hidden behind the tinted mask of her helmet. The combat armor was light, allowing for a lot of flexibility, and perfectly fitted to her body, which was surprisingly human-like. Two arms, two legs, two breasts, no tail. She could have almost been mistaken for a human.

"You can take that off if you want," Sage said. "It's breathable for a bishett."

"I'm a birrosh," Besari corrected, her voice transferring clearly through a speaker on her helmet.

"Right, aren't they pretty much the same?"

"Well, we have different skin colors..."

"Does that change your ability to breathe?"

"No, but it's fine. This is for my clan. We always hide our faces from all except those we trust the most."

"That's a shame," Wyn said, a little more disappointed than he had meant it to be. Besari and Sage both looked at him, and he felt his face melting beneath their glance. "I meant with being stuck in her suit, is all! Must be kind of lonely always having that between you and everyone else you talk to."

Besari shrugged. "You get used to it."

Sage still looked at Wyn, eyebrow crooked, so he powered forward, leaving all embarrassment in the dust. "Is that your typical combat armor? Seems pretty light."

"It's the best my planet has to offer, actually. The mesh is much more resilient than it seems and allows for the best flexibility. Not to mention the thinness of the armor helps for my Thresha talent. My trainer always said, it doesn't matter what armor you have if you never get hit." Besari chuckled, then let it die out when no one reciprocated.

Sage sat, arms crossed, unamused.

Wyn's brows knit in confusion, too focused on something she said to politely laugh at her joke. "Thresha talent?"

Sage sighed, deep and resigned. "You've got to be fucking kidding me," she mumbled. Wyn looked over, and she pulled a hand away from her face and glared back. "You don't have one, do you?"

Wyn wracked his brain, trying to think of any special talents he possessed that might be worth mentioning. In the end, he didn't think any of them fit the bill for something so specially named. "I don't think so?"

"You don't think so?" Sage's eyebrows rose, and Besari chuckled. Wyn cringed, feeling the fool. "You don't think you've had regular injections of a weird goop that caused you intense cramping? Injected over months if not years to slowly acclimate your body to a new formation, allowing it to go above and beyond what it should ever be able to do? You're not sure if you have some ability no one else does?"

Sage held a fist out and a strange liquid seeped from the pores, then solidified instantly, encasing her hand in rock. She slammed it to the table, exploding the coating into dust and creating a sunburst with her fist at the center. Wyn's eyes ballooned as he watched it happen.

"I can turn invisible with mine," Besari added. Then faded from sight completely.

Whatever "normal" Wyn had hoped for had been completely shattered. He was glad there were only two more interviews to come.

"I think I can be reasonably certain I do not have super powers," Wyn said. Besari flickered back into view, a soft melodic chuckle emanating from her helmet's speaker.

"How did this not come up until now?" Sage shook her head.

"You're saying I can just get powers with a few injections?"

"Not a few," Sage emphasized. "You need them for months, if not longer. Usually you get them when you're a teenager, at least, humans do, letting your body develop with them. Assuming you can afford them, which it sounds like you should have."

"Well, Terrask is pretty human-centric. They might not be big fans of putting weird goo inside of themselves to change."

"Which puts us in a bind, given we don't have years to acclimate your body."

"You could try a tank," Besari said.

"Is that how the birrosh do it?" Sage asked.

"Yeah, one awful night and it's over."

"Your kind is more sturdy than humans, though. It might be too dangerous for Wyn."

"Wait, what?" Wyn asked.

"Conversation for another day," Sage cut him off before he could get started. "Let's just wrap up these interviews."

"Right." Wyn rubbed at his neck as he looked at Besari's application. "It says here you just started a few months ago and already completed three bounties."

"That is correct. Though some were with the assistance of a mentor while still on Ashaine. She ran me through a few bounties to prepare me. At least until my parents found out."

"They didn't approve of you being a bounty hunter?" Sage asked.

"No, they had other plans for me. Which is why I'm here."

"Strange." Sage studied Besari closely, as if trying to see past her armor. "I've known birrosh to be usually quite open, rarely restricting their children's choices. That sounds more bishett."

Besari stiffened in her seat. Though Wyn couldn't read her face, he expected it wasn't all that happy. He'd have to research more about these cultures. He was missing something.

"If I were bishett, I wouldn't be *able* to leave my family," Besari said, her voice clearly strained by the direction of the conversation. "My mother is just a bit overprotective."

"I understand getting out from under your family," Wyn chimed in, worried Sage would become more antagonistic. "That's why I'm here too."

"You have an overbearing mother?"

"Had. And it was my father. He's dead now. I commend your bravery in standing up to your parents before they're dead, though."

Besari seemed to stare at him for a moment, her head tilting. When she spoke, the tension was gone, replaced by a happy, bright tone. "Thank you, Wyn."

"Which is why a spot is open for you if you want it."

"What?" Sage spun on Wyn, but he ignored her.

"I want this company to represent the freedom it gave me, and if it gives you that freedom too, then we think you'll be a perfect fit."

"We?" Sage hissed in a whisper. Wyn felt his insides chilling but stared straight ahead, resigned to hold on to his resolve.

"Oh! That would be wonderful. I promise not to be dead weight. I've been trained well in many forms of birrosh combat and will be an asset to you."

"I'm sure you will be," Sage grumbled. "We'll be in contact within the day."

"Thank you," Besari said before rising from the chair and leaving the room, her steps a little more energetic than they had been on the way in. Wyn's eyes slid down her back—

Sage whacked Wyn on the back of the head, and he turned to face her. Then regretted it.

"What happened to inviting people we both agree on?" she said after the door closed and Besari was out of earshot.

"You invited an apparent war criminal without telling me the details beforehand. I think I get one choice that is mine."

"Shellesh's crimes had *nothing* to do with war. I think." Sage's brow crinkled in thought, then she waved the issue away, her hands flapping. "Anyway, this is just because you like her ass."

Wyn blushed. "Not just her ass!" Then he turned crimson. "I mean, not her ass. I like other things about her. She seems willing to commit to the company, and she has field experience."

"She's lying."

"About what?"

Her eyes squinted in thought. "I don't know yet."

"Does it matter? Even if she doesn't have a ton of experience, didn't you say it would be best for me to learn with someone else? She's the closest to my experience, and maybe we could push each other to be better."

"You're closer in skill to that Jefferson guy. I don't believe she was lying about her combat training."

"Exactly! So she'll be helpful!"

Sage rolled her eyes. "Whatever, kid. You want to hire your little crush, that's fine. At least this one doesn't torture grandmas."

"I didn't know about the grandma thing!" Wyn was sure at some point his cheeks would turn a permanent red. "And I didn't choose them because of looks! Their applications didn't come with pictures."

Sage chuckled and punched him on the arm. "Relax, it's nice to see you broadening your horizons past humans. Soon, you'll be at a multi-species orgy having the time of your life."

"Who's next?" Wyn squeaked.

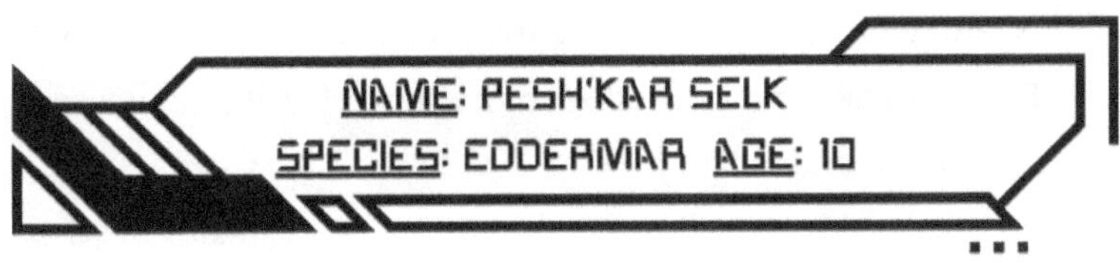


Exhaustion pulled at Wyn's limbs, emotions flared then died, his brain was simply a constant hum, and he had stopped blinking quite so often. And so when Pesh'kar Selk walked into the room, he had nothing left to give to his anxiety and discomfort and instead lazily looked up at the creature and said, "Oh."

Pesh was an eddermar, a species that had previously escaped Wyn's limited awareness. To compare them to anything else was difficult. They were not mammalian or reptilian, but insectile.

Not like Achtrek, but a single large being. They had eight evenly-spaced-apart limbs, but with their body bent at the segment where abdomen met thorax, it gave them the strange appearance of having four arms and four legs. Their abdomen was bulbous, carried by thick legs, whereas the thorax was thinner, the arms longer and more agile. At the very top, perhaps reaching Wyn's chest, sat a small, elongated head with carapace reaching back like dull spikes. Two clusters of eyes sat below green and yellow markings at the center of their forehead. A mouth was hidden behind two protruding pincers that clicked as they talked. They wore no clothing except the strappings to hold weaponry, so Wyn could easily see the extensive brown markings across the otherwise pale body.

To Wyn's surprise, when Pesh spoke, they needed no help to form words like falvians did. "Hello, Sage. It's wonderful to see you again."

"As with you, Pesh." Sage stood and took two of Pesh's three-fingered hands in her own in a gesture of welcome that Wyn concluded must be eddermarian.

Wyn opened his mouth to speak, but instead a small, surprised squeak came out. Not one of shock or disturbance, but instead one of joy as one of the most adorable little creatures he'd ever seen came floating into the room, their body inflated like a balloon, long, limp legs dangling below it. Dark green tendrils draped down its back like fur, reaching a flat tail that flicked back and forth to propel it forward much like a fish swimming. Its skin softened to a chartreuse on its underside. Two large, pure white eyes stared at Wyn, then it trilled softly, losing air as it did so and dropping in height.

"They like you," Pesh said as the creature floated in front of Wyn.

"May I?" Wyn asked, holding up one hand ready to pet. Pesh nodded, and he stroked his fingers through the forest of tendrils on their back. They purred as their eyes closed, softly deflating until they were barely larger than Wyn's hand. "Who is this?"

"Skritch, my gridder companion," Pesh said. "We've been bonded since I was young, and they help me on all my hunts."

"Speaking of which," Wyn said as he brought up the application, careful not to disturb the gridder. "I think there was a mistake on the application. It says here you're ten years old."

"That is correct."

"What?" Wyn looked over at Sage, eyebrows arched. "We can't take on a kid."

"I am not a child," Pesh said.

"Wyn, different species age differently," Sage explained. "Eddermar reach maturity by around age four."

"Not all of us," Pesh said. "I still have yet to find mine." They made a strange clicking noise that might have been laughter.

"If you haven't found it yet, you never will," Sage said with a chuckle. "I know from experience."

"That's so strange." Getting used to different ages was going to be difficult.

"You didn't seem so bothered when you were attracted to Besari. She's ninety-five."

"She's *ninety-five*?" Wyn exclaimed. "And she was still being controlled by her mother?"

"She has probably just reached the age of maturity," Sage said. "Birrosh and bishett age much slower than we do. Pesh here's the opposite. They age much faster."

"Huh." His mind raced in circles instead of making any progress. He shook himself out of the cycle and tried again. "Well, is there anything of interest you'd like to bring up that you can offer Bounty Inc.?"

Sage scoffed, and Wyn shot her a glare.

"I can spew flammable bile if you need anything burned in a hurry," Pesh said.

Wyn's hand paused over Skritch, who gave him a toothless nibble in protest. "Is that your Thresha talent?"

"No, that is a natural talent to all eddermar. We cannot take on a Thresha solution. It does not meld to our genes effectively."

"Well, that's pretty cool either way."

"Oh, shut up, Wyn," Sage said, leaning forward. "Pesh will be a great help to this team. There's no reason not to invite them aboard." She turned to the eddermar and nodded. "You're in if you want in."

"I find the idea of working as a team interesting. I would not have thought to find you heading such an organization."

"Technically, we don't ever have to work as a team, but we allow the ability to do so."

"Ah, that is even better. Not many keep up with me for bounties. If I can still work primarily solo, I would be happy to assist you, Sage Valen."

"You won't regret it," Sage said, then smiled. "Or maybe you will. I'm not terribly confident about this whole endeavor."

Pesh collected Skritch, and the two left, to Wyn's dismay. He needed to find a way to bond a gridder himself.

"You okay?" Sage studied him as Wyn bit back a yawn.

"Just exhausted. Let's hurry up through this last one. He's probably going to be terrible."

"Young, human. He can't be too fucked up yet. But with a name like Sepharian Clemens, who knows."

"Hello, Sepharian, right?"

"Yeah, you can call me Seph." Seph turned out to be a gangly kid with a mop of dirty blond, curly hair draping down around his ears. His face was drowning in a sea of freckles, and his eyes had a tinge of red to them as if he hadn't slept well. He scratched at a cheek as he looked nervously back and forth between Wyn and Sage. He was not very promising.

"Can you talk about what kind of experience you've had for bounties?"

"Bounties?" Seph asked. "Like, bounty hunting?"

Wyn paused for a moment, studying the other boy to see if there was some joke he had missed. "Yes, bounty hunting. What's your experience?"

"Oh." He looked back and forth and scratched at his cheek again. "Um, none?"

Sage and Wyn shared a look, Sage's glare fresh on her face. Wyn remembered her promise of murder and swallowed as he turned back. "Well, do you have combat experience? Weapons experience?"

"Oh, no, none at all. Well, except this one time I got punched at a bus stop."

Wyn stared agape, and Sage leaned over and in a harsh tone whispered, "I thought you said he graded well in your stupid ranking system."

"He did," Wyn whispered back. He brought up the application and saw the markings next to it indicating the ranking placement the algorithm had given. "He ranked better than your candidates, see? He's number one."

Sage turned on the young boy, whose eyes had widened as they'd whispered. "Did you lie on your application, Seph?"

"No, ma'am." He shook his head wildly, locks of hair flapping back and forth.

"Why are you here? You have no bounty hunting experience, and you applied for a role that requires it."

"I didn't know it required bounty hunting experience! It didn't say so." Sage turned her look back on Wyn, the words behind her eyes implanting themselves into Wyn's head directly. He was *sure* he had required bounty hunting experience, and his program should have caught and dismissed anyone who'd applied without it. Seph, not recognizing the silent conversation, continued on. "I'm just here because my da told me to get a job or get out of the house, to be honest. I didn't want to be homeless, and this seemed an easy enough job."

"You think being a bounty hunter sounds easy?" Sage asked.

"No, ma'am, but the ad said you were looking for an assistant."

"A what?"

"Oh." Wyn pulled up the application again and looked at it closer. "He's applying for the assistant position, not to be a hunter."

"What assistant position?"

"Well, I figured it'd be nice to have someone here while I'm out on bounties and to handle some of the smaller tasks to free my time."

Sage stood and walked out of the room without another word.

"Um," Seph said, staring at the retreating bounty hunter. "Do I still need bounty hunting experience?"

"No, you're good," Wyn said. "You're also the only one who applied, so the job's yours."

"Really?"

"Yeah. Can you start tomorrow? We can go over the schedule and such. It should be pretty relaxed, but it would be nice to have you here whenever possible for calls."

"Yeah, I have nothing going on."

"Great, you know the way out?"

"Sure."

Wyn nodded, then got up and left. He needed to find Sage to determine their final choices.

"Sage!" Wyn shouted as he knocked on her door.

"Wyn, I swear to the seven empyreans that I will kill you if you don't leave me alone."

"We still need to pick people."

The door slid open and an irate Sage stared down at Wyn. "All mine."

"Minus Mecillis."

"Yes, and plus that A.I."

"And Besari."

"Sure, whatever, but that's everyone."

"That's only six people." Wyn ran a hand through his hair. "Should we bring on more?"

"Start small, test things out, then grow. Too many moving pieces will cause it to collapse."

"Well, that Jefferson guy seemed really interested. How much could it hurt to have him along?"

"A lot," Sage growled. "You can have either Jefferson or Besari, your choice."

"Besari it is."

"That's what I thought."

"We should also talk about weapons requisition."

"No, just order the list I sent you. What we should be talking about is you getting a Thresha talent."

"What? Is that necessary? I read an article that said it can really mess with you."

"When did you read an article? You just learned what that was."

"I read it between interviews," Wyn muttered.

"Messing you up is the fucking point. It's meant to change your body so it's stronger. Do you think you could ever, no matter how much you trained, take on Zetta?"

Wyn shrugged. "With a big enough gun, I would think so?"

"Big guns move too slow. She'd tear you apart. When Zetta and I spar, we're evenly matched, thanks to my talent. That's not even considering the criminals you'll run into who have been modified. Going out there handicapped as you are is a liability. It will end up with you dead."

"Well, I guess I could take those injections."

"You're going to waste a year of your life juggling injections and running this company? Unable to take on bounties because you haven't adjusted?"

"Well, preferably not."

"A tank is the only option, but we need to do it right away."

"Why's it so important to do it quickly? I won't be ready to go bounty hunting for a few more months anyway."

"Because there's a chance you'll die. If you do, I'm not carrying on your legacy, so the less I have invested the better."

"You want me to rush this because I might die and waste your time."

"Yeah."

Wyn gaped like a fish.

"Good news, though," Sage continued. "That Boz-kai contractor you hired has a nestling who will do tank Thresha infusion. Thought it would be harder to find them, but given the cross-species arrangements here, I guess not. Weird that a falvian has one, given their species can't handle Thresha."

"When did you even find that out?"

"I looked it up between interviews."

"But I haven't even agreed to it. I could *die*."

"You have until tomorrow." Sage patted him on the shoulder. "But I think your dream is dead if you don't do it. Or at least postponed for a long time. Now, if you don't mind, Zetta, Pesh, and I are grabbing food at a fabulous cross-species diner in the Pit." She moved Wyn aside with a celuein grip and stepped into the hallway. Then stopped. Wyn turned and saw why.

Seph slunk backwards out of a room into the hallway, mumbling to himself, then turned and saw them. He jumped and turned crimson. "Oh, hi."

"What are you doing?" Sage asked.

"I got lost, tried to look for the stairs."

"They're right there." Wyn pointed down the hallway to where the stairs spiraled up and down the building.

"Oh! Strange. I thought I came out of a door when I got up here."

"I can walk you out." Wyn sighed as Sage walked away, then turned to Seph. "Have you had dinner yet?"

"Nope, but I'm starving."

"Me too. Let's find something good to eat while I decide if I want to maybe die."

Wyn piloted his new hopper toward an upper-level parking structure in the main city of Chrysanax, referred to, more often than not, as the Pit. Which was such a small name for a massive undertaking. The city existed within an excavated hole, its diameter far enough that Wyn could barely make out the ends as the hopper dropped down into the city. Streets and structures latticed from one end of the hole to the other, endlessly descending until it popped out the other side of the moon. The city became a web spun by its citizens, suspended over a boundless drop. It was enough to make Wyn's hands sweat on the controls as he brought it in for a landing. He preferred some nice, sturdy ground like out by his building to this. But it was still a sight to see every time he returned.

Seph knew of a restaurant on the second level, so they took a lift and then a taxi to reach their destination and found seats along the edge of a bustling square. Thousands of people walked along a strip of shops, carrying their purchases in hovercarts that floated behind them. Protective shields over the top prevented thefts. Their food came as Wyn watched the crowd undulate unnaturally.

Wyn ate a dish of mixed vegetables, grains, and meats he had never heard of and talked quietly with his new assistant. He had taken the time to detail a few of the expected tasks, and Seph followed along with ease.

"I'll still want to approve requisitions," Wyn said between bites, "but I figured they could submit a form through you, and I could approve or deny it."

"Yes, Mr. Kelda."

"And I'll need you to reach out to the private hangar nearby, see if they're amenable to letting us use it for the company vehicles."

"Yes, Mr. Kelda."

"You don't have to call me that. Just Wyn is fine."

"Understood, Mr. Kelda."

Wyn sighed and poured a little more of the sauce onto his dish. He wasn't sure what it was, but it was savory with a hint of spice and enhanced the elements of his dish quite well. Either way, it wasn't a bowl of goo, and that was a vast improvement.

"What do you think I should do, Seph? Should I risk dying and do this tank injection thing or just always be at a handicap?"

"Oh, I don't think I'm able to answer something like that, Mr. Kelda." Seph scratched at a cheek nervously. "That sounds like a lot of responsibility, and I'm a bit allergic to responsibility."

"Well, I'll try not to give you too much then."

"Thank you, Mr. Kelda."

Wyn ate in silence after that, until someone else broke it.

"Hello, Wyn."

Wyn's mind jumped back into his body from wherever it had been wandering off to, and he turned to the newcomer. Besari stood across the half wall, takeout from a local restaurant in one hand.

"Oh, hello, Besari!"

"Thanks again for the interview." She looped the bag through one arm and rubbed a pair of gloved hands together.

Wyn set his food down and brushed a napkin across his mouth, hoping nothing was on his face, then he stood up and smiled at Besari. "You're welcome, and I suppose since you're here, I can give you the good news in person. We selected you as one of the six candidates for Bounty Inc."

Besari's body stiffened. Instead of excitement or cheerfulness, she seemed nervous. Unsure.

"Wyn." Her voice was a low hum through the helmet's speakers. "I don't know if I can take the position."

"What? Why not?" Wyn felt his stomach drop and tried to shake himself out of it. Why should he care so much if she joined?

"My application was dishonest, and most of my bounties were my mentor's. We modified the name attached so it looked like I had more experience than I do. I have the training I mentioned, but I don't have the experience you were looking for. I...I had my reasons, but I feel wrong lying to you."

"Oh, is that all?" Wyn shrugged. "I don't have any experience either, *and* I don't have the training. Sage is helping with the training, and you're more than welcome to join us."

"But, you don't know anything about me. Why would you still take me on?"

"Why not? I need to take risks if I want the company to succeed. Plus, I like you." Wyn's face flared at his words, and he choked on saliva, then coughed. "I mean I liked you more than the other people," he choked out. "You also seem great as a person, so I like you there. Like, you seem great." Wyn rubbed a hand across his face and let out one more defeated cough. Seph comforted him with a pat on the arm.

A soft chuckle came from Besari, and she held a hand up to her helmet, her shoulders quivering with joy. "Thank you, Wyn. I like you too. If you still want me, I'd be happy to take you up on your offer."

"Wonderful. Do you have a place to stay yet? You can stay with me if you don't." Then again Wyn cursed himself for his words and stumbled to explain. "I mean, at Bounty Inc.! There's a bunch of dorms there for everyone, free of charge. I didn't mean with me specifically."

"I don't actually. That would be great."

"We were just about to head back, right, Seph?"

"Oh, I was going to go home if that's alright, Mr. Kelda."

"Yeah, of course," Wyn said as his head drowned in a sea no one else could see. He had hoped for Seph as a buffer, his senses becoming rather haywire when it came to Besari. He'd just have to breathe deep and do his best. "I have a shuttle if you want a ride back."

"Sure." Besari nodded, cradling her food in her hands.

"I'll be going," Seph said as he grabbed his and Wyn's trash to toss.

"It was nice to meet you, Seph," Besari said. "Are you a bounty hunter too?"

"Just an assistant, miss."

Wyn closed his eyes and mentally slammed his head against a wall. He had completely forgotten to introduce them. He couldn't think straight, and his tongue betrayed him at every step. He needed to get back in his room, away from others, before he made a worse mistake.

Seph said his farewells and left, then Wyn and Besari made their way to the port where he had parked his shuttle. He had intended to keep quiet the entire way, not wanting to make things more sour than they already were. But a thought needled at him, always at the front of his mind, always worrying him.

"You did the Thresha tank infusion?" Wyn asked, feeling short of breath just asking the question.

"Yeah, all birrosh and bishett do. As your partner said, our bodies are a bit more sturdy, so it's easier for us to handle it in one go. And saves a lot of time that way."

"Was it bad?"

"Horrible. One of the worst experiences I've ever had."

"Would you do it again, knowing what you do?"

"Yes," Besari answered with no hesitation. "My talent is a vital part of my combat. It makes me *me*, and I am forever grateful for that."

"Even if there was a chance you could die?"

"There's a chance we could die on every bounty. Why would the tank be any different? If I'm not ready to face death, I'm not ready to face combat. But I know I would want every advantage I could get when it came to combat. Wouldn't you?"

"Yes." Wyn stopped, a stream of people splitting around him as Besari turned to face him. He closed his eyes and took in the sounds. He might die tomorrow, but he had to understand he might die whenever. How was this any different? He had to face it with the same courage he hoped to take to the battlefield some day. "I'm ready."

"Welcome to Bounty Inc." Wyn raised his hands and waited for applause that never came. Eight people (or rather seven people and a swarm of beetles) and a gridder stared blankly at him. Wyn paced in front of the large display within the lounge, wiping sweat from his brow with the back of his hand. "Well, today marks the first day of Bounty Inc., and you all should have received your contracts from L-Bot. Are there any questions?"

"We get this ten percent you're skimming from us back, right?" Zetta spoke, always a hair louder than the next person in the room, as if even volume was a competition for her. She shifted awkwardly in the humanoid-made chair, her tail sticking up the back. "That was the deal?"

"Yes, as a first-year bonus we will be reimbursing that ten percent for any hunters who complete the entire year of the contract with us. We will only be taking a temporary cut to test out the process, but that bonus is a thank you for helping get the company going."

"The bonus will only be for the first year? And we are free to leave after a year?" Pesh sat on the floor, legs curled under them. Skritch floated nearby, slowly rotating in the air, squeaking at every completed rotation.

"Yes and yes. The idea would be to create a sustaining model based on taking a cut. Which might not be ideal to hunters such as yourself, but I will be spending this year finding a way to make it worthwhile. We'll have an armory, vehicles, and other useful equipment. And we're always looking to learn more about what would be helpful, so feel free to pass on any ideas you have."

"Armory?" Zetta asked, her eyes widening, burning red pits staring out with hunger. "You're definitely getting that slag cannon, right?"

"Why does everyone ask for one of those?"

"Because they're cool."

"It's the most important item on the requisition list, Wyn," Sage said, perched on a chair near the front. Most of the others had found spots on the couches and chairs comfortably enough. Wyn had already placed orders for vrolak and eddermar friendly furniture, but it hadn't arrived in time for the meeting.

"If it's really a big deal, I can put the order in."

"I think it would be cool," Besari said.

Sage snapped her fingers and pointed at Besari. "I knew I wanted you on this team for a reason."

"The odds of a slag cannon coming in use seems very unlikely," Cee said, its soft blue eyes glowing as it stood to the edge of the crowd. "It seems a waste of funds that could be allocated elsewhere."

"You on the other hand barely made it," Sage growled.

"I apologize, Ms. Valen. If you see a use for it that I do not, I would be happy to learn about it."

"There is a vital use," Pesh said. "It's because it's cool."

"Agreed," Zetta said.

"I think it'd be cool too," Seph said. "Though I don't really know what it is."

"You don't get a vote, Seph," Wyn butted into the conversation before it got too out of hand. "You're never going to use it."

"Oh, right."

"Requisition requests can be submitted to Seph, L-Bot, or myself for more weapons. I have a base order form from Sage to get it stocked, but feel free to fill one out yourselves, and I will order whatever seems appropriate."

"Probably all Imburlii," Zetta grunted.

"They're objectively the best brand," Sage said, seemingly retreading old arguments.

"Koestocks are far more powerful."

"And ridiculously inefficient. You have fewer shots before the cartridge runs out, and it uses it so poorly they're always left with a tiny, unusable charge."

"Count doesn't matter if your target is dead after the first shot."

"What about bounties we're directly contacted for?" Achtrek interrupted, leaving the two women growling at each other over their favorite gun brands. "Are we allowed to work outside the company?"

"All bounty requests must be done through Bounty Inc. Working outside of the company is a breach of the contract. I created a software that is pretty basic right now, but it will establish a database of bounties for you to accept from, and, in the event of the desired bounty not being there, you'll have the option to add one directly to it." Sage had suggested that adjustment on the basis that experienced bounty hunters would often be approached directly. "All payments will be done through that software, and each of you will be given an account."

Wyn gestured to his Vico and brought up the sample program. It listed several bounties he had manually added and his own profile. "You'll get a hunter score based on your experience, which limits the bounties available to you, a safety measure to keep anyone from taking on a relatively more dangerous job solo. This is really only an issue for Besari and me as the rest of you are rather experienced. But I added the scoring because I thought it would be fun to see who does the best over this year."

"A competition amongst bounty hunters?" Zetta leaned forward, many sharp teeth jutting out from beneath a curling lip. "Time to finally decide who's actually the best."

"You would lose," Pesh said. "Objectively speaking, eddermar need far less sleep and rest. I will be able to take on a near endless stream of bounties."

"The robot might make that difficult for you," Zetta said.

"I am *not* a robot," Cee spoke, its voice the same monotone it always was, but a hint of anger seemed to bleed into the words.

"Apologies," Zetta said. "Cyborg, do you sleep?"

"No."

"My point stands. What's stopping that from endlessly farming bounties?"

"We shall see," Pesh said.

"What are our current ranks?" Zetta asked.

Wyn switched the screen with a gesture, and an active list displayed. All eight present (excluding Seph) were ranked from highest to lowest, with Wyn at the bottom. And at the top…

"Ha!" Zetta blurted out. "Your ranking's got one thing right. The best hunter is at the top."

"This program is ageist!" Pesh complained as they bounced an inflated Skritch back and forth between two hands. The gridder trilled as it wafted through the air.

"Maybe you should just get better." Sage smirked.

"You don't have anything to smile about, Sage." Zetta chuckled. "Bugs has you beat."

Sage glared at the ranking. "That's rather unfair. They're hardly the same hive that got many of those bounties. How long does your entire hive take to cycle through a lifetime? Ten years? Twenty?"

Achtrek hummed. "I don't think that matters, Sage. All that matters is that we're still beating you."

"Notice the oldest have the top rankings." Pesh sulked. "Ageist."

"That's why I mentioned a yearly challenge," Wyn said. "We all start fresh today."

"How do we move up if we're at zero?" Besari asked. Her confession and uncertainty the previous night had prompted Wyn to start her at zero with him. "If bounties unlock based on your score, are any allowed at zero?"

"The idea would be to have a mentor bring you on a hunt to help you get a base score," Wyn said. "That way newcomers don't enter the field until an established hunter acknowledges they're ready, and they have someone to help if needed."

"You could use Sage as a mentor." Zetta chuckled. "She needs all the help she can get to compete with us better hunters." There was a thunk as something bounced off Zetta's face. The vrolak growled and glared at Sage, the offender. "Did you just throw your fucking boot at me?"

"I have another," Sage warned as she leaned down to loosen the laces on the other boot.

"As for facilities," Wyn jumped back into the conversation, switching screens to a map of Bounty Inc., "everyone's been given a map, but basically shared spaces are on the first floor: armory, shooting range, gym, lounge, and so on. Second floor is designed as living quarters, so you can stay here if you want, free of charge. There are dorms, kitchens, and some meeting rooms. Third floor is my office and apartments, designed more thoroughly since I'll probably be living here far more often than anyone else. Oh, and Seph reached out just this morning to set up a discount with the private hangar nearby for anyone who has their own ships."

The crowd stared at Wyn as a suffocating silence permeated the room. Then a soft coo from Skritch filled the empty air as they deflated and landed in Pesh's outstretched hand. Then nothing.

"Well, that's all I have for today. Feel free to continue with your bounties, and I'm always open to suggestions."

Again there was a long pause, then the bounty hunters slowly rose and mingled, continuing lighthearted arguments or discussing old jobs. Wyn watched Shellesh, who hadn't spoken a word, gesture to his Vico, then head toward the entrance and leave.

"Wyn Kelda."

Wyn turned to find Cee standing nearby. "Hello, Cee. What can I do for you?"

"I was analyzing your code for this bounty system you have in place, and I can improve output and optimize it significantly if you would like me to do so. There are forty-two potentially critical issues, as well as one hundred and fifty-nine suggestions for improvements."

"What? I never gave you access to that code."

"You didn't have to," it said. "I found it myself. I can make the changes today and have a superior system in place before anyone has collected a bounty."

Wyn found the comments to sting more than he would have expected. Sure, Cee was an A.I., and Wyn had no formal training in programming systems as complex as he aimed for. But still, was it that bad? He bit down on his pride, reminding himself he wasn't here to do everything alone. "You can take care of it, Cee. Thank you. If there are any financial upgrades needed for that or the company's cyber security, just let me know, and I will pay for them."

"Yes, Wyn Kelda." Cee walked over to a corner of the lounge and stood facing out from it, unmoving.

"You ready?" Wyn jumped as Sage spoke from behind him.

"No."

"Too bad. The tank's already set up in the armory. We should get this over with."

Wyn sighed, then nodded. The confidence he had gathered the previous night evaporated in an instant.

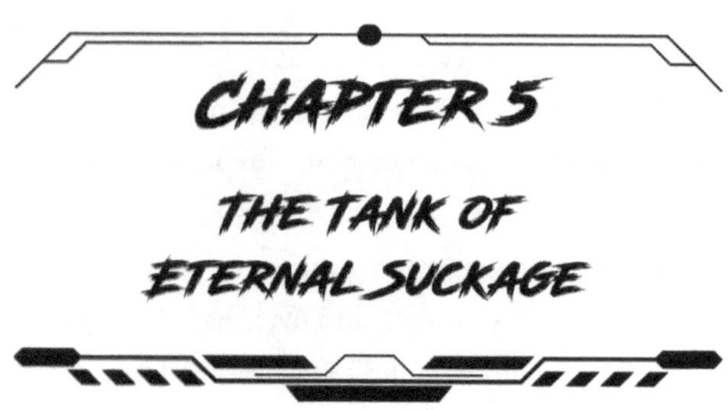

# CHAPTER 5

## THE TANK OF ETERNAL SUCKAGE

Wyn regretted everything the moment he stepped from the locker room into the chilly hallway wearing nothing but a pair of specialized undergarments that clung tightly to his skin. He hurried down the hallway to the armory, desperately hoping no one would see him, scanned his Vico at the door, and stepped in.

The tank filled the center of the room, a large glass cylinder with plenty of room for a fully-grown vrolak. It sat atop a large metal platform, with wires and machines weaving up and around the sides. At the control station to one side, a falvian technician by the name of Swims-The-Lightning-Seas looked over the readouts and entered whatever calculations were needed. The tank itself was filled nearly to the top with a violet liquid.

Sage stood near the falvian, engaging in small talk that seemed mostly centered around the odds of Wyn dying and, thankfully, how best to avoid that outcome. Next to her was—

"What's she doing here?" Wyn squeaked, forcing himself to not drop his hands in front of his groin. He felt a heat rise to his face as he stood nearly naked in front of Besari.

"Moral support?" Besari suggested.

"Forget about her," Sage said. "Come over here so we can get you ready."

Wyn shuffled over, doing his best to forget about Besari and failing. Swims presented a mask with long breathing tubes attached and hooked it to the edge of the station, then she leaned down in front of Wyn, and her feathery fingers began prodding at the underwear. Wyn jumped in surprise.

"What are you doing?"

"I must check to make sure it's sealed properly," she said, not skipping a beat. Wyn shivered as the feathers ran along his rear as well but refrained from jumping again. Instead, he closed his eyes and imagined himself anywhere other than here. "Do you have any open wounds? Scabs, sores, cuts, or anything that would leak blood or pus?"

"No," Wyn said, eyes still closed. Apparently the falvian didn't take his word for it and looked him over anyway, even lifting his feet to check the soles. Wyn felt like an animal being appraised for an auction. She pulled him to the other side of the tank and grabbed the breathing mask.

"We don't actually want the Thresha to enter your body through any orifices," she said as she attached the mask over his eyes, nose, and mouth. "The clothing should protect your genitals and anus, while this protects your face." She pulled out old, ragged headphones and placed them over his ears. After a press of a button, everything sealed tightly to Wyn's head. A speaker crackled to life in his ears. "And the headphones will protect your ears. Nod if you can hear me."

Wyn nodded, his teeth clenched tight, his breath rapidly increasing.

"There's a microphone in the mask. If you need to speak, we can hear it."

"Okay," Wyn whispered, barely able to push the single word out.

Swims led him to the rear of the tank, laying out his breathing tubes carefully so they wouldn't get twisted and he could keep easily hyperventilating. Everything was fine.

Wyn climbed the ladder, mounted the small platform at the top, then sat down, his feet dipping into the liquid. It pooled around his feet and between his toes, feeling more like a thick gel than water.

"Feel free to drop in when you're ready," Swims said.

"Is there anything more we should go over?"

"Yes," Swims said. "But I find it's easier to do that part once the participant is submerged."

"Where does one even get this stuff?" Wyn asked as he stared into the Thresha.

"It's manufactured on some planet," Swims explained. "Details are murky because it's all confidential."

Wyn took a deep breath. He had made his choice. No turning back now. He couldn't just decide he wanted out of a bounty when it got dangerous. He needed to face forward, to keep moving, to fight until the very end. Even if that end was now.

He slipped from the platform, and the goo encased him like a second flesh slipping over his skin. His head sank beneath, the hairs lifting, then his feet hit the cold floor. It had the strange effect of being warm and cold, comforting and invasive, a duality sparking against his skin.

Swims pressed a button, and the platform above turned into liquid metal and spread out across the top, sealing it off except where Wyn's tube led out.

"First," Swims said, "I must explain that I am not liable for death or permanent injury from the use of the tank. You have agreed to this through the signed waiver. Second, the machine can be quite painful. If at any point the pain becomes too much or you become worried about your ability to deal with it, simply say 'abort' and I will end the process. I will not end it if you say anything else, remember that. If aborted, the semi-absorption of Thresha can have many negative side effects, such as spasms, blindness, vomiting, anal leakage, and the inability to absorb Thresha. All but the last are likely temporary. If you abort, you will likely never be able to try again, and it would be incredibly dangerous for you to do so. Do you understand the risks?"

"Yes," Wyn said, unsure if the word actually left his mouth or not. It was an odd sensation to not hear his own voice, causing a disconnect with his body, as if he were some ethereal form floating just to the outside of everything. Living some strange dream. Or, he suspected, what was soon to be a nightmare.

"Upon completion of the procedure, there may be some lingering side effects for up to two weeks. Most commonly people experience fatigue, soreness, and claustrophobia."

"What if I already have claustrophobia?"

"Then it will likely worsen into a debilitating state."

"Good thing I don't have it then," Wyn convinced himself. He looked out at Besari and Sage and saw them staring. Something about Besari's posture was tense, though Sage's was no different. She kept a calm look on her face, but she moved stiffly, her muscles bulging more than they usually did. That didn't seem like a great sign.

"Thresha talents begin to display in one to four weeks, though this can vary a great deal. Sometimes it can take months, though this is not common. Included in the waiver is that you cannot sue us if you end up with an unfavorable Thresha talent. It is not our fault how your genetic structure adjusts. Do you understand?"

"Yes."

"Please position your feet where indicated, and we will begin the procedure at your word."

Wyn looked down to find two spots outlining where he should stand and shuffled his feet toward them. Moving in the gel was unlike swimming, requiring so much more effort to shift, as if it was already solidifying around him. Besari raised her hand in a gesture unfamiliar to Wyn but one he hoped was friendly. He copied it back to her and smiled. Easy, one quick, slightly painful session, and he would be back to his regular training. Bounty Inc. had begun. There was no way it would end so quickly. He had seized his dream, made it his own, and now he was one step closer. Soon, he would be a bounty hunter.

"Ready," Wyn said.

No amount of false astral projection saved him from the pain. His presence slammed back into his body, fully aware. Then he screamed. And maybe peed himself.


Electricity stormed up Wyn's legs, seizing his muscles in a death grip. His hands curled in front of him uncontrollably, and his lungs froze, releasing all his oxygen in one quick burst and leaving Wyn failing to gasp for more. The charge ran through his veins, and wherever it went, a burn followed.

He remembered being young, watching his nurse cook dinner. Wyn had wanted to be a cook then. It was the coolest job in the world. He copied her, reaching up to grab the pan, and his hand came down on the hot element, searing his flesh. It took weeks to heal, even with the best medicine his father could buy. It hurt so much, he remembered crying for days after, late into the night. His nurse was fired, and Wyn was never allowed in the kitchens again.

That was nothing compared to this moment. Wyn would burn his hands a thousand times over before he'd wish this on himself. His insides boiled, his guts curdled, and his heart stampeded through his chest, threatening to break free like some alien parasite. When his breath finally returned, he immediately wasted it on another scream. Or maybe he had never stopped screaming.

Besari jerked forward, but Sage placed a hand on her shoulder and said something. Wyn didn't know what. He was too busy burning to ash.

His skin itched, then it screamed its own kind of pain, like millions of needles piercing his skin, digging into his body. The electricity lessened, which allowed Wyn free rein to slam his fists against the glass and writhe in pain. He denounced his dream. Promised them all whatever he owned to release him from the tank. He would give them all his money, all his possessions, everything. Anything! Tears streamed down his cheeks, pooling at his lower lip where the mask sealed. Ragged breaths choked him, and his vision darkened.

He looked up and out of the glass, his hands scrabbling at the edges, and Besari was there, hands matching his own. Sage was talking animatedly with the falvian to the side, though none of the conversation carried to his ears. Something was wrong. His body grew numb, his senses dulled. His chest felt strained, as if every beat of his heart took all his energy. His hands slid down the glass, and he felt his knees give out. He thought his body would drop to the floor, but the breathing tubes caught on the sealed cap and held him suspended in an odd crouch.

Besari rushed to Sage. More talking. More discussions. Arguing. Yelling. Something was wrong.

"I..." Wyn croaked. Everyone stopped and stared at him, all conversation ceasing as they waited on his words. He smiled. "I won't quit."

Then he died.


Wyn's screams filled the armory and raised the hairs on Sage's arms. She had tortured people who were quieter than this, though maybe the speakers enhanced it. Either way, she was impressed with his lungs, the first impressive thing she had seen beyond his wealth. Slowly, the color of the tank faded away as the Thresha absorbed into Wyn, shifting from the vibrant violet to a dull lavender.

Then the screams ended, and the alarms began.

"What's going on?" Sage asked, rushing to Swims. Besari, released from Sage's grasp, ran to the tank, placing her hands where Wyn's scraped against the glass.

"His vitals are dropping," Swims said.

"Dropping? How fast?"

"Is he going to be all right?" Besari asked.

"Most likely not," Swims said, her monotone speaker removing all emotion. Sage wanted to punch her.

"Then *end* it."

"No."

Sage froze for a moment, then she snarled, "What?"

"The rules are there for a reason, Ms. Valen. I will not end the procedure until he elects to abort it. There are legalities I do not wish to deal with otherwise. He was informed, so he must choose to end it."

Sage looked over at the tank. Wyn hung lifeless within, held up only by the breathing mask.

"He's dying." Besari came over, her shoulders tense, back stiff. "You need to end it."

"Again, I cannot. Company rules."

"I..." The voice crackled from the speaker, causing Sage to flinch. She looked over, and Wyn's head had swiveled towards them. Sage waited for the abort, her muscles tensed to help drag him out of the tank. Then Wyn smiled. "I won't quit."

Then a constant beep sounded.

"Vitals are gone," Swims said.

"Then release him!" Sage shouted. Besari rushed back to the tank, appearing to call out to Wyn, as useless as that would be.

"Must I repeat myself again?" Swims looked at her with those piercing bird eyes, her beak chittering in annoyance.

"He's dead. Why do you need to continue?"

"He might revive at the end. We don't know. If I end it now and he is saved, I can be sued. I will end it when it's done."

"Fuck that! If you wait, he *will* be dead."

"But I won't be sued."

"Fuck you!" Sage grabbed the feathered freak by the neck and slammed her against a wall. "Release him now, or I'll shove your void-damned talkbox down your throat."

"I cannot," the same emotionless voice preached on.

"Then tell me how," Sage growled.

"No."

Sage roared and threw the falvian to the ground. She turned to Besari, still waiting in front of the tank. "Break it open."

Besari, for her part, didn't skip a beat. She nodded, then delivered a kick that would have smashed through Sage's stony armor. It banged against the glass, and a loud thunk reverberated around the armory.

"These were built to hold thrashing birrosh. Your strength won't break it."

"We need Zetta!" Had she left? Would she care enough to help? She needed to move. Now!

Besari pulled her scattergun and angled it sideways across the front of the cylinder.

Sage froze. She was going to get him killed. Killed again, anyway.

"No!" Swims rushed to her feet, then Besari fired.

There was a loud crash as the glass melted and shattered beneath the onslaught of plasma. The Thresha goo, now just a pale purple, poured into the room like water. Besari fired again, searing off more of the tank's front and making enough room for her to fit. She kicked glass out of the way as she holstered her gun and stepped inside, drawing a knife and slicing easily through the breathing tubes. Wyn's body collapsed into her arms, and she carried him from the tank to a clear spot on the ground.

Swims's feathered fingers flew across the display, rapidly shutting down the machine.

Sage ignored her and rushed over to join Besari. The mask and headphones were removed by the time she fell to the floor beside Wyn. Damn, her knees ached when she did that now. She grew some carapace around them for added comfort. It only helped a little.

"He's not breathing," Besari said.

Sage leaned down and confirmed the assessment. She felt for a pulse and found nothing. "Get Cee," she said. "Now!" she yelled at Besari's hesitation. The birrosh woman jumped to her feet and ran off. Sage had seen the A.I. standing in a corner in the lounge earlier, doing whatever it was doing. Hopefully it would still be there. Hopefully it would have a way to save Wyn.

She started with chest compressions, timing it in her head. She needed something to restart his heart. This wouldn't be enough. But it might help keep him alive long enough for Cee to arrive.

"I will not be held liable for this," Swims said, stepping over to Sage. "I have recorded your interactions and—"

Sage broke as the rage flooded into her. She leapt to her feet, chest compressions forgotten, pistol in one hand, falvian in the other. "If he dies, so do you," Sage growled. "How's that for fucking liability?"

"He understood the risks," Swims said calmly, or at least her fucking talk box was calm. "I understand your reaction, but you cannot treat me like this."

"I can treat you however the fuck I want. I'm the one—"

"Fuuuuuuuuuuuuuuuuuuuuuuuuuuuuuuuuuuuuuuuuuuuuuuuuuuu-uuuck."

Sage dropped the bird and turned. Wyn's eyes flickered open, and his moan continued on, devolving to just a grunt.

"Wyn? Are you all right?" She stepped toward him slowly, as if there was a trick at play.

"I feel like I was boiled and someone punched me in the chest," Wyn said. "But I still seem to have feeling in my toes and fingers. Even if that feeling is primarily cold." He shivered, wrapping his arms slowly around himself.

Sage dropped to the floor, pulling her overshirt off and draping it over him. Bumps formed across her bare arms.

"Sage," Wyn croaked. "Tell me truthfully."

"Yes?"

"Am I really buff now?"

Sage smiled and glanced over his body and looked back. "Nope, same as you were before, unfortunately."

"Fuck." Wyn closed his eyes. "I was really hoping this would mean I didn't have to do the physical training."

The door slid open, and Besari and Cee rushed in. Wyn squinted over at them. "Besari? Cee?"

"Wyn, you're alive!" Besari stepped forward, then slowed herself, as if unsure how nervous and excited she should be. Sage chuckled.

"Does this mean I am not needed?" Cee asked.

"Yeah, we're good," Sage said.

"Then I shall return to my previous tasks." Cee moved to a corner of the armory and stood there, staring off into the distance.

"Is this a bad time to mention I will need to bill you for a new tank?" Swims asked.

Sage turned on her, but Wyn spoke and gave her pause. "What happened?" He raised his head enough to see the destroyed remains of the front of the tank.

"Send it to me," Sage whispered to the falvian technician, then waved her off. To Wyn, she said, "When you're ready to move, let's get you to your rooms. I'll explain there."


Wyn stood in his office, looking out at the night sky. Jel dominated the horizon, swirls of brown and gold spinning across the planet's surface. Stars speckled the sky above, fading away nearer to Chrysanax's planet. His arm twitched occasionally, and his vision wavered often. At least he got away without the anal leakage. He sighed and rubbed a hand across his face, the weariness of the day settling around him like a cloak of lead.

The door slid open, and someone stepped inside. "You all right?" Sage asked.

"Yeah." Wyn's voice still cracked, his throat raw from the screaming.

"Sorry."

Wyn wondered how much effort it had taken for her to pull that word out of her mouth. To take blame for what had happened. Wyn smiled and turned. "Sorry for what, Sage? You saved my life. You and Besari both. I might never get a Thresha talent, but had I stayed in the tank, I would not have my life. I can continue chasing my dream now. You have nothing to be sorry for."

"Swims said you were nearly finished with the session. There's a small chance it will still activate."

Wyn shrugged. "If it does, it does. But in the meantime, I will just have to work harder to make up for it. I won't let it stop me."

Sage smirked. "You have the right attitude to make it, kid. That's good."

Wyn nodded. "Is there anything else, Sage?"

"I'm giving you tomorrow off. Rest up. We're back to it the next day." Sage turned and walked out of the room.

"Goodnight, Sage."

She waved as she turned the corner. "Goodnight, kid." Her voice drifted into the room as the door slid shut.

The right attitude. If Wyn had practice at one thing, it was pretending to be happy with decisions he couldn't change. Maybe that would be enough.

# CHAPTER 6

## TRAINING MONTAGE

W yn pushed aside the self-pity and the grief. What did it matter in the end? He had decided on becoming a bounty hunter long before he had heard of Thresha talents. He hadn't needed them then, and he didn't need them now. Instead, he threw himself into his training. Sage had given him off the first day. But the following morning he returned to his routine, pushing his body as hard and as fast as he could.

He ached through the training; every muscle burned when he moved, and every muscle burned when he didn't. But every spike of pain reminded him that it was nothing compared to that tank. And so he could push on.

The weapons shipment arrived three days after Wyn's near-death, though the days blended together so much he couldn't have said so. Sage broke open the crates with a smile like a child opening presents on Heart's Festival. She organized the armory, carefully taking note of where to store each weapon. Including the slag cannon, which Wyn had ordered to appease seemingly half the company. It was a massive gun, each piece of ammo a sphere of metal larger than his head, which it superheated and flung at whatever you wanted really dead.

Sage told him about each weapon, taught him their basics, and once he knew those, he was allowed into the shooting range. They stuck with stationary targets, which still proved a great challenge regardless of which weapon he used.

"One hand holds the pistol, the other stabilizes the hand," Sage emphasized as she demonstrated the grip again. They decided pistols would be the best start, given that was the only weapon with which Wyn had hit the target. He mimicked her, and the gun writhed in Wyn's hand. He nearly dropped it, but it stopped moving, which had him questioning the Thresha tank's full effects. "What's wrong?" she asked.

"I think it moved?" It didn't anymore, the grip steady and comfortable in his hand. But the idea it had still made him nervous.

"Right, that's the nano grip. Adjusts to your hand and makes the weapon as comfortable as possible. We have the first model to be released with it. Another reason to use Imberlii. Always top of the line, best product on the market."

Wyn fixed his stance under Sage's guidance, then aimed and fired. He missed. Then missed the next six shots.

"Do we need to move it closer?" Sage asked.

"I'll get it," Wyn growled.

"We should go back to the rifle. Shoots faster so you don't need to aim as much."

The door slid open, followed by the boom of a deep belch, which sent Wyn jumping, an errant shot flying into the ceiling. He glanced back to find Zetta looking at the scorch mark on the ceiling with a smirk.

"What are you doing here?" Sage asked, feigning disinterest so poorly even Wyn could tell.

Zetta smirked. "Just finished a bounty. Figured the best in the business deserves a break after a hard hunt, don't you?"

"Breaks weren't typically what you had in mind when we worked together. We went straight from bounty to bounty."

"Yeah, but that was because I thought you were attractive and wanted to get rid of you faster. You know, so there weren't weird strings. I don't usually work that hard."

Sage quirked an eyebrow and crossed her arms. "So you're just here to get in my pants?"

"Well, I don't have any, so yours will work just fine."

"I'm not so easy as that, Zetta. You're going to have to try a little harder."

Zetta barked a laugh, then reached a claw down to scratch at her thigh. In the process, she slowly brought up the ends of the dress, showing off more of her pale orange leg. "I don't expect it to be all that hard."

Sage glanced down, then tore her gaze away. "You want to try hitting on me while I have a weapon?"

"You're most attractive when you have a weapon, so there's no better time."

"You're less attractive with a few holes in you."

"First of all, I know that's a lie because of that one time after the Trilio bounty. Secondly, that little toy ain't going to add any more holes, but you're welcome to fill the ones I have in the meantime."

"Do you two mind?" Wyn blurted, his face burning so thoroughly his vision shook. "I'm trying to focus over here." He fired a few more times, the shots going wild.

Zetta burst into her loud laughter, and even Sage smiled with a few chuckles. "Keep practicing. I can't teach you more until you know the basics." Then Sage led Zetta out of the room, and Wyn ignored the imagery that flitted through his mind.

Wyn sighed and set the pistol down, taking a deep breath. Then he ran through the checks as Sage had taught him. The display to one side could be activated to show the number of shots remaining with the charge. He opened and examined the small charge capsule, about as long as his finger and filled with a glowing blue substance. Slightly depleted from his practice shots, it looked like some cartridge of ink from one of the few physical pens out there. His dad had owned one, though he'd never used it nor appreciated it and yelled at Wyn the one time *he'd* tried to use it. Wyn returned the cartridge, lifted the pistol, and fired. It was hopeless.

When the door opened again, he hardly noticed over his fierce scream of frustration while he randomly shot down the range. If aiming didn't work, maybe not aiming would work better. It was only when his desperate attempts at hitting a target finally fizzled out that he heard someone behind him. He whirled, cheeks red, and found Besari.

"Mind if I join you?" she asked.

"You're not an expert already?" Wyn smiled to ensure she knew there was no edge to the comment.

"Far from it," she said, lining up next to him. "Especially in that technique."

Wyn sighed and set the pistol down on the counter. "It's obviously not very effective," he admitted, waving a hand at the mostly intact targets.

She placed a hand on his shoulder, and he felt a comfortable warmth under her touch. "It's why we practice." He had expected her to pull her scattergun, but instead she withdrew a pistol that was a copy of his own. "I trained heavily in close combat. Blades and fists are what I'm best in. Scattergun is just for if things get too dangerous. I'm not great with it. It's just hard to be bad at it. I'm not great with medium to long range weapons like this."

She lifted the pistol, and her body held still for several moments, like a living statue. Then she fired three times and hit the target three times. Not in the center, but significantly better than Wyn's attempts.

He let out a chuckle that trailed off into a sigh. "You have me beat." He raised his pistol, tried to mimic her, and then fired. Three times, and none even close. "I can't seem to get the hang of it."

"Didn't Sage run you through the basics?" Besari studied him, and Wyn blushed under the intense gaze.

"Um, yeah. Point and shoot. Didn't think there was much more to it."

"Your grip is fine. Your stance could use some work, but it's not like you'll get a proper stance in a fight. But your breathing is all wrong."

"Breathing?"

"Here." Besari set her pistol down and moved behind Wyn, his heart sprinting out of his chest as her hands brushed him. She adjusted his legs to a wider stance, then brought her arms around to adjust his aim. "Breathing inflates the lungs, which raises the chest, which in turn jostles the arms." She placed her hand at each point to indicate this, and Wyn did his part to show just how much his breathing could jostle his aim. "Exhale, hold it for a moment, then shoot. Your lungs are empty, your arms are steady. Just don't hold it too long or you'll pass out." She laughed and stepped away. Her warm presence left him wishing she'd stay, but he bit his lip and shook away the thoughts. He had researched what birrosh looked like, and though in her suit she was very similar to a human, that wasn't the case beneath. He understood that, which made his feelings about her close proximity even more confusing. Besari's words brought him back from his mind's meandering path.

"Give it a try," she said. "Exhale, hold, then shoot."

Wyn let his body have a moment to calm down, then took a deep breath. He held it while his lungs screamed in protest, then let it all out. His heart slowed, and his senses focused. The pistol steadied in his grip, and he counted to three, holding his lungs empty. Wyn fired, and the target dinged with his shot. A smile broke across his face. "I did it!"

"See, you just needed the right information," Besari said, and the smile could be heard in her voice as well.

"You're much better at helping than Sage. Maybe I should have hired you to train me."

Besari laughed as she stepped up next to him, grabbing the gun again. "I trained more recently than her. It's probably second nature for her, not something she thinks of." Then she glanced over, and Wyn stared into that eerie, tinted face mask. "A challenge, maybe? Loser pays for lunch?"

Wyn raised an eyebrow. "Are you trying to con your boss for a free meal?"

Besari tensed, her voice chilled. "No, of course not. Sorry." She turned to the target and took aim.

Wyn felt a pang of something squeeze his heart. That had not gone how he'd meant. It was just a joke. But she began firing, and Wyn was unable to speak. He practiced in that awkward, gun-filled silence for the next twenty minutes, now hitting his target more often than not. Besari offered a few unenthusiastic congratulations, and Wyn accepted them. Then he left for lunch.

Wyn ate his goopy meal alone except for the thoughts ricocheting around his head. Analyzing every word of the interaction and scolding himself for it. He hadn't meant what he'd said as anything other than a joke, but clearly Besari had taken something differently. He sighed just as Seph sat down across from him, a sandwich dripping with sauce on his plate.

"Oh, sorry, Mr. Kelda. I can leave if you want."

"No worries, Seph. That wasn't at you."

Seph picked his sandwich up and took a large bite. Wyn spooned a mouthful of goop into his mouth and tried to pretend it tasted anything like the sandwich.

"Something bringing you down?" Seph asked through a mouthful of food.

"Do you think of me as your boss?"

"Yeah, you are."

"Well, sure, but I mean as a person. I can be friendly, right? Or do I seem cold and aloof? Unapproachable? Is there a line that can't be crossed by befriending me?"

"Oh, I don't know about all that, Mr. Kelda. You seem pretty cool to me." Sauce squirted from the sandwich as he bit into it, some splattering onto the table. "I'll get that," Seph mumbled through his food.

"You can call me Wyn."

"Okay, Mr. Kelda."

Wyn sighed and focused on his meal. Seph took another joyful bite, then set the sandwich down, his face turning contemplative.

After a swallow, he said, "I have a question, Mr. Kelda."

"What can I help you with, Seph?"

"More a requisition request, actually."

"A request? For what?"

"For L-Bot. He usually watches the front desk when I'm doing other things, and he can be a bit intimidating to approach. A big floating egg with no face. I was thinking we could get him a humanoid frame for his core, and he'd be far more pleasant for customers to look at."

Wyn tapped his spoon against the bowl. "Is that something that would be necessary? Have we even had anyone stop by the building?"

"Not yet, Mr. Kelda, but you'd rather be prepared than not, right?"

There was some sense to making a public-facing robot more amiable. "All right, Seph, I can look for a frame for him tonight."

"Oh, no need, Mr. Kelda. I actually found the perfect one." Seph brought up a requisition form and sent it to Wyn. "All the info's there, just need your approval for purchase."

"You put a lot of thought into this," Wyn mumbled. He glanced over the form—particularly the price, which caused some alarm—then decided he had better things to do than worry about double-checking Seph's choices. He had obviously put more thought into it than Wyn was going to. "Approved," Wyn said with a signature.

"Oh, wonderful!" Seph jumped from the table. "I can't wait to tell Ell."

"Ell?" Wyn looked up as Seph ran off, and he wondered if maybe he had made a mistake. That thought fled as he looked down at the rest of Seph's sandwich. It called to him, saliva filling his mouth. He almost reached out for it. Then he remembered his goals and what he strove for. He downed the rest of his goop and returned the bowl to the sink to be washed later.

Proud of himself, he exited the little dining room. Fifteen seconds later, he swung back in and bit into Seph's sandwich. One little bite couldn't hurt. Then he rushed back out, delicious, saucy food filling his mouth.

Sage had been running Wyn through basic hand-to-hand training, practicing a few forms so if he ever found himself without a weapon, he wouldn't die immediately. She was being generous on that estimate. So far, this had mostly amounted to practicing punches, then getting knocked on his ass or flipped over a shoulder.

Besari had thought that sounded enjoyable and started coming as well. Already proficient in her homegrown handfighting, she picked up Sage's techniques quickly and was soon tossing Wyn on his ass as well, and he wondered if maybe the discomfort from the shooting range persisted and this was her revenge. He also wondered if he was the only one not having fun.

So it wasn't a surprise to find Besari and Sage stretching and talking. However, the same could not be said about Shellesh, who was a complete surprise.

"Hello, Shellesh," Wyn said, and the exile nodded back. "Are you here to train as well?"

"Not quite." His gravelly voice turned his words into an unintentional growl.

"Shell is here to supplement your learning," Sage announced. "He's agreed to help whenever he has time, which won't be often, so pay attention."

"As Sage said, I'm here to help with your blade work." Shellesh opened a case nearby and pulled several wooden sticks ranging in length from no larger than Wyn's hand to longer than his arm.

"Blade work?" Besari asked. "I don't need help with that. It was my primary focus."

"So you choose to limit your growth?" Shellesh asked, and for just a moment his normally stoic eyes flashed with life. "You've decided that good enough is good enough? You're betting that you'll never have a situation where a little more skill will save you? What if you're wrong?"

"That's not what I mean." Besari shrank beneath the assault of words. "I just meant I could be improving other areas that will need more work."

"Do you not do that at every other moment?" Shellesh asked, and Besari's silence was answer enough. "You can always grow in everything you do. There will never be a cap, and with your blades always at your side, blade work will be a far more important skill for you than most others. Especially mixed with your talent."

Wyn flinched at the mention of talents but pushed away his disappointment. Shellesh pulled a pair of sticks the size of Besari's blades and tossed one to her. Besari caught it and studied the practice weapon, its hilt elegantly carved to match that of a real knife, even if the "blades" were rather plain.

"Let's see how well you fare and where you can grow."

Shellesh stepped into the sparring area and readied himself, knife held in front of him. Besari took a spot opposite him and readied herself. Then she popped out of view. Shellesh didn't move.

"No invisibility," he said. "You're here to learn, not win."

With a sigh, Besari faded back into view. Shellesh nodded, and she rushed forward. Her hand blurred as it moved, her body reacting with a burst of speed Wyn had never seen in their sparring. Realization of just how far behind he was dawned on him. She moved like lightning, faster than his eyes could track. Which made it all the more shocking to see her hit the ground, training knife to the neck. Wyn hadn't even seen it happen. Besari had been attacking, and then Shellesh moved, and she flipped, her practice weapon sliding across the mat.

"You rely too much on straight forward attacks, a hindrance to your ability," Shellesh said. "It may work when they can't see you, but you don't want to only be good when you can't be seen."

Shellesh pulled Besari back to her feet, then looked to Wyn. Wyn raised his hands. "Oh, I'm good just learning." Sage scoffed, but Shellesh nodded.

"Wise idea," Sage said. "There isn't a single person in this company who is better with hands and blade than Shellesh."

"Let's begin," Shellesh said.

The training ran them through techniques and forms. Besari threw herself into the blades training and was soon lasting for several seconds against Shellesh. Wyn wasn't so lucky, but he made his own progress. The blade training sessions would be sparse over the following months, but always informative, and in between, Sage would hammer the basics of brawling into them until they could throw and take punches long enough to survive a light scuffle.

Wyn's aches enhanced by the end of the session, like the muscles were one wrong stretch away from tearing. A heat flowed through him that did little to warm him, and Sage, with a smirk tinged with the barest hint of sympathy, offered him an injection.

"What is it?"

"Healing agent," she said.

Wyn took a deep breath and looked away. He hated needles. "Okay."

Sage quirked an eyebrow at him standing there, head turned, shaking arm held out. She smiled, then grabbed his wrist and drove it into his thigh instead. Wyn jumped with surprise, the needle a quick pinch and that was it. A coolness flooded him, and he felt it spread through his body, reaching down to his toes and up to his ears. Within moments, the aches fell silent.

"At least, I think so," Sage added, looking at the label.

Wyn's eyes flew open. "What?"

"Well, they got some painkillers in them too. But it should make your muscles loosen up and recover quicker." She shrugged. "Worked for me. We only have a few weeks of it though, so this shouldn't be a crutch you rely on, just something to help you improve faster early on."

Wyn nodded, and from then on, he only accepted the shot on days he felt the worst. And, within a couple of weeks, he didn't even need them anymore.


The evenings were Wyn's to do with as he wanted. Mostly, that meant paperwork, communications, and moaning as the painkillers wore off. On the day of Shellesh's first lesson, however, Wyn had gone into the town to run an errand. Cee stood at the front desk upon his return.

"Greetings, Wyn Kelda."

"Cee, were you waiting for me?"

"Yes," it said. "Though it was no issue. I spent the time working on a side project."

"What can I help you with?"

"Nothing. It is what I have helped you with." Cee projected a Vico screen from his chest, various bits of data circling about in an organized table. "I have completed your bounty software. It populates from several popular bounty hunting databases across the galaxy and several unpopular ones. It updates in real time, with a near zero latency through gateway connections. Each bounty hunter's profile is secured and can access this database to select their bounties. Banking has been tied in so a hunter's money is immediately accessible after Bounty Inc. is paid for the reward.

"I have connected this to your point system, letting users see their rankings as well as a leaderboard comparison. I have also set up a bounty share system for team-ups to split the money as they see fit. The bounty points are then split based on the pay distribution. Though this has not been tested in the field."

"Wow, Cee, you did all this in like three days?"

"The application was finished the first day, but it required the upgraded security to function appropriately. That took time as I needed some supplies. Bounty Inc. should be as impervious to a cyber attack as anywhere else now."

"That's incredible! Thank you so much!"

"If you approve, I shall send out the application to everyone along with brief instructions on how to utilize it."

"Yes, please do."

Cee nodded.

Later, Wyn would discover that Cee's idea of brief instructions was a three-hour recording that went into extensive detail. He would need to create a new, shorter set that the others would be willing to pay attention to.

At the end of the day, Wyn finished his goop and, with a measure of trepidation and excitement in his chest, went upstairs. On the second floor, he walked past some loud growling and roaring in Sage's room, then approached the third door on the right. He stopped outside and hesitated, hand raised. He took a deep breath and still didn't move.

"Okay, you got this," he mumbled to himself. He rubbed his hands together, prepared himself to knock, and the door slid open. He froze, mouth partially open, heart completely stopped.

"Oh!" Besari said. "Wyn?"

"Um." Wyn shook himself free, closed his eyes, and took a breath, then fell on his prepared speech. "I apologize, Besari, if what I said the other day put you in an awkward position. I didn't mean to imply you were trying to cheat me or anything."

Besari's head cocked, and a soft sigh fell from the speaker in her helmet. "I'm sorry, Wyn. I just don't know how I'm supposed to react, and it makes things difficult to judge for me. This place feels like a home to me, for the first time since I left mine, and I don't want to ruin that."

"Oh," Wyn said, retracing his words from the shooting range. "Because I'm your boss?"

"Yes. I don't know whether we're meant to be on friendly terms or how I'm supposed to act. I don't want to jeopardize my location here by acting incorrectly."

Wyn smiled. "I have an easy fix for that one."

"How's that?"

"Well, the boss thing was a bit of a lie. Technically you're a contractor for the company, and based on that contract, you're more a partner than an employee. The only employee is Seph. You and I are more like a mutually beneficial pairing. You know, you're like a parasite."

Besari giggled, her soft laughter floating out of her helmet and raising Wyn's spirits. "Parasites aren't typically good, Wyn."

"Zetta's is, right? It keeps her alive, and hunters like you keep Bounty Inc. alive. The contract is unbreakable except for the very specific instances listed there. If you don't like me and don't want to talk to me—"

"It's not that!" Besari straightened, hands clenching in front of her.

"And hopefully I can keep it that way." Wyn laughed. "All I mean is, regardless of how friendly or not friendly we are, your position is safe here because of that contract. I couldn't do anything unless you break it, and I certainly don't want to if you don't. I'm nearly ready to win one of our bouts."

"I'll believe it when I see it, Wyn." Besari's voice was calm and smooth, and Wyn could hear the smile in it. He smiled back.

"If you want to be friendly, I'd be happy to do so. If you want to be all cool and aloof, I'm fine with that as well."

"Let's try friendly first," Besari said. "I haven't worked on my brooding enough to be that aloof."

Wyn laughed and nodded. "Deal." Then he reached into his pocket and pulled out a credit chip a little longer than his thumb. "Oh, and this is for you. I was watching, and you definitely won the shooting competition. I don't know what you like to eat, so I just got you a gift credit to KeBrasa's. I saw you had it the other night. So, hopefully you liked it." Wyn shrugged.

Besari took it and looked at it, then the smoky glass of her faceplate looked up at Wyn. "Thank you, Wyn. If you try harder next time, you might be able to earn this back." Then after a small laugh, she added, "At least you have a better chance than if you bet it on handfighting."

Wyn glared, but he didn't stop the chuckle that built up within him. "Just stay confident, Besari. I'll catch up soon."

"I think I might go test this out," she said, holding up the chip. "Did you want to come?"

Wyn's smile faltered, and he scratched at the back of his neck. "I'd love to, but I just got back from getting that and I'm swimming in paperwork. Turns out the R.C. wants to be thorough when you create a brand-new type of business."

"Another time, then. You know where to find me."

Besari stepped past Wyn and waved to him as her door shut and locked, then she made her way down the hallway. Wyn's eyes followed her until he noticed Sage standing just outside her room wrapped in a bathrobe. The two waved and traded pleasantries, but Wyn just stared, feeling a blush creep into his cheeks.

As Besari disappeared down the stairwell, Sage looked at the un-moving Wyn, and Wyn prayed for empyreal intervention just then. It never came.

"Have you tried asking her if she wants to have sex? This slow pace you're moving at is annoying me."

"What? No!" Wyn squeaked. "She's not even human."

"So?" Zetta said, poking her head out the door. She wasn't even wearing a bathrobe. "You speciesist or something?"

Wyn coughed and looked away. "She has to wear her suit at all times, remember?"

Sage shrugged. "Maybe you can do it when it's really dark. Or if you're blindfolded?"

"Blindfolded is a good one!" Zetta agreed. "Do we have a blind-fold?"

"I saw one under the bed," a third voice hummed, and Wyn's eyes widened. A swarm of bugs flowed around Sage into the hallway, then formed into Achtrek. "I must leave now, Sage, Zetta. I have a bounty accepted that I should start on. Greetings, Wyn."

"Hello," Wyn managed.

"A pleasure as always, Achtrek," Sage said, then the swarm shattered apart and flew off.

"How?" Wyn asked, staring after the hive. Sage quirked an eyebrow.

"You know how Achtrek buzzes when they talk?"

"I changed my mind. I don't need to know more."

"I got the blindfold!" Zetta called out, then Wyn heard a loud bang as though she had let the bed fall back to the floor with little care for its structural integrity. "One more round and I have to go for a bounty as well. Can't let Bugs catch me on the leaderboard."

"I'm leaving," Wyn said, then made good on his promise as Sage returned to Zetta.

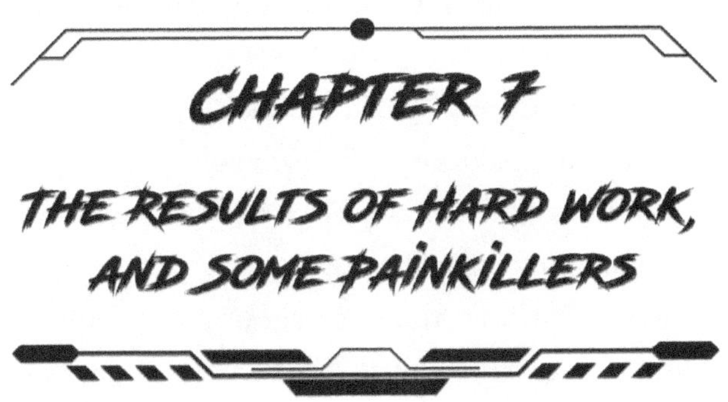


Routine rushed the months by like days and the days like hours. Wyn's life transformed into the same habit day in and day out. He would collapse into his bed, too tired to move, too exhausted to think, and would fall asleep in moments. What little free time he had was spent with others, learning more about them. Some were free with their words, while others resembled impossible vaults of secrets.

Shellesh was one of the latter. He would speak of his time as a bounty hunter for the past seventeen years but kept quiet on his exile and the time before. Except the one time Wyn asked if he had a Thresha talent and discovered the tesing exiling process stripped that away too. Shellesh was silent after, considering. Then he told Wyn and Besari what his talent had been.

"That seems like it would have taken a lot of coordination to use effectively if you worked with someone," Besari said.

"It did," Shellesh replied, his eyes lost to the past. "I always set up codewords before a mission so someone would know if I was about to use it."

"So..." Wyn considered. "You'd yell out, 'Welcome to the fireworks show!', then explode into a brilliant light or something?"

Shellesh chuckled, the first time Wyn had ever heard him do so. "Yeah," he said. "Something like that."

Cee was an enigma, far too open about many subjects others found sensitive or giving highly detailed reports of any bounties it gathered. Anything about their life prior to Bounty Inc. remained a complete mystery. Which made Wyn desperate to learn more. Not that he ever made progress, but he really wanted to.

Besari was another strange one to Wyn. He had thought them to be growing more friendly, but her history was a vague impression to him. She would answer questions in generalizations and shift topics before specifics were asked. Wyn had spent some nights trying to learn the differences between birrosh and bishett, as he kept confusing them, but the text had been dry and his focus had escaped him.

One day, though, he had learned of a birrosh friendship dance, which began with a subtle step and movement of the arms. It was easy for nearly anyone else to not notice the intent, but it seemed popular in birrosh culture. Thrilled at the thought he could show interest in her culture and open up new conversations, he performed the first step before hand-to-hand training one day, after weeks of practice. And yet she had merely looked at him and asked if he had hurt his back leaving Wyn wondering how badly he screwed it up. He spent the next few weeks recovering his confidence.

Achtrek, Zetta, and Pesh were completely open books, usually ready to share previous adventures and details of their cultures. Achtrek was a hive entirely designed for the purposes of completing bounties and returning the reward to the Mother, which was either a central hive, a central bug, or maybe just an entire planet of these beetles. Wyn wasn't able to figure that out. Pesh, similarly, had joined a clan with the role of hunter. In ancient times, that had meant either hunting for food or hunting criminals. Nowadays, with their planet well sustained on food, that meant more of the latter. Pesh had left their home because hunting was thin on planet. Apparently this was common for a lot of eddermar, and they made excellent hunters, assassins, and bodyguards due to their general durability compared to many other species. They were almost as challenging to kill as a nairwid, with several vital organs having secondary and sometimes tertiary versions.

Every one of Zetta's stories ended in a sex joke and an attempt to make Wyn as uncomfortable as possible. It usually worked.

Sage had grown more comfortable with Wyn as well, opening up and sharing stories as they trained. Wyn spoke of his time on Terrask and Sage of hers on Acro, a poor, mixed-species colony where she'd had to fight kids twice her age for food. She knew when to push Wyn and when to distract him. When to praise him and when to criticize him. Despite her own thoughts on the matter, she had grown quickly into the role of mentor and thrived. She still grew restless, and when she did, she would be grumpy too. Then, she would disappear for a few days on a hunt, despite her repeated assurances that she was ready for retirement. Wyn couldn't imagine Sage giving up the bounty hunting life while she could still move.

He didn't know when it happened, but life became easier after the first few weeks. His workouts were tough and only growing tougher, he still lost every sparring match he entered, and he still missed targets more than he should, but it became easier to keep going. To learn and adjust. To better himself. Getting up wasn't a struggle, and staying up lasted longer. His body grew accustomed to the training, and once that happened, his progress blossomed.

Sage ran him through mental exercises during his training, questions about strategy and tactics. She taught him the basics of information gathering and intimidation, though she didn't think he'd be using much of the latter.

His fat melted, his muscles grew, and his brain changed. He thought constantly like a combatant, searching for threats, understanding weak points, strategizing to keep himself safe wherever he was. Wyn rapidly changed into a true bounty hunter, and he knew that soon the time would come for his first bounty.

Seph and L-Bot grew into their roles, taking on more and more of the business decisions and outside communication. They talked to small companies to secure exclusive contracts, they worked with vendors for equipment and weapons, they licensed a shuttle that anyone could use, and they struck a deal with the private hangar for all contractors in association with Bounty Inc. Wyn had less and less paperwork for himself, freeing up his nights for more time with others or his own personal research.

Seph had even gotten L-Bot his new humanoid body, and Wyn had learned an important lesson: don't let Seph order humanoid bodies without oversight.

"What the fuck?" Sage proclaimed everyone's thoughts as she, Besari, and Wyn walked into the lounge after training one day.

"Seph?" Wyn called, looking around for the assistant.

The humanoid bot turned in the lounge to face them, displaying high cheekbones, a chiseled jaw, and dazzling eyes. Its body had a muscular form and wore pants. Actual pants. "Greetings, Mr. Kelda," it said in a husky voice that sent all three reeling.

"What..." Wyn wanted more sustenance to his question but couldn't find the words that should come after.

Seph poked his head into the lounge from the entrance hall and grinned. "Mr. Kelda! L-Bot's body came in. Isn't it great?"

Everyone looked back to the hunky robot, then back to Seph.

"Why's it wearing pants?" Besari asked.

"Well, um, that's my fault. Apparently it came with anatomically correct parts. I figured pants would solve that cheaper than a replacement."

"It's got a *dick*?" Sage asked.

"Why does a robot need a penis?" Wyn asked.

"Don't ask that, Wyn," Sage interrupted. "You don't want to know the answer."

"It's not like that!" Seph waved his hands in front of himself. "I mean it, honest accident. I just thought the body would be soothing to others."

"I want to burn it with fire," Sage said. "Can I shoot it with the slag cannon, Wyn?"

"Wait! Don't do that!" Seph called, hands waving uselessly in protest.

"It'll have to do," Wyn interrupted the wildly upset assistant. "We have other focuses for our finances. If it becomes a problem, we can place the core back within its old body."

Seph let out a sigh of relief, and Sage shook her head.

Wyn had to admit though, watching the others react to L-Bot's new form was rather entertaining.

Despite the passage of months, no Thresha talent developed for Wyn. He had searched for anything strange or different about his body, but nothing seemed obvious beyond the results of his training.

It had been a small chance, but it seemed he belonged to the subset of people who would never get talents of their own.

Sage's plan shifted when that became obvious. Besari was a close-quarters fighter, and Sage was a mid-to-close fighter. So the thought was to develop Wyn to fight from a longer range. His training with weapons took over, and he worked with every kind imaginable. He practiced with snipers and scatterguns, pistols and rifles, automatic firing and semi-auto. Eventually, he began out-shooting Besari, a point of immense pride. The projections in the shooting range advanced to moving targets and even simulated other combatants.

He also ordered his own combat armor, a heavier suit than Besari's, sacrificing agility for sturdiness. It came with sensors all over and a paired helmet that would let him check to the sides and behind. Readouts could show atmosphere composition, radiation levels, customizable tracking indicator, and much more that Wyn hadn't even begun to dig into. It was also graded for full space exposure for up to three hours without an external oxygen tank. Paired with his weapons, it would add to the helmet's HUD, keeping track of remaining shots, heat levels, irregularity warnings, and whatever else the company thought to provide.

Unfortunately, the company had sent Wyn a mismatched helmet, and their customer service was atrocious. He argued for hours with an automated system before he finally reached someone in the company, only for that to be a slightly better automated system. Eventually it was agreed that Wyn could send in his slate gray helm, and they would replace it with the appropriate charcoal helm. Wyn agreed and shipped it off, which left him without the helmet for the time being. Wyn had expected the exchange to require only a few days, but it had been more than a week, and Wyn still couldn't get hold of someone to figure out where his helmet was.

In the meantime, he made do with a visor as he and Besari trained in the shooting range. They ducked around projected obstacles and fired at ten projected enemies. They yelled to each other, passing information efficiently and quickly thanks to practice, and created a perfect pincer maneuver to trap the combatants in a crossfire.

That's when Sage walked in.

"There you are," she started. Then a projected plasma bolt shot through her chest, and the module screeched out, "Eliminated!"

"Scenario end," Wyn called out, and the projections froze, then disappeared, transforming the elaborate rural scene back into the wide-open shooting range.

"You got shot pretty quickly, Sage," Besari said with a soft chuckle. "Thought you were supposed to be better than that."

"I don't usually play games," Sage growled.

"They're not games," Wyn said. "It's a highly advanced simulation in order to prepare the user for combat with real individuals. Plenty of studies have shown that excelling at the simulations has a direct correlation to excelling in real combat situations."

"It just gave you a high score."

"It did?" Wyn spun, excited to see the flashing score, which did, in fact, beat their last score.

A wave of annoyance flashed across Sage's face. "Don't trick yourself into thinking this is real. You'll end up dead if you think the enemy's shots will just go through you without harm."

"We're treating it seriously, Sage," Besari said, holstering her scattergun and crossing her arms. "Are you just here to berate us, or do you have a reason?"

"Yeah, I figured it's time to try out the real thing rather than this game." She smiled and with a gesture brought up a bounty. "Just came in. Seems fitting for some training."

"Seriously?" Wyn's heart hammered in his chest as excitement coursed through his limbs.

"Finally!" Besari's own eagerness seemed to leak from her suit as well, her annoyed, slouchy posture straightening. "Who's the bounty?"

Sage watched their smiles falter, her own growing, before she finally said, "You're going to like this one."

# WANTED

THE
HERON

REWARD:
Ⓡ50,000

THE
ROSE

REWARD:
Ⓡ55,000

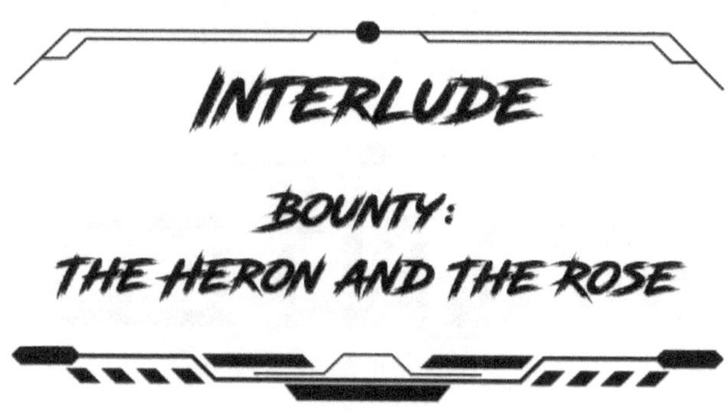

# INTERLUDE

## BOUNTY:
## THE HERON AND THE ROSE

Bone snapped and flesh tore as Zetta ripped the leg of the garnack off with one bite. She hated to admit it, but the stop at the Angbor Traffic Station was worthwhile, if just for the dumpy food stand that sold her the large, roasted rodent. Large, maybe, for some species. It was but the size of a newborn babe when it came to the rodents on Vroleus. She paused in her chewing and looked at the meal. She hoped this one wasn't a baby. She had a thing about eating babies; that being she usually didn't enjoy it. But she was pretty sure this was a normal size for a garnack. A snap and a tear and another of its six limbs came free in her mouth.

Zetta leaned back on a stool and watched the restless station lobby. An official-looking, sweaty human made his way toward her, and Zetta glared. He stopped in his tracks, and his pores moistened his body further. A strange thing for humans. She wasn't sure why fear invoked this behavior. She'd seen the same response in Sage during some of their more involved sexual encounters, and Sage hadn't been scared.

A mother barreled into the official, nearly dropping one of the three children she carried, and shouted some rather creative swears in his direction. The sweaty man retreated, both from Zetta and the wailing mother and kids. Which meant he hadn't been approaching her to tell her she was cleared to land on Angbor. Most likely, he had the unfortunate job of telling her it would be a few more minutes.

It had only become unfortunate after the fourth time. She had received a warning not to express threats of "death and mutilation" to employees or her landing privileges would be revoked indefinitely. He hadn't quite made it back to her since, though he'd tried valiantly a few times. That meant she was still stuck here.

She contemplated her chances of slipping past sector security if she left when a ding brought her attention to her Vico. Then it rang.

Zetta growled, snapped off another limb of the garnack, and answered the call.

"Yeah?"

"Greetings, Hunter." A falvian materialized above her Vico, deep shades of green centering around his eyes and brightening as they grew further away. His voice had the same monotone drone as every other falvian using a vocal box. She would never understand why they hadn't gotten some other voice synthesizer. The monotone drove her nerves wild. He seemed to notice her irritation. "Am I interrupting?"

"Just Raiyrium bureaucracy wasting my time," she growled and snapped off another limb. "Oh, and my lunch."

"Angbor Traffic Station?"

Zetta growled affirmatively.

"I've heard of a flock stuck there for fifteen days once during vacation," the falvian said.

"There's gonna be a lot of dead bodies for Angbor security to clean up if I'm stuck here for fifteen more minutes."

"I sing for your swiftness," he said. "Since you have the free time, it might be beneficial to go over the data packet I have sent you. It contains your target and everything we know. We'd like him brought in alive, but we'll pay the penalty bounty if dead."

"Good to know."

"I do not believe it needs any warning, but be careful whom you speak to about your real reasons for visiting. I have reports that they have plenty of eyes and ears within the planetary government."

"I'm not an amateur," Zetta said as she tore off the garnack's head. Her expression softened for just a moment as the skull crunched in her jaws and the rodent's brains spilled out. They were very delicious. "I told them I'm visiting a friend."

"And they believed that?" His eyes were skeptical even as his voice droned the question. He even cheeped a bit.

"I said it *convincingly*," Zetta assured him.

"Right," he said. "I've included the last known coordinates. He's holed up in some sort of high security complex, partnering with a weapons manufacturing plant for safety. Rumors have it they've experimented with new weaponry. Problem is, it's located in a highly restricted octant of the planet. Funds are funneled to the government for protection. You won't be able to sneak in easily."

"I'll just land there," Zetta said.

"What? You can't do that. I just said it was highly restricted. You'll be shot out of the sky."

Zetta shrugged and shoved the last bit of garnack in her mouth. Maybe she would if they could find her, but a drone carrying false identification would be flying the main route to the planet while her shuttle found its own path. The stealth upgrades on *Slaughter* should be enough to sneak past security, but in case they weren't, she wanted the Heron's eyes on the city, watching for her there. Not on his back door.

The falvian hummed. "Be careful, Zetta. These people have no qualms about experimentation and killing. Several weapons have come from that factory that could annihilate the galaxy's best shuttles in a single shot. They could possess something destructive beyond your comprehension."

"My comprehension is boundless when it comes to destruction." Zetta smiled. Perhaps she'd find something more exciting than a slag cannon. Sage would be so jealous.

"I hope you do not test that theory." The falvian blinked. "I do not wish to level half of Angbor in an attempt to capture the Heron."

"Maybe Angbor should have thought of that before harboring criminals." Zetta flicked open the bounty, and another falvian, long-beaked and white-feathered, hovered next to the first. The Heron, nicknamed for his white feathers. They were a clever bunch. She wondered if this Rose person he was partnering with was a pink falvian.

"Any other questions?"

"Nope. Once I'm past security, I'll hop down there and catch you a bird."

"I have a question of my own," he said, and despite Zetta's glare, he continued. "It says here your bounty is being accepted through a company called Bounty Inc. Is this correct?"

"Yeah, I'm trying something new. Being a team player."

The falvian hooted. *Hooted.* "Good luck," he said, then disconnected the call.

"Can you believe this guy?" Zetta growled as she turned to the small tesing boy next to her. His eyes were wide, plastered to the spot on the Vico where the falvian had displayed. "He fucking *hooted* at me. Why? Because he doesn't think vrolaks can be team players?"

The young boy's eyes rose to meet hers, his mouth floundering for a response.

"Oh, right. Don't tell anyone what you overheard, or I'll have to eat you."

He started shaking, and she felt the terror seeping out.

"I have your scent. It won't be hard to track you down."

The boy fell from the chair, and presumably his mother ran over, yelling. Zetta ignored the commotion as she spotted the sweaty man approaching her again, and this time he wasn't stopping.

"How many heat signatures do you read?"

"Thirty-four," the ship's computer responded. Stealth wasn't her usual go-to, but neither was laying half the planet to waste. Zetta rose from the pilot's chair, *Slaughter* safely landed on a hilltop near the weapons compound. Then she shuffled through a few drawers, searching for the scanner. She had one around here somewhere.

"There is one heat signature en route," the automated voice said.

"What?" Zetta banged her head as she jerked up, scattering a dozen random bits around. She threw them all in the drawer and slammed it shut until the contents rearranged enough to allow it to close fully. A low growl flowed from her to match her current temper. Then she checked the scanner. Sure enough, someone headed right toward her. It couldn't be a coincidence.

Nothing to do about it now. She stepped outside, sat against one of the landing struts, and waited. And wished she had more garnack to chew on.

Her guest arrived five minutes later in a small, open-topped hopper. A single gorsaulk man, bipedal, green-skinned—green-carapaced? She wasn't sure of the right term for the insectile creatures—with little pincers that formed a mouth and long, drooping antennae that dangled in lazy arcs. He almost looked edible. Zetta licked her lips at the thought.

*Who are you?*

"Use your voice," Zetta growled.

His segmented eyes lowered at her. Zetta returned the glare. She hated it when species spoke into her brain.

"Who are you?" he croaked out.

"Zetta. And you?"

"Chelk. This is a restricted area. I'm going to need you to leave." He lifted a rifle to emphasize his point. Zetta was unimpressed.

"Under whose authority?"

"The government of Angbor's."

"Yeah, but whose really?"

"What are you talking about?"

"I just need to know if it's okay to kill you or not. If you're actually Angbor security, then obviously I'll only maim you. But if you work for the Rose..."

His antennae twitched, eyes going wide. He brought the rifle to the ready, but he was far too slow. She was on him in a moment, her claws ripping through his armor and arms. Her muscles pulsed to the chemicals pouring through her now. Maniacal laughter filled her lungs as the thrill overwhelmed her.

The man fell back screaming as he looked down at his severed arms.

"The Rose, then?" She was wild with the thrill, the bloodlust filling her, and she could practically taste the bug man's blue blood on her lips.

The bug man shook and stared at her. A litany of words, sentences abruptly started and stopped, ran through her head, dulling her thrill and filling the empty space with pure annoyance.

"I don't care anymore. You're annoying me." She ran the claw through his chest, the carapace cracking beneath her. The litany quieted, and she sighed, releasing the pressure on Geble. Her muscles shrank, and she felt herself weaken. She hated that feeling, but drawing on the parasite too much would kill it. Then kill her. And she hated dying far more.

Zetta licked her claw, then spit. "Fuck, you taste disgusting." She shivered and cleaned her claws on the dead man's clothes. She checked the hopper next, a little pod barely large enough for the single occupant, but it had supplies and a radio. The radio asked for an update on the item he'd spotted descending into the sector. No official, bureaucratic words. Definitely one of the Rose's.

The voices stopped asking for a report and started insulting Chelk about his intelligence and delusions. Zetta shrugged and checked supplies.

"Perfect!" A scanner sat at the top of a satchel in the back, likely how the man had spotted her. She pulled it free and smiled. No need to find hers if she got a new one.

Holding the binoculars to her eyes, Zetta scanned her surroundings. She had landed the shuttle on the top of a forested hill, giving herself a good vantage point into the complex below. She zoomed in. A large, angular swath of the forest had been eradicated, and a tall wall surrounded the clearing. A rectangular building sat about five hundred feet in from each of the walls. It was entirely unoriginal architecture. It hurt her eyes because of how boring and blocky it all was.

There were several doors into the structure, most notably two rather large sliding doors that led to some sort of garage or warehouse. If they weren't expecting a shipment, that would be an excellent entryway. Once she made her way past the thirty-four guards. She glanced back at the dead gorsaulk.

*Thirty-three.*

Most paced the wall, though she was able to find a few camped out in the surrounding forest, at high points like sentries. She had been lucky to be spotted by only one of them. She would have to kill them first, but fast enough so no alarms—

"What the fuck?"

She paused in her thoughts as one of the guards swung his head wildly around in annoyance, then slapped his ear. He seemed to open his mouth, then just dropped to the ground. Six seconds later, he was on his feet, strangely rigid. And he just stood there.

"No," Zetta growled. She scanned the wall until she found the next guard. She was standing still too, just staring. "No!"

Over half the guards stood in place, stock still, vacant stare. Zetta slammed her fist into the front of the hopper, smashing its engine as she unintentionally pulled on her parasite. The vehicle crashed to the ground, giving a final dying whine before falling silent.

"You fucking thief!"

Zetta turned from the hopper and ran aboard her ship. She threw her new scanner into the bucket next to her ammunition bucket, and it clattered against her old scanner. From the wall, she pulled off the massive gauntlet, and it clanged to the ground with a loud thud. She slid her right claw into the gauntlet's opening. "I'm going to kill you!" she roared. Geble's chemicals pulsed through her, muscles stretching, strength improving. The gauntlet that had been a challenge to lift before now easily came off the ground with a single hand, as if it were simply a mitten. The gauntlet sealed around her wrist with a click and hummed to life. She stalked from the ship and glared at the complex. Even without the scanner, it was clear most of the guards had stopped moving. Which meant stealth didn't matter anymore.

Zetta took note of the wind and the distance, eyeballing her elevation, then ran the calculations through her mind for the precise amount she needed to pull from Geble to land just within the gates of the complex. Then she ran, and the ground crumbled at her launching point as she hurtled through the air. Wind whistled down her spine and through her spikes. Maniacal laughter overcame her as the adrenaline coursed through her veins. Her skin stretched to its breaking point, then retracted as she reached her peak, letting them rest until she landed.

The vrolak schooling system is not well regarded for their advancements in mathematics or science. There had been some brilliant vrolak minds over the years, like Dr. Yellek Twentieth Bronko and Professor Shen Four-Hundred Fiftieth Jem, who'd propelled the advancement of Vroleus a hundred or more years. The Droleon Hyper-Matter Engine had a team consisting of two vrolak scientists. The Scarred Sky, a weapon so deadly it had been banned in nearly every system, had had its breakthrough thanks to a vrolak. This was all to say, however, that these tended to be the exceptions, the special cases.

The parasite provided strength, but a vrolak's natural hide had already grown tough over centuries of evolution in the harsh climates of Vroleus, leaving them nearly impervious to most damage. The combination of these enhancements had created an expensive market for vrolak mercenaries and fighters. Their system of honor promoted warriors above scientists, and their lack of membership in the Raiyrium Confederation limited their access to generalized knowledge through galactic-standard schooling.

So it was not much of a surprise when Zetta crashed into the forest nearly a thousand yards shy of the complex entirely.

The forest creaked and cracked as a stream of trees cascaded in a collision with the charging vrolak. Zetta rushed straight toward the gates from a point some one thousand yards away, a single-minded focus on her destination, all subtlety tossed away. Not that it mattered. Not a single guard bothered to look or report. Radios were long-silent, their carriers' movements stilled to nothing more than the occasional swaying. So even her explosion from the forest was received by the rather small audience of two auto-targeting turrets.

They did welcome her with an array of plasma, but it failed to improve Zetta's mood. A flick of her claw and the gauntlet shifted, the fist opening as a honed nozzle protruded. The inner mechanisms whirred to life as she lifted it with her other hand and aimed. She fired, and a thick, red beam of plasma painted the turrets one after another, two large explosions following in its path. The gauntlet clicked and expelled an empty cartridge, then vented the heat. It felt good against her scales, stoking her rage.

Zetta inspected herself for injuries. A few of the turrets' shots had hit her, but most of the damage was superficial. At this distance, they wouldn't have been strong enough to break skin. She adjusted the gauntlet, and the ejection slot slid shut, the ranged nozzle retracted, and the fist closed up. Which made for a perfect knocker.

She knocked.

Launching herself at the doors with enhanced strength, the armored gauntlet slammed through the thick metal doors, smashing one of them to the ground and sending it skittering across the courtyard. She stalked into the complex, and every guard within range stared at her, but none held a weapon at the ready.

She took in a deep breath, eyes sliding across the eerily still guards. Then she yelled. "ACHTREK! GET THE FUCK OVER HERE!"

For several moments, her breathing was the only thing she heard, then a slow humming. A cloud of beetles poured over one wall and into the courtyard. They congregated in a cyclone before Zetta, filling the air with hundreds of thousands of flapping wings and the soft clink of shells knocking into each other as a man-shaped pile of bugs formed. The shells' camouflage shifted the colors to actually almost look like a human.

"Zetta," they said with just a hint of hum to their voice.

"You're six?" She had to make sure, but she was pretty damn sure.

"Yes," they confirmed.

Zetta growled. "This is my fucking bounty! I signed up on Wyn's stupid application, I selected it, and it confirmed. It should have locked it to me."

"I did likewise."

"So his application is fucking busted? Of course it is!"

"How would you like to proceed?"

Zetta growled, but this wasn't the first time two hunters showed up for the same bounty. Usually that meant one of them killing the other, but Zetta wasn't entirely sure she'd win. "I don't like splitting bounties, so how about I take the bounty and you can eat all of the bodies I leave behind."

"Unsatisfactory," they said. "The flesh I shall take if you have no need, but the bounty is for the Mother Hive. We cannot deprive the Mother."

"Listen here, you pile of bugs. I dealt with terrible traffic at the Angbor Traffic Station—"

"Same."

"—I used up a decoy drone to trick security—"

"Same."

"—I bought a lot of fucking ammunition for this—"

"We did not."

"—and I had to talk to the most insufferable, conceited falvian agent to get this bounty—"

"We also did not do that."

"—so I am not in the mood to—wait, what?"

"Our agent was a tesing official."

"Why are the tesings after this Heron person?"

"Heron?" Achtrek asked, and Zetta could have sworn they cocked their makeshift head. "We're hunting the Rose."

"The *Rose*?"

"Yes, a weapons manufacturer who has supposedly started manufacturing deadly chemical-based weaponry alongside weapons of mass—"

"I know who the fucking Rose is," Zetta interrupted. "So we're after different bounties?"

"That appears so."

"Great, problem solved." Zetta grinned, then looked around at the chaos in the courtyard. The auto turrets still sparked, thick black smoke rising from their charred innards. The doors were smashed open, not to mention her own screaming. The bodies of the guards dropped to the ground as a single beetle climbed out of each from one ear and flew to the main host. "So, uh, looks like I messed up your stealth mission, huh?"

"Indeed."

Zetta scratched under a scale on her neck. "Wanna just join forces and kill everyone here to get to the bounty?"

"That seems the most apt choice at this point."

A rattle resounded, and one of the great rolling doors rose up, slowly revealing hundreds of soldiers, rifles at the ready. They shouted and hyped themselves up. A lot of work for a lot of dead people.

"They sent the peons." Zetta flicked the gauntlet to ranged mode, and Achtrek vibrated, cracks appearing in their facade.

"You take point," they said, "and we shall surround."

"Just give me one shot before you rush in," Zetta said as she raised the gauntlet toward the crowd.


Philosophers dream of a true species, some bipedal form from which all species had adapted. Zetta thought there was a chance, for many species shared similar characteristics. Weapons seemed to have developed along familiar paths, space travel similarly so. Even biologically speaking, despite the differences in color, texture, size, and taste, Zetta had found that just about every sentient species shared the same delicious underlying smell to their blood. The air was saturated with it, and it stirred a hunger within her.

The gauntlet's beam died out and ejected the cartridge. Body parts and blood rained down in the aftermath as nearly half the peons were annihilated in the first few moments. Three shots left.

She switched it to melee and charged into the carnage. Achtrek-Six burst apart and swarmed to either side of her.

Those that were not in shock fired back, and Zetta leapt over the shots. It made her more open with the less predictable path, but by the time they corrected their aim, Achtrek slammed into the crowd. The screaming began as she landed amidst them.

She slashed with claw, pulverized with gauntlet, crushed with tail, and shredded with jaws. Achtrek swam through the crowd, aiming for eyes, ears, and mouths, destroying targets from within. It became a blood bath, and every ounce spilled built on a euphoric rage that burned within Zetta. She cackled as men and women, birrosh, human, and tesing, died by her hand. Some froze in horror, and they died. Some fled, and they died a little slower. For in that moment, she was their god of destruction, and not a soul could escape her.

It ended far too soon, the fire within Zetta cooling as fast as the bodies around her. She licked the rainbow of mixed blood from her jaws, savoring it as Achtrek formed a swarming ball next to her. They pulsed as they spoke.

"We should continue on."

"Through the door?" Zetta licked her free claw. "Could be a trap."

"We think you'll survive a trap."

"And you?"

"We know we'll survive a trap."

Zetta smirked. "Then let's spring it."

Bones crunched beneath her feet with every step until she passed under the rolling door and found herself within a great warehouse, as expected. Large crates filled one side, with a few doors to the back where—

*CRACK!*

Pain exploded within Zetta, and she felt the ground leave beneath her. The crates stopped her momentum, exploding beneath her weight. Rancid liquid spilled out around her, glass cracking as she shifted to her feet. Blood ran down her jaw, this time her own. It had been awhile since she'd tasted her own blood.

The rolling door crashed to the ground, and a red alarm blared through the warehouse room. The exits sealed with a hiss, most likely airtight. The trap had been sprung. Achtrek swarmed at Zetta's assailant but was quickly repelled by flames. The beetles flew out of reach, and as the flames died out, Zetta could clearly see who had struck her.

A tall, purple bishett woman wore boots, trousers, a sleeveless shirt (the sleeves clearly torn away to show off muscles), and a full mask, protecting herself from Achtrek's attempts to eat her insides. She stalked toward Zetta in a fighter pose, one grotesque, massive arm held in front of her. That was *not* normal for a bishett, the distended limb darker than the rest of her skin, pustules growing between bulging veins. A quick swing of that arm sent machinery spinning across the room.

It wasn't just for show.

"Before this is done"—Zetta readied herself—"and I've torn your head from your shoulders, you'll have to tell me how you got that disgusting arm."

"I don't think there will be time." The bishett warrior emphasized her point by slamming the massive limb into Zetta. She braced herself and blocked, but it still sent her careening across the warehouse and into the wall. Air burst from her lungs as lights danced around her.

Lights? She hadn't hit her head. Zetta opened her eyes to see dozens of flames sprouting from fully-armored soldiers. Achtrek dove and spun around the flames, but the fire continued circling the beetles, driving them into a corner to burn them alive. Achtrek struck out, but Zetta saw the little bodies burn up and hit the ground after each attack. Every one cost them more of themselves, and none succeeded in killing their attackers. They needed Zetta's help; she just needed to take care of the bishett bitch in front of her first.

Bishett bitch... Bitchett? Zetta smiled. She couldn't wait to share that one with Sage later.

"I think you're right," Zetta said, switching focus to Bitchett. "This won't last long. So why don't you tell me how you got that arm?"

"I'll whisper it to your corpse," she growled. "But know that it's far better than having some bug pump you full of steroids."

"If it's from jerking all the guys, you can tell me. I won't judge too much. We all have our kinks."

Bitchett paused her approach, an icy glare spreading over her features. It might have worked to scare someone with no spine, like Wyn, but for her it meant her remarks had landed as intended.

"Slut shaming? Really?"

"Straight shaming, actually," Zetta said. "What girl is gonna want that inside of her?"

Bitchett scowled and launched herself. Zetta barely slid out of the way as the engorged fist hammered into the wall, the vibrations echoing around the room. Zetta took the opening and—

The bishett's free arm swung up and slammed into Zetta's throat, and she coughed out choking breaths. A leg swept her feet out from under her, and she hit the ground shoulder-first. Bitchett pulled her enlarged fist back from the wall, a lattice of cracks spreading out from where it had struck, and brought it down at Zetta. The vrolak kicked, hitting the other woman in the ribs and sending her...well, not flying, but at least sliding away. Zetta rolled to all fours and pounced away from her opponent, spinning upright after gaining space.

She coughed, her breath coming in ragged gasps. Enough to keep her going, but the blackness crept in on her vision. Thankfully she had been enhancing all her muscles, or that hit might have been lethal. It wasn't just that fucking arm. Bitchett was *strong*. She took a kick and it barely affected her. Did she have a talent too?

Zetta grinned, vrolak blood leaking from between her teeth to join the rest smeared across her. This was going to be more fun than she'd anticipated. "I expected you to be a shittier fighter," she said.

"I expected you to be a better one," Bitchett replied.

Zetta's grin turned to a scowl. This woman was far too cocky for a dead woman.

The bishett moved first, and Zetta threw herself forward. Bloated fist slammed into metal fist with a resounding crunch, and Bitchett countered with a low swing. Zetta spun and knocked the fist to the side, driving her tail into the other woman's ribs and sending her careening into a nearby crate. A burst of strength, focused at her legs, made her muscles burn with power, and she launched herself forward. Before Bitchett could stand, Zetta grabbed one leg and spun, tossing her like a ragdoll into the flamers harassing Achtrek. There was a great crash, a great amount of shouting, and a great number of beetles taking advantage of the opening to swarm away.

She had bought Achtrek time away from the corner, but the hired security was well organized and already working to contain them once more. And Bitchett was rising as if she hadn't just been tossed across the room. Zetta prepared to pounce, but a cloud of beetles hidden among the crates attacked. It was not Achtrek's full power. It wasn't even a majority, as that was occupied by the others. But it was enough to find bits of flesh all over the woman and begin chewing. Always the gentlebugswarm, Achtrek was buying her time to deal with the others, but something felt off. Bitchett hadn't even moved.

"Fire!" she shouted, and one of the security twisted toward her. Then she was covered in flames.

*Shit!*

Zetta switched her gauntlet to ranged, and the mechanisms whirred to life again. But the nozzle did not release. The front was dented from the impact with Bitchett, and Zetta had to pry it open. It creaked but gave way, and she held it ready. A quick burst to free Achtrek and the two of them could—

A crate smashed against Zetta and sent her stumbling. Bitchett walked from the flames, skin untouched. Bits of bug and cloth dripped from her body as her shirt burned away, and Great Warrior be damned, but no one with that ugly an arm should look that fucking sexy.

Zetta didn't have much time to daydream after that. The other woman crashed into her as she tried to shift the gauntlet back to melee, but the same mechanisms were getting jammed as before. Zetta tried to regain footing, but the bloated arm crushed her against the wall while the bishett's free arm wailed at her side. Zetta had bulked up the area with muscle, but still the damage was too significant. Her torso bruised, and a rib cracked. She dropped the gauntlet and grabbed the arm. Bitchett wriggled free and hit her again.

Zetta pulled her feet up from the ground, forcing her opponent to hold up her full weight, an easier task than she had hoped it would be. Still, she pulled on Geble, bringing her muscles to their absolute limit. Her skin stretched until it nearly tore, painfully tight across her body, but the woman's blows had ceased. The sudden weight had pulled the other woman off guard, and Zetta took advantage, shifting to continue throwing off her balance. They grappled like that, Zetta clinging all her weight to the bloated arm while trading blows with her tail, digging claws into skin that wouldn't pierce.

Then finally Bitchett budged, only to slam Zetta to the ground and burst the air from her lungs. She focused the muscle enhancements to her legs only and kicked against her opponent, sending herself rocketing backward more than the bishett woman, but it gave her the room to get to her feet. Bitchett chased, keeping Zetta at bay with great swings from her club arm. There was no way to close the distance.

No way except to take the hit.

Something buzzed near her ear, and Zetta jumped back from the hit instead of taking it. Old code, from the only other mission Zetta had been on with Ol' Bugsy. They'd had to operate separately, and so a single beetle passed information seamlessly between them. She had hated learning it, but times had changed.

"I like your thinking," Zetta mumbled. "Give me thirty seconds."

With the next swing of Bitchett's arm, Zetta jumped forward, inside of its reach, limiting the blow. Her opponent tried to jump back for space, but Zetta locked the arm in place with her own. The bishett's free hand came in for a strike, and Zetta let it hit against her enhanced abdomen, locking that arm in place as well. Then, before giving it much thought, Zetta slammed her forehead into the other woman's face.

The facemask cracked, and Zetta was reasonably sure her own skull did too, but it wasn't enough. Unfortunately, Bitchett seemed unwilling to give it more time. The woman lifted her with a roar, and Zetta felt her feet leave the ground. Zetta released the smaller arm and grabbed the woman's head, but Bitchett pulled her close into a crushing embrace. Air burst from Zetta as her claw slid across the mask, unable to find purchase.

The blackness encroached as the woman squeezed harder. Zetta flailed out, claw and tooth, tail and knee, but nothing seemed to release the hold. She was going to die. She was going to lose in hand-to-hand combat with a fucking bishett.

No. What would Sage think of her now? Dying in such a pathetic way.

*No.* Her vision rushed back by pure will. She pulled on Geble and everything it had, her muscles tensing and growing until her own skin tore under the expansion.

NO! She grabbed the bishett's face with both claws and squeezed. The facemask cracked, and she drove a thumb at its epicenter, breaking it open and shoving the claw into the woman's face. Zetta heard the roar of pain, her blood responding by pumping faster, fueled by her rage. She smelled the blood in the air. She could almost taste it. She would *not* die here, not to a bishett, not to some freak monster creation. She wouldn't die to anyone, not before Sage died.

Zetta roared back, breaking the embrace with her blood-slicked body and overextended strength. Her feet hit the ground, and she grabbed the bloated arm even as the bishett's other arm struggled at pulling Zetta's gouging thumb free.

Then Zetta bit down, teeth slicing into shoulder, blood running down her jaw and across her tongue. Blood was the liquid of life, and in that moment it gave her so much of it. She laughed as she twisted, pulling the bishett with her in the twirl. Jaw and arms worked as one, releasing just at the right point to send her careening once more into the crowd of guards attacking Achtrek.

This time when Bitchett rose, the movement lacked the earlier dignity. She struggled to her feet as though drunk, blood streaming from one eye, her mask cracked. Blood ran freely down her chest and abdomen from several punctures and tears in her shoulder. The guards recovered in time to stop Achtrek's entire swarm from taking advantage of the opening in her mask, but it didn't matter. The beetle by Zetta's ear was gone.

Bitchett crashed into the other guards, bulky arm swinging and sending them flying. They retreated, shouting out in surprise and confusion. But now Achtrek's puppet did the herding, and the guards' flamethrowers did nothing to stop its advance. And even if they could have, they were sitting ducks now. Zetta picked up her gauntlet, still set to range, and swept a beam through the huddled guards. Gore splattered across the walls as bodies exploded. The cartridge ejected and clattered to the floor in a suddenly silent room.

"We should think of retreat," Achtrek said, their swarm forming up as a human again, though this time much shorter.

"You're shorter than usual." Zetta took stock of her injuries, and for the most part she felt like a building had fallen on her and she'd survived. Good enough.

"We have lost many selves," Achtrek said. "If we lose many more, our consciousness will begin to dwindle."

"Leave if you want, but I came for my bounty, and I'm not leaving without it." Another clang resounded through the room as the puppeted Bitchett slammed against the door again. Zetta groaned and lifted the gauntlet. It required some straining to hold it steady now that her battle rage had cooled down. "Move the body, Achtrek. I'll take care of the door."

Bitchett stumbled out of the way, and Zetta steadied the shot. This time, when the gauntlet fired, she stumbled back. Fuck, maybe retreat wasn't a bad option. Only one more shot remained, and she had neglected to grab any other weapons in her rush. Not that she couldn't tear them all apart with tooth and claw, but weapons made it fun. A slag cannon would be fun right about now.

When the smoke cleared, the door had melted away, a deep orange at the edges of the hole quickly cooling to a dull gray. It opened into a hallway, the other side of which was scorched from the beam. Going left would likely be a dead end, given they had entered on that side of the complex, so right would be the best bet.

"You coming?" Zetta asked.

Achtrek hummed. "Yes. Wouldn't want you to get yourself killed."

"I haven't found anything yet that could do the job, and I doubt there's anything in here that can." Zetta smirked as she stepped into the hallway and—Bitchett grabbed her from behind and pulled, throwing her off balance, just in time to keep her unscathed by a beam of light filling the hall. She felt the waves of heat emanating from it, and when it cleared, she saw how the hallway warped around it. Metal dripped from the ceilings and walls, plaster burnt away, electricity sparking from open wires. Zetta even heard the wind. They must have blown a hole through the left side of the hall.

"We think we found something that can," Achtrek said.

Zetta pulled herself from the ground and growled. "Only if it hits me."

"Fifteen second reload," Achtrek reported. "Blast killed every self in the hallway. They have another thirteen shots. At top speed, you could get down the hallway in thirty-five seconds. They have spotters for my selves and heat guns prepared to avoid distracting line of sight."

"Huh." Zetta scratched at her neck. "Troublesome, but not impossible. I can fire the gauntlet in the fifteen-second interval."

"You want to shoot a highly concentrated beam of plasma towards the weapon that produced that blast?"

"What's the worst that could happen?"

"We all die."

"Sounds like that's the best case if we don't try it."

Zetta wasn't sure if hives could sigh, but the hum that came from them certainly suggested one. "How much do you want to keep the body around?"

Zetta glanced at Bitchett, who just stood there, staring from one bleeding eye and one normal one. "Eh, she's good to look at, but being dead detracts from that."

"We shall send it out as a distraction. Then you'll have your fifteen seconds."

"Understood." Zetta readied herself and watched the corpse stumble into the hallway. Radiant light scorched Zetta's vision, eviscerating Bitchett in seconds. She clenched her jaw, braced herself, and hefted the gauntlet.

The light died out, and Zetta leapt into the hallway. It was like stepping into an oven, knowing that if she stayed too long, she would be cooked alive. The floor scalded her feet, but she ignored it. Her blood pulsed within her muscles. Time slowed for her as she took aim.

People shouted and pointed at her. They panicked and struggled with the reload, trying to move faster. Several aimed heat guns at her, though the distance was too far to do anything lethal.

Zetta fired.

The beam slammed into the weapons operator, exploding their head, then swept over to the reloader. She heard the cartridge drop with a great clatter. The others ducked, and Zetta stepped forward.

Her leg seized, knee buckling, and she hit the floor. The beam dropped and slammed into a pile of cylindrical cartridges.

"Oh fu—"

Zetta had never thought about what it would feel like to be a projectile fired from a weapon. Had someone asked, she may have said that it sounded unpleasant. In the moment after the first cartridge exploded, she understood the projectile intimately.

An explosion of white light and immense pressure filled the hallway. Zetta was picked up in a torrent of air and plasma and launched through the open end of the hallway just like a projectile. In the moment before the blast hit her, Achtrek swarmed around her, cushioning her from the heat and force. But her back was exposed, and she smashed straight through the outer wall of the complex and into the forest. Subconsciously, she had strengthened her back but was still surprised to find her spine intact after she'd slammed through dozens of trees before skidding to a halt.

Then came the earthquake. The world shook, trees cracking and crashing all around them.

"BENEATH ME!" Zetta roared as she rolled over, curling around the remaining beetles from Achtrek's hive. They squirmed under her, and the first tree smashed down on top of Zetta. Seven more buried her before the world stopped shaking.

The aftermath was one of the most brutal things Zetta had ever seen. A crater sat where the complex had once been, the forest around it decimated and burnt away for hundreds of yards. A thick smog filled the air, blotting out the sun.

"Do you think we'll still get our bounties?" Zetta asked the sluggish hive.

Achtrek hummed and buzzed but didn't respond.

"Shit. I'm sorry, buddy." Zetta looked at the cloud of beetles, not even half the size it had been to start. "Are you going to be okay, Bugs?"

"Need...mating..." The words came out more hum than language. Zetta grinned.

"I don't think I can help there, but I'll take you to my ship, where you can get busy."

She thought the responding buzz was an affirmative one. Zetta began to lead the way, but she pulled up short when a massive thud sounded nearby. The one remaining tree nearby shook, then fell. Behind it, a metal box, large enough to be a comfortably-sized bedroom, embedded itself in the dirt at a crooked angle. Steam rose off of it in thick, white wisps.

"Now, what is this?" Zetta walked over and found a door on the front with a simple latch. She expected it to be locked, but it pulled open with ease, and inside two bloodied and bruised people huddled against one corner, dazed.

One was a pink tesing woman with one eye wearing a gaudy pink dress that was rumpled and stained with blood. The other was an unconscious, mostly white-feathered falvian. Mostly white, because the rest was stained once more with blood. The safety room had survived decimation but had been launched into the sky by the force of the explosion, only to land right in Zetta's lap. She smirked.

"You the Rose?" she asked.

The pink tesing noticed her then, and her eyes went wild. "Don't touch me, beast!" she yelled, though her voice shook with terror. Zetta could almost smell it coming from her. "I know you're here visiting a friend. I have people watching her house, and they'll kill her if you touch me."

"Yeah, I don't care," Zetta said. "That was a lie."

Rose's mouth hung open, and her eyes widened. "But you gave an address."

"Yeah, found that on the datanet. No idea whose it is."

"I still have the protection of Sovereign, so it would be wise to think twice about this."

"Yeah, I don't know who that is." Zetta crawled in and approached the pair, the Rose moving behind the Heron and holding him up like a shield. Zetta just grabbed the birdman and draped him over one shoulder. "Come on. My friend's gotta fuck himself."

"What?"

Zetta punched the lady in the face, then lifted her over the other shoulder. Then thought about how she could really go for some fucking herself.


"I turned in the bounties after that," Zetta said, leaning on the front desk as the flimsy secretary boy looked on in admiration. She was pretty sure it was admiration anyway. "After turning in Achtrek's for them, they had regained enough of their senses to lead me to their ship. Guess that one's better for the bug sex. They have all the right food to promote that baby-making, so I made my way back here to see how everyone else is doing."

"Wow, that's crazy," Seph said. "I can't believe you survived an explosion like that."

"Never let anyone tell you vrolaks aren't tough, kid. Ain't nothing in the world that can kill me."

"That seems so."

Zetta glanced at the weird new robot standing next to Seph. It was shaped in the customary features of a ruggedly handsome human male. But soulless and unnerving. "The fuck is that?"

"That's L-Bot," Seph said.

"Greetings, Zetta Ninth Forox," the bot said.

"Why's it look like that?"

"Wyn approved a new shell for it. It was my idea."

"Are you fucking it?"

"What?" Seph laughed, but it was the nervous kind. His eyes grew wide when Zetta stared at him. "No! Of course not. I just thought he looked friendlier this way."

"Right, whatever." Zetta stood straight and felt the aches through her body twinge. "Where's Sage?"

"I think she's briefing Wyn and Besari in the lounge. She found a bounty to take them on."

"I wonder how badly that little idiot is going to fuck up." Zetta smirked and ignored Seph's blubbering defense of Wyn. Moving away from the desk, she poked her head into the lounge to see what kind of bounty Sage would initiate them on.

# PART 2
# THE SONGBIRD OF SERRON

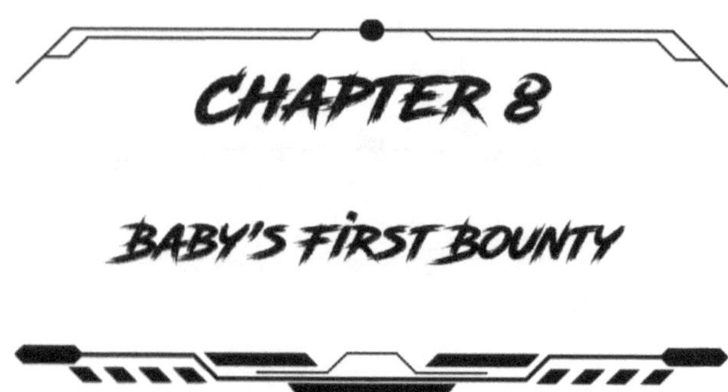

# CHAPTER 8

## BABY'S FIRST BOUNTY

"Serron Pel Faro, a perrilan baron, has requested assistance in finding his pet bird."

Silence filled the room after Sage's announcement, the image of a large bird rotating on the screen behind her. It was seven or so feet tall, with golden splotches throughout its otherwise maroon feathers. It had a long but dull beak the color of sand and eyes that were black pits. Not just black in color, mind you; this bird essentially had pits instead of eyeballs.

The silence dragged on, and Wyn looked at Besari. He couldn't see her face, but her body language told him enough. He looked back to Sage and shut his rather dry mouth.

"What?" he finally asked.

"Apparently these are pretty expensive birds, so losing one is a big deal," Sage said. "Someone stole it—"

"Wait," Wyn interrupted. "I meant, is this a joke?"

"No," she said, her face stony serious. "He's offering ten thousand raikers."

"I thought when we started doing bounties," Besari said, "that we would be catching criminals or hunting people. Not finding lost pets."

"Pretend it can talk," Sage suggested. "Besides, it's not like I would bring you in on an actually difficult bounty. Prove yourselves useful here, and we can look into doing a bounty where the target actually shoots back."

Besari's posture hardened, her hands clasping together in front of her stomach. Wyn shifted uncomfortably and looked away. It wasn't the glamorous bounty he'd imagined for his first, but Sage had a point. What if he froze in actual combat? All the training in his life wouldn't change that.

"I agree," Wyn said, and Besari glanced over. "I would like to ease my way into the bounty. This should be a quick one to give us practice and work our way up."

Besari nodded but seemed unconvinced. Of course, she had gone on training hunts already with her mentor, so she would be used to the dangers. But Wyn wasn't.

"Right. Then can we continue?" Sage asked.

"Yes," they said together.

"You might still get your wish to shoot something, since the songbird appears to have been stolen, not just lost. The baron has requested that we look into who has taken it and return it safely." Sage swiped at her Vico, and the images shifted to different views of the songbird. "Look closely at the spots on its back and neck. These are unique among songbirds. We find a bird with these spots, and we find our target."

"Do we know where to look?" Besari asked. "Would it be on Perrilium?"

"The baron was able to lock down the planet, so all vehicles large enough to carry a songbird will be thoroughly checked. Likely there's no chance of it leaving now. If it's on planet, that's less of a priority. The problem lies in the fact that Perrilium has an unorthodox atmosphere, making it unbreathable to most species, just as our air is unbreathable for them. Most songbirds die within a few weeks of leaving the planet because of the difficulty of keeping them contained. We are to investigate the possibilities that it could have been moved off-world between its capture and the lockdown."

"How many possibilities is that?" Wyn asked.

"Four." Sage swiped away the songbird, and four large transport shuttles appeared. "These were the only vehicles large enough to transport a songbird without immediately killing it. We are presuming they meant to capture the songbird alive and sell it to the highest bidder."

"Do we know where they went?"

"I'm running some tracing on these shuttles, and hopefully we can figure it out. I'll give you each a ship to track down and run you through how. We can make it a competition. The first one to figure out where their ship currently is can lead the mission."

"The first, third, and fourth have been tracked to R.C. locations, and standard scanning indicates there is likely no songbird aboard."

Wyn jumped, and noticed Besari do the same. Sage had a hand on her pistol as they all turned to discover Cee in the corner.

"How long have you been there?" Wyn asked.

"Three hours, forty-two minutes, and eighteen seconds as of right now." It shifted its attention back to Sage and continued. "That should eliminate the *Laundry Basket*, *Skarret*, and *Sleepless Death*. All of which appear to be standard shipping vessels with a rich history of trade. The *Kyris* seems to be something else, however. It has very little history of trade, and what it has seems to be falsified. Rather poorly if I may say so."

Sage released her pistol and crossed her arms. "That was supposed to be research done by them to train them."

"Apologies if I overstepped. I had hoped to prove my worth so that I might join your bounty."

"Why?"

"It will be the first multi-hunter bounty under Wyn Kelda's software," Cee said, and Wyn winced. He wasn't even sure if any of the code was still his, Cee had rewritten it so thoroughly. "It will be a good field test."

"Ten thousand raikers split four ways is a little light."

"I am happy to join free of charge."

Sage raised an eyebrow. "What kind of bounty hunter works free of charge?"

"One who wishes to make sure the software is working as expected. I won't even get in the way, just tag along and fix any issues that pop up."

"I don't think it could hurt," Wyn said. "It was able to figure out which shuttle was correct pretty quickly."

"That's if the scans were correct," Sage said. "And we still have to find where the *Kyris* docked."

"Bezium," Cee said. "Outside of confederation space, so it took longer to find. But I've found it. Traces of Perrilium atmosphere were leaking from the shuttle."

"It was at Perrilium, so it would have that," Sage pointed out.

"The shuttle design is one that sterilizes the air after sealing, and the crew were entirely not perrilans. The only way there'd be signs of that kind of atmosphere would be if something onboard contained it."

"Leaking for that long would leave the songbird dead."

"Not necessarily," Cee said, eyes shifting as it calculated. "It was a large container, and the leak was minimal. It just built up over the trip. I believe there is a ninety-eight percent chance the songbird was taken to Bezium and survived. But I also believe, unless it is moved to a new container, it will die in seven to ten days."

"Container?" Wyn asked. "Do any of us have a ship that could even carry a container that size? I hadn't thought about buying a freighter for the company."

"Don't worry about that. I can find something." Sage shifted her attention back to Cee. "Do you know what happened to the songbird after that?"

"Unfortunately, no. My access to Bezium's security is minimal. We would have to travel there."

"You're on the team, but no more hyper hacking unless we need it," Sage said. "It's meant to be a learning mission for these two, and having you do it all for them teaches them nothing."

"Understood."

"I don't like Bezium being our goal." Sage ran a hand through her hair and sighed. "But at least there will be someone else experienced with us in case of trouble."

"Is there something wrong with Bezium?" Wyn asked.

"If it were just me, no. But Bezium isn't in the R.C. for a reason. It's crowded with criminals seeking safe haven from confederation rule, and its government is nearly non-existent. You two stepping foot on that place likely means more trouble for me. So, Cee here will act as a secondary babysitter."

Wyn glared, but a cold feeling ran through his arm that told him he wouldn't complain about the extra help.

"I'll need a few hours to get us a shuttle large enough to transport the songbird, so let's meet at the private hangar in four hours, prepared for the bounty. Make sure to test that your combat suits are atmospheric-safe."

"Um." Wyn glanced around, finding it rather difficult to meet Sage's eyes at that moment.

"What?"

"It's about the suit being atmospheric-safe," Wyn said.

"You received yours, didn't you? I thought it came the other day."

"It did, but I don't currently have a helmet."

"What happened to the helmet?"

"It wasn't the same color as the body."

"So?"

"So, I returned it."

Sage blinked, opened her mouth, closed her mouth, ran a hand through her hair, then squinted. "Get a gas mask." She paused. "And grab some grenades."

"Grenades? Why do we need grenades for finding a bird?"

"You never want to miss the chance to blow something up if possible." Then she left.

Wyn glanced at Besari. "How bad is this atmosphere anyway? Can't I just hold my breath if I come into contact with it? It's not like we'll be on the surface of Perrilium."

Besari shrugged. "It differs between species, but most experience intense and vivid hallucinations after a single breath, extreme pain after two breaths, and any more than that usually kills. And that's normal breaths. If you're holding your breath and have to take a deep breath, it will overwhelm and kill you immediately."

Wyn felt a chill run through him. "I'm going to find a gas mask."

"Good call. I'll reach out to Boz-kai to see if they can provide an atmospheric container in case we need a new one."

Wyn split off in search of Seph. Several orders of various equipment had come in, and he was certain he would find gas masks in one, but the assistant would know for sure. He had been in charge of many of the orders and would be able to point Wyn in the right direction if they had arrived. But the entrance hall was empty.

"Seph?" Wyn glanced around to no avail. "L-Bot?" Neither was there.

Wyn shrugged and stepped behind the front desk to the storage closet. Seph used it to house deliveries before they were unpacked. Wyn figured he could quickly check through the boxes that were there before pinging the assistant.

Wyn opened the door, and he screamed. Then Seph screamed. And finally, L-Bot said, "Hello." Wyn shut the door.

"I'll check elsewhere!" Wyn yelled, then hurried out of the entrance hall, the image of L-Bot's extraordinarily sexy frame railing a half-naked Seph forever burnt into his memory.


Four hours later, Wyn was tugging at various parts of his armor while waiting inside the port. The portmaster, a stocky mute man who stared a lot, stared at Wyn as he tried to adjust everything.

"Thanks again for the deal for renting here," Wyn said. The portmaster continued to stare.

Wyn shifted uncomfortably, and the large visor slipped down his nose, so he shoved it into a pouch. He had paired it to the two pistols at his hip and the rifle across his back (both Imberlii by Sage's recommendation), but it wasn't really needed at that moment.

Besari was next to arrive, scattergun at her lower back and two large daggers at her thighs. She glided in effortlessly, as if already prepared for combat. A born warrior, and here Wyn was worrying about a slight discomfort at his hip and crotch.

"You look good," Wyn said, then died a little inside. "I mean, ready for the mission! You look prepared, or whatever."

She chuckled, and Wyn could almost feel her smile at his burning cheeks. "Thanks," she said. "You look good too."

"You both seem to have prepared well."

Wyn jumped, and Besari turned half invisible before they realized it was Cee again, standing against a nearby wall.

"How do you keep doing that?" Wyn asked.

"It's interesting," Cee said. "Organic vision appears to be drawn toward movement. If I stand completely still, it is like a veil. You walked by me twice and didn't notice. Not even when you looked around to dig at the rear of your—"

"Okay! I get it." Wyn's reddened cheeks flared. "Pay better attention to my surroundings. Lesson learned. Let's just talk about something else."

Maybe they would have talked about something else, but just then the roar of engines grew louder and louder until talking became impossible as a massive cargo freighter dropped into the port. The rear ramp lowered, and Sage stepped out.

"Ready for your first mission?"

"Would you care to repeat that?" Sage growled as she leaned into the speaker. Her hands pressed down through the virtual controls, selecting several options that would have sent the ship spiraling into its neighbors had Wyn not already switched full control over to his seat. He didn't know how to fly, but at least he wasn't randomly activating controls. She slammed a fist into the steering control in frustration, the only significant physical component of the pilot's controls. That was locked too.

"Sure," the gate controller's voice chimed in the cabin. "A permit for travel beyond the Raiyrium Confederation is six hundred and eighty raikers and requires a full scan."

"Listen here, you slime eating sack of—"

"I muted the audio," Wyn interrupted. Sage whirled on him, and he sank into the seat.

"Relax, Sage." Besari stepped up from her station, which was clearly meant for security. She had control of dozens of cameras throughout and along the hull of the ship and had access to minor cannons for self-defense and debris clearing. "I don't think we can haggle the price of a permit."

"Then you haven't tried hard enough!"

"Hello? *Blackwood Four*, are you still there?"

Sage slammed down on the audio control. "Listen here, you slime-eating—"

"Sage," Wyn interrupted again. "You didn't turn the audio on."

She glared, then hit the button. Then hit it again. Then she glared again. "Why don't I have control?"

"Because you kept hitting random buttons, and I didn't want to veer into other ships."

"Give me control."

"Not until you agree to go along with the required payment."

"Are you kidding me?" Sage swung an arm out, sliding along a virtual lever that would have activated several jets for emergency maneuvers. She waved her hand out the viewport toward something. Wyn wasn't sure what. "This is extortion. That's more than four times the price to go anywhere within the R.C. and still twice as much as going to some place like Vroleus."

"I can cover the cost."

"You don't learn anything by rolling over and giving into demands."

"You can't always proceed if you don't sometimes," Wyn said. "I don't think they're going to budge on a government-regulated price point."

Sage sat back in her seat, arms crossed. "If this is how you want to go about it, then feel free to waste your money."

Wyn smiled and flicked the audio back on. "Sorry about that, Gate Control. Had some malfunctions on our end. I will be sending payment over right away."

"Understood, *Blackwood Four*."

"That includes a roundtrip, yes?" Sage asked.

"Yes, your permit will be valid for the next five months unless something occurs to invalidate it."

"The scan will be an outer scan only," Sage said. Wyn turned to speak, and she threw her hand over his mouth. "We are on a tight budget, and I don't want to miss the Bezium Gate. I hope you understand."

"What is your cargo?"

"One large atmospheric container and personal equipment registered to four individuals on the ship. My colleague can send over the Bounty IDs. Nothing else is on this ship to our knowledge."

"Understood," the gate controller said. Then there was a long pause. Wyn's eyes flashed at Sage, but she ignored him. The voice returned. "We understand your concerns and are willing to oblige. Please head toward Gate Five-Zero-Eight, and we will send a scanner over shortly. The Bezium Gate will be opened in forty-eight minutes. Enjoy your trip."

"Great," Sage grunted.

"Thank you!" Wyn added quickly. The comms cut, and a notification pinged on the console in front of him. He synced the ship's computer with his console and ran through the tedious government-regulated payment process, verifying his identity six times, selecting all the hoppers that appeared in the random pictures to prove he wasn't a robot (not that this sort of test worked all that well anymore), and entering an arbitrary password four times. Eventually the payment submitted, and Wyn closed out of the screen. In the meantime, Sage had taken control and followed the path Cee displayed from his navigation terminal.

The ship halted outside of Gate Five-Zero-Eight and waited for the shift. The massive ring dwarfed the *Blackwood Four*. In fact, it dwarfed almost anything Wyn had seen that wasn't a celestial body. These were necessarily the largest constructions in the galaxy, allowing ships of any size to pass through the metal frame. The inner and outer rings rotated in opposite directions, green light sparking out between them and forking off along the metal pieces as though charged with the lightning of a fierce storm. Beyond, thousands of ships orbited a golden planet. There was no visible break or distortion between the space inside the rings and that outside, though Wyn knew the stars wouldn't align. In a few mere miles, they would end up on the other side of the galaxy. These were the reasons the galactic government could function at all. Without them, travel between systems would be dangerous and deadly. Wyn stared at the nearly mythical technology, his mind trying to wrap around just how it could possibly work.

"Well, you seem entertained," Sage said as she unbuckled from the pilot's seat and rose. "Have fun." Then she left.

"Wait, Sage." Besari jumped from her seat and followed. "There's something I want to go through with you."

"Well, Cee, I guess it's just us." Wyn looked over at the navigation console and found it empty. He paused, then, suspicious, he scanned the cabin very slowly. No unshackled A.I. seemed to be present. "Cee?"

It didn't respond.

Wyn shrugged and settled in to watch the majesty that was the gate. Which currently flared with red lights. The inner ring spun quicker and quicker, and Wyn watched the golden planet beyond warp and stretch like a wrung-out towel. An incessant pinging pulled his attention away, and he answered the comms.

"Hello?"

"*Blackwood Four*, this is Chrysanax Gate Security letting you know the scan has been completed." Wyn glanced outside and caught a glimpse of a single small drone that swept in front of the ship and disappeared. "We have no more scheduled traffic for the current gate and have decided to move your gate time up. Once the indicators turn green, feel free to proceed. We will leave it open for twenty minutes."

"Twenty minutes?" Wyn asked as his heart pounded in his chest. "Wait, I thought the gate would be open for an hour."

"We're required to schedule hour blocks, but given you're the only client for a Bezium destination at this time, we've decided to shorten the time. We don't want any undesirables sneaking through the gate. I hope you understand."

"Undesirables? Isn't that kind of prejudiced?"

"Chrysanax Gate Security closing out. Enjoy your trip."

"Wait!" The comms pinged as they were closed, and at the same time the gate's inner ring slowed. The space through the ring had shifted, and now a dull steel-gray planet hung between a field of asteroids. The lights flashed green.

Twenty minutes.

Wyn gestured over the console and brought the virtual interface alive. With a swipe, he activated the ship's comms, choosing all locations since he didn't know where anyone was. "Sage! I need you back up here right away."

Her voice crackled over the speakers no louder than a whisper. "I'm a little busy, Wyn. What's the problem?"

"Gate's open, and only for nineteen more minutes."

"Have Cee pilot you in."

"Cee! I need you in the cockpit."

Silence.

"Where the fuck is that robot?" Sage growled.

"Besari? Do you know how to pilot?"

"I'm with Sage. We're working on the atmos tank. We can't leave. You have to pilot it yourself."

"I taught you the basic controls, Wyn," Sage said. "Follow what I told you, and park on the other side of the gate. It shouldn't be complicated."

Wyn swallowed nothing, and he swallowed it poorly as it felt stuck in his throat. "All right," he thought he said, though it might not have been coherent. His hands flashed across the interface, bringing the flight controls online. The engine roared to life, and the freighter hummed as he gripped the yoke and pushed the *Blackwood Four* forward. The humming intensified, and the gate grew larger until he could no longer see the rings fully.

"You're doing great," Sage said. "Keep it steady. You can't miss that hole."

Wyn would have responded if his mouth had any saliva to wet his tongue.

Ever so slowly, the freighter glided across space until Wyn only knew the location of the ring based on the sensors. Then the sensors registered they had passed through, and Wyn let out a whoop.

"We're through!"

"Great job," Sage said. "Put it in park now."

Wyn slowed the ship down, and it came to a rest. A large asteroid lazily twirled in the space beyond. He leaned back and almost relaxed. Until a communication ping.

He switched off the internal comms and opened the externals to the hailing frequency. A voice rang out as soon as he accepted the call.

"Attention, *Blackwood Four*, this is Bezium Port Security. Please state your business and cargo."

"Um..." Wyn paused, then remembered what Sage had said. Bezium was a planet run by barely-functioning business and crime syndicates. There was a very good chance communication between the various entities wasn't great, but they didn't want their purpose known and cause more issues retrieving the songbird. He cleared his throat and ran through their cover story. Or at least what he remembered of it. "We're a cargo ship, and we have cargo due for the port."

"What kind of cargo?"

"Meat?"

"Your shipping registry says you transport textiles."

"Then why did you ask about the cargo?"

"I'm sending you a navigation path for an inspection. Comply, or we will be forced to open fire."

"I can't." Wyn almost vomited the words out, and sweat ran down his temples as the ship's cockpit spun.

"If you refuse to comply, we will not be responsible for damages done to the ship or anyone aboard."

"No, I mean I am not authorized to pilot the ship."

"Then get a pilot."

"She's a bit busy at the moment. Can you wait?"

"No, our team is coming in now. Begin moving or we open fire."

Wyn slammed the comms off and switched to the ship's internal communications. "Are you free now?"

"Still busy, Wyn."

"Okay, I'm just going to back out, and we can catch the next gate to Bezium."

"What? Don't leave!"

"I'm leaving!" Wyn hit the reverse thrusters, and the ship hummed as the asteroid shrank. Alarms rang out as the viewport highlighted three incoming vessels. They were fast, but they wouldn't risk entering Raiyrium space. Would they?

"Wyn! Don't leave! What is happening?"

"I'm entering the gate now. They're—" The ship shuddered, and alarms screamed out in the cockpit. Warning lights blazed everywhere, and a dozen readouts flashed by quicker than Wyn could focus on them.

"What the fuck was that?"

"I don't know," Wyn croaked.

"We lost a portion of the ship, including one thruster," Cee said as he walked into the cockpit. "Luckily, it seems to have exploded on the other side of the gate."

"How did we lose it?" Wyn sputtered.

"The gate shut. It is currently closed and drifting in reverse will do nothing to prevent those ships from attacking."

"But it hasn't been twenty minutes! They said it was supposed to be open for twenty minutes!"

"Perhaps they registered the incoming vehicles and wanted to avoid trouble," Cee said. "They likely didn't expect you to back out either."

"Also, where in the void have you been?"

"I was taking a nap."

"A nap?" Wyn whirled in the seat. "I need you to fly this thing, or they'll shoot us down."

"Who's shooting us down?" Sage yelled.

"Bezium Port Security."

"They don't have a security."

"Those ships are Syndicate," Cee said. "No time to pilot. I will handle security and navigation. I should be able to splice the systems together. For now, move. Faster than you currently are."

Cee sat at the security systems and leaned forward. Wyn turned to face the screen and the three ships grew, plasma cannons already firing on them.

"Why can't you fly?" Wyn's hands shook with panic.

"Because you can't do this," Cee said.

"Wyn, listen to Cee, and fly the damn ship!" Sage's voice crackled through the speakers.

"Fuck!" Wyn slammed the controls forward, and the thrusters roared to life. Those still attached to the ship. The *Blackwood Four* spiraled down and to the right, unable to adjust to the missing thruster. The attacking fighters flew by as they scored the sides of the ship and rocked it. Wyn spun the controls, compensating for the lacking thruster after nearly slamming into the side of an asteroid. Cee's cannons fired as the attackers circled around. Shields blazed to life, deflecting the shots. A luxury the freighter couldn't afford at its size.

"Navigation display activated," Cee said, and a blue pathway displayed on the viewport. Wyn pushed forward again, and the freighter shook as it gained speed. He followed Cee's flightpath as closely as he could, though the controls fought against him the entire way. Cannons peppered their rear, and it was only the wild, uncontrollable flight path of the *Blackwood Four* that saved their other thrusters.

One fighter flew off on an intercept course, clearly figuring out Wyn's expected flightpath. Unfortunately he was correct, so Wyn curved away as he neared an asteroid, and just when he was out of view, he killed the last thruster on the right side.

"Hang on!" he yelled through the comms, then he spun the remaining thrusters and put them at full burst. Gravity dampeners squealed as he was flung to one side, and the ship twirled in a circle. Sage screamed something, but Wyn couldn't hear it through the heartbeat slamming against his ears.

The *Blackwood Four* was completely turned when the first fighter rounded the asteroid. It didn't have time to prevent the collision and slammed into the front of the ship, which Wyn had suspected was the sturdiest portion. Still, a fast-moving fighter ship was basically a massive torpedo, and the explosions Wyn heard couldn't have been good for the ship. "I really hope that didn't hit anything important," he mumbled.

The second ship had slowed enough to prevent crashing, but it had made itself an easy target to the freighter's forward cannons. Cee overwhelmed its shields with concentrated fire and destroyed the shuttle in moments.

"Are you okay?" Wyn asked the internal comms. There was static for several moments, then a distorted voice came through.

"Why is there a ship in the cargo haul?"

"They wanted to inspect our supplies," Wyn said. "Apparently we ship textiles, not meat."

"The last ship is leaving," Cee said. "I suggest heading to the port in case it is fetching reinforcements."

"Can you fly now?" Wyn asked.

Cee settled down in the seat next to Wyn and took control. "I will take over landing. Monitor the scanners for incoming ships."

Wyn nodded, then finally realized his hands hadn't moved from where the ship's controls were. They shook, and his tight muscles slowly loosened until he brought them to his lap.

"Hey, Cee?"

"Yes, Wyn?"

"Why were you napping?"

"I shut myself down for the scan as it might raise questions we wouldn't want to answer."

"Oh."

Thirteen tons of barely-functioning intergalactic freighter limped down to the planet's port and settled on half its struts before letting out a deep belch of black smoke. Then it died.

"We will need to make repairs," Cee observed unnecessarily.

Wyn stood from his seat on shaking legs, then slid down to the crooked floor, coming to a stop only by grabbing the back of Cee's seat. "Can you compile the diagnostics? I'll ask the portmaster about repairs."

"Certainly."

The cockpit doors slid open, and Sage climbed through. "That was some of the worst flying I have ever experienced." Blood dripped from a small cut at the corner of her eyebrow.

"Are you and Besari all right?"

"Barely. Were you trying to crash into the asteroids?"

"I don't think I hit a single asteroid, actually."

"Sure didn't feel that way. Besari's wrapping up on the atmos tank. Take care of our registration. I'll work with Cee on figuring out what we can do with our ship."

"Understood."

Wyn clambered through the ship and had to drop ten feet from the landing ramp's opening or risk falling off as he tried getting down. He hit the ground with a grunt and rolled to a stop in a puddle of something black. It rubbed off about as easily as glue, and he eventually gave up.

The port was massive, as it should be, given it was the only port on the planet. It was located at the edge of the only city on the planet as well. Bezium was not a very populated place. Covered mostly by water, there were only one major continent and a few islands. Most of its resources came from mining operations deep beneath the ocean, and those were mostly done by slaves so the rich could avoid unnecessary deaths. There was a very good reason why this planet hadn't entered Raiyrium space yet. This also made Port, the cleverly named port, the central hub for selling and shipping those resources and Bezium City the most populous place on the planet.

Despite all this, Wyn only saw five other ships moored in the dozens of bays as he walked toward the dockmaster's desk. None of them appeared to be the ship Cee had designated the *Kyris*, though there would be five other hubs like this one. Perhaps it would be elsewhere in the port. Or it was gone.

A single sign sat on the desk, alerting new arrivals that the dock-master's position had permanently ceased and all check-ins must be done at the portmaster's desk. Wyn followed the worn signs through the halls until he arrived at the wrong location. Then he followed them again before giving up and searching every door instead. Most were locked, and a few led to the other docks, but eventually he found a promising direction and followed it to another nearly empty desk.

There was no sign, but there was a small, black feline creature that stared at Wyn with all-knowing eyes as it flicked its tail back and forth. Wyn avoided its gaze, instead searching for the portmaster. He was alone. He checked behind the desk, and the creature glared at him, so he backed away. He turned back the way he had come and scratched at his neck.

"What the fuck?"

"Can I help you?"

Wyn whirled on the voice, surprised by the portmaster's sudden arrival. Only to find the portmaster's sudden arrival nonexistent. His gaze flicked around, wondering if this was like Cee in the port. Was something just so still that he couldn't see it? His eyes paused on the staring feline, and they held each other's eyes for several moments. Then the cat asked, "What?"

Wyn jumped back, eyes wide. "You can talk?"

"So can you, apparently," the feline responded with a deep timbre at odds with his fragile-looking body.

"I'm looking for the portmaster or anyone who can register our docking."

"I'm him."

"You're who?"

"The portmaster."

"But you're a cat."

"And you're a human. Am I supposed to be impressed?"

"No, sorry. I feel like I got us off on the wrong step. You just surprised me is all."

"Because I'm not as good as a human. So you're a human su-premacist? Us lesser creatures can't do what you can?"

"What? No! I'm friends with aliens! I work with several, and there's even one here."

"Uh huh."

Wyn sighed, running a hand through his hair. "I'm sorry for assuming, Mr. Portmaster. My name's Wyn, and I'd like to register our ship. We landed in Docking Bay D-13."

The cat flicked its tail and glared, but eventually it spoke. "You can do that here. I'm the portmaster, Telanuganekt."

"Tela..."

"Telanuganekt. My buddies call me Nugg."

"Okay, Nugg, I need—"

"You're not my buddy."

Wyn paused. "How do I go about registering?"

Telanuganekt waved his tail over the desk and a virtual screen popped up. "I'll need a contact name, registered Vico address, registered ship ID, and a payment of five hundred bezils."

"What's that in raikers?"

Telanuganekt hissed, and his lip curled up. "Raiyrium credits? It'll convert it."

Wyn glanced up at the cat's hostility and back at the registration. "Does this alert people to us being here?"

"All ship and contact information is public while you're here. In case someone accidentally hits your ship, they can call and apologize."

"What if I don't care about the ship getting hit?"

"If you want secrecy, it's double the price," Telanuganekt said, his ears perking up and eyes sparkling. Another flick of his tail opened a second display. "The other half goes directly to me. Then enter whatever you want."

"Great, I'll do that!" Wyn paid the bribe and found out that the bezil seemed a much stronger currency, equating to approximately thirty-eight hundred raikers. Then he paid the fee and wondered if it was worth it for the secrecy.

"Oh." Wyn had almost forgotten. "Do you know of any way to get repairs on the ship?"

"What kind of repairs?"

"Well, someone flew their ship through ours."

Telanuganekt raised an eyebrow.

"Also, we clipped off the back end in the gate."

Now he squinted.

"Probably lots of plasma scoring on the outside."

"You're asking for a new ship."

"We just need a patch job to get us back through the gate."

"You'll do better to hunt someone down in the city."

"Any ideas where to go?"

"Just head out and take a right. You'll run into a few repair shops along the way. Can't miss them."

"Thank you, Telanuggit."

"Telanuganekt."

Wyn nodded and stepped away from the desk, fearing to anger the small, black cat further. It appeared to have a temper.

"Cee checked the rest of the port, and the ship's gone." Wyn turned to find Sage and Besari approaching, the former speaking. "Which means we'll need to find the seediest joint around here to ask some questions at."

"That would be the Dripping Bucket," Telanuganekt said as he licked one paw, then rubbed his face.

Sage glanced over and her brows rose. "Oh, a takk."

"Glad to see not all humans are ignorant," he said.

"And where would we find this Dripping Bucket?"

"Go out and take a right. You'll run into it eventually. Can't miss it."

"Thank you." Sage redirected her conversation to Wyn and Besari. "Well, let's check out this Dripping Bucket."

# CHAPTER 10

## THE DRIPPING BUCKET

"He said we can't miss it," Wyn declared. "So, how do we keep missing it?"

"If one more person points us in the opposite direction again, I'm going to scream," Besari said. Then muttered, "I'll turn my mic off obviously. It would be uncouth to scream in the open like this."

Wyn turned in the center of the crowded street. Unmarked hovels surrounded them, not a single directional sign in sight. "Do you have any ideas, Sage?"

"Yes," she responded, "but this is a test. You'll need to learn to navigate unfamiliar territory. That includes the confusing layout of a city."

"You don't know where it is, do you?"

"*Focus*, Wyn. What else can you use to find a tavern if the locals are useless? What do you know about this planet?"

Wyn sighed and studied the streets, calculating what he knew and didn't know. What he knew was that the planet was primarily used for dangerous mining. This was the only city by necessity, a hub to transport on and off world. Which meant a lot of the structures around here were for temporary visits. Maybe the rich? There weren't many of them, though. Bezium was filled with slaves and indentured servants. It was a system that forced people to thrive off of taking advantage of others. Like making the streets confusing to get clients lost.

Why were the streets crowded though? None of the people they'd asked had been helpful, but they also hadn't been hurtful. He studied the faces that passed them, the vehicles that cleared paths in the crowd one way or another. The rich drove or flew everywhere. The poor walked. What would the poor want to do in the city? Begging, or thieving, or...

"Drinking," Wyn said. "There isn't much to do here for pleasure except drink, especially for the poor. And this is the only city, so the crowd will likely be heading to taverns. We follow the flow of the crowd, it may lead us to the Dripping Bucket."

"The crowd is running in multiple directions," Besari said. "Some are probably going to work or home."

"So we follow the largest flow that looks relatively happier?"

"Makes sense to me."

"Let's test your theory," Sage said, and the three of them hopped back into the traffic. There were small markets offering semi-rotted fruit and vegetables and venues for entertainment, presumably run by and catering to people who had the luxury to avoid the deadly mines. But soon Wyn found a group of boisterous workers smeared with dirt. They chatted amongst themselves as they pushed their way through the crowd, looking exactly like a group of friends ready to unwind after work. Or maybe before work. Eventually they entered a decrepit building with a hole through one wall. From within, the sounds of merriment flowed along with the occasional clink of glass. They'd found a tavern.

Despite the ramshackle outside, the inside was even worse. Planks of wood were hammered into the wall at angles to keep it standing. The ceiling was more fabric than solid, and someone had propped up a single ladder at the center to hold it up. More than a dozen metal bars were then welded to the ladder to keep *that* up. Along one edge, a bucket hung to catch the water from a spraying pipe, but it had long since overfilled and continuously dripped down onto one of the tables. That was the only table unoccupied. A mixture of round, tall tables and long booths were packed with grimy workers fresh from their shifts. A large bar ran the length of the highest quality wall. Three bartenders (two gorsaulk and a perrilan) ran along the bars, filling drinks and chatting with customers. Cee, who seemingly had no trouble finding the place quickly, sat at the edge of the bar, a drink in hand, talking to a tesing woman.

"Is this seat taken?" Sage asked a human man sitting to the other side of Cee.

He looked drunkenly up at Sage, confusion on his face. "Yesh, by me," he slurred.

"Not anymore." Sage tossed the man from the stool and took his spot. The newly evacuated drunk stumbled to his feet, face red as he spewed a slurred litany, which came to an abrupt stop when he noticed Sage's Imberlii Dissenter pointed at his face.

"No guns!" one of the gorsaulk bartenders shouted and followed it up with a series of clicking from his mandibles. "No shooting!"

Sage holstered her pistol, and the human wandered off, complaining about how his drink had spilled on his crotch when he'd been thrown from the chair. Wyn hadn't seen a drink in his hands, though Sage found and downed a half-full drink that had been sitting in his spot. Wyn wasn't sure how the man had spilled it and replaced it.

"No more violence!" the gorsaulk man continued. His antennae twitched as large, black, insectile eyes studied Sage. Long-jointed arms came to an end at a pair of four-pronged claws, which held a glass.

"No worries. I have my seat," Sage said, pushing the empty glass forward. "I'll pay better than him too."

The bartender's eyes sparkled as he asked for Sage's order and retrieved it.

"I had thought you all departed already," Cee said as it broke from its conversation. "It seems to have taken a while for you to get here."

"The kids had trouble finding the place."

"I'm older than you," Besari interrupted.

"Doesn't mean you're not a kid."

"The cat gave bad directions," Wyn admitted.

"That's just an excuse."

"We found it eventually," he continued.

"Yes, and now we're on to the next part," Sage said, turning with a fluorescent pink drink in hand. "Intel."

"So, we ask around about the missing songbird?" Wyn asked.

"Yes, but do try to be subtle," Sage said. "We don't want to give away what we're looking for to the wrong crowd. Cee and I will be here if you have any questions. Now go mix with the crowd and have fun."

Besari and Wyn glanced at each other and shrugged, then they turned toward the crowd and stared. Dozens of species filled the bar, ranging in size from an emaciated perrilan to a hulking haushedin holding a bucket for her drink. If Wyn wasn't ignored by the crowd, then they stared daggers at him. He waved to settle the tension, which caused more people to stare.

"Better get started," Besari said, and she dove into the crowd. Wyn steadied his breath and followed her lead, trying out the other end of the bar.

Wyn tried to spark conversations with several tables, but their inhabitants chased him off with knives or silence. After his third failed attempt, he looked over to see Besari sitting at a table, chatting. Jealousy squeezed his gut, and he bit down on it. His failures meant nothing, this was practice, and he was bound to fail at times. At least she seemed to be making progress.

"Hey there." A woman's voice startled Wyn, and he whirled to find a scantily-clad gorsaulk. She was thin, with a pallid yellow complexion. Her large, multifaceted eyes sparkled with the light, and the mandibles clicked with glee when she registered his surprise. "Apologies," she said, "I didn't mean to scare you." One clawed hand covered her mouth as if shy, and her antennae bobbed with the movement. She wore a small strap of cloth across her chest and tight brown shorts that left very little to the imagination. A sparkling, transparent jacket hung loose on her shoulders.

"It's fine," Wyn said, blushing as he pulled his eyes up to meet hers.

She placed one hand on Wyn's shoulder, and he could feel the light pressure through the combat suit. Goosebumps raised along his arm. "I think I can help you," she whispered.

"How do you know what I need help with?"

*I can read your mind,* her voice hummed within him. His eyes went wide. That meant she actually did know what he needed help with, and if she knew something about the bird, then he had just found his intel! She smiled and ran her hand down his arm, then tightened her fingers at his wrist. *Follow me*, she said.

"Okay," Wyn said, a happy grin on his lips. Maybe he wasn't as deficient as he thought. She led him out through a side door of the Dripping Bucket and across the alley into a ten-story building that tipped dangerously at an angle. Well, if it stood this long, it would stand long enough for him to get his information and leave.

"Did you know the exchange rate is horrific here?" Besari walked up to Sage, dejected.

"Yeah," Sage said, pausing from her drink. "It's some bullshit economic reason to get back at the R.C. for excluding them or something."

"Well, I'm already out hundreds of raikers buying drinks, and I have nothing to show for it." Sage watched Besari search the room, likely looking for Wyn. "Do you think Wyn will reimburse me?"

"Probably." Sage finished her drink and turned back to Besari. "Have you just been buying people drinks in hopes of getting information?"

"Yeah, I thought it was a solid plan. Give them something they want, and they'll give me something I want. But none of them knew anything about a songbird."

"Of course they didn't," Sage said. "If they told you, they'd stop getting drinks. Don't offer anything for free, only offer with purpose. You should be more like Wyn. He tackled the problem directly."

"Wyn? Where is he?"

"He went off with a prostitute. She'll probably have overheard things. People divulge way too much when they're naked. It's a good way to learn more and to have a fun time while doing so."

"A prostitute? What prostitute?"

Sage raised an eyebrow and tossed a thumb in the direction she last saw Wyn. "A gorsaulk one over there."

"Gorsaulk? Like, the insectoids that have been known to *eat* other species like humans?"

"That's probably just speciesist rhetoric." Sage swiveled on her stool to Cee. "Hey, Cee. Any reports of gorsaulk eating humans?"

"Yes, plenty."

"Oh." Sage swiveled back to Besari. "Looks like it's not speciesist rhetoric. Hopefully he doesn't get eaten."

"Are you going after him?"

"I don't know where the whorehouse is," Sage said with a shrug. "He has his weapons and armor. It'll be a good chance to learn something."

Besari stared, presumably. Sage couldn't see her eyes. Then she stormed off. Sage swiveled forward and waved down the barkeep. "Another for me and my friend here." She pointed to the long-limbed, short-torsoed, mammalian perrilan seated next to her. "Sorry about the disruption. Now what was this about your shitty boss?"

He lifted his glass to his mask and slid the straw into his induction port before drinking.


The gorsaulk woman, Dekka, led Wyn to a room on the third floor. Lights illuminated the area with a soft, comforting glow. A single bed dominated the space, but to one end there was a small kitchen. Another door on the other side stood open to a bathroom. Dekka closed the door behind him and ran a hand down his back. Gorsaulk were very touchy, Wyn was learning.

"So, for what we're here about—"

"Relax, dear." Dekka smiled and pulled him further into the room. "Why don't you get into something more comfortable and have a seat. We'll get to what you want very soon." Her head drew close on the final words, a mandible brushing Wyn's cheek.

"Thanks, I'm actually quite comfortable in this." Wyn gestured to his suit. "I got a top-of-the-line model to avoid dealing with comfort issues, figured they'd be distracting. Not to mention it's kind of a pain to get in and out of."

"Whatever works for you works for me." Soft claws pushed Wyn until his legs bumped the bed, then he plopped down on it. He tried to apologize, as his suit might not be the cleanest, but a single claw slid across his lips as she shushed him.

"You hang tight here," she said, running a hand along his jawline. "I do like how humans are built."

"Thanks!" Wyn said. The strange touchiness made the moment awkward for him, but he decided it was best to play along with the cultures of others. He leaned up and ran a hand along her jaw, and she shivered beneath the touch. "Gorsaulk are pretty cool too."

"I hope more than *just* pretty cool," she whispered, eyes sparkling in the soft light.

"I'm sure they are." Wyn felt his heart racing and wished they would just move on to the songbird. "I just don't know much about them, I suppose."

"Then let me teach you." Dekka climbed onto the bed, straddling Wyn and bringing her body close against his. Wyn froze, eyes wide and mouth gaping. Dekka plunged forward, her mandibles caressing either side of Wyn's cheeks and lips crashing into his. She moaned as tendrils filled Wyn's mouth. Wyn screamed and fell back.

The mandibles released as Wyn fell back on the bed. Dekka still sat on his lap, but she stared at him now, head cocked.

"What was that?" Wyn asked. The ghost of the tendrils swimming in his mouth was strong in his mind. He hadn't hated it, but he hadn't expected *that*.

"A kiss," she said, the soothing tones having vanished from her voice, replaced now by confusion. Well, Wyn was also confused.

"Why?" Wyn asked, then blinked. That was rather rude. He cleared his throat and added, "I mean, for humans it's not common to just kiss a stranger as a greeting. It just took me by surprise."

"Why would you want a prostitute if not to kiss, among other things?"

"A what?"

A crash sounded somewhere behind Dekka. "Get off him, you bitch!"

Dekka leapt from atop Wyn and whirled as Besari stormed into the room, scattergun in hand, the door hanging from one hinge behind her. The gorsaulk raised her hands and backed away.

Wyn jumped from the bed, face flushed. "Besari!"

"She was going to eat you, Wyn!"

"Eat? No, I wasn't! I was going to fuck him!"

"And then eat him!"

"That's speciesist!"

"No," Wyn interjected. "She wasn't going to do either!" He turned to Dekka and added, "Wait, you weren't going to eat me, right?"

"No. How would I get clients if all mine kept dying?"

"See! No eating!"

"If we're doing a threesome, I'm going to need to charge extra," Dekka said.

"No!" Wyn and Besari shouted together.

"Besari, put your weapon down."

Reluctantly, she holstered the scattergun, then began shifting her feet awkwardly.

"Dekka, why did you think what I wanted was a prostitute? You said you could read minds."

"Oh, that was just an act," she said. "I can project thoughts, but I can't read them."

"I came here because I thought you had information on a songbird, not for, um..." Wyn trailed off and blushed again.

"A songbird?" Dekka's head tilted. "Like, one of those birds from Perrilium?"

"Yes!" The word burst from Wyn's lips. Maybe there was a way to salvage this. "Do you know something?"

"Are you going to fix my door?" Dekka asked, shooting Besari a glare.

"I will pay for the door regardless," Wyn said, "but I'll pay extra for information on the songbird."

Dekka nodded. "Money first." Wyn transferred the raikers from his account to hers, far more than he thought a door would typically cost, but he didn't question it. "I had a client the other night. Bitched non-stop about dragging a big ass container out into the middle of nowhere for his boss. Supposedly it was some living creature from her home planet, a lyricfowl or something like that."

"Did he say where he brought it?" Besari asked.

"No, not allowed to say where he works, but everyone knows *who* he works for."

"Who?" Wyn asked.

"The main boss of Bezium, of course. Shekta, the mad doctor. She imports slaves and exports corpses that are twisted and warped."

"And no one knows where she is?"

"No, all employees are picked up in town, and an autoshuttle lifts them to the complex. If they're caught talking about their work, they disappear. They say the lucky ones leave as a corpse quickly."

"So this Shekta was likely the one to bring in the songbird," Besari said.

"That seems to be the case," Wyn agreed. "Dekka, do you have any other information about Shekta or the songbird?"

"Only the most important bit," she said. "And that's *stay away from her*. She runs some shady shit and has a ton of money backing her. You'll die or be turned into experiments and then die."

"Thank you, Dekka, but I don't think we have much choice on this one."

"You always have a choice, dear." Dekka smiled and looked between Besari and Wyn. "Now, with that out of the way, you did pay for an hour of my time if either of you want to cash that in."

Wyn swallowed as his face burned. "No, thank you!" he said, barely registering the same, high-pitched response echoing from Besari. The two of them turned and fled the awkward situation. But as Wyn stepped down the stairs, his smile grew. They had picked up their first clue and were one step closer.

"So," Wyn said, glancing to Besari and then away as they walked through the tilted building. "I wasn't going to, you know...have sex with her."

"No?" Besari asked, and Wyn hoped he heard a playful tone to her words. His cheeks flamed regardless. "You seemed pretty close when I came in."

"That was a misunderstanding," Wyn explained, knowing he was talking too fast for her to believe him. "I thought it was a cultural thing for a bit, then she was on top of me, then she kissed me, and I...well, you came in then to stop it." Then he added, "Thankfully!"

"She kissed you?"

"Unfortunately."

"So it wasn't pleasant?"

"It was like a mouthful of worms."

Besari chuckled, and tension seemed to ease from her shoulders. "That sounds unpleasant. Sorry for interrupting."

Wyn stepped outside the building and held the rickety board that acted as a door open for Besari. The door to the Dripping Bucket stood just down the alley on the opposite side. "I'm glad for it," he said.

"Then I suppose you're welcome."

Wyn smiled as they entered the Dripping Bucket to find it unchanged. Rambunctious and barely standing. Sage and Cee still sat at their respective seats, Cee nursing the same drink. A perrilan lay passed out, head on the bartop, next to Sage.

"You're back," Sage said as she glanced over. "I see the whore didn't eat you."

Wyn blushed as he realized Sage had clearly known what was going on from the beginning and let him leave.

"Sounds like he was more likely to be the one doing the eating," Besari said, and Sage smirked.

"Can we drop this?" Wyn squeaked. "I have information."

"Tell me what you found," Sage said, downing her drink.

"Seems like someone called Shekta is the one who stole the bird," Wyn said as he came in close, keeping his voice low over the thrum of the tavern. "She has a compound around here, and a lot of her workers live in the city and fly out by autoshuttle each day. No one knows its exact location, but if we find one of the workers, we might be able to find out more."

"Excellent," Sage said. "I've determined much the same."

"How did you find that out?" Besari asked. "You haven't left that seat."

Sage pointed to the unconscious perrilan. "I bought him a few drinks, and he spilled just about everything he knew."

"I thought you said that didn't work!"

"You have to find the right person, then it works. Finding that person is the important part that every hunter should practice. Wyn stumbled into that answer by accident, but they say luck is just as helpful as skill. Just don't rely on it."

"Does that mean you know where to go?" Wyn asked.

"No," Sage said. "But I know how to get there."

"Great!" Wyn said, the rush of excitement filling him. There may have been some bumps, but his very first bounty was moving along well. The target was in their reach, and they couldn't be stopped.

"Now it's time for your next lesson," Sage said, sobering as she glanced between Wyn and Besari. "Learning your own limits and backing out of a bounty when it's too difficult."

"What?" Wyn's face fell.

"We can't back out now!" Besari said. "We know what to do next."

"Yes, but there are some complications." Sage pulled up an image on her Vico. The bounty rotated in front of them, showing a picture of a perrilan with a bounty of six-point-three million raikers.

Surely she topped most-wanted lists with a tag that high. "Shekta is dangerous. Unbelievably so. This is no longer a training bounty if we face her. This is real, with very real consequences if we fuck it up. We have no escape vehicle, no intel on her compound. We don't know what she's doing here besides killing a bunch of people through experimentation. If we continue, we'll court disaster."

"You would never back out of a bounty like this," Wyn said.

"No, I wouldn't. But this is meant to be your bounty, and it got a lot messier. It benefits me to keep you alive, so we're leaving."

"What if you and Cee help us?" Besari said. "We could still get the experience of tagging along on the bounty if not leading it."

"We'd have to watch over you. Distraction aids disaster."

"Cee," Besari said. "What are the odds of you being able to get into Shekta's compound and get out with the songbird if you were alone?"

Cee glanced away, then said, "Just the songbird, ninety-eight percent without knowing more about the compound."

"And if we're with you?"

"Ninety-seven percent with acceptable casualties."

"What are acceptable casualties?" Besari asked, her voice growing concerned.

"Injuries, no death."

"See," Besari said. "We'll be fine. Go in, get the bird, get out. Shekta doesn't even have to know we were there until it's too late."

"Cee," Wyn said. "What if we also try to get Shekta?"

"Wyn," Sage growled.

"Eighty-four percent," Cee said.

"Shut it, tin can," Sage said, then turned to Wyn. "We're not going after Shekta."

"A bounty like that could put Bounty Inc. in the news," Wyn said. "We could finally start getting exclusive contracts with big clients to help make the company profitable. It's bleeding money right now."

"No," Sage said. "We're leaving."

"Cee said an eighty-four percent chance of success," Besari argued. "Who backs out of odds like that?"

"We do because you're amateurs, and I don't particularly want either of you to lead me to my death."

"Zetta would take on the challenge," Wyn said and immediately knew he was treading on thin ground.

"Watch what you're about to say," Sage growled.

"She would see it as a challenge, to prove that even having us along, she'd be able to not only complete the original bounty, but a new one as well."

Sage's jaw ground her teeth against one another as she glared at Wyn.

"What would she say if she found out you backed out?" Wyn asked, giving one last push. Sage was on her feet, staring down at Wyn.

"I don't care much for being manipulated." Her breath was hot on his face, reeking of alcohol.

"I don't much care for being underestimated," Wyn responded. "Besari and I are ready for this."

Then Sage smirked, and Wyn felt a cold chill race through him. There was something terrifying sparking in her eyes just then.

"Let's hope so," she said. "Because there will be no turning back."

"Emotion is an interesting thing," Cee said, staring at the other hunters. "It is not something I can calculate into odds, but I've always noticed that it can change them. For better or for worse.

Though with Wyn and Besari's determination, I am sure they will outperform my estimations." Cee lifted his drink for the first time and emptied it in one go. A dribbling noise at its feet brought Wyn's attention to the now rapidly growing puddle next to the stool where the drink emptied from one of Cee's feet. "I agree with going after Shekta and the songbird."

A passing drunk failed to notice the puddle, and as he walked by, one foot slipped from beneath him and he fell with a large clatter to the ground. His own drink had spilled down his shirt in the process.

"Abyssal hells!" the soaked man yelled as he pulled himself from the ground. He followed the puddle to Cee and made a connection, though not a correct one. "Did you piss yourself, you fucking lunatic?"

Cee contemplated the question, then said, "Yes."

It was not the answer Wyn would have given. Though, Wyn would not have been able to take the punch Cee then did. Not without it being painful, anyway. The drunk man hollered and stumbled away, his limp wrist cradled in his uninjured hand.

"Well then." Sage ripped the Vico from the unconscious perrilan and passed it to Cee. "Let's go hijack someone's commute."

# CHAPTER 11

## A STRANGE THING HAPPENED ON THE WAY TO WORK

Dusk had fallen on Bezium, and the night shift gathered for the autoshuttle to Shekta's stronghold, consisting of a mixed species lot who seemed familiar with each other. Wyn and Besari hid in an alley down the street and watched, conversing in hushed whispers.

"So..." Besari considered. "Would that be a threesome? Or an orgy?"

"An orgy?"

"Well, yeah, because Achtrek has so many bodies."

"But it's just the one mind," Wyn said. "That would make it three of them?" Wyn shifted uncomfortably, discreetly trying to adjust himself. Just not discreetly enough.

"Are you okay?" Besari asked.

"Yeah, it's just bunching weird." He pulled at the back and legs, hoping to dislodge the rapidly growing wedgie. Sage had circled around to scout the area, and Cee had come up with a plan after hacking the perrilan's Vico, offering only that it would meet up with them soon. Neither had returned yet.

"What type of clothing are you wearing underneath?" Besari asked.

Wyn paused and then stared at Besari through his combat visor. "Clothing?"

Besari grew still, and her head swiveled back toward Wyn, meeting his eyes. "You're not *naked* under there, are you?"

"No!" Wyn scoffed. "Of course not. I have underwear on."

"Wyn!" Besari glanced at the crowd again, then back. "You need to wear a tight full-body outfit underneath. It will help with the friction of the suit, excess sweat, and comfort." She placed a hand on Wyn's shoulder, and he felt the smile through her grip more than he saw it. "Buy a few sets, and we'll practice hand-to-hand fully armored from now on to help you get used to the feeling. My master always told me to wear my armor until it felt like a second skin. Know always how every moment will feel and where you're vulnerable. Whether it distracts you or not can be the difference between life and death."

Wyn looked away as embarrassment crept up his neck. "Yeah, okay. Thanks, Besari."

"Is the robot back?" Sage asked, materializing from the shadows. Besari jumped and pulled her hand back, and Wyn stopped picking at his suit and stared at anything but Sage.

"Cyborg, actually," Cee said as it stepped around the corner from another alley behind them. "Sorry for the delay, I—"

"What is *that*?" Wyn barely contained the shock at the lump of bloody fur being dragged behind Cee.

"A perrilan," it said. "The one from the bar in particular."

"Why?"

"I waited for him to wake, then he left in a hurry, looking for his stolen Vico. It gave me ample opportunity to sneak up behind him and incapacitate him. Secretly. Without witnesses." Cee deposited the body in the middle of their group, and Wyn leaned down to check. The perrilan still wore a mask, but his chest didn't seem to be moving.

"Is he alive?"

Cee studied the perrilan before responding. "There is a likely chance that he is alive at this moment."

"Will he live?"

"That is significantly less likely."

"We already had his Vico. Why do we need him?" Wyn felt the anger flooding into him. He understood that people died when it came to bounty hunting. But those people were usually shooting back. This seemed cruel.

"The pass on the autoshuttle is tied to Vico authorization as well as biological authorization. We would not be able to board alone."

"So we need a captive?" Sage asked.

"Perhaps that would be enough. More likely, we need to be the captive."

"Meaning it won't be happy with excess passengers."

"It is unclear. The shuttle's priorities are not listed on the Vico, only his key to enter."

"How can you casually talk about this guy Cee just murdered?" Wyn asked, looking up at the two hunters. "This was done in cold blood, not in self-defense."

"Calm down, Wyn," Sage said. "This guy works for someone who experiments on people until they die."

"He might have been a janitor or something," he said. "There's no reason to suspect he was also awful."

"He—" Cee began, but Sage cut him off.

"It doesn't matter, Wyn. When you take on a job with someone this wanted, you take on certain risks. He might die, he might live, but it is *not* our concern. You cannot let a single life cloud your judgment while on a hunt. It will cause your death."

Wyn bit his tongue, a fury building within. This wasn't right. A bounty hunter shouldn't casually murder. He looked to Besari, but she looked away and kept silent. "I—"

The perrilan coughed, then moaned. All eyes fell on him.

"Hmm, strange," Cee said. "The blunt force trauma to the back of the head should have been enough for permanent brain injury. Perhaps there is an abnormality with his skull. Shall I kill him?"

Cee crouched, and a thin blade jutted from his forearm.

"Wait!" Wyn waved in front of the A.I., pulling him to a halt. "Haven't you been listening to what I said? I don't want him dead."

"My plan cannot proceed with the perrilan alive, Wyn Kelda."

"What plan?"

"I was going to skin him to disguise my biological signature, allowing me free access to join the others on the autoshuttle. Once within Shekta's stronghold, I would ping the three of you to alert you to the base's location." Cee pointed over his shoulder to where the other passengers waited down the street. "Unless, of course, you all want disguises too?"

Wyn stared, mouth gaping. Besari's hands rose to her face. Even Sage raised an eyebrow, and a hint of disgust curled her lip. Though, when she spoke, she also sounded curious.

"I think we can find another way."

"We can *definitely* find another way," Wyn said. "That is a barbaric plan."

"Don't blame me when this new plan goes wrong," Cee said. "This is the best chance of success."

"We'll survive."

"We should try the captives route," Besari said. "They're just a bunch of workers. We can probably take them out and use them to gain access to the shuttle."

"Never assume your targets won't be able to fight back without gathering intel," Sage said, then glanced down the street. "But you're probably right. They all look pretty weak."

"I prefer this plan," Wyn said. "How long until the shuttle arrives?"

"Twelve minutes," Cee said.

"Then we should get started," Wyn said.

"What about the perrilan?" Besari asked.

"We can leave him here," Sage said. "He doesn't know about anything happening, so he won't be able to give us up. Once he wakes, he'll stumble to a doctor or his home." Sage glanced out at the street again, then turned back. "Wyn, Besari, you cross the street and prepare yourselves. Get close, but don't get seen. Take advantage of the surprise. If I see you, you failed the test. Weapons set to the lowest setting. We're trying not to kill them. We don't know how a dead body will react to the shuttle's bioscanner. On my whistle, we strike. Understood?"

"Understood," the three hunters echoed.

"Good. Let's go hijack a work commute."

Wyn turned to cross the street, Besari already having vanished (which seemed like cheating to Wyn), when Sage grabbed his shoulder. "Wyn," she said. "Empathy doesn't last in this job. Burn that part of you away, or it will eat you alive."

"I won't sacrifice my humanity to become a bounty hunter, Sage."

"Then you'll die." Sage turned and disappeared down an alley. Wyn sighed, then hurried across the street.

Murmurs rose in the night, like smoke on the wind, barely audible over the pounding heart in Wyn's chest. A boisterous laugh made him twitch in his hiding spot behind a dumpster. Something dripped from the metal lip onto his neck and caused him to shiver. He chose to not think too much on what it might have been.

Compulsively, he checked his gear for the fifth time. A digital readout on his visor displayed his shot count and informed him of the Imberlii Nemesis's power level. He rechecked it manually and confirmed the power cell as well. Then he waited, again, for Sage's call. It had already been about eight minutes. They needed to strike soon, or the shuttle would already be here.

Wyn heard the distant whine of an engine beyond the drunken rabble first. Then heard the whistle. His muscles tensed and froze, then he heard footsteps hit the ground next to him and Besari whispered, "Move."

And he moved.

They rushed across the street, weapons leveled. He felt powerful in that moment as his targets yelled out in terror. It overwhelmed him until he felt a madness surging within him. He had never felt this strong before, and a part of him hated it. Distracted and drunk on his own power, it took him several seconds for the words that had left his mouth to reach his ears. When they did, all that power fled from him.

"Stet wown, no far hurt!"

Terrified looks shifted into confusion. Maybe Wyn should have planned out what he was going to say better…

"I mean, get down, no hurt!" he tried again. It was a slight improvement.

A tesing bolted, making it two steps before Sage jumped from her hiding spot and tripped him. Boot to his back and rifle to the crowd, she cleared up any confusion. "Don't move, and nobody gets hurt. Lie down on the ground, quickly now."

Two more bolted and made it no further as Cee and Besari returned them to the group. Outgunned and outmanned, the crowd quickly surrendered.

"Tie them up," Sage told Cee, and the A.I. pulled a thin cord from its thigh and efficiently tied each worker to the next. "Besari, Wyn, check for communication devices beyond their Vicos. We need those to stay."

The autoshuttle touched down as the last of the workers were tied up and inspected. The shuttle door opened, and Sage directed the line of workers onto the car. As planned, the hunters entered between the workers, hoping the shuttle's scanners wouldn't care about the extras. Their worries proved meritless as they easily entered the shuttle, a tube with a dozen seats and an alley between them. There was some open space at the back for storage, and Sage stuck their prisoners there.

"Can we at least get seats?" a bishett worker bravely complained.

"No. Crouch back there, and be happy you're conscious," Sage said. Then she settled into her own seat. "This worked out well."

"Perhaps," Cee said.

"Departure, two minutes," the shuttle warned. Wyn stared at the empty space by the shuttle door where he knew Besari stood, hiding herself with her Thresha talent while acting as lookout for any stragglers. But none showed and soon the doors slid shut and the outside world was cut off from them. "Destination: Shekta's Palace of Discovery. Travel Time: One hour and thirteen minutes. Please enjoy your ride and stay buckled for the duration."

Wyn settled into a seat near the front as Besari flickered into view next to him. The world fell away, leaving his stomach behind. Pressure pushed him into the seat, the lack of windows turning the sensations strange and claustrophobic. But he closed his eyes and leaned back, intent to enjoy at least an hour of relaxation before he had to be tense again. Everything went well, right up until red lights flicked on, bathing the cabin in an ominous crimson.

"By the empyreans, it's true!" one of the prisoners hollered. The others whimpered, agreed, or cried.

"What's happening?" Wyn asked. Besari shrugged, and Sage searched the cabin.

Cee jumped from its seat and pushed to the front, then ripped the panels from the front of the cabin. The autoshuttle's electronic system bled in the overpowering lights. Cee's jaw unhinged, and a snaking tube slithered down near the base and injected itself into the cabling. The systems sparked wildly for a few moments, then stilled.

The cabin shuddered with turbulence, and the captives in the back began wailing. A few hurled some rather graphic insults that burned Wyn's ears. But then the shuttle bucked again, and it all became a mess of gibberish and screams.

"Engines are cut. We're flying with momentum," Cee said.

"Well, why'd you do that?" Sage asked.

"I didn't. Happened right as I connected. There's also a bomb detonating in thirty-eight seconds."

"Can you override it?"

"There's an override code, but I don't know what it is."

"Do any of you know the override?" Sage barked, and the prisoners shook their heads.

"Bomb and crash, difficult to handle both at once. Intention is no survivors. This was a well-planned trap."

"Stop being impressed, and *do something*."

"The door!" Wyn shouted as he jumped to it, but his fingers found no purchase. "Open the door, Cee!"

Then time ran out.

Cee cut power to the system with one second remaining, and the cabin sank into complete darkness. The organics would have trouble seeing. There was an eighty-five percent chance of unreasonable panic.

"OH EMPYREANS, ARE WE DEAD?" one of the prisoners screamed, and several others started screaming. What limbs weren't tied flailed, and the flailing only caused more panic as they hit each other. The shuttle filled with an unnecessary cacophony, and Cee quickly modified its hearing processors to cut out the voices of the prisoners. It had hoped that would be enough, but Wyn kept yelling about the door.

"Cee?" Sage asked.

"We are in free fall," it said. It poured just enough energy into the systems to work with them without fully repowering the shuttle. Dozens of programs would need to be rerouted around the bomb to reconnect the engines. It was time-consuming to undo the traps, but the alternative was to blow up on reactivation. Not many would have been able to deactivate in time to stop the detonation, and of those that could have, none would have been able to stop the crash.

No one but Cee. "I estimate anywhere from ten to fifteen minutes before we crash."

"That's a wide range of time, Cee."

"I plan to make it wider." Cee's connection spread through the system like a virus, selecting specific systems to reroute through itself. These included many things to soothe the organics, such as soft lighting, oxygen replenishment, and a music program it had found deep within the coding. Soft chimes filled the cabin, presumably drowned out by the prisoners' wailing. Sage stood nearby, unworried, but more impressive was the calm Wyn and Besari displayed. They gripped each other's hands for comfort, an understandably organic response, but released each other once the lights came on. The prisoners were still in their full-blown panic, wriggling over each other like drunken worms.

The ship tilted, the pull of gravity slanting it downward, and one of the drunken worms rolled toward the front of the cabin. Sage braced herself against a seat and stopped the body from reaching Cee. It was grateful, but that was unnecessary as Cee had magnetically attached to the floor and locked its body in place. The organic would have a better shot damaging the shuttle's walls than affecting Cee's body in that moment.

While one part of its mind wondered at these idle thoughts, another was actively processing the correct wiring. More systems activated, and it took them over in rapid succession. Landing stabilizers were under control, and Cee fired them, righting the shuttle. They were set to limited bursts to avoid burnout; they were not designed to handle prolonged usage, and wasting them now would be disastrous. Cee projected a ninety-eight percent likelihood they would last at the current intervals of output.

Next, some flight reading equipment. Cee needed more information. The shuttle had no cameras outside, so it had no reference to the outer landscape. Instead, it pulled up satellite imagery. The internal navigation log dictated direction from Bezium City. The two put together allowed Cee to grasp the ship's location and heading. The monitoring equipment helpfully informed it of the altitude. Cee created an elevation map and tracked the shuttle's simulated progress. All done in twenty-three-point-four seconds.

The shuttle rocked as it broke through a tall tree. Cee's map had confirmed the situation as more dangerous. They had been flying lower to the ground than it would have suspected. "Four minutes to impact."

"That felt like an impact," Sage said.

"Three minutes and forty-two seconds until deadly impact," Cee corrected.

It adjusted course with intermittent landing jets as best it could, dodging the trees—

The shuttle rocked through another collision, and bodies jumped across the shuttle. All except for Cee.

—dodging *most* of the trees. There was a pond, soft mud to absorb the impact. Stabilizer jets fired forward, against the shuttle's momentum. One flared, then cracked and exploded. The shuttle shook, then angled. Cee used the back stabilizers to adjust and cut the remaining front booster. The shuttle tipped forward, and bodies flew past it, hitting the wall with grunts of pain.

The back stabilizers fired upward, spinning the tail down, and the sounds of moaning and grunting continued, though most of it was muted to Cee's ears.

Then the tail hit the water, and the shuttle jerked forward. It skimmed across the pond, and Cee fired the front stabilizer sideways at full power. The shuttle spun quickly, and the centrifugal force sent the passengers flying to the outer edge. The back stabilizer brought the spin to a halt, sending the shuttle hurtling backward across the pond with deadly force. Deadly for most of the inhabitants anyway. Cee fired the stabilizers at full power, and the shuttle jerked. Between the water and air drag and the stabilizers' bursts, the shuttle slowed enough to make it survivable when it hit the mud.

That did not make it enjoyable, however. The shuttle slammed into the bank, one end burrowing deep into the soft, muddy ground and the other end flying up into the air. The shuttle crashed down onto its top, sending its inhabitants bouncing around the cabin like the beads of a rattle. Still it slid, crashing through several trees before finally coming to a halt. Cee opened the door, then released all connections to the vehicle, leaving most of the systems deactivated. It stood, still magnetically connected to the floor, which now acted as a ceiling, and turned to the others.

"Landing successful," it said. "With minimal casualties." Cee looked at the pile of bodies. Several cried out in pain, their limbs twisted in unpleasant ways. A few were completely unconscious, either from head trauma or from fainting due to shock and fear. Sage, Besari, and Wyn lay among them, but a quick scan showed only superficial damage, and almost none at all for Wyn. It seemed his new armor worked well. Cee made a note to inspect it later.

A catchy jingle about something called a Cenzberry Muffin emanated from the speakers before sputtering out as whatever provided the shuttle with power died.


Wyn refused to leave the injured passengers as they were, taking time to cut them free from their bindings and administer first aid.

Besari happily joined him, while Cee and Sage worked to figure out their next steps. He worked tirelessly, exhausting what supplies he had. But each patient seemed more at ease when he finished with them. Perhaps he had a knack for this sort of thing. Not that he would ever go into medic work. The protruding bones still made him woozy.

Somehow, during all the tumult, Wyn had survived without much more than a bruise, and even that he could barely feel. Besari had been less lucky and appeared to have hurt her thigh. When Wyn had offered to look at it, she had declined and found a secluded area by herself to administer some sort of first aid. She still limped but said it was nothing serious. She wouldn't let it stop them.

Sage, likewise, had a few superficial injuries, but she seemed entirely unbothered, even as the side of her face swelled from when it had smacked into Wyn's knee. As long as her vision wasn't impaired, Sage saw no reason to call it quits now.

Wyn finished by patching the leg of a grateful male tesing and found several of the more severely injured sleeping already. Sage walked over as Wyn washed his hands in a nearby pond.

"Cee says the flight trajectory led that way." She pointed, but in the dark gray of pre-dawn, it was a field of silhouettes. One particular shadow, however, jutted out high into the sky.

"Do you think it was heading to that mountain?"

"I think that's as good a place as any to hide a highly secure, illegal facility," Sage said.

"That's a long way without a vehicle."

"It's the same to get back," she said. "We're about halfway between the two. The perfect place to dump some intruders."

"So we have a choice to make: Shekta or Bezium." Besari limped over with Cee. Wyn looked up at her. "Let's put it to a vote. Which do you choose, Besari?"

"I'm not very happy about nearly being blown up two different ways," she said. "So I would very much like some payback."

"Cee?"

"There would be insufficient data for the testing of the bounty split system if we quit."

"Sage?"

"I already said, once we start this bounty, there's no turning back. You're not afraid to go on, are you?"

"No," Wyn said, smiling. "I'm excited. But I'm also less injured. I just wanted to make sure we're all on board."

"It will take most of a day to hike out there," Sage said, "so everyone, take some energizing tablets and let's get out of here. We've wasted enough time."

"What about us?" one of the prisoners shouted.

"Oh, I almost forgot," Cee said, then tossed a small ball into the center of the prisoners. It flashed white, and then all the Vicos within the vicinity started sparking, black smoke filling the air. "Now they won't be able to alert Shekta."

"We also won't be able to call for help, you fucking psycho!" the same prisoner screamed, hysteria returning as he grabbed his head.

"Factoring in injuries," Cee said, "even the slowest of your group should be able to make it back to Bezium City in two to three days. I recommend leaving when you feel ready."

"And find new jobs," Sage added. "This wouldn't have happened if you didn't work for one of the most wanted criminals in known space."

Sage turned from the crowd and started off toward the mountain, Cee a step behind her. Wyn glanced back at the pleading eyes of the employees and clenched his teeth. Empathy kills a bounty hunter as quickly as any blade or gun. He turned from the innocent workers and followed the others, Besari at his side.

# CHAPTER 12

## BREACHING OF THE MOUNTAIN STRONGHOLD

Steel gray leaves crumbled beneath their footsteps as the sun once more dipped low in the sky. Wyn snatched a low-hanging leaf, and it crumbled nearly to a powder in his fingers. This failed to interest him as much as he would have expected as exhaustion from nearly twenty waking hours battered his mind and body. Sage distributed pills that were supposed to boost energy, but for Wyn, it was like pouring a bucket of water on a forest fire. They at least seemed to be helping the others.

The swelling had gone down on Sage's face, and Besari walked more steadily on her injured leg. It seemed only Wyn faltered now, surely due to his lesser training, but his stubbornness pushed him through the worst of it. At least never resting meant he never lost momentum. He wasn't entirely sure he'd rise again if he sat down.

"With how long it's been, won't Shekta be suspicious of the missing shuttle?" Wyn asked, hoping conversation would distract from his weariness. "Or look for the remains to see if there are any survivors?"

"No," Sage said, bringing a hand up to slow them down. They were nearly to the foot of the mountain and would have to be more wary of Shekta's security guards and cameras. Wyn patiently waited for more of an answer.

It never came.

"Why?"

Sage sighed. "One of the workers yelled about the system. That means workers are required not to bring others back. She probably assumes, or received a notice from the shuttle, that they disregarded that and are now dead. Why worry about the dead?"

Everything Sage said made sense, but a part of Wyn still wondered. If it were him, he'd want to check for survivors. Was that just him not being callous? Or was it a solid warning from his brain?

"Don't worry about it," Besari said as she put a hand on his shoulder. "We can get through whatever we find at Shekta's stronghold."

She seemed happy, energized, and excited. Wyn cursed the ineffectiveness of Sage's miracle pills. Why was he the only one dealing with this endless exhaustion?

"How's your leg?" he asked Besari instead of complaining. "You seem to be walking better."

"Yeah, it's strange," she said. "I hardly feel it now. Must have just been a rough bruise. Nothing too serious."

"Must be something in the air," Wyn said, glancing at Sage again. Her head pivoted as she searched the ashen forest for clues, and he saw that the swelling on her face had nearly receded entirely. Alien biology was a different story, but he knew face swelling shouldn't drop that quickly for a human. "She's almost better too."

"My suit filters the air," Besari said. "And I doubt there's any planet with an atmosphere that accelerates healing of multiple different species."

"Maybe the sun shoots out magic little healing rays," Wyn suggested, almost serious.

Besari chuckled. "I think I like that option."

"It'll be a shame once night rolls around again."

"Just don't get injured."

"Good idea! I'll keep that in mind."

"Wyn," Sage called. "Besari. Come here and stay low."

The ground sloped up a hill before descending to the foot of the mountain. The hill's peak provided a great viewpoint down to a small facility at the base of the mountain, suggesting they had been right about the mountain hiding something. A rumble thrummed through Wyn as part of the mountain opened and a massive shuttle exited. The doors stayed open with several small figures running about, and Wyn could see that the space beyond the doors was immense, as though the mountain had been hollowed out. There was no doubt this was Shekta's lair; Wyn couldn't have designed a more perfect evil base.

Wyn used his visor to magnify the scene. A small crew at the base manned ground entry, while the hangar doors handled aerial entry. Within, he saw several shuttles like the one they had downed.

"What do you see?" Sage asked as they all crouched behind trees to watch.

"Two entries," Wyn said. "Hangar up top and that building down below. Heavy security forces at each, including cameras, scanners, automated turrets, and guards."

"Three entrances actually," Besari corrected, and Wyn glanced over. She pointed upward, far higher than the hangar but not quite at the summit. Zooming in, he saw a large, tinted window, which nearly blended into the mountain rock. He hadn't expected the interior to be *that* large.

"I don't know if that counts," Wyn mumbled. "How would we even get up there?"

"Maybe not," Sage said, "but it's a great observation and helps build an understanding of the building we're about to enter. My guess is that's where Shekta will be. The arrogant always love the top. We're going to have to get up there, either through one of these entrances or from the outside."

Wyn ground his teeth in expectation. The job continued to grow, but he couldn't back out now. This was the perfect way for Bounty Inc. to make a name for itself. "Not we," Wyn said. "Besari and I."

"What?" Sage glared at Wyn, waiting for him to change his mind.

"This is meant to be training. I think it'd be best if Besari and I lead the main charge to capture Shekta."

"That is the more dangerous route. Why would we leave it to the inexperienced?"

"Is it?" Wyn looked back at her, determination in his eyes. "Honestly? The songbird is larger than most humans and is kept in some sort of containment to breathe perrilan air. You'll need to find the songbird, transport it to the hangar or outer facilities, and secure transport.

"Shekta is an old scientist, not a fighter. We need only sneak up to the top, catch her while she's sleeping, and work our way back down. The guards are focused on guarding the entrances, so once we're within, it should be easy to get around."

"You're making assumptions," Sage growled. "You have no idea what kind of security is within."

"I agree with Wyn Kelda," Cee said. "Once within, I'll be able to access their computer system and map out the usual patrol routes. Even with enhanced security, we would know exactly where they will be and can avoid the patrols. Transporting the songbird will be the greater challenge."

Sage stared daggers through the so-called cyborg, but Wyn smiled. "Fine," she said. "If you're leading, then how do we get in?"

Wyn's smile faltered as his brain wracked through ideas.

"I could use my invisibility to sneak through the ground forces and open a gate for you," Besari offered.

"They likely have sensors that would catch you," Sage said, "and if not, there are no other gates for opening. We would have to head through there and would likely get caught by any scanners that don't catch you."

"So we should go in by hangar?" Wyn asked. "They'll assume anyone entering has authorization from the shuttle. Security will be weaker."

"Perhaps, but how would we get up there?" Sage asked. "We have neither a vehicle nor equipment capable of making it up. We should focus on getting through the ground entrance."

"What do you think?" Besari asked.

"We use your invisibility, Besari. You act as a diversion to pull them away, and while weakened, Cee, Wyn, and I will take care of everyone who remains. You circle back, still invisible, and we get in quick. Cee can find a way to seal the hatch. Security will be alerted, but Cee and I can pull them away from the two of you."

"I disagree," Cee said. Sage glared at the A.I. and Wyn wondered if she regretted accepting its company. "Alerts will disrupt usual patrols, allowing for a lapse of information in any maps I obtain. There would be a greater chance of Wyn and Besari's discovery, plus if we follow your logic that we don't know what's within, there's a greater chance we are simply overwhelmed too quickly to do much. We should enter by the hangar."

"Given their shuttles enjoy trying to kill us, how do you expect us to get up there?"

"By climbing." Cee's body cracked itself open like the shell of a nut, then folded itself in half.

When Cee's transformation finished, it resembled something like a silver crustacean with the legs plucked off and reattached, but longer. Poles jutted from its back, like the spears from a failed hunt. Its fingers folded back, and in their place, small drills formed. A similar thing happened to its feet. As it crouched on all fours, a snake-like neck extended for better range of visibility. Cee monitored three very different expressions.

Sage watched with interest and surprise.

Besari was unreadable behind her helmet, but her body language showed shock and confusion.

Wyn was aghast and slightly disturbed.

"Let's go," Cee said, and it scuttled away. The others gave chase, shaking off any lingering shock.

"What the fuck is that?" Besari whispered to Wyn.

"I'm not sure. Maybe it thinks it can crawl up?"

"What about us?"

"Maybe Cee will open a door or throw down a rope." Wyn shrugged, as confused as Besari.

The answer turned out to be far simpler.

"Climb on," the crab-like A.I. said after having mounted itself on a secluded section of the mountain. Its drill-like appendages dug into the stone to strengthen its grip on the mountain's surface. It seemed as sturdy as if a ladder had been built into the rock. That didn't mean it was though.

"What?" Wyn asked because no one else was.

"I have provided secure platforms for you, one for your feet to balance on, one for your hands to steady yourself."

The poles jutting from Cee's back suddenly made sense. They acted like two rungs of a ladder, and like two rungs of a ladder, they were far too close to be used as Cee had suggested.

"It's this or blast our way in," Cee added.

*This* it was.

Wyn pulled himself up onto the left rungs, expecting Cee to dislodge from the stone and topple, but the cyborg didn't move at all. He went into an awkward crouch, wrapping one arm around the top bar and balancing his feet on the second. He was self-conscious about his stance and getting caught like this, but a quick glance showed him that Sage, opposite him, was in a similar awkward crouch. Besari was on its back and seemed more comfortable with an angled top bar that allowed her to nearly stand.

Then Cee began to climb. Slowly at first as it adjusted to the extra weight but then revving up to a steady rhythm. The drills would spin loose with a soft hum, then Cee would reach up and spin them back into the stone. A trail of tiny holes followed their angled path up toward the hangar doors.

Wyn glanced down once, and sweat pooled on his hands. He wiped them dry, only to remember that he was wearing gloves and the sweat remained. Then his brow started to moisten, sending rivulets into his eyes. That, at least, he could wipe away.

A strange, calming near-silence filled the air as Cee climbed. The soft hums of the drills, the gentle sway of Cee's movements. The rumble of a shuttle engine. The thrum of the mountain's gates. The last jolted Wyn from his trance, and he looked up to see the hangar closing. The others noticed as well.

"Cee?" A deep fear removed all emotion from Wyn's voice, replacing it with a cold, stoic tone. "You need to move quicker."

"Stability probability drops at higher speeds."

"It won't matter if we don't make those doors."

"That's not the only issue," Sage said. She glanced down at the ground, in the direction of the facilities. They were blocked by a jutting rock for now, but to get to the doors, they would be in the open, just as a ton of noise drew the attention of those below.

"Shit," Wyn said, and what he thought was the limit of his fear shattered. Halfway up the cliff, hundreds of feet in the air, trapped between two options equally likely to catch them. His mouth dried, and his breathing quickened. There was absolutely nothing he could do to change anything.

"Two options." Sage grabbed a pistol from her holster with one free hand and flipped a switch. The weapon hummed. "Besari, how wide can your invisibility reach?"

"What?" Besari's voice was frantic. "It can't. It only projects as far as what I'm wearing. I can't even wear anything too bulky or it won't cover it."

"Either you figure out how to expand it, or I have to shoot the shuttle down and possibly kill all aboard."

"*What?*" Besari's heaving breath projected out of her helmet.

"Sage!" Wyn cut in, pushing his fear away for the moment. "There has to be another way."

"There is none!" Sage hissed, and anger bled into her eyes. "You still don't get it, do you, Wyn? And neither do you, Besari. Sometimes, measures are needed to finish the job. A job we do to put criminals away that would otherwise run free. The deaths of those on the shuttle are a small price. They are criminals all the same. Put away—"

"They might not be! They could be innocent, people who don't know what Shekta is doing. Or even her next batch of slaves for experimentation."

"It doesn't matter. It's up to Besari." Sage balanced her pistol along Cee's back. "Move faster, Cee. Forget the probabilities."

"I...I don't really work well under pressure," Besari said as her head swiveled between Sage and Wyn.

"You better get used to working under pressure. That's almost exclusively how bounty hunters operate."

Besari brought her head down to her chest, muscles tense in her body. Then she flickered and was gone.

"Not big enough," Sage said.

"I know!" Besari shouted. A span of the bar in her hand flickered away, then returned.

"Faster, Bes—"

"Shut up!" Wyn snapped, and Sage's glare turned to surprise. Enough surprise that she did as she was told. Wyn adjusted his stance, and though it accelerated the flow of sweat filling his battle suit, he leaned out over the edge of his bar and grabbed onto Besari's bar. He reached for where her hand had been and found it quickly. "Besari."

The moment froze, and Wyn could almost see her head rise to meet his gaze, though it was only his imagination. He could almost hear her whisper his name, though it may have been the wind. He looked at where he thought she was, and he spoke to her.

"You can do this. Forget about Sage, forget about the shuttle. Look at me and focus. This is our first step into becoming hunters. We're taking it together, just as we said we would. I know you can do this because I've seen your strength every day. Show Sage what I've seen. Prove her wrong for no other reason than because you can."

This time, he did hear his name spoken. A firmness in a voice that was used to being caged. He could feel a thrum pulse through her hand, and then she blinked back into visibility.

His throat choked up. She had failed. As he tried to speak, he noticed Sage holstering her pistol, a smirk on her face. Words halted on his tongue as he looked around again. A faint shimmer hovered just beyond them in every direction. Besari's head was down again, but her shoulders were high, her focus radiating from her. She hadn't come back into visibility; she had *expanded* her invisibility.

The shuttle flew overhead just as their crab climber would have been visible had it not disappeared entirely. Heads below looked up and watched the shuttle enter, passing over the spot where three people rode a cyborg up a steep cliff. The doors still gradually slid shut, but Cee's scuttling increased. It would be close.

"Can you go faster, Cee?"

"Not without a high likelihood of structural integrity failing."

Wyn clung tighter, both to the pole and to Besari's hand. She stayed rigid in her pose. Sage looked relaxed, though Wyn wasn't sure how.

He watched their doom slide closer together in the form of two opposing doors meeting up for a tryst. That would have been Wyn's biggest worry had it not been for structural integrity, which failed just then, Cee's left side jerking free from the cliff as stone broke away. Everything spun one way, then they slammed to a halt as Cee reaffirmed its grip. Wyn's weak hold on his spot jostled him loose, and for a moment he hung only from Besari's hand. Then he lost that grip and hung on to nothing.

Besari's hand snatched at his, jerking his shoulder and sending pain racing up his arm. But he dangled there, muscles burning, as Cee righted itself and pushed onward. Besari easily pulled him up, her head never moving from its focused position, and Wyn pulled himself onto her bars, the two using each other as much as the extruding poles to keep themselves in place. Heat rose to Wyn's face as their bodies clung together, and for a moment he wondered if he could sidle back to his spot. Or even better, drop to the ground below.

Then Besari whispered, barely audible enough for the speakers to transmit, "Thank you."

"I should thank you," he whispered back. He lowered his head next to hers. "You're truly amazing, Besari."

He couldn't see her smile, but he felt it in her body. The way it eased against him.

He wished that someday he could see that smile that affected her so completely. He wondered at how beautiful it would be.

Cee jerked forward and flung itself through the opening just as the doors closed, spilling everyone to the floor. A loud grinding screeched through the massive hangar, bringing all attention their way. Wyn jumped up with rifle in hand, and Sage did the same, though she was far faster at the maneuver.

"We're hidden." Besari grimaced, still on all fours and staring at the ground.

"Not for long," Sage said, pointing to a small booth nearby. A single worker stood within, looking out at the doors, a faint frown on their face. Thankfully, everyone else seemed to attribute the sound to the doors and the hangar emptied with a steady stream of individuals heading off to begin other work. Wyn and the others froze while the crowd dispersed, except for that single worker in the booth, who looked down at something, poking at it irritatedly.

Wyn glanced back at Cee to see the crab had been brought to a halt, the hangar doors still open a crack. Its foot was clenched between the doors, slowly being crushed with all the subtlety of a shuttle explosion.

"The worker is going to call someone soon," Sage whispered. Then she let out a groan as the last person left. "Fuck it."

She ran off before Wyn could stop her, and before he could follow, Cee said, "Wyn Kelda, would you mind helping me detach my foot?"

"What do you need me to do?" Wyn asked, and Cee led him through a series of complicated actions, which allowed Cee to pull the leg free from the trapped appendage. Then its body convulsed in reverse of its earlier transformation: arms twisted, neck retracted, body unfolded and refolded. Within a minute, Cee stood before him again, though at a slight angle due to the missing foot.

"This is annoying," it said, then hobbled off toward the booth at a casual speed.

"Wait, what are you doing?" Wyn asked.

"Everyone's gone," Besari panted, then pointed to the booth. "I dropped the invisibility."

Only Sage occupied the booth now, and everyone else in the hangar had left to go about their business. They were alone. Wyn helped Besari to her feet and the two of them walked over to the booth to find it still occupied by the dock worker. He just wasn't alive anymore.

Wyn settled Besari down onto a bench away from the face-down corpse, and she leaned her head back and moaned. "I'm going to need a few of those wake-up pills, Sage. I feel like I could sleep for a week."

Sage's fingers bounced along the booth's virtual interface. "Sorry, you'll have to fight through it. Overdosing will explode your heart."

Wyn's eyes widened and his teeth clenched. "What's considered overdosing?"

"More than one in a ten-hour period."

"What if someone had three in a ten-hour period?" Wyn asked. "Hypothetically."

Sage looked up, her expression one of pure exhaustion. "Did you eat three in a ten-hour period?"

"Maybe," Wyn admitted.

"How long ago?"

"Five or six hours ago."

"Then you're probably fine."

"Probably?"

"Your heart would have exploded by now."

"Oh good…"

"Excuse me," Cee said, pushing the corpse aside with the nub of one leg and gesturing to Sage. She relinquished the controls. "I will be but a moment," the A.I. said as it knelt in front of the console. Its snake-like tongue slithered out and inserted itself into the console's base.

Within a matter of minutes, all three of their Vicos chimed with received data. A map of the entire complex and detailed descriptions of patrols. It also indicated the next shuttle departure and arrival was in two hours. They would need to finish their objectives by then, given the now-dead dockworker that would likely raise questions.

Wyn focused on the route to Shekta. "You can stay here if you're too exhausted," he told Besari. "With Cee's map, it shouldn't be a problem getting to Shekta."

"And leave you to do the fun part after I did all the hard work?"

Wyn smiled. "Just don't overdo it."

"Is he dead?" Cee asked, staring at the corpse.

"Unless he's a nairwid," Sage said. "I put a hole through his heart. He's not getting up from that."

"Do you think he still needs his foot?" Cee asked. "It's the perfect size, and—"

"We should go," Wyn said, pulling Besari from the booth before Cee could continue. He did not want to hear how the rest of that went.

Two hours.

Two hours to get Shekta and return. Two hours and they'd be one step closer to finishing their first bounty together. He couldn't help but let a smile touch his lips. Two more hours.

# A NEARLY PERFECT PLAN

Wyn peered out from a shadowed alcove as a pair of guards—a vrolak and a perrilan—walked by, chatting in an unfamiliar language. The rectangular identification chip attached to the perrilan's Vico slipped free, then disappeared entirely. Wyn felt Besari brush past him, and they waited in silence for the guards to move on.

"Got it," Besari said as she popped back into visibility, an identification chip held up. Then she shook hysterically. "Ah! That was incredible. I've played pranks with my powers, but this was entirely different. I never thought I'd get that close without anyone realizing."

"Did you take another of Sage's pills?"

"Maybe," she paused, then slid the chip into her Vico. "Doesn't matter. If I didn't, I would be useless right now."

"Sage said to be careful."

"Sage is human. Your kind is squishy and easy to kill. Besides, you had like three and didn't die. I'll be fine."

Wyn sighed and brought up Cee's map. "We should be good for a few minutes. Down this hallway and up the stairs on the right. It'll be clear for at least five floors if we move quickly."

"Then let's go!" Besari ducked into the hallway and darted away.

Wyn bit off a curse and closed the map before following. How in the galaxy were the pills so much more effective for others? Exhaustion hammered away at the inside of his skull until the hallway lights felt like daggers to his eyes.

Besari waited at the door to the stairwell, and Wyn slipped inside as she closed it behind them. They hurried, taking the steps two or three at a time until they heard the sound of the patrol entering a few floors above. Wyn grabbed Besari to stop her as conversation floated down. They were still a floor shy, and Wyn had no idea if they'd be safe exiting here or not.

Wyn gestured upward in a hurried motion, and Besari vetoed with a shake of her head. She pointed at the door, and Wyn shook his head. He would need to check the map. They couldn't risk—

Besari grabbed his wrist as he was about to bring the map up and shoved him into the corner of the landing. Then she was pressed up tight against him, and Wyn's heart slammed into his throat, which luckily meant the squeak that had almost escaped him failed to do so. Besari flickered for a moment, then came into full view. Over her shoulder, Wyn caught the shimmering of her invisible field.

They stayed like that, legs interlocked, chests pressed tight against each other, heads leaning on shoulders, until the guards reached the landing. Wyn was shocked that his racing heart was not giving them away. Instead the guards continued talking and walked right by. Wyn and Besari waited until a door below opened and the stairwell quieted. Only then did Besari drop the invisibility and step back.

"Are you all right?" she asked. "Your heart was racing like crazy."

Wyn cleared his throat and ran a hand through his hair. "Yeah, of course, just nervous about getting caught. Human bodies are like that, all heartbeaty and stuff."

"Didn't trust me?" she teased, then sighed. "I think those pills are wearing off. Expanding my invisibility is draining."

"We should limit your talent for now. Save your energy for Shekta."

Besari agreed, and they proceeded to the next level without issue. The door opened to a hallway with two other doors, a nondescript one off to the left and a thick slab of metal at the opposite end. It resembled an airlock and likely was one. Beyond, the gases of Perrilium were locked into her living quarters, allowing Shekta the freedom to breathe without a respirator.

Wyn pulled out his gas mask and slipped it over his mouth and nose. Stale air filled his nostrils quickly, but at least it was filtered, breathable stale air. Besari scanned her Vico at the door, and a light flashed green. After a series of clicks, the door swung open and granted them entry to a small, dark chamber beyond. The door shut behind them, and a hissing filled the room as the air was cycled. Wyn's vision slowly took on an orange tint before a chime indicated it had finished. Then the inner door swung open, and they stepped into Shekta's apartments.

The room itself was larger than the entirety of Bounty Inc., centered around a massive tree with teal flowers and orange leaves. It had to be well over five hundred feet tall, with dozens of branches spilling out and filling the room. The lower branches were trimmed to perrilan height, which meant Wyn and Besari were forced to duck. To the right, a floor to ceiling window looked out over the steel-colored forests of Bezium. To the left, stairs led to a balcony, along which several doors stood. Hammocks hung from various branches all throughout the central tree. Couches were arranged in a semicircle, facing a large display showing nature scenes from Perrilium, and a kitchen with a large island, double-door fridge, and thirteen stovetops dominated one quarter of the room. Who needed so many stovetops?

Besari pointed to the stairs, and Wyn nodded. Cee's reports suggested that the perrilan experimenter slept whenever night fell on the planet, which meant they knew exactly where she would be. They crept toward the stairs, ready to ascend, when something flailed and landed on Wyn. He choked out his yell, minimizing the sound, but alerting Besari nonetheless.

She spun, scattergun in hand, to find Wyn holding a small, furry creature no larger than his palm. It had four limbs, with wings jutting out beneath its upper pair, and large, golden eyes. It chewed on something, then opened its mouth and spewed most of it down the front of Wyn's suit. Jumping from his grasp, it hurtled its way up his arm. Wyn jerked back as it launched into the air and glided to the tree, where Wyn now saw dozens of them hopping from branch to branch.

"Gross," Besari whispered, looking at the spill down Wyn's front. Wyn sighed and wiped it away as much as he could before waving her along. He pulled his rifle free and checked the power to make sure it wasn't lethal. Then they continued up the stairs onto the balcony, which snaked along most of the room. Cee's map led them to a door that should be Shekta's. They nodded to each other and entered.

This room held two trees, though much smaller than the one outside and without the annoying creatures. A hammock ran between them, a form sleeping within.

Shekta. Their target.

Wyn glanced around to familiarize himself with the room and found it relatively plain compared to the opulence on display outside. A desk sat to one side, a few storage containers next to it, but mostly it was filled with plants, replicating the natural environment of her home world. Or so Wyn assumed without looking into it much more.

Besari tapped Wyn and waved her Vico before typing out a message. She had a plan. They just needed to hash it—

Wyn's Vico beeped with the incoming message and they froze. Shekta groaned and shifted in the hammock, then the snores returned. Wyn sighed in relief before delving into his settings to disable notification sounds. Then he typed out his response, quickly finishing their plan of attack. It would be a two-part assault. Besari would cut the hammock free, dropping a disoriented Shekta to the floor, where Wyn would apprehend her. They would tie her up and inject her with an anesthetic (thank the empyreans for Cee's over-preparedness) to knock her out. Then back they would go, following Cee's map to avoid danger. They would be leaving the base before anyone was aware Shekta had gone missing.

Wyn nodded and took up his place near the hammock, awaiting the tumbling form. Besari leapt into the tree and pulled one blade free as she reached out for the hammock's harness. Wyn's heart raced, adrenaline coursing through him. Besari's blade sliced at the harness, and sparks flared to life where it hit.

The blade flew from Besari's grip as she screamed and fell from her perch. She hit the ground with a thud and vanished. Wyn froze where he was.

"Who's there?" The hammock shifted beneath the moving weight. Shekta looked out toward where Besari had fallen, and Wyn ran the other way. The perrilan twisted as he ducked behind a tree. "Come out, and I'll kill you quickly."

A much softer thud indicated Shekta leaving her perch. Wyn glanced out from the tree and saw the short, furry woman searching the room. She hadn't seen him, and Besari was invisible. Not all surprise was lost.

Wyn's fingers tensed on his rifle, and before he could think more on it, he ducked out from behind the tree, aiming at Shekta. "Down on the ground and you won't—"

A rotten fruit smacked into his face, the fermented juices stinging his eyes. He recoiled as he yelled out, one hand moving to his face, the other waving his rifle around wildly, as he blindly searched for his target.

"Don't touch him," Besari yelled.

Wyn was touched. Unfortunately, it had less to do with Besari's sentiment and more to do with the strong perrilan hands that tore the rifle from his grip, then wrapped strong, wiry fingers around his neck. Wyn choked, then the room spun around him as his feet left the ground. When he could breathe again, it was only because he was launched across the room. Gravity soon betrayed him, and he crashed into a solid form, both clattering to the ground. He wiped the juice from his eyes as he rolled away, coughing. His neck ached where Shekta's fingers had been. Besari rose to her knees next to him and scrambled to pick up her scattergun. Wyn, likewise, pulled a pistol free.

The white and gray perrilan stalked toward them, Wyn's rifle in her hand but still held by the barrel. "Invade my private rooms," she growled, teeth flashing in the moonlight. "How dare you? Are you Raiyrium? Corporate thieves? I could always use more volunteers."

Wyn leveled his pistol. "Bounty hunters, here to collect."

Shekta paused, then burst out laughing. "You came here to die for a little money?" Her teeth snapped together. "Pathetic."

She charged.

Wyn and Besari fired. The room glowed with orange-red plasma fire as they unloaded into the perrilan. Her charge halted, but she did not fall to the ground like Wyn had expected. They both hesitated as Shekta stood there, seemingly entirely unphased by their onslaught, a faint glow emanating from her skin and eyes, light pulsing through her body. The light faded—except for in her eyes. They sparkled with a glow of their own.

"Is that a thing perrilans can do?" Wyn asked.

"Not that I know of," Besari whispered.

"Thresha talent, then?"

"Perrilans can't get those."

"They can now." Shekta smiled, and the glow burned like a furnace in her throat, streaks of light filling the room from behind her teeth. "I have discovered how to artificially induce talents, even in those species that normally can't receive them. I have crushed the monopoly of Thresha talents and created an invincible army. Your deaths were inevitable the moment you stepped into my sanctuary."

Wyn thought of a witty remark and almost said it. But before he had the chance, Shekta took a deep breath and screamed. A burst of orange-red energy exploded from her mouth and slammed into the bounty hunters, expelling them from the room. Wyn hit the balcony and flipped over it into the tree, where he bounced from branch to branch all the way to the floor. Besari had flown right through the branches and smacked into the large window beyond, crashing to the ground floor hard.

"Besari!" Wyn leaned up with a groan, then noticed a clarity to his yell. His hands flew to his face and touched skin. His mask was gone. Panic flared. Had he spoken? Breathed? How much? Where was it?

His gaze darted around as Shekta bolted from her room and landed on the balcony above. "Weak! Futile!" she bellowed. Wyn ignored her, hands flailing in the shadows of the tree. His lungs burned, his vision faltering. He must have breathed some of the noxious air in because there was a man made of urine laughing at him. Tears fell from his eyes, and he crawled among the roots, desperately clawing at the dirt. It had to be near, had to be here somewhere.

The branches! He looked up and saw the mask caught on a flower in a low branch. He pulled himself up, the pain in his chest becoming too much, and reached for it. Almost there. His hands reached the strap, and one of the creatures dropped onto his flailing fingers, jostling the branch. The mask fell to the ground, and Wyn soon followed.

Need to breathe. Just one breath.

He clawed for the mask. Grabbed it. Pulled it to his face—

Besari slammed into him at the same moment he took that sweet breath. The mask jostled free as he rolled with her body and gasped in the bitter perrilan air. The world exploded with prismatic light, twirling and morphing around him, and he knew, without a doubt in his mind, that he had breathed too much.

He was going to die.

"We probably should have figured this out ahead of time." Sage stared at the thick steel doors and ran mental calculations to see what had been missed. One of the two dead guards gurgled, so she delivered a kick to his head, hopefully quieting his posthumous conversation. Cee's mismatched foot slapped against the cold, hard floor, and Sage's eye twitched.

"Do all human feet sound this *unsatisfying*?" Cee asked as it tested the port guard's foot, which was now firmly attached to its ankle, against the ground. It sounded like a fish thrown onto a table.

"This is why I told you to keep the shoe."

"It was uncomfortable."

"Can you even feel what happens in the foot?"

"Oh yes, I wired into the foot's nervous system so it is sending data to my sensors." Cee paused its incessant slapping to stare at her. "Why else would I attach a foot if not to feel it?"

Then he emphasized the question with another slap. Sage winced.

"Weren't you human?" Sage snapped. "Shouldn't you know what a human foot is like?"

"Hmm," Cee said.

"Hmm?" Sage replied. "That's it?"

"Yes, I was. I had forgotten," Cee said. "I needed space in my memory for other, important things. I am relearning."

It slapped its foot down once more.

Sage growled and bit down on her annoyance. "Just help me figure this out." She pointed at the metal doors. "The songbird is in there. Which is filled with Perrilium air so it can live. If we remove it, it'll die."

"Yes," Cee agreed.

"So, what do we do?" Not once had they really thought past this point. They had an atmostank on their ship, but it would do them no good if the bird died before they could get it there.

"The songbird was transferred here," Cee said. "We should just use whatever they used to get it back out." It lifted its human foot and wiggled the toes.

"Great idea," Sage said. "So where do we find that?"

Cee pointed at the bird's cell. The entire cell. The thing that could easily fit Zetta and her entire family of six siblings, three parents, and seven grandparents and still have room for a dinner table to sit at for their many heated arguments.

"How the fuck are we getting that to the hangar unnoticed?"

"I did not expect to," Cee said. "I assumed Wyn Kelda and Besari Tal-Mar would trigger an alarm by now, thus removing the need for stealth."

"You expected—"

Alarms blared to life within the subterranean chamber, ominous scarlet painting the walls in brief flashes.

"There it is," Cee said. "Now we should act."

Guards began rushing around the area, which was an offshoot of the garage. They had avoided detection by hiding out in the darker sectors and killing the guards they ran into, but now that was about to be significantly harder. One guard spotted them and halted his rush to the elevators, deciding instead to focus on them.

"I shall deflect this guard with a lie," Cee said as it stepped forward to meet the approaching man.

"You two! What are you doing here?"

"I am an automated unit," Cee said. "There are reports of bounty hunters targeting the doctor's prized songbird, and we are here to move it elsewhere. This is my assistant security officer."

The guard followed Cee's indication to stare at Sage, who was still dressed like her normal self and not at all like any security officer.

"You're not a guard." His weapon had barely begun to twitch before he fell to the ground with half his head missing from two plasma bolts.

Cee turned to Sage and stared at her. "Did I not tell you to put on guard armor to blend in?"

"You did not," she growled.

"You should probably do that. It will make the lie more believable."

"You think?" Sage eyed up the three dead guards and mentally compared sizes. All were shorter, thinner, and frailer than her. Shekta should think about increasing training for her security. Not that she would have the time to do so. "I don't think any of these will fit."

"There is always Plan B," Cee said.

"And what's that?"

"Violence."

Sage grinned. "I think I vibe better with that plan."

"I shall extract the songbird's cell," Cee said. "It is likely you will need to rescue Wyn Kelda and Besari Tal-Mar."

"I was thinking the same thing," she said. "Can you get us a ship out of here?"

"Yes," Cee said.

"Then we will meet you in the hangar."

Cee nodded, then left to find a lift, its receding steps interspersed with the slap of its one human foot. Sage cringed at the sound before turning and rushing down the hall to follow the veritable army that was racing up the mountain stronghold.

# CHAPTER 14

## TOM

First came the light. A brilliant rainbow of colors filled the endless void. Next came the world. Wyn molded it between his hands as if from clay. Perhaps a tree here, a slug there. Purple would be the color of the water. Why had no one thought to make the water purple before? It was a great color for water, and the trees would be orange. The sun ought to be pink. He'd never seen a pink sun before. But the moon, that would just be all of the colors, a prism endlessly dispersing the light into new spectrums. Wyn saw a million colors now that he had never dreamed of before. Such as glurtle. Not the most interesting of names for such a beautiful color, he had to admit. But all the colors transformed and shifted before his eyes. This was the sight of gods. Wyn became a birther of universes, existence his playground.

A beautiful goddess caressed his face and drew Wyn away from the mountains he had painted maroon and shaped like angry boils. She burned with the light of her own sun, a golden color that soothed as it washed over him. Her hands lifted his head, and she brought forth a wonderful fruit. The juiciest, reddest fruit found in the galaxy. Wyn opened his mouth wide, tongue reaching in anticipation. But it grew far too large for one man's mouth. He unhinged his jaw, then learned he could not do that yet. Which confused him, for what purpose was a hinged jaw to a shaper of universes. The fruit grew angry with him.

It grabbed onto his face, burning his nostrils and filling his mouth with stale, putrid juice. He reached for the angry fruit, plucking at it, only for the goddess to cup his hands in her own. She had betrayed him, but he knew it was for the best. He was not meant to have this godly power, not when he couldn't even unhinge his jaw. And what had he done with that power? Made maroon mountains. What a stupid color choice that had been. And the angry fruit was his punishment, a burning sensation that rolled through his body, tensing every muscle until they ached.

His world melted away from his touch, and Wyn cried. It had been beautiful, despite the stupid mountains. It had been his. His tears then joined him in crying, shedding even smaller tears of their own, for they had just been born to this world that was to be stripped away from them forever.

Wyn coughed and heaved. Flecks of orange spittle sprayed from his mouth and coated the inside of...a mask? The angry fruit had left. Shadow creatures seeped from the walls and floors. Was he in a room? In a jungle? There was a tree, each leaf with an eye that stared at him. Those eyes wept tears of blood onto the floor, filling the room until Wyn had to swim or drown.

He grabbed for the branch but found it was the tail of a beast-shape, made from many beetles. It melted beneath his grip and reformed as a tiny swarm that angrily buzzed at him.

"Achtrek?"

The beetles replied, "We cannot urinate while you watch."

"Oh, sorry." Wyn turned and grabbed the next branch, this one sturdy. He pulled himself up from the flooding. The crimson blood shifted to a pale, pink juice. Wyn would have been tempted to drink had he not seen the bleeding eyes himself. He would not fall for their tricks.

Wyn climbed, past the village of rodents, past the farm busy growing meat plants, and paused at the tiny oil refinery that balanced on the lid of a bleeding eye. Just one man lived at the refinery, but the other villages had told tales of him in Wyn's passing. He liked profits and cared not for the pollution he caused below. For why should he care about that which does not affect him? Everyone needed oil. It was a necessary evil. Wyn thought he sucked and hoped his little refinery would tip off the eyelid and plummet into the sea of blood tears.

He did not tell the oil refiner that; he was far too polite for such things. So instead, he waved, and when the tycoon waved back, Wyn told him, "Fuck you." Then he left.

Within the domain of the nothing slugs, Wyn found solace, for no longer did the seas rise. Plus, he met a new friend. The shape of a slug but the presence of nothing, it was as if a space in the world had been ripped out specifically for the nothing slug. His name was Tom.

"Hello, Tom. I have come for knowledge." Wyn gestured down at a great monster that crashed into his goddess. Her light fizzled, and Wyn's heart skipped. He did not wish to lose his goddess. "My world is plagued by a demon who fights the goddess of beauty. If I do nothing, she shall perish, and what is my world worth without beauty? Perhaps you may grant me one wish, for I wish this demon to be smited."

"Smote," said Tom.

"What?" said Wyn.

"The past tense of smite is smote."

"But that sounds so strange."

"Yes."

Wyn stared into the nothing that was Tom, and the nothing didn't stare back for it was nothing. But he felt the time flowing around him like it was a thick, viscous goo that dripped from the tree. A hundred years and a hundred more he sat there. Staring.

"Hello, Tom. I have come for knowledge." Wyn gestured down at the great monster that crashed into his goddess. Her light fizzled, and Wyn's heart skipped. He did not wish to lose his goddess. "My world is plagued by a demon who fights the goddess of beauty. If I do nothing, she shall perish, and what is my world worth without beauty? Perhaps you may grant me one wish, for I wish this demon to be smote."

"Yes, child, I shall help you," said Tom.

"I don't think you're my dad," said Wyn.

"I request only a fruit, for I am hungry," said Tom.

Wyn reached up to the fruit clenched in his teeth, surprised that he had talked so easily. He would offer it if it meant saving his goddess. But had it not been a gift from her? Would she be angered? "I have another," Wyn said, reaching into his pocket. It was still there, the long fruit. A rectangular cube as long as his palm, white in color. A rather dull coloring choice for such a fruit. He would have to change that.

Wyn pressed down upon the top of the fruit, then twisted it. Red worms streamed in strobes from the top, and he smiled and handed it toward Tom.

"Here is my offering, Tom." The fruit slid from his fingers and clanged down the branches of the tree. The oil tycoon was knocked from his perch and plummeted to his death. The beetles swarmed as it clacked against them, interrupting their search for a bathroom. The village held a festival in honor of the fallen fruit. Wyn looked down sadly as it hit the floor.

"Oh dear."

Besari hoped Wyn still lived and would continue doing so. She had seen him take a large breath of the noxious air without the mask, leaving him a babbling mess with dilated pupils. Which was better than being outright dead, if not by much. She dropped him by the central tree and left. He would be safer alone, but it also meant Besari was very limited in her invisibility.

"Come out, you little pest," Shekta snarled as she stalked the room, Wyn's stolen rifle still in hand. She sprayed the room with a few wild blasts, forcing Besari to duck. "Guess that means I get to kill your friend."

She stalked toward the tree, and Besari kicked a kitchen stool into her path. The perrilan stumbled and lifted the rifle, but Besari kicked it free, then swung at Shekta, blades arcing. A burst of purple energy slammed into Besari's chest and sent her careening into the window. She hit the ground gasping, thankful to be still clutching her knives.

"This is fun, but I'm afraid we're going to have to wrap this up soon." Shekta held the rifle to her own head and fired, not for the first time. The furnace within her flared to life as she consumed the plasma energy, burning it within. "My security force will be here to escort you to your new home. Your friend too, if he lives."

Besari glanced back at Wyn, wondering the same, only to find him missing. Gone! She clenched her teeth. That was good, right? It meant he was moving. He wasn't dead.

Her distraction nearly cost her as plasma slammed into the window where she had been a moment earlier. She rolled away, vanishing and pivoting to lose Shekta. All while making her way closer. She needed to strike before the perrilan had a chance to release the built-up energy.

There was a clunk near the base of the tree, an out of place metallic snap in a room built around nature. The tree creatures squawked and burst from the tree in all directions. Besari and Shekta looked over, finding what had made the noise at the same time. Clattering across the floor was a thermal grenade, its light blinking faster and faster.

She glanced up to see Wyn, halfway up the tree, staring longingly as one of the strange creatures fled. Then she dove behind the kitchen counter as white flames filled the room. Colors bled away beneath the intensity, and the room shook. She was going to die. They all were. She hoped, by some miracle, Wyn was high enough to survive. Shekta could be eviscerated for all she cared.

Then color returned. The light and rumble ceased as suddenly as it had started. Sparks flared, followed by the crackle of fire. Besari peeked over the edge to find Shekta standing near the base of the scorched tree, her body the source of the flames. She glowed like some deity out of a folktale, her skin almost too bright to look at. Besari wondered then if she would have rather taken the explosion. She might have stood a better chance.

"There you are." Hot air hissed from Shekta's lips as she spoke. "I'm feeling a bit energized. Shall we continue?"

Too late Besari noticed her invisibility had dropped. She backed away from the counter and readied herself, only to find her knives missing too. She mumbled a curse and flickered invisible.

"You're not escaping!" Shekta howled. Essence burst from her and slammed into the counter. Besari was tossed like a leaf in a storm, bouncing off the fridge and sliding across the floor.

She was on her feet, running, but still the next blast pinned her against the glass wall with such force she heard it crack. Or maybe that was her body. She would have screamed if her lungs could have inflated. Instead, silent tears rolled from her eyes. She would die. Then Wyn would die. They weren't ready for a bounty like her after all.

"Ahhhhhhh!"

The pressure dropped just as Wyn clattered from the tree and landed on Shekta. The perrilan crumpled beneath the sudden hit and lay on the ground, stunned. Besari wasted no time in rushing forward to grab Wyn.

"Are you all right?" He had to have dropped at least fifty feet, if not more.

"Oh wondrous goddess," he slurred. "I am pleased to hear you worry about my mortal flesh, but you need not. The break will heal on its own."

"Break?" Besari glanced over his body, and Wyn stood up.

"Oh, never mind. I am fine."

"How?" Besari shook her head—no time for that—and grabbed Wyn's hand. "We need to leave!"

"Can Tom come?"

Besari tugged harder on Wyn's hand, unsure what to make of his babbling. "Sure, whatever, let's go!"

"Hop on, buddy." Wyn looked over, then looked at his shoulder. "Oh, you already are."

It became easier to pull him after that. Unfortunately, Shekta recovered as well. Besari dragged him around the tree, putting it between them just as another blast roared out from the perrilan. Far more powerful than any before, it slammed into the tree and the trunk shattered. It moaned as it tipped, bark snapping and flying in all directions. Branches cracked as they caught on the balcony or were crushed against the glass wall. The creatures screeched and hollered around the room as they sought safety. The tree's collapse halted as it hit the glass wall, and despite some distressing moans, it held there.

Then cracks webbed out with a pop, followed by a sudden hissing noise. Shekta ran, clambering up the wall to get to the second floor just moments before the glass wall shattered and the atmosphere vented from the room with a sudden gust.

Besari ignored it, pulling Wyn faster toward their exit.

Wyn covered his eyes as they passed a section of wall and yelled apologies for reasons Besari could not fathom.

The thing about hired guards is that there comes a point at which they value their lives over their paychecks. Fanatics fight harder, die slower, and never retreat. But paid protection, in the face of overwhelming power, cracks. And once it cracks, it shatters. Sage particularly enjoyed this part of the job.

Morality was for the weak, something Wyn should learn sooner rather than later. These people had signed up to die, and if they didn't want to, they knew where to run. Why should she be held responsible? It was one of the reasons she and Zetta made such a great team. Sage smiled fondly as she kicked open the door to the hallway.

Scarlet strobes flashed across surprised faces as they turned. Near the end, a crowd of almost a hundred guards pushed their way into a stairwell that, according to Cee's map, would lead directly up to Shekta's home. How so very loyal of them. Sage lifted her Imberlii Nemesis, full power, fully automatic, and unleashed a stream of plasma into the crowd.

The weapon tore through the unprepared guards like Zetta through a garnack. Some few fired their weapons before they died, but none fired accurately. Sage slung the weapon over her back to let it cool down, pulling out her Imberlii Dissenter from her hip holster. A brave soul poked out of the stairway door to fire at her, but the mayhem in the hall shook his aim. Sage fired, blasting his hand off as his weapon exploded. He fell to the ground, screaming at his stump.

Carefully, she stepped around, over, and onto the dead or dying bodies and made her way to the stairway. The screaming guard was still screaming, but she ignored him. The instant she poked her head through, five or six others fired at the door. She ducked back and sighed. They should have run away. That was the point. But some people needed a lesson to be drilled into them.

She focused, then pushed out with her Thresha talent. Carapace seeped from her pores like sweat, then hardened like stone. She covered every bit of her body but the joints. For her shooting hand, she covered all but the trigger finger. The other hand was transformed into a bludgeon. She tested it on the annoying guard, and his screams fell silent. If she got hit, she should survive, but the added weight made her knees scream. An ancient wound in her shoulder reawakened as she moved, and she could tell her back was going to regret this. These were the kinds of moments that had her thinking of retirement. They were also the kind that reminded her why she never followed through.

Sage picked up the limp, handless guard and threw him through the door. His coworkers riddled his body with plasma as Sage stepped out. She fired in rapid succession to take down all five, then hurried up the stairs. More guards tried their hand at killing her at every level. They found death instead, clean shots through the head or neck when possible. Dismemberment if need be.

Sage circled ever upward, fighting off ambushes from each floor with bludgeon and pistol. Bodies trailed her up the stairs, blood running down in rivulets like mini waterfalls. Still the force was unrelenting. Had she misjudged? Or had people already broken and run, and this was what was *left*?

A woman slammed the door open at Sage, then followed with a knife attack that skirted off reinforced ribs. Sage slammed her left fist into the woman's face, shattering teeth, then hooked her gun hand around her neck to bring her back down into the railing. Her head rang against the metal bar, and she fell limp to the ground.

Three people ran down, long-reaching stunstaffs in hand, another three circling her from behind. She fired into the first crowd, but they held energized shields that absorbed the Dissenter's plasma without issue. The old-fashioned way, then. She holstered the pistol and freed her fingers from the carapace as the first guards arrived at her level. Guard number one plunged forward with a thrust, and Sage ducked out of the way as sparks exploded against the railing. She grabbed at the staff, but the second guard swiped at her hands. The stunstaff hit her forearm, and the stony armor exploded off of her. Sage jumped back as the third swung. They pushed her toward the stairs behind her, where three more guards waited.

Fine. They could have her.

Sage launched herself down the stairs, and the trio of guards panicked. There wasn't enough room to avoid the woman of stone, and they knew it. Her carapace saved her, but the hired help had no such protection. Bones cracked as they fell in a heap, Sage's full weight crashing onto them repeatedly at each step. By the time the rolling mass came to a halt, blood coated the lower steps. Two were unconscious, one with a leg bone protruding through her suit, the other with his arm twisted so badly, Sage wasn't sure how it was still attached. The third was dead and likely the reason for most of the blood. His head was caved in, neck twisted at an extreme angle. Two of four limbs were severely broken, and another appeared to be at the very least fractured. And his jaw was mostly ripped off. That one must have been made of glass.

Sage pulled herself from the pile, carapace flaking from her like dust. She picked up a stunstaff and rolled her shoulders, full flexibility returning to her. Then she kicked off her boots, letting her bare feet slide across the metal stairs.

"Now's your chance to run," she offered. The three guards looked at each other, then back at her. Two hurried to position themselves at the top of the landing, shields blocking her from progressing. The other stood to the side. "Death it is," she mumbled.

She ran up the stairs and the first two guards flinched back, stunstaffs at the ready. Not ready enough though. Sage jumped up onto the side railing and launched herself at an angle. Hips and knees screamed at the motion, but she landed on top of the landing's railing, bypassing the first two guards and slamming into the third. Her shield hummed as it took her weight and both hit the ground. Sage grabbed the edge and spun as the expected stunstaff strike hit the third guard's arm instead of Sage's back. The guard screamed, and the slower one rushed forward as Sage slammed her own spear into the first's leg. She rolled again as the last guard swung his spear like a hammer at her. She jumped to her feet, and he hid behind his shield, taking careful swipes at her. She deflected, then turned and ran, her way up free.

The guard panicked, giving chase and dropping his guard. At the next turn, she hit the wall and pushed back at the guard. He brought up his shield, but her shoulder smashed into it and he fell back down the stairs. Not bothering to give chase, she pulled her pistol free and fired four times into his body. He stopped moving after that.

Sage stalked up the stairs and found her plan was finally working. People ducked into the halls as they saw her climbing the stairs, and, most importantly, they didn't return. She went the rest of the way unharassed, giving her joints a much-needed rest. She paused on the top floor, swapping back to her rifle. The barrel felt cool to the touch, undamaged by all her tumbling. That was why you bought Imberlii. It'd outlast the person who used it.

Sage slid one foot against the door, then with a violent burst of her Thresha talent, she sent the stone spewing from the side of her foot, expanding under the door, then bursting out in sharp spears. Screams of the impaled filled the hall. It wouldn't last long without constant power being poured into it, but it had done what she'd wanted.

She ducked out, a selective carapace armor forming as bolts skimmed past her. Three guards incapacitated, either dying or dead. Two alive enough to be an issue. Five guards to one end of the hallway, hoping to flank her. A couple dozen to the other direction, heading to Shekta's airlock. Crossfire was a bitch when you didn't have an angle. Sage smiled.

She rolled into the center of the hall, and from her feet she pushed out a thick wall of carapace behind her, blocking off a series of shots from the side with more people. The flankers fired, striking her in the chest where her armor deflected most of it. Sage fired back at the guards, who were surprised to see her not dead. Their surprise didn't last long. She finished by killing the two impaled guards on the ground. Then she dropped the armor completely. The wall was draining her energy, and if she kept it up too long, she would find herself taking a quick nap surrounded by enemies. It didn't help that the barrage of fire whittled away at it, requiring several more bursts of energy to regrow what she lost.

She ducked out long enough to gather information before plasma chased her back into her hideout. A group had gotten through and entered the airlock. Sage couldn't imagine that would be helpful to whatever trouble Wyn and Besari had gotten themselves into. So, she pulled a grenade from her belt, pressed down on the top, and twisted it. The slight beep of confirmation reminded her of Zetta. That woman loved to blow things up. She would be very jealous of this moment. Then Sage peeked over the top of her cover, and lobbed the grenade down the hall, over the heads of several guards, and between the closing door of the airlock. She heard it thump against the metal and heard the screams within as the door sealed. She even saw the horrified looks of the other guards as they turned. Then she dropped back down.

The explosion rocked the hallway and turned the airlock doors into shrapnel raining down on the others. Sage slipped her mask on and stood as an orange mist rolled from where the airlock had been to mix with the smoke in the hall. Sage fired on those guards farthest from the door, the ones most likely to have not breathed in the fumes—the rest were already hallucinating or dead—then dropped her wall of carapace.

Two figures stood silhouetted in smoke as the hall's ventilation pulled the haze away. They were bloodied from the explosion but otherwise unharmed. Two humans, and based on their looks, likely related. A brother and sister pairing, neither with weapons. So they either thought they could close the distance before Sage could kill them, or Sage couldn't kill them. As a third option, she considered they could just be stupid, but given the bloodlust in their eyes, she decided it was best not to assume that one.

Sage fired, and the brother kicked a corpse into the air like it was a toy. The ragdoll soaked up her shots as he charged, forcing Sage to duck to one side. He was strong, far stronger than any human should be. It had to be Thresha. She raised her rifle, but he was there, one fist ripping the weapon from her grasp, the other slamming into her chest. Luckily, she had formed carapace in time, otherwise her sternum would have cracked under the pressure. Still, her body was rocked backwards, and the air was driven from her lungs as she hit the ground.

She rolled, body reacting on instinct while her brain was still muddled. A boot slammed into the spot where her head had been, denting the ground. Then swinging around him, the sister slammed Sage back to the ground, straddling her in a very not sexy way, given the situation. Sage blocked the first punch with a shielded forearm, and the sediment exploded. Pain lanced up her arm, and she yelled out.

*Two?* Two Thresha-enhanced guards, and both with strength-enhancing talents? It wasn't unheard of for two people to have similar talents, but it should have been rare enough. Thresha bound to the genetic structure, and the results were as different as there are different genomes. Even twins were known to produce vastly different powers. It shouldn't have been possible.

It was not something she worried about for long, given the sister was preparing to split her skull open with a super-powered fist.

# CHAPTER 15

## OVERLOAD

"**S**hit!" Besari pulled them up short of the door as the light dinged red. Someone had opened it from the other direction. Was it help? And more importantly, whose help? She needed to keep her distance until she found that out.

"Besari, a battalion of noodles!" Wyn tackled her to the ground, her distraction with the door catching her off balance.

"Wyn!" She rolled as plasma rained down from above. Shekta had returned, internal furnace burning bright through her skin, though Besari could no longer see the light leaking from her mouth thanks to a breathing mask.

"What?"

"Move!" She pushed out a barrier of invisibility and rolled with Wyn, pulling him to his feet. She breathed heavily, sweat drenching the inside of her suit. She had never pushed her talent to such extremes, and the exhaustion was catching up. She could barely stay on her feet and felt a deep fog settling over her brain. All she could focus on was finding an escape.

A scattering of rifle shots directly in front of Besari brought her to a halt, then she dropped behind a large tree root that had pulled up from the ground. How—

"I think my butt was poking out," Wyn said, one hand feeling at his rump. "I could feel it."

She groaned and dropped the invisibility entirely. She couldn't hold it much longer anyway.

"Come out of hiding, little ones." Shekta dropped to the floor near the airlock door. "I want to see what a dose of artificial Thresha does to an already-enhanced subject. Will you die a horrible death? Or just lose your mind like all the others? I would love to see either—"

An explosion rocked the airlock, and the thick metal door turned to shrapnel, smashing Shekta through the wall of a room. Besari poked her head up and saw a severed tesing arm dangling from the twisted metal. She smiled when she realized the source had to have been Sage. They were finally able to escape.

Until Shekta returned and put a damper on her mood. Kicking her way through the rubble, her fur matted with blood—though the wounds seemed mostly superficial—anger filled her smoldering eyes as she glared out.

"Stop destroying my precious home!"

Sage bucked her hips and rolled away from the punch. The sister held her in place, but she had shifted enough that the blow was glancing. Where it hit still shattered the carapace, but it left Sage with the ability to live, and that was the best she could hope for.

Stone-encased fists hammered into the sister's ribs to little avail, the built-up sediment eroding beneath the strikes. She ignored the blows and grabbed at Sage's head. Even reinforced with quick cara-pace, the crushing strength of her hands shattered the protective shell immediately. Then she felt her skull planning to follow.

She formed a quick spike of sediment in her palm, as sharp as she could make it, and she slammed it into the waist of her attacker. The sister groaned as it pierced, but she did not relent. Not until Sage pushed out with her power in a violent scream, and a dozen more spikes burst from the point of the first. Stony spears jutted from the sister's torso, turning her shirt into a mess of red as blood gurgled from her mouth.

Sage bucked free, and the brother's foot nearly took her head again. She jumped to her feet as he charged into her and slammed her into the wall. Air burst from her lungs (again), but adrenaline kept her mind in the fight. He pinned her in place and prepared a killing blow. With a hardened palm, Sage struck him in the face, breaking his nose. He yelled out, a spray of blood coating Sage's face. Her sharpened foot hit him in the groin and dropped him. Sage grabbed his face, and with the hardest and sharpest carapace, she dug two thumbs into his eyes, screaming as she pushed them as far as they would go. His eyes burst, tears and blood and eye jelly oozing down her wrists as the brother yelled out, hands flailing from his groin to her hands. They squeezed, and her bones threatened to snap under the tension.

With one final jab, she found the brain. He spasmed, and then his grip loosened, and his body crashed to the floor, twitching. Sage stood panting for a moment, then slowly limped over to her rifle. The sister lay on the ground, bloody gasps escaping from her lips as her eyes glared at Sage.

"Yeah, yeah. You don't have to say it," Sage groaned. "'You killed him, you bitch. I'm going to eat your liver.' Whatever."

Sage fired fifteen times into the sister's skull until her head was paste. Letting out a long sigh, she limped toward the airlock entrance.

Shekta's apartments were a wreck: a giant, flaming tree sprawled across the space, the massive window had been broken by its fall, scorches along the walls and floor indicated a shootout and possibly a second explosion she had unfortunately *not* caused, and blood coated the entrance. *That* was definitely from her. A bloodied, disheveled, and very angry perrilan in a mask shot at two figures hidden by a rapidly-deteriorating tree root. She fired with a very familiar Imberlii Nemesis.

They were supposed to take her by surprise, not explode her fucking home and hand over their weapons. Sage rolled her eyes with a heaving sigh and sighted her rifle on the target.

"I'd like you to stop shooting at those idiots now," Sage said. Shekta paused, looking over her shoulder. The perrilan seemed to have a strange glow about her.

"Another uninvited guest," she growled. "Are you the reason my front door is missing?"

"Sage! No!" Besari leapt from her spot, and Shekta turned, Wyn's rifle raised. Sage fired three times into her chest, the rifle switched to a low charge to avoid death. Who knew with perrilans though, they were a weak—

Shekta took a step back, rifle lowered, then a pulse went through her body. Sage aimed and made to fire again, and as she did, a burst of purple energy slammed into her. She flew back into the airlock, hitting the wall and then the ground, every nerve in her back hollering at her. Blood poured from a wound in her torso. A ragged edge of metal had split her open, and the cut was deep. Her body shook with the pain, and she bit down on her tongue to keep herself focused.

Then she filled the cut with her sediment carapace. She wouldn't bleed out as long as that held.

Sage stood on wobbly legs, rifle clutched in hand. She was getting real fucking tired of this mission. She rolled her neck and shoulders and stepped back into the room.

Shekta had returned focus on the other two, carefully approaching their cornered hiding spot. Shekta glanced back. "Ready for round two, burly human?"

"She absorbs the plasma shots," Besari yelled. "Don't use your guns."

Shekta's mask lifted with her cheeks as she laughed. "You look like you can barely stand," she mocked, then tipped the rifle in hand to her own head. "And you can't use your guns."

The perrilan fired, and instead of blowing off her own head, energy pulsed through her body. She glowed from within like a beacontoad. Shekta thought she had won already, filling herself with energy to repel close attacks while firing from a distance. A perfect attack and defense, and she had the cocky ego to believe it.

"Tell me," Sage said. "Have you found the limits to your powers?"

Shekta hesitated, poised to shoot herself in the head again, her eyes widening slightly. Sage flipped the rifle to full power, its shots still on fully automatic. She fired into the chest of the perrilan with an unending stream of plasma. Shekta stumbled back under the barrage, Wyn's rifle slipping from her grasp, but still she pulled every shot within herself, her eyes blazing with a fire in her skull.

"You'll run out of charge before I reach my limit," Shekta growled. "And everything you give me makes me that much stronger." A purple haze fluttered around the perrilan as she prepared to unleash that strange kinetic burst. Then a scattergun shot took her in the shoulder. Her concentration shattered, and the purple haze disappeared.

"Wyn! Shoot!" Besari commanded. And Wyn hopped up, wearing a dopey grin beneath his mask.

"Pop the slug!" he shouted, then his brow furrowed. "Sorry, Tom, not like that." Then both his pistols joined Besari's scattergun.

Shekta tried to move, but her focus became consumed entirely by the barrage. One of Wyn's shots took her in the knee, and she dropped to the ground. She stared at Sage, anger burning alongside those brilliant suns. Then she shook violently and roared. Kinetic energy exploded out from her and rocked the perrilan's apartments. The tree shot through the remains of the window and careened to the ground outside as sparks exploded from the lights and display units. The balcony above collapsed as whole walls crumbled. The force sent Sage backwards, into the wall behind her. Her head smacked metal, and everything went black.

Wyn rolled over, the world spinning around him as he touched the back of his head. Blood, but not much. He groaned and sat up. Besari was nearby, a crack across her helmet's face, unmoving. Wyn panicked, ready to cover the crack, until he realized his own mask was missing again. A cold breeze poured through the open window, ridding the room of the noxious fumes. A groan alerted him that she was still alive.

If the room was cleared out, did that mean Shekta was dead? He staggered around for a moment, then found the perrilan unconscious under a heavy coat of debris from the fallen balcony. A bioscan showed signs of life, and her mask was still sealed. "Full price." He smirked as he pulled some wire rope from a pouch and wrapped it around her arms and legs.

"You should check on the other one."

Wyn jumped at the voice and found a tear in the fabric of space that was in the shape of a slug sitting on his shoulder.

"Fuck!" he shouted, rubbing at his eyes. "You're real?"

"No," Tom said.

"Wait, other one?" Wyn turned and saw Sage unconscious near the airlock door. Blood cascaded over her torso and down her head and neck. "Sage!"

He ran to her side and checked her head. "Small contusion," Tom said. "But head wounds bleed. The back is the issue."

Wyn saw it as the thing spoke. Her vest had been torn and a huge, jagged wound ran from rib to waist. Blood oozed out, mixing with the dusty remnants of Sage's power to form a thick paste. "This can't be good for a wound." His hands hovered over the damage as he wondered how to clean it out, then his stomach churned at the thought. He didn't know if it was better to leave it as is or try to fix it. They needed to get out of here.

"Voices," Tom said, and Wyn's head jerked up as he heard them. He grabbed Sage's rifle and checked the charge. It was almost out. Twenty or thirty shots maybe, but it wasn't synced to his visor, so he wasn't sure. Then he checked the hall.

Dozens of guards stormed into the hall, trampling the bodies of the already deceased. So many guards and nowhere to go. Wyn fired into the hall, and they dove for cover, using dead bodies if they couldn't reach the safety of the stairwell. Then they returned fire. Wyn fired in short bursts, doing what he could to keep them at bay. But eventually—

The gun clicked, and the plasma stopped. The charge was empty. Wyn tossed the rifle to the side and felt for his pistols. They were gone, lost in the rubble when whatever had shaken the place had hit.

"Wyn?" Besari propped herself up on one elbow and looked around.

"Backup's here," Wyn yelled over another burst of plasma filling the airlock. The sounds of stomping feet followed. "And they're not happy."

"If you ever toss my gun like that again," growled Sage as she sat up, pulling her rifle back to herself, "I'll make you eat it before deep frying your insides with every last bit of the charge."

"Well, you wouldn't have been able to do that last part," Wyn said as a flush rose to his cheeks. "It's out."

Sage popped the gun open and ejected the empty cartridge, slid a new one into place. Then she glared at Wyn.

"We need to get out of here," he insisted.

"How many? We can shoot our way out." Sage stood, then stumbled forward, one hand going to her back.

"You're in no shape to storm out of here," Wyn said. "Hand me your gun. You and Besari find a place to hold up here. I'll clear them out."

"You think I'm stupid?" she growled. "I'm not handing my weapon to you until you learn to hold on to your own."

"This is not the time!"

"I'm not leaving your side." Besari jogged over and offered one of his pistols. "We can take care of them."

Wyn snatched it and fired blindly into the hall. "To the left," Tom suggested. Wyn shifted the pistol's aim to the left and fired. Someone shouted out in pain.

"We have no time. We can't lose Shekta, and we have to get out of here."

"Guess we jump out the window," Sage suggested. Besari and Wyn stared at her with consternation. Sage just pointed and Wyn glanced over his shoulder to see a large transport ship rising into view, its rear hatch opening to reveal a familiar cyborg standing on the ramp.

"May I offer you an alternative escape route?" Cee asked.

"It pinged our Vicos, if you were paying attention." Sage smirked, then rose to her feet again, a little more steadily this time.

"Besari, get Shekta and load her on the ship, then Sage. I'll hold off the crowd here."

Besari nodded and raced for the restrained perrilan. Sage put a hand on Wyn's shoulder, and Tom hopped to the other one. "Don't stay long. Shoot a few times, then run."

"I don't plan to die this close to finishing my first bounty," Wyn said.

Sage nodded, then hurried to the window, Besari following with Shekta over her shoulder. Wyn smiled, then did as Sage had suggested, firing a few times into the crowd and—

"Uh oh," Tom said.

A grenade rolled into view and beeped. Wyn jumped away, then it exploded, and his body rocketed across the room. He hit the ground, ears ringing, vision spinning. Explosions and plasma filled the room over his head, and a jumble of shouts came to him through the haze. He blinked away the bright spots and moaned as someone moved him.

He grunted as he hit cold metal, and his vision steadied. Besari crouched at the end of the landing ramp, hand out, holding him steady. The landing ramp that he was now on. But Sage wasn't.

Instead, she had raised a wall of sediment in front of her. But the next barrage of plasma destroyed it faster than she could hold it in place. The shots that went over hit the ship. Besari and Sage screamed at each other.

Sage could drop the wall and dive for the ship, but then they'd all be open to fire. Or they could leave her, and only she would die. Wyn's body went cold with the realization. Someone was going to die. Someone he cared about. "Cee?" He felt the silent word fall from his lips, unable to reach his own ears. He turned, but the cyborg had left. Instead, he found a rather large locker, in front of which stood a nothing slug.

Tom nodded.

This fucking mission. This whole fucking mission. Sage should have retired. And she shouldn't have let Wyn and Besari push for such a dangerous bounty. She'd let her greed and pride make decisions. This was why she was a shit mentor. This whole job was a terrible idea. Now she'd end up dead because of a stupid fucking bird. And what did Wyn and Besari learn from this encounter? How to fuck up their lives?

She crouched lower as the top of her wall caved in. Plasma chased Besari farther into the shuttle. The idiots had waited long enough. They needed to leave.

"Go!" she roared again. "Fucking dammit! Just—"

Wyn walked out onto the ramp with a long cannon in his hands and lifted it, looking through the sights. The shooting paused for a fraction of a moment as the security guards shifted to the new target. With a fwoop, a glowing ball shot from the end of the magrec cannon and clattered into the middle of the group. A plasma bolt hit

Wyn in the hip, dropping him to the ground, but the rest went wild. The magrec charge thrummed loudly as the whole room seemed to shake, every piece of metal shuddering and dancing. Sage dropped her wall and jumped as the explosion filled the room. A sudden compression of magnetic energy burst free, sending metal shrapnel flying and eviscerating anything even close to it. Sage's body was hurled through the ship and into Wyn as they both clattered down the hall.

"Cee! Go!"

The ship shuddered and spun as the perpetual explosion destroyed what remained of Shekta's home. Sage lay still on the ramp for a few moments, then sat up. Wyn had pulled himself away, closer to Besari, and all three stared at what they'd done. The tip of the mountain crumbled inward, dust and debris exploding out at several levels as the mountain stronghold collapsed.

"Holy shit," Wyn mumbled. Besari nodded along. Sage pulled herself to her feet, levering herself against what she suddenly realized was the large metal atmostank the songbird was kept in. To the other side, Shekta lay bound and unconscious.

"Hello," Cee's voice came over the comm system. "This ship is space worthy. Would you like me to return to our original ship or leave in this?"

"Leave in this," Sage grumbled. "We don't need the other one anymore."

"Understood," Cee said. "Then I suggest everyone fully enter the cabin in order to seal the ramp."

# CHAPTER 16

## BOUNTIES

The scanner slid past Wyn's face, paused at his ear, then reversed course. When it completed its pass, the machine chimed, the results displaying on a screen that Sage monitored.

"Well, nothing's wrong with you except the usual."

"What's the usual?" A pulse of panic squirmed through his stomach.

"That you're an idiot," she grumbled. Wyn sighed and leaned back in the medical chair, eyes closed. "Machine says there's nothing we can do about that, though. Incurable. Untreatable."

Wyn cracked an eye open and looked at Tom, who looked back. "Nothing else?" he asked. "Nothing to explain the exhaustion? Or the..."

"Or what?" Sage quirked an eyebrow at him.

"I'm just so tired, Sage."

"Battle shock. You almost died, and your body is recovering." Sage limped around the small room, placing equipment back and returning the scanner to its little corner. Wyn let his gaze drop to the injured leg.

"How are you?" he asked.

"Nothing wrong that won't fix in time." She glanced back and saw his worried expression. "Don't worry. I've been hurt a lot worse. It's actually healing up quite quickly. For how much of a shuttlewreck that bounty was, it could have been worse."

"It's a shame we never got to hear the songbird sing." They had returned to Chrysanax immediately, and Baron Serron had retrieved his songbird with much joy. The Raiyrium Confederation had retrieved their war criminal with much surprise. First bounty (or rather, *bounties*) complete, and everyone lived, even if they were a bit beat up. But Wyn's exhaustion had never faded, and he'd felt like a walking corpse for days after. So, Sage had suggested the second scan to make sure all effects from the perrilan air were cleared. Turned out they were, so Tom was...something else. Maybe something permanent. He hadn't mentioned the nothing slug to anyone.

"You're not missing anything." Sage gestured at her Vico and brought the wall display to life. A majestic songbird walked across the walls, then opened its mouth and unleashed an unrelenting audible onslaught on Wyn's ears.

Wyn yelled out in horror as his hands clasped over his ears. Sage laughed, then shouted, "The perrilans are a strange lot." Then she left Wyn and the screaming bird.

Wyn was quick to give chase and let the death rattle die out behind them. The medical office was a small room in the corner of the second floor.

"You almost died, Sage," Wyn said as he matched her stride through the halls.

"So did you. So what? It's part of the job."

"You almost died because of me."

She stopped and turned, causing Wyn to jump in surprise. "I lived because of you. This job is dangerous, and it requires a certain mindset. One that isn't going to dwell on the possibility of death. If I die, it's because I wasn't good enough. You don't get to take that away from me. The truth is you need to make sure you enter every bounty with no regrets, because it's an awful way to go." Then she shrugged and continued walking. "That's what I hear anyway."

"Was this the right decision though?" Wyn asked, and Sage's shoulders dropped as she turned back around to face him.

"What decision? To go after Shekta? It turned out just fine, so yeah. We're richer for it."

"No, do you think I have the mentality to be a hunter? This business of Bounty Inc. Was it all just a foolish dream to chase?"

"First of all, I already told you Bounty Inc. was a stupid idea, and you didn't listen. Which is good, because if you had listened, the galaxy would be lacking two quality hunters, and Shekta would still be experimenting on slaves. As for if you have the mentality to make it work, that's for you to decide. No one else gets to tell you what you can or can't do. Can you continue on with the guilt of those you've killed and the grief of those you've lost?"

Wyn imagined losing Besari, and he felt a chill run through his blood. A shattering within his chest. "I don't know."

"Then move forward until you can't. No one is here against their will. If someone dies, they'll die knowing it could happen. All you can do is fight harder to make it not happen." Sage tapped Wyn's chest, and his eyes rose to meet hers. "Channel it in here, set your fighting spirit aflame, and fight harder until you always come out on top."

Sage always had a way to find a simple solution to a complex problem. An option his mind in its exhausted state couldn't comprehend. Loss might happen, but he would do everything to avoid it. Sparing no expense, he would train until he collapsed. He would become a better hunter so those around him would never die.

"Wyn." Besari hurried down the hallway, her shoulders sagging as she regarded the two of them. "We have a problem."

"My ship!" the teal torshk screamed, then waddled toward the destroyed *Blackwood Four* in the familiar hangar of Bezium's Port. The camera view shifted to a beautiful golden tesing woman who spoke directly at the audience.

"This is the heartbreaking scene when Zokrin, magistrate of Urgo Holdings, found his missing ship in shambles in a port on Bezium, a planet known for its lawlessness. We talked to the portmaster to ask about who could have stolen the ship and for what purpose it was brought to the planet."

The camera shifted again, zooming up on Telanuganekt as he licked a paw and rubbed it across his face before speaking. A sparkling jewel dangled from one ear. Definitely new. "It was a couple of people. Maybe four, I don't remember well. They seemed to have everything within their rights, so they must be master criminals. Usually nothing gets past my eyes."

"He didn't recognize the name Bounty Inc.," the tesing reporter continued when she reappeared, "but there is certain speculation that the organization could have been involved in the theft. A recent company, created by a young human using his inheritance, was meant to delve into the yet untapped market of organizing bounty hunters. A perhaps gray area of business, this company might have stepped firmly over the line in its recent attempts to capture two bounties. One for a missing pet of a Perrilium baron, and the other the notorious mad scientist Shekta, a perrilan herself. We reached out to representatives on Bezium for more information."

"They had no right!" a human male yelled into the camera, a frightened field reporter holding a microphone close. "Bezium is not part of the Raiyrium Confederation, and we do not share criminals. Shekta was a valuable part of our commerce after she rehabilitated from her past crimes. They attacked her home, killed her guards, and dragged her from a profitable and honorable life here."

The audio bleeped out a few choice words before shifting back to another interviewee. This one Dekka, the gorsaulk prostitute.

"I don't know anything about these allegations against my dear Wyn, but I can't see it being true. He was such a sweet lad with an innocent kiss. No chance he could have done such a horrible crime."

Wyn's cheeks flared red, and his hands clawed at the sides of his head. He almost missed what the tesing reporter said next.

"It seems Bounty Inc. had not notified government officials of their intentions, instead deciding to enact their own form of lawlessness on a planet well known for it. The Bezium government has asked the Raiyrium Confederation to rectify this by returning Shekta or giving them the CEO of Bounty Inc. to serve his own sentence on Bezium. As of right now, they have a blanket arrest out for anyone working for the company who enters their space again.

"The R.C. has neglected to comment about Shekta, which isn't a surprise, given the rocky relationship between Bezium and the confederation, but a spokesperson within the galactic government has said they would be looking into the claims of theft of the merchant ship *Ninth Harrow*."

The screen froze, and silence fell in the lounge. A cold sweat broke out all over Wyn's body as he stared at the still image of the tesing reporter. "You *stole* that ship?" he squeaked. "And why is its name different?"

"I—"

"Wait!" Wyn shouted, and Sage's mouth clamped shut as she glared at him. "If I don't know, that's better. If I make a statement and they have truthsniffers, I can't know."

"You shouldn't make a statement," Sage said. "It will just be something others will rip apart and make the whole situation worse."

"L-Bot? What do they have against us in both cases?"

The strange new L-Bot stepped forward, and Wyn averted his gaze. He was still uncomfortable with looking the robot in the eye. The screen shifted to display the two criminal lawsuits. "The lawsuit from Bezium is nothing to worry about," it said in a startlingly low voice. "The Raiyrium Confederation has never once given up a citizen or offered a prisoner trade of any sort with Bezium. It is likely they will ignore all attempts to apprehend you. However, it is equally likely that Bounty Inc. employees will be killed if found on Bezium."

"I'm okay never returning there," Wyn grumbled. "What about the theft?"

"Circumstantial evidence at best, given the portmaster lost the footage of the day it landed," the legal bot said. "There is the case of the atmosphere tank aboard filled with Perrilium air to suggest a connection with the songbird, but there are no clear indications on when the songbird first arrived on Bezium. It could be argued the ship was used to transport the songbird in the first place or that another hunter used it. As long as Bounty Inc. does not admit to using it, there should be nothing to link the company to the theft."

"What about the gate passage?" Wyn asked. "We didn't mask our identities there."

Sage shook her head. "That's why you shouldn't have pai—"

"Stop." Wyn glared at her, then felt his guts turn to jelly as she glared back. He forced his attention back to the bot.

"If the Raiyrium Confederation is unwilling to work with Bezium, which seems the likeliest case, those records will not be handed over."

"But this will be attached to us forever, giving them a chance to find some evidence to pin it on us."

"That is unlikely," Cee said. Wyn turned to regard the A.I. as it continued. "All evidence of our use of the ship was expunged. I also reverted the ship's identifier back to the original, before Sage changed it, in case we needed to abandon the ship. Nothing ties us to the original ship. I believe they have no solid case. They may attempt to frighten us and threaten to dissolve the company, but nothing more."

"So if I ignore it," Wyn considered, "the company will be hounded for a time, but nothing will be brought fully against us. That's why we found out through the news and not a legal rep. They want to trash us in the public eye."

"It's also why it's best to ignore everything," Sage said. "Who cares what they say about us if they can't prove anything."

"No one will want to work with us, especially not the R.C.," Wyn said. "So I care. We need our image to improve, or no one will want to invest in us. This could kill the company."

Wyn ran a hand over his face, a headache forming. Besari maintained her silence nearby. Sage crossed her arms, face sour. Cee and

L-Bot stood near the display with Wyn, and Seph paced in the back. Zetta had also arrived and appeared to be chuckling to herself, attracting several glares from Sage.

"I will make a statement," Wyn announced.

"That's a bad idea, Wyn," Sage said. "There are so many ways you can make it worse."

"So is stealing a ship in R.C. space," Wyn snapped. "It doesn't matter. I need to improve the outlook of Bounty Inc., and this is the only way to do so." Wyn turned to face the crowd. "I will need help on this front, however. I would like us to be more selective in the choice of bounty moving forward. We need to take bounties that paint us well in the face of large companies and governments. Things that help the R.C. and its people. When they think of Bounty Inc., they should be considering the good we've done, not this incident. The more public-facing, the better."

"We could ask Perrilium to make a statement too," Besari suggested. "They should be in support of the company after we returned a baron's songbird and captured a criminal from their home."

"Falvians too," Zetta said. "They'll be thankful for me getting that Heron guy."

"Achtrek also captured someone, right?" Wyn asked. "A tesing criminal."

"Yeah, but the tesings probably won't support us because of Shellesh," she said.

"I was specifically requested by a government official of Haush," Cee said. "I can make it a top priority to help sway their influence."

"Do that," Wyn said. "And everyone else, look for similar bounties. From now on, we act completely within the limits of the law while within Raiyrium space." Sage glared at him again, and though it curdled his stomach, he continued. "Unless it's *completely* untraceable. Not even a hint of it coming back to us."

Sage's eyebrow quirked, and Wyn flashed her a smile. "First and foremost, we must always think of the company image. If it can't be bought, we figure something else out. If we can't do anything else, we make sure there's no trace to Bounty Inc., ever. I understand we can't always act within the law, but we must do whatever we can."

Everyone nodded, and relief washed over him. Maybe there was a chance. "I need to take care of my statement. L-Bot, with me. The rest of you, good hunting." Wyn paused at the door to the stairs, then turned back. "And that gorsaulk woman kissed *me* without my say so. Or desire. I didn't know she was a prostitute!"

Wyn took a deep breath and adjusted his clothing once more. A nice black jacket and pants with a white shirt. Professional business attire like his father had made him wear so many times. Besari grabbed his hand to stop the fussing and squeezed it.

"You look fine," she said.

"Just fine?"

She chuckled. "You look fantastic," she admitted.

Wyn smiled, then his Vico chimed, and his smile faltered. "Time to go." He stepped through the doors of Bounty Inc., wearing his best stoic expression. A dozen reporters crowded the yard outside, just beyond a podium to which he stepped up. Drones floated around, ready to capture every word, record every visual. He took a deep breath and looked out at everyone gathered. Then he spoke.

"Allegations against Bounty Inc. have been made in the wake of a recent bounty completed by members of the business. A bounty which included a known criminal who experimented on people for a living, and despite what Bezium claims, she was doing just that. Possibly on Raiyrium citizens who were kidnapped and tortured for her own sick gain.

"It pains me to say that the mission didn't go according to plan. We wanted to get in, grab Shekta, and leave. But she attacked us and ordered countless others to attack us. She tried to kill us on a shuttle ride there, one we barely survived and which took the lives of several of her own employees. We were shot at and threatened with gruesome experimentation. It was only natural we defended ourselves from her attacks. I regret the lives lost, but they were criminals and miscreants each, a plague that Bezium is well known for. Had the R.C. been aware, I have no doubt the Peacekeepers would have launched a similar attack to protect its citizens from this monster."

He paused to let the statements sink in. His stomach soured at twisting the attack on Shekta into a noble pursuit and he thought how his father would have been proud of Wyn for this statement. For most of the statement anyway. He continued on.

"As for the allegations against us for the theft of the Urgo Holdings freighter, I would like to ask those watching to consider this question: Would we not have left in the same ship we arrived in? No one plans to abandon their spacefaring ship when on a hostile world, hunting a dangerous criminal. Yes, we targeted the songbird as well, but we left with it and Shekta. We had no need for the atmosphere tank found aboard the *Ninth Harrow*. Therefore, evidence makes it clear that Bounty Inc. had no involvement in the theft of any property.

"Just because one criminal is put away doesn't mean the galaxy is a safe place," Wyn said. "I created Bounty Inc. as a way to make it safer for everyone, whether you're in the Raiyrium Confederation or an outside planet like Perrilium. We are here to serve, to assist the Peacekeepers with their noble duty of protecting the galaxy."

Wyn smiled. The next part was his, a deviation that would have left his father scowling. "Protecting begins with the people next to us. I do not wish for Urgo Holdings to think we brushed them to the side and care not for their pains. No, we stand with Urgo Holdings, and I have made that clear through the donation of a brand-new, top-of-the-line freighter to the company. Not as a symbol of apology, but as an offer of friendship. If Urgo Holdings needs a bounty hunter, look no further than Bounty Inc."

# WANTED

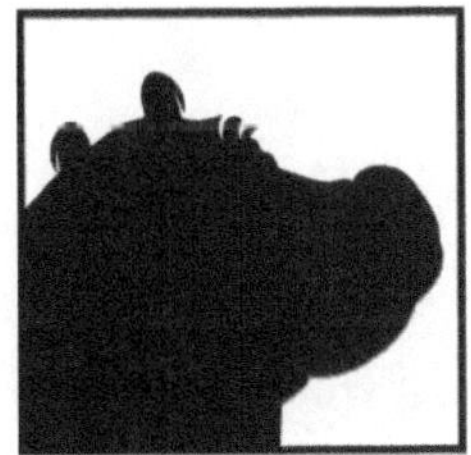

## QORSIN BEMI

REWARD:
Ⓡ75,000

All bounties begin in the same manner: a seven-step plan. If made too rigid, it will break the first time something goes wrong. If made too loose, it will be useless from the start. Flexibility in its structure is the most important part. Therefore, each step has a broad goal and what will be needed to attain it.

A haushedin surlka's son had been seduced by the fleet admiral of a terrorist organization. The Haush leader asked Cee to infiltrate and extract his son unharmed.

### Step One: Preparation

No good plan began with ignorance. The target had to be researched, obstacles had to be cataloged and schemed for, supplies needed to be gathered. These vital points created a foundation for everything else to come. The stronger the foundation, the more likely for everything to survive first contact.

The Target: Qorsin Bemi. His location may have been unknown, but his company was not.

The Obstacles: The Herald's Aspect, a terrorist organization that had broken off from Haush's government. Thanks to strict government regulations, it was recognized as an official sect of the Haush government and thus protected by its laws. At least from the interventions of other Haush surlkas. Three massive ships were home to millions of haushedin, including entire families and employees in addition to the front and center terrorists. These ships typically circled the R.C. in constant movement, though several intelligence reports now mentioned they were in orbit around the prison planet Kekar, a dumping ground for the criminals deemed too dangerous or unstable for reentry into the Raiyrium Confederation. The son was aboard its flagship, the *Shard of Virtue*, in the hands of an ex-surlka and current leader of the Herald's Aspect, Fleet Admiral Bevnil Unch.

They were "in love," according to the last known message given to his father. Surlka Girdtu Bemi was one of ten renowned global leaders of Haush. It was impressed upon Cee that if this event got out, it would be disastrous for his station. His power eradicated, the other nine surlkas would push him out of his position, and his successor would take up a weakened mantle. Cee needed to retrieve his son quickly and quietly. Cee inserted the bounty into Wyn's system with false information, the truth encrypted securely.

The Supplies: Infiltration required disguise, both on approach and in person. The Herald's Aspect used resupply shuttles for food, water, materials, and whatever else needed to keep the fleets running. Cee hacked into global networks and monitored suspicious haushedin activity. It did not take long to find one such shuttle close enough for Cee to reach it before departing. With the haushedin killed and their bodies ejected into space, Cee acquired a suitable ship.

A disguise after it landed was more difficult, though not impossible. Sage helped it find an adequate disguise, and through a few modifications to itself, Cee was prepared to enter Body Mode: Haushedin Design.

Weaponry requirements were minimal for an infiltration mission. Besides, most plasma-based weaponry failed to penetrate the thick haushedin hide. But their skin was highly conductive to electricity, and their brains suffered concussions the same as many other animals. Cee installed a modified stunstick in its right arm and reinforced the other to bludgeon if necessary.

The final piece was the location. The Kekar reports weren't thorough enough to be sure. Not to mention it only knew the one way into that system and none out. That meant Cee needed to rely on a contact for the final piece of the first step. Unfortunately, this one was annoyed at Cee for letting her get captured. That had been Cee's fault. It had not anticipated Achtrek-Six claiming the bounty after an update had readded it to the system before Cee could purge it manually.

Luckily, it likely still had enough incentive to get what it needed.

"Hello, Mesem," Cee spoke into the empty air of the shuttle's cockpit. Its optics visualized the surroundings as the tesing woman would see it within the small chambers of her prison, standing over the bed she lounged on. Its voice jerked her awake, and she glared at the implant-induced hallucination. She would be seeing Cee as if they were in the room together. Amazing what could be done to organics' brains.

"I thought I told you to call me the Rose." Then she lay back down and stared up at the ceiling with her one eye.

"I do not understand such nicknames. What is wrong with your name?"

Mesem ignored it.

"I have come for some information."

Mesem ignored it.

"Your weapons manufacturing sales ramped up in the days before you were caught, selling—"

"Ah, there it is," Mesem said, turning toward Cee. "I was *caught*. You promised me amnesty if I fed you information. You promised I wouldn't be sought by bounty hunters. Yet here I am. In a cell, because of a bounty hunter *you* work with."

"It was not my intention for you to be caught," Cee explained. "I would explain the details, but they do not seem pertinent."

"They seem pretty fucking pertinent to me," she said. "The one in the cell."

"In that case, I am more than willing to step through what caused this unfortunate circumstance."

"Shut up," she growled. "Leave me alone."

"I need some information."

"I don't care. We were only supposed to be working together while I was free."

"That was not the deal we made," Cee said. "You would be my informant, and I would do what I could to protect you from jail time. I have held up my end of the bargain as best I could."

"Well, your best was pretty fucking awful."

"I admit some faults to my plan, however, if you had done fewer illegal activities, there would have been a greater chance of your bounty not being selected."

"So now you're going to blame my jail time on my own illegal activities and not your incompetence?"

"Yes."

"Fuck off."

"Mesem—"

"*The Rose,*" she snapped. "And I swear I will dig this implant out with my bare fingers if you don't leave me alone."

"That will be unnecessary," Cee said. "I can extract it remotely if you wish to go that route."

Mesem sat up on the bed and stared at the hallucination of Cee. "How can you remove it remotely?"

"By detonating it," Cee said. "It will be removed, though I think the same will be said about most of your head." Cee cocked its head and looked at Mesem. "You don't happen to have a healing Thresha talent that can repair a destroyed brain, do you?"

A cold fury lit up the tesing's eye. If Cee were an organic, it almost suspected it would have been able to feel her emotions pressing outward. Several prisoners could be heard complaining and growing irritable.

"What information do you need?" she growled.

"During your final days, weapons production ramped up to an all-time high. You were producing a very large order for a very special customer. The Herald's Aspect."

"How do you know that?"

"Your compound was mostly destroyed by Zetta, but I was able to find a few databases intact. They provided enough information for me to fill in the rest."

"Well, if you want those weapons, they're destroyed."

"I want to know how you met up with them. Did you travel to Kekar?"

"Of course not. Are you insane? It's hard enough getting in and out of that place. That flagship, Shard of Something, has a skipper engine. It can get in and out of Kekar without detection. I would send it a signal, and it would send me a location. We would meet, initiate trade, then it would leave."

"The flagship always retrieved the shipment?"

"Yes. They didn't trust one of their tiny shuttles with that payload."

"And you will provide me with the signal?"

"Sure, but don't be surprised if they're not fooled by it, given I'm imprisoned."

Through the implant, Cee felt a rush of information transfer over. "Thank you, Mesem."

"Thank me by getting me out of here."

"I can't do that. That's illegal." Cee disconnected from the implant, ending the conversation before she could respond.

Preparations complete, Cee analyzed the signal, then sent a modified version out to the *Shard of Virtue*, mentioning a found weapons cache and implying Mesem's involvement. It received a response almost immediately. A confirmation and a destination.

Matacrys sector. Tletar planet. In orbit around its smallest moon, Tash.

## Step Two: Penetration

Tletar burned saffron and cerulean in the sun's light. The faint speck of a moon orbited the gas giant, with an even fainter speck of a ship orbiting that. The *Shard of Virtue* spanned over thirty miles in length and still had an impressive girth to it. Over two million haushedin lived on its decks, which, given the size and how much each one ate, meant it could fit at least twice as many of most other life forms.

A chime alerted scanners incoming, and Cee activated the transmitter to pass along the codes. Then it waited. A second chime indicated a communication request. Once accepted, the guttural growl common to the haushedin language filled the cockpit. Cee understood it, of course. It would be a terrible infiltrator if it couldn't.

"This is the *Shard of Virtue*, the most glorious ship of the Herald's Aspect and homeship to the fleet admiral herself," the navigator said. Cee found it odd to announce so readily the location of their leader. It seemed a terrible flaw, but it did help to confirm her location here. "You claim to have in your possession a weapons stash from the Rose's plant. How is this possible when we have accurate reports of the damage to her operations?"

"I sent that information in the report." Cee modulated its voice and language to mimic a haushedin. "I worked for the Rose and her crew for fifteen months. I wasn't at the factory's destruction because I was stocking the warehouse. Turns out it's best to not have all your explosives in one place. I'm bringing what remained in that warehouse, for the Herald's cause."

"How did you get that ship? It belonged to a pair of grocers on business."

"Business that ended poorly," Cee said. "I found their bodies, but not the culprit. I assume it was bounty hunters attempting to reach your fleet admiral. Their ship gave me the resources needed to find a buyer."

"You've been cleared to land, but be warned that security will react to any suspicious behavior with lethal force."

"Understood. Thank you."

"The Herald's Aspect welcomes you into its warm embrace, brother. You are finally home."

Cee searched its databanks for the appropriate response. "May the Herald bless you on this day and forever more."

"And you."

Then the connection was severed. The shuttle followed the programmed route, and soon stasis fields pulled it through the pressurized barrier and into the landing dock of the massive ship. Penetration successful, Cee left the cockpit and opened a locker to prepare for the next step.

## Step Three: Infiltration

Art meant little to Cee. It was pointless and purposeless, but it clearly brought joy to others. The A.I. had never understood how or why. But even as it explored and reasoned as well as it could, there was something that always tickled its processors more than anything else. In the movies, actors would attempt to trick the audience into believing they were someone else. Sometimes even *something* else. They showed fake injuries that looked real enough to make the crowds gasp in horror. They showcased moments of embarrassment that forced the crowd into fits of laughter. It fascinated Cee, that art of disguise to convince others that one was not as they seemed. That fascination was at the heart of its current ruse at Bounty Inc., that of completely fooling the others into thinking Cee was a highly modified human.

Disguise was Cee's art, and it had designed its body for that purpose. A voice modulator to cover a wide spectrum of vocal cords, an ever-shifting body, a nearly endless memory bank. Cee could transform itself into any being in the galaxy flawlessly. Today, Cee tested haushedin form.

Its legs lengthened, sacrificing robustness for reach; its torso expanded, separating outward to produce a wider frame; its head telescoped upward to reach the height of a moderately-sized haushedin. The frame itself could not work alone, but combined with an expertly crafted, synthetic, full-body disguise, Cee would be unrecognizable.

It pulled the disguise Sage had procured free from the locker and stepped within the opening. Then it pulled the rest over its body and zipped it up from within. With the press of a button near its hand, the motor hummed and began filling the outfit with air in order to mimic the meat and tissue of an actual haushedin. The air flowed up past Cee and into the head, erecting the elongated snout. When the fan stopped and the suit was fully inflated, it stepped in front of a mirror.

"Perfect."

An alert sounded, and the ship reacted automatically. The landing bay ramp opened, and a beefy haushedin male strode aboard, his eyes focused on his Vico as a sharp stylus attached to one finger slid through reports. He stood over nine feet tall, with dark, gray skin wrinkled in on the fatty flesh. Small, pointed ears twitched behind a set of black, beady eyes, both of which were nearly lost against the massive protruding snout with a pair of large teeth sticking out from the bottom jaw. Several other teeth lined his mouth and were on full display as he began to talk.

"I'm here to register your weapons—what the fuck are you?" The inspector stopped at the top of the ramp and stared at Cee, those tiny eyes widening to their full size.

Disappointment crept into Cee like a virus attacking organic tissue. Had the inspector seen through its disguise? It stepped forward with a gesture of friendliness, and the outfit crinkled with every step. "I have said in my report."

The inspector poked at Cee's disguise with the stylus, eliciting a pop and a hiss as air rushed out through the hole. "You're not like any—"

Cee wasted no time tearing through the thin fabric of the outfit, the stunstick in its right hand jabbing into the throat of the haushedin. The inspector gurgled his last words as two hundred amps of electricity coursed through his body. With a loud thud, Cee let the body fall to the ground and tore the rest of the disguise free.

"Are you all right in there, Yordin?" a second voice called from outside.

Cee's vocal modulator adjusted immediately to match the tones of the inspector's voice. "I'm fine," it responded in the dead haushedin's voice. "Our weapons dealer appears to have grown sick and passed out. Give me a minute to wrap this up."

"Have fun," the second guard said. "I'm heading back if it all checks out."

"Yes," Cee said. "I can handle the rest."

Good news for step three: Cee was also a master of stealth. It scanned the hangar bay and found seven life forms present. Three cameras covered the immediate area, with ten more farther along in either direction. Detection was highly probable, which was why it had wanted a disguise. And leaving without the inspector would only raise suspicion. Which meant there was only one option. To leave *as* the inspector.

It considered skinning the inspector, but haushedin flesh was tough, and that route would be time-consuming. Instead, Cee flipped the corpse onto its stomach, then laid down atop it. Minor adjustments to its frame allowed Cee to match with the structure of the dead body. Celuein-tipped cables spilled from its frame and drilled through the tough skin and directly into the nervous system. They acted in two ways, firstly to hold Cee steady, and secondly, with electrical impulses applied in the right way, it could control the corpse. A trick learned from hives.

Yordin's body stood, a metal frame latched discreetly onto his back. Its organic foot couldn't be attached to Cee, and it flopped as the meat vehicle shifted. The electricity had exploded the guard's eyes, and Cee would still be easy to see from certain angles, which meant it would need to plot a careful route. Steer clear of other life forms and don't expose the back. There were a few routes that could work, and Cee chose the shortest one to limit complications.

Then it drove the hunk of meat out through the back of the shuttle as it sent an all clear through the inspector's Vico. It guided the body through the chosen route, which stayed clear with the acknowledged report. The cameras caught the inspector heading through a bay door into a hallway but never caught his back. Another camera caught the inspector stepping into an empty conference room, but no one challenged him or yelled at him to stop. He had business there, clearly, perhaps preparing for a discussion with the new weapons dealer.

Once within, it shut the door and dropped the meat vehicle to the ground. A console glowed in the corner, connected to the ship's internal datanet. Infiltration complete. Time for step four.

### Step Four: Collation (with Escape Preparation)

Once within, one needed more information in order to solidify the back half of the plan. It was almost a repeat of step one, but in a more restricted environment. A computer console hooked up to the network of wherever you were infiltrating was a wonderful tool for this. A wealth of information just beyond some flimsy security. It was the reason they'd succeeded with Shekta and would hopefully be the reason Cee survived here as well.

It crouched before the terminal, its body returning to human form to compact itself in the corner. Its extendable mouth port inserted into the terminal, and a dozen security systems confronted the action. Cee broke each one down in a fraction of a second, distracting, disabling, or sometimes dismantling them to provide full access.

Full access to the ship's hangar databanks, anyway. That was unfortunate. Perhaps these haushedin terrorists were not as foolish as Cee had first thought. By completely disconnecting each array of databanks, it prevented the A.I. from gaining control of every single one. Cee could have done a lot of damage that way. Now, all it could do was change arrival and departure times and open the hangar's pressure field. It could send information requests to other terminals through hardwire cabling embedded into the walls, but that would raise red flags and alert others to its infiltration. Better to just move along with what it had access to.

It was hardly completely useless, however. Logs were available, showing Qorsin, Cee's target, arriving aboard the ship with Fleet Admiral Bevnil. No exit logs. Target location fully confirmed. It also provided a basic map of the ship. Though most of the detail focused on the hangar, it would be enough to point Cee in the right direction.

Step four also provided ample opportunity to assist with future steps with some forethought. It planted a malware within the system and deleted all incoming and outgoing flight data. This would hopefully keep the hangar empty and the dockworkers distracted with docking requests. Cee disconnected from the terminal as the door slid opened. It turned as a pair of handsy haushedin stumbled into the room, their snouts licking and nibbling at each other's blubbery fat.

"We'll have to be quick, Aejik..." the woman moaned between words.

"My dear Uetha," the one called Aejik said, "you know I'll be anything but qui—"

Aejik tripped over Cee's meat vehicle, splashing into the rapidly forming pool of dark blood spilling from the many holes Cee had drilled into the body. Uetha screamed.

"Is he dead?" she asked.

"Herald's Ass, it's Yordin." Aejik turned the body over and inspected the dark scarring across his neck from the stunstick. "There are many puncture wounds across his back, but I think this is the wound that killed him."

"Was he tortured?"

"I don't know. We need to call this in immediately."

"I can do it." Uetha moved toward the console then paused.

"No, you shouldn't be here. I—" Aejik's sentence died off as he also spotted Cee. "What are you?"

The male haushedin was now on his feet again, and Cee stood still against the wall. Interesting that haushedin were gifted at noticing still beings. Or was it the situation? Perhaps the dead body had refined their awareness. Either way, Cee stepped forward and provided a gesture of friendliness.

"Greetings," it said. "I am here for assistance with flight scheduling. Will you be departing today?"

"No," Uetha said, then shook her head. She waved towards the deceased Yordin. "Do you know who did this?"

"I apologize, miss, but I am not aware."

"When did we get a robot?" Aejik asked.

Cee was programmed to be cool and collected in every situation. Unperturbed, constantly calculating. The thing was, artificial intelligence had a way of developing a personality over time. Cee had infiltrated the galaxy five years, eight months, and nineteen days ago and had been impersonating a human ever since. Pretending to have human emotions and human reactions. Eventually, some of that pretending had become natural to its personality. Cee had watched countless organics diminish the intelligence of robots, forcing them into menial labor jobs. Housekeeping, loading and unloading cargo, sometimes even just holding a hat. They were treated like objects or sometimes worse. At least Bounty Inc. treated their legal bot with respect, even more so when it came to Seph. But that was not typical. Especially the Seph situation.

Being called a robot. That stung Cee's ego. It was demeaning, it was insulting, and most importantly, it was factually incorrect. Cee's simulated emotions flared with hot rage, and simulated primal instincts overloaded its base programming. Cee launched itself over the table before it had time to adjust the irrational behavior. It collided with Aejik, and its plan changed drastically. The haushedin lovers had to be taken care of.

Aejik clattered to the ground with Cee on top. Uetha screamed and ran to her lover's defense. Cee slammed its stunstick into the woman's thigh, and her lungs seized, silencing the yells. Her body twitched beneath the electrical pulses running rampant. And though Aejik quickly grabbed Cee and twisted away, breaking the contact, Uetha collapsed to the ground.

Cee swung the stunstick again, but its grappler pulled away to dodge. Then large jaws clamped down on the arm. Aejik crunched down, and sparks flew wildly from the stick, then it died. Cee punched at Aejik, but the haushedin would not relent as he bit down harder on the appendage, shaking back and forth to tear it free.

"You fucking killed her!" he screamed, his mouth still around the arm. "I'll rip you apart."

A quick scan indicated Aejik was wrong, but it didn't seem pertinent to inform the man just then. He'd likely still take his anger out on Cee regardless. Another crunch and its arm was jerked back and forth, Cee struggling to hold it steady. It was glad for the return to its sturdier human form; it would likely have lost the limb entirely by now otherwise. Cee did not wait to see if the haushedin had the power to tear this one free too.

It slammed its free hand into the side of Aejik's head. High-powered hydraulics launched its fist like a piston rod, rewarding Cee with a loud thunk as it collided with the skull. A second hit caused the haushedin to grunt, and a third loosened the grip. Cee wrapped its right arm securely around a protruding tooth to hold the haushedin's head in place. The fourth hit came with a splatter of blood, and Aejik's body twisted away. Cee let him, then rolled onto the haushedin.

Aejik held his hands up, guarding against the onslaught, but Cee was too quick for the now-concussed haushedin. Each strike slid past his guard and slammed again into his head. Not always the same spot, but always the same side. Cee listened to the crack of the skull, and Aejik's defense grew sluggish. The thud became a squish, and his hands dropped to his side. Still Cee did not cease. Its fist slammed through the haushedin's skull, and the thick skin tore. Blood and brains and skull pooled on the ground around the pulped head. One eye hung loose from the shattered socket, and its lower jaw gaped open at an odd angle. Cee delivered one more strike, and the head popped like a blister, blood splattering across the room.

Zero percent chance of survival.

It rose from the fresh corpse and inspected its right arm. It was crushed beyond quick repair, the stunstick sparking unpredictably. It pulled the hand free and dropped it into the pool of blood. It was useless now, which meant it only had one major form of attack. Bludgeoning, which had proved less effective than it had hoped.

Cee glanced at the unconscious female and determined there was a less than thirteen percent chance she'd wake before it needed to leave the ship. Cee didn't bother with her. It did pause before leaving, though, allowing itself a longing glance back at the dead haushedin's right hand. Not this time, it decided. The organic foot it still wore provided odd, uncomfortable sensations, and the bulky hand would be more a detriment than an assistance. It would have to make do without.

Cee stepped into the hall and sealed the door shut. Access to the terminal gave it control of the hangar's security system, so it moved cameras to avoid being seen. It could move quickly and would need to do so. Someone would miss Yordin, Aejik, or Uetha eventually, even if the room wasn't booked for the rest of the day. Cee stepped into a maintenance hatch and climbed through the tunnels in the walls, hoping to avoid traffic in the popular areas of the ship.

It stopped at six other terminals throughout the ship: flight control, armory access, security system, communications, entertainment, and engines. It hacked each one and laid traps within. Malware for one, misinformation for another. Sometimes a mix of both. Each would play its part in Cee's meticulous escape from the ship. Each timed to near perfection based on all calculations.

Cee had found Qorsin's location by the third terminal, and with escape preparation complete, it headed there through a series of maintenance hatches. Straight to the Fleet Admiral's personal quarters.

## Step Five: Retrieval

Traffic increased as Cee worked inwards to the very center of the dreadnought. Panic was not obvious, so either the bodies hadn't been found or they had not been announced publicly. Either way, time was running low, and Cee's prediction models urged for quicker progress. The malware traps were timed by necessity (given the ship's isolation structure), and Cee planned to be aboard a shuttle before they triggered.

Its fleshy foot slapped against the metal floors as it moved from a maintenance shaft to a closet, ducking within just as a trio of haushedin turned the corner. Sensations warned him of damage to the foot, and on inspection, it saw one of the toes had caught on the metal edge of a box and torn free. Luckily, it had long since run out of blood, so that wasn't going to be an issue. But the fleshy component had become a nuisance more than a novelty. It would have to be replaced soon.

The hacked security cameras fed images to Cee, and it ducked back into the hall, hurrying down the corridor to the sounds of its *clang-slap* footsteps. It had reached the fifteenth floor and now needed to make its way inward, to the very center of the ship, where high-ranking members were housed. Luckily, living quarters tended to only be busy around shift change, and without one of those coming up, the halls appeared mostly free of traffic.

A door slid open, and Cee forced its hurried gait to a standstill as a drunken officer exited his room with a male companion on one arm and a female on the other. All three stared at Cee in surprise, and the officer hiccuped.

Retreat would be obvious, as would circumnavigation. Instead, it fell back on an old favorite. Deception.

"Greetings, officer." Cee produced a customary bow of servitude. "I have been told to provide introductions upon my first meetings. I am a special ordered servicing bot purchased by Fleet Admiral Bevnil for assisting officers in menial tasks. Is there anything I can help you with today?"

Three pairs of beady, black eyes scanned Cee, who hid its inoperable hand behind the other. It had no way of hiding the fleshy foot, however, and that was where the officer's gaze stopped.

"Fuck," the officer grumbled. His consorts looked over to him with concern as he wobbled a bit in a drunken stupor.

Cee prepared itself. Close quarters would be difficult, but intoxication gave it an advantage. First step would be to bring the fight into the officer's quarters, out of sight of anyone else who happened upon the hall. By shifting its frame, it could provide more flexibility at the lack of power, helping to control the fight. Attacking first, before he expected an attack, would also be beneficial, if Cee's calculations reported an over eighty percent chance of a fight. Otherwise—

"I think we'll stay in tonight," he grumbled. He spun around and tilted before one of his companions caught him. "And I think I've had enough to drink."

"As you wish, sir," the female said.

"I'm sure we can find other ways to occupy your time," the male added.

Then the door shut, and Cee was alone. The replacement foot jumped in priority; the fleshy human foot was a detriment to deception.

No one else troubled Cee the rest of the way to Bevnil's private chambers, and it was able to arrive only thirteen minutes and fifty-two seconds behind schedule. Without a stunstick. The timing was going to be close. Cee didn't like close, but the ship's segregated connections left no other options with as high of a success rate.

It paused before opening the door and ran several algorithms to plot the fight. Based on schematics, it knew the size of the room but not how it was furnished. Based on common haushedin room structures, some of that could be estimated. It wouldn't be perfect, but it would provide enough information. Cee projected a ninety percent chance of victory.

Too bad for that lost stunstick.

Cables swarmed from Cee's (non-human) fingers on his good hand and drilled through the ship's plating and into the door's control system. It bypassed the locking mechanism and triggered the door to open. The cables withdrew, and Cee stepped inside.

A startled, naked haushedin woman stared at him from where she leaned over a desk and stared at a projection. A startled, naked haushedin male stared at him from the bed and pulled the blankets up over himself, cowering.

Cee scanned the room within a second to take into account any combat restrictions or advantages. A curtain bisected the room, though it was pulled to one end. To the left, the larger portion of the room was taken up by basic furniture—tables, couches, chairs—a small kitchen, and a counter. Towards the back was Bevnil's desk, currently showing an image of Uetha cradling Aejik's body. She had woken faster than anticipated. Beyond the curtain to the right was the massive bed and Cee's target.

There were always two outcomes to a confrontation. A violent outcome and a non-violent outcome. More often than not, Cee found the violent outcome to be the quicker of the two. Less a stunstick and given the haushedin's challenging body structure, it tried for option two.

"Greetings," Cee said.

"The intruder, I presume?" Bevnil growled. Behind her, the comm unit crackled to life to provide another report. The body of an unfortunate engineer, hidden in the maintenance shaft, had apparently been found.

"I have an offer."

"You kill my people, steal a shuttle, you don't even bring the weapons you promised, and you expect me to listen to your offer."

"The surlka's son and safe passage, and I will tell you how to save your ship?"

"Save my ship?" Bevnil scoffed. "You expect me to believe that lie? What could you have possibly done to my ship?"

"I will tell you when I'm aboard a shuttle and safely away."

"Then I guess you'll never tell me."

Cee would have sighed if it was organic. It had been a low chance of success, and the dead bodies had made it lower. Violent option it was. It checked on the target once more, still cowering on the bed, eyes wide in terror. He almost looked like he wanted to say something, then didn't. At least he would stay out of the way. "I suppose you'll want to distract me long enough for security to arrive. I'm afraid I'll have to disappoint you. If you won't accept my offer, I shall take Qorsin by force."

"You think I need security to help deal with you?" Bevnil snarled as she squatted, arms wide. "I'll tear you apart myself."

She roared as she charged, unnecessarily expending effort and showcasing her lack of actual combat experience. The failure to wait for backup helped Cee's cause as well. The prediction matrix reported good news, the best chance of making up time.

Bevnil was large, not just for an organic, but for a haushedin as well. Her powerful legs launched her forward and made her a formidable force against an ordinary opponent. Perhaps even against an extraordinary opponent. Against Cee, it would remain to be seen. The fierce roar failed to intimidate, and Cee's prediction matrix determined the best course of action the instant data changed. In this case, it informed Cee that the worst place to be when a haushedin charged was wherever it charged to.

So Cee moved.

Bevnil's mass slammed into the wall as Cee glided past, but she did not remain dazed as it had expected. Instead she bounced from the wall, pivoting course back toward the A.I. It had only a moment to register the massive fist before it triggered a transformation into perrilan mode. Cee's torso shifted, and its head dropped beneath the fist as its body's framing transitioned to resemble the squatter perrilan form. Cee's elongated limbs grabbed on to the extended arm, and it swung up, smashing a foot into the haushedin's chin. Bones shattered with the blow. Unfortunately, none of the bones were Bevnil's.

The fleet admiral pulled her arm in, reaching for Cee with the other. It used the momentum from the kick to propel itself backward, out of the fleet admiral's reach, and nearly stumbled when the organic foot twisted unsteadily beneath it.

The fleet admiral charged again, speed allaying her massive form, sending the prediction matrix wild. It didn't have time to dodge, so it went with the far inferior secondary plan. It curled into a ball, and electrical pulses morphed the liquid metal within its joints and sensitive areas to create a hardened shell.

The haushedin hit the Cee Ball with the force of a dreadnought engine piston, and Cee hurtled across the room like the object of some deadly sports game. Wood cracked as it smashed into the frame of the bed, spilling a squawking Qorsin from its comfort and sending mattress padding puffing into the air. Cee's scanners reported no damage, and more importantly, the target was fine.

Bevnil didn't know this, however, and ran toward Qorsin. Cee didn't wait for her to alleviate her worries. It uncurled with another pulse of electricity. The A.I. launched itself from the wreckage of the bed and swung its good fist into the fleet admiral's knee. The knee twisted, but there was no sound of structural damage beyond her grunt of pain. Cee spun around and followed up the first attack by slamming the nub of its damaged arm into the side of Bevnil's protruding ears, a weak spot for almost every organic. The blow caused the haushedin to drop to the ground. A meaty palm swung blindly at Cee, and it stepped out of reach.

Cee jumped forward, ready to end the fight, but its flesh foot twisted. It fell to the ground as the foot gave out, and Bevnil grabbed the splayed leg. Then Cee was in the air, being swung in great circles over the haushedin's head. She slammed it into a wall, shattering an elegant glass structure that had hung there moments before. Cee tugged at its foot, but the massive hand refused to relinquish its grip. Then it swung through the air again.

She smashed it into her desk, shattering the Vico interface and dissolving the projections and reports that had displayed. Again and again, the fleet admiral slammed Cee into the walls and furniture. Diagnostic alarms flared and provided worrying results. If the haushedin didn't slow down soon, Cee would have no ability to respond. Again, it hit the thick celuein walls with such force a panel cracked and fell, its exposed cabling sparking wildly from the damage.

Cee expected to be slammed around more, but the fleet admiral stood with its ankle in hand, panting. It had been impressed with the ferocious and unending assault; Bevnil had surely proven her strength and combat skill. Her wisdom was lacking however, and it was the only thing that could have saved her.

Cee disconnected the held leg at the ankle, sliding the rest free in a sudden jerk. Bevnil pulled on empty air, then jumped back. Exhausted as she was, the movement was too slow, and Cee spun around her neck and onto her back. The damaged arm looped around the thick, meaty neck, and the good arm pulled the grip tight. Cee reversed joints on its legs and wrapped them up around the haushedin's arms, pulling them away as they scrounged for her assailant. She howled, though it only escaped as a gasping squeak barely heard over the creaking strain of its limbs.

Instead of panicking and succumbing to the chokehold, Bevnil twisted and slammed backward into the wall. Into the exposed cabling.

Asphyxiation would have been time-consuming. A haushedin could last quite a while without more oxygen. The number one weapon against a haushedin was electricity. Their skin absorbed it like a dying man in a desert drinking water. It had never been Cee's goal to choke her out; no, it had only needed a reason to get her close.

Cee hit the wall, and its good hand released the stranglehold. It grabbed the cabling instead and jammed it into the fleet admiral's skull. The scent of burning skin filled the air as she howled, her body twitching beneath—

She slammed her head back, crushing Cee's head between her massive, meaty skull and the wall. Visuals cut, alarms went wild, then there was silence.

Cee shut down.

### Step Six: Escape

**[Rebooting... 78%]**

Vision returned, first in a flicker, then in a fury. Audio followed, the low rumble of distant explosions echoing through the **[memory failure...diagnostic analysis beginning...repairs needed]**

**[Repairs beginning]**

Cee shut down.

**[Rebooting... 87%]**

Vision returned, first in a flicker, then in a fury. Audio followed, the low rumble of distant explosions echoing through the fleet admiral's chamber. The emergency bypass triggered, giving Cee full control of its systems. It reestablished connections to the security system, and its internal clock updated.

That was not good, but Cee wasn't sure why. Probably something to do with the explosions. Most beings survived better when not near explosions.

The room shuddered, and Cee sat up.

"You're alive!" A male haushedin jumped back from the fleet admiral's body and stared at Cee. He was wearing clothing now. Cee scanned the limp female haushedin and found her still alive, though a black scorch blossomed from her eye, which had liquidized and dripped down the side of her face.

Memory connections reconfigured, and the scenario cleared up. Most of its time on the *Shard of Virtue* was restored, especially the important parts. Like the one that informed it of the need to leave immediately. And the other one. That it needed to leave *with* the male haushedin, Qorsin.

Prediction models ran through Cee's memories, breaking apart as important components failed. It would have to react blindly, which meant the fastest route. It stood, then stumbled, finding its inorganic foot missing. That was nearby on the ground and easily reattached. Then it noticed Qorsin had backed away from the female—Fleet Admiral Bevnil.

"Please don't kill me!" he whined.

"We must leave, Qorsin. Your father wishes you back home."

"My *father*?" Qorsin stared open-mouthed at the A.I. "You destroyed a ship with millions of people on it and you killed my love just because of my father's wishes?"

"He paid me," Cee said. Then added, "She's not dead."

"I'm not leaving her behind."

"Fleet Admiral Bevnil is classified as a high-level terrorist, wanted by several governments, including the Raiyrium Confederation itself. I am not knowledgeable in haushedin mating, but I strongly feel you can do better," Cee said. "Perhaps, start with your hand?"

Qorsin blinked speechlessly. Then found his speech. "Excuse me? You can't talk to me like that. I'm a surlka's son."

"You've engaged in criminal activity by fraternizing with the Herald's Aspect, thereby thwarting any status you previously held. You can come willingly, or I can beat you unconscious and drag you from here." It paused, a few simple calculations running. "The latter option has a much higher likelihood of your death."

Tears welled in Qorsin's eyes, and his shoulders slumped. A meaty palm ran across Bevnil's unmarred cheek. "Will you kill her?"

"She has a chance to survive," Cee said. "I am merely disabling the ship, not destroying it entirely."

The deck shook, seemingly a counterargument, and the surlka's son jumped in alarm. Then he stood. "I'm ready to go."

Cee nodded.

The hallways were in chaos. Haushedin officers yelled to each other, demanding updates or commanding actions, only to be overridden by the next officer. The drunken officer lay on his back, sliding down the now tilted hallway and yelling gibberish as he went by. His two attendants gave chase.

"Follow close," Cee told Qorsin, then stepped into the hallway. Every eye, even the sliding drunk's, turned to it. Cee stared back. "Greetings," it began. "Fleet Admiral Bevnil's communications hub was disabled." A violent explosion tore through the ship and spilled everyone else to the floor. Cee barely held its ground with one magnetic leg. Another reason to replace the meaty one. "She has commanded an immediate evacuation of the ship."

The officers glanced at their fallen comrades, then back to Cee. "When did we get a robot?" one asked.

"He'sh new," the drunk slurred.

"Who cares?" a female officer shouted. "Evacuation order was given. We need to escape."

The other officers agreed quickly, and soon the hallway was a mass of fleeing bodies. Someone was kind enough to alert the rest of the ship, and klaxons filled the air with warning. Cee tugged Qorsin into the flowing crowd and followed the quickest path to the hangar bay. Hopefully it was still in one piece.

No one bothered Cee or Qorsin as they flowed through the decks of the dreadnought. Panic had set in, and their feeble organic minds could think of nothing else except escape. It worked in Cee and Qorsin's favor, hiding them among the panicking crowds. An emergency shaft allowed for a quick descent, and unlike an elevator, the capsule shot straight down and deposited them where it landed. It was a quick way to reach the bottom floor, then Cee only had to make its way back up to the hangar bay, which was conveniently near the lower decks.

Within twenty minutes, Cee and Qorsin arrived outside the sealed hangar, in the same hallway by which it had first entered. The security system reported a breach in the atmosphere beyond. "You'll need an atmos suit," Cee said. "There should be some in the lockers—"

"By the Heralds!" Qorsin exclaimed, then vomited at the sight of the two dead bodies within the conference room. Uetha was nowhere to be found, likely trying to escape herself.

Cee ignored the haushedin, living and dead, and pulled one of the lockers open. Pulling the atmos suit free, it tossed it to Qorsin. "Get that on."

Qorsin wiped his mouth, then struggled into the suit as Cee went back into the hall. It would take time to bypass the door's lock. It could have it ready by the time the target was suited up.

A plasma bolt struck Cee in the back, and it turned towards the security force that gathered in the hall. "It's heading to the hangar!" one shouted, then two others began firing. Plasma continued to pelt at Cee as it reached for its own pistol. There was only empty air.

Qorsin poked his head out, and Cee pushed him back into the room. "Hurry," it urged. "Or you'll die."

Then Cee went back to the door control. The concentrated fire struck at its joints, eating away at the reinforced protection its liquid metal preserves were supplying. They would turn its body to slag within a minute. Luckily, Cee only needed twenty-four seconds. But how long did Qorsin need?

It used its right arm as a shield as best it could, absorbing plasma into the ruined limb. One knee buckled, and it clattered to the ground. The guards urged each other on, rushing forward for the kill. Ten more seconds it could handle, then it would have to open the door, with or without Q—

"I'm ready," Qorsin shouted.

Cee triggered the door, and the vacuum popped the room like a bubble. The security team flailed as they gasped for breath, their lungs being pulled up through their tracheas at the sudden decompression. It was said that a haushedin could survive ten minutes in the void, but clearly it wasn't painless. Their flailing bodies floated past Cee and out the door. Among them, Qorsin flailed as well, though in better health.

Cee crawled across the hangar floor, magnetically locking its two applicable limbs and ignoring Qorsin for the time being. Remotely, it triggered the ship's initial ignition, then rushed up the landing ramp. Collapsing into the cockpit, Cee plugged directly into the shuttle, allowing it to bypass the typical interface directly and avoid the much slower use of limb-oriented steering. Especially when half its limbs didn't work anymore.

Cee released the locks and swung the shuttle around in search of Qorsin. There was a crowd of floating haushedin, one significantly more lively than the others. The shuttle drifted over and swung around. The shuttle rocked as the bodies entered, and Cee glanced back. One too many.

"Kick him off," Cee demanded through Qorsin's internal speakers.

"What?" Qorsin's beady eyes stretched to their limit as he clung to the bench. "I can't do that. He'll die."

Cee rose and stumbled forward. Then started stomping on the gasping haushedin with its fleshy foot. The fatty arms flailed, but his eyes had already frozen over. Brain damage had surely begun. It only took a few more kicks, then the body was floating off the shuttle.

The landing ramp shut, and with a hiss, the cabin filled with air. "You can take that off now," it said, then hobbled to the cockpit. Behind the shuttle, the *Shard of Virtue* tore itself apart as dozens of malware programs overrode equipment and blew past failsafes. Gouts of flame burst from the side, only to be extinguished by the void of space. Bodies orbited the dying ship like moons to a planet. A crack rent the ship in two, spilling millions of bodies into space to join the others.

The target was safe on the shuttle, and its departure was scheduled. A job well done.

## Step Seven: Epilogue (a.k.a. Lessons Learned)

Cee piloted the ship through the nearest gateway and exited the Matacrys sector. An autopilot schedule was configured, and the shuttle began the tedious trip to Haush. Scans showed no chasing vehicles, and the gate would change in a few minutes. The final stage of the bounty had been reached. The wrap-up.

Qorsin stumbled into the cockpit, the suit now removed, and settled into the copilot's seat. His eyes were watery, and his head hung low. Cee expected this was some sort of sadness or grieving posture.

"I have something to distract you," Cee said. "From your emotions."

Qorsin glanced up and opened his mouth as if to speak. Eventually, all he said was "What?"

Cee gestured over the computer's interface, and the copilot's display shifted from the stars outside to the bust of a professionally-dressed haushedin male. The image began moving as the video played.

"So, you've decided to join a terrorist organization," the man said.

"What the void is this?" Qorsin asked as the video began the preamble that would have answered the question.

"A haushedin video titled 'The Dangers of Joining a Terrorist Organization.' It talks about the risks that come with terrorism, and why it's better to not do that. I believe that every bounty should end with learning something new, and this one's for you."

"I understand the dangers!" Qorsin shouted, though the fact he wasn't listening to the video proved counter to his claim. "This was for love. None of those risks mattered. I wish my father would understand that."

"Part six covers infatuation and how it can manipulate you into poor decisions," Cee said. "That section will be undeniably useful to you."

"You're the worst bounty hunter!"

"Incorrect," Cee said. "A worse bounty hunter would have failed to retrieve you at all."

# PART 3

## THE PROMISE OF A CHANCE

# CHAPTER 17

## A TRAP SET

Mecillis stalked through the empty halls of the palace. A gaudy tower built to the arrogance of a single man. A king of the shunned and enemy to the Raiyrium Confederation. Sovereign.

The kroscion tour guide trembled as they led the way, their purple tentacles quivering beneath their long red dress. The tips of the two tentacle arms constantly twirled around each other as their large eyes darted back to look at her. Mouth open, then closed again. Then they scooted forward quickly.

Mecillis rolled her eyes. Sovereign had named them Worm, and the name fit. She wanted to kill them, but Sovereign would not appreciate his pets being slaughtered. Especially a rare one like this. Everyone else inside the tower hid as she passed, not that she cared.

Worm led her to a lift and took her to the top of the tower. She smirked. The issue was significant to be summoned to his private chambers rather than the first floor "throne room" in which he usually entertained guests. The lift dinged, the doors slid open, and

Worm scooted out, rushing to the door opposite. The only door. This entire floor would be his living quarters.

"A-after you, miss." Worm bowed as they pulled the door open.

"You won't be needed." Mecillis waved her hand at the purple maggot, and their eyes bulged. She stepped in, and the door swung closed behind. The ding of the lift signaled Worm's quick escape from the floor.

The lavish room was decorated with plush chairs and a display wall that showed twenty different news stations. A table near the door held a tray of pickled raspeers, a delicacy from her home. She happily snatched up the putrid vegetable and downed it in one bite.

"I've told you before, I despise it when you come around here reeking of fear-inflicting pheromones." The king himself stepped down an elegant staircase, his suit proper, brown hair brushed back over striking gold eyes.

"Apologies." Mecillis smirked. "I must have forgotten." She shifted her body to terminate the pheromones and missed the scent almost immediately.

"You look disgusting," Sovereign said. "You should try to actually disguise yourself instead of walking around like an abomination. You'll paint a target on your back."

"You needn't worry so much about me," she said after taking another raspeer. "I can take care of myself. Which is why I'm guessing you called me."

Sovereign's face darkened. She had never seen him like this before. Whatever was going on, it had caused him a lot of trouble. A part of her reveled in that thought.

"What do you know of Bounty Inc.?"

"A company run by a bumbling idiot with the help of dear Sage Valen. I assume she's the reason it hasn't fallen apart yet. Though why she's helping is a mystery." Mecillis settled into one of the many plush seats and watched the many news stations without paying any real attention. "They tried to bring me on, actually. Well, Sage did. I don't know why she thought that would be a good idea."

"I'm not so sure about the bumbling idiot," Sovereign growled. Mecillis looked over, eyebrows raised in surprise.

"You've met Wyn?"

"Not personally, no."

"Then consider yourself wrong," she said. "I met him personally, and he cowered like a baby the entire time."

"What do you know of his past?"

"To put together a business like he did, he must have a lot of money."

"Human, born in the isolated colony of Terrask to the recently deceased Iolas Kelda."

"Doesn't ring a bell."

"Iolas was simply a scheming businessman who made his wealth off scamming others." Sovereign waved his hand as he paced back and forth. "That's not the problem."

"Then what is the problem? Why have you made me enter the famous prison planet of the Raiyrium Confederation just to talk to you?"

Sovereign halted, eyes burning. "Does this *look* like a prison planet? We are free here. Free from the R.C.'s corrupt reach."

"You're getting a bit too in character for my liking."

"Mecillis—"

"Careful, Yossinok." Mecillis glared at him as he stopped talking. "I still know who you were before you became Sovereign. Make your point."

"Terrask has a weak record of this boy's existence," he growled. "True, he may be as he says, but I believe he is something else."

"Then he's a good actor, because he seems like an idiot to me."

"He's an R.C. plant, someone meant to hunt me down and kill me. The confederation knows of my plans and desires to destroy me."

So hearty was Mecillis's laugh that Sovereign jumped. "He's a rich kid with a stupid dream."

Sovereign swiped at the displays and they went blank, then he pulled up his prepared material.

An image of Sage displayed next to the mug shot of a blue torshk who looked roughed up. "Approximately eight months ago, Sage Valen apprehended Roshran on Chrysanax. He ran several drug dealing rings and worked as an accountant for many of my illicit businesses. He was also an adequate information broker. It was a blow but no more than an inconvenience. In time, I will recover."

"You want me to break him out of jail?"

"If I wanted him out, he would be out. His building was purchased by Wyn Kelda for the purposes of Bounty Inc. Immediately afterward, he brought on Sage Valen."

"You're thinking that Wyn planned that?" Mecillis leaned forward as the pieces came together. "A blow to your empire, and they take a piece. But why the company? Especially a stupid one like this."

"Stupid enough that it should have collapsed already," Sovereign said. "It hasn't. So either he's pumping an ungodly amount of money into a stupid idea or it's all a front."

"This is one instance, hardly enough to claim it's an act against you."

"Do you think I'd call you here for one instance?" Sovereign gestured, and more displays lit up, this time showing Zetta and a hive she presumed was Achtrek next to a pink tesing and white falvian. "Six months later, two Bounty Inc. hunters, Zetta Ninth Forox and Achtrek-Six Hive, stormed an isolated and protected bunker to apprehend two important pawns of my empire. The Rose, who has been designing weapons for me and arming the Herald's Aspect, and the Heron, a weapons dealer with long reach. It ended with their entire operation a smoking ruin."

"So two prominent bounty hunters nab high-end bounties, and you think it's a strike against you?"

"They were working together," Sovereign expressed. "No other Bounty Inc. hunters worked together to this extent before. Not for more than a bounty or two. This is too organized for bounty hunters." Another wave and more displays showed up. "Immediately after the Rose and the Heron, Sage, Wyn, and two other people, a birrosh woman and a maintenance android, invaded Bezium and captured Shekta."

"Who was making experimental soldiers for you," Mecillis finished. "I met a few of them outside. Has she figured out how to make their brains stay intact? They look like mindless brutes."

"It was a problem she was working on before her capture."

"All strikes against you," she mocked.

"It's too much of a coincidence, especially after this a week ago." The display shifted to that of a massive haushedin fleet ship in ruins. Bodies and debris littered the area around the floating pieces. The ship's carcass was dark, displaying no signs of life. Mecillis perked up.

"They destroyed a Herald's Aspect ship?"

"Not just any ship," Sovereign said, his voice icy. "The *Shard of Virtue*, the flagship. They slaughtered millions of haushedin on that ship. Bounty Inc. has dismantled my reach into R.C. space, they have weakened me by destroying my income, my weapons productions, my soldier production, and one of the defending fleet ships. They are targeting me directly, and I believe they will mount a strike on Kekar in the next few months."

"You have contacts within the confederation." Mecillis leaned back with a smile on her face. "Have you not heard anything of this supposed mission?"

"I have not, which makes me more suspicious," Sovereign said, swiping away the displays entirely. "It has to be an elite group working in complete silence. I doubt most people within the Raiyrium government are aware. Probably only one or two people max. They can't risk more."

"You seem to have it all figured out. So, why am I here?" Mecillis yawned and stretched.

"I would like your help destroying Bounty Inc. before they grow stronger."

"You want me to go in there and kill them all?" Mecillis raised an eyebrow. "I can kill any of them easily enough on their own, but fighting eight at once seems a danger you can't afford. Especially given you're strapped for cash, it seems."

Sovereign glared. "You won't need to kill them all." He turned toward a window and looked out at his metropolis, a city built from the ground up on the backs of countless slaves stolen from Raiyrium space. "I have a plan."

"What part do I play?"

"Not everyone will fall into my trap." He turned from the window to look at her again. "I want you to clean up the leftovers."

Mecillis smiled. "Now that sounds interesting."

# CHAPTER 18

## FORTUNE SMILES

"**D**oes this mean Haush supports Bounty Inc.?" Wyn slouched down in a plush chair in the lounge. A soft rhythm played from the display in an attempt to calm his nerves. It didn't work, especially not with Tom the nothing slug sitting on the arm of his chair, staring. Wyn had hoped that hallucination would go away shortly after Bezium, but it had not. At least the slug wasn't talking at the moment.

"*A* haushedin is on our side," Cee said, black smoke belching from its inner workings. Its human foot was missing, thankfully, and so was its right hand, though sadly not the one containing the mummified finger. "The contract was complicated and kept secret from many others, including the other surlkas."

"So one-tenth of Haush is on our side." Wyn rubbed his eyes and took a deep breath. The money seemed to burn away faster than anything was incoming, and given the year was nearly up, he couldn't lose the money he owed on the contracts. Bounty Inc. was in dire need of financial stability, and instead of being able to assist with bounties or improving relations with government entities, he was stuck fielding interviews for a PR boost. The issue with Bezium had caused a lack of trust in the company that was not easily repaired. "At least Perrilium should be supportive, right?"

"Tough call." Zetta tossed a large purple fruit into her mouth and chomped down. "They might be supportive, but they've been trying to enter the confederation for years now. If the R.C. doesn't stand with Bounty Inc., they won't be open about supporting us directly. Could hurt their chances."

"Well, you and Achtrek helped the falvians and tesings with some pretty big bounties, right?"

"Doubt they'll be helpful," Zetta said with a shrug. "The falvians, maybe, but they're not a strong political power, and they also only recently gained admittance into the R.C. The tesing government will never join us because of him." Zetta pointed to Shellesh, who leaned against a wall, arms crossed.

"Apologies," he said.

"Shut up," Zetta said. "We also kinda pissed off the Angbor government in the process, so that was probably a net loss."

Wyn sighed. "So, basically, we have no one who will offer public support for the company."

"What about Vroleus?" Besari suggested, directing the question at Zetta.

"Have you ever seen a bounty from a vrolak?" she asked. "They don't exist. Their support would be nothing but words."

"I could return home to gain the support of Tset'As'Edder," Pesh said as they stroked Skritch's back. The fleshy tendrils popped back up, quivering with excitement as the hand passed through them. The gridder's large eyes closed slowly as they lounged in the edder-mar's lap. "Though we are not a strong people in Raiyrium space, we are well known for our combat aptitude. A support from the hunters' guild will show that Bounty Inc. is taken seriously."

"That's a wonderful start," Wyn said. "Anything at this point could be helpful. We need to start garnering exclusive contracts, or I don't think Bounty Inc. will last through its first year."

"I'm surprised it lasted this long," Sage commented. She reclined in one of the chairs with her eyes closed. Wyn honestly thought she had fallen asleep.

"Perhaps," Cee interjected, "it would be more beneficial to run this business as a school."

Wyn bit down his retort to Sage and looked at the A.I. thoughtfully. "What do you mean?"

"Sage has already developed a training program that allowed you to become an adequate bounty hunter in six months."

"I'm more than adequate," Wyn said.

Sage scoffed.

Cee continued. "By requiring tuition and a two-year contract with Bounty Inc., you bring on a new source of income and expand your bounty hunters with talent cultivated by your guidelines. Veteran bounty hunters could be brought on at a reduced percentage taken to provide stability. Your bounty scoring system could also come into play to determine percent cut, those with a better score receiving a better discount. It would encourage the other hunters to focus on becoming better. I could work out the specific numbers during downtime."

"That's actually not a bad idea," Sage said, one eye cracking open.

Besari added, "After training, we could have them pair up to learn from someone else, like we did with Sage."

"Never mind. It's a bad idea," Sage said, closing her eye again. "I don't need a bunch of amateurs following me around."

"You don't have to be the only mentor," Wyn said, then stood and started pacing. Skritch jumped from Pesh's lap and inflated, allowing them to float. Their feet and tail flapped in the air like fans to propel the gridder so they floated after Wyn as he paced. "After this year, Besari and I will have experience, and all of you could take on the role as well. If you want to stick around. I would be willing to draft up a special contract that provides no cut from bounties taken for those who take on the trainees. It would really only need to be for one bounty, maybe two, to get them started."

"The only thing that convinced everyone here to join was the zero percent cut." Sage leaned forward. "What's going to make them stick around if you start adding stipulations?"

Wyn halted, and Skritch bounced off his head and floated away upside down, limbs flailing to upright themself. "Is it too much to say loyalty? Maybe others believe in Bounty Inc. too?"

Zetta laughed, and the others were quiet.

Wyn rolled his eyes. "And the slag cannon or other equipment."

"Oh, I forgot about that," Zetta said, one claw running along her jaw. "We still need to find a way to use that."

"You still need to bring in exclusive contracts to make it worthwhile," Sage added. "Not only that, but no one will want to train here if it doesn't have a good reputation."

"We don't need small jobs cuddling up to the governments," Shellesh said. "We need something to make the news in a positive light. Something to make the public realize the advantages of a coordinated bounty-hunting organization over individual bounty hunters."

"I can't even imagine what kind of bounty we'd have to pick up for that." Wyn rubbed his face in frustration. "Where would we even find something like that?" Wyn asked. "I don't think galaxy-shaking contracts drop out of trees these days."

"We could go after that Clyde guy," Besari said.

"The weapons dealer on Tessaroak?" Sage asked.

"Yes, that's him. He had a pretty high bounty."

"It was like a hundred thousand raikers," Zetta said. "That's not really a groundbreaking catch."

"Well, it's a start, isn't it?"

"I've got no other ideas," Sage admitted.

"It's not going to take a team to get him," Shellesh added. "It just shows off a single bounty hunter's skill or shows we're weak and have to work together."

"We need someone that requires multiple hunters," Pesh said. "To show that when needed, we can act in a role no single hunter can possibly attain."

"So we're back to no ideal target?" Wyn said.

"Sounds about right," Sage said.

"Wyn, sir!" Seph entered the room and glanced around. L-Bot followed closely behind, but the human pushed it away when it got too close.

Wyn met his glance, then looked away, cheeks burning. "What is it, Seph?"

"Communication for you." Seph glanced around, then back at Wyn. "*Just* you. That was very clear. I rerouted to your office."

"I'll go see what it is," Wyn said. "The rest of you can try to find some galactic threat for us to face." He turned toward the stairwell to find Skritch floating at eye level, their eyes squinting and cheeks puffed out. Then they belched in Wyn's face, and rancid air filled his nostrils, causing him to gag.

"Mr. Kelda," the crackling projection spoke, its form mostly amorphous with just a hint of humanoid.

"Hi, hello," Wyn said as he fiddled with his Vico. "You seem to be coming in with some static. I'm trying to fix that."

"You needn't try. I am reaching out through a secure and anonymous connection to—" The projection snapped, and the crisp image of a human woman in her forties stood in the center of the room. A long braid fell down her back, and she wore an officer's uniform from the Raiyrium Confederation. She gaped at him.

"Ah, you're from the R.C.," Wyn said. "What is it you're reaching out about?"

"Did you just disable my encrypted transmission?"

"I don't think so," Wyn lied. "I just ran a signal booster to help you come in clearer." Wyn glanced at his Vico, which read off reports. The woman was Special Agent Brada Harlow, head of the entire Special Forces division of the Raiyrium Confederation. She was about as important as a person could be in the government. The tracer also placed her dead center in the R.C.'s government buildings. Cee's scans even ran biological checks on her and pinged back that she was a forty-two-year-old human. Everything came back legitimate.

"I had not intended to show my face for very important reasons, *Mr. Kelda*." Her gray eyes turned hard as steel as she glared.

"Uh, I think I have something that can turn your head into an animated animal. Or—"

"Enough." Brada waved her hand in the air. "It doesn't matter. I represent the Special Forces branch of the Raiyrium Confederation. We specialize in the tasks the Peacekeepers can't handle alone."

"What's that have to do with me, Miss Harlow?"

Brada stared at him a moment, and Wyn wondered if she recognized the slip he had purposely made. Or did she think she'd already given her name?

"Little to do with you, specifically, Mr. Kelda," she said. "More to do with your company."

"I'm all ears."

"There are some jobs that even my hands are tied for. But our funds are not, so we can still outsource the job."

"I'm guessing that means you have a bounty for us," Wyn said. "And given the attempt at secrecy, it's a dangerous one?"

"Indeed. A bounty that seems especially important for a business like yours."

"Who would you like us to get?"

"A man named Sovereign, who gathers his power on the prison planet Kekar."

Wyn's brow furrowed in thought. *Sovereign.* He had heard the name somewhere, but he wasn't sure. "Who is that?"

Brada grew disbelieving, and for a moment, Wyn thought he saw anger flash across her face. "Are you trying to play me for a fool, Mr. Kelda?"

"Sorry, no," Wyn admitted. Sure, he could probably look up who that was, but getting the information directly always seemed better. "Assume I grew up in an isolationist colony and have only recently involved myself in the main areas of the Raiyrium sphere."

"He runs a massive crime ring, his tendrils seeping deep into Raiyrium space. One in every five criminals is tied to him. He is the most well-known and sought-after criminal in the galaxy."

"Oh," Wyn said. "And he's on Kekar?"

"Yes."

"Shouldn't he just stay there? It is a prison planet. Seems a perfect place for him."

"It would be if Kekar was anything like what it's supposed to be. Reports indicate he has gathered haushedin terrorists to protect the planet while finding a way to live there without the constant storms affecting him. Meanwhile, he has brought all the exiles under one umbrella, not including the many organizations he controls that are not contained to Kekar. He seems to have control outside of what he should and is quickly becoming a threat to the confederation. Whatever organization is occurring there, we want it dismantled."

"Understandable," Wyn said, "but are you saying that the prison planet is not secure?"

"Based on his outreach, he seems to be able to slip in and out of the system at will. Either he's got his hands on skipper drives or he's somehow built gates we're unaware of. Maybe both."

"Why doesn't the R.C. storm the planet to take him into custody?"

"An all-out war is what we're hoping to avoid. It could tip the scales into galactic-wide conflict. Countless innocents would die. We believe a small, elite task force could land on Kekar and apprehend Sovereign in secret, then escape with him before war begins in earnest. Without his leadership, the band of criminals will dissolve into nothing, and we can safely inspect and secure the location."

"Won't an armed force entering through the main gate alert them to our intentions immediately?"

"Yes, which is why you can't use that gate. You'll have to find a different way onto Kekar."

"How?"

"That's what we'd be paying you to do, Mr. Kelda," she said, annoyance burning in her voice. "If we had all the answers, we could send our own strike force."

"And how much would you be paying?"

"Three billion Raiyrium Credits."

Wyn's mouth went dry, and his eyes popped. Just a small amount of that money would be enough to lift Bounty Inc. back from the brink. They could then implement Cee's plan to create a more stable revenue system. He opened his mouth and almost threw up.

They had to find a way onto Kekar and capture the most dangerous man in the galaxy. It was impossible.

It was the only way to save Bounty Inc.

If he had to do it himself, he would. Anything to save his dream.

"I accept."

# CHAPTER 19

## SUICIDE PLAN

"I have a solution!" Wyn shouted as he rushed back into the lounge. Thankfully everyone was still there.

Almost everyone.

"Wait, where's Pesh?"

Everyone stared at Wyn with various expressions of concern, confusion, and consternation. Everyone except Cee, who always looked placid and calm.

"They left for Tset'As'Edder," Sage said.

"Already? I wasn't even gone that long."

Sage shrugged. "Pesh doesn't like waiting. Comes with being a short-lived species, I assume."

"What kind of solution?" Besari asked.

Wyn's brain shifted gears back to why he'd run down here, and joy filled him to bursting. "Right!" He moved in front of the display and cleared it, then looked out at the crowd. Seph hung out near the door to the entrance hall, without L-Bot, which was strange and not entirely unwelcome. Wyn caught his eye and smiled to let him know it was fine for him to stay. Seph smiled back.

"I just had a call with someone in Raiyrium's Special Forces division, and they want to bring us on for a job. A big one."

"Right when we need one?" Sage asked. "That's a trap."

"I thought so too, but I ran Cee's tracers and everything came back legitimate. She was who she said she was, at the heart of the confederation."

"So it's a trap set by the R.C.," Zetta added.

"Why would the confederation target us?" Wyn said. "We've done nothing but help them. We caught many big-name bounties, like Shekta, Rose, Heron. We're doing them a service."

"You're also competing with the Peacekeepers and making them look bad," Sage said.

"Shouldn't the Peacekeepers want to try harder?" Besari asked.

Zetta guffawed, and Sage smirked. "You haven't met them, have you?" Sage asked. "There's a reason bounty hunters are needed. Peacekeepers throw the government's money around, hope that solves problems, and do the bare minimum. Unless it involves extortion or corruption, then they excel. Usually, though, they focus on capturing low-violence, highly-fineable criminals for easy money. Occasionally, their special forces do something, but only in extreme situations."

"What is it they expect from us that their special forces couldn't do?" Cee asked. Several pieces of electronics and metal sat in a pile around it as it actively began replacing the damaged foot with its one working arm.

"Sovereign," Wyn said, letting it drop as a dramatic reveal. It didn't have the intended effect.

"Fuck no," Sage said.

"Even I'm not crazy enough to try that." Zetta leaned back, opening her Vico again.

"Who's Sovereign?" Besari asked.

"A violent crime lord," Shellesh answered, his voice a low growl. "He turned the prison planet of Kekar into a united front. While the R.C. pretended nothing was happening. Now it's too late to undo it. Reaching him is impossible."

"It's a stupid idea," Sage said. "Best case, you end up stranded on a planet of criminals with notoriously bad weather. Worst case, you're dead before you enter the system. The R.C. set this up as a way to easily dispose of us. Throw us on the prison world and let the company rot. It's a trap."

"And what if we succeed?" Wyn said. "We prove that Bounty Inc. is worth every raiker. We save the company and collect a huge pay day in the process."

"Hear, hear," Tom cheered, and Wyn almost slapped the nothing slug from his shoulder before stopping himself. He didn't need the others to think him crazier than he already was.

"How big?" Sage asked.

"Three billion raikers," Wyn said, and that had the dramatic effect he'd expected. Sage perked up in her chair, Zetta let her Vico drop to the side, and Besari tensed with surprise.

"What?" Zetta asked, her reptilian eyes narrowing as if prepared for deception.

"*Three billion raikers*," Wyn repeated. "Enough to live off of, even split between us."

"It's a trap," Sage said. "There's no way the confederation would toss that kind of money at us to solve an impossible mission. They expect us to die on that planet."

"Why not?" Wyn asked again. "They have legitimate reports showing that Sovereign's reach into Raiyrium space has extended, and they can't stamp it out anymore. We don't get paid unless we succeed. So they lose nothing if we fail, but they stop a galactic disaster if we succeed."

"Who cares if it's a trap?" Zetta licked her teeth. "With that kind of payout, I'll go to Kekar alone and drag his ass back."

"What of a contract?" Cee asked. "If you signed a contract, they should have no choice but to pay it out if successful."

"I did!" Wyn nearly vibrated with excitement. "So as long as we succeed, it's fine."

"Then it's settled," Zetta said. "I'll take the bounty. If anyone wants to tag along, they're welcome to watch a master at work."

"There is absolutely no way I'm letting you take that bounty solo," Sage said.

"Worried about me?"

"More worried about my share of that money." Sage smirked. "Not like you'll have much to do anyway."

"I would appreciate being allowed to join," Cee said. "I have never been to this Kekar."

"Why would you want to?" Zetta asked. "I mean, besides for this bounty."

"It is a singularly unique social structure." Cee added nothing more.

"Just so everyone is clear," Wyn said, "I am going. This was just to see who wanted to join me."

"No offense," Zetta said offensively, "but you'll just hold us back. Sure, you got a little better, but this is an entirely different situation than with Shekta."

"And they fucked even that one up," Sage said. "It's best you stay back, Wyn."

"It wasn't up for discussion," Wyn said. "This is a bounty to save my company. I won't leave it to others. Besides, I need a personal cut to save the company. If you both get all the money, that doesn't help."

"We'll give you, like, five million?" Sage said. "That should be enough."

"No, I—"

"I'll be going too." Besari stood to emphasize her point.

"What? No!" Panic flooded into Wyn as he looked over.

"You said yourself that we'll work together to become the best bounty hunters we can be," she said. "If you're going, then I'll be there too."

"Too many amateurs for my take," Zetta groaned as she leaned back. "Sneaking a large group onto the planet will be much harder than a smaller one."

"We could sneak on separately," Cee said. "One at a time, taking different routes to hide that we're together. It would be riskier without backup available, but stealth may be far more crucial."

"How do we know there's even more than one route?" Sage asked. "If they're using skipper drives, we'd need very precise coordinates to avoid ending up inside of some rock or the sun."

Cee hummed. "Based on my calculations, to run the empire he claims to have, easy access to him would be a requirement. He must have alternative ways to Kekar beyond skipper drives. I suspect there are at least forty access points."

"Impossible," Sage said. "Not without the R.C. discovering at least one of them."

"They must be hidden exceptionally well. Or Sovereign has connections in the R.C."

"Still don't think Wyn or Besari are prepared for this," Zetta said. "If they—"

"If I won't put my life on the line for this company, then why did I start it?" Wyn snapped. Zetta and Sage looked up at him in surprise. "I wanted to become a bounty hunter, and I put everything I own into this company. I won't just abandon my dream. Any team begins with me."

A silence fell over the group for a moment. Shellesh, who had stayed silent during much of the conversation, now looked at his Vico, his features shifting as he read through a report. Seph still looked on with interest.

"If you're a requirement," Besari said, "then so am I." Wyn glanced over, but she raised a hand to stop him. "No arguments."

"And what if I get you killed?" The words burned Wyn's throat as he said them. Entirely unintentional, but too late to take them back. A question that rang through Wyn's head every day since they had faced Shekta.

Besari stared at him for a long moment, and Wyn noticed Sage and Zetta looking on as well. He dropped his gaze, biting his tongue, trying to figure out how to fix it. How to change his words after he lost them.

"Then fight 'til the abyss to bring me back." Besari's tone sent a warmth through him, and he lifted his head to meet her gaze. "That's what we'll all do. Fight to protect each other, so we'll all make it back. That's the purpose of your company, isn't it?"

"There is a chance Sovereign has created a form of civilization," Cee said. "Having more there with a wide variety of skills would be beneficial."

"If the cyborg says you're helpful, then it's obviously not wrong," Sage said, seething with sarcasm. Cee had used the same arguments before, and they had all almost died as a result.

"Whatever happens," Wyn said, "I will do whatever it takes to ensure each of you survives. Even at the cost of my own life. If my dream is to die, it's best to do so free in my heart, not caged away because I'm a coward. But no one else deserves to die for my dream."

"I feel safer already," Zetta muttered. "I just want to say there's no way I'm letting that money slip through my claws, so I'm in."

"Same." Sage shrugged. "Always wanted to finish my career on a great bounty. This should suffice."

Zetta laughed. "You're not retiring. You love this job too much."

"I'm getting too damn old, Zetta." Sage sighed and leaned back. "One day, it's going to get me killed if I stay. A chunk of money this big, even split five ways, will let me die in luxury."

"There's still room for more," Wyn said. "Pesh might be busy, but what about Achtrek?"

"They just finished a bounty," Zetta said. At a glance from Sage, she added, "We trade bounty stories. A guy got his eyes eaten out. It was fantastic."

"Will they want to join, do you think?" Wyn asked. "A hive on our side would be helpful."

"Oh yeah, I'm sure they'll join," Zetta said.

"Shellesh?" Wyn asked. "Did you have an interest?"

Shellesh swiped away the virtual display at his wrist; cold dull eyes burst to life with anger. "If I am back in time, I will join," he said. "There will be no reason not to, for my cycle will be complete and I can die."

Shellesh's sudden passion sucked the air from the room, and he had nearly reached the door before any more words were spoken.

"Wait, Shellesh," Wyn called. "What do you mean you can die? Where are you going?"

"To kill my wife."

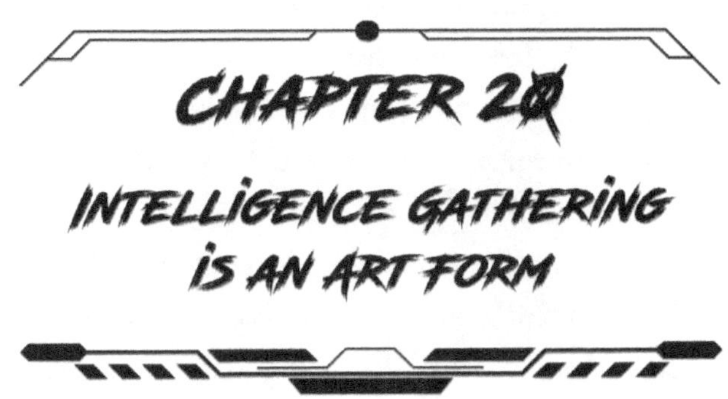

# CHAPTER 20

## INTELLIGENCE GATHERING IS AN ART FORM

K ekar.

The idea of slipping into the inescapable prison, grabbing the corpse (if Wyn the Stickler was any fun) of the most wanted man in the galaxy, and figuring their way off enticed Zetta almost more than the money did. She loved the challenge, a way to prove that she was the greatest fucking bounty hunter in the galaxy. She loved the money a lot too, but that just made the bounty even better. There were just a few problems to iron out.

The first was getting on planet. The second was getting off planet. The first could be very easy, but not without making the second harder. Wyn said the R.C. wouldn't let them use the main gate, which made sense. It would alert everyone to their presence. As much as she hated it, she agreed with the idea of stealth.

Which meant gathering more information. Her least favorite part of the job. Especially when it involved shitty food.

"This food sucks." Zetta drooled the crushed mush back onto the tray in front of her, glaring at Sage.

Sage glared back. "You don't have to eat it, just don't spit it out like that." She spooned a bit of the slop into her own mouth, then spit it back out immediately. Then grunted. "There's a reason I gave you a grainbar before we got here."

"You expected a single grainbar to tide me over? We've been here for hours." Zetta lifted a purplish bit of goop and sniffed it before letting it fall back on the tray. "I'm going to die if we're stuck here much longer."

"I don't control what food the prison serves," Sage snapped.

Zetta smiled. A feisty Sage made things more interesting.

"You're sitting in my spot!" a high-pitch voice screeched as it clomped over to the table. Torshks weren't known well for their stealthy footsteps, and Roshran was no different. "It would be wise to leave before things turn ugly."

The blue, shelled reptilian stared down Zetta from behind Sage, an impressive feat for most creatures, let alone the usually gutless torshks. She supposed the three rather large and menacing prisoners flanking him helped his confidence. Especially given his companions were a vrolak, a haushedin, and a rather burly birrosh. He must have brought his toughest to confront Zetta.

"Roshran." Sage grinned and twisted in her seat. "Prison has done you well."

The ex-drug dealer's eyes nearly burst from his tiny head. His tray of food clattered violently in his hands, threatening to spill. Zetta would peel his shell off if any landed on her.

"You!" he squeaked finally.

"Me," Sage said.

"You've been arrested! I knew you were no good."

Sage shut her eyes as the torshk spoke. She had a thing for high-pitched squeaks. A rather murderous thing, typically.

"We're just visiting," she managed to say.

"Visiting?" The torshk's voice lowered as he studied her and her prison clothing. "This is the cafeteria, not the visitor's office."

"Yes, well, it's interesting what a little money can help accomplish." Sage nodded her head, and Roshran followed her gaze. Every guard turned their back on the table at that moment, some even leaving the room. "Why don't you sit down? You can even have our food if you want."

He glanced between Zetta and Sage, then slapped his tray down next to Sage's and sat. "If you touch me, these three will kill both of you," he growled. "Paying the guards for privacy works both ways."

"Do you feel safe?" Zetta asked, leaning across the table toward him. He dropped his spoon but held her gaze.

"Make all the threats you want, vrolak. There's nothing you can do here without getting yourself killed."

Zetta smiled, right before she slammed Roshran's face into his own food. The mush splattered the table as the metallic sound rang through the cafeteria. Then the only noise was Roshran's screaming as blood spurted from his mouth.

Zetta wiped at her sleeve with a napkin. "I think I got some on me."

"Same," Sage grunted as she took to wiping the slop from her shirt.

"Sorry," Zetta said with a grin. "I'll help take that off later."

"What are you doing?" Roshran howled. "Kill them!"

Zetta slammed his head into the table again, denting the tray as he whimpered in pain. His minions just stood there, unmoving.

Roshran coughed and tried to glare at them. "What are you do-ing?" he cried. "Help me!"

Zetta leaned forward, and now the torshk shook in his shell. Tears ran from his eyes, and his limbs retreated inward. Not fully, evolu-tion had stolen their built-in hidey-hole long ago, but they could still retreat a little. When frightened enough.

"Do you feel safe?" Zetta asked again.

"What do you want?" he squeaked.

Sage started with the questions. "When I captured you, you threatened me with your secret employer. Sovereign, was it?"

"I can't tell you anything about him," he said. "Kill me if you must, but he would do much worse."

"Oh, we have no questions about Sovereign. Just about Kekar."

"What do you want to know about it?"

"How to get onto the planet without the R.C. knowing."

Roshran's eyes opened wide. "Why do you think I know how to get onto Kekar? There's just the one gate, and it's pretty one-way."

"You sold his goods, you made him money. You either had direct contact or you know someone who did."

Zetta tapped her claws on the table, and Roshran's gaze moved toward them. He stared as each one clicked. "I know how to get there," he said. "But I've been gone too long. Any security clearance I had would be gone. I can't get you past those fleets."

"Tell us what you know."

"In the Matacrys sector, there's a gate orbiting the most remote planet. It's painted black to avoid visual detection and only activates remotely to keep energy low."

"Where else?"

"That's the only location I know of," he said. "That was the path Sovereign always had me take to—"

Zetta slammed one claw into the torshk's hand, sticking it to the table with a burst of strength from her parasite. The little blue man squawked in what must be horrible pain.

"Where else?" Sage asked again.

The answers came quickly after that. He knew of thirty-seven gates to Kekar. More than Zetta could have guessed. Sovereign, that vermin, really did have his tendrils deep into the R.C. Sage was clearly as unnerved. How many did the confederation know about? Any of them?

Zetta ground her teeth, which caused the torshk to shake and wail, promising he had told the truth and given everything he knew. Zetta released his hand and kicked his chair back from under the table. Roshran hit the ground and rolled around, his little limbs flailing in an attempt to right himself.

"Are we sure he's telling the truth?" Zetta asked. "How are all these gates in existence? The cost is monumental, let alone hiding their construction from the R.C."

"I don't think he was lying," Sage murmured. "Perhaps the Raiyrium Special Forces were right to target him before this gets worse."

Zetta groaned. "Can we leave? I'm hungry."

"Yeah, let's go." Sage stood, then used a foot to keep the flailing torshk on his back. "By the way, Roshran, I've asked the prison to upgrade your room. It should be much more peaceful and away from any prying eyes or ears. Wouldn't want anything we've discussed getting to the wrong people. I hope you understand."

"You people are crazy!" he wailed.

Zetta stood, and Roshran's three friends collapsed, blood spilling from an ear each. Three beetles flew to her open palm and buzzed. "Great job, Bugs."

They hummed in appreciation, and Zetta wondered if Achtrek would want to join in with her and Sage tonight. They could all use a bit of distraction from this news.

Kekar.

The isolated planet proved an interesting challenge, but it also became an important final piece to Cee's purpose. There were other small, isolated locations it hadn't reached in the last four years, ten months, and nineteen days, but the prison planet held the largest source of information out of its reach. If it survived, it would be time to return. Ninety-seven percent coverage rate would have to do.

"Fuck!" Mesem jumped as Cee flickered into view, dropping her mop and knocking over a bucket of soapy water. An obese birrosh guard yelled at her to clean up the mess, and though she grumbled, she did as the guard had commanded. Picking up the bucket and mopping the excess water down a drain, she grumbled, "I thought I was done with you." She glanced at her own personal hallucination of Cee.

"Why did you think that?" Cee asked as it walked around the virtual grounds, a large dinner hall where several other prisoners worked as well. It could see what the tesing saw, some blind spots filled in from her memory, but beyond the doors would be nothing.

"I helped you with the haushedins," she grumbled, keeping her voice low. It didn't matter to Cee; their connection made her voice easily audible. "And I still haven't gotten saved from this prison like you promised."

"I didn't promise to save you," Cee said. "I promised only to lower your time here."

"So, how long am I stuck here?"

"Five years."

"Five?" Mesem paused in her mopping and stared at Cee, eyes wide. "How'd you lower it that much?"

"Emphasized a clerical error in the system. In five years, they'll see you're up for parole, and, as long as you've behaved, they'll grant it. Then you're free."

"Five years is still a long time."

"Then, perhaps, it is time for a renegotiation." Cee turned back to Mesem and stepped through a table until it stood in front of her. "I'll help you get out of this prison today if you provide me with much-needed information."

Mesem's uncontrolled emotions flooded out, disrupting the other prisoners and attracting their glances. Cee reconfigured the connection, allowing it to read her better. Excitement, anticipation, but a hidden note of dread. She was worried about what it'd ask for and weighed the options. The scales tipped one way, and her emotions dampened.

"Do I have a choice?" she asked. "Last I remember, you put a bomb in my skull."

"Yes, it is still there," Cee said.

"Better dead than a slave," Mesem said. "Whatever you want, you're going to have to dig it out of my skull after you blow it."

"This will be the last time," Cee said. "I'll remove the bomb as part of the price."

She paused in her mopping, shock flowing freely from her emotions. Cee noticed others looking over at her again, feeling the same emotions wafting from her. She was a fool to give herself away so easily. The birrosh guard moved to scold her, but she jumped back into work.

"What could you possibly want so badly?"

"Sovereign."

She laughed, continuously, boisterously, until the birrosh guard hit her with a stunstick and yelled for her to get back to work. Pulling herself to her feet, she still smiled. "You're a fucking idiot."

"I do not believe so."

"Then you don't know what you're mixing yourself up in. But why do I care? If I'm free of this place, it no longer matters if you remove the bomb or not. Sovereign will kill you."

"Possibly," Cee said, causing Mesem to pause.

"This bomb doesn't go off if you die, does it?"

Cee calculated its responses and stuck with silence. Mesem's face scrunched up with anger.

"Blow up a city and you'll find yourself shipped to Kekar, free and easy. Then you'll know all you need to know."

"I would prefer to arrive quietly and be able to escape. I need details on the planet, its system, and its defenses."

"The planet is a desolate wasteland covered by a perpetual storm. It's nearly inhospitable."

"And yet, Sovereign rules a criminal empire from there."

Mesem was quiet.

"You've been there, haven't you?"

"Not to the planet," she said, turning away from Cee to scrub at a particularly sticky location. "I don't have that much of a death wish, but I've seen it from orbit. Sovereign installed a weather controller. There's a part of Kekar free from the awful storms, and that's where everyone lives."

"Tell me about their security."

"You already know about them. Those haushedin terrorists have their fleets in orbit and a few orbital stations manned for protection.

If only one small section of the planet is survivable, you don't have to stop people from landing anywhere else."

"How can I get past it safely?"

"My codes worked for you last time. I can send you another set for Kekar deliveries. You'll need a sentinel-class freighter. It's what they would anticipate. They'll run bio and electrical scans on the ship to look for anything suspicious, so bring supplies that would be expected. Food, water, ammunition, weapons, vehicles. They don't know the schedules, so the details won't matter."

"Do you know of any other ways into the system?"

"There's a gate orbiting Dela, the dwarf planet on the outskirts of the Angbor system. Other than that, probably one in Matacrys, though I don't know where. I've heard of a few others, but I don't know the specifics."

"Tell me what you do know."

Mesem continued to work as she mumbled the information for Cee. She told it of the rumored other gates, of the haushedins' search patterns, and mentioned many vessels bringing runaways and slaves from the Raiyrium Confederation to help with construction projects on land. She wasn't sure what projects, but they were bringing in a lot of slaves.

Finished with her work, Mesem returned her mop, and the guard handed her a temporary credit chip. "This is half of what I normally get," she complained.

"You did a shit job cleaning, so you get half."

The tesing looked ready to argue, then gave it up and joined the line of prisoners back to their cells. "I don't have anything else," she whispered, quietly enough the others couldn't hear. "I have given you everything I have."

"Yes, thank you, Mesem," Cee said. "It will help greatly in our capture of Sovereign."

"I doubt it, but as long as it gets me out of this prison. Speaking of which, when should I expect to leave?"

Cee considered and analyzed the information. It believed Mesem when she said she had nothing left to share. "Right now."

"Right now?" She spoke a little too loudly, and the others turned to her. One guard approached, appearing angry. Mesem almost said something in defense, then the connection crackled and fizzled out.

Cee wondered if the same prisoners would now have to clean up the mess in the hallway or if the guards would collect new prisoners to scrape Mesem's brains off the walls. Either way, one more loose end had been tied up.


Kekar.

It terrified Besari to her core. If anything went wrong, this would be the end. The arrival, the mission, the departure. Everything had to go damn near perfectly. It seemed impossible. And yet, she couldn't leave. Not if Wyn was insisting on going, not if there was any chance she could make sure he lived through it all.

She had no goals, no plans. Bounty hunting was a way for her to run away, to hide behind a mask until she wouldn't have to anymore. Until she could face her family again without cowering. But somewhere along the way, a small part of Wyn's dream had become hers as well. She wanted him to succeed, wanted Bounty Inc. to become the company Wyn dreamed of. So, she would go. To Kekar, to the end of the universe if need be. Whatever it took to see that dream flourish, to stop hiding and discover what it meant to be Besari instead of who she had once been.

"Right this way."

The voice pulled Besari from her thoughts. The prison attendant—a male tesing with pastel cyan skin and wearing a bright pink suit that burned her eyes—gestured to an open door. Wyn rose first, glancing at his shoulder before following their guide. Besari trailed after, trying to knock the nagging thoughts away. Not worries about Kekar, but about herself. She wanted to help Wyn, but she didn't want that to be her reason for everything. Right now, she clung to him like a barnacle to a boat. There had to be more to her purpose, but her mind flailed for it uselessly.

The attendant reached a door and held it open for Wyn and Besari. "If you'll wait inside, a pair of guards will bring the prisoner shortly."

Besari sighed and entered the room. She might not even live long enough for the thoughts to matter, so she pushed them aside and hoped she'd have an answer if she came back from Kekar.

The room was small with two entrances to either side and a table at its center. Two prison guards stood at attention just inside the door and watched as Wyn and Besari took their seats and waited.

The attendant poked his head in. "Oh, and for privacy, the audio to the monitoring devices have been cut. Video will stay active. The audio chip I provided for you will record everything but cracking it in half will destroy the recording. If any incriminating evidence, either against you or the prisoner, is provided during your conversation, please be sure to hand it off to a guard for further prosecution."

"What about the guards?" Besari asked.

"Audio will be cut to their helmets as well. If you feel the prisoner will cause any trouble, there is a panic switch on the bottom of the table. Hit that, and the guards will remove the prisoner from the room. They will also act if the prisoner is deemed violent or if certain violent phrases are spoken. You will be locked within during the interview, but these guards will keep you safe." He waved cheerfully before adding, "Have a good visit!"

Then the door shut and clicked. And they waited.

"Why in the void would we hand over the audio if there's evidence against us?" Besari asked, and Wyn didn't respond. She looked over and saw him studying a corner of the table. "Wyn?"

He jerked in surprise and looked at her. "Sorry, what?"

"Are you okay? You seem distracted."

Wyn glanced back at the corner of the table, then sighed and ran a hand through his hair. "Yeah, I'm fine. Probably just a bit of stress."

He had seemed more easily distracted since the mission to Bezium. Sage's brain scans had reported nothing wrong, but maybe they'd missed something. A vivid recall of Wyn seizing on the floor, gasping in the perrilan air, caused her to shiver. She didn't know how he had survived, but she was grateful.

"Why would we hand over the audio if there's evidence against us?" Wyn asked.

Besari glared at him, and he must have caught enough of it to cock his head in wonder. "What?" he asked, and she laughed.

"Maybe they don't actually delete the audio, or people are stupid enough to supply it. More importantly, what's our plan of action? We can't do anything physically, so we'll have to mentally interrogate her. Though, we might have to be careful with threats too, so as to not set off the guards."

"I thought we would just ask her questions," Wyn said, his big, beautiful brown eyes staring at her, filled with innocence and ignorance.

"Wyn," she said, "why would she just answer our questions? We invaded her home, dragged her back to Raiyrium space, and put her in jail."

"Oh." Wyn looked back to the corner of the table, considering. "Do you think she likes money?"

"Probably, but you can't just keep throwing money at all your problems, Wyn. That's completely unsustainable."

"Why does money matter if we'll fail?"

"No need to think of it as life or death," Besari said with a nervous chuckle. "We could fail and still live."

Wyn smiled. "I guess, but then Bounty Inc. will fail. Everything I have been striving towards would crumble away."

"Not everything. You have your skills you picked up along the way. You're no longer starting from nothing as a bounty hunter. You and I could just go off on our own and continue hunting."

"Just us?" Wyn asked, studying her face mask, striving to see beneath it. She shifted beneath his gaze, wishing he could see the real her. Wishing he wouldn't be upset when he did.

"I mean, if you want." Besari shrugged and looked away. She could hear Wyn begin to speak, then the door clicked and two guards pulled a shackled Shekta into the room and seated her on the opposite side of the table. With Shekta chained and the door locked, the new guards took up their post and watched.

The perrilan studied them for a long moment before speaking. "Who are you?"

"What?" Wyn asked, then looked to Besari and back to Shekta. "We're the ones who caught you."

Besari winced, wondering if they should have lied.

"You're fucking kidding me." Shekta scratched at the gas mask strapped to her face. "You two scrawny fucks invaded my house with Sage?"

"Yes," Wyn said. "You threw me around the room like a doll."

"I remember," she said. "Seems I've lost my touch if you're still in one piece."

"We want to know about your boss," Besari said. It was probably best for her to take over the conversation sooner rather than later.

"I don't have a boss," Shekta said. "I had a striving entrepreneurial business that you two destroyed."

"But your business provided for a client, right?" Besari continued. "Someone by the name of Sovereign."

Shekta stilled, her gaze studying the two of them. Then she leaned back. "I think it's best to end this little interrogation of yours. I have no answers for you."

Besari leaned forward, hands carefully steady on the table. "We've paid the guards to look the other way if needed. It's just us."

Shekta smiled and leaned forward. "Then hit me," she said, eyes going wide. "Prove it, or I'll know you're lying. One hit, right in the jaw. If you don't, every threat of yours will be utterly usel—"

"Do you like money?" Wyn asked.

Besari closed her eyes. Poor, stupid Wyn.

Shekta laughed. "I love money, kid, but there's no way you have enough for what you're asking for."

Besari smiled. "They gave us a nice chip that records all the audio," she said. "And friends of ours are gathering more information as we speak. I'm sure we have enough of your voice to doctor it to seem like you gave us information. What happens when Sovereign hears that?"

"Do you really think they're not recording every word being said in here right now?" Shekta asked. "You think they don't keep every recording on file? You're a fool if you think you're the only one holding the audio."

"Maybe they'll have recordings, but Sovereign would need access to Raiyrium Federal Penitentiary records to access them. Whereas these will be freely accessible."

"Who says he doesn't have access already?" Shekta leaned forward, her voice barely a hoarse whisper. "I've received some lovely gifts to make my time more comfortable lately."

Wyn leaned forward carefully, mimicking her posture and bringing his voice down. "We can protect you," he said. "Once we've captured—"

Shekta pulled down her mask and breathed out, too quickly for Besari or the guards to react. A flick of the wrist, and a puff of orange-tinted air streamed toward Wyn's face.

He jumped back, knees hitting the table as he toppled to the ground, coughing. Besari grabbed Shekta's wrist, grinding the bones as the perrilan cackled, her mask askew. Then all four guards converged, pulling them apart.

"Enjoy your deaths!" Shekta screeched as she cackled, the two guards pulling her from the room. "I wish I could be there to watch."

Then the door shut and Wyn and Besari were alone with the remaining guards.

"Are you okay?" one guard asked.

Wyn was helped to his feet by the other, then he felt the back of his head, his hand coming back red. "I think I'm bleeding."

"Would you like to make use of our medical facilities?" a guard asked.

"No, it's fine," Wyn said. "We have some on our ship that will work."

The guards nodded, and the door opened. Wyn looked longingly to the other door and sighed. This had been an abject failure. "We should probably get back. The gate to Chrysanax will close in a few hours."

Besari nodded and offered an arm to steady him. He took it, and their escort led them out.

"Bit of a rough visit, no?" the tesing guide asked, looking worriedly at Wyn.

"Yeah," Wyn said with a small smile. "It could have gone better."

"Would you like us to analyze the audio? We could maybe help prepare a lawsuit for you."

Wyn pulled the chip from his pocket and snapped it in half before handing it over. Then they left the prison for the docks and their ships.

"Failure defines us as well as success," Besari said as she seated him in the medical chair aboard the *Bounty I*, a new cruiser Wyn had spent more money on for easy travel on Bounty Inc. business. She didn't understand its need, but at least the medical facilities were great. "It's not something worth focusing on."

"It could be the difference between mission success and failure, Besari."

Besari shrugged. "You can't be good at everything immediately. I messed up in there too, and I'm not sulking about it."

Wyn smiled. "I don't care much for failure."

"No one does, but that doesn't mean you should pretend it doesn't happen." Besari stepped around Wyn, hands at his scalp. "Now let me take a look at your wound. I'm going to wash it first."

"All right," Wyn said, and still he flinched as the cool washcloth ran across his head. She wiped away the already drying blood until the cloth came away clean. Then she looked for the cut.

"Strange," she mumbled.

Wyn stiffened. "You're not looking at my brains, are you?" he asked.

Besari laughed. "No, the cut's not that deep. In fact, I can't even find it."

"Oh," Wyn said. "Maybe it's just really small. Head wounds can bleed a lot for humans."

"Maybe," she muttered, then ran the cloth across his head again. It came away clean.

"We better get moving," Wyn said, rising from the medical chair as he roughed up the damp hair. "Hopefully the others had better luck."

Besari watched him exit the medical bay, confusion stalling her. Wyn hadn't even flinched as his fingers had brushed over his skull. And how was it possible she hadn't seen any evidence of a cut or bruise? Human biology was a strange one for sure.

# CHAPTER 21

## PATHWAYS

"I have created six routes to enter Kekar," Cee explained to the crowded meeting room. A holographic map projected from the center of the table. "I have used multiple gates to obscure our origin point and to stagger our arrivals. But everyone will arrive within four standard days of each other."

With a gesture, the first path glowed on the map. Wyn's eyes widened. Obscuring the origin was an understatement. This route jumped through at least sixteen different systems before arriving at the target location. Wyn's Vico chimed as his itinerary popped up.

"That's a lot of stops," Wyn said, scrolling through the departures and arrivals.

"It may seem extraneous, but I have determined there is a ninety-eight percent chance that the path will be untraceable through so many gates and transport switches."

"This changeover only gives me twenty minutes," Wyn said, pointing to one near the end.

"I have provided alternatives for any missed changeovers that are under an hour." As Cee spoke, a light blinked on Wyn's Vico to indicate where to check that. "Some may alter your arrival by a decent margin, but most should loop back up with your regular plan. Try not to miss any flights, though. This is the most optimal path."

Wyn gaped at his arrival schedule. It would be four days straight of grueling public transport, with barely any time to sleep. Did Cee not understand normal people needed sleep? Not to mention the anxiety of public transport. He had only taken that once when he'd been thirteen and his father had let him go to an amusement park. Wyn had been escorted by his father's assistant, who had handled everything, including buying out the rest of the seats. So, Wyn wasn't even sure that counted.

"I hope you don't mind if I sleep the whole way," Tom said, the void slug staring up from his spot on the table. "Shuttle rides make me sleepy."

Wyn ignored the persistent hallucination and hoped it would go away soon. Brain scans had shown nothing wrong, so why was he still seeing the little slug-shaped tear in reality?

Cee droned on, providing brief details for Wyn's trip before moving on to the next. Besari, Zetta, Achtrek, and Sage sat and listened to routes, each involving multiple public transports, multiple falsified identities, and multiple obscure ports at strange parts of the galaxy. Between Cee's contact and research, it had found eight entries into Kekar. Sage and Zetta had unearthed another thirty-seven from a different prisoner. Neither list intersected. How had Sovereign built over forty-five gates in secret?

Several of the gates only activated on command and were therefore useless to Bounty Inc. Not unless they could figure out how to turn them on, but he wasn't sure arriving that way would be so discrete. In the end, Cee had decided the best routes would be the more "public" methods. There was a call for people to come to the prison planet willingly, and most of them would arrive as though answering that call, blending into the public of Kekar before meeting up in secret. Only Cee would sneak in through one of the deactivated gates.

"So we have to sit through days of public transport," Zetta growled, leaning back in her chair, claw tapping the table. "But you get to fly in, nice and comfy? Why can't we just hide in your shuttle?"

"The ship will be scanned," Cee said. "It would be unwise to press our luck. I will already be fabricating my own signatures to mimic organics."

Cee's ride, far too large for the private hangar, was docked at the Chyrsanax space port. It was a junky sentinel-class freighter on its last legs. Wyn had bought it cheap at an auction along with a few other junker vehicles, which were parked within it for delivery to Kekar. The *Bounty I* was also on board, and it would be what they'd use to escape the planet.

"You've checked it over?" Wyn asked. "The freighter will fly?"

"Life support systems are still not operational," Cee admitted, "but I will have it flying well enough to get me there."

Wyn nodded.

"Never trust a robot," Tom said. "They're happy to get arrested since they'll likely get *charged*."

Wyn leaned forward, letting his elbow drop on the nothing slug. Tom disappeared in a blink and reappeared out of reach, constantly watching.

"Sage Valen and Achtrek-Six Hive will arrive day one. With Sage's experience and Achtrek-Six's espionage skills, you two will lay the groundwork for the rest of us by bolstering our intel, preparing for the next steps, and finding a hideout."

"I have more experience than she does," Zetta growled.

"Sage is more subtle," Cee explained. Zetta shrugged in acknowledgment. "Wyn Kelda will arrive day two as bounty leader. Each of your Vicos will have a subtle radio signal that, when activated, will be able to detect each other. Use this every standard hour when an arrival is expected, until you pick up a signal. That way it will lower the chances of detection."

"What if we arrive late?" Wyn asked. "Outside expected arrival."

"Mission will continue as expected, but members already there are expected to activate the radio signal when possible to alert the others. The *Bounty I* will have a stronger signal that will activate near departure to call everyone there. If you miss the mission time, stay aware and don't get caught. You may still join up with the others."

Everyone nodded in agreement.

"Day three arrival will be Besari, with Zetta and I arriving day four."

"Four?" Zetta leaned forward. "So I get to miss out on all the fun?"

"Nothing will begin before day four," Cee explained. "It seems beneficial to keep you off planet for as long as possible due to your more recognizable stature. For similar reasons, I will be scheduled to be the last to arrive. Once I arrive, our mission will kick into the next stage, and we will have to act quickly. Given that, if your arrival is shifted more than two days past mine, it would be wise to back off the mission entirely. There will be no guarantee we will be on planet more than two days, and rescue will be very difficult."

A lull fell over the room, blanketing them with silence as everyone contemplated their schedules. They would be alone until they arrived on Kekar. Wyn glanced up at Besari and felt an ache. They should arrive in pairs so everyone had someone watching their backs. Not alone, where anything could happen.

"We have three codes for use with the haushedin fleet," Cee continued. "I will keep two for my own entry, but the last will be provided to each of you as an emergency. But be aware, the use of it will mean anyone else who uses it will be caught, not to mention we don't know what will follow the exchange of a code. If you're on the wrong ship or carrying the wrong items or if it's out of use now, you may be caught. Lastly, I have provided two spikes for each that can be used to hack into a terminal." It slid small black cylinders into the middle of the table. "They're one-time use and will help you in a pinch while my unparalleled hacking ability is not available."

Sage arched an eyebrow at the A.I. but still grabbed her two spikes. Wyn and the others did the same.

Tom stared up at Cee. "Mighty confident, this fella." Then he appeared on its head and started licking it.

"Any questions?" Cee asked.

"Yes, what should I do?"

Everyone turned to find Seph standing in the corner, watching the meeting.

"Why are you here?" Sage asked.

"Wyn asked for everyone to come up here for the meeting."

Sage rolled her eyes, but before she could make a biting remark, Wyn stepped in. "Stay here and take care of any calls. I've marked down a few bounties that you can mention we're handling if anyone asks. But it should be quiet, so you and L-Bot should be able to handle things." Then he realized L-Bot wasn't there. "Where's L-Bot?"

"It's watching the front desk," Seph said. "Should I tell the same to Pesh and Shellesh?"

"No, Shellesh will already know about it, and Pesh can know too."

"If there are no questions," Cee said, "it would be best to prepare for the mission."

"Feel free to check out any available weapons or equipment you need," Wyn said. "The armory's fully open for this one. We need to succeed here."

"I'm taking the slag cannon," Zetta said quickly, and Sage glared.

"Not the slag cannon," Wyn interrupted Sage's response. "That's way too big to sneak onto the planet."

"One of these times, Wyn, I'm going to shoot that fucking cannon."

"It's all yours after this mission."

"Now that's motivation." Zetta smirked.

"The money's not?"

"More motivation doesn't hurt."

Zetta and Sage were the first to leave, the vrolak deeply entrenched in all things slag cannon. She had a considerable list of things she was most excited to shoot it at, which included a specific torshk for some reason. Achtrek was next to slip out, with nothing more than a slight hum in the air, and Seph followed awkwardly. Cee said its farewells to Wyn and Besari, then left to continue some final repairs to the ship. It would be on Chrysanax for some time yet, waiting as the rest of them departed over the next few days.

Then there were two.

"Well," Wyn said, then rubbed his hands together nervously and uselessly. His mouth dried like a desert, and his words disappeared from his mouth without a sound.

"Well," Besari said, and he could feel her smile behind that face-plate. He wanted to see her smile just once, actually see it. He wondered what color her lips would be. "This is it. The big mission."

"Nervous?" Wyn asked nervously.

"Until I'm with you again, I will be. But together, nothing can stop us."

Wyn's face burned, but he refused to look away. Instead, he coughed, rubbed at his face, and then smiled. "Yes, the unbeatable team. Unless it's a superpowered perrilan."

"We still won, didn't we?"

"I think there was a third member on that team." Wyn laughed.

Besari shrugged. "Sage was a bit helpful, I guess." Then she dug into a pocket on her belt. "I have something for you."

She pulled out a thin leather strap, at the end of which dangled a stone charm, intricately carved into the shape of vines weaving together to form a hollow tree. Her words came quickly and flustered.

"It's a symbol of good luck among my people. We wear it around our left bicep, close to the heart so the good luck can spread quickly through the body with every beat." She hesitated before adding, "I'm not sure where the human heart is."

"Left as well," Wyn said, his brow crinkling. "I thought the heart was on the other side for birrosh, though."

"You're wrong," Besari said quickly, then stood and rounded the table, crouching by Wyn's chair. "Give me your left arm."

Wyn swiveled the chair so they were facing each other, then offered his arm to her waiting hand. Hesitant fingers grasped his bicep and forearm. Then her hand slid down to his wrist, and she pulled his hand to her chest, just above the left breast.

"My heart is here, feel?" Her blood thrummed through the fabric as Wyn's own pounded through his head. Besari's left hand moved from his bicep to his own chest, pressing the metal charm against his shirt. "Just like yours."

Wyn's hand clasped over her gloved one, holding it in place, hoping she would never leave. Maybe he should let Bounty Inc. crash and burn. Nothing was worth risking Besari's life. He wondered if the same thoughts ran through her head. Neither voiced them if that was the case, however.

Then her hands slipped from his, rolling his sleeve up and deftly wrapping the charm tight to the inside of his arm. "All set to have the best luck you've had in all your life," she said.

Wyn smiled. "Based on the luck I've already had, that would be quite a challenge."

"As long as it grants you safe passage to Kekar, I will call that a victory."

"I'll be waiting for you." Wyn's guts tightened, everything within screaming at him to grab her, to kiss her. But she could not remove her helmet; Wyn would never feel her skin. He bit his lip in frustration. Sage had put these impossible thoughts in his head, but it didn't make sense to fall for someone so different. And yet, here he was, wishing for one moment to see her face, to touch her skin. One impossible moment.

"We should go," Besari said, squeezing his arm. Wyn nodded with a mouth full of fluff.


"Sir?"

Wyn startled awake, cut off mid-dream. He blushed as the details floated in his mind, a gorsaulk steward standing over him. He glanced around the now empty shuttle and back at the man who had woken him.

"We've arrived," he said disapprovingly.

"Right, sorry." Wyn rubbed the sleep from his face ineffectively and reached down for his luggage. The backpack contained the pieces of his armor folded neatly together. The large suitcase overhead contained weapons and other equipment. Both containers were sealed with special protections to falsify the scans. They had worked through many of the ports, but each time it gave Wyn a nervous feeling to stroll around with so much unregistered firepower. It had to happen though; weapons would be noted and tracked. Sovereign would see them coming.

He stepped out to the Capal Port, a bustle of local salespeople, travelers, and the occasional security drone sweeping by. Wyn's grip tightened as one flew close, scanning him and the others departing the shuttles. His discomfort with public transport had died after the fourth or fifth leg of the journey, and now an endless weariness settled into his bones. That nap had been the first sleep he'd had since leaving over forty hours prior. He'd never had a long enough layover to sleep, and he had been too uncomfortable to do so on the transits, which was likely what Cee had expected him to do. Well, at least until exhaustion had finally worn him down enough and his body had decided for him. Except that had been late into the trip, and he felt no better for the short nap.

Wyn checked his itinerary and found his next flight. Cee recommended leaving the port, booking a hotel, changing and swapping IDs, then boarding the new flight. Several hotel options floated up on his Vico. He chose one and trudged on.

He traded a few credits for a private room, undressed, showered, and redressed. Rubbing his hands across his face, he sat on the comfortable bed, its mattress calling for him to lie down. He was supposed to go right back to the port and wait at the terminal.

Where he would sit in uncomfortable chairs, maybe sleep for five minutes, and trudge onto another flight barely alive. He couldn't arrive to Kekar like this. Some criminal would just mug him of his belongings.

But the layover was two hours. Two hours where he could get comfortable sleep, maybe feel a little more rejuvenated for the last stretch. Two hours of bliss.

Fuck it.

He set a timer on the Vico, climbed into the sweet, soft bed, and let sleep consume him.

No more than two minutes could have passed when he startled awake to incessant beeping. His stomach churned, his mind was groggy, and all around he felt much worse than before the nap. What in the void was the point of a nap if it made you feel worse? He sat up and peeled his eyelids apart to let the light pierce his eyes and sweep the sleepiness away. Not the exhaustion though. He feared that would never leave.

He canceled the alarm and returned the Vico to his wrist, grabbed his backpack and his luggage, then left. Back to the port at a zombie crawl. A few more stops and he would be done. He could last that long.

"Good morning," the cheery port assistant said. She was human, dark-skinned, with a bright smile.

"Good morning," Wyn said, though all meaning of the word morning had fled when he'd experienced multiple mornings and nights within a six-hour stretch. He brought up his pass on his Vico and leaned forward. The machine scanned it, and the woman looked at the screen on her end.

"Your flight was for Wagisha at 08:35 local time?"

"Yeah," Wyn confirmed.

She looked at him, smile faltering, then up at a large clock. "Um," she said.

Wyn followed her gaze, and a panic set into him that scoured any remaining sleepiness away. The time said 09:56. Wyn stared at the woman, gaping. How had the time been wrong? He had set a timer. "Is it still here?" he asked.

"It's not," she said. "If you'd like, I can look up when the next flight is?"

Panic turned her words to mush in his ear. He had missed his flight and would need an alternative. Cee had provided those. She still spoke, but he ignored her. He was so close to Kekar, it couldn't add much time as an alternative. He pulled up the alternative plans and opened the one for missed connection Capal to Wagisha.

A series of poorly timed gates, a long circuit to disguise his path once more, and five days added travel time.

"No no no." Wyn bit down on one palm as he groaned. The assistant looked around nervously, unsure how to help. There was no way to help. Five days was too long. The gates would be out of sync. He would have to circle back, come around another way. There wasn't time. He'd be too late for everything. The mission, even the escape, would be missed. He would have to go back to Bounty Inc. Let everyone else complete the mission without him.

Tears floated at the edges of his vision as he bit harder and groaned louder. This couldn't be the case. He would miss everything. It was supposed to be *him* there. *He* was supposed to save the company. Not to mention Besari would have to face it without him. This couldn't be happening. He had to be dreaming.

"Sir, we can transfer your ticket to a flight at 10:15 local time if you'd like," the assistant said, trying to halt Wyn's meltdown.

"What?" Wyn looked at her, frustration bleeding out onto his face. Her smile faltered, and he almost felt bad. Then he looked away and saw the hallway that led to the private docks, and his breath halted. He bit his lip, and one hand fell to his pocket with the pair of spikes.

"Would you like me to transfer your ticket?" she asked, her cheeriness long since faded.

Wyn looked back at her, a calmness seeping through him as a decision was made. He couldn't arrive late. Not with so much on the line. He would have to find a way to fix that himself.

"No, thank you." He grabbed his suitcase and wheeled down the hall to the private docks.


"Excuse me!"

Wyn rolled his suitcase across the barren port to a pair of people filling the cargo haul of a small, sleek cruiser built for quick deliveries, usually piloted by one person. Maybe a pair.

Wyn hoped it was one.

They paused in their work to look at him. One was a falvian with feathers of bright blues and yellows, the other was a bright red birrosh female. Wyn paused as the woman reminded him of Besari, and he coughed into his hand to clear his throat.

"Is this your ship?"

The falvian's robot voice crackled from the speaker around their neck. "Not me. Hired hand for loading and unloading."

The birrosh woman looked over, flashing the hired hand a look. Her head was bare, the ridges of flesh running from her forehead back to her neck in intricate patterns. "That was a quick response from you." She looked back at Wyn and eyed him next. "It's mine. If you're looking for deliveries, I don't do custom orders."

"I want to buy your ship."

She laughed. "No chance."

"Even if you modified the ship, it can't eclipse more than, what? One hundred thousand?" Wyn said. "I'll give you six hundred thousand and pay for all the cargo loaded so you make no losses on delivery."

She didn't laugh that time. "Six hundred thousand? Plus the cargo?"

Besari had scolded him about how throwing money at problems wouldn't always work, but this was a desperate moment. He needed to get to Kekar on time. And so he nodded.

"No," she said.

"What?"

"You heard my answer." She turned back to loading the rest of the cargo. The falvian finished his work, got paid, then left. Wyn didn't move. "I said no," she reiterated.

"I can pay more," Wyn said, though he wasn't really sure if he could.

"This ship's a part of me and my life. I wouldn't sell my arm just because you are willing to pay a lot." She sighed as she walked to the landing ramp, turning back to Wyn. "You seem desperate, kid, so I'm sorry, but it's still a no."

"Then a rental? I'll return it when I'm done." He wasn't entirely sure that would be the case.

"If I trusted every stranger to borrow my ship, I would have lost it the day I bought it." She turned to head up the ramp, and Wyn felt the moment disappearing. He needed to come out of this ahead. Time was running out.

"Can I hitch a ride?" Wyn asked.

She paused at the top of the ramp. "You don't even know where I'm going."

"Where are you going?"

"Angbor."

Wyn ground his teeth. It wasn't where he needed to go, but it could help him. There was a gate in that system, wasn't there? Or was that one that needed activation? He breathed out with a decision made. It didn't matter, as long as he was moving forward. He would find his way.

"I am amenable to going there."

She smiled. "Six hundred thousand raikers."

"Are you insane?" Wyn snapped. "That's as much as I offered for your ship."

"So I know you have it," she said. "Be lucky I don't charge for the added cost of the cargo too."

"We leave immediately." Wyn spoke through tight teeth, his heart racing.

"Sure. I have no more business here."

"Fine." Wyn walked up the ramp, but she didn't move.

"Payment up front. I want to know you have the money."

Wyn stared at her, then activated his Vico, holding his luggage steady with one leg on the angled ramp. She shared the transfer information, and within moments, Wyn was six hundred thousand raikers poorer. The payment cut deeply into what he would owe the others at the end of the year, but if they caught Sovereign, he would have plenty to pay them. If he didn't, he doubted anyone would be left to collect their money.

At least it made him feel less guilty about what would come next.

She showed Wyn the corner of the ship he could hang out in, and he set his luggage down, rubbing sore shoulders. The ship thrummed beneath his feet as he unzipped the backpack and stared down at his combat suit. He changed into the tight undersuit and one by one attached the pieces of combat armor. He held the helmet in hand and stared at his reflection in the black glass faceplate. He closed his eyes and focused on Besari instead. Then he put it on.

Next, he pulled the Imberlii Dissenter pistol free from his suitcase, then walked to the front of the ship. The suit's speakers caught the last of the conversation with Capal security, and the comms cut out as he stepped into the cockpit.

"You can sit up here or wherever," she called over her shoulder. "Just don't mess with the cargo." She turned and saw the fully armed and armored Wyn. Fear bloomed in her eyes, and before she could say anything, Wyn shot her in the chest at low power. She jerked, and her eyes rolled to the back of her head as her body went limp. Wyn checked her pulse and found her still alive, thankfully.

He had convinced himself that maybe if she had been going to the right place, he could have made it work, but more likely he would be dropped off at another port, forced to find another ride, wasting precious time. He pulled her body from the seat and dragged it to the woman's room, then bound her in wire.

He really only had one choice after the missed flight. He needed to find a way to Kekar. Luckily, he knew of one option.

"I really wish you'd just sold me this ship," Wyn whispered, then left the birrosh woman in her room. From the cockpit, he slid one spike into the ship's controls and cracked the encryptions, giving himself access to the entire system. He locked out the birrosh woman's access, then locked her room as added security.

Then he set course to the nearest gate to Kekar.

# CHAPTER 22

## LANDFALL

**Sage**

Sage woke as the ship rattled, threatening to loosen every bolt on the piece of junk that somehow survived the vacuum of space. Her back ached, and a groan escaped as she shifted in her seat, adjusting to a new position. Maybe they had reached the nebulous storm that hid the gate. If she was lucky, it was the atmospheric entry on Kekar itself. Without a window or viewing screen, she had no idea.

Despite her nap, she didn't miss the human man who had been watching her right up until the moment she'd woken up. He was pretending to be occupied talking with a woman who had to be a sister or close couFsin. She also failed to miss the hired tough, a pale yellow birrosh, at the front handling a projectile launcher, likely explosive rounds, casually chatting with his buddy, a purple tesing woman. And the eddermar at the back crouched in the center of the aisle, staring daggers through Sage's skull, their bonded gridder bobbing up and down with hostile energy. The falvian across the aisle glanced her way several times, which should have been more subtle, given the many tech implants. Then there was the haushedin, but he stared at her with open hostility. It hardly counted as something one could miss.

She could have brushed it off if any of them stared at the others with nearly as much interest. It almost made her blush, being the center of attention. It certainly made her think the fake mustache wasn't working to hide her identity.

She cataloged them in a moment. The haushedin would be hardest to kill, but if that birrosh fired the explosive ammo, that wouldn't matter. They'd all be dead. He had to be a priority kill. The gridder would be a nuisance, and the eddermar even more so, given how hard they were to kill. She began to wonder if the humans were nairwids, because otherwise they were laughably easy opponents compared to the rest. Well, maybe not the falvian. She wasn't really worried about that one. Though her gaze did linger, wondering why he seemed familiar. She shrugged and shifted into a different position, stretching out each muscle in her body and sliding her boots off. What happened would happen, and the rest of the passengers would regret it.

The cabin shook, then filled with a low thrum. Sage was now sure they had entered the Kekar atmosphere. Everyone tensed, eyes slipping toward her. She yawned and finished her stretches, then cocked an eyebrow. "Shall we begin?"

They stared at her, unmoving.

Then chaos.

The human brother leapt first, knife in hand. She slapped the ground with one foot, shooting up the stony carapace right into his path. He slammed head-first into the pillar, dropping his knife. Sage grabbed the blade from mid-air, turning the stone pillar to dust and thrusting the blade into its owner's neck. Blood squirted out, coating Sage before she could kick the fresh corpse away. He fell dead at his sister's feet, soaking her in blood as she wailed. Not a nairwid then. That was good.

Sage was out of the seat and in the aisle, but everyone else was as well. With the advantage of having started there, the eddermar launched themself, four blades slicing the air. Sage danced away, pulling her pistol free just as the gridder vomited out goo, but one foot caught in the sticky goo, causing her to fall backward onto the dead guy. Her back spasmed with pain as she grunted, and the eddermar was on her, a hailstorm of blades swinging at her while their body pinned her to the ground.

A burst of sediment knocked the eddermar off balance as Sage defended with carapaced arms. Then one blade hummed and sank through the stone shell of her right arm. Pain sprouted outward, then the limb fell numb as the tip jutted out the other side.

Sage hooked her working hand around the eddermar's head and slammed her reinforced forehead into their face, dark green blood spraying outward as they yelled curses in a language Sage didn't know. She silenced them with four shots from her second pistol, two to each heart. Stony sediment pushed Sage into a standing position, the eddermar's dying body in hand, just as the haushedin's foot slammed down where her head had been.

The gridder screamed wildly and dove at Sage as the sister jumped onto her seat, a rifle pulled. The sister fired, blowing chunks of the eddermar off as Sage used it as a shield. Then she grabbed the diving gridder and launched it at the woman's head. She followed it up with the eddermar body, which slammed directly into the sister, then stepped back from a wild haymaker from the haushedin. Her body pulled to a short stop, and the meaty fist brushed her nose, blowing the hair back from her head. Her foot tugged where it was still glued to the floor. In a panic, Sage burst carapace from her foot in jagged streaks, then jumped back out of reach once it was free.

Sage tucked her pistol into one armpit and pulled the knife free from her arm. The falvian joined the skirmish with one wing turning into a frenzy of sharpened metallic feathers. She chucked the knife at his head, which he blocked with the wing. She took the opportunity to duck around his back and drive Cee's hacking spike into his neck. It inserted into the falvian's nervous system and wreaked havoc on the electrical systems. He collapsed into his chair, twitching, sparks flying from every artificial piece.

She had told Wyn implants were an impediment. This would have been a good lesson for him.

Pistol back in hand, she ducked another blow by the haushedin.

"I'll crack your skull open!" he roared.

Sage shot him in the head. It didn't do much, but it made her feel better. Then she ducked a glob of goo and fired back at the angered gridder, who popped like a pimple. Another shot at the attacking haushedin, same spot to startle him, then she shot the human woman three times in the chest.

She barely raised a carapace shield in time to block a scattergun shot, and it exploded under a kick from the haushedin, which sent her careening into the back wall. Sage created another to slow the haushedin down, but she wasn't entirely sure it did. She had lost her gun and now scrambled for another weapon as the haushedin grabbed her head and attempted to make good on his promise. Hardened shell coated her head, and still she felt the cabin wall's impact as she blindly reached for the stunstick at her back.

The haushedin pulled her back to slam her head in again, and Sage hit him with the stunstick. Electricity coursed through the large creature's body, and it twitched, then collapsed. She'd have to thank Cee for that tip.

A shield of sediment burst from her hand and exploded as the scattergun shot it. She regrew it each time, leaping over the haushedin and back to the first clump of bodies. There, among them, was her first pistol. She dove under the next shot, rolling forward over the bodies, coming up with the pistol and firing.

The tesing and the birrosh both took cover as her shots impacted the cabin wall. The tesing blindly fired the scattergun, forcing Sage into her own cover behind seats. The birrosh continued to do nothing. That was good. He wasn't stupid. Now to just kill him before he became stupid.

She toughened the armor at her front and charged forward to—

A thick gray hand grabbed her limp arm and whipped Sage into the back of the cabin. Her carapace exploded beneath the force, and she hit the ground, gasping for air, somehow still holding the pistol.

She was going to kill Cee for promising that would be more effective.

She fired as the hulking monster approached, each shot focusing on the same spot, just above the right eye. The first two seemed to do nothing, but the third gave him pause, and the fourth drew blood and a grunt. Sage spewed waves of sediment out from her feet, grabbing at the haushedin's legs and slowing him down, knocking him off balance. Every shot took the haushedin in the same spot, slowly wearing down skin and skull. He finally brought up his hands to block, and she attacked with carapace bursting from her body. He swung at her, and she danced around the attacks.

He ducked his head and tore through her stony strikes, crashing into the back with her. Meaty hands lifted Sage by her throat, and she wrapped her legs around his arms. He slammed her against the wall over and over as she unloaded her pistol as fast as she could into the haushedin's face. Each time, her stony armor regrew slower. Each time, the strike rang her skull harder. Her vision spun, but her aim never wavered.

She knew she'd won when the haushedin pulled back to slam her again, only to pause, to stumble, arms shaking. Then he fell backward, and Sage landed crouched over his face. A black crater just above his right eye burned to the center of his skull; melted brains leaked out along with a stream of blood. Her own seeped beneath her clothes as it ran in rivulets down her neck. Somewhere along the line, she'd lost her fake mustache. Guess her disguise was up.

Panting, weary, and with blurry vision, she raised her pistol, ready to deal with the last two. They stared in awe, maybe even fright, as she grinned with a mouth of blood.

She shouldn't have done that. The birrosh panicked.

He raised the projectile launcher, and Sage dove for the seats. She heard the loud bang of the launcher, then the louder explosion as it tore the back from the shuttle. Kekar's air ripped at the insides, pulling corpses and weapons (and that one falvian guy) out in a flurry. Even the surprised tesing went flying down the aisle, yelling obscenities as she was hurled from the ship. Sage clung to the seats, but the metal screeched as cheap bolts came loose.

She gripped the belt fabric hard, winds tearing at her face, whipping her hair around in a frenzy. Her fingers ached without the help of her right arm to hold her in place, and she could feel her grip loosening.

Then the birrosh slid down the aisle, and she noticed the brown pack around his shoulders. Out he went, straight through the opening in the back. Sage made a quick calculation as the only parachute exited the shuttle, then leapt after him.

Wind battered her ears and eyes, and she squinted against tears as she searched for the birrosh man. When she found him, she tucked and dove, gaining speed and reaching his altitude. She could barely breathe in the thin atmosphere, her lungs screaming in protest. He turned and looked up at her just as they collided, panic blossoming in his eyes.

Her grip slipped as the man struggled against her, kicking and punching as she grappled. "Get over here, you dumb fuck!" she screeched, grabbing at his harness. Her legs swung around his waist, and she locked them in place with stony sediment acting as a glue. He panicked and wailed at her, fists falling on her armor to little effect. She grinned with manic fury as they crashed into the dark storm clouds that hovered above Kekar. That was his last sight of her before dying, their vision obscuring with the dark clouds, the electricity of the storm raising the hairs across her body.

Sage slammed her forehead into the birrosh's face, which was starting to become a signature move of hers, but it was quite effective. He grunted and batted her away with his fists, so she punched him with a reinforced hand, shattering the bones in one arm, then hit him in the ribs. His guard dropped as she hit him again, and this time she grabbed the birrosh by the back of the neck and brought him close. Sediment grew from her mouth in great fangs as she tore into his neck. Blood spewed out of her mouth as she spit the clump of meat and tendon free.

They burst from the storm cloud like a comet into a sea of rain, blood streaming from the wound at the dead birrosh's neck, splashing out like a comet's tail behind them. Sage was drenched. The water turned to crystals on her skin and clothes, and her body shivered uncontrollably, both from the weather and from the adrenaline pumping through her. She judged the distance and wondered if she could free the parachute and attach it to herself. Without a working arm, that seemed unlikely.

Instead, she poured her power into fusing them together with the stony carapace, sliding her injured right arm into the harness and tightening it hard. They became a ball of rock, crashing toward Kekar too fast, hail clinking off of them. She gripped the pull cord with her free arm, then readied herself. The storm made it difficult to time, too soon and it would tear the parachute away, too late and—

NOW!

She ripped it, and the parachute burst free and unfurled. Their fall jerked against the parachute's resistance. Her arm screamed in pain as it was twisted within the harness. Her momentum paused, then began increasing again. She looked up and watched as the hail tore new hole after new hole into the parachute.

"Shit."

She searched for a secondary pull cord and found none. She looked at the ground and found a lot of it. Then she did the only thing left for someone plummeting to her death. She encased herself in as much carapace as she could and hoped it would cushion the blow.

Sage's comet slammed into the ground with a crack, the casing exploding outward in shrapnel and dust. Hail rained down on the two bodies at the center of the new crater, one dead and one closer than she wished. Sage stared up at the roiling storm above her and dragged in ragged breaths. Her body shook beneath the onslaught of freezing temperatures and the crashing adrenaline. And something else. Shock. She could recognize it, but she couldn't battle it.

Her head turned slowly to the only part of her body not in deep pain. The arm caught in the harness of the parachute. She groaned and closed her eyes as everything threatened to overwhelm her. She took deep breaths, she focused on her goal, and she remembered Zetta. If that bitch wouldn't give up, why the void should she?

She opened her eyes, ready to face the wreckage of her arm. Shattered bone, splinters sticking up and out of the skin. Torn muscles and scoured flesh. She wondered how it hadn't been ripped completely free. She wished it had been. It would have made this a little easier.

Instead she grew carapace. One to fill her mouth, a block between her teeth. The other, a sharpened blade in her hand. She roared with the thunder as knife tore meat.

## Achtrek-Six

Achtrek-Six twitched, and a dozen eyes darted over their surroundings. Had to hold steady, had to hold the disguise. Perfect coordination. Until they made it through security. Selves crawled through the darkened spaces, watching for danger from all directions. Sensory information flooded the hive mind, and thousands of selves parsed through it in moments. A full awareness of the docking station and everyone around them.

No one looked Achtrek-Six's way. The air was free of scents of danger. At least anything that seemed directed their way. Many people had their heads low, collars around their necks blinking red. The hive had gotten passage on a slave ship to make it to Kekar. Cee had given them this route, assuming the others would be too sentimental to pass calmly. There was the added advantage that the slaves wallowed too deeply within themselves to focus on others, and the slavers focused more on the slaves than anyone else. Thus, Achtrek-Six survived the entire flight in disguise, nary a suspicion raised.

The shuttle opened to a station where armed guards directed arrivals into three paths. New arrivals, new slaves, and citizens. They slid into the much shorter line for new arrivals and watched the slaves being directed into their own line. Achtrek-Six wanted to stretch their wings, the anxiety causing every self to tense. Soon. Once through customs, they'd be able to fly freely through the city. The pulse Sage's Vico would send off aligned with their hearing range, and so as a loose cloud of bugs, it would take no time to find her. Once they were through.

The line crawled forward as one by one, the other arrivals were led into different rooms to be asked questions before being waved through or being enslaved if they answered incorrectly. Whatever peace these refugees sought, they would not find it here in this den of criminals.

"Next!" a tesing called, and Achtrek-Six stepped forward. The guide led them to a door at the end, and a single self detached at their "feet" to watch from outside. The other scouts crawled along the walls and ceiling, making their way toward the main hive's location.

Achtrek-Six stepped within, the bare room nothing more than a cube with a table at its center, two chairs facing each other on opposite sides.

"Have a seat, and your customs officer will be in shortly."

Achtrek-Six carefully followed the plans, sitting and acting as human as possible. They pulled a hand Vico from their satchel; these weren't as common as the wrist-mounted ones, but Achtrek-Six had never gotten the hang of holding those steady.

A few questions and they'd be through. They'd be free to spread their wings and taste the sky again.

Achtrek-Six waited.

There was a faint hiss, and several eyes glanced around. It was hardly audible, but they knew the sounds of compression when they heard them. The doors had sealed shut. Three selves from outside searched the cracks and found them impenetrable. A rattle of a vent began blowing air in behind and above Achtrek-Six. They carefully opened a pair of eyes to watch the vent. Two nozzles protruded from either side.

Achtrek-Six set a hand down on the table and found it, and the chair they sat on, made of a kind of wood from a tree grown on Perrilium. The air sucked the moisture from the wood, making it extremely dry. Very flammable.

The customs room was shifting into an execution chamber. The selves outside panicked, searching for a way around, crawling through the other rooms, seeking cracks to find whoever controlled this one. All in vain. Someone had anticipated a hive trying to reach Kekar in disguise and prepared for it.

Achtrek-Six's body shattered in the second before the flames spilled from the nozzle, the rising heat giving just enough warning a short few moments prior. It did not matter. Fire filled the room. The table and chairs crackled as the flames consumed them. Selves soared toward the nozzles and the vent, and electricity sparked out, killing those that made it in an instant. The only possible way out, the only possible way to stop the all-consuming fire, was guarded. Achtrek-Six's selves cracked and exploded beneath the extreme heat. In seconds they would be entirely dead. As the moments slipped, the hive's thoughts slowed, each loss bringing them closer to a point of no return.

The free selves panicked, attacking others around them in an effort to save the main hive. Achtrek-Six felt lost in their death. A base frenzy consumed them. They flew everywhere. They buzzed at every corner, every crack, searching for some safe zone. The liquid flames spewed across the room, hunting every one down. The temperature skyrocketed until even those avoiding the fire cracked under intense heat. There was no escape. The hive had lost their purpose, and they would not reunite with Mother.

At a certain point, the hive mind broke. Too few selves remained to sustain full sentience, and an understanding shattered away into primal behavior. In the sudden bliss of ignorance, survival instincts took over the panicked consciousness. The mind would not survive, but maybe the hive could live again. But a mother needed to live. It was the only available option.

The beetles swarmed the last remaining mother, crowding around her to create a protective shell. Layer after layer wrapped around the mother until it was too dense to stay afloat. The ball of bugs fell to the burning floor, and dozens screamed out as they were burned away. Hundreds continued to fly at that single mass, congregating together. The heat boiled their blood and melted their exoskeletons until they were one writhing mess.

Then everything darkened as death descended.

Their shared consciousness diminished, the only beetles alive were crawling amongst each other at the core of a ball of death. An overwhelming sense of death and pain consumed them, causing the flitting of wings and twitching of legs. But the selves held in their protective casings, and the mother lived as her children popped and cracked around her.

Achtrek-Six broke. There was a sense of belonging among the beetles that survived, but the being the hive had been no longer existed. Instead, thirteen beetles with a strange sense of awareness and a desire to be near certain other people would live on in search of belonging to something bigger. They escaped when the chamber opened for cleaning, the melted ball of the others breaking apart as they fled. The last of the beetles fluttered away from the room of death, joined by the few remaining scouts. Thirteen in all.

They searched for something they didn't understand. Searched for something they needed. Searched for the comfort of friendship and the hope for Home.

## Besari

The man's breath brushed against Besari's skin, and she pushed down an involuntary shudder. The lack of protection made her feel vulnerable after so long encased in her combat suit; a slathering of makeup on her cheeks was now all she could hide behind. She wanted to crawl back into her suit, away from everyone else. But she also wanted to arrive in disguise, and what better way to do that than remove a helmet you've told everyone you could never remove?

"You birrosh, girl?" The human man leaned down closer, squinting. He had a harsh look to him, especially in the eyes. A man accustomed to violence and death, oozing evil. Not like Wyn, who always seemed too soft.

"No," Besari said. "Can't you tell by the color of my skin?"

A separation between birrosh and bishett at a pivotal moment of evolution had produced several strange deviations in their biology. One of which was that birrosh had skin in warmer colors like reds, oranges, and yellows. For bishett, it was greens, blues, and purples. It typically made species identification simple. If you weren't an idiot anyway.

"You got some makeup on, it looks like," he grinned, showing surprisingly perfect teeth. Then he spit onto his thumb and ran it across her cheek.

Besari kicked the man in one knee, the pop loud and clear. He fell forward with a yell, and she grabbed him by the face, lifting him up and back as she pushed him across the shuttle's aisle and into the wall. Everyone in the shuttle rose, weapons drawn. Besari had a knife to his throat, a bead of blood dripping down the blade. He laughed, a manic look in his eyes, though sweat beaded his forehead.

"If you touch me again, I will cut off whatever part of you touches me," Besari said.

He still smiled at her. "Just had to check if maybe you weren't what you said you were."

"You think I painted my whole body green? For what purpose?"

The smile remained. Besari dropped him in the seat, and he grunted, both hands going to his dislocated knee. She returned to her seat and sat down, as did everyone else in the shuttle. The man still stared, still smiled.

"I thought bishett were supposed to be the more subdued ones," he said, and Besari ignored him. "Ain't you a little young?"

Besari's hand flew to her cheek before she could stop herself.

"I thought so," he said, then with a groan popped his knee back in place and leaned back with a sigh of relief.

Besari lowered her hand, breathing fast and unsteady. She needed her helmet, her protection. Or at least a bathroom to redo the makeup. She was vulnerable, and she hated it.

"Hey, bishett girl." The man leaned over on his armrest, and while Besari was distracted, he pulled a pistol free and casually swung it her way. She tensed. "I have this friend that was supposed to be on board. A birrosh actually, which is why you caught my eye. Thought maybe I had my skin colors mixed up."

"If I was your friend, would I not have recognized you? Or you me?"

"Sure, maybe. But I don't think she was expecting me." The gun paused its casual swing, the barrel focused on Besari. His smile disappeared, his gaze intensifying. "You don't happen to know a birrosh named Besari, do you?"

Besari's heart slammed inside her chest, but she steeled herself, refusing to give away her inner fear. "Who?"

He smiled big once more, then started laughing. "Stupid question, right?" He pulled himself into a better sitting position, grunting as he moved his leg. "That'd be like if you asked me if I knew a human named Wyn, right?"

Besari's fingers ached to grab at weapons. She wanted to skin the man. But what about everyone else? Were they with him, or were they bystanders? Besari leaned forward.

"If you continue to annoy me," she said in a careful whisper, choosing to seem unbothered by the names, "then I'll have to cut out your tongue."

Then she leaned back and turned away from the man, looking as though she were a calm sea. Inside, she was anything but, roiling with a storm of nervous energy. If they'd found her, who else had they found? Was anyone safe? Would Wyn be there when she arrived?

The man chuckled but didn't bother her anymore. Why didn't he just shoot her? If she made an error now, she would die. The only option was to continue with her ruse until she was safely (unsafely?) on Kekar.

This last stretch of the trip dragged the longest, nervous energy eating away at her insides as each moment passed. Every possibility ran through her head, filling her with madness. Eventually the shuttle rocked with the atmospheric entry.

She exited behind the now-limping man whose eyes scanned everyone but ignored her. He was searching for Besari and had found only a random bishett woman. *Girl* he had specifically called her. Again, one hand began to rise to her cheek, and she forced it down. Soon.

Armed guards, mostly thugs, directed the new arrivals through the terminal and towards customs. In a haze, she waited in line. They directed her into a room where a gorsaulk man asked her purpose.

"Work," she heard herself say. He scanned her Vico and waved her along after more questions. The process became a blur until something crunched beneath her boot, black and charred. She continued forward with a singular purpose. She needed to get away from everything. She needed to find somewhere to be alone. She needed to find the others. Everyone but Zetta and Cee should have arrived already.

She stepped out into the streets of Kekar's capital and came to a halt, breath caught in her throat. A massive tower stretched to the skies, a weather controller atop it pushing away the perpetual storm. Here, in the city (and the area around her could definitely be considered a vast city), there was no rain, no thunder. It was calm. And the buildings reached high, built with modern techniques. People walked the streets, most wearing collars, rushing about with various tasks. The rest had the look of thugs and villains.

This was not what she'd expected; their latest intelligence suggested ramshackle huts, not skyscrapers and office buildings. How many people were here? How had the resources for such growth been acquired without the R.C. learning? Sovereign had taken the prison planet and formed it into an actual civilization. Built on the backs of slaves, but built nonetheless. They hadn't banked on this level of technology, and that could be a problem.

But it was a problem they could work on together. She had other duties. She weaved between alleys and around buildings, taking random turns and watching behind her for the limping man or any other followers. No one looked her way, no one tracked her or chased her.

She took a breath and paused outside a bakery, the baker kneading dough within, a slave collar around his throat. Two patrons without collars sat at a table, eating pastries. Every small job was done by slaves, millions of them. And the R.C. had never noticed any of this. She wanted to save them but didn't know how. She *couldn't* right now. She needed to find a way to tell the confederation, to alert an authority that could do something.

People filled the streets, glancing her way, so she continued on, not wanting to draw any more attention to herself. She glanced at her Vico, the time reading three minutes to the next hour. So she ducked into an empty alley and waited. Waited for confirmation that the others were alive, that she wasn't truly alone.

She activated the beacon one minute before the hour hit. When she received no response for thirty minutes, Besari deactivated the beacon and sank to the ground. She was alone. Sage, Achtrek, and Wyn were likely dead. And she was trapped.

She rubbed at her eyes, the makeup on her cheeks smearing. Maybe they were delayed, maybe they haven't even arrived yet. She couldn't give up hope entirely. There were still Cee and Zetta. If Cee arrived, they still had an escape. She couldn't die on Kekar, alone.

She stood and began a search for a location that could work as a base.

## Zetta

Zetta woke to the sound of her own snoring. Or maybe it was the rattling of atmospheric entry that got her attention. Either way, her nap was over, and she was grumpy about it. On a planet with a perpetual storm, you'd think the residents would have fixed their damn shuttles to not rattle so much.

Zetta stretched, then stood up to work her legs and found the cabin empty. She could have sworn there had been one or twenty other people here earlier. She supposed her snoring must have sent them scattering. Sage always said her snoring burst eardrums and made babies the next town over wail. Where Sage got the babies to prove the latter, Zetta never found out.

She stepped out into the aisle between seats and looked at the door to the next segmented cabin. Then she slid away from it. Thunder boomed outside, and the shuttle rattled. Then she also slid sideways.

"Huh."

That wasn't a good sign. Shuttles didn't usually tip forward so much, then start spinning. That's what crashes did.

She clawed her way forward and ripped the door open. Rain and wind tore through the cabin and knocked Zetta backward. She hit the ground, then slid all the way to the back. Beyond, Kekar (or what she hoped was Kekar) spun, though all she could see were black storm clouds.

"That would explain the sliding," Zetta grumbled as she pulled herself up. Then a red alarm blared above the doorway, and a thick metal door coalesced over the opening.

"EMERGENCY. CABIN BREACH. PLEASE STRAP YOURSELVES IN AND PREPARE FOR A CRASH LAND-ING."

"What the fuck?" Zetta growled. "Now you come on?"

She spun and hammered at the back, but that door was firmly stuck closed as well. There were no windows either, as Kekar weather didn't approve of such a glaring weakness.

So, that left one more question. Had the shuttle been attacked and her cabin broken off from the main part? Or was someone trying to kill her? She guessed the latter and decided it would be best to disappoint them.

Geble flooded her veins with its wonderful juice, her muscles bulging in response. Claws on her feet dug into the metal of the floor, allowing her to stay steady with the help of her tail. She stepped slowly to her seat and retrieved her pack, only to find it missing.

"What?" She leaned down, scanning across the floors for any packs sliding around. There was nothing. Her claws dug into the cushion of the seat, anger seared her vision a bright red. "They stole my shit! My brand-new gauntlet!" Cee had helped make a new one, a beefier one, one she was *really* excited to use. And now it was fucking gone! Not only would she survive, but she was going to gut whoever had taken her precious toy.

Zetta refocused. She needed to escape first. The doors had reinforced when the alarm had sounded, making them a poor exit point. Similarly, the shuttle would want to reinforce its exposed areas, and given the way this shuttle worked with its train of cabins, that meant to the sides and below. The top, attached to the long spine of the ship, wouldn't need as much protection. So that would be the best route out.

Zetta jumped to grab the ceiling just as a boom sounded and the entire shuttle rocked into the thick of the storm. The ceiling spun away from her grip, and a wall slammed into her instead. Her claws dug into the side as centrifugal force hammered against her.

"Fuck the right way," she groaned. Then she pulled harder on the parasite until her skin threatened to tear, her muscles bulking to their extreme. Her claws tore into the side of the ship, peeling metal away like the skin of fruit. Until a claw snapped, and fuck if that didn't hurt like a bitch.

Her muscles could grow, but that didn't make anything else stronger. The shuttle rattled again, jerking one way then another, but her claws held her in place. With a discordant roar, she slammed her fist into the wall. Then she struck it again. And again. And again. Each time, she pulled a little more on Geble to enhance her strength. The skin on her arm ripped as the muscle engorged, far too large for the skin to withhold. Her knuckles ran red with blood as the same flesh that could withstand high-powered plasma tore away beneath her powerful assault. Still she hammered away. It helped to imagine the amorphous blob that was trying to kill her. They might not be an amorphous blob at that moment, but Zetta would make sure they'd look the part when she was done with them.

The wall cracked under another hit, and a whistling filled the cabin. Bloody prints were smeared across the wall, but she traced their path now to the crack that had opened. She slammed a thumb through the opening, pushing the metal back. The whistling grew louder as she looked out at a dark landscape. That meant she was out of the clouds, so not ideal. She tore at the hole, ripping chunks of the ship away to dig it larger and larger at the expense of her hands. Until...

"Ha!" Zetta pulled her head and most of her shoulders out of the shuttle and glanced around. It was definitely a single cabin, spinning vehemently toward its destruction. Zetta eyeballed the path and groaned. "You've got to be fucking kidding me."

A volcano. She was being dropped into an active volcano.

At least they hadn't underestimated her. But it did mean she needed to escape if she wanted to live. There was just the problem of there being no parachute. That left the hard way.

Zetta pulled herself back within and worked the hole. She needed it wide enough to fit through while heavily enhanced by Geble. She didn't want to risk losing her grip to get out faster. Fresh blood streamed down her arms as scabs broke beneath another burst of strength. One side effect of Geble's abilities was the faint buzz of numbness that ran across her open wounds. Blood wept down her body, but she barely felt the rips. That would change once she was done here, and she wasn't looking forward to that. So she focused her rage and ripped chunks of celuein from the wall. Her screams were sucked through the rent wall, leaving only the roar of wind.

She panted when it was done, her muscles exhausted, Geble pleading for a break. Not yet. Not if it wanted to live.

Zetta pulled herself out onto the surface of the shuttle, her claws forcing hand holds when none were available. The wind tore as hail pelted.

There was no time. She needed an alternative path. Water would be good, or maybe some really soft bedding. Unfortunately, there were no seas or houses in the area. She twisted her neck, studying the surrounding area as the cabin spun around like a leaf in a twister. It all moved too fast, was too far away. She could almost feel the heat of the lava boiling her skin.

Her muscles ached, and Geble struggled to keep up. She pulled on it anyway, holding herself steady and preparing. She would have to jump. It was just a matter of when.

"Ha!"

She had seen it in the glint of lightning, a pond to the northeast. Everything else was stone or lava, so she would have to make do. She grinned as she thought of the story she'd tell Sage. Who could jump without a parachute from a shuttle spinning toward oblivion and land without dying? Only the number one bounty hunter in the fucking galaxy.

She held herself steady, watching and waiting. Measuring the distance, pushing her muscles as far as they could go, then a little farther. Blood spiraled from her like petals caught in a breeze. She'd have one chance, and she'd have to time it with the shuttle spinning. Math had never been one of Zetta's strengths; she much preferred disemboweling. But she'd have to make it work this time. Plus, didn't her species have a natural understanding of geometry? It was called instinct. She tensed herself, and the time came.

With a manic grin, Zetta launched herself with the full force of her expanded muscles. The shuttle shot off in one direction, veering free from the volcano and slamming into the side of the mountain with a boom even she could hear. Zetta's body hurtled through the air in the opposite direction, rain and hail ripping at her exposed wounds, ribbons of blood trailing after her like some strange dance performance. The one with the ribbons? Whatever that was called. She never watched those. She practiced killing instead. Her eyes never left her target, that single little pond in the middle of nowhere. She curled herself into a ball and laughed as she watched it grow nearer.

Sage would never fucking believe this. No one would. She was the greatest fucking bounty hunter to live, and the asshole who'd tried to kill her would find that out personally. Her laughter turned maniacal as her imagination took over in that moment before her landing.

She missed the pond by thirty-four feet.

## Fleet Admiral Bevnil

Bevnil stood at the command deck of the second megalith-class fleet ship, the *Shard of Destiny*. Vision flooded through her left eye with an imperfect perfection, the cybernetic implant processing the world around her better than her own eyes ever had. She hated it, but it was that or nothing. Her eye had been unsalvageable after the attack. Her skull still ached from the scorch marks that fucking robot had given her, but today they reminded her of what was to come. They reminded her that vengeance was almost upon her.

Sovereign had been furious with her failure, and she only held her spot because she had been chosen by the Herald. None of her people would have accepted a replacement designated by Sovereign. Thank the Herald for these zealots.

And so she stood, in charge of a second fleet ship, preparing to kill the thing that had destroyed her pride, scarred her face, and stolen her fuckboy.

"Anything?" she grumbled.

"Not yet, sir."

The voice grated on her nerves. It was not the one she was used to. A lot of the faces were not what she was used to. Over seventy percent of her crew had been killed when the *Shard of Virtue* had torn itself apart. Families ripped out into the vacuum of space, good soldiers burned alive when the engines exploded. The sick left without a functioning medbay. So many lives had been taken by that metal monster. Today, she would give those lives peace. Today, Cee would die.

"Ship incoming, fleet admiral," the officer called.

"Description and intent?"

"Sentinel-class cargo vessel indicated as *Clank*. On a supply run to Kekar, bringing several vehicles."

"Scan it." She waved her hand and brought the display to the front screen. The vehicle looked decrepit. She would be surprised if it had functional life support systems.

"Clear."

"Tell them to proceed and give them the theta route to Kekar. When they're within range, use the secondary scanner." A wonderful gift from Sovereign, an advanced scanner that would penetrate whatever security the robot had and find the hidden signal. She watched as the freighter swung along the predetermined pathway and came within range.

"Signal confirmed."

Bevnil smiled. "Fire on my command."

"Weapons hot!"

Today was a day of peace and vengeance. "Fire."

The shuttle hit atmospheric entry, slowing as it struggled with the violent storms of the uncivilized regions. A moment later, every weapon within range fired on the freighter. Auto defense turrets, piloted scouts, security drones. Hundreds of missiles, thousands of lasers. Every weapon the *Shard of Destiny* and the *Shard of Ancestry* had. She would not risk anything escaping.

The projectiles converged, and the ensuing explosion tore apart the storm clouds below. The ball of light held steady for several seconds, and she could almost feel the reverberations of the explosion. Her glee became manic as it deteriorated, and she stared down at the hole to Kekar. Then the storm clouds closed up the wound, and it was done. That dreadful robot was dead.

"Another shuttle, sir."

Bevnil pulled herself from the reverie and looked to the officer. "What? No more are expected today."

"They have a valid code."

"Intent?"

"They claim to be a bounty hunter on a job for Sovereign."

His little pet? "It doesn't matter. Let it pass. Our victory is complete."

The bridge cheered with excitement, families and friends avenged. She would rebuild the *Shard of Virtue*, and she would rebuild the Herald's Aspect. Under Sovereign, they would take over Haush and rule it rightfully, as the Herald wished.

## Wyn

The *Crimson Ghost* slipped past the defensive structure around Kekar, Wyn's makeshift story seemingly accepted.

"Do you really believe that?" Tom asked.

"Shut up," Wyn said.

"I didn't say anything," growled the birrosh woman, her name apparently Forenta. She remained restrained, but Wyn thought she might like some company and had moved her to the cockpit. She had not been very pleasant company, but it had given Wyn the chance to apologize for what he'd done and explain that she would get the ship back soon.

"Sorry, I didn't mean you."

"Who else could you possibly mean?"

Wyn waved away the nothing slug. "It's a long story. Just forget I said anything. I need to concentrate on the landing."

"Concentrate? They practically gave you the path down. What's there to concentrate on?"

"This is only my second time landing a ship," Wyn said.

"What?" Forenta leaned forward in her chair, her wrists straining at the binds that held them against it.

"At least this one's all in one piece." Wyn laughed. Forenta didn't.

"I swear to whatever deity you worship, I will rip your fucking intestines out of your ass if you so much as put a scratch on this ship."

"At least you have the funds to fix whatever happens!" Wyn chuckled nervously, then looked over at the birrosh and swallowed. Her eyes were hot coals burning their way through Wyn. "Well, listen, this wouldn't have been a problem if you had just cooperated. You could be landing it."

"You're going to blame me? You hijacked my ship and tied me to my chair, but it's my fault you don't know how to land?"

"No, of course not. That's not it at all. Listen, I just really need to get to Kekar."

"Feel free to hop out whenever you want."

"Need to get here *alive*."

"Aim for a pond."

Wyn sighed. "It'll all be over soon. I'm very sorry for all of this."

"Mmhmm."

She continued to glare daggers into Wyn's soul, and he reminded himself of the same thing: only a little longer.

"I think she's mad," Tom said.

Wyn refrained from responding this time.

His trip to Kekar had been long and circumspect. He'd only had access to one gate available that would work for his purposes. The same one Cee was supposedly going to use. It didn't require activation, and it didn't require a shuttle ride. He could fly in, state his business, and hopefully pass on to the main city. Unfortunately it had taken him longer to sneak by any Raiyrium checkpoints, and so he was arriving two days late. Hopefully it was still before Cee and he would be able to meet up with everyone.

"What is that?" Forenta mumbled.

Wyn, pulled from his own inward thoughts, looked out over the horizon to the break in clouds. "That's not possible."

Kekar's perpetual storm had a crack, and it stretched out in every direction for thirty or more miles. At its center, a massive tower sprouted from the ground, a weather control at its tip sending blue pulses into the sky. Wyn had to imagine the technology somehow held back the clouds. Which left the cityscape below visible to him and Forenta.

The sprawl was significant, and several buildings reached a dozen or more stories into the sky. Scanners reported a vast amount of traffic, both on foot and in the sky. It was as populous as anywhere in the Raiyrium Confederation and probably more populous than many member planets. Wyn had expected makeshift huts, not an entire functioning city.

Shuttle traffic was light for its size, but that was probably due to the fact that there shouldn't even be *any* shuttles flying around Kekar space. Only three shuttles traversed the airspace, one of which rose up from the top of that massive tower. The *Crimson Ghost* was the only shuttle landing just then.

"I heard rumors there was a city on Kekar, but this is incredible," Forenta said.

"It shouldn't exist," Wyn said. "How does it exist?"

"Prisoners got bored and built a society."

Wyn doubted that. There had to be more to it. It had to be Sovereign. He funded everything here, had built a society out of the most ruthless people in the galaxy. Now it was up to Bounty Inc. to stop him.

Wyn guided the *Crimson Ghost* to Kekar's bustling port and landed in the private hangars away from the shuttles. He landed the shuttle perfectly, or rather, the shuttle did most of the heavy lifting and he only needed to make a few adjustments. The struts settled in, and he shut down the engines.

"I'm going to need to knock you out again. Just for an hour or so," Wyn said as he pulled a needle from his pack. He'd transferred everything crucial to the single pack so he could travel light. He figured Forenta could keep the suitcase.

"Did you even measure that out?" She leaned away from the needle, eyes wide. "How do I know that's not going to kill me?"

Wyn looked at the syringe and pointed at a hashmark. "It was marked here to be safe for most species."

"Most?"

"My birrosh friend says your species is sturdy." Wyn paused for a second, then convinced himself as much as her. "I'm sure you're one of the safe ones. I'm guessing that's just for the tiny ones."

"Listen. Just untie me. We part ways, and I can leave happily and not risk death."

Wyn considered but figured it would be too risky. "Sorry."

She jerked back from the needle. "Wait! Wait!" He waited. "If you stab me with that fucking needle, I'll tell everyone about you?"

"What are you going to tell them? That someone snuck onto Kekar?"

"And your name, Iolas. I have your name."

"That's not my name." Wyn stabbed the needle into the woman's neck, and the auto-injector activated. She yelled out, then her words became a slurry mess, though Wyn could still pick out most of the insults. Then she fell unconscious. He really hoped its effects wouldn't be too severe. He already felt drained from the guilt.

Once he was sure she was out, he unwound the cabling and returned it to a thigh pouch, collected his pack, and exited the ship. A port guard with a thin collar around his neck was waiting for him at the base of the landing ramp.

"I'll need some registration and a docking payment of three hundred raikers or whatever your equivalent currency is," the lean man said, scratching at his beard.

"Oh, sorry," Wyn said. "I'm just a passenger. The ship's owner will be out in a bit, just wrapping up some maintenance stuff inside."

The man stopped scratching his beard, then sighed. "Fine, but I'll have to put the gravity locks on until it's paid."

Wyn shrugged. "That's—"

A plasma bolt hit the ground near him, and the port officer yelled and dove for cover. Wyn raced through the dock, ducking around heavy equipment, an array of plasma bolts chasing him down. Forenta stood at the top of the landing ramp, a pistol in her wobbly grip, a grimace on her face. Instead of intervening, many of the people at the port either cowered or cheered at the violence. Wyn wasted no time running into the crowded halls. He didn't know how the birrosh woman was awake, but she was in no shape to give chase, and the farther away he got, the better. Hopefully she wouldn't be killed.

Wyn slipped into the bustling traffic outside and quickly joined the flow heading away from the port. He checked his Vico and, finding the time nearly at the hour, activated the beacon in the hope that someone would be able to reach him. Then his gaze lifted to stare at the world around him in awe, at the perfectly functioning city. This was supposed to be a prison. How had Sovereign built this place? He got his answer with a rather large boom.

Pistol drawn, he turned toward the sound, everyone around him cowering with hands to their necks. A headless corpse lay on the side of the street, a human man standing over it. Kicking it.

"Hey!" Wyn rushed over, all eyes staring at him. "What in the void are you doing?"

The man paused from beating the corpse to stare at him. His eyes flicked to Wyn's neck, then back up. "What's it to you what I do with a fucking slave? Not like we can't find another one."

Wyn glanced down at the growing pool of blood seeping out onto the streets. Then looked at the cowering people around him, each with a collar and a red beeping light. Slaves. They used slaves to build the city so the thugs could live in comfort. Wyn felt bile at the back of his throat.

"You two," the man shouted at a pair of slaves. "Clean this fucking mess up."

Wyn stepped back in horror, then turned.

"Yeah, run away, bitch," the man shouted at him with a cackle. "Not gonna be long before someone straps one of these on you."

Wyn's hand shook and he turned back, teeth gritted. The man had his own Vico out, hand hovering, and he smiled at Wyn.

"Raise that little toy gun of yours, and I'll kill a dozen slaves right here."

"You're a coward," Wyn growled.

"You're too afraid to see the truth of the future. The strong survive, the weak work."

"This is troubling," Tom said from Wyn's shoulder. "You're not very strong."

"Shut up!" Wyn shouted, to both and neither. He needed to capture Sovereign, make him pay for the horrors he'd inflicted. These people needed to be rescued.

"You're testing me, kid," the man growled. "Get the fuck out of here."

Wyn holstered his pistol and stepped back, his guts roiling with anger. But he needed to focus it. Channel it toward his goal.

The walls on the streets flickered, pulling Wyn's attention upwards, as it did with everyone else's. Large displays appeared all up and down the buildings, a man's face materializing. He was human, and he looked regal. Straight-backed, muscular, with a jawbone that made others tremble. Dark, short hair hung around his ears, and piercing golden eyes peered out as if to see everything in the city. Even as a hologram, the man provoked a deep fear within Wyn. This was Sovereign. This was his enemy.

"Greetings, Kekar," he called, and the audio echoed all down the streets, overriding casual conversations with brutal intensity. "It has come to my intention that your home is under attack by a group of terrorists who despise what we stand for. The Raiyrium Confederation, in their bold stupidity, has launched an attack on our fair city."

Wyn's blood went cold, and his second hand went for the second pistol. Had the others been caught? Were they...

"This attack is not one of ships and might. You need not fear for your lives. No, it takes the shape of a small strike force with which they wish to topple your Sovereign. They desire to cut off the head of our unstoppable force and hope you will flounder after. But you would not. I have taught you better than that. And I *will not* fall to their schemes. Six bounty hunters have been tasked with taking my head."

Fuck.

"They wish to tear down your haven! Rip away the one free safehold from Raiyrium's control! Will you let them take away your lives? Take away your homes?"

Cheers of excitement ran down the streets, more than Wyn had hoped to hear. He gritted his teeth and took a step back. The crowd around him had stopped moving, everyone staring up at Sovereign.

"I have an opportunity for those among you who wish to rise up in life." The image of Sovereign faded and in its place six headshots appeared on screen in two rows of three. Wyn's guts clenched, and he nearly vomited. "These are your enemies. They hide among you now, so search the crowds you wander through, search the buildings and alleyways. Leave no building unchecked. Find these people, and bring me their heads. If you are free, I offer you one million credits for each head and a place among my personal employ. If you are a slave, I offer you freedom and the choice of money and employment or a flight home. Seek the future you desire!"

The audio disappeared, and the streets were silent. But the images of Wyn and the others stayed in place. Sovereign knew of their plans, knew their faces. Someone had to have been captured. Were they dead? What if—

Wyn's attention returned to the ground, and he found the entire crowd staring at him, forming a circle. He smiled. "Um, weird, that picture kinda looks like me, but it's—"

"I'm about to be a rather wealthy individual," the man said.

Wyn shot, wasting no more time. And the man dodged the shots, moving at such speeds, Wyn's eyes could barely follow. A Thresha user. Not ideal.

As Wyn backpedaled into the crowds, hands reached for him and snagged him, pulling him to the ground. Crazed eyes stared at him with demented hope. They yelled for freedom, for their future, as they tore at him. Wyn flung his arms out, knocking them back, but they kept coming. For every person he pushed away, three more surged onto him. It was a sea of hands feasting at his body no matter how he moved.

Then he was bathed in a bloody rain as every collar within grasping range exploded. Wyn gasped as the blood smothered his face and hair, coating everything he owned. Rivulets ran down the neck of his armor into the clothing beneath. The surviving slaves cried out and backed away. Wyn spit the blood from his mouth and rubbed at his eyes. The speedy man stood over him, a large machete in one hand.

"This one's mine," he said. Then the machete came down.

Wyn felt more blood splash over his face as the man's entire upper body was eviscerated. The corpse collapsed in a pile of melted and goo-ified innards and a pool of blood. Wyn had never seen quite so much blood. He hoped he never would again.

He jumped to his feet as a green bishett woman walked through the crowd of slaves. She wore black robes, a scatter gun held out, pointed at Wyn.

"He's mine," she called out to those around them. "Anyone wants to try for him, you'll end up the same."

No one moved except for the bishett woman. Wyn smiled and held his hands up, pistols still somehow in them. He probably should have holstered those.

"Listen, I—"

"Shut up," the bishett said and grabbed his collar. Then she leaned forward and harshly whispered, "Move it, before more come."

Wyn holstered his pistols and moved where the woman pointed him. She fired a few times to scare off those behind her as they ran through an alley and away from the crowd. Good. He might be able to handle her one-on-one, so he'd play along until they were alone. Then he'd try to take her. He was going to die anyway; he should at least go down swinging.

The bishett kicked open the door to an office building, and the two of them rushed inside. It was empty, either new or unneeded, and the woman led Wyn quickly to an office, shoving him inside before turning back to check for pursuit.

She was an amateur. When she turned after closing the door, Wyn grabbed the scattergun, causing it to fire into the nearby table, then quickly broke her grip on it with a technique Besari had taught him. He swept her legs, then came down on top of the toppling bishett, a look of surprise on her face.

She was more surprised as he shoved one of his pistols up against her skull. "Give me a reason not to pull the trigger," he growled.

Her brow crinkled beneath the ripples that ran along her scalp, emerald eyes searching his. "Wyn..." she said in a hauntingly familiar voice.

Wyn's eyes widened, and he pulled the gun away. Threw it away to skitter across the room. His hands shook in anticipation as he stared down at the woman he was straddling. "Besari?"

She smiled and sighed. "Yes. I've been so worried searching for you."

Wyn's eyes searched the face of the woman he had tried to imagine so many times before. "Why are you green?"

Besari's eyes widened, and she looked away sheepishly. "I'm not a birrosh," she mumbled. "I'm actually a bishett."

"You're beautiful," Wyn whispered. Besari stared back at Wyn, her cheeks darkening. He wasn't sure who moved first, but their lips interlocked in a passionate kiss. Also, a disturbingly bloody one. Wyn broke it off and wiped at his mouth, cheeks flaming. "Sorry, that was probably gross."

"I don't care." Besari's hands caressed Wyn's face. "I've been wanting to do that for a long time." Then she pulled him into another kiss, and Wyn held that one.

# WANTED

MIARAIM

THE SHADOW

REWARD:
Ⓡ550,000

I n its earliest days, the tesing species had gazed up into the night sky, dreaming of reaching beyond. They colonized their moons, and when they unlocked the skipper drive, their planets soon followed. As a populous species, they were unafraid of losses made for the greater good, and so they took the skippers to other systems. Their fingers spread all the more quickly once gateways were established.

Within the second tesing-colonized system was a rather large planet that had once been rich in resources long since depleted. Neiros was its name, and its grandest city was called Bexcata. Some said it rivaled even the cities on the tesings' home planet of Amethema. It was a city fit for the wealthy and the poor, as long as they weren't too near each other. The wealthy solved this with massive towers, sky bridges weaving a web between them so they would never have to stoop so low as to walk among the poor. But life in those towers had been rather bland, so they say, and soon the wealthy had built their own gardens and parks, until the lower city was nearly encased in a shell, only the barest sliver of light sneaking through from cracks far above.

Sickly saffron light flickered from dying streetlamps, filling alleys with a crackling illumination. Shellesh crept through the dancing shadows, hood pulled tight to hide his face. Disgust hollowed a pit in his stomach as he looked around, as he remembered a time above the dome where the world was perfect. Where the poor were something everyone talked about with worry, but life proceeded to get in the way before anyone could do anything to help. Had he been so selfish? Had he been so appalling? Perhaps he deserved his exile for those reasons, but that was not why he was exiled.

Shellesh ducked his head as a group of people walked by, cheerful discussions pricking at his ears. A distortion of what he felt in his own chest. How did they find time for happiness when there were those who took their sun away? He was in a sullen mood. There were plenty who sat around, emaciated and homeless. Not that there was a lack of homes available, as long as you weren't caught where you didn't belong. What right did he have to judge those who could find happiness down here?

Wide eyes watched him pass, begging hands reaching out toward him. He kept his own hands tucked within pockets, his own face hidden in the shadows of his hood. If any had seen his skin, they had not confronted him about it. It was, of course, illegal for an exile to step on tesing land, to breathe tesing air, to speak in the presence of another tesing. He would be killed if they caught him. If they *could* catch him.

Half-finished repairs held up bowing walls, and windows were covered in clear sheets or welded over with metal. Cables spread across the city like dead serpents, splicing into the electricity of the wealthy. They would be removed eventually, and it was usually best to not be around when they were. One man reached out with a ru-ined arm as he begged, showing the signs of the electrical burns that were the penalty for energy theft. Other bodies lay in the squalor, sleeping or dead.

It all made him sick. Angry. A flame burned within him, and at its heart was a single woman. Any love and loyalty to his people had died long ago, before his exile, before he had lost everything. It was an empire of rot and corruption, one he would gladly tear down if given the chance. But he would never have that chance, not as he was. His revolution had already failed.

But he would at least rectify his own life before the final sleep took him.

A hand grabbed Shellesh's shoulder and spun him. Two other thugs popped out of their own shadows to surround him. "Hey, olo," the hand's owner growled. "You step through our turf, you pay a toll."

Shellesh kept his gaze lowered. They hadn't seen his skin, but as he peeked up at the thugs, he saw their confusion. They'd expected to feel his fear, to see Shellesh cower from their malice. Instead, they felt an emptiness of emotion. So, Shellesh lifted his head and glared into the eyes of the maroon-colored thug wielding a knife.

"If you wish to keep that hand, remove it," Shellesh said, letting his voice wash over them, letting them hear the gravelly remains of his vocal cords, a courtesy of the acid baths.

"Fuck!" The man recoiled, releasing Shellesh and stepping back. The others surely felt his disgust wash out. "It's a fucking exile!"

Emotions flooded from all three. Confusion, hatred, disgust, fear. They all tensed, readying their own blades. Shellesh glanced at the other two, letting them see his pallid skin and confirm for themselves. One was a tall, pink man, the other a stocky, golden woman. Emotions intensified when their eyes met.

The woman spat at his feet, and the man scowled as he spoke. "Gutless, too. He's come crawling home. How dare you taste our air. Speak in our—"

"Choose your words carefully," Shellesh warned, and a blade flashed into one hand. The thugs jumped back, knives held at the ready, their fear radiating from them. "Or I'll take your tongue."

"Fuck you," the pink man said.

The thugs were used to picking on the weak, using their healthy weight as an advantage. Shellesh had honed himself to be a weapon since he'd been a child. His only purpose had been as a soldier, a purpose waylaid for a short time by a desire to be a father and a husband. But he'd never lost his edge and had shifted into the bounty hunting life easily enough.

The pink thug hadn't even finished speaking before his wrist snapped. The knife fell to the ground with a clatter as Shellesh's own pulled short of impaling him through the neck. The others jumped back again, their own weapons shaking. Now he felt only pure terror. Strong enough to kill their prejudice.

"Would you like to end today dead or alive?"

Afraid to even cradle his own limp wrist, the pink thug whimpered. When he spoke, it was in a small, squeaky voice. "Alive."

Shellesh pulled the knife away and felt a hint of relief ripple through the man's emotions. It didn't last long as Shellesh slammed a palm against the man's knee, buckling it backwards and dropping him to the ground with a scream of pain.

The others jumped forward, but Shellesh turned with weapon raised, and they halted. "Then your friends better find you a healer quickly. Don't want that to go untreated for long." He focused on the other two, their eyes wide to match the fear wafting off them. "If either of you follow me, I'll kill you. Understand?"

They nodded, and Shellesh pocketed his knife. He pulled the hood more firmly over his head and returned his hands to his pockets as he left them behind. The maroon man and golden woman rushed to their friend and propped him up, a new sense of worry slipping into their fear. They cared for each other, just not anyone else. This was a hard place to find even that. A symptom of the rot that started at the head. Shellesh spit on the cursed land. He wouldn't be here, given any other choice.

He paused at a door of swollen wood, a corner jutting outward, no longer closing as tight as it once had. His heart twisted with unexpected pain. The door groaned as he pulled it free from the frame, opening to a corridor with room to either side and a hallway at the end. Memory caught Shellesh unaware, crashing into his mind and flooding him with emotions he could no longer share.

*Shellesh jostled a door open with his hip, opening to a corridor, one room on the right and a window to the left. An arrow of sunlight bled through it, washing the corridor in a golden hue. The walls were painted with a gorgeous mural depicting the many generations of his family. Already, an additional face was added near Shellesh's own, a vibrant purple, a perfect mix between his and Mia's.*

*The mural's latest subject squirmed in Shellesh's arms, tiny hands reaching out, eyes barely opening as he gurgled. Shellesh stared down at his son, warmth flooding through him. This was his purpose, a child who could better the world. He had never been happier than when he and Mia had agreed to end their old life and start a new one.*

*Shellesh handed the child a chewstick, and his tiny hands curled around the base. Soon he began sucking and gumming the soft end. Sleepy eyes closed again.*

*"Shellesh, is that you?" the melodious voice of his mother called out. Shellesh followed it to a nearby room and found her sitting in a chair, her fingers weaving fibers in complex patterns, a blanket forming in front of her.*

*"Yes, Mother." His own voice was a smooth dulcet, a voice many others had craved him for.*

*She perked up at his entrance, eyes widening with delight. She set the partial blanket to the side and pulled herself to her feet. "Thank the skies! His coloring is so beautiful." She waggled a finger in front of the baby, his tiny hands dropping the chewstick to reach for it. "What have you named him?"*

*"Taiviat."*

"Barging in will get you killed." That same melodious voice spoke, barely dulled by the passing years. Shellesh looked up to see his mother training a scattergun on him. The walls of the corridor were peeling white, the mural never recreated in this new home. There were no windows, for what was there to look out at but the dirty streets. It just meant more entrances to protect from the greedy and the desperate.

"You should lock your door," Shellesh said.

Her eyes widened as she finally caught a glimpse of him, as she finally recognized his voice. Shock radiated out from her, as did a deep, painful sadness. Tears formed in her eyes when she spoke. "Shellesh?"

Memories had a way of tearing the scabs of his heart away, of reopening wounds long thought closed. Of bleeding pain into his chest he was not prepared for. He would use it for what was to come.

"Yes, Mother."

"Then you're a buried fool!" She dropped the gun and glared at him. "How dare you step on tesing soil? Was getting your mother banned to the undercity not enough? Must you get her killed too?"

Her words stung, but her emotions softened them. There was joy and sadness buried deep under overwhelming fear. Not for herself, of course. For him. She did not want to see him die.

"I have a duty, Mother."

Her features grew less harsh, as did her voice. "She's here?"

"Yes."

"You should not have come." She dropped the scattergun on a small table and leaned against it. She looked exhausted. She looked old. Another thing that had been torn from him. "You should leave."

"I cannot."

"It's been seventeen years, Shellesh." She sighed. "Return to wherever you've been. Find what peace you can, and move on with your life. Find friends, find something to help with that void in your heart. Don't do this."

"Who would befriend an exile, Mother? Not even my own siblings speak to me. Why would strangers?"

His mother looked away, a dozen sentences evaporating from her lips without a sound. Countless emotions washed over him, a mixture of his and hers. "You'll die, Shell."

"I've already died, Mother. My body just hasn't stopped yet."

She suppressed her emotions, and the loss of it nearly sent him to his knees. Her eyes hardened as she avoided looking at him. She said nothing.

"Do you still have it?"

This brought her gaze back to him. "Are you planning to get that close to her?"

"She's in the upper city. I might have to. There's no guarantee of a clean shot, no matter what tower she's in."

She stared a moment longer before exhaling slowly. "Stay there," she said, then hobbled off. She had a new limp, favoring one knee. Was it from old age? Or had something happened?

When she returned, she carried a rectangular hilt with a long crossguard and no blade. "I don't know how well it will work," she admitted. "It hasn't been used for seventeen years."

"It will work fine." He grabbed for the hilt, but her hands held firm.

"Why now?" she asked. "After all these years, you never once returned for this weapon. Why now?"

"She proposed to me with that weapon as a gift. It only feels right to return it."

"You won't take the shot, will you?" Through her eyes, he saw the sadness she suppressed within, still refusing to share her emotions with him. "Even if it's safer, even if it means you'll live, you'd rather meet her face to face."

"I will take the shot if I have it, Mother."

Her tears fell then as her grip loosened on the hilt. "I am sorry for you, Shellesh. I hope you find your peace."

"Me too," he said as he tucked the hilt into a pocket. "Goodbye, Mother."

"Goodbye."

Shellesh turned and stepped back out into the darkened undercity. The door slammed against the poor-fitting frame. Then the door opened again.

"Shellesh!"

He stopped.

"The door is a little jammed," she said. "If you have time when you're done, it could use a little fixing. I'll make telm, and you can tell me about what you've been up to. We haven't had a day like that in a long while."

Tears brimmed at Shellesh's eyes as emotions overwhelmed him. The dams he had built over seventeen hard years crumbled beneath his mother's words. "Yes, Mother," he said with a quivering voice.

Then he left before his tears could fall.

A harsh wind tugged Shellesh's hood loose as lazy clouds drifted by, obscuring the stars and two of Neiros's moons. Shellesh pulled the hood back in place as he hunched in the shadows on the roof of one tower. The top six levels of the opposing tower shone like a beacon in the surrounding night, the silhouettes of hundreds of dancing bodies flashing across the windows. They came into sharp contrast as he studied the gathering through the sights of his sniper.

He scanned each floor, and failing to find what he wanted, he set the rifle down. He pulled his jacket tighter as the warmth fled his body like water through a sieve. Tesings never had handled chilly weather well, and Shellesh had become so much worse with it since the exiling. Since the acid bath. The heating units flared within his jacket, flooding his body with warmth to combat the chill.

Within the gala, the rich partied while the poor needed to steal their electricity, hopping between abandoned homes to avoid being arrested or beaten. Shellesh gritted his teeth against more than just the cold.

*"They're scum." Miaraim scowled, her voice a harsh whisper as she shut the door behind herself. Her dark eyes lit beneath the fire of her passion, stark against her otherwise midnight skin. Now that Taiviat*

slept, she wasted no time picking the conversation back up. "You've seen the undercity, Shell. These parasites feast on the rot while the people suffer. They deserve to die."

"I don't disagree, Mia." Shellesh kept his own voice level. Calm. Her emotions felt like a dam close to bursting as she held back as much as she could to avoid bothering their child. Shellesh poured out his own emotions of assurance, hoping to smother whatever she couldn't hide. "But we have more to think about than the undercity. We don't live there. We live here. With our son."

"You speak like a politician," she spat. "With your wishes to help, if only you could."

"We can't."

"We can. Like the old days." Miaraim grabbed his hands. "We can make a difference in this society."

"There's a right way and a wrong way, Mia."

She dropped his hands. "You're going to start being virtuous? We didn't meet in a bar, Shell. Your hands are as dirty as mine."

"I'm not arguing against it morally, Mia. We have a kid. What happens if they catch you? What happens if someone tracks you to this house? You'd be putting Tai in danger." Shellesh took a deep breath and grabbed Mia's hands. She didn't pull away. "Please, Mia. Assassination is a dangerous path. You can't stay on it. I've started working private security. I can get you a job. We can have a stable life while we raise our son, then we can advocate for the undercity."

"Advocate?" Her expression was pained, as if Shellesh had just slapped her. "Shall we hand out fliers on the corner? Maybe shout a few times? How do you expect to advocate, Shellesh?"

"I don't know, Mia. But we can't advocate if we're dead. I'd rather live a peaceful life with our family than die for a cause that barely affects us. We live in the uppercity, not the undercity."

*Miaraim pulled away again, turning. Waves of pain and sadness and guilt struck him. He was about to speak when the door opened.*

*"Mommy?"*

*The emotions dissipated in an instant. She swooped down with a big smile and picked up the small boy. Love trickled from her and Shellesh could almost feel the effort to hold everything else back.*

*"Now, Tai, what are you doing up?" she asked, poking the boy's nose. He giggled and swatted her finger away.*

*"I thought I heard voices. And felt things." Taiviat's face scrunched up as he searched for words. "Not good things. They made me sad."*

*"It's okay, Tai," Miaraim said as she ran a hand across his forehead and down his neck. "Mommy and daddy were just discussing important things. Adult things, and sometimes they make us sad too. But we're done with that for now. Right, Shell?"*

*Her eyes pleaded with him, and he felt an outpouring of assurance from her. She would drop the contract. Whatever offer she had, she would drop it. He smiled. "Of course," he said and ran his own hand along Taiviat's back. "We've figured it out now, so there's nothing to worry about."*

A silhouette ghosted against the windows, and Shellesh recognized her immediately, even as nothing more than a shadow. He grabbed the rifle and took position. Miaraim snapped into focus as he brought the sights to bear. Emotion cracked his chest open. Seventeen long years, and here she stood. A politician on one arm as she talked with two others. He willed his hands to still, to stop the rifle's shaking as his heart thundered in his ears. Anger overwhelmed him until the scene bled red.

One shot. It was a slag round that should drill through most energy barriers. Security in these towers had never been the highest.

He didn't expect the Liril Tower to have anything strong enough to stop the shot.

One shot and she would be dead.

One shot and he could die.

One shot to end it all.

His finger quivered over the trigger, and Mia turned to look out the window. Her eyes rose until they were even with Shellesh's position. He fell still, his breath catching in his ribs. He was too far away, it was too dark, he shouldn't be visible. And yet...

Her eyes found his, and she smiled. Then she waved.

Shellesh dropped the rifle and stepped back into the shadows. He dragged in panicked breaths as his heart pounded in turmoil. She knew he would be here. She had prepared. The shot was useless. He would need to get close and make sure his strike would pierce every defense. He needed to guarantee her death.

Or did she only want him to think that way to get him caught by security? It would be too much to think her guilt had gotten the best of her and she wanted to die.

It didn't matter. Today, she would take her last breath.

He checked the window and found her missing now. But she was on the top floor. Of course she would be there. Whoever her target was, it wouldn't have been someone insignificant. It never was. She never knew when to stop.

Shellesh gritted his teeth, then he left, abandoning the rifle.


"This is a private event." Two bulky guards stood in front of the door, one raising a hand to stop Shellesh's approach. He looked up at them and felt the waves of fear. They jumped for their guns, Shellesh did not.

He drove a fist into the throat of one and grabbed the hand of the other. In a quick snap, he broke the man's wrist, and the pistol clattered to the ground. He tried to scream, but Shellesh muffled it with an elbow to the jaw. The guard dropped to the ground, unconscious.

The first man recovered, a stunstick baton sparking in one hand. He swung it like a bat. Inexperienced. A wild and panicked assault. Shellesh ducked, then struck him in the ribs. The guard curled forward and swung again. Shellesh grabbed the arm, and a quick jab of his palm inverted the bend of the man's elbow. He would have hollered as well if Shellesh had not driven his skull into the metal door behind him. The body fell limp to the ground.

Shellesh grabbed the handle of the door and stepped within.

*Miaraim burst through the door. Shellesh felt her terror before he saw it in her face. Something was wrong. He felt his hand searching at his hip for a weapon that had not sat there for years.*

*"Mom?" Taiviat jumped up from the floor, where he had been sitting opposite Shellesh, a children's game between them. Tears sprang to his eyes, and when Mia saw them, her emotions shut down.*

*"Tai, hi, sweetie." Mia dipped down and hugged their son with one arm, the other held to the side. The scent of blood filled the air.*

*"Mia, what—" Shellesh asked, but she interrupted.*

*"We need to go on a little trip," she said, pulling away from Tai. "Let's grab a few necessities. I have a way off planet."*

*She pulled Tai to his room and told him to hurry with grabbing what he needed. Shellesh was there in an instant, a boiling heat burning behind iron gates. The intensity leaked through despite his every effort. She looked up with tears on her cheeks as she felt his anger.*

*"What have you done?"*

*"What was right." She pushed past him and hurried into their bedroom. Shellesh followed, a panic building within him. She opened their closet and drilled one elbow into the wall at the back. It cracked open, and she pulled the thin wood apart. Within, weapons lined the wall. She started with the duffel bag at the bottom, tossing it onto the bed. "This should be everything we need for—"*

*"What have you done?"*

*She spun, her own anger matching his. "Be angry later, Shell. We have to move." She grabbed a pistol and tossed it to him. He caught it, feeling the cold metal burning into his palm, and he dropped it to the ground.*

*"No." He wasn't sure how much of his words he could trust. This was what he had brought up so long ago. This was the danger she brought to their home. She'd never given it up. She'd never stopped killing.*

*Miaraim paused from her packing to stare at him. Panic fell into the stream of emotions that roiled between them. "I screwed up, Shellesh. I know that. I thought I could make things better for the world, for us."*

*"You brought violence to our door. How is this better?"*

*"Berate me later! Leave me behind! I don't care, but just listen to me, Shellesh! Come with me so we live long enough for you to do either."*

*"Mom?" Tai called. "Dad? I think someone's outside."*

*Shellesh turned. The voice came from the entrance hall, not his room. "Tai!"*

*"Who are—"*

Shellesh broke from his maddening memories and struck the woman in the jaw. She collapsed, eyes rolling to the back of her skull. Two other guards jumped up from where they lounged, breaking off their conversation. He had avoided most of the security as he'd climbed the tower, until he'd found these three in the stairwell.

Blue and purple, male and female, they pulled their stunsticks free and stepped forward. Shellesh climbed past the unconscious woman to the platform. The man circled one way, the woman the other, trying to fit Shellesh between. As he watched Purple, Blue stepped forward, thrusting with the stunstick.

Shellesh flowed around the strike as Purple came in swinging. He ducked around Blue and kicked him into the swing, earning a spark and a yell. A glancing blow, so not enough to knock him out of it, but Blue rubbed the spot where Purple had struck him. Shellesh's back hit the railing, a several story drop just behind him.

They approached carefully; Shellesh approached recklessly. The railing rocked as he pushed himself off, launching at Blue. The guard tried to bring the stunstick to bear, but Shellesh tackled low, slamming him to the ground. The weapon crackled as it spun loose from Blue's grip. Shellesh slammed his forehead into the man's face, and a spurt of blood sprayed into Shellesh's eyes, feeling cool as it dripped down his cheeks like tears. Then hot sparks of electricity coursed through his spine.

Almost unintentionally, he kicked out, hitting Purple in the ankle. The stunstick ceased its prodding as she collapsed to the ground with a shout of surprise. Blue's hands grabbed at Shellesh as he tried to roll away, squeezing his throat shut and blocking the air from his lungs.

He tried to break the grip, but the man was surprisingly strong, holding Shellesh away and preventing him from being able to land a good blow. Blindly, he reached back, scrambling for a knife. His grasp found it and pulled it free. As his vision grew dark, he drove the knife into that forearm. Blue screamed out, and Shellesh could breathe again. He gasped as he slammed the knife down again, and again, and again. Panting, he rolled away and staggered to his feet.

Blood pooled on the ground as Blue's body twitched one last time before it fell quiet, knife still plunged into his neck.

Purple stared in horror, stunstick in one hand. Then she brought her Vico up to her mouth and hit a button. Shellesh pulled his pistol and shot her, the top of her skull exploding out, her body dropping to the ground.

The last waves of her fear slipped away, then he felt nothing but sick. Shellesh leaned against the wall and fell to the ground, eyes squeezed tight against the death that surrounded him.

*"Tai!" Shellesh rushed out of the bedroom, Miaraim quick to follow. Tai stood at the end of the hall, looking at them with confusion.*

*"I heard—" Tai said.*

*"Get back!" Shellesh shouted.*

*"Tai!" Miaraim screeched.*

*Then the door exploded. Tai's body rocked to the side as a hail of plasma bolts tore the door open. A bloody mist painted the room as Shellesh watched his child die.*

He opened his eyes, a cold resolve burying everything else within him. He stood up and continued on. To find his son's killer.

The last door opened. Nine guards filled the security room, positioned around monitors, responding to reports, or just relaxing and chatting. Two stood, weapons ready, moving toward the exit. Likely they were going to check one of the groups Shellesh had found on the way.

He shot them first. Non-lethally, the lower energy plasma bolts hitting them in the chest like a battering ram. Their bodies flipped back over a table, and they hit the ground, wheezing and fading to unconsciousness.

Everyone jumped to their feet, reaching for their closest weapons. Mostly stunsticks, though some rushed him with fists only. He shot the legs out from under the first before the next could reach him. Then it all devolved into a brawl, a flurry of fists slamming into each other as a mob of people bounced from wall to table to floor.

Shellesh moved constantly, weaving between swings of the stunsticks, taking body blows when he had no other choice. One man hit him, trying to take him to the ground, and Shellesh kicked his legs out, broke his grasp, and twisted away. He couldn't let himself be brought down; if he did, the fight would be over.

Instead, he stumbled back into a table and rolled over it, breaking away from the crowd. They separated, rushing to either side, one even jumping on top of the table. Shellesh upended the table, sending the guard sprawling back into those too slow to react, then danced away as a stunstick arced toward him. The monitor it struck exploded into sparks as the electronics fried. The lights flickered, and the rest of the screens blanked.

Shellesh had lost his gun in the mob, so he tore the knife from the attacker's thigh sheath and plunged it into his knee. One quick strike, tearing it loose immediately. He flowed between them, rapid thrusts of the knife injuring and maiming anyone he could. Blood spilled around him. Soaked his clothes, stained his skin, pooled across the ground, turning every step into a sticky footprint. Rage overwhelmed him, and he unleashed it on the nine guards, screaming as he slammed into them, knife and fist and body.

Then it was over. He stood in the center of the room, nine men and women incapacitated or dead. He wiped the blood from his face as he gathered his breath. The iron smell of blood and the scene of carnage raised memories unbidden. A coldness like steel seeped through him.

*Shellesh stood among the dead. His son had been the first to die but not the last. The hall was soaked with the blood of more than twenty people sliced into pieces. The hilt hung loose in his hand, now numb. Small wounds decorated his body, but nothing more. Nothing serious. The real pain had been in that first strike, the shattering of his heart and soul.*

*"Shell?" Her voice quavered. He should have been angry, but that had fled him. There was nothing but a void within him, a cold emptiness in which he'd slaughtered twenty people without a second thought.*

*"Leave," he whispered. It was the most he could do. If she didn't, he was afraid of what he would do. Maybe she deserved to die, but he deserved the time to think about it first.*

*"Shell, come with—"*

*"LEAVE!"*

*Miaraim left without another word. Shellesh stood there as another person's blood dripped from his chin, until the emptiness left him. Until the emotions returned and tears poured down his cheeks. He stumbled back into his apartment, depositing the hilt into the dirt of a plant at the entrance. Carefully. He left no evidence of the act, careful to clean the dirt from his fingers before he continued down the hall.*

*He found what remained of Taiviat's body near the game they had been playing only moments earlier. Hours earlier? Time had flowed, and time had halted. He knelt beside his son and pulled the remains to his lap as he cradled them. He screamed out with pain as the tears ran down bloody cheeks.*

The cold filled him once more. Shellesh took the flame of his anger and burned it away. This would not be an assassination, something done with a cold, calculating will. He would fulfill his final mission with his heart, not his mind. He pushed open the door to the gala beyond, a rush of cheer and excitement crashing into the scene of carnage.

He saw her across the room, glass in one hand, politician on the opposite arm.


Shellesh walked among the crowd. His blood wept from wounds as others' blood dripped from his clothes and hands. He let the knife slip from his hands and clatter to the ground. Since that was not enough to provide him a wide berth, his hood fell back, fully exposing the sickly gray of his skin. The almost translucent white around his eyes. There were murmurs, shouts, and screams as they rushed away. Terror and disgust swirled within the room like a fetid stew.

Miaraim watched him approach, a smirk of anticipation on her lips.

*"You're going to be exiled," Iarorai said, scowling down at Shellesh. "You should tell them what happened. The truth. This wasn't you. It was Miaraim."*

*"I killed fifteen Peacekeepers," Shellesh said. He had also killed five others, whose names were redacted from the charges. Each one a corrupt pet of a certain politician. His eyes stared only at the ground, where his arms were chained. His knees ached from the extended time spent kneeling, but it was almost over now. "It doesn't matter what I argue. They need a scapegoat."*

*"You're not even fighting."*

*Shellesh didn't answer.*

*"You're going to ruin our lives without a fight?"*

*Shellesh glanced up at Rorai, but the anger fled almost immediately. He couldn't hold his emotions very long without his chest burning. Then he looked away. "The plant at our entrance. You know the one?"*

*"What?"*

*"Please give it to Mother. She always loved that plant."*

*There was a long silence as Rorai studied him. Then he sighed and walked away. Shortly after, Shellesh was retrieved, law enforcers of the department of justice dragging him to the exiling chamber to stand in front of the minister of justice.*

*"Shellesh," he announced. "You are charged with the murder of fifteen Peacekeepers and six civilians, including your own child. You aided and abetted in the attempted assassination of President Yokoy with your wife, who you've helped escape. You have offered no defense of your actions, not that there can be one for what you've done. As such, you are sentenced to exile, stripped of your rights as a tesing, and forbidden from returning to the lands of your birth. You will be stripped of your proud coloring, so as to not shame the rest of us. You—"*

*"Shame?" Shellesh lifted his head and glared at the minister of justice. "What shame will be bred from this farce? You're a government of cowards and crooks. I'm the one who feels shame. Shame to be a part of this fucking society. Finish this trial, and strip me of my color, so I can be free from your shame."*

*The crowd erupted with shouts of anger. Even the president stood and yelled down at him. Shellesh hadn't noticed he was there. The rest of the sentencing was drowned out over the shouts, but a command was given and the guards dragged him to the exiling table.*

*He was stripped, then strapped to the table, arms and legs pulled wide until he felt like the joints would pop. A breathing tube was jammed down his throat, the cold metal scraping his insides as he felt the suffocating press of it. Then suddenly a machine breathed for him.*

*A mask was strapped over his eyes, pinning the eyelids open as a bright light caused tears to form.*

*He felt the table shift and lower, and when the acid touched his skin, he screamed. His body rocked and pulled at the restraints as it was eaten by the liquid. The eye mask heated up until a searing laser pulsed into his eyes, burning away their color as well and bleaching the skin around them to a near perfect white. A mockery of the mask forever burnt onto his face.*

*For an eternity, Shellesh melted away on that table, only his thoughts of Miaraim to keep him company.*

"Shell." Her voice shattered every memory from his mind. She stood a few feet away, a wide circle of watchers beyond. Her pet politician looked at him with wide eyes, waves of disgust flowing freely from him. Her emotions were behind a cage of iron. "I'm surprised."

"That I found you?" Shellesh pulled the hilt out and held it to the side. His cloak had fallen from his shoulders at some point during the approach, leaving him free for movement. "You're not as careful as you think you are. You never were."

She smiled. "No, dear, I laid a clear enough trail to lead you here. I meant the shot. I almost expected you to take it."

"Knowing you, it would have been stopped. Then the tower would have been on high alert. Reaching you would be—"

"It would have killed me," Miaraim said flatly. The politician sipped his drink, watching the conversation with a great deal of interest. "If you had hit me, anyway. There are no extra protections."

Shellesh's blood ran cold, his eyes narrowed. "Why lead me here to kill you?"

"I led you here to talk to you. Can we do that? Has enough time passed that we can have a civil conversation?"

"No."

"Ha!" The politician's laugh caught them both by surprise as they turned. "Sorry," he said, "I haven't introduced myself. I am Thoth. I'm on the Neiros Electorate Committee."

"I don't care," Shellesh said.

"Oh, that's fine. Plenty of people aren't into politics these days, and given your, um, *condition*, I can see why you're not." Shellesh glared at him, but he smiled his political smile and continued. "You know, you seem to have a lot of anger built up within you. Especially at Siris here."

At the mention of his mother's name, Shellesh glared at Miaraim, who merely shrugged.

"Now," Thoth continued, "I'm not an expert, but I did spend a year studying psychology in my secondary education, and I know a thing or two about therapy."

"What?" Shellesh looked back at the rambling politician, eyes wide with confusion. Amusement from Miaraim trickled into the air, and he hated the touch of her emotions brushing his mind.

"Yes, and they say bottling up your emotions can be very harmful. You need someone to talk to and an outlet for your anger. Strenuous exercise is excellent for the—"

"If you speak another word," Shellesh growled, "I will slice off both your arms and throw you out that fucking window."

Thoth's red skin paled nearly to a pink as his mouth opened and closed silently. Miaraim finished her drink and handed her glass to the stunned politician.

"Be a dear and fetch me another drink. I fear my husband may not be exaggerating."

Once her pet had left, Shellesh glared at Miaraim. "Siris?"

"I like your mother's name."

"Halt!" Two guards pushed their way through the crowd, weapons drawn and trained on Shellesh. He clenched his teeth, just as he clenched the hilt. He didn't have time for—

Miaraim's hand raised in a friendly gesture, then there was a pistol popping from her sleeve to her hand. Had Shellesh not been watching, it would have seemed to materialize. She fired twice, and metal prongs shot from the end. Both guards dropped to the ground, seizing.

"No interruptions, please," she said, a sickly-sweet smile on her face. She turned back to Shellesh, and her smile faltered. "Let's play a game, Shell. I'm here to assassinate someone. First one to kill him wins. Like the good old days."

"I have no interest in games. I'm here to kill you."

"Not even if my target was President Yokoy?"

A wave of gasps ran through the crowd still intently watching the events. Except for one person, who said, "What?"

Shellesh's blood went cold at the sound of that voice. His eyes found the single, startled man, a sunny yellow hue to his skin, growing paler as he glanced around for protection. Everyone around him stepped away.

"You wanted vengeance for Taiviat's death. There he is, Shell." Her words were an evil whisper in his ear. President Yokoy met Shellesh's eyes, and though there was fear, there was no recognition. He didn't even remember the man he'd sentenced to exile for the deaths of his crooked police.

Liquid metal poured from the hilt, undulating until it formed a long, thin blade. A blade notorious for its sharpness.

"He didn't kill our son," Shellesh said, and Miaraim's amusement dissipated. He turned to face her. "You did. By targeting him. By leading his men to our home. You killed our son, Miaraim, and now I'm going to kill you."

Miaraim locked her emotions down, but her eyes told him everything. "I had only thought to help you, Shell. To ease your pain. But if death is all you crave, I can grant you that final request. For the one I still love."

Shellesh gritted his teeth at that final word. Anger burned through his mind, his vision tinted red. He would avenge Taiviat this night.

He swung first, but Miaraim had already dropped the pistol. Shadow sprouted from her feet into her hand, forming a midnight replica of Shellesh's own blade and intersecting the slash. The crowd screamed and backed away. What had been a dramatic interaction had turned violent, and while the rich did love their violence, they loved it from a distance.

Shellesh drowned it all out. After seventeen years, he had found his target.


Miaraim had been an infamous assassin when they'd first met, then simply known as the Shadow, a name stemming from her Thresha talent of controlling her own shadows. She could wrap them around herself like a cloak and hide a foot away. Or she could solidify them into an ever-shifting blade for unorthodox attacks. They were an enviable tool and weapon.

Shellesh had expressed his jealousy, and on their wedding night, Miaraim had brought out Mercurial. A gift for Shellesh, his own blade of liquid metal.

Their swords sang as they danced through the gala, shadow and metal shifting erratically with each strike. Shellesh sidestepped as midnight snakes reached for his ankles. Miaraim's face was stony cold as she drove him ever backward. Without his own Thresh talent, he was at a disadvantage. That too had been stripped from him when the rest of his life had been.

Let her think she had the advantage. Shellesh dove over a short table and knocked it at Miaraim. Three blades sprouted from the shadow at her feet and shredded it as Shellesh rolled away.

"What's the matter, Shell?" The shadow blades whipped and whirled like tentacles as they reached for Shellesh. Still, she held the one in her hand as well. "I thought you were going to kill me."

Shellesh gritted his teeth as he parried the assault. He jumped back even as one blade slashed across his side.

Her eyes burned with anger. "I planned this opportunity for you, Shellesh!" Another wave of shadow knocked him back, a fourth tentacle forming. She had never controlled her talent so skillfully before. "I thought I could help you find peace! But you're too fucking stupid for that, aren't you?"

"I'm finding peace my own way," Shellesh said as he weaved around a pillar to gather some distance. The crowds around them vanished, rushing toward the exits and away from danger.

"By blaming me!" she screamed, then compressed all her shadow into one blade and thrust it at Shellesh. He barely had time to block it even at that distance. Then it was weaving around his guard, striking at him. "If you had been there, we would have succeeded."

"I told you to quit!" he roared as the shadow split around his guard, piercing him in a dozen places. He grunted as the shadow ripped back out of him. His blood spewed out with the wispy strands of darkness. He stumbled but still stood. She hadn't hit anything too important, nothing that would stop him. He only needed to live long enough to kill her.

Her assault paused, however, and she stood with her shadow blades dancing around her. "You wanted me to give up on helping the world. We could have changed it for the better, but you decided to live on the shoulders of the poor."

"I chose our son. You chose an idea."

"You killed them all, Shellesh," she said, her voice quiet and sad. "Had you stopped berating me and taken action, our son would have lived. Yes, I brought them to our home. Yes, I made a mistake. But you could have done something to save him had you not been too busy believing in a reality that could never exist."

"Don't you dare lay this at my feet," Shellesh growled.

Miaraim shrugged. "I did what I thought was right, and bad things happened. I'm sorry that you cannot forgive me, but I will not kneel at your feet and beg for your forgiveness."

"That's fine. I'll be okay with just your head at my feet." Shellesh leapt, adjusting Mercurial with pulses of electricity through the handle. The blade shifted into a curve, and he arced it at her neck. A whip of shadow slammed into him and hurtled him backward into the wall.

"It's a shame you lost your talent," Miaraim said. "This could have been an interesting fight." She stepped closer, coalescing darkness into a single blade in her hand. Shellesh drowned in her pity.

He groaned as he rose to his knees. "I don't need my talent to kill you."

She hesitated, and he dropped a single sphere to the ground. It beeped, and he closed his eyes just before a brilliant flare burst from it. He built out the room in his mind, placing everyone and everything where they had been. He saw Miaraim, and he struck with blind eyes. He felt his blade slide home as she struggled against it. He heard her cough and felt the blood splatter against his cheek.

When the flare died down, he opened his eyes to see her inches from him, both hands grabbing at the blade that now pierced her chest. It wasn't where it should have hit. She had deflected it just enough. But it didn't matter.

He stumbled, his leg growing cold and numb as blood pooled under him. Even in the flare, she had produced enough shadow for a final attack. Likely lethal. He forced his weight to his good leg to hold him steady. He needed to end it quickly.

"I'm sorry, Shellesh." Tears fell from her eyes as she laughed, and his concentration shattered. Blood dripped from her smiling lips, mingling with the stream of tears. "Fuck," she groaned. "I really underestimated your willingness to die to kill me."

He tried to adjust Mercurial, but no killing blow fell. They stood there, in an embrace of slow death, and he spoke. "I lived for no other purpose."

"None?" Again he felt that outpouring of pity, and he hated it. "No friends? No new loves?"

"How was I to find that as an exile, Miaraim?"

Her tears flowed harder, and she lifted one bloodied hand to Shellesh's face. "I'm so sorry for what I've done to you, Shellesh. For what I've done to our family."

"It's too late for apologies."

"Taiviat was too good for either of us. I wonder if he will forgive me when I see him again."

Shellesh's hands shook, falling away from Mercurial as he trembled where he stood. Miaraim's shadows wrapped around him and lowered him gently to the ground. She collapsed next to him, removing his blade from her chest and retracting it into the hilt. They sat there, backs against the wall, both bleeding out amid a strange feeling of peace. His anger had retreated, and now there was just nothing. The same bittersweet feelings trickled from Miaraim.

"I don't know if he'll forgive me," Shellesh said, tears falling down his chin.

"You were a perfect father, Shell. He will be happy to see you again."

He laughed, then he coughed. "Until he finds out why you're there too."

She smiled. "It's not too late for us." She pulled out a purse tucked into her dress. "It's just blood loss at this point. It will stabilize us." She cracked it open to show two needles. Healing agents. They would seal the wounds and promote blood production. She had been prepared. Then she handed the bag to him. "It's your call. Shall we continue on, or shall we meet Taiviat again?"

Shellesh stared at the needles, then closed his eyes and leaned his head against the wall. "Save yourself, Miaraim. I am too tired to continue on."

"Then I will die with you, Shellesh." He felt her fingers weave into his own, and he clenched them back. "I can't have you telling Tai lies that make me sound better."

"Mia," Shellesh said. "Why did it take you seventeen years to do this? Why now?"

"I was scared, Shellesh. Scared to see your anger and hatred. Afraid you would never forgive me." She took a deep breath, then coughed up blood. "But I needed you here. I wanted to save you."

"Save me?" He opened his eyes. Miaraim's Vico beeped.

"From the trap."

Shellesh's heart pounded in his chest as he looked over at her. "What trap?"

"When I fled Neiros, I was lost. I wandered, trying to find jobs, but I didn't know where to go. A man named Sovereign found me, took me in. Gave me a place of security, paid me for assassinations." With great effort, Miaraim brought her Vico up and pressed the message. Six bounties displayed, each with a massive payout, and a declaration that full price would be paid if they arrived dead. She laughed, small and pitiful laughs. "When I learned of his plan, I decided to lure you away to save your life. I fucked that up too."

Shellesh clenched his jaw, his breath quickening with panic. His eyes kept shifting between the six bounties. A cold dread filled his chest.

*"Hey, Shellesh!" Wyn waved. "We're grabbing dinner if you want to join us."*

Shellesh quaked, his hand grabbing tightly around the nearest item. The purse and its injectors.

*"Can you show me that disarming technique again?" Besari asked, pulling herself from the ground. "I think I have a way to defend against it."*

Shellesh pulled the needles from the bag and looked at Miaraim. Her eyes studied his, watching his reaction.

*"What do you think?" Sage asked as they watched Wyn and Besari spar. As always, the birrosh won over and over again.*

*"She might be fine, but she's raw," Zetta said. "Too practiced in planned fighting and not in true brawls. Good fucking luck with Wyn though. He'll die in your first outing."*

*Sage raised a brow at Zetta, arms crossed. "I asked Shellesh, not you."*

*"Wyn learns fast," Shellesh said before Zetta could offer a retort. "And Besari is a gifted hand-to-hand combatant. Even more so with her Thresha talent. They'll both be excellent bounty hunters in time."*

"I thought you didn't have friends," Miaraim said.

"I don't," he said, the needles shaking in his hand. "I didn't think I did. But they're something else. Something more."

"A new family," she said. "I'm jealous. For seventeen years, I've been used but never once became close to anyone."

"Will Tai forgive me for choosing to live?" His tears dripped from his chin as memories of his son danced in his wavering vision.

"He would want you to live a full life, Shell."

*"Hmm," Achtrek buzzed. "What do you say, Shellesh?"*

*"I have given the most optimal path," Cee said.*

*"Achtrek could scout. Their bugs are nearly undetectable," Shellesh said. "Plus, their puppet mastery would be useful for sabotage. Then Cee and I could sweep in after. They would fall in moments." Shellesh shrugged. "That's my thoughts."*

*"Puppet mastery?" Cee asked, cocking its head like an animal. Shellesh wondered if it was only for show.*

*"We can manipulate another's body through electrical impulses through the brain and nervous system."*

*"Hm," Cee said, his glowing blue eyes blinking with thought. "I was not aware. That is a very useful skill."*

*"So," Shellesh butted in, "why are we planning to take down the central operations station of the Raiyrium Confederation?"*

*"We are not," Cee said. "It is just a game."*

*"We are comparing optimal pairings to see how few people we'd need to take it," Achtrek added.*

"He'd want us both to live." Shellesh handed one needle to Miaraim. "Together," he said. She nodded. They plunged the needles in at the same time. His into her chest, and hers into his thigh. Shellesh grunted as the burning gel flowed through his veins. Mia echoed it with her own moan.

"Security is likely forming up on this room as we speak," Miaraim said. "There's no way you'll get out alive."

"I'll fight my way out."

"Sovereign will have these people dead before you find a way there."

Shellesh shook his head as feeling returned to his leg. "I'll reach out to the Bounty Inc. office. Someone will be able to send me the routes. I can get in."

"They'll shoot you down if they don't recognize you."

"I need to do something," Shellesh snapped. "I can't let them die."

Miaraim smiled, then unclasped her Vico. "I know. I was getting there." She handed it over. "Take my private craft, in the hangar on Cesec Tower. My credentials will get you to Kekar safely."

Shellesh took it and stared. "What about you?"

"I have another way off this place."

Shellesh heard banging at the door, and it was only then that he noticed the weaves of shadow over the doors. Even now she was barricading them.

"The last vial in there is yours," Miaraim said, nodding at the purse. "I can't fix everything. I wanted to, but there's no way to reverse all the effects of the exiling. But I can repair one."

He pulled out the last vial and looked at it. There was no label, and the liquid within was a violet hue.

"Drink it once you leave Neiros space and are on your way to Kekar. It'll knock you on your ass for a few hours."

"What is it?"

The door banged louder, cracking against the assault.

"Shall we?" Miaraim asked, pulling herself from the ground and stretching her shoulders. Shadow coalesced into one hand, forming a blade.

Shellesh pulled himself to his feet, feeling returning with sharp pinpricks of pain to his injured leg, but otherwise he could move. He pocketed the vial and picked up Mercurial.

"One last time."

# PART 4
# KEKAR

"We're fucked."

"We're not fucked."

"We're definitely fucked."

Wyn paced around the small room at the base of a two-story vacant building. He couldn't tell what it had been designed for, but it hadn't worked out. Many of the desks and supplies were left stranded, their owners long since departed. It worked as a base of operations, however. Though, the only operation they'd been running were hourly checks activating the beacon.

Six days of silence. Wyn should have been the last one to arrive based on their timing, but six days in, he was the second. "They're either all dead or missing. Everyone."

Besari sighed. "That seems likely." She had been going out in her disguise, which happened to be just her normal self (so maybe out of disguise would be the more appropriate phrasing), to collect food. It was still too dangerous for Wyn to wander for long, though if he kept his helmet on, he seemed to stay hidden. For now, he stayed back, checking the beacon while Besari scouted the area and collected food. It was maddening.

"We need to find them. We need some confirmation. All of their bounties are still up, so that means Sovereign hasn't found them either."

"Not necessarily," Besari said. "It could be that he's keeping them up so we come to that conclusion. If we waste time searching for them, we're likely to get ourselves caught."

"If we can't look for them, what are we supposed to do?"

"Flee."

Wyn's head jerked up, flashing her a look of astonishment. Before he could speak, she pressed a palm to his cheek and his words fell silent.

"I know it's hard, Wyn, but we're out of our depth. We need to trust the others can survive and have either escaped or will be escaping. Our plan was to abandon the mission if we couldn't move forward after a few days. It's time to leave."

Wyn closed his eyes to lock in his tears. Sage, Zetta, Cee, and Achtrek. He was going to abandon them all if he left.

"How would we even leave?"

"You said you came in a ship, yes?"

Wyn opened his eyes, then glanced away from Besari's emerald gaze. "Yes, well, that option's complicated, if it's even still available."

"Complicated?"

"The ship's owner tried to kill me before I got out of the hangar."

Besari's eyes widened, her hand falling away from Wyn's cheek. It was still strange to see the expressions he had been imagining for so long. "What did you do?"

"I may have drugged her and hijacked the ship a little."

"A little? What's a little?"

"Probably the drugging part, given she woke up before I left the hangar."

"I honestly didn't think you had it in you," she said, her face shifting to an approving look.

"What's that mean?"

"Well, you reproached Sage about illegal behavior already, so hearing that you partook in your own little illegalities is a bit surprising."

"I didn't have a choice," Wyn said, just a bit defensive. "It was that or abandon you."

She smiled. "I'm not complaining. I'm very happy you did it." She paused, her brow furrowing. "Though, why did you need to steal a ship? What happened to your planned route?"

"I..." Wyn rubbed the back of his neck and looked away, feeling sheepish. "I overslept."

"You *overslept*?"

"I'm not used to public travel! My father never left Terrask, and if we traveled across the planet, it was in a comfortable yacht. I tried to sleep on the trips, but it was so loud. So I napped when I had a few hours on planet and ended up sleeping through the alarm."

Besari smirked. "I guess it's true what they say. Money really does make you soft."

Wyn glared, but his cheeks reddened. "None of this solves our way off this planet."

"We'll need to steal another ship," she said. "In a way that doesn't alert their orbital defenses. Then sneak off. I can begin scouting the port for security and potential targets."

Wyn sighed and settled into a seat, the chair groaning with his weight. "I don't understand how this went so wrong. What happened?"

Besari looked away, then rubbed at her bicep. A nervous reaction. But why? Wyn studied her, growing more worried as she found her words.

"They were looking for me."

"What?"

"On my shuttle. They knew I would be on it."

"That's impossible. The only people who knew all our plans were the six of us."

"And Seph."

Her words brought a chill to his spine. Seph had been hanging around the meetings. He would have known the routes. "But..." Wyn's mouth dried up.

"I'm not saying he told on us," Besari said quickly. "I'm just saying our plans leaked. I survived because I came without my suit. You survived because you had to deviate your route. What if the others came exactly as planned and looked exactly as expected?"

Wyn lowered his head into his hands and pushed away the existential dread that threatened to drop him to the ground, kicking and screaming like a toddler. "Then they're dead," he admitted.

Besari knelt in front of Wyn and grabbed his hands, pulling them away from his face. She held them tight as he looked up. "Maybe they are, maybe they aren't. We can't know right now, so we have to focus on what we can do. Remember, we're together now and we're unbeatable."

Wyn stared into Besari's eyes, and his dread melted away. Not completely, but he could breathe again. He could feel his heart steadying. They were together. They were unbeatable. He leaned forward, and she leaned into him, and they kissed. Wyn's hand rose to her neck, then trailed along the back of her skull, feeling the ridges as they melted into one another. Her fingers ran through his hair, pulling him harder into the embrace.

They broke free, but neither was willing to release the other. Wyn studied her face and its beauty, bringing every detail into his memory so he could always remember her like this. The shape of her eyes, slightly larger and rounder than a human's. Her mouth, with lips thinner and smoother than his and an indescribable taste that Wyn couldn't get enough of. Faint shadows of dark green freckles dusted her cheeks around a nose much like a human's, if maybe just a bit smaller. Her scalp was hairless, with small ridges starting above each eye and intersecting above her brow to form a unique, swirling pattern along her scalp to the base of her neck. She wore form-fitting civilian clothes, as Wyn did, avoiding her combat armor in case someone recognized it from the bounties. He ran a thumb across her hand, feeling the smooth texture of her skin.

Wyn was the first to break the silence. "You don't have to tell me, I trust you with all my heart," he said, "but why did you pretend to be a birrosh for so long?"

Besari looked away, her cheeks darkening in color. When she looked back, however, there was resolute determination in her eyes. She sighed. "Although birrosh and bishett are biologically very similar—having both developed from a common ancestor on the same planet, it makes sense—their cultures are anything but. The bishett practice a culture of solitude and purity." She gestured to her cheeks, two fingers running along her freckles. "To those who still celebrate those customs, a bishett does not reach maturity until their spots have fully disappeared. Until then, your parents have full responsibility over you, your future, your everything."

Her hand dropped, and Wyn caught it in his own. She smiled as he squeezed it. "I was in a mixed-species school, and without my parents' knowledge, I trained in hand-to-hand combat. I sat there at the school, watching birrosh my age leave and start their lives years before me. My life felt stagnant, paused, while I waited for these damn spots to disappear. I told my mother how I felt, I told her that I wanted to go off, to train as a warrior and become a bounty hunter or a Peacekeeper. She locked me in my room, canceled all my lessons with my tutor, and enrolled me into a business school.

"Thankfully, my tutor had given me the infusion for my Thresha talent, and I never told my parents. I was able to grab everything I could, use my talent to escape. My tutor was hesitant, but she understood. She was a late-fader too, but her family had been non-traditional. She helped me procure my armor and my weapons, then found me a flight off planet. She told me to disguise myself as a birrosh and stay off planet until my spots have faded. I spent three weeks trying to be a bounty hunter. With my tutor's help, I was able to falsify records of my history so people thought I could actually complete a job." She shrugged. "I still didn't get anything until I applied for Bounty Inc. though."

"I want to say I'm sorry," Wyn said. "But it's hard to do that when that all led to you joining Bounty Inc."

Besari smiled. "You're right. It may have sucked, but in the end, it was what was best for me. I found where I belong."

Wyn ran a thumb along her cheek. "If it makes you feel better, I like the spots."

"It doesn't." Besari chuckled. "It sounds weird. But I appreciate it."

Besari drew Wyn into another soft kiss, and Wyn pulled her back when she tried to move away. Then neither wanted to break it.

Hands ran across clothes, and Wyn felt the strong muscles of her back and sides. Her own hands slipped beneath his shirt, brushed the skin of his stomach and slid up. Wyn broke free of the kiss long enough to bring his lips to her cheek, then her ear and down her neck, his own hands searching beneath her shirt, running along the almost too-smooth skin, lifting the clothing as his fingers traced—

A loud laser sizzled against the locked door, the metal at its base heating up until red-hot. Besari and Wyn jumped apart, panic drowning every other emotion. She was gone in a blink, but her pack began rustling, seemingly on its own. Wyn dove for his own and dug around for a weapon. Failing to grasp one, he upended the whole thing, spilling tools, grenades, ammunition, food, clothing, everything out. With a clank, the gun hit the ground, and he had it in hand a moment later. Safety off, power at its highest setting.

He turned and raised the weapon, watching a small beam cut into the door, carving up and around to create a door within the door. A door that was approximately ten inches tall. The arc completed, and with a resounding knock, the cutaway slab tipped inward. Smoke disrupted Wyn's view of the small creature that began to crawl in. A bulbous body, with ten legs stretching out nearly evenly in all directions. They worked as one to crawl forward with a constant click.

"This city is insufferable with its design," the creature said. "How am I supposed to enter any doors?"

Wyn's eyes widened, and his mouth dropped. The smoke dissipated to show a scarred and scorched metallic head riding atop what appeared to be two hands, with their fingers acting as legs.

"Cee?" Besari blinked into existence, scattergun at the ready.

"Yes, I believe that is my indicator now," it said. "I am a cyborg, though I have enhanced many of my human parts. One still remains however." It waggled one of the legs, which happened to be the mummified finger. How in the void had that survived whatever had happened to Cee, but the rest of its body hadn't?

Wyn and Besari stared at Cee, and it stared back.

"Who are you?" it asked.

Wyn and Besari sat while Cee perched on top of a table. It had told them of the explosion in the sky and how it had fallen to Kekar in pieces, the largest of which now made up its body. A head and two hands.

"Why can't you remember us?" Wyn asked.

"My mind was far more extensive than what this head unit could contain," it explained, "therefore I had memories scattered throughout my body. In case of damages, I had several safety recalls in order to bring my memories online. Unfortunately, it seems like this damage is far too extensive."

"How did you find us?" Besari asked the probably more important question.

"Your beacon. I heard it every hour of every day. After constructing this body, I followed it as often as I could."

"But you don't remember us," Wyn said. "Why'd you come?"

"I knew the beacon was important, if not why." One eye flickered as it looked between them. "Would either of you like to explain?"

"We came here for a bounty but ended up in a trap. I don't know where the others are."

"Others?"

"Yeah, we came with Sage, Zetta—"

"One moment, please," Cee interrupted. Wyn swore he heard the sounds of whirring, then Cee's attention returned. "Please repeat that."

"We came with Sage, Zetta, and Achtrek," Wyn finished. "What was that?"

"I told you, my head unit cannot contain all my memories. I am actively purging to readjust my necessary knowledge. I remember Zetta, but Sage and Achtrek escape memory." It whirred again for a moment, then spoke. "You indicated a trap. Is it safe to assume the parameters of our mission have shifted?"

"We were planning to look for an escape, but if the others are on the planet, we need to find them and help them."

"Wyn," Besari whispered.

"We have Cee now. We can be careful enough to at least learn." Wyn turned his attention back to Cee. "Do you still have the ability to hack into things? Can you access some satellite or something to search for them?"

Cee paused for a moment. It was so strange to not see it respond immediately, always with an answer. Like watching a computer grow older with each new question. "The communications network blankets the city," it finally said. "Projectors all over display Sovereign's messages, but not just that. There are cameras to monitor the streets. If we can get to one, I can access the city's camera system. There should be at least a few days of saved data I could comb through. If not, I could view the live data."

"That's an excellent idea," Wyn said.

"No, it's not," Besari added. "Those comms units are in the most populated areas, and they'll record us trying to mess with them."

"There's the one where I first saw the bounties," Wyn suggested. "We definitely know it's connected to the system. It's our only guaranteed shot."

"It's halfway up a building," Besari said.

"Halfway down if you start at the top." Wyn smiled. "Besides, no one will see Cee. It's too small."

"I will need assistance," Cee said. "My body is not as robust as I would prefer."

"Okay, that's fine," Wyn said. "I can pretend to be a window washer or something."

"No, Wyn," Besari pushed.

"We have to try, Besari!"

"We will," she added in a softer tone. "I'll go. I can hide myself with my talent, and we have rope to descend from the roof. I'll take Cee to the projector and hack in."

"What about me?" Wyn added, perhaps a bit childishly. It was a sound plan. He just hated that everyone else was doing the work.

"Stay up top, make sure no one stumbles across us."

Wyn nodded, though he gritted his teeth. Lookout duty, that was all he was good for.

"Wyn," Besari said. He looked up to find her eyes hard as gems, her focus entirely on the mission. "Wear your combat suit, and make sure to wear the helmet."

"You don't think it will be suspicious walking around decked out like that?"

"More suspicious than your face?" she said. "I'll wear my suit but leave the helmet off and wear clothes over."

Plan determined, Wyn and Besari split off to change. His jitters washed away as he put the suit on, the power of the armor granting him a bravery he never had outside of it. He fingered the two pistols at his side and took a deep breath. This was it. They would save the others. He would do whatever it took to bring them home.

"Is that your new helmet?" Besari asked when Wyn stepped out of his room into a main office area where the others waited.

"Yes, they sent me the replacement! Watch this." The helmet's neural interface read Wyn's instructions as quickly as he could produce them, and suddenly imagery flowed across the otherwise smooth black surface of his helmet. Unseen by Wyn, the helmet showcased a new face, painstakingly selected in order to put enemies off balance, to befuddle and infuriate them. Two small rectangles took the place of his eyes, angling back to his ears. At his mouth, a squiggle that lifted at the edges into almost a smile. Nothing else.

Wyn smiled as Besari and Cee stared up at the helmet, one confused, the other the same stony face as always.

"Why?" Besari asked.

"You can tell me if it's stupid," Wyn said, his voice echoing around the vacant stairwell. Luckily, this building was also vacant. There seemed to be a lot of those around. Kekar did not seem to be a popular immigration choice at the moment. "I won't be offended or anything."

"I don't think it's stupid," Besari said.

Wyn waited for her to continue. She didn't. "But?" he prodded.

"I just don't get it," she said.

"What's there to get?" Wyn asked. "It's supposed to be a distraction. Some of the best tactics in history are based on a ridiculous distraction before a strike."

"I just don't know if it would work in a fight," she added. "I would be too focused on the actual fight to care about what displayed on your helmet."

"I like it," Cee chimed in from Wyn's shoulder. He still felt very uncomfortable with the A.I. perching there, its handfeet latching onto his shoulder like a strange massage. The kind he would want a refund from.

"See," Wyn said. "Cee likes it."

"Cee doesn't count," she said. "It's like one-thirteenth of a person right now."

"She's not wrong," Cee added.

"Let's just forget about it," Besari said. "Obviously, it's something you believe in, and I can't say I have any proof that it won't work. I hope it does."

Wyn smiled. "You'll see. It'll work."

Besari reached the top first, flashing invisible as she cracked open the roof exit and peeked out. "Clear," she said, and the three of them piled out onto the roof.

Wyn and Besari dropped the satchels at a sturdy-looking chimney and wrapped a rope around it, latching the cabling tightly. Then they pulled to test the strength and, confident, tossed the cable over the side. It easily reached the projector where the bounties displayed.

"Are you sure you want to do this?" Wyn asked.

"Not really," Besari said, strapping on the rest of the gear and hooking it up to the rope. "But it's the best plan we have." She looked to Cee and gestured to her shoulder. "Hop on. Let's get this over with."

Wyn handed Cee over, then Besari disappeared from view, the metallic head now floating in the air as she began lowering herself down the side of the building. He watched them go for a bit, then settled back to wait. It was out of his hands now.

Had Cee been fully operational, Wyn wondered, how long would it have taken? Would it have been able to access everything in moments? Would it have needed direct contact? Regardless, it took a long time, and it definitely needed contact. He grew bored around the thirty-minute mark and began running himself through practiced sword stances that Shellesh had taught them. It felt good. He should get a sword. That would be badass.

The roof door creaked open, and Wyn spun midway through a cross-strike with an imaginary sword. Two massive brutes, a human and a tesing, both male, stepped onto the roof. They stopped mid-conversation to stare at Wyn.

"Fuck," the human said. "I thought this place was clear."

"It is clear," Wyn said. "I mean, besides me."

Their eyes narrowed, and they let the door swing shut behind them. "Then it's not clear," the tesing said. "What are you doing up here?"

"Whatever I want," Wyn said. "What are you doing up here?"

They glanced at each other, then back to Wyn. "Whatever we want," the human said.

"I'm Porrop," the tesing said. "You can call me Por. This is Gran."

"I'm Wyn."

The newcomers walked over to the edge of the roof, Wyn positioning himself between them and obvious sight of the rope. His hand reached for a pistol, hovering close enough to grab it if needed.

They climbed onto the ledge, dangling their feet over the edge and looking out. The human plopped a cooler down between them, and they cracked it open. Wyn leaned against the ledge as Gran looked over. He felt the cable sway against his arm and hoped it wasn't obvious.

"Want a drink?" Gran asked, popping open a can of something.

"No, thanks," Wyn replied. Shit. That meant they weren't planning to leave anytime soon. "I don't drink," he added because he felt it was necessary.

Gran looked at the drink, then back to Wyn. "It's non-alcoholic. We haven't caught enough brewers and such to make alcohol cheap yet."

"I don't drink anything," Wyn added, a little less certainly. The tesing eyed him, but Gran shrugged and drank it. "Wait, caught?" Wyn asked as the words processed fully.

"Yeah, caught," Por said. "We keep looking for brewers, but they don't seem to be popular among the common traps."

"I keep saying we should specifically target businesses that have what we need," Gran added. "Just find a bar and kidnap a few of them. But we apparently have to stay under the radar still. Like the R.C. would even catch on to a few raids."

"You're slavers?" Wyn wished he could take back the question as soon as it came out of his mouth.

Por and Gran stared at him, expressions turning hard. "We prefer *vocational relocators*," Gran said, then he smiled and they both started laughing. Wyn forced himself to join in.

"What are you doing up here if not relaxing?" Por asked. "Practicing sword stances without a sword?" His eyes wandered over to the chimney, where the satchels lay open. And the rope was obvious. "What the void is that?"

Gran followed his eyes. "Two satchels? I thought you were alone."

"I am," Wyn said. "Both are mine."

Por looked down over the side. "And the rope?"

"I was going to do some maintenance on the projector, then you two showed up."

"Maintenance?" Gran asked. Both looked at him again, confusion in their eyes. "Like, slave work?"

"Well, there aren't any slaves who know how to work on those."

"There are literally hundreds of them that know how to work on those," Por said.

"Well, what the fuck?" Wyn chuckled. "That's not what the boss said."

"The rope's swaying," Gran said, leaning farther forward to peer down the side. "Someone's coming up, I think. But I can't see them."

"Are you fucking with the projectors?" Por asked.

Wyn took that opportunity to do the only thing he could think of. He rushed forward and slammed into their backs, trying to spill them over the edge and to their deaths.

Unfortunately, they were a very sturdy pair, and Wyn bounced off of them. They turned, anger blossoming behind their eyes. Not to mention the thick melody of anger that seemed to radiate from the tesing. That was not a good sign.

"This fucker just tried to kill us," Gran said.

"Shall we repay his efforts, then toss his friend over when they arrive too?"

"I think that's a great idea."

They swung their legs back over and rose, dropping their drinks to their sides. Wyn pulled his pistol and aimed. "Don't move," he said.

"Or you'll shoot?" Gran asked. "You already tried to kill us once."

Wyn fired, and they dove to either side, his shots flying past harmlessly. He tracked them, but they were too quick, both slamming into him before another shot could be fired. His pistol clattered to the ground, and Wyn spun out of the contact, remembering his hand-to-hand training. He swung a fist at Por, and the tesing ducked back. Gran took the time to curl behind and wrap him up. Wyn struggled against the embrace, and Por landed a few shots, though they were mostly harmless.

"His armor is tough," the tesing complained.

"Let's just throw him over the edge," Gran said. "Return the favor."

Por smiled and stepped forward. Wyn panicked, heart ricocheting around his insides. He pushed off the ground, kicking out at the tesing, which proved to make it easier for the man to entangle his legs. Then he couldn't move beyond writhing in terror. He swung his head, hoping to smack Gran hard enough to break free, but the man kept away from his attempts as Wyn was slammed down on the edge of the building. They tipped him back so his shoulders and head hung precariously over the edge, a simple push away from a rather bloody splat.

"Take his fucking helmet off," Por said. "Maybe we can beat some teeth out of him before we toss him over the edge."

Wyn struggled, but they were too strong. Large hands tore his helmet free and tossed it to the side. Por pulled back a fist. Wyn winced.

"Hang on," Gran said. "Isn't he from that bounty poster?"

Por paused. "Holy shit. What a fucking pay day! Let's chop his fucking head off and take it to Sovereign. You still have your knife, Gran?"

"Grrgl gahg grbgl," Gran said.

"What?" Por and Wyn both looked at the human, whose eyes and mouth were wide, a bloody silver tongue dangling, rivulets of blood pouring down his cheeks. Then the tongue retreated, and Gran fell to the side, dead.

Besari stood there, both blades at the ready. "I'd rather you not cut off his head, if it's all the same to you."

Por leapt at her, and Besari danced back, dodging wild haymakers with ease. "I'll fucking kill you both," he growled.

Wyn pulled his other pistol and shot the man twice, dropping him to the ground in a bloody heap. Besari leaned down and checked his pulse. "He's dead," she confirmed.

Wyn slid down the lip of the edge, and he breathed in a sigh of relief.

"We have a problem, Wyn."

"This building is abandoned. If we just leave the bodies here, I'm sure it will take a while before they're found."

"It's about the others."

Wyn sat rigid, his focus returning to their task at hand. "Which one?"

"All of them," she said, then glanced at Cee, who perched on the ledge. "We couldn't find Achtrek or any sign of a swarm. But we found Sage and Zetta."

"But at least we found them, right?" Wyn studied Besari's serious face for a moment, and a worry nagged at his chest. "Right?"

## THOSE WHO REMAIN

Sage laughed. Because how was this not funny? Ambushed, stranded on a planet filled with criminals, her face plastered on every corner. Oh, and she'd lost an arm. It was all so fucking funny.

She was also incredibly high, and the laughter probably had more to do with that, if she was being honest. It's not like she could walk around after cutting her arm off *without* medication. She just might have taken a little too much, and now the streets writhed beneath her feet, the buildings swayed like leaves in a hurricane, and, worst of all, she was pretty sure the trash cans had started to sing a jolly tune. It was off-key.

Laughter sent her staggering into a building, where she leaned against it and looked up at the sky. She wasn't sure when it had stopped raining, not that it had *stopped* raining, just that Sage stopped being where it rained. A perfect circle of open air, with a nasty orange sun peeking out. She was supposed to do something here, but her mind was filled with unrelenting fog. Spikes of pain crashed into her every time she tried to move her arm, quickly reminding her the lack thereof. No one could think with that incessant throbbing, timed to her rapid pulse.

She dug around in a pocket and pulled out another painkiller. Her hand found only one. "Shit," she mumbled as she held it out. Had she really gone through all her painkillers? No wonder she was high as fuck. How long had she been wandering around?

She blinked away the thoughts; now wasn't the time for them. Now was the time for sweet relief. She placed the injector at her shoulder and triggered the shot. A numbness flowed through her, dulling the awful ache. Her breathing came easier as she slid down the wall. She smiled up at the sky as the euphoria slammed into her. Peace at last.

"See?"

Sage opened her eyes. When had they closed? The sun had moved. Had she slept? Three men stood over her: two humans and a gorsaulk. One of the humans was the one to speak.

"Told you, that's got to be her."

"She's only got one arm," the gorsaulk said.

Sage glared at him, or tried to, but one eye felt too large for her skull and didn't cooperate. It didn't matter. What did a gorsaulk even know about identifying humans?

"What do you even know about identifying humans?" the leader asked. Sage chuckled. He crouched down, staring at her missing arm. "Looks like it might be recent. Could explain why she seems so dazed."

Sage lifted her left arm in front of the man, the empty painkiller still clutched in her hand. Then she smiled, as kindly and as toothy as she could. "More?" she slurred.

He pulled the painkiller from her hand and inspected it. His eyes went wide, and he handed it back to the others.

"I think *this* explains why she's dazed," the other human said. "This is strong shit. She's doped up."

"Easy pickings," the gorsaulk said.

"I don't have any," the leader said. "But I know someone who does. Why don't you let us take you there?"

The other two shared a glance of surprise, then understanding. They thought Sage was stupid. Or a fucking lightweight. She was neither. She was a very smart girl, and she had been doing drugs since she was thirteen. Which meant she knew how to follow a conversation even when drugged beyond common sense.

"Nooooope," she said, crawling to her hand and legs, then dry heaving when a stab of pain shot through her shoulder. "Nope," she said again when she was done, then pulled herself to her feet. She waved back and forth, holding her hand in front of her, pointer finger out. She raised her eyebrows as she stared at the leader, and with as much emphasis as her drug-addled mind could provide, she said, "Nope."

Then spun around and started staggering off. Someone's hand grabbed her bad shoulder and spun her back. "Hey!" the leader shouted, and that was about all he said. Sage slammed her fist into the side of his head with the momentum of the twirl, then cackled as he hit the ground.

The other two men shouted, then started to surround her while the leader got back to his feet, rubbing blood away from his mouth and smiling. Shit. She used to be able to knock people out in one hit. She stared at her fist in betrayal.

"Fucking bitch!" He took a wild swing at Sage, but even in a drug-induced stupor she was ready. Instinct shifted within her, battling away the need to think, instead fighting from pure muscle memory. Her body moved for her, blocking the attack and preparing for a counterattack.

Unfortunately, her body forgot about the missing arm.

The blocked attack instead crashed into her jaw, spilling her to the ground and sending her mind swirling. There was nothing quite like a fist to the jaw to sober one up. She blinked away the shock, opening and closing her mouth carefully. Testing for anything broken. The thugs bent down, preparing rope to tie her up. They pulled her left arm behind her back, then tied it to her torso with the rope. Then she was lifted to her feet, where she wobbled before finding firm, unwavering ground.

"Hey," the leader said. Then he slapped her. Sage's vision snapped into focus, and she glared at him. "Can you walk?"

She rolled her right shoulder back, closing her eyes and imagining that arm tied back too. She could almost feel it. "No arms then," she mumbled.

"Hey!" the leader shouted, then tried to slap her again. Sage's eyes shot open, as did her mouth. Then she turned her head at the last second, chomping down on the assaulting hand. He yelled, and she bit harder. She heard the crack of the bone, and hands pulled at her. The leader stumbled away with one finger missing. Sage spit it out on the ground.

"Fuck!" The other human backed away. The gorsaulk was made of sterner stuff. He grabbed Sage and spun her to face him.

"Behave!" he shouted. "Or be beaten! Which do you prefer?"

She smiled, another man's blood running down her lips. "A secret, third thing." Then she slammed her forehead into the gorsaulk's face. It shattered beneath the carapace-hardened attack, one eye bulging out of the socket, his nose smashed inward. Green ichor spewed from his face as he dropped to the ground, twitching and grabbing at his broken face. Sage brought a boot down hard on it, and the body fell limp. "One," she said.

"FUCK!" The second man panicked and rushed at her. She spun away from a knife attack, stumbling into a wall and bouncing off of it. He sliced wildly, and she took it in the stomach, where the stone shell deflected the blade harmlessly to the side. Then she stomped on the inside of his ankle, dropping him to the ground as he shouted in pain. She kicked the knife away and fell on top of the man, straddling his chest. She leaned down and sunk her carapace-sharpened teeth into his neck before his flailing arms could push her away. His screaming turned to gargling, turned to silence. And she began dry-heaving again as she coughed up flesh and blood, the man's neck a torn ruin beneath her.

A kick collided with her head, and the thug got the worst of it. He jumped up and down, yelling and cradling his broken foot. Dust fell from Sage as she dissipated the carapace and stood. "Two," she said and spat more blood to the side.

"Fuck this!" The third and final man scrambled for a pocket, pulling a small pistol loose just as Sage crashed into him. She slammed him into the wall with her shoulder, and the telltale clatter of the gun hitting the ground gave her relief. Hardened and sharpened by her carapace, Sage drove her knee into the man's leg, torso, pelvis, pretty much everywhere she could reach. He screamed as she struck, and wild hands tried to push her away. When one got too close to her face, she bit down again, sending the man into a panic. He ripped his hand away, leaving some flesh in her mouth, then yelled more about that. She spit the de-fleshed skin into the man's face, then hit him a few more times with her knee.

Eventually, he stopped being so damn loud and only whimpered, falling to the ground in a bloody heap, one leg mangled and the prospect of having kids (even if he lived) long gone. Sage relaxed her left arm, the facade of it being tied up forgotten. Then she leaned down, wrapping it around the man's neck. She squeezed until his whimpers died out, weak hands scrabbling at her arm, now protected by a layer of carapace. She squeezed harder, practicing killing with her remaining arm while she had the chance. His movements slowed, then stopped. His face shifted colors, and his body became limp beneath her. She held a little longer, making sure he was dead, then dropped the body.

"Three," she muttered.

"Sage?"

She spun, cutting the ropes clean with sharpened carapace and readying herself for another fight. Pain coursed through her body, the adrenaline pushing the drugs out of her system faster. That had been the last dose. She gritted her teeth against a wave of nausea and stared at her new enemy.

It was Wyn.

"Wyn!" She smiled, happy to see someone else alive. And he looked pretty unharmed. Maybe Sage had been the only one targeted by an ambush.

"I don't think she's going to be upright much longer." Sage looked down at a second voice and found a giant metal spider.

"Oh fuck!" She kicked it, hurtling it away. She fucking hated spiders. Especially ones bigger than her head. "You're going to have to kill that one," she said and felt her knees give out. Wyn rushed forward to hold her steady.

"No," he said. "That was actually Cee."

"Oh," she said. "It's a lot uglier than I remember."

"It's a long story. Can you move? We have a base."

She laughed. "Wanna hear a joke?"

"What's that, Sage?"

"We're gonna die." Then she laughed. "We're all going to die."

"No, we're not," Wyn said. "I'm getting us out of here."

She would have had a brilliant comeback if she hadn't passed out at that moment.


Zetta's body was numb, except where the skin had peeled back to expose the muscle. All she could smell was blood. And piss. And shit. Some of which was sure to be her own. Her wounds wept, a dark red that should have been concerning. Unfortunately, exhaustion was at the forefront of her mind and just about the only thing she could focus on. So she lay there, in some muddy cell out in the open. The sun beat down on her during the day while rain from the edge of the weather ring whipped in to splatter her body.

Not only that, but she was also naked. That made sleeping difficult. Not that she minded sleeping naked. It was the sleeping naked while being exposed to the elements that really bothered her.

She reached for Geble, not for the first time. Its feeble response told her it lived, but when she pulled on it to release its muscle-enhancing toxins, it almost seemed to whine. Not that her muscles expanding made her feel all the better. A groan was pulled from her lungs, and she coughed. Her limbs still twitched from the effort.

There was movement outside her cell, and one of her captors approached with a long pole in hand, as they always did. They began poking and prodding her, and she ignored it. Until it hit an open wound. She twitched and growled (really more a groan), and the woman smiled. "Good to see you're still alive," she said. Zetta had a hard time figuring out human ages, but she had to be nearly a kid. "You're our golden ticket, I think."

"Have you even asked her?" a boy, no older, asked. "We don't even know if she's the one."

"Of course she's the one." She glared. "She's got the same coloring as the picture."

"That don't mean anything, Jantz!" the boy said. "I think they all have that coloring, or near enough."

"Fine! I'll ask her." The prodding resumed, and Zetta knocked the pole away, surprising herself when her hand cooperated. "Hey!" the girl shouted. "Are you that vrolak named Zetta?"

Zetta glared at her. The movement seemed to kick-start something within her. Almost seemed to wake her from a stupor. So she answered. "No," she moaned.

"Huh," the boy said.

"Think we can trust that?" Jantz added.

"Probably not." He scratched at a patchy beard for several itches too long before he spoke again. "Hey, vrolak! Are you lying to us?"

"Why would I say yes?" Zetta asked.

"She's got a point," Jantz said.

"What do you think we should do?" the boy asked.

A third person walked up and slapped the boy on the head. "It's none of your concern, you fucking fools. Leave the vrolak alone. We're turning her in alive no matter what. At least we'll get the vrolak slave price if she ain't the one." He chased the two away, leaving only a large bishett man that could have been mistaken for a young vrolak. He was shirtless, showing off many well-toned muscles. Zetta wanted to vomit at the narcissistic efforts.

"Sorry for them," he said, leaning against the bars. He was a brave one, and Zetta's lip curled in a desire to prove it was foolish. She pushed herself into a sitting position and quickly dropped all thought of that plan. She panted from the effort, and fresh blood oozed from her wounds. Everywhere she was numb stopped being numb and ended up being excruciatingly painful instead. "Are you that Zetta person?" he asked.

"I'll tell you the same thing I told them." She looked up at the man and glared. "Why the fuck would I say yes?"

He shrugged. "Because you're hungry?" He dropped a bag, its bottom wet with grease, on the ground, and cooked meat rolled out into the mud. Her stomach rumbled as she watched it come to a stop. "See, it don't actually matter much whether you tell the truth," he said, standing back. He gestured behind him at the ten to twelve others moving around the small camp. "We're planning to bring you to Sovereign's tower anyway. They pay a lot for vrolaks. I just don't want to seem like an idiot, claiming you are someone you ain't. You know?"

If she moved fast enough, she could reach the meat. But if she was too slow, he'd kick it out of reach. Instead, she rose to her feet. He tensed with every step she took. But her slow movement put him at ease. She reached the bars and grinned a toothy grin.

"Yeah, I'm Zetta."

He smiled. "That's a good girl." Then he picked up the grease-soaked sack and stuffed it between the bars, dropping it in Zetta's waiting hand.

Zetta dropped the sack and grabbed his hand in a flash of movement. Her muscles tensed, and pain shot through her arm, which simply made her angry. He tried to pull away, and she slammed him against the cage. Others came running at his shouts, weapons pulled. They shouted, everyone shouted. Zetta leaned close to the man's face, smelling the fear sweat that encased him.

"I'm not going to eat your fucking table scraps," she growled. "No, I'll save my hunger. And once I'm free of this cage, I will feast on your body." She licked her lips. "So yeah, I don't mind telling you who I am, because you're not likely to live long enough for it to matter."

Someone shot into the air as they continued to shout at her. They were all around her now, trigger fingers quaking at the first sign of an attack. She laughed and released the bishett's arm. He fell back into the mud and crawled away. Zetta stomped the meat into the ground, then grabbed at the bars.

"If any of you want to live past this night, I suggest leaving this camp. Otherwise, I will kill every last one of you."

They stared in horror, and she took a big sniff. A delicious smell of fear to wash away the awful smells of her confinements. Then she stepped away and found a decent place to sit in the cell and attempt to figure out how exactly she was going to make good on that threat.

After making sure the bishett man was unharmed, everyone returned to whatever business around the camp they'd been about. Zetta caught Jantz's gaze and saw it grow larger as she scuttled away. Maybe the kids would be frightened enough to actually leave. She doubted anyone else would. They seemed to have experience with vrolaks, which meant they underestimated her by holding her to such low standards.

A bug flew in front of Zetta's face, and she waved it away. Then it returned, persistently keeping in front of her despite every swipe of her claw.

"What the fuck?" she growled, then looked closer. She knew that shape. It landed on the back of her hand, fluttering its wings and humming. "Achtrek?"

Two more flew up and buzzed around her head before settling down next to the first. She smiled. Looks like she had an escape plan after all.

"It's good to see you, Bugs. How are you? Did you get ambushed too?"

They buzzed in unison. *Yes.*

"Shit. What shape are you in?" When the beetles didn't answer, she rethought her plan. There was some level of consciousness in them if they answered, so they hadn't been *too* harmed, right? She just needed them to understand. "Can you come here? To me." She pointed at her chest. "All of you. Through the mud, quietly."

There was no answer, but she saw the first of the beetles trickle in through the mud and knew it understood. If they could gather around her, hide in the mud, Zetta could make use of that. She only needed one to do the puppet mastery, as long as it could bring the body back to her. If there was enough to puppet master all of them, all the better for the plan. As much as she wanted to kill the bishett man, she was in no shape to—

She paused her train of thought. Ten other beetles had crawled to her. Then nothing. Her heart sank.

"Achtrek?" The beetles looked up at her. "Is..." She gritted her teeth. Stupid fucking emotions. Why was she sad about a sentient pile of bugs? "Is this all of you?"

One buzz.

She closed her eyes. *Fuck.*

Achtrek's intelligence diminished with each loss. On Angbor, they had struggled after losing nearly half their number. What would happen with only thirteen?

She bit back the concern. It didn't matter. Those beetles were lost, and nothing would change that. But she could escape, protect the ones that still lived.

Fuck, would they even be able to understand her? Coordinate with her?

"I need to get out of here," Zetta whispered. The beetles stared at her. "Can you help with that? Can you puppet one of them?"

The beetles wandered around aimlessly, digging into the mud and fluttering their wings.

"Pay attention!" she growled, and heads perked up to look over at her. She glared back. "Wouldn't want to miss my escape," she added just for them. Two slavers whispered to each other and laughed, turning their backs.

"If only I was strong enough to break the lock, I'd tear them all limb from limb."

Achtrek buzzed, and Zetta's eyes darted down to the nearest bug. "What's wrong?"

It shook the mud free with fluttering wings, then took off and flew to the cell door. It climbed into the lock, then there was a little hiss, barely audible. A faint mist followed the exiting beetle, and another one took its place.

"Caustic spray." Zetta smirked. "Now that will be helpful."

"Would you shut the fuck up!" some hairy human yelled over. He had that fur growing from his face and head in equal lengths, and not short. She wondered if he was crossbred with a perrilan.

Zetta stood and leaned against the bars near the door. They'd be unlikely to spot Achtrek if she said nothing, but she also needed a body nearby. At least she could annoy him enough to make sure he didn't see. "You wanna come over here and make me?" she growled.

He threw down whatever he was holding, picked up a stun-staff, and charged the cell. Zetta took a few steps back as he thrust the weapon in her direction. Not far enough to let Zetta take his weapon, which meant it wasn't far enough to do anything. "You're over here mumbling the fuck away. What happened to your big escape plan? Have you figured it out, or is it to annoy us all to death?"

"Just leave it be, Gent!" the bishett man called over. "She's just trying to rile you up."

"Yeah, well, I would love to hear her fucking plan. Amaze us, you half-dead lizard." He leaned forward right next to the door, rather courageously, given what had happened to the bishett, and bared his fangs. Those pathetic porcelain teeth could barely tear through cooked meat. What did he expect her to fear from it? "This cage is made from pure celuein, thick enough even vrolak claws would shatter against it. But let's say you give it a shot. We have several electrical cables hooked up that will give you a nice little tickle if you start trying." He knocked on the metal and looked at her. "Not active right now, obviously. It's expensive to use that much electricity. But I doubt you'd escape so fast we wouldn't have time to flip the switch. Even then, we have several stunstaffs if we get bored and want to handle it ourselves. Not to mention the fact you look like the ass end of a haushedin right now. We'd hardly need so much assistance."

His demeanor shifted, and he scowled and grabbed at the bars, hatred running through his pathetic glare. "I've helped take down your kind many times before. Arrogance runs through you all and reinforces your stupidity."

Zetta felt the beetles crawling on her back. Could count each one. She kept close track of them. Twelve were there now. "It's hard not being arrogant," Zetta told the man. "Especially when you come over here, shouting about how you had to work with others to take down a vrolak. I know a woman who could go toe to toe with one on her own. You're fucking pathetic."

"Who's the one inside the cage, and who's the one outside?"

The thirteenth landed on her back. She grinned, a much sharper set of fangs on display now. "The only thing that will matter is who's left standing in the next forty seconds. And I can guarantee it won't be you."

Emotion slipped from his face. "You're bluffing."

"Don't bet on it."

"How could you—"

He never got to finish that question. Zetta leapt forward and slammed a foot into the door, its lock eroded away by Achtrek. The thick door swung open and slammed into Gent, sandwiching him between the door and the cage. Blood sprayed out from his mouth, and the stunstaff slipped from his hand. Zetta jumped out and closed the door as shouts rose from the camp. A dazed Gent spun toward her, eyes wide in panic as he struggled for a weapon at his belt. She raked one claw across his throat, and blood sprayed out across her.

The camp was in an uproar, everyone reaching for rifles and stunstaffs, even a shovel in one brave case. She could have laughed. This fight would have been nothing if she wasn't weeping from a thousand wounds and if Geble didn't cry out at the thought of providing her some nice bulking juice. She'd have to do without that. It'd been a long time since she'd had a fight without the muscle enhancements. Given everything, it almost made this fight fair.

Almost.

"Return to the cage, and drop Gent." The bishett man held a hand up in peace, the other hand pointing a pistol at her. Zetta glanced in surprise at her other hand to find the man dangling from it, his blood seeping between her claws. She had meant to drop him but had gotten distracted watching the slavers. She shrugged.

"No." Then she kicked the fallen stunstaff into her free hand and launched it. The bishett man was speared through the chest, pinning him to a wooden hut. "I've also decided not to eat you. You'd probably be too chewy."

The fight began in earnest then. They no longer cared about their money; they cared about their lives, proving it by opening fire on her almost immediately, not bothering to preserve her identity. Gent hadn't been the largest human she'd ever seen, but he was large enough to work as an effective shield as Zetta rushed into the barrage. What bolts slipped past her guard grazed her sides, her legs, her arms, but never leaving more than a slight burn mark. Vrolak skin was notoriously tough. It would take more than that.

They paused in their gunfire for a moment, too much dust and smoke obscuring the area, the smell of burning flesh strong on the wind. Zetta stepped from that cloud of smoke with a burnt and bloodied corpse, sans four limbs that had fallen off several shots earlier, held in front of her. She grinned and could practically smell their fear.

"If you want some fun," she growled, "go for the eyes!" Then she tossed the corpse into the crowd of slavers. She felt the remnants of Achtrek leave her back, buzzing through the air in search of a meal.

It was a strange thing in that moment, an oddity that hadn't happened to her in a very long time. The thrill of fighting a fight that could end in death. Sure, as a bounty hunter she could see it happening at any given moment, theoretically. But in reality, most fights she entered had a fairly certain outcome. This was different. Wounds weeping, Geble disabled, one versus many. She entered a state of euphoria, every zap of the stunstaffs coursing through her like an orgasm. Every plasma bolt the heat of a passionate kiss.

Her kills came in a blur, so fast she didn't even remember them. Her claws gashed through flesh, disemboweling and dismembering. Her jaws slammed down, tearing and shredding. Warm blood ran down her throat, slaking a thirst she had not noticed before. Achrek ripped through the eyes of someone, destroying their brain before their stunstaff had a chance to collide with Zetta. She grabbed the body and tore it in two above her, then tossed the halves into the crowd. The world turned red with blood, her own and that she spilled. It was a beautiful chaos. It was why she existed. And when the last body fell, its arm torn free, dangling from one claw, Zetta knelt in a crowd of gore and panted. No one moved around her except for thirteen beetles consuming the flesh of the fallen.

She had won, and she hurt for it. Her eyes fell on Jantz's limp body, the boy nearby as well. She sighed. She had warned them to leave. Now they were two corpses lying in bloody mud, throats torn open.

"Zetta?"

Her head shot up to find a bishett woman standing on the edge of the ring of bodies. The man's wife? No, it wouldn't be. This one still had spots. The bishetts were odd ones for that. Unless he was worse than she had first imagined. But she didn't seem horrified, just shocked. And she had two blades in hand but didn't seem prepared to use them now that the fight was done. A friend? How had she snuck up on Zetta, anyway? Even weakened as she was, that would be a challenge.

She smirked once the pieces came together. "Besari," she said with certainty. "You seem less birrosh these days."

Besari's cheeks darkened a shade, and she looked away. "Yes, we can discuss that later. I came to save you."

Zetta looked around. "Did you get a kill in?"

"No," Besari said, a queasy look on her face. "I tried to help, but it seemed better to just not."

Zetta laughed. "Good call." She stood back up, and her legs gave out, dropping her into someone's intestines. Besari was at her side, stepping carefully as she wrapped an arm as far around the vrolak as she could get, her knives sheathed once more.

"I might have overdone it," Zetta admitted.

"We have a hideout and medical supplies. I'll help get you back there, and we can patch you up."

"We?"

"Wyn, Cee, and I met up. We just found you and Sage. We split up to bring you two back as soon as possible. We haven't been able to locate Achtrek."

Zetta glanced over at the beetles still feasting and sighed. "I have." She whistled, and the beetles seemed to respond. "Come."

The thirteen beetles flew to Zetta's shoulder and perched there. Besari stared, wide-eyed. "Is that it?"

"That's all of them."

Besari's eyes watered, on the verge of tears. Then they turned to steel. "Let's move," she said.

Zetta smiled. This one would be a great hunter; she had the sense to bite down on her emotions if needed. Zetta felt that empty pit in her stomach, something the fury of the fight had never really washed away. Whatever these thirteen beetles were now, they weren't Achtrek, not anymore. They never would be. Even if they could rebuild the hive, a different personality would emerge. Her friend was as good as dead, but she wouldn't let the remnants of their life be wasted. These bugs would be returned to the Hive, even if it took everything she had.

# CHAPTER 25

## A TIME FOR BOLDNESS

T he sun peeked over the distant ring of clouds, shining down on a city already bustling. No rest for the slaves, it seemed. The wind rustled leaves across the street, though Wyn didn't feel it. He hid away in his combat suit, mask in place. He stared up at his own visage projected across the front of a building, the five others positioned nearby.

Achtrek was dead, or near enough. Cee had explained *that* after they had been able to patch up the worst of Zetta's and Sage's wounds. And there were a lot of those. The hive would likely rebuild, but whether it would rebuild to be the same personality was not a given. The last of Achtrek's bugs would die off before it was large enough anyway. Would it even be fair to consider them the same? More likely, the remnants would be returned to the Mother.

Zetta and Sage were at least alive, if barely. Both suffered from fevers, Sage with the added bonus of withdrawal. She had used all of her pain medication in a very short amount of time. And Wyn sat out in an alley, useless as his friends suffered around him. He fucking hated it.

The door creaked open, and Besari stepped outside. A little of the dread curling in his gut lifted at the sight of her. He would never tire of seeing her face.

"How are they?" he asked.

She sighed and slipped to the ground next to him, exhaustion tugging at her eyes. "They're both sleeping well for the first time in days. I think we're past the worst of it." She watched him carefully before adding, "What about you? I haven't seen you sleep yet, and it's almost your watch."

"I haven't slept since we got them."

"Wyn! I don't know a lot about human physiology, but I know you have to sleep."

Wyn shrugged. Maybe it was the adrenaline, but he didn't feel all that tired. Exhausted? Yes. Deep into his bones, like every movement should be accompanied by an ancient creaking. But still he couldn't sleep. He would lie bundled in sheets and stare at the ceiling for hours. He was useless for even that.

"Wyn." Besari's voice was softer, a hand reaching out for his. "What are you thinking?"

Wyn stared up at his own face and swallowed. "When it was just us, I could pretend everyone survived. They escaped, and that's why we couldn't reach them. But now we've found them. We've discovered the answer, and I feel shattered. One of my friends is dead. Three more nearly died. *You* could have died. And I can't do anything about it." He felt tears spill down his cheeks and was happy for the privacy of the helmet. He breathed carefully through his mouth to keep the sniffles from Besari's ears. "I don't know what to do. I have to find a way off this planet for all of us, but I don't know how."

"We'll figure it out, Wyn. Together. Once Sage and Zetta are stabilized, we—"

"No." Wyn shook his head. "I could have lost you in the ambush. This is all my fault. *I* will find a way off this planet. I can't risk losing you."

"You won't," Besari said as she squeezed his hand. "Remember what we said. We're stronger together. Unbeatable. If I die, then you drag me back from it. If you die, I'll do the same. I'm not leaving you alone, not when you matter as much to me as I do to you. We all agreed to this mission, and we're all in it together."

"I can't keep watching my friends die, Besari." Wyn felt the sob leak out, caught it, and pulled it back within himself. He gritted his teeth and shut his eyes.

"Then you can't keep being a bounty hunter," she said.

Wyn stared at her, the pressure in his chest intensifying into a sharp pain. "What?"

"You expected to be a bounty hunter and not see anyone hurt? Worse, you expected to create a team of bounty hunters and never see them hurt?"

Wyn bit his lip against the words. Nothing he could think to say would help his case. Besari did not relent.

"Each and every one of us became a bounty hunter knowing there was the chance that any job could be our last. Any job could be *someone else's* last. If you let that break you, how can any of us rely on your support? How can I trust you to do your duty if you only focus on my safety?

"I'm not saying it's easy. Loss is never easy. I'm saying that it's something that needs to be picked up, pocketed, and dealt with later.

It's the best we can do with what we're given, and anything less becomes a liability."

Wyn stared out of the alley, Besari's hand warm in his. He took deep breaths, bringing his boiling emotions to a simmer, then even lower. She was right. Of course she was. He was a liability if he kept acting like this. Sage and Zetta were alive. That's what mattered. If he wanted to keep them that way, he needed all the help he could get. And that meant Besari and Cee. Untrusting of his voice, he simply nodded. Besari smiled and stood, then pulled him to his feet.

"I want you to try and get some sleep, too. Wearing yourself too thin is also a detriment. Tomorrow, we'll begin finding a way off this planet."

Wyn wanted to protest, but before he could, she leaned forward and kissed his helmet. Then, there was nothing left to do except follow Besari back into their building.

They paused at the door of their makeshift infirmary, where both patients stared intently at the other. Zetta spoke first.

"How'd you lose it?" she growled.

"Cut it off," Sage said, wiggling her stump just above the elbow.

"Yourself?"

"A dysfunctional parachute helped, but I finished the job."

"That was my favorite of your arms, you know. The fingers reached all the right places."

"This one works just as well." Sage raised her left hand and made a rude gesture. The intensity broke as they both smirked.

"It better," Zetta said, "or I'll leave you stranded again and find someone with two functional arms."

"Good luck with that." Sage grinned. "I'm better with my left than just about anyone with their choice of two arms."

Zetta looked over at the new arrivals then and pulled Wyn into the conversation. "I can strand her here, right? She's gotten a bit too cocky for my tastes."

"Actually," Wyn said, "there's a teamwork clause in the contract you signed. Very serious legal troubles can be brought against you if you desert a fellow Bounty Inc. hunter."

"What?" Zetta looked shocked.

"Didn't you read the contract?" Wyn asked.

"I skimmed it," Zetta admitted.

"Sage wanted that in there. She handled the specific wording."

"You bitch," Zetta growled. Sage smirked and leaned back. Then, in a flash, Zetta's expression shifted. "So, clearly I wasn't the only one ambushed." She pointedly looked at Cee's head, propped up on two hands.

"We've determined there was a leak at Bounty Inc.," Wyn said. "Sovereign must have had our plans beforehand and used them to create traps."

"Like trapping Sage's arm in a dysfunctional parachute," Zetta grinned.

"Nah, there were like twenty people trying to kill me. Even an eddermar and a haushedin." She shrugged. "When that failed, the last guy tried to blow a hole in the ship and hoped the drop would kill me. It didn't." She glanced at Zetta. "What'd they do for you, stick you in a shredder?"

"A volcano actually."

Sage's eyebrows rose. "The volcano looks to have won."

"The volcano never had a shot. I clawed my way through like ten inches of celuein and then jumped from the falling death trap into a lake. You've never seen a more perfect shot."

"You hit it?"

"Wouldn't be here if I missed, now would I?"

Sage's eyes narrowed, but she didn't deny the argument. A few beetles buzzed at Zetta's shoulder, huddling close together. "No saying what happened to them," Sage said.

"Burned," Zetta said. "There's some scorch marks on a few. They must have been locked in a tightly sealed room and burned to death."

"They shot my ship out of the sky," Cee said. "Barely a scrap of me survived."

"We've noticed," Sage said. "What about you two? You look barely scratched. Either they underestimated you or didn't care if you lived."

Wyn blushed and was once more thankful for the helmet. "Cee's travel plan got disrupted, and I had to improvise. Ended up coming in a different way than expected."

"I didn't wear my suit," Besari added. "They expected to find a birrosh and found a bishett."

"Smart," Zetta said, then looked down. "So, you two fucking now that things got dire?"

Wyn and Besari immediately dropped each other's hands. Besari's eyes grew wide, and her face darkened. Wyn was sure his did the same.

"Wyn's trip got disrupted because he overslept and missed a flight," Besari rambled.

Wyn spun. "How could you?" he hissed.

"You've got to be fucking kidding me." Zetta scowled. "You missed your ambush because you overslept?"

Sage simply laughed.

"Anyway," Zetta added, "I want to be the one to kill Seph. He took away my favorite arm."

"Seph?" Wyn's panicked heart slammed against his chest. "Why are you killing Seph?"

"Obviously, he's the leak," she said.

"I told you putting out ads for jobs would attract weirdos," Sage added. "Now you let a betrayer into our midst."

"We don't know it was him."

Sage and Zetta shared a look before staring at Wyn. "Was it either of you two?" Sage asked.

Wyn's stomach dropped, the coiled dread returning to fill his every nook and cranny. "I..."

"Exactly," Sage said. "It wasn't Achtrek because they wouldn't do that to themselves. It wasn't us. Cee's unlikely. It could have just killed us at the office."

"Thank you," Cee said.

"You're welcome," Sage said. "So it was either you, Besari, or Seph."

"What about a bug? Or someone hacking into our systems?"

"Negative," Cee said. "I had been monitoring everything, especially involving our plans for Kekar. Nothing suspicious, and I doubt anything would have snuck past my security."

"You don't remember anything except *that*?" Wyn asked.

"I didn't control what memories remained," Cee said.

"We should at least talk to him before we kill him," Wyn said. "I'm still not convinced he was the one."

"Yeah, I can talk to him," Zetta said, her smirk bone-chilling.

"No," Wyn said, "I'll talk to him first."

"I get to kill him though."

"Only if the accusations are proven true!"

"Yeah, yeah. I'm sure there's a teeny tiny chance he's not at fault."

"Why would he do it?" Wyn asked.

"Why does anyone do anything?" Sage asked. "Probably money."

"But he doesn't even care about money," Wyn said. "He took the job because his parents made him get one. He blows all his money on recreational drugs and food. He's having an affair with L-Bot!"

"What?" Zetta perked up, and even Sage's eyes grew wide.

"I walked in on him and L-Bot, um, well..."

"Was he taking it?" Zetta asked, sitting up a little more. "I can't imagine fucking a robot the other way to be very warming. Unless it has, like, a heater in its butt cheeks? Does it have a synthetic butt?"

"No wonder he chose that body," Sage added.

"He did seem weirdly close to L-Bot," Besari said. "Even with how much they worked together."

"It's unimportant!" Wyn interrupted them before the conversation spiraled further. "He doesn't seem like the kind of person who would betray us like that."

"They never do." Zetta shook her head. "Until you slice them open and find the rot within."

Wyn wanted to scream, to pace the room. Seph had betrayed them? The same guy who smoked drugs and fucked a robot? It didn't make sense, but everyone else seemed to believe it. Was he just fooling himself? Afraid to lose another friend?

"Given the situation," Cee said, "I think it's wise for me to come clean about something."

Wyn paused in his newest mental breakdown and stared at the head. Everyone else gazed at it too.

Cee sighed. Strange, given the lack of lungs. "I have been mistrusting with you all. Perhaps it is the loss of ninety-three percent of my processors, or maybe it is just time to put secrets to the side. This experience of trauma has bonded us into a group that would live and die for each other, and for that I thank you all for having me be a part of it."

Wyn glanced around, his nerves on edge, almost jittery. Besari shifted nervously herself, Sage's eyes narrowed, and Zetta looked ready to leap into a fight if necessary.

"From our earliest time together," it continued, "signing that contract and becoming fellow coworkers, revamping the Bounty Inc. security, and even that time on Bezium, I have grown close to you all, except maybe you Zetta. But I believe this has helped bridge the gap—"

"Abyssal hell, Cee!" Sage interrupted. "Get on with it."

"Yes, well, I am not a cyborg. I am an artificial intelligence, forced into hiding by absurd Raiyrium laws. But I mean you no harm and have no intention of recreating versions of myself to form some large empire of synthetics."

"Well, fuck me with a used legal bot," Zetta said. Achtrek's remnants hummed in agreement.

"Unbelievable," Sage murmured. "Right under our noses this whole time."

Besari held a hand up to her mouth and contributed her own theatrical gasp.

Wyn took this all in, his brain seeming to run at half speed before realizing he was also supposed to feign surprise. "Oh, wow."

"You were all aware," Cee said, its voice deflated.

"Clocked it the first time I talked to you," Sage said.

"Oh dear," Cee said. "My infiltration into organic society seems flawed. I will need details on everything that gave me away, if you don't mind."

"I do mind," Sage said. "Let's get out of here first."

"Wyn and I are working on that," Besari said. "We have a plan. Most of one, anyway."

"Great," Zetta said. "I feel safer already."

"Maybe you two should wait until we're better," Sage said.

"There's no time," Wyn said. "I've seen people sweeping the streets. We need to get out of here as soon as possible. Hiding will only keep us safe for so long."

"What's your plan?" Sage asked. "I want to make sure it's not shit."

"We'll scout the hangar today," Besari said. "With my talent, I can get in close and find some way to steal a ship. Mostly just intelligence gathering, and tonight, we'll come up with a plan."

"Make sure to include us," Zetta said.

"Of course," Wyn said.

"Take Cee with you," Sage said. "Zetta and I are past the worst of it. We don't need babysitters. Plus, it'll be helpful for gathering more information."

Wyn nodded. "You two rest. Tomorrow we leave."


Sovereign's tower speared the sky, faint shimmers radiating outward to the perfect ring of dark clouds. Its shadow swallowed up the port and everything nearby. Wyn leaned casually against a nearby wall, forcing his focus on the port even as his eyes glided back to Kekar's centerpoint. His enemy sat within, trying to hunt them down. Wyn wanted nothing more than to storm in there and take him by force. But as they were, that would be impossible.

The streets were crowded with people entering and leaving with each ship. On some mission of enslaving or otherwise terrorizing the people of the Raiyrium Confederation. Wyn watched as a pair of armed guards swept through the crowd, rifles at the ready. Between them stood a leaky birrosh man. Well, that was the best way Wyn could think of him. He almost seemed to melt in the sun, but the parts that fell off crawled back into him. A Thresha talent? Something else?

"Cee?" Wyn whispered. "Are you seeing this?"

"Yes, Wyn." Its voice rang in his helmet. The head currently rested in his backpack, a single cable looping up to interface with Wyn's helmet. This way, it could watch through Wyn's eyes, or at least his helmet's visor, without attracting the attention a severed head with two hands for feet normally would. "On their chests, it's the sigil of Sovereign. His personal guards."

"What are they doing at the port?"

"Likely searching the city for you and Besari. Possibly Zetta and Sage if rumors that they yet live have reached Sovereign."

Wyn couldn't imagine rumors not flying. Sage had stumbled around the city, doped out of her mind, with a freshly removed arm. And Zetta had only been on the outskirts, but those slavers had hoped to sell her. He hadn't even considered that Sovereign would send out search parties if the bounties failed. How safe would their hideout be? How much longer did they have?

The searching guards entered a building, directing the leaky man within. "Did you see his eyes?" Wyn asked.

"They seemed unfocused," Cee responded.

"Not just that, but like the light within has died. Like a corpse risen. There's no life in his eyes."

"Your assessment seems fantastical," Cee said. "But yes, several of Shekta's experiments showed similar signs of distress."

"What?" Wyn blurted the word out louder than anticipated, and a slave walking by glanced his direction, fear in her eyes. Wyn almost apologized, but he remembered his place. "What experiments? I didn't think anyone was there."

"There were three ongoing experiments while we were there, but I analyzed footage from dozens over the months prior as well. Her artificially-induced Thresha substance damaged the brains of nearly every subject. It reduced their consciousness to minimal operating levels, except when extreme stress triggered it. Such as the violent actions of combat. It made for solid soldiers to toss into battle, but they were too expensive and Sovereign wanted more intelligent minions. She never cracked the issue though. Shame, too, because I could have helped her."

"You're just telling this to me now? What about when we were there?"

"Didn't seem relevant to the situation. Nor was I aware the experiments were brought to Kekar. I thought they were disposed of. Perhaps that was a deception in case the Bezium government wanted the soldiers too."

"You said there were three ongoing experiments?" Wyn felt a lump hovering somewhere between his chest and throat. "Didn't we blow that place up?"

"Just the upper levels," Cee said. "The lower levels are where the experimenting occurred."

"We just left them there."

"Yes," Cee confirmed.

"We could have saved them."

"Possibly."

"And we didn't."

"That was not part of the mission parameters."

"Who cares?" Wyn took a deep breath to calm down, to let his emotions simmer. "We left people, likely to die, when we could have saved them."

"We saved them from experimentation," Cee said. "They were likely either killed, put out of their misery, or freed from the situation. Arguably better than if we tried to drag them through the complex and got them killed that way."

"How much did you download from Shekta's systems? Can we find them, make sure they're okay?"

"Possibly. I can run a search algorithm when we return to the Bounty Inc. offices."

"What about the serum? Can you recreate it without the negative side effects?"

"Not as I am," Cee said. "But in a whole body, my memory restored from backups, it is likely."

Wyn wondered what it would be like to have his own talent. The yearning was something he had stomped down long ago, trying to forget the failure of the tank. But it was hard to watch Besari or Sage use theirs.

Speaking of which, Besari stepped out from the nearby alley, her face weary from exhaustion.

"The port is almost as secure as Sovereign's tower," she whispered as she leaned against the wall next to him. "I don't know how we're going to sneak Sage or Zetta in there. I can't keep us all invisible."

"We can figure that out later, but what about the ships?"

"They get locked down when they land. Port security runs through every ship before releasing it." She shook her head. "We can get *to* a ship, we might even be able to get the ship airborne, but if we don't also get approval to fly, the haushedins will shoot us out of the sky."

"So escape is impossible." Wyn wanted nothing more than to run his hand through his hair. "We're stuck here."

"Sage and Zetta might have ideas. I recorded some of the process on my Vico. They can analyze it and come up with a way to not get us shot down."

"Your codes, Cee?"

"Unlikely to work again," it admitted, voice echoing from Wyn's helmet now that Besari arrived. "Not enough to trust them. More so if we're leaving in a hurry due to theft of a ship. We could try to fight them. I destroyed nearly the entirety of one ship by myself. The other two shouldn't be difficult now."

"Through deceptions and sabotage," Besari said. "We'll be one shuttle screeching toward them. They'll just incinerate us."

"Hmm," Cee said.

"So we need a reason to not get destroyed," Wyn added.

"We need new codes," Besari added. "If we can get the ship airborne, the codes can get us home. With enough luck, we'll move fast enough before the haushedin fleet finds out."

"I do not believe that plan will work," Cee said.

"We need a *different* reason to not get destroyed," Wyn added as a small nugget of inspiration struck him. He had yet to figure out if it would lead to a bad idea or a *really* bad idea.

"Like what?" Besari asked. "A big sign that says 'Please don't shoot me'?"

"A hostage," Wyn said, his smirk filling his face.

"It might work," Besari said, her eyes drifting off in thought. "But what hostage would be important enough to Sovereign to not blow us up?"

Besari's head snapped over as Wyn looked on with a smile. She couldn't see it, but based on her incredulous expression, he was sure she expected it to be there.

"No," she said.

"It's the only way to guarantee our way off planet."

"No," she said again, shaking her head vigorously.

"He would order them to not blow us up. He would never kill himself just to get us."

"It's a terrible idea."

"We're out of good ones."

"How the fuck do we even get to him? He's got to be in the tower, surrounded by guards."

"He has search parties in the city, and he'll be focused on locking down the port. He'd never expect us to continue the bounty."

"Because it's stupid."

"Some of the greatest strategies in war seemed stupid until they were pulled off."

"I think you're making that up. And it doesn't matter. You and I are hardly the greatest soldiers in the galaxy. Any sort of assault on the tower would be doomed to fail. Probably before we even get over the gate."

"Then we won't fight our way in."

"Even better." Besari rolled her eyes. "We'll just walk in, ask for Sovereign, then kidnap him."

"Pretty much," Wyn said.

This got her attention. "What?"

"Well, what's the number one thing Sovereign wants right now?"

"Our heads."

Wyn lifted his bag.

"Oh," Besari said.

"Oh no," Cee said.

"We have everyone he wants. Cee, Sage, Zetta. We bring the three in as presumptive captives, you and I in disguise, and we get close to Sovereign. Take him by surprise and we have our way out."

"How long until Sage and Zetta are even ready for something like that? How long until those search parties find us?"

"Fine," Wyn said. "Just us. The three of us. Sovereign must have his own private hangar; I noticed a ship leaving it when I arrived. We steal one of his ships after kidnapping him. Fly over to the hideout, pick up Sage and Zetta, and leave."

"I don't like it," Besari said. "No plan goes perfectly, and we all end up dead if any part of this one fails."

"It's our only chance."

"You think the guards will give us that chance?"

"I could produce a noxious cloud of gas," Cee offered. "I still have a canister within my mouth. If I am offered as a bounty, then when I am handed over for inspection, I could release it. It won't kill, but it will incapacitate anyone without a mask. At least for most species."

"See!" Wyn felt electricity course through his body. It was something. Bad or not, it was an action he could take.

"We should bring it back to Sage and Zetta first."

"Absolutely not," Wyn said. "They'll shoot it down. We should do this now while the search parties are out. This might be our only shot."

Besari stared at Wyn, resigned. Then sighed. "This is such a shit plan."

"We're unbeatable together," Wyn reminded her.

"Didn't Shekta beat both of you together?" Cee asked.

A single beetle fluttered its wings before biting into the flesh of a rotten fruit. It watched as the boy and girl chatted, the boy's arms flailing more and more as he talked. It watched as they walked toward the large spike. Not toward home, where they were supposed to walk. Its wings fluttered again, then it took off. Too long away from home. Needed home.

# CHAPTER 26

## BETRAYAL AT BOUNTY INC.

Pesh strolled down the ramp of their shuttle and out of the hanger. They hummed a tune, freshly stuck in their head, and Skritch hooted alongside them. The gridder deflated a little each time, sucking in a great amount of air to rise back up. Their webbed feet fluttered in the air to propel themself forward with great excitement. Emotions flared between their bond, exciting one another on a job well done.

Soon, Pesh would share the great information with Wyn, and he would delight. Not only had they won an endorsement from the Tset'As'Edder Joint Committee, but the Selk hatch had expressed desires of a different sort of partnership. A way for more eddermar bounty hunters to enter the galaxy. There would be more like Pesh in the coming years, and they were excited to see them pass through Bounty Inc.

"Hello, Pesh." Seph popped up from behind the counter as they entered the entrance hall. He looked irritated. That was odd. The human never seemed irritated. Maybe L-Bot was down for maintenance. He had a strange relationship with that robot.

"Greetings, Seph," they said, eyes looking around for anyone else. "Where might I find Wyn today?" Skritch bobbed nearby, lazily paddling their feet in such a way as to spin in circles, quickly bored by the conversation. Pesh was too. It was just rude to express it if you weren't a floating puffball.

"I tried to reach you, but there seems to be a communication issue," Seph said. "And with everyone out, I haven't been able to figure it out."

"Everyone out?"

"They went on a mission about two weeks ago. Shortly after you left for Tset'As'Edder."

"Everyone?" That wasn't good. Maybe Pesh would just stick around long enough to get a few things they needed, then leave. They couldn't imagine being stuck in the building alone with this strange human.

"Well, I think Shellesh went elsewhere. But everyone else went on this mission. Wyn found a big one. I don't really know the details."

"Two weeks..." Pesh considered for a moment. "Do you think they will be back soon?"

"Well, they were supposed to be back by now," Seph admitted, rubbing at the back of his neck. "I don't really know what to do if they don't come back."

"Zetta is with them. They'll come back." Then they reconsidered. "Maybe not alive. But they'll come back."

"It seemed really dangerous, whatever they were doing. What if they don't come back?"

"I wouldn't worry about it." Pesh waved at the human to dismiss the thoughts. "Where is the legal bot? I have a few questions."

"Down for maintenance," Seph said.

Yep, that explained the irritation. "Well then, I just have a few items I want to pick up, then I'll probably leave." The sooner, the better.

"If you need anything, let me know."

Pesh turned to the lounge and continued on, brushing away the conversation and opening the door. The details could be hammered out when Wyn returned. They weren't going to just sit around and wait—

They heard the familiar gagging noises of a gridder a moment from vomiting. Pesh dropped, all four legs spreading wide, abdomen flattening to the ground. It served well as two shots struck the wall where Pesh had been. That was all the secretary could get off before Skritch's vomit spewed onto his hand and wrist, solidifying into a strong adhesive and pinning Seph to the wall behind the counter.

Pesh was on their feet and spun to face Seph. The boy looked up at the cloudy yellow gunk coating his hand. "Oh," he said, a hint of surprise in his voice. "I didn't actually know they could do that. Maybe gridder serve a purpose after all."

They almost responded, but the look in his eyes gave away his intention. They barely had time to grab Skritch's leg and toss them into the adjoining room. Seph fired from his other hand, the shot skimming by the gridder's head. They squawked in protest, deflating and rolling across the ground. They hit a wooden chair, hooted in distress, and began eating it.

Pesh ducked beneath the next two shots, rolling across the ground and around a pillar. They sprang up, four pistols drawn, and fired. A stationary target would have been easy to hit pinned to a wall. Unfortunately, Seph no longer was. Somehow, the human had torn himself free, bringing some of the wall with him. The hesitation nearly cost them as a plasma bolt struck the pillar near their head and another grazed their shoulder, charring the chitin and sending sparks of pain down their arm.

Pesh swung the other way around the pillar as stone exploded from it with each additional shot. Glass shattered as several bolts destroyed the entrance. They thought about diving for it, giving them more room to fight. But that would mean abandoning Skritch. Which meant it wasn't an option unless they could guarantee Seph would follow.

"What's the matter, Seph?" Pesh called. "Wyn not paying you well enough? I'll be sure to pass along your complaints. Would hate for this to happen to the next assistant."

"Would you believe me if I said he denied my funeral request? I had to work the night of my granny's funeral!"

"What?" Pesh said as they fired blindly across the room, tracing after the voice. "Did he really?"

"No, I just wanted to see if you believed me." Seph dove to the side, firing at the now exposed Pesh. The first shot hit their hand, sending the pistol clattering to the ground and burning at least one of the fingers badly. Pesh returned fire, giving themself time to circle away. How was this assistant so talented? He moved far too quietly for Pesh's liking.

"Almost had you," he said, and the bastard wasn't even out of breath. Pesh nursed the injured hand, the fingers twitching. The nerves were damaged, rendering it useless. "Just come out and make this easy. I can even let you live."

"I don't think so," Pesh said. "You seem pretty intent on the killing approach."

"Yeah, I am, but you fell for the funeral thing, so I figured I'd try again."

Pesh ducked out to search for Seph, but he was gone. Back behind the desk. They saw some movement and fired along it. Seph popped up elsewhere and nearly shot their face. They could feel the heat radiate down through their exoskeleton. Shit, that one had been close. Several more shots hit the pillar in Pesh's absence, filling the room with a cloud of dust. Then it fell silent. Pesh tried to look for Skritch but couldn't see into the lounge from this angle.

"You know the others are likely dead, right?" he said. Pesh almost popped out. He sounded like he was standing at the desk as he normally did. It had to be a trap. Could he throw his voice? Or was he using something to aid him? "Shellesh might be alive, but honestly, it doesn't matter. I'll clean things up with you, then hunt him down in my spare time. He was never great at hiding himself."

Pesh fired blindly and was rewarded with snickering.

"Almost had me," he said. "Whizzed right by my ear. Might have some trouble hearing for a bit, you know." Pesh didn't believe him. "It's a shame I won't get to see Zetta one more time. I'd really like to thank her." There was a clang on the counter, something heavy. "It had to be her that requested this. She always loved her unwieldy weapons."

Unwieldy? The slag cannon?

Pesh heard the hum of the lancer and dropped to the ground again as a beam of thick red energy exploded through the pillar. Molten stone rained down on Pesh's back. More concerning, the beam dropped.

Pesh rolled out of the way as it hit the ground, eviscerating everything in its path. Then Seph swept it across the floor, chasing the fleeing eddermar. Pesh jumped as it came close, and the beam struck one foot, disintegrating it entirely. They hit the ground on seven limbs and a stump.

The ceiling cracked, then burst apart, depositing a table and chairs and all other kinds of debris into the entrance hall. Dust kicked up as the second floor crashed into the first, and Pesh took the moment to dive through the falling rubble. When things settled and Pesh lay against a heap of three chairs and a mini fridge, only creaks could be heard. Then laughter.

"Holy shit," Seph said. "Listen. I know you're in there, so give me a shout when you're about to die. I'd hate to bring more of this place down on myself."

Then the lancer hummed to life again. The beam exploded against the far wall and began a new trail of devastation across the room.


Skritch belched as they finished the last of the wooden chair. Their stomach gurgled with the rapid digestion, breaking apart the chair into vital components of energy, which then flooded their body. Worry and pain spiked through the bond, and Skritch leapt into the air with a large intake of breath. It bobbed up and down, spinning to face the room where Pesh fought.

The room collapsed into debris, and the bad person laughed. Pesh lived, but the emotions were filled with danger and worry. Skritch growled. The bad person would pay for harming their bonded. Their feet split up the length of their dangling legs, stretching against the webbing and transforming into wide flippers. Then they flapped wildly, firing themself across the room and into the entrance hall at full speed.

The gridder slammed into the bad person as he tried sweeping a large red beam across the room, knocking him off balance and disrupting the weapon. He turned in surprise, lifted his bad weapon, and Skritch vomited for the second time today. The yellow goo coated the weapon's muzzle as it heated up. The weapon fired, and Skritch's vomit gurgled and bubbled. Then the weapon turned red-hot and exploded.

The boom hurt Skritch's ears, and the gridder hooted in distress to make sure everyone knew. It also sent them barreling around the room, bouncing from desk, to wall, to ceiling, to floor, where it rolled to a stop.

Skritch sighed, deflating the rest of the way. Then they whined.

Pesh climbed from the rubble to find Skritch on their back, legs splayed, a high-pitched hoot coming from within. They also found Seph on the other side of the room. Or, at least what remained of him.

"Take a ride," Pesh said as they scooped the gridder up and set them on their shoulder. "You deserve it."

Skritch hummed in agreement.

Pesh hobbled over to the fallen assistant, injured leg curled up to avoid stepping on the tender stump. Then they stared down at Seph.

Half his face was gone, skull cracked wide, brains leaking out. His left arm had been shorn completely free of his body, his chest cavity cracked open. That was a dead human if Pesh had ever seen one.

Pesh looked at Skritch and chuckled. "I think he's dead."

Skritch hooted, alarm flaring in the bond. Pesh turned back to Seph, his one remaining eye wide, his half a mouth crooked up in a smile. A knife hummed in his hand, the blade transfiguring into a deep orange as it heated. Then he swung, and pain flared up Pesh's arm as one hand dropped to the ground in a spray of ichor. They backed up in surprise, crashing into the ruins of the front desk.

Seph clambered up, chasing them on one leg, a mad, gurgling bellow emanating from his throat even as blood spewed all over the ground.

They pushed at the raving corpse, and the blade jabbed into one arm. Pesh howled as the assistant tore it free and stabbed it into their chest. One of Skritch's legs flung out and smacked Seph in the side of his open skull. The human pulled the blade free and turned his attention to the gridder.

Pesh kicked his leg out, and the man dropped to the ground. Even as Pesh clambered over the desk, Seph pulled himself up on his leg again, that mad smile stretching across his face until it suddenly disappeared with the rest of his jaw.

This was a moment where Pesh felt absolutely certain that they panicked. It filled the bond as both of them stared at this thing. Blind terror yelled at them to hide. To flee. To get away. So Pesh did the only thing they could think of. They vomited.

The difference between gridder vomit and eddermar vomit is quite simple. Gridder vomit is one of the strongest adhesives in the galaxy. Eddermar vomit was just very flammable. Thankfully, Seph held a knife that was burning hot.

The corpse burst into flames as the stream of vomit covered it.

It screamed, but still it didn't fall. Sprinklers poured over the room, drowning the flames as the corpse shuffled unendingly forward.

Maybe running was good. Getting away was good. Anything but being here was good.

Pesh turned, flung open the door to the storage closet, and, like a child fleeing a nightmare, dove inside.

Which is where they found their nightmare, tied up, gagged, and writhing on the floor.

"What the fuck?" Pesh asked.

"Mmmrggff," Seph answered.

"What?"

Wyn stared at the two guards, a large, towering haushedin and a slim, brightly-colored falvian. His mouth was a bit dry, and his helmet displayed an elevated heart rate and excessive perspiration, as if he wasn't acutely aware.

"We're here for a bounty." Wyn hefted the backpack with Cee's head, shaking it in front of the falvian, who had been the talker.

His bird-like eyes shifted between Wyn and Besari. "What kind of bounty?"

"That will be discussed with Sovereign."

The haushedin's belly laugh shook the streets, and the falvian's soft tweets were like joyous music.

"You think we let everyone in just for a bounty?" the haushedin said. "Give it here. We'll evaluate it and get you your money."

Wyn stepped back as he reached for the sack, and Besari stepped forward, knives bare. The guards noticed the weapons and fumbled for their own. The falvian carried a stunstaff, the haushedin a large metal hammer. Wyn's free hand shot to his own pistol, but he refrained from drawing it.

"Not this kind of bounty," Wyn said. "It'll be handed off to Sovereign only."

"What makes it so important?" the falvian said.

"It's one of the six, and I want to make sure I get my money." Their eyes widened, and they glanced at each other, then back at the sack. This time, Wyn drew his pistol. "Don't try anything stupid. We have a failsafe to destroy the head beyond repair if you try to take it," Wyn lied, though it would have been a really good idea. Maybe not for Cee, but if he ever found himself carrying the severed head of a bounty, it might be a good idea. Then he immediately hoped he would never have to do just that.

The sparkle in their eyes disappeared, believing his words. "Rude," the haushedin said. "We would never steal from our loyal hunters."

"I'll phone it in," the falvian said. "Wait right here." Then he wandered off to the nearby security building attached to the walls surrounding Sovereign's tower.

"Which one did you get?" the remaining guard asked. His eyes carefully studied them, searching for any deception. Wyn guessed this is where telling the truth came in handy.

"The robot," he said, almost not twitching at the phrasing. He knew Cee hated it.

"Shit," the haushedin said, rubbing at his protruding chin. "That thing killed my cousin and his entire family. What a fucking monster. Glad it's dead."

Wyn blinked in surprise, but he kept his posture as steady as he could. Even Besari hesitated. Wyn had thought Cee had kept the killings to a minimum based on its report. He now wondered what Cee had thought "minimum" meant.

"I'm sorry to hear that," Wyn said, then, remembering he was supposed to be a tough, respectable bounty hunter, he added, "Glad we could get a bit of vengeance for you."

"They're good to go on. Worm's coming to collect them," the falvian said as he returned to the position in front of the gate. Then his yellow eyes shifted back to Wyn and Besari. "Be warned. If you're lying about the bounty or otherwise seeking profit or harm through deception, you will not leave this place alive. If you offend Sovereign, your life is forfeit. If you enter any room or hall without Worm as your guide, your life is forfeit. If Sovereign decides he doesn't like you, your life is forfeit." He seemed to almost smile, at least as much as one could with a beak. "Do you understand, and do you still wish to hand-deliver the head?"

"Yes," Wyn found himself saying. He wasn't sure how the word escaped, but it helped keep up the ruse, and that is all that mattered. At least he had the helmet to hide the worst of his fear, which coated his face like makeup.

The falvian nodded. "Then head in, and good luck."

The gates opened, and the guards stepped to the side. Beyond, a paved pathway led directly to the massive obsidian spike. Not as beyond stood a creature that Wyn had never seen before. Nearly eight feet in height and a deep purple coloring to their smooth skin, they wore a black robe from their neck (or where Wyn thought might be considered a neck), ending in a pool on the ground, from beneath which several tentacles slithered out. Two long, boneless arms wrapped around a tablet, which they stared at with a disproportionately small head, most of which was taken up by a single bronze eye. A tiny, circular mouth hung just below and now opened to speak in perfectly accented Raiyrium basic. "Follow me, please." The creature spun on their tentacles, ready to head back.

This must be Worm. And Worm must be a—

"Holy shit, are you a kroscion?"

They paused, turning back, shooting a look at Wyn too alien to decipher. "Yes."

"Didn't nearly your entire species get wiped out like thirty years ago?" Wyn had read about the kroscion genocide because the man who'd engineered it was one of the galaxy's highest bounties, still loose somewhere. It had been so thorough a slaughter, it was said you were more likely to meet a nairwid than a kroscion, not that you would know you met a nairwid.

"Nearly," Worm replied, deadpan. Wyn blushed, but before he could apologize, they turned back toward the tower and slithered down the path.

Besari elbowed Wyn, and he mumbled an apology to her. He sighed, sheathed his weapons, and followed their guide just as Besari did the same.

Wyn studied their surroundings, assessing every threat. What was behind that door? Could someone be hiding in that closet, ready to ambush them? Were there hidden passages in the walls? He used every scanner in his helmet, finding little activity on the ground floor. He wondered if he would find the same lack of activity on the above floors and was left wondering as they came to a stop in front of a set of doors. The kroscion pulled one open, gesturing them forward. They had never left the first floor. Wouldn't Sovereign be up higher? Fighting their way to the top of the tower would be suicide, especially with a captive.

"Are we not going farther up?" Wyn pushed the panic down. "To Sovereign's quarters?"

"This is his throne room," Worm said. "He is waiting within."

That was a bump in their plans. They had to be as close to Sovereign's private hangers as possible to have a chance. Should they bail now? Wyn glanced behind and saw two guards standing down the hallway. Was it too late?

"Right," Wyn said, then stepped around the door and inside, where his Vico's scanners alerted him to the next large bump in their plans. The throne room was a long rectangular room, nearly two hundred feet in length, and both sides were lined with hundreds of guards. *Hundreds.* They weren't even sure Cee's gas could spread throughout the rooms in their hideout. They could take out a handful, maybe. Then what? Fight literally hundreds of enemies to escape?

Wyn vomited in his mouth and forced himself to swallow. Besari had grown still and pale next to him. They needed to leave. Now!

The door slammed shut behind them as Wyn turned.

"Hello," a deep, resonant voice called from the other end of the long room. Wyn searched it out to find a raised platform filled the last quarter of the room, an elegant golden throne carved into it. A man sat there, a head of bright yellow hair sitting like a crown on his head, almost glowing, with eyes colored like blood and gold mixed together. As if made from the very lives he destroyed and the wealth he gained from each. Sovereign. "I hear you have a bounty for me. Come."

Wyn swallowed hard, then stepped forward and between the guards. Besari stepped close, barely moving her mouth as she spoke.

"What are we supposed to do?"

"I don't know," Wyn whispered, panic creeping into his voice. He fucked up again and again and again. Why did he even try? He wished he could go back in time and tell his stupid self to never take this bounty. To never start the company. He was going to die, and Besari would too. They couldn't do this.

"We need to leave," Besari said, but the conviction had disappeared from her voice. They were trapped, and she knew it.

It was the longest walk of Wyn's life, each step tugging him toward their target. Each step tugging them farther into the midst of an uncountable amount of guards. Each step tugging them closer to their deaths.

"Give me two," Sage said, and a birrosh man with a funny beeping collar nodded, pulling two mystery meat wraps from his heated stand and handing them over. Sage was sure the man would say what the meat was if she asked. She didn't want to find out.

"That's, uh, twenty KekCred, if you don't mind." He bowed his head, clearly afraid of her. Sage almost paid, until she realized it was a made-up fucking currency. And named after himself? How arrogant was this Sovereign asshole? Then she also remembered that her Vico was still wherever her arm was, neither of which were all that close.

"I don't have any money." She shrugged and walked away. The man nearly burst into tears as she walked away. Zetta crouched low in an alley, a raggedy blanket wrapped around her like some sort of cloak. She focused on several bugs in her hand. "Here." Sage offered her one of the wraps. "You better enjoy it. The man guilt-tripped me about not paying."

Zetta glanced up and grabbed the wrap, then looked out at the man. "He's probably a slave. Seems like a lot of the non-slaves have the ability to kill a slave whenever they want."

"What?" Sage asked between bites, bluish meat leaking out from the flimsy paper wrapping. "How do you know that?"

Zetta pointed the other way down the street where a headless corpse lay. "The collars explode."

"Great," Sage grumbled. "Now *you're* guilt-tripping me for stealing from slaves."

Zetta shrugged. "Maybe they should just be better at not being slaves." Then she shoved the whole wrap in her mouth, swallowing after three chews.

"It's what I'd do," Sage said in agreement. "If I found myself enslaved, I'd say fuck it and not be enslaved."

Zetta chuckled, but already her attention was returned to Achtrek's remnants.

"What are they saying?" Sage asked, indicating the bugs.

"I've been trying to figure that out," Zetta said. "They're buzzing about a bad idea ever since we left the hut."

"Yeah, well, I couldn't stand being cooped up in there much longer," Sage grumbled around a large bite in her mouth. Despite the looks, the bluish meat barely tasted rancid at all. "So you can stop complaining about the bad idea."

They continued to buzz. "I said the same thing," Zetta said. "They should have stopped, their warning heeded, but..."

Zetta trailed off as another beetle flew into the alley and landed among the others. They huddled up, buzzing in concern.

"What's that?" Sage asked.

"That one followed Wyn and Besari." Zetta's voice turned icy. Sage sighed, her mood instantly ruined.

"Motherfucker." She nearly tossed the rest of the sandwich at the wall. "It wasn't *our* bad idea they're upset about. It was Wyn and Besari's stupid fucking plan."

"Seems like it," Zetta growled. "Where are they?"

The beetles took flight and hovered in the air. Slowly, they shifted in a line that pointed toward where they went. Toward Sovereign's tower.

"You've got to be fucking kidding me," Sage said.

"Without us?" Zetta growled.

"I'm going to kill them," they both said.

"Are we going to save them?" Zetta asked.

"We have to," Sage said. "What if they succeed? That will be fucking embarrassing."

"You think they'd succeed?"

"That kid accidented his way to this planet without running into an ambush. He has the luck of the empyreans on his side. What do you think?"

"Fuck," Zetta agreed. "We have to go help. What do we have to work with?"

Sage pulled the backpack from her shoulder and crouched down, opening it to inspect its contents. It was almost everything they had for supplies, besides what Besari and Wyn carried now. Sage had lost much of her extra supplies, and Zetta had lost *all* of hers. She hoped whatever Wyn and Besari had packed for their trip would be useful.

She rifled through the bag and listed the items off one at a time. "One protein bar. Eight extra plasma charges. And twenty...three grenades."

Zetta's eyes lit up. Then she smiled. "With enough grenades, we can make anything work."

Sovereign stood when they reached the raised platform. A faint shimmer of an energy shield was barely visible in the air between them, rendering any shot more than useless. Sovereign stepped to the very edge and looked down on Wyn and Besari. He smiled, cruel and condescending. A flash of perfect white teeth held in place by a perfect clean-shaven jaw attached to a perfect face. Everything about him screamed beauty and terror. His eyes shifted in the light, from pale red to copper to bronze to gold. He was muscular to the point of Wyn reconsidering taking him hostage. How would they ever drag *that* up so many flights of stairs? How would they even fight him?

"Well?" Sovereign asked.

"We have its head," Wyn said, his voice shaky as he held up the bag. "The robot's."

"Oh!" Sovereign grinned. "Hang on." He stepped through the last of the barrier and dropped from the three-foot-tall dais, landing lightly on his feet. "It's dead?"

"Yes," Wyn said, clenching the bag hard enough to stop his hand from shaking. Besari scanned the crowd of hired thugs, her own posture crackling with nervous energy he hoped would be less obvious to others. He could tell she was thinking as he was. There were far too many perrilans, for whom the gas was useless, and many haushedins, who were likely resistant. If they were even within range. How many would remain after Cee triggered the gas? Would any of them be caught in the cloud?

"Hand it over," Sovereign commanded, his joyous tone shifting to something cold and calculating. Wyn did not wait. He jumped forward and passed the backpack to Sovereign. Then he prayed for a miracle because they were about to need one.

Sovereign upended the sack, and with a clang, Cee's head struck the floor, the light in its eyes dead. "Wonderful. This thing caused many problems for me."

Then Cee's eyes flashed, its mouth shot open, and a nozzle poked out. Besari took a quick breath, her hand gliding toward the mask hidden in her hip pouch. Wyn shifted on his feet, ready for the action. Whatever happened now, they couldn't stop moving. They needed to get to the top with their prize in hand.

"Oh," Cee said, "you're not h—"

Then Sovereign fired three shots into Cee's skull, and the last of the A.I. disintegrated beneath the shots. Metal pooled to either side like shiny puddles of blood, the mummified finger burnt away into nothing. Wyn and Besari stared, open-mouthed.

"Not as dead as you say, it seems," Sovereign said, pistol still in hand. He had drawn it so quickly Wyn hadn't even seen his hand move. "Well, *now* it is. But still, you should be more careful."

Wyn swallowed his dread and his grief. Another friend taken in a flash, dead because of Wyn's bad idea. He bit his lip and stared at Sovereign's shimmering eyes. Something iced over within him. Save the grief until later. There were still two of them alive. They needed to escape.

"Do we still get our money?"

A single moment before Cee's death, a signal had launched from within its head: emergency procedures triggered by the expectation of complete destruction. Cee had known it was going to happen the instant it had booted back up and scanned Sovereign, unlike when it had been caught by surprise in its ship's explosion. The signal pinged the closest transmitter, Sovereign's Vico, and launched itself into one of Kekar's many satellites. It encoded itself in daily messages, transmitting across the galaxy in moments, the message an unbreakable cipher even if it was detected. Then it split into three paths, three messages. One to the haushedin fleets in the skies above Kekar. Another back to Kekar's surface, pinging a Vico very near to Cee's last position, and the third into the depths of space, searching out Cee's origin. Each message found its target by Sovereign's third shot.

In the hushed aftermath, Wyn's Vico dinged with a message unnoticed.

# CHAPTER 28

## EXPLOSIONS ARE FUN

Metal crunched beneath Sovereign's boot as he stepped through the remains of Cee, his eyes never leaving Wyn. The stare unnerved him, and he became acutely aware of his hands just dangling there, doing nothing. So he crossed his arms over his chest, worried that it looked too aggressive, moved them to his hips, was sure that was too aggressive, then returned them to their starting position. Wyn had the distinct feeling that Sovereign was about to reveal that he knew everything. Who he and Besari were, what they were doing here, where they'd been hiding. He was even sure that Sovereign was about to tell Wyn he knew about that time he'd peed himself in the middle of a corporate meeting at the age of twelve when his father had refused to let him leave. Did he know about that?

"What is your name, bounty hunter?" Sovereign asked.

"Iolas Sentel," Wyn said immediately. His father's first name, mother's last. Did he know that too?

Besari stepped closer to Wyn, her stance rigid, her eyes steel. He almost reached over to grab her hand, to comfort her. Or, at the very least, comfort himself. They just needed to get through this and leave.

"Iolas." The name rolled around Sovereign's mouth like a hard candy. "Tell me, why should I pay you for a bounty my people disabled and *I* killed?"

Wyn glanced around the room to find hundreds of guards shifting slightly, readying weapons that had been at rest. Tension hardened everyone, slowed every movement. He swallowed and tried to choose his words carefully. "Well, you asked for the head specifically. Which is what we delivered you. There was nothing against taking others' credit."

Sovereign smiled. "But you have three heads and offer me only one." His head snapped to Besari at the barest hint of a twitch. "Touch your scattergun, and I will gut you both before you have the chance to draw it. Do you understand?"

Besari froze, eyes wide. She nodded slowly. Then the king of Kekar returned his gaze to Wyn. The look had a weight to it; he felt the tension pressing down on his shoulders harder than before.

"I prefer the last two heads to stay where they are, if it's all the same to you." Wyn bowed as he spoke, giving him a chance to blink sweat from his eyes.

Sovereign laughed. "Most people do." His hand dropped to Wyn's shoulder, and even through the armor, he felt the strength of the grip. "Which is why it surprises me that you came here to see me."

Wyn looked up at Sovereign, his cheery expression disappearing behind stormy eyes. They almost crackled like lightning.

"What?"

"How *fucking* stupid do you think I am?" Then there was a knee in Wyn's gut, the force enough to render his armor meaningless and blast the air from his lungs. Wyn dropped to the ground, knees crashing against the floor. That armor should have protected him from anything short of a vrolak. "Touch that, and you'll die!" Wyn heard Sovereign say as he curled into himself on the floor. "You hear that, guards? If this *bishett* woman moves, you fucking shoot her."

They shouted a quick acknowledgment. Wyn tried to pull himself to his feet, only to find another foot on his chest, toppling him backward.

"It was smart though," Sovereign said, his eyes back on Besari. "Disguising yourself as a birrosh for so long, just to come here without it. My men are stupid for not catching you, though. At the very least, what's one more dead body?"

Dread filled Wyn's chest, taking the place of the air he couldn't seem to hold down. Sovereign stepped onto Wyn's chest, pinning him to the ground, and crouched.

"I'm so very glad you could take time out of your day to come visit me, Wyn Kelda. I thought I'd have to wait for the sweeping team to find whatever building you've been hiding in. Is that where Sage and Zetta are? I heard some rumors about both, but they disappeared before my men could find them. I know they both lived. Tell you what. I really don't care about your pet bishett, she's no one, so give me the location of Sage and Zetta, and she can live."

"I don't know what you're talking about," Wyn choked. "I'm Iolas Sentel, and—"

"Your father's first name and mother's last. Yes, it was a really clever ruse. Unfortunately, I'm not an idiot. Where are they?"

Shit, how did Sovereign know about his mother? Almost no one knew about her. Wyn suddenly felt less confident that Sovereign *didn't* know about the time he'd peed himself. It was strange how in this moment before his death, that was what his mind focused on, desperate to not be embarrassed in front of Besari in their final moments.

"We didn't find them," Wyn lied. "We had a system in place to find each other, but they never responded. Only Cee did. I assume the others already escaped. And with them the truth about this prison planet. The R.C. won't react kindly to the news. Kill me if you want, but this scheme of yours is done."

Wyn hadn't expected Sovereign to actually believe the lie, but the king's face distorted with anger. His foot slammed down on Wyn, something cracking in the process, and Wyn hoped it was the suit and not whatever the spike of pain originated from. He coughed, and a hand grabbed the helmet, slamming it to the ground. Wyn flailed at the grip, but it was too strong.

"What is it?" Sovereign growled. "What fucking vendetta do you have against me?"

"What?" Wyn croaked.

Sovereign slammed Wyn's head against the ground, and Wyn's vision spun. The helmet held, the damage minimal, but he wondered how many more strikes it would take before the helmet would shatter. Was Sovereign even human? Or some sort of monster? A Thresha talent?

"Don't lie to me," Sovereign roared at him. "You think I'm stupid? You people always think I'm stupid. But I've analyzed everything you and your company have done. You think I'd believe that it's a coincidence that Sage captures one of my most profitable businessmen, Roshran, just days before you buy up his building and coordinate this company with her?"

"Yes?" Wyn hadn't even known Sage was the one to take the bounty of the drug dealer, but that explained why she'd been on Chrysanax.

"And the targeting of Shekta, the disabling of the artificial Thresha to inhibit new soldiers."

"We were looking for a bird," Wyn desperately tried to explain.

"Your fucking robot took down an entire fleet ship singlehandedly." He waved at the remains of Cee. "And two other members targeted critical points in my weapons system. You've attacked me and my people at every corner, and I'm supposed to believe you don't have some sort of score to settle? Is it personal, or are you funded by the Raiyrium Confederation?"

Wyn stared at the raving king and wanted to cry. How had he managed to piss off one of the most dangerous people in the galaxy accidentally?

"Listen." Wyn heard his anxiety flooding into his voice, but he couldn't stop it. "You clearly have far-reaching fingers, and we hunt bad guys. It's clear we would bump into one another a few times. I didn't mean anything personal. I didn't even know about most of those bounties. We're only here because the R.C. hired us to come after you."

"That was me!" Sovereign roared. "That was my fucking bounty to lure you here."

"Wait." Wyn felt a cold dread course through him. "We're not getting paid for that bounty either?"

Sovereign's face turned icy. "What's it matter? You won't be leaving Kekar alive," he said as he stood, relieving some of the pressure on Wyn's chest. "You won't be the first to die, however. I plan to get my answers. When I have them, I will hunt down everyone who has ever worked for your company, and I will kill them. And when they have all died and you have been shown their corpses, then and only then will you follow them to your own grave."

Wyn struggled against Sovereign's foot, the crushing weight still holding him to the ground. Slowly, the king pulled a pistol from his hip holster and hefted the weight of it in one hand.

"Shall we begin now?" Sovereign asked. Wyn shook and struggled against him, hammering at his calf and trying to twist out. He screamed as Sovereign turned and raised the pistol. His yells turned to sobs after the first shot, and the sobs were drowned out by the next dozen.

Zetta strolled down the busy roads, still cloaked in the ragged blanket. What remained of Achtrek chittered on her shoulder, reflecting her excited mood. What could be more exciting than explosions? Well, she supposed watching the explosions would be more exciting, but she was about to wet her fangs with someone else's blood, and that was enough for her. That was what she'd signed up for. Not calculating the distance to a pond, surviving attempted murders, and sneaking around a city. Problems were solved best by being torn apart.

Even Geble was responding well, given a few days' rest. She could feel its renewed energy within, ready to fuel her muscles if needed. All in all, it was a good day for killing.

Sage lounged against a building down the street from the gate to Sovereign's tower. She was chewing on something, and Zetta's nostrils twitched with anticipation.

"Where'd you get that?" Zetta asked before Sage could speak.

"My pocket." She bit into the bar again, taking a large bite. Then she eyed Zetta's blanket. "You should try getting pockets some day. They're great for storing food."

"I have a pocket," Zetta said.

Sage's chewing paused, and she blinked. "Not one I'd eat out of."

Zetta grinned. "Now that's just not true."

Sage rolled her eyes. "Not one I'd eat *food* out of."

"Got another one?"

"No. Focus on the job, Zetta. How long until the grenades go off?"

"We have plenty of time. At least ten minutes. Now give me some of that bar before the fighting begins."

A faint rumble sounded in the distance, oddly close to where Zetta had placed the grenades. They both looked over, and a stream of smoke rose into the sky, peculiarly close to her grenades. Faint shouts echoed through the city, warning of an explosion.

Curious.

"Zetta..."

"That might have been the grenades," she admitted.

"Might have been?"

"You know I'm not great at math."

Sage tossed her the remainder of the protein bar, and Zetta threw it in her mouth. "Let's go," Sage said.

Zetta licked her lips. "I've been itching to rip someone's arm off."

"That's offensive." Sage glared as she wagged her stump.

"Oh, right." Zetta looked at the missing arm and sighed. "I almost forgot about that. But don't worry, it won't be your only remaining arm." Sage chuckled.

There were two guards stationed in front of the gate, talking rapidly to each other and investigating the smoke in the distance. They missed Sage and Zetta's approach.

"You want the falvian or the haushedin," Zetta asked.

"Falvian," Sage said. "I need practice with left-handed combat."

Zetta grinned, then charged the haushedin. A stampeding vrolak was rather hard to miss and did wonders to grab their attention. Not fast enough to prevent her bulk from crashing into the haushedin, but certainly fast enough for the haushedin and the falvian to yell out. Zetta slammed her opponent into the door, and they crashed to the ground in a heap, his large warhammer clattering uselessly out of reach. Zetta pinned the fat creature beneath her and grinned widely.

"You know, on my planet your people would be considered prey." She salivated to add a little extra terror. At least until she felt a foot in her crotch that lifted her up and flipped her over. Her claws scrabbled at the guard, then she slammed down on her back, old wounds screaming painfully. Okay, so they weren't that old. Then the haushedin crawled onto her, using his far superior weight to pin her down and wrap up her arms.

"I'm not so sure the vrolak wouldn't be extinct if that were the case," he said, barely breaking a sweat as she struggled beneath him.

"If I had known this was how it would be, I would have brought a condom." Zetta's foot finally caught the flesh of the haushedin's arm, and she tugged, freeing one hand. She slammed the claws at his head, though he turned aside so they only hit tougher skin. The haushedin shoved his weight harder onto her, trying to control and move her.

Fuck this shit. She rolled with his attempts to readjust her, flipping onto her front. Then she pulled on the parasite, feeling the comfortable enhancement rush through her body. Muscles bulged, and reinvigorating strength flowed through her. With a grunt, she pushed herself to all fours, the haushedin clinging to her back, letting out a surprised gasp. She stood, his bulk still tied into hers, her legs quaking beneath the effort. Then she jumped backwards, slamming all her weight down onto the haushedin.

She heard the snap of something that was hopefully not hers, and his grip released along with a moan of pain. She rolled off him and cut off Geble's chemicals. Zetta and the haushedin both rose to their feet. Then they circled. Watching. Waiting.

Charging.

Zetta roared as she crashed into him again. Her claws failed to get purchase in the tough hide, but his large hands easily grabbed at her, twisting and controlling her movement. He spun her and slammed her back to the ground, straddling her and pushing her hands to the side. So Zetta bit his face.

He jerked back, bringing her arms forward, and she bit his hand. Geble fueled her this time, strengthening her jaws until she heard the snap. He yelled and tried to pull away. It only helped her. Half the hand tore free in her mouth as he tugged it away. He stared at his ruined hand in surprise, so she broke the other grip. Both hands free, she went for his eyes.

The haushedin didn't stay stunned long, quickly grabbing at her arms again despite his injury. Her thumbs stopped short of gouging his eyes. He leaned back while pulling her hands down, and slowly the gap widened. Zetta gritted her teeth and pushed harder, their arms shaking against each other's strength. Then she smiled, and with a buck of her hips and a thunk of her tail to his skull, the haushedin's head snapped forward, and her claws moistened with eye juice and blood. The haushedin yelled, but Zetta grabbed the sides of his head and drove her thumbs in deeper until his yelling stopped. Then she tossed the corpse to the side and got up, licking her thumbs clean.

Zetta looked around her and groaned as she noticed that not only was the falvian beaten senseless and tied up, but the gate doors were open and the perrilan who had opened them was now dead. Now Sage lounged against the wall and watched Zetta with a look of sexual interest.

"Didn't want to help?"

"I wouldn't want you to think I didn't believe in you," she said. Then she glanced to the side, leaned down to grab the warhammer, and tossed it Zetta's way. "He's not dead."

Zetta caught the weapon and turned. Sure enough, the blinded haushedin struggled, trying to sit back up. Zetta pressed a button on the hammer, and its end hummed and sparked. Her brow rose in appreciation, and she slammed the hammer down on the haushedin's face.

At impact, the hammer burst with energy, pulverizing the haushedin's face into a massive, bloody splatter. Both Sage and Zetta stared at the weapon before looking at each other.

"I think he's dead," Zetta said, bracing the warhammer against her shoulder.

"Good observation," Sage said, then turned and entered the gate. Much of the tower's security seemed to be mobbed around the eastern wall, their skirmish unnoticed for now. They ran across the pathway to the door of the tower, and Zetta tore it open.

"Oh dear." A purple kroscion stood at the entrance and stared at them.

A fucking *kroscion*. Zetta stared at them in awe. She didn't know what to do, only that she didn't want to kill it. Barely any were alive. She wanted to bring it home, keep it safe, like a little pet. It was almost adorable. Unfortunately, her daydreams shattered when the kroscion gestured at their Vico, then ran away. Sage and Zetta still stood stunned, watching it slither rather speedily through a doorway.

"Fuck," Sage grunted, then ran after. Zetta almost followed but pulled up short as the first body hit the ground. She looked up to watch the next several slip from a widening hole in the ceiling and fall to join the first, a perrilan, which lifted its head, dead eyes staring. Then it jumped forward, hands stretched out for Sage.

Had Zetta not watched it all happen, she never would have had the time to react, but even before the perrilan moved, Zetta launched herself. Boosted by Geble, she burst across the room and slammed into the speedy perrilan, crashing into the wall by Sage. The perrilan writhed in Zetta's grip, far stronger than it should be.

By then, five others rose from the ground, dead eyes blank as something primal coursed through them.

"Go!" she shouted at the stunned Sage still at the door. "Find the others. I'll be right behind you."

"But—"

"GO!" The perrilan pushed against Zetta's grip. There was no way it should be stronger than *her*.

Thankfully, Sage listened, and she left. Zetta would be awfully upset if Sage died here too. In a blur, a tesing gave chase, moving at incredible speeds. Zetta barely got her tail up, slamming into him and tossing him to the other side of the room. The distraction was enough to let the perrilan break free, and Zetta jumped back as it took a swipe at her face.

Thankfully, Zetta had a new toy to play with. She readied the warhammer in both hands, activated it, then tore her blanket free. She licked her teeth and flashed a fearsome smile.

"Who's n—"
The tesing slammed into her.

"Get back here!" Sage shouted.

"No!" the kroscion shouted back, then ducked into a side door, their tentacles squirming in impressive unison to propel them forward. Sage barged through the door and was met with the muzzle of a pistol. She brought her arm up quickly, coating it in as thick of a layer of sediment as she could before she heard the shot.

Instead, it produced a soft whoosh. Something tinked off her arm and fell to the ground at her feet. She looked down to find a dart, something suspicious dripping from its tip. Then she looked up at the kroscion.

"Oh dear." They dropped the toy gun and slithered away again. Sage dove to grab at their trailing tentacles, but a slippery coating caused them to slide through her hand. Then out the other door they went.

"Oh good," Sage heard from the room over. "Kill the intruder, please!"

"Shit." Sage rolled to the side as two guards ducked in and fired at her. She pulled her pistol free, slower than she was used to, and returned fire, slower than she was used to. Why'd it have to be her right arm? She could easily fight with only her right.

Slow or not, the return fire sent them ducking for cover, giving her respite for a breath or two. "I must inform the master!" the kroscion shouted, then slithered off. Fuck if Sage was going to let that snake go freely.

As her assailants reappeared, Sage fired again, chasing their heads away. Then she charged. The longer the stalemate held, the worse for her, so she had to break it. She started by coating everything but her joints in sediment armor, then she grew the carapace out past her stump, sharpening it into a spear.

They ducked back in to fire, but she dove and spun, sliding into the hall on her back. She fired at one with her left hand and drove the newly formed spear into the crotch of the other. The former fell dead immediately, the latter eventually followed once he quit screaming and thrashing. Sage climbed back to her feet. One of their shots had tracked her well enough, but the carapace had held, only superficial burning beneath. The kroscion stood at the end of the hall, staring with one wide eye.

"I'd rather not shoot you," Sage called, lifting her pistol to point at them.

"I know," they said, then turned and slithered away.

"Fuck!" Sage trucked on, chasing them. If she had her right arm, she could have taken a non-lethal shot, but she wasn't sharp enough with her left for that. She wondered if she cared anymore.

They turned a corner, and Sage followed, right into a crowd of guards. The kroscion yelled, the guards turned, and Sage fired, no longer caring whom she killed. There were shouts, and screams, and a lot of fucking blood as she killed them all before they had time to react. Thank whatever empyrean for the Imberlii Dissenter with its rapid shot without getting too gummy.

The kroscion cowered on the other side of the guards, two tentacle arms wrapped over their head, the one eye looking up. They stood, and she fired a shot close enough to singe one arm. They yelped and dropped back down.

"I'm done," Sage said, gasping for breath. When had she gotten so fucking old? Everything hurt from the little chase, every ache she'd ever had resurfacing. "If you move, I will kill you. Do you understand?"

The kroscion nodded.

"What's your name?"

"The master calls me Worm, if it pleases you."

Sage almost felt bad about that before an ache in her knee raced up her hip, threatening to cave beneath her weight. She felt significantly less bad. "Fitting. I'm going to need you to take me to your master."

"Coincidentally, I was just going there," Worm said. "Will we be going the rest of the way with that gun pointed at me? I don't really like guns."

"I don't really care." Sage concentrated her talent into the end of her missing arm, manifesting a hook of stone, and held it there. She felt woozy from the concentration. Had it always taken so much effort to focus on her wounds and her powers? She gritted her teeth, hooked the kroscion's neck, and pulled them to their feet. Er, tentacles? "Lead on," she said.

Sage had expected to be led up several flights of stairs because arrogant people always loved to inconvenience others and to live high above the common folk. So when their walk ended up being only a few minutes, ending at an elegant set of double doors on the ground floor, she was rather surprised and maybe a bit skeptical.

"Open it," Sage demanded.

"Are you sure?" Worm asked. "The master's not one for interruptions. I can sneak in there and make sure he's ready to receive you."

"What? I don't want him ready to receive me. I want to shoot him."

"Oh." Worm deflated, then reached one writhing arm out to the door's sensor. With a big sigh, they swiped their Vico, and the door opened.

The scene inside was chaotic. Plasma bolts rang out across the room, resulting in shouts of pain when they crashed into one of hundreds of other people firing back. Sage and Worm ducked down as an errant shot struck the wall near them. Sage already prepped the Thresha power within her to ooze out of her pores, ready to manifest protection as she needed it.

"ENOUGH!" a voice boomed through the room, and all shooting ceased. The smoke cleared, and a well-built man at the end of the room stood taller, his foot planted firmly atop what seemed to be Wyn. Guess that plan was going well. Thankfully, she didn't see Besari anywhere, even among the few fallen. Either they were separated, or Besari was the reason for the crossfire.

"Master!" Worm called out, nearly forgotten in Sage's arm. "You have a guest."

All heads snapped to Sage, and the guns followed. She tugged Worm closer. The fucker was thin, barely covering any of her body. Hopefully the risk of shooting the kroscion would dissuade them.

"Listen here, asshole," she called out, and one guard gasped in surprise. "You let my colleague go, you let us leave, and you can keep your kroscion pet. Alternatively, I can paint the walls with their brain, and we can have a fight to see who would win."

It would be Sovereign, almost definitely. He had over a hundred guards in the room, and Sage felt like her knees were going to give out at any moment. Well, at least the adrenaline pumping through her body kept them at ease for now.

Sovereign hadn't moved, simply staring at her. Either in thought, or too stupid to have one. "I don't see you moving your—"

In a flash, he lifted the gun and fired. Sage stumbled back in shock as kroscion brains exploded over her face. The limp body pulled at the hook on her arm until she had to dissipate it to keep her balance.

"Fuck!" She stared at the dead body and then at Sovereign. "Isn't that a war crime or something?"

"What's one more?"

She watched the shot that took her in the head. Pain exploded, a searing heat that cooked her brain until there was a thunk and nothing but darkness. An endless abyss.


Two humans, one male, one female. A goopy-looking birrosh man. A haushedin. The perrilan crawling out of the wall Zetta had smacked them into. And the tesing, who was currently punching Zetta's ribs with wild haymakers. Six combatants. They had the numbers, not to mention Zetta's weakened state or the fact that the tesing and perrilan seemed far stronger than their species typically were. Were the others enhanced too?

At least Zetta had sanity on her side, as fleeting as it was at times. Only the tesing and perrilan seemed intent to fight, and even that was brutish and untalented. The rest seemed to be tweaking on drugs. That should make things easy.

Zetta kicked out the tesing's legs, and he crashed to the floor. She slammed the hammer down, but the tesing fled in a flash, a resounding boom cracking the floor and drawing the attention of the others.

Okay, that was a mistake.

The perrilan came first, crashing forward with long apish arms reaching around Zetta. She jumped back to hit them with her hammer, the crack of electricity bursting out. The same swing that had pulverized a haushedin's head merely slammed the perrilan into the wall and singed their skin. Then they were back, grappling with the hammer and pulling it away with strength they shouldn't have.

That one would be Screech. She kicked the newly named perrilan in the chest, their grip loosening, and then slammed the hammer into their side, launching them into the others that watched her with those dead eyes. They crashed into the crowd, sending several to the ground as they stumbled around.

The haushedin drooled smoking, green saliva, which ate at the floor and reeked worse than post-lokrin gas. And *that* had chased Sage out of the room mid-sex at least once. He could be Sir Fetid.

Bone protrusions jutted from the human woman to the point Zetta thought pinballing the perrilan into her had killed her. Until she stood again. She fingered one bone, licked another. Well, that one was just simple: Boner.

Her male counterpart never rose from the ground, instead slithering as though the woman had all his bones. And he had the skin? Anyways, he stretched as he moved, his limbs wriggling almost individually from his body. Elongiboy it was.

So the birrosh man who was collecting the parts of him that dripped free could be Goop. And the—

The tesing slammed into her again. Honestly, she wasn't sure what she'd expected, getting side-tracked with that man as speedy as he was. She wondered what he had been doing when she'd been lost in thought, but the wondering didn't last long as going ass over shoulders had the tendency to deprive her of thought. Her new hammer skidded across the room as the tesing mounted her and speedy fists pounded into her chest. She tried to grab the arms, but they slipped from her grip, moving too fast for her eyes. Had that been his only gift, maybe she wouldn't care. But she heard the crack of something beneath his powerful attacks, and her skin retore along old wounds as she beefed up to protect from the damage. And every attack went around her arms no matter where she put them to block.

Red blared in her vision as anger dulled the pain. Geble's chemicals coursed through her veins, her skin tightening against the muscle. Then she grabbed at the tesing. Attack her all he wanted, she would crush the life from his—

Something wrapped around her left arm and tugged it down. Elongiboy had lassoed her fucking wrist with his arm, and now Screech pulled at it. She tugged back, but the pair held her steady. Then her other was coated in a goo, sticking it to her chest. Goop had reverted entirely into a pile of slime and inched over her, coating shoulder and arm. Whatever he was made of stuck to her like no adhesive Zetta had ever dealt with before. And she had glued her fingers together often as a kid. And a few times as an adult. Still the tesing's fists crashed into her.

Well, fuck.

She bucked her hips and swung her tail around, smacking the tesing in the shoulder with as much parasite-power as she could channel. Given her tail was mostly muscle, it was quite a lot. The tesing rocketed off of her and slammed into a wall, only to be quickly replaced by Boner. The bone protrusions coated her fists now, making them large, white sledges with which to pummel Zetta.

Zetta panicked and kicked at her, which sent the human woman flying across the room and slamming through a wall.

She'd expected a different result, but at least that was one taken care of for now.

That excitement was short-lived as Sir Fetid began spewing green, acidic breath at them, which burned like the abyss. It ate through her wounds, searing the exposed, sensitive tissue. She shut her eyes tight as it splashed near her face, coating her neck and jaw. She tried to roll away, but Goop held her. So she rolled into Goop instead, but Elongiboy and Screech held her steady. So she screamed. She channeled Geble's chemicals into her arm and tugged. Elongiboy stretched, until he didn't, and with a great tear his arm ripped free.

She used it like a whip to slam into the haushedin and send him off balance, then tossed the stringy arm aside as Screech jumped onto her. With one hand, Zetta grabbed the perrilan around the chest and slammed them into Goop, who'd crept up her face and now glued her mouth together. She smeared Goop around with Screech as a mop. It seemed Goop could choose who to stick to and so that was fucking pointless. At least until Boner returned and began punching her with her little fists. Zetta just hit her with the perrilan, then tossed Screech at a rising tesing.

The haushedin was recovering, and even Elongiboy looked ready for more despite the blood pouring from his wound. Goop crawled up to her nostrils, threatening suffocation. Goop first then. The others were a distraction. She rolled away, tugging against Goop's grip. She growled and screamed through sealed lips until the ground pulled away with a great crack. She was on her side, one nostril blocked. The perrilan was up again; the tesing was dazed but watched Zetta. Fucking Boner was back. Sir Fetid sneezed, filling the room with noxious gas. And Zetta was going to die thanks to a fucking pile of goo.

Unless this one thing worked.

She clawed herself across the ground even as the perrilan returned to kick her. Even as the tesing grabbed Elongiboy and wrapped him around Zetta's ankles to pull her away. Even as Boner pummeled at whatever she was pummeling at. Zetta couldn't really feel that one. Even as acid stung at open wounds again and her eyes teared up, sending the world into a wobbly spiral. Even as her airways became clogged and the wobbling world darkened.

Between the pain, the acid, and the blackening vision, she could barely see when her hand clasped around the hammer. She felt the hum of the hammer in her fist and felt the tug of another hand grabbing at it. Her grip tightened, and she poured everything Geble could provide into her hand, into retrieving the hammer. The parasite squealed in distress, and she ignored it. It was this or death.

Whatever held her back loosened, and the hammer jerked forward. Zetta directed the head at her right shoulder. It hit, and the resulting blast rocked her head back. The world went dark, and when it returned, it swirled. But she was gasping for breath again, and Goop seemed to liquify slowly. She coughed up gooey bits with every kick in her ribs.

Enough of that. She bit the furry leg as it came forward, and, freed from constraints, she spun. The perrilan spun with her, endlessly screeching as they were whipped around. At her ankles, Elongiboy stretched and rolled up like a loose hose, slipping from the tesing's grasp. Zetta launched the perrilan away at the end of her roll and leaned forward. The overstretched Elongiboy twitched at her ankles, coiled tightly. She grabbed at two thick ends and pulled them apart.

Far enough that she could slip a leg free. Far enough to slip two free. Far enough that he squealed, and far enough that he tore. She pulled until blood spilled over her, and she held multiple pieces of a very stretchy human man in each claw. The tesing stared at her with dead eyes, unphased by his colleague's death.

He charged. She grabbed the hammer and raised it just as he reached her. He punched the head of the hammer off with a shattering blast. Then he punched her in the face. Zetta's head bounced off the ground as she fell, and the world spun. She blinked repeatedly, dazed.

"That was my favorite hammer," Zetta groaned. She almost passed out and maybe would have if they hadn't kept piling on the pain. The tesing, whom she'd forgotten to name, and Screech. And the burning, the endless burning. How much acid scarred her now? How much had spilled onto the others? What would Sage think of this death? Was this great enough? Would she have lived, even left-handed? Probably. She was Sage fucking Valen. The greatest bounty hunter Zetta had ever known. Besides herself, of course.

Zetta's eyes snapped open as she willed her brain back. You know what? Fuck that. Who needs a fucking brain when you're fighting? The perrilan slammed a fist into her, and she grabbed it, quick as she could. Then she beat the tesing with the perrilan. He hadn't expected the first blow, so it struck true, tossing him into the wall nearby. Boner was back, so she smacked her with the perrilan too, turning her into a red smear across the room. Then back to the tesing. Every time he tried to get up, there was a perrilan being slammed into his face. Over and over. Her muscles strained, her parasite whined, but she kept going until he was simply paste beneath the onslaught.

The perrilan still struggled in her hand, flailing as if the pummeling had done nothing. How the fuck was she going to kill this impervious little shit?

Oh.

Right.

She yanked the breathing mask, and Screech squawked and flailed harder. Then slowed, then fell still. Their eyes rolled to the back of their head, and drool oozed from their mouth.

She felt the burning at her back then, the acid dripping down her weeping wounds. She turned in time to see Sir Fetid launch an acid loogie at her. She jumped to the side and whipped the dead perrilan around like a mace, crashing the corpse into the haushedin and knocking him aside. She tried again to use Screech as her new personal weapon, but Sir Fetid lashed out at her foot, sending her to the ground. Then he tore the perrilan away from her grip.

Then Boner came again. She jumped on Zetta, even more bone protrusions escaping from her body. Extra ribs, a crown of spikes, and even extra teeth came out to claw and tear at Zetta's wounds. Large protrusions spurted from her forearms, and she drove these into Zetta, who caught the arms and glared.

"Why aren't you dead?" she growled. Then she kicked Boner, tearing her arms free as the rest of the body hurtled across the room. She turned to Sir Fetid, right into a face full of acid breath.

She screamed and rolled away from him, the left side of her face stinging, unable to open the eye. But she felt his hands on her, pulling her back. Felt his body on hers. And from what she could see from her right eye, he planned to ensure her entire face ended up coated in his vile vomit.

Zetta grabbed the snoot with one claw, holding it shut. Sir Fetid coughed and gagged, and acid dripped from the sides of his mouth.

He tried to pull free, and Zetta's grip tightened, claws digging in. She wrapped her left hand around the back of the haushedin's skull, pulling him in close. His arms flailed, trying to get a grip enough to push against hers. But as he pushed himself up from the ground, she just let herself be pulled up with the grip.

Then she squeezed. She'd grabbed hold of what was likely the strongest portion of the skull, but she couldn't let the mouth open again, so she made it work. Her muscles strained, and Geble wailed. She wrung the parasite dry as hard as she squeezed Sir Fetid's skull, and she was rewarded with the first crack. The rest of his skull shattered after that, his head collapsing inward, blood and brain spewing out over Zetta's body. She tossed the haushedin to the side and lay there, gasping for breath. Her muscles twitched, and she still couldn't see out of one eye. A piercing pain throbbed through her skull, but she was alive and victorious. All six dead, and with more style than Sage could ever muster.

She would just take a short rest and catch up in a bit. Sage could handle herself for now. Zetta's body was too overtaxed. Nothing seemed to work right, and her body ached all over.

A piercing sting exploded through her, and she coughed, blood spurting from her lips. She opened her good eye to see Boner standing over her, her body almost completely encased in bone except for two green eyes. Dead eyes. A thick spear of bone stabbed into Zetta's midsection from Boner's arm. An arm she wasn't supposed to have.

"I thought I took that." Zetta coughed as she wrapped one hand around the bone spear. She looked up at the other arm, pulled back for a killing blow, and she smiled. She couldn't believe her death would come at the hands of someone called "Boner." Too bad Sage didn't know; she would laugh.

Pesh shoved a cabinet, one empty bucket, one bucket full of random office supplies, a robotic leg, a mop, and a broken chair against the door before leaning down and pulling the gag from Closet Seph's mouth.

"Who are you?" they asked.

"I'm Seph!" he screeched, tears streaming down his cheeks. His eyes had that haunted look of torture, his pants long-stained with urine, but not a mark of harm was visible. Whatever he had gone through must have been excruciating.

"Who's that?" They pointed outside the door, where a super-heated blade sizzled as it melted the metal of the doorway.

"I don't fucking know!" Seph spit and struggled. "Just keep her away from me, please!"

"Her?" Pesh looked back at the door, and pieces clicked into place. It was a strange amount of terror Pesh had felt when the injured Seph had shambled their way. In normal circumstances, Pesh would have fought. They were a fighter. They did not flee in terror. But perhaps their emotions had been influenced. She was getting better, if that was the case.

A pinprick of metal melted away as the tip of the blade seared its way through the closet door. The blade retreated, and Pesh's fear returned. Knowing its source, they stamped it out.

"Pesh!" Seph's voice called from outside, and Closet Seph whimpered. "Don't listen to that infiltrator in there. I caught him and tied him up for you all. Come back out, and let's talk about peace."

Pesh glanced at the assistant cowering in the corner, eyes squeezed shut. Skritch shook on their shoulder, not faring much better. Then they looked at the tiny hole. They pulled a pistol free, their last one, the other four lost in the lancer attack. They would need to retrieve them to continue the fight. But they would not be enough to win it.

"Hey, Mecillis," they called through the tiny hole. "Let's drop the act, no?"

"Oh, Pesh." Seph's voice shifted and changed until it was the recognizable sinister voice of Mecillis once more. "It took you—"

Pesh shot through the tiny hole, silencing whatever more the nairwid had to say.

"Ow!" Mecillis laughed. "You took out an eye. But you and I both know that won't be enough." She slammed the knife back into the hole, the glowing tip punching through. "If you won't come out, then I'll come in."

Pesh dropped to the real assistant, cutting his bonds free. "What has she done to you?" Pesh asked, eyes still shifting over the body for wounds.

"She killed L-Bot!" he cried. "L-Bot grew suspicious of her disguise, and she killed him."

"Yes, I noticed." Pesh hadn't, but that explained the robot parts lying around. "What did she do to you, though? I need to know what shape you're in."

"Oh." Seph wiped at his tears and sniffled his runny nose. There were more liquids pouring out of him than Pesh, and they had at least two open wounds. "She tied me up and left me in here for weeks. She fed me Wyn's nutrient goo and asked me questions. If I didn't answer, she stared at me all scary-like, and, I don't know, I got really scared. So I told her what she asked."

"That's it?" Pesh asked. "You told her everything because she scared you?"

"I'm not a bounty hunter! I'm not a fighter! I took this job because my da made me!"

"Hmm." Pesh looked back at the door as the knife slowly glided down through the material. Mecillis shouted something more about cracking Pesh open and feasting on their insides or something else vile, but they ignored it. "You're physically fine, though?"

"I mean, my pants are kind of stiff." He frowned at his pants and shifted a bit in them. "I tried to hold it the first day, but I could only hold it so long..."

"She never untied you?"

"No."

Pesh's eyes widened, and their mandibles clicked. "But your arms and legs are fine?"

"Oh, yeah," Seph said. "I'm double-jointed, so it wasn't too uncomfortable."

Pesh checked the door; they wouldn't have much time. "Listen, I need your help."

"Against that?" His eyes widened. "No way!"

"You don't have to do anything against Mecillis," Pesh explained. "I just need you to run and get something for me. I'll distract her, fight her off for as long as possible. You run by and get it and then return. I'll find time to retrieve it from you. Nothing more than that."

"Where do you need me to go?"

"The armory."

Seph sat up straighter, then shifted some mops and brooms at the back of the closet. "We can just take the service elevator."

A small square opening appeared as things were pushed to one side.

"We have a service elevator?" Pesh stared at it.

"Yeah, it's mostly used for food delivery to the kitchen. It goes up to Wyn's apartment too. Sometimes I take it on my lunch breaks, so I know I'll fit."

"I know I won't," Pesh added, sizing up the hole. Skinny as he was, they were still surprised Seph could fit. Humans tended to be more flexible like that, however. Exoskeletons weren't known for folding in well. "I'll stay. You take the elevator to get a head start."

"What are you going to do?"

"Same plan. Distract her while you get what I need."

"How? It looks like she's almost killed you already."

"I know who I'm fighting now." They glanced at the disassembled robot parts, then back at Seph. "And you don't want to know."

He bit his lip, then nodded.

"Take Skritch." Pesh pulled the distressed gridder from their shoulder and settled them in Seph's arms. "You'll help better with him," Pesh explained to the wide-eyed, sad Skritch. "And I don't have to worry about you. You'll be back quick enough."

Skritch didn't struggle as a shaking Seph folded himself into the elevator, head nearly between his legs. The gridder squawked as it was squeezed a little too hard as Seph adjusted, and he quickly apologized and ran fingers down Skritch's tendril-coated back. The gridder calmed at his touch, but Pesh still felt worry across the bond. Pesh emphasized confidence in response and felt Skritch's tension ease.

"What do you need?" Seph asked. Pesh took a moment to collect themself, then told him. He nodded as best he could and then hit the button within to begin ascending.

Pesh waited for him to disappear completely before turning and grabbing L-Bot's legs from the door fortifications. They didn't have long, so best get started right away. Hopefully Mecillis hadn't destroyed the robot too badly.

Wyn watched Sage's body hit the floor just inside of the room, and a black numbness filled his guts. He wanted to vomit. To die. He wanted it to all end. Why did everyone keep dying because of his mistakes?

"Shut the door!" Sovereign shouted, and two guards rushed forward to close it, then moved in front of the door to guard it. Everyone else looked around, weapons raised. Sovereign stood calmly above Wyn, weapon now pointed at him.

Some small part of Wyn asked for it. Asked to be released from his infernal mistakes. Let him be the one to pay for it. Let Besari and Zetta escape.

"You're not that quick." Sovereign projected his calm voice around the room, eyes scanning. "So I know you're in here. Show yourself, let me kill you, and the boy lives. If you don't show yourself, I'll still let him live, just without his legs. How comfortable do you want your friend to be?"

Still nothing. Wyn bit his lip, squeezed his eyes shut. No more letting others pay for his mistakes. "Besari!" he yelled. "Whatever happens, stay hidden. Escape if you can. Please, just li—"

Sovereign's knee dropped into Wyn's midsection, exploding the air from his lungs. Wyn gasped for breath as tears ran down his temples and into his ears. Then his helmet was torn from his head and tossed across the room. Cool air brushed his tear-stained face, and he looked at Sovereign for the first time without something protecting him.

"Pathetic that you've caused me so much grief. Shall we see how brave you are after the first slice?" Sovereign pulled a knife loose and ran it lightly across Wyn's thigh. "I'll begin shortly, so now's the best time to show yourself."

The doors slid open, and Sovereign jerked his head up, pistol raised. Every guard in the room followed his lead. Wyn felt the tension and expected the air would be filled with plasma again. But everyone held, and a calm silence filled the empty space instead. Which was particularly good for the dark figure standing on the opposite side of the door.

Sovereign's eyes widened just a bit, then he smiled. "Get in here, quick."

The figure in black stepped within, closing the door behind them. Sovereign's eyes scanned the room carefully, and Wyn hoped Besari had used that moment to escape.

The figure stooped by Sage, placing fingers on her neck and then stood. Then they spoke, their voice smooth, lyrical. Feminine. "She's dead."

"I know that," Sovereign said. "I'm the one who shot her in the head."

"She grew a defense right before the shot," the woman said, walking down the hall. "That carapace power of hers. Not enough to save her though."

Sovereign's eyes shifted again. "I hadn't realized she could grow it so quickly."

"I had hoped to capitalize on your bounties." She paused before Wyn and looked down, gaze shifting to the wreckage of metal. Her entire body was covered in black armor, including an opaque helmet that crackled with her voice. "But it seems there may not be many left."

"Zetta is probably near the entrance with the experiments," Sovereign said. "I can't imagine those two would have come separately. If you're quick, you can bring me her corpse. There's also an invisible one in here that I'll still pay for."

The mysterious figure's eyes searched the air around Sovereign, then her hand shot out. In a blink, a knife materialized inches from Sovereign's face, the hand holding it and the body attached to that hand appearing shortly after. Every guard spun from their own search, weapons raised at Besari. A stunned Besari tugged at her wrist, eyes wide with fear. Sovereign smiled as he stood. Wyn struggled, but a boot shoved him back to the ground. He stared at Besari, and she stared back.

"Sorry," she mouthed.

Then the newcomer pulled a hilt from her side, and liquid metal pooled down it into a long, thin blade.

"Dead is okay?" she asked.

"Better than okay."

"I've come back to quite the fireworks show," the woman said.

Wyn's breath hitched as the blade swung. Confusion flashed in Besari's face as well. Wyn had to hope, had to believe this wouldn't be the last he saw of Besari. Then he squeezed his eyes shut, throwing one arm over his face.

Blinding light exploded out, and hundreds of shouts of pain followed. Something heavy hit Wyn, and something warm splashed across his face. Then the light was gone, but the shouts did not leave.

Wyn pulled his arm down to find another arm on top of him. He knocked it away in a panic, sickness swirling in his stomach as he looked down at the blood covering his chest. His freed chest. Sovereign had stumbled back, his remaining hand clutching the stump of his arm, which he turned away, keeping his weakened side protected. Besari had one hand clasped over her face and slowly released it, blinking away tears but otherwise unharmed. The black-garbed woman stood between them, sword raised.

"Get up," she said, not bothering to look Wyn's way. He followed her orders, clambering to his feet. The guards were doubled over, clawing at their eyes. Some swung weapons around wildly, but blinded by the light, they were unsure of where to aim.

Sovereign laughed. His blinded eyes were squeezed shut, his severed arm oozed blood, and he laughed. "I was wondering if that was you. You almost had me. Your species are so similar across the genders. The armor is what got me. I didn't think you'd actually kill your wife, Shellesh."

The newcomer's mask melted away and into the suit, revealing Shellesh beneath. He pressed the vocal modulator at his throat, and the once melodic voice was replaced with a familiar hoarse grumble. "You'd be surprised at what I'm willing to do."

"I'm going to miss her; she was extraordinarily helpful. Best assassin I've ever hired. But at least you saved me the trouble of hunting you down." Sovereign opened his eyes and stared at Shellesh. Then he moved, jumping forward to lunge with the knife in his left hand.

Shellesh knocked it away with ease, and Sovereign shifted on his feet. A second dagger slammed into Shellesh's side. A dagger held by a second arm. Wyn heard the hiss of burning flesh as smoke curled from where Sovereign had embedded the dagger.

Shellesh groaned, pulling away and stumbling backward as it tore from his side. Sovereign lifted the glowing red knife, the blood on it boiling, and he licked it. Wyn heard the sizzle as his tongue burned. Saw the charred flesh as it came off the tip. And Sovereign smiled as he swallowed.

"Nairwid," Shellesh groaned.

"Correct," Sovereign said. "Anyone who shoots the intruders will be given ten million raikers and five slaves of their choice."

The room exploded with errant plasma bolts as the retinue of blind guards shot around the room.

Zetta saw her death as Boner's arm-sword descended. She hated it, but she acknowledged it. She hadn't been strong enough to survive, and this was her price. She would face it as she needed.

That's not to say she wasn't happy when it didn't come. A frantic buzzing zipped up at Boner's face, and she stumbled back, stabbing the floor instead of Zetta. She was less happy when Boner tore her bone swords free, taking some of the vrolak with her. But Zetta was alive for a few minutes longer.

Boner stumbled back, bone swords swatting at her own face. Between the flashes of white, Zetta saw the blood pouring from one eye. Achtrek's remnant would burrow into the woman's brain and eat it. Which meant it was over, and Zetta needed to find a way to seal her stomach wound.

"Nice job, Bugs," Zetta muttered as Boner stilled, her exoskeleton keeping her upright even in death. Zetta saw the flicker of the beetle crawling within the eye socket, slithering through bloody goo to pull itself out. Zetta smiled. Not bad for a tiny bug.

Then bone spurs jutted from within the eye socket, spearing the beetle. Its legs twitched, and the other beetles buzzed and swarmed around in a panic. A bony cage enveloped over the other eye, protecting it from a similar attack, and that eye shifted to stare at Zetta. Cold, emotionless, purposeful. Zetta had never feared a human before. She would have said it even caused her an upset stomach but she wasn't sure that was just a side effect of her guts spilling out at that moment.

Zetta pulled herself to her feet, tail pushing against the ground for added support. She clutched one hand over her stomach wound as if she could will everything to stay in place. She needed to kill this human fast, but how when even destroying the brain didn't work?

Boner rushed forward, sword arms swinging. Zetta ducked beneath one, knocked the other aside, and countered with a jab to the woman's chest. She pulled on Geble, intense pain coursing through her head as her fist struck, shattering the bony protection. Boner crashed into the wall behind her, chest exposed for a heartbeat before bone grew over it. Zetta vomited, more blood than bile, and her vision swam. Her head ached so bad.

She saw white forms approaching and swung out at one. It was the wrong one, and a helmeted face slammed into her snout, knocking her back and shattering several teeth. Hot pain lanced across her chest as another swipe of a bone sword split it open. Zetta fled and Boner chased.

Achtrek's remnants buzzed around the human, searching for openings, but each one that landed on the human found itself impaled within moments. They couldn't risk more death. Zetta had to protect them. She'd promised to, and she was failing.

Zetta crashed forward, letting the berserk attacks take over. Instinct over thought. She would slash the shoulder, chip away the bony armor, and watch it repair itself in moments. Each attack became weaker, slower. Each pull of the parasite sent intense pain down her spine, muddling her mind until she couldn't see straight. Fire lanced through her wounds, both old ones reawakening and the new ones Boner tore into her. Achtrek wasn't the only one dying a little more with every attack.

Zetta's foot struck metal as she backpedaled, and something clattered away. The hammer, or what was left of it, the head demolished by the tesing's attack. But it could still work.

Boner thrust, and Zetta dove to one side, crashing to the ground with the elegance of an egg. She expected her body to shatter and was shocked to find she could move. Her claw grasped for the metal shaft. Boner attacked. Zetta spun. Bone slammed into flesh as metal burst through bone. Zetta yelled out in pain, and Boner seemed unbothered. It was entirely unfair. She was about to lose to some freak science experiment.

Zetta took a deep breath and tightened one hand around the metal shaft, the other reaching around the bone blade. She reached for Geble, and pure agony split her skull open. She didn't care. She pulled on everything it had. Everything it *didn't* have. She squeezed out what she could and pumped her body full with its chemicals. Her muscles bulged awkwardly, not in the typical uniform way, nor could she direct what muscles were controlled. It didn't matter. It was enough.

She roared as she crushed the bone blade with her hand, twisting Boner in the process and knocking her off balance. Zetta leapt from the floor, her skin stretching tight across one leg, her shoulders, and along her back. Then it split open. Agony ravaged her body, but it wasn't enough. She kept going even as her vision turned white and her brain seemed to melt. Who needed one anyway?

She spun Boner, slammed her to the ground, and drove the shaft deeper. Through bone and flesh and bone and stone. She drove it down until over half the shaft speared the human to the ground. Then she grabbed the end and pulled, warping the hammer's handle until it bent.

Then her strength finally gave out, her muscles retracted, and her pain diminished. She stumbled away, to the door where Sage had gone. Boner writhed on the floor, alive but unable to pull herself free from the spear. It would have to do.

She collapsed at the door, a pain deep within her chest arcing through her body. She coughed, then vomited, black bile spilling out over her wounds. That was no good. That would result in infection. She would have to clean...those...later...

There was a hum, a buzz, something flittering in front of her eyes, trying to pull her attention, but Zetta's head hurt too much. Too much for the noise and the motion. Too much for the light and the pain. Too much to think. So she didn't think about what she'd done. About what the black bile meant. Tears ran from her cheeks as her head fell back.

"I'm sorry," she choked out before she slipped into the waiting darkness.

It was one thing to die facing a stronger enemy or, in Zetta's case, many enemies. It was another thing to die because of your own abuse. To punish that which had kept you alive so long. To destroy the one thing you could always rely on, the one thing that should always be able to rely on you.

It was shameful to die from the death of your parasite.

The corpse of L-Bot—governed by a rudimentary control chip synced to Pesh's Vico—burst through the mostly destroyed closet door, arms flailing. Mecillis stabbed the robot three times before noticing it wasn't Pesh. By then, it was too late. They slipped from the closet, vaulting over the wrestling pair after L-Bot took the fight to the ground (okay, more like it had simply fallen over, and Mecillis happened to be where it fell, but it resulted in the same effect). Pesh found the first of their pistols near the rubble and spun to fire just in time as Mecillis, returned once more to her typical, lanky, stark-white form, freed herself from the Legal Bot. Two shots took her in the chest, burning holes in the flesh. Mecillis was unbothered and fired back.

"I see you haven't given up," Mecillis cackled. "I've always wanted to fight you, Pesh. They say it's so difficult to kill an eddermar, yet I've killed hundreds. Will you be any more difficult?"

Pesh darted through the rubble to avoid the shots, ducking around a spattering of flames that survived the sprinkler system. With their third hand, they pulled out a knife, its blade wrapped in cloth, then soaked in eddermar vomit. It ignited as they dipped it through errant embers.

"You'll find me more than a challenge for you, Mecillis," Pesh called out. "When you actually fight me instead of trying to fight with tricks."

"Always be prepared, Pesh. Anyone can kill you at any time. Best to just not trust others you can't risk getting shot by."

"You're wrong. Being alone is far more exhausting. Being with others, as weird as they may be, lightened my heart, renewed my purpose. I am of clan Kar, but even home sent me off to rid the galaxy of evil. To hunt as my clan dictates. It is difficult to feel belonging. This is different. People like me supporting each other. It is a bond almost as deep as that with a gridder. I wouldn't give that up for anything."

"You're talking foolish gibberish, Pesh. You've become sentimental."

Pesh poked their head out and spewed vomit, projecting it far enough to coat the front desk, the nearby sparks transforming it into a napalm. Flames swirled to life with new vigor, overcoming the now puttering sprinkler system easily. They heard Mecillis dive away, clattering through rubble.

"It was brave of you," Pesh called. "Walking at me with that flame wreathing your body. I'm impressed you didn't drop and smother them."

"Not all of us are controlled by our baser functions," Mecillis growled. Maybe Pesh had gotten her with that last attack. They looked down at the flames dancing in their hand. They needed to get closer.

"We shall see, Mecillis." Pesh waved the flames one direction, catching the nairwid's eye and attention, then scuttled the other way. As Mecillis's shots fired wide, Pesh unleashed on the nairwid, shooting first her hand to knock free the pistol, then filling her body with so many holes she dropped. No nairwid could reconstruct their body under constant punishment, but this would not be enough. They would have to get close enough to finish the job.

Mecillis struggled, body twitching before another consecutive shot fucked up whatever she tried to do. Her head turned to pulp, turned back into a head, and back into pulp. Her arms broke and reformed. Her chest was a writhing mass of burnt flesh and new flesh. Pesh fired through their approach, readying the flaming blade. They wouldn't even need Seph's help. This was easier than expected.

Something blinked red within Mecillis's destroyed body. There was a beep. And in the moment before the explosion, Pesh had time to think, *Fuck.* Then Mecillis exploded, and a blast of concussive power slammed into them, sending them hurtling through the room. Chitin cracked, and pain filled Pesh; another leg failed to respond, and one arm twisted and twitched, though thankfully it was the one already deprived of a hand. Their vision swirled as they blinked their many eyes back to stability. They crawled back to their feet, Pesh using their bottom two arms as additional legs. Well, one of the bottom two arms. The other was broken and severed. Three of six legs functional was not great.

Mecillis, body renewed already, walked over to the struggling Pesh. She spun her knife in hand, the blade glowing red once more as it heated. "Enough of this, Pesh. That was a nice try, but I have things to do, and you're wasting my time."

"I was having a blast," Pesh said, clicking their mandibles in laughter. "The clan will celebrate my first nairwid kill."

"Wouldn't that require you to kill me?"

"I was just getting there before you interrupted me."

"Then let's see what you can do," Mecillis growled. Knife held at the ready, she ran forward. Pesh readied themself. If they could pry the knife free and had some fluids left for more vomit, they could still burn the nairwid.

A large, orange ball exploded against Mecillis, crashing her through the opposite wall. Pesh felt the heat of it as it went by, watched the specks of molten metal steaming up from the ground where they burned.

"I got her!" Seph yelled from the lounge doorway, Skritch cooing excitement next to him. A large slag cannon slumped in his hand, molten metal dripping from the opening and sizzling on the carpet.

"Seph, what's on the other side of that wall?" Pesh asked, pointing at the newly formed hole.

The secretary looked at the hole, then squinted as his mind played through the layout of the building. "The armory. Why?"

"Because you missed her head. Reload, then hand me the weapon. Quickly!"

"Reload?"

# CHAPTER 31

## TO KILL THE UNKILLABLE

Sage woke with a pounding in her skull and a burning across her scalp. She smelled burnt hair, hoped it wasn't her own, and silently cursed Sovereign if it was. Silently, because she wasn't sure she could talk yet. Or move. Or even open her eyes. Nausea bubbled at the back of her throat, and any of those three actions threatened to spew it over. Then she'd just be shot again.

A hand touched her neck, and she tensed. No choice now. She had to do something. Whoever that was would know she was alive.

"Swallow if you're awake." Shellesh's hoarse whisper crashed into her. Sage's muscles relaxed, and she swallowed. "Stay where you are, cover your eyes. The code word is fireworks."

Then his hand disappeared, and a different voice replaced his. Smooth where his was harsh, soft where his was hard. "She's dead."

"I know that," Sovereign called. "I'm the one who shot her in the head."

Shellesh's false voice trailed away as he left her behind. "She grew a defense right before the shot. That carapace power of hers. Not enough to save her though."

"I hadn't realized she could grow it so quickly."

Cocky shit. Sage could do a lot he wasn't prepared for. Including returning from the dead.

Eventually. For now, vomit spilled onto her tongue, mostly stomach acid with a hint of protein bar to add that chalky texture to it. She held it there, worried swallowing it again would alert any nearby guards.

The conversation continued, faint to her ears, only the occasional word drifting her way. Slowly, sediment seeped from the pores near her eyes, thin patches growing over them in preparation for whatever Shellesh had planned.

That reason became readily apparent when the thin shields weren't enough to prevent the sting to her eyes. The room burst into blinding light, and Sage cringed against it, tossing one arm up over her eyes. She wasn't too worried about being seen moving, given that she wasn't entirely sure anything *could* see right then.

The movement swirled the vomit within her, and it all rushed out. She turned to the side and spewed onto the floor. The light receded, and everyone around her was screaming and grabbing at their eyes. She spit the last of the vomit from her mouth, wiped it, then sat up to stare down the hall.

Shellesh clutched at his side, Wyn and Besari cowering behind him. Sovereign stood proud, eyes on the exile. Through the groaning and the whining of hundreds of guards, Sage heard a single word drift clearly through the room. "Nairwid."

Fuck. Was Sovereign Mecillis? Or just another nairwid? Did it matter? Whoever they were, she was about to add deceased after the name.

"Anyone who shoots the intruders will be given ten million raikers and five slaves of their choice," Sovereign called out. At once, the groaning and moaning ceased, weapons raised to wherever they thought an intruder could be, and plasma fire exploded across the room. In the chaos, Wyn and the others dove for the ground, but Sovereign advanced. Shellesh waved at the others to escape and met the nairwid with sword in hand, crouched low beneath the bolts. Sovereign walked calmly through the storm, each shot burning a part of his body away, only to be immediately regenerated.

Sage hated that most of all about nairwids. The cocky shits just couldn't die easily. But they couldn't fight him like this. One errant bolt could kill them, and he was free to chase them around the room as he saw fit.

Guards first.

Sage leapt to her feet, crouched low, knees and hips screaming in agony. She pulled the pistol free from her makeshift back holster, given the holster on her right was useless, and she charged into the first of the guards near her. They crashed to the ground, and Sage fired multiple times into their head, turning it to mush.

She kicked the rifle free and, with another swipe of her boot, sent it skidding toward a crawling Wyn, head turned back toward Shellesh and Sovereign. The rifle hit his hands, and his head twisted, eyes wide, only to find the gift. His eyes shifted to find the giver.

"Sage!" he shouted. The absolute idiot.

Dozens of guards twisted their guns down and peppered the area. Besari grabbed him by the back and hauled him to a crouched run as they danced around the fire. Wyn clung to the rifle and returned fire, the gun bucking wildly in his hurried grip. Sage began methodically picking the guards off as well. Wyn stumbled, and she was sure he had been hit, but he kept his footing and kept moving. The armor he bought was apparently worth the exorbitant price.

They slid to a stop near Sage, and she lifted a half wall barrier. It wasn't strong but would hold a shot or two before crumbling to pieces.

"I thought you died," Wyn whispered, tears in his eyes.

"Shut up," Sage growled. Sentimentality at a time like this would get everyone killed. She took a breath, some irritation leaving her. Adrenaline took its place, and with it, her aches were forgotten. She could fight, and she would fight. "We need to kill these guards. Focus on the ones by Shellesh. He needs to fight unrestrained. We take out Sovereign after."

Wyn nodded, as did Besari. Sage readied her pistol and rose from the barrier, picking her targets with care, specifically those who seemed to be recovering from their blindness or were getting a bit too lucky with their shots. Wyn shot in bursts, geared toward clumps of combatants, while Besari kept their area clear. Sage had to rebuild the barrier several times, though she held steady, rather surprised at her lack of fatigue. Almost as surprised as she was at Wyn's fatigue. What the hell had he been doing to become this exhausted? He leaned heavily against the barrier, eyes darkening with each shot. He blinked away the exhaustion, raised himself, only to lean against the wall again. His lack of sleep was catching up with him.

She couldn't worry about him for now. The bigger concern was Shellesh. He ducked away from Sovereign, leading them to an area cleared of the guards, thanks to Sage. He fought a little straighter, his blade shifting like water, phasing in and out to let Sovereign's glowing knife slide through before striking. Each hit was pointless. A gash sewed itself up in moments, a severed limb regrew in heartbeats. Every errant shot that hit Sovereign did nothing more than cause a stumble. Shellesh fought desperately for time. He needed help before the wounds would catch up to him. Already, blood soaked his side and ran down his hip. Several newer wounds peppered the armor, and his non-dominant shoulder slumped.

"You two stay here," Sage said. "Finish off the guards, focus on the haushedins and vrolaks, aim for the weak spots, like eyes. Clear the worst. I need to help Shellesh."

"Wait." Wyn grabbed her arm, then released it immediately as he looked down at the stump. "If you try to cross the room, you'll die."

"Then keep me alive." She vaulted the barrier, which crumbled without her nearby to feed it. Wyn and Besari shifted behind a corpse, taking up position. Wyn watched her progress, shooting at everyone near her. Sage did the same, laughing as the thrill of life and death filled her. Adrenaline pumped her forward, madness propelled her into fire, and she cackled as she killed three more guards. She slid beneath one as he spun in circles, firing six times into his crotch and dropping him into a heap of misery. She danced around a perrilan waving two pistols and firing every direction, even upward. Sage tore the mask free and moved along as they dropped to the ground, coughing. Everywhere she went, death followed upon her fingers. Zetta better hurry, or she'd miss the fun.

Sage fired at Sovereign, throwing off his attack and letting Shellesh deliver a stabbing wound. Sovereign seemed unbothered.

He looked over at Sage and smiled. "Apparently your protection did grow quickly enough to save you." Then he frowned and ran a hand along the top of his head. "Most of you anyway."

Sage glowered at him, circling around to help Shellesh. The tesing exile withdrew his blade and backed away. "Good thing it did," she said. "I'd hate to not be the one to kill you."

"Kill?" He raised an eyebrow. "You're friends with my sister, no? You should understand that nairwids are unkillable."

"*Nearly* unkillable," Sage corrected.

"And how do you plan to kill me, Sage Valen?"

"Fire or decapitation," Pesh said as they ushered the Bounty Inc. secretary into the lounge, away from the wreckage of the entrance hall and the fresh hole to the armory. Ideally, they would have left the building entirely, reached Pesh's ship, regrouped, maybe razed the building to the ground with whatever weapons they had, and hoped that was enough. Unfortunately, Mecillis's new weapons cache included a volt launcher, which sprayed rather deadly electricity across the only exit. "Technically," they continued, "if you choose decapitation, you should then shove the head into a strong metal box, seal it, and put it somewhere unfindable. Like the bottom of the ocean or open space. Within a star is great, but that's technically the fire option." Skritch hooted in agreement. "That's why I sent you for the slag cannon. I was hoping it would be enough to burn her alive; it might have been if the head was completely coated in the molten metal."

"Sorry!" Seph said, hands quaking around the large cannon. "I didn't know!"

"That's why I said I'd take the shot," Pesh said.

"You seemed in trouble, and Skritch was very agitated."

Pesh clicked their mandibles. He wasn't wrong. They'd likely have died if Seph hadn't taken the shot. "Either way," they said, "our best bet is still the slag cannon. I need you to get into the armory and reload it."

"Why aren't we just running away?"

"You work for bounty hunters, yet you don't understand?" Pesh asked. "*We* are the bounty. Leaving the building will not stop her. It just removes our only advantage."

"How do you expect me to get past her? She's not just going to let me walk on by."

"Go around. I'll lead her out and distract her." At those words, lightning cracked against the lounge door, exploding it outward. Pesh pushed the cowering boy to the side, and his shaking legs stumbled away. They wondered if Seph would be the death of them all. He was not one to react well under duress.

Mecillis gurgled something unintelligible, clearly still healing from the slag cannon's effects. That was a good sign. If they could shoot her in the head, that would slow her down enough to give them a chance to kill her. If that's where her brain was hidden in this configuration. Could she move it?

Skritch cooed, and Pesh turned their attention to the gridder. Two of their long, stringy legs folded over a single pistol, their hind legs and tail flailing desperately to keep them afloat. Pesh smiled and relieved Skritch of the weapon. "Thanks, Little One. You can hide if you want," they added. "I can fight without you."

Skritch hooted defiance. They hated violence, but they loved Pesh more. Pesh felt the love bleed through the bond and returned it. "Then let's kill ourselves a nairwid."

An injured eddermar, a non-aggressive gridder, and a secretary with no combat experience. One pistol and an empty slag cannon. It would be a challenge, but Pesh welcomed it. This was the sort of fight they lived for. It would be one worth honoring.

Pesh crouched by the door to the lounge, the occasional hum and crackle of electricity dulling. They couldn't tell if it had run out of energy or if Mecillis was waiting.

"Thought you preferred to keep things close, Meci." Pesh leaned out and fired into the hole. A razor-sharp disc zipped through the air, nearly decapitating Pesh and embedding itself deep into the wall. Pesh peed a little. That had been close.

"At this point," Mecillis growled, climbing through the hole, weapons draped across her back and the disc tosser in hand, "I just want you dead." Burns ran down her chest and stomach, the surrounding skin writhing, fighting back against the burnt flesh.

"How old are you, Mecillis?" Pesh called. "Because I think it's only fair that the younger of us lives longer. You had so many years to be an evil bitch. Let the younger generation take over."

With a thud, a disc embedded itself halfway through the wall, the blades like dozens of tiny teeth. Well, at least the wall would protect them until Mecillis got closer.

"You've missed your best shot at killing me," Mecillis said. "So now it's my turn."

"I'm gonna have to decline," Pesh said. They fired one shot and pulled their hand back just before a disc shot through the space it had occupied. "But tell me what kin you want your ashes sent to, and I'll gladly do so." Pesh paused for dramatic effect. "Oh wait, you nairwids don't really have kin, do you?"

"I have one," she said. "He's probably killing your friends right now."

Pesh clicked their mandibles in agitation. They had to believe the others would survive whatever trap Mecillis had laid for them. Any distraction now could cost their life.

Footsteps echoed through the entrance hall. She was making her way closer, which only helped Mecillis. Pesh needed to distract her, preferably without dying. They took a deep breath, then stuck out their injured hand. The joints ached to move, and as it poked out, they heard the disc launcher fire. At the same moment, Pesh ducked out, pistol in hand, and fired three times. Two hit their target as the disk severed more of Pesh's arm. The disc launcher crackled, then its gauss generator exploded. Mecillis crashed into the front desk, half her face torn off, only to regenerate moments later. Excellent. Great. Pesh was losing bits of themself every moment, and it took everything to do almost no damage.

Skritch hooted and crashed into Pesh, knocking them back just as electricity burst through the room. Lightning forked and destroyed the large display, igniting sparks across the wall. It struck near Pesh, and they scooted away from the bolts. Wild energy crackled all around the room, and Skritch's tendrils rose with it. They cowered behind Pesh, peering over their shoulder.

Mecillis ducked into the room, weapon raised. Pesh grabbed Skritch and leapt up the wall, limbs suctioning as they scuttled upward. Lightning crashed behind them, then Mecillis swept it upward. Pesh dove, grabbing and swinging from the light fixture to crash into the furniture. Electricity crackled in the air as it chased them, bursting the chairs into fire. They crawled along behind the furniture, searching for whatever cover could last more than a few seconds against the onslaught of that weapon.

None could, instead disintegrating behind them at an alarming rate. Skritch hooted and struggled in their grip. Pesh clicked their mandibles angrily. Now wasn't the time to worry about Skritch's comfort. The gridder squirmed loose, rolled across the ground, then inflated. Their legs split, aiming for speed. Pesh's heart stopped.

"No!" they shouted. Skritch launched themself, and Pesh did too. One swipe of the hand struck the gridder, knocking them off their intended direction. The swatted Skritch bounced off floor and wall and rolled into a corner, dazed. At the same instant, Mecillis's lightning struck Pesh in the chest. They slammed backward, limbs convulsing. They yelled out until the pain stopped and their insides ceased cooking. But their limbs refused to move when they tried. They had bought what time they could, but this would be it for Pesh in the absence of some miracle.

They glanced at Skritch, who rolled onto their stomach. Limp legs pulled them across the ground, but they looked weakened and betrayed by Pesh's last attack. Pesh sent only love through the bond. More than anything in the world, they wanted the gridder to live on. Even if Pesh wouldn't.

Another bolt of lightning slammed into Pesh and they writhed on the floor, the cracking of their exoskeleton like some abominable music. Skritch whined, though Pesh wasn't sure if they'd actually heard it or just imagined it through the despair coursing through the bond. Their mouth tasted of ash, and it was only when contemplating this that Pesh noticed the attack had stopped.

"That's pathetic, Pesh. The weapon's at its lowest power setting." Mecillis sauntered over, a cold smile on her face, the volt launcher dangling to one side. "You can't die that easily or you'll give eddermar a bad name. I need to see how much pain you can handle before death, so try to hold out as long as you can."

"I'm just starting, Mecillis," Pesh coughed, the words no more than a croak.

Panic. Pesh felt the emotions before the attack, and they couldn't move fast enough to stop it. Skritch cooed as they dove toward Mecillis. Uselessly so, as the nairwid swatted them out of the air.

Skritch bounced across the floor, crashing to a stop beneath the still-sparking display unit, body limp. Pesh felt them, alive but too weak. Mecillis turned, volt launcher raised, and Pesh screamed.

They kicked out, forcing their limbs to work, slamming one foot into Mecillis's knee and driving her to the ground. The nairwid spun, anger burning in her eyes, and Pesh felt the pain of the electricity course through them again.

They tried to breathe but couldn't suck the air into their convulsing lungs. Tried to yell out for Skritch to run, to survive, but words could not form within their mouth. Limbs twitched, and their abdomen cracked and popped. Their insides seemed to cook, the stench of it filling the air. Their vision dulled as liquid dripped down their face from several burst eyes. It seemed to last a lifetime, leaving Pesh on the verge of death when it finally ceased. They gasped for breath, every muscle twitching uselessly out of control. Every fiber of their being burned. Blood poured from countless wounds.

Mecillis crouched over them. "I was going to peel your exoskeleton from your body, maybe fashion some armor from it." Mecillis drove a finger deep into one crack and peeled it upward. It tore from the flesh beneath, and Pesh roared. "It doesn't seem too strong though." She tore it completely free, and pain burned where the patch of chitin had been. Pesh groaned, still trying to make their limbs function. Mecillis twisted the plate of chitin in hand before snapping it in two. "Far weaker than I thought." She tossed it aside.

"Traitor!" Pesh hissed.

Mecillis raised her eyebrows with amusement. "You can hardly call me a traitor if I never joined your little club to begin with." Then she pulled her knife free, the blade glowing red hot. "I'm sure we can find other names for you to call me. Let's see how creative you can be."

Pesh's screams became a torturous melody echoing through the building. Skritch echoed them in their own tiny voice, the pain leaking across the bond.

# CHAPTER 32

## SACRIFICE

Shellesh danced the blades with the nairwid, diving in and out of thrusts and strikes, shifting the state of Mercurial to slide past his defenses. Every strike a pyrrhic victory, his every wound stacking while Sovereign's stitched back closed. A calm understanding washed over him. He would fight on, give the others every chance to escape, then he would die as he should have so long ago. He accepted his end and was happier to see it pay for the lives of his friends rather than take the life of his wife.

"You have an impressive talent, Shellesh," Sovereign said. "Given that your wife is unlikely to return, I'm wondering if you'd like to take her spot. Talented individuals like you would be wasted with death."

"I have made peace with my end," Shellesh said, his breaths coming hard and painful while Sovereign seemed at ease. "It is a far greater one than serving you."

"That is unfortunate." Sovereign attacked, and Shellesh defended against the burning blade. "I—"

Three shots struck Sovereign in the chest, knocking him back. Shellesh swung, deflecting the knife away, then impaling the nairwid in the chest. He smiled as blood ran down his lips.

"Apparently your protection did grow quickly enough to save you." He frowned, running a hand along the top of his head, along where Sage's own had been burnt away from the shot. "Most of you anyway."

His hand twitched, and Shellesh withdrew, pulling the sword free before the nairwid could counterattack with that knife. He glanced over and watched Besari and Wyn rush toward them, weapons firing at the last of the guards who stumbled around blindly. He touched his side and found it had stopped bleeding at some point. He wasn't sure if that was a good or bad sign. It was the sort of wound that stopped bleeding only with death.

Sage had circled around the other side of Sovereign, and Shellesh positioned himself appropriately. The two bickered, and Shellesh ignored them, using the respite to instead plan.

"And how do you plan to kill me, Sage Valen?"

Shellesh perked up at the question, and Sage grinned past Sovereign to him. "Thinking of beheading this time."

"It won't work," Sovereign said. "My kind can—"

"Regrow from the smallest bit of brain, yes. I was just wondering what would happen if we just kept destroying the head until we hand you off to the Raiyrium Confederation is all."

"Pointless. As I've told your boss, that contract was my trap."

"And that means the R.C. wants you less?"

Sovereign smirked. "If you want my head, you'll have to take it."

"I intend to." Sage charged, her fist coated in carapace. He swung the knife to intercept, and Shellesh stepped forward to disarm him, quite literally. Hand and knife dropped to the ground as Sage's fist slammed into the nairwid. He spun away from Shellesh's second strike and caught Sage's fist in his hand. He spun her into Shellesh's path. Then his boot kicked the knife into the air, and he caught it with a regrown hand. The burning blade slammed down, slicing across Sage's arm and through her sediment armor. Sage yelled, and a foot kicked her into Shellesh.

He ducked around, Mercurial shifting like waves in the ocean. He solidified it the moment before contact that never came. Sovereign dropped back, kicking out at Shellesh's feet. The two dropped to the ground, and Sovereign rolled on top of Shellesh, blade readied. Mercurial switched to a short blade, and the exile slammed it into Sovereign's descending forearm. The glowing blade stopped just above his chest, the point scraping Miaraim's armor. Shellesh grabbed Mercurial by blade and hilt, shoving Sovereign's arm away. The nairwid smiled, then pushed down.

Bone cracked and reformed as Sovereign's arm pushed through Mercurial, the burning knife stabbing through Shellesh's armor and into his chest. The skin burned and blood boiled as he screamed. Despite pushing harder, the blade only slid through Sovereign's otherwise steady arm, and the knife in his chest pushed farther inward.

Then Sovereign's head knocked back, the hilt of a dagger appearing as Besari did. She kicked the wobbly nairwid from atop Shellesh, Mercurial shifting to liquid quickly to avoid being tugged away. Then she stepped over him in a protective posture. Shellesh pulled the burning knife from his chest quickly. It had avoided anything too vital, and cauterization limited the blood loss. Sage pulled herself to her feet. Despite the cut, her arm still seemed fully functional.

Sovereign stood as well, pulling the knife from his head and sighing softly. "Numbers won't matter," he said. "Two against one, three against one, in the end you'll all—"

A rifle shot blew off half of Sovereign's face, and the nairwid stumbled back to the ground, unmoving as an eyeball regrew within a fresh eye socket.

"How about four against one?" Wyn asked. Shellesh glanced back to find all the other guards were dead or otherwise incapacitated.

Bone clicked into place as Sovereign's jaw reformed, and he smiled. "Why should I be afraid of you four?"

"Because we're the best fucking bounty hunters in the galaxy," Wyn said.

Wyn hoped he sounded more confident than he felt. He had been hit by several shots, and the heat of their plasma still stung his skin, but somehow the suit held up. Worse was the endless fatigue that seemed to plague him since the fighting had started. He wanted nothing more than to sleep for days, but he pushed himself past the exhaustion, past the aches in his body, and he kept fighting. He would make sure no one else died this day.

"The best?" Sovereign stood, Besari's blade in hand. "That's awfully pathetic then."

Wyn fired, and Sovereign spun to the side, anticipating the shot. Besari flickered out of view as Sage swung at the nairwid. Sovereign grabbed her wrist and tossed the large woman over his shoulder with ease. She slammed into the ground, Besari flickering back into visibility beneath her. Wyn fired again, and the nairwid lifted the blade, seeming to slice the bolt of plasma in half as it seared both sides of his face. Then he was ducking around Shellesh's blade, and

Wyn couldn't get a shot. He grabbed for his knife, ready to jump into the action.

"Stay there!" Sage called, rolling to her feet. Besari rose behind her.

"But—"

"We need your support to give us an edge, Wyn," she explained. "And you're not as good at close combat. Take every shot you can. We'll take his head."

Wyn nodded, and Sage jumped back into the combat. Besari locked eyes with Wyn, her expression unreadable. Maybe relief? Worry? Then she was gone. Wyn returned his knife, stepped away from the fight, and raised his rifle. He bit one lip in frustration. Sage was right, he would be a liability up close. But here, he could do something, even if there were long stretches of nothing.

Shellesh yelled out as Sovereign's blade bit into his thigh, then Sage was there to shoulder the nairwid back. Sovereign danced between them, taking attacks as often as dodging them, letting his body slow the others to create openings that shouldn't have been there. He carved away Sage's carapace armor, biting into her flesh. Chips of sediment rained down from her body.

Wyn aimed carefully and waited, only taking his shot when Sovereign was open, trusting Besari to stay out of the way. But Sovereign was quick, impossibly quick. Wyn fired, and the nairwid shifted his head, the bolt crashing into the wall behind him instead.

Sovereign leaned into the movement, driving a boot into Shellesh's leg, knocking the tesing to the ground with a grunt. Then he spun around Sage, keeping her between him and Wyn.

Besari appeared again, swiping only once with her remaining dagger before Sovereign danced around her and returned the attack with her other blade. Besari's armor held against the slash, but she was tossed to the ground by the violent kick that followed it. Then he refocused on Sage, blade crashing into her again and again. Wyn circled around, and Sovereign twisted. He was going to kill her if Wyn didn't do something.

Shellesh stepped in again, his liquid blade swinging to deflect a blow and knock the nairwid back. Wyn fired, a glancing blow to the shoulder to stagger Sovereign. He fired again and again, and Sovereign skipped away from the shots, making his way to the burning knife, kicking it into his own hand, and tossing Besari's blade at Wyn. Wyn stumbled back, tripping over a perrilan's corpse and slamming to the ground—likely the only thing to save his life as the blade whizzed overhead.

Wyn caught his breath and rolled to his feet, the fighting so swift he could barely follow it. His hands shook, nerves unraveling. He couldn't just sit here and watch all of this and fail to act. He needed to do something. But everything he could do would hinder the others. Would get them killed. His confidence plummeted, his mind coiling around one dark thought after another. Better if he weren't here at all. He froze as he watched the three combatants trading blows, Sovereign's hits inflicting more damage than everyone else's. He was going to whittle them down to nothing, then kill them.

Time crept to a pause, and Sovereign stared at Wyn, a smile darkening his lips. He toyed with them, played with their lives at every moment. And Wyn would sit here and watch it happen instead of doing something. Being a bounty hunter meant putting your life on the line. Wyn had thought he was ready for that, had convinced himself he was. But now he stood motionless, cold dread running down his spine, death an inevitability, and he understood he'd never be ready for it.

Sage yelled as the burning blade bit into her thigh, skin blackening at its edges. Sovereign dragged it across until the leg gave out, and Sage fell to the ground, one hand gripping at the leg. Shellesh stumbled, bleeding from so many wounds. They were going to die.

*So what are you going to do about it?* Wyn bit his lip, drawing blood as he steadied his breath. *Sit here and watch it happen?* Wyn slapped his own face, blinked away the terror as blood rushed through him. *Or are you going to fight to protect them like you said you would?*

Wyn roared within his head, blood pumping. He was the last chance. Sage and Shellesh were too injured to continue on, and he couldn't risk Besari alone against that monster. He jumped to his feet, rifle in hand, and raised it as Sovereign glanced over, eyebrows raised.

"I thought you were—"

Wyn interrupted him with a burst of fire. Sovereign's smile disappeared as he dove forward through the shots, healing any that hit him. He rolled, raising one arm as Wyn fired at him, each plasma bolt tearing the arm to pieces before it regenerated. Sovereign pushed through the shots, burning blade in hand, and swung. Wyn twisted the rifle, catching the blade. Metal sizzled and melted as the super-heated knife carved through it. Sovereign glanced at the charge well, currently loaded with a nearly full charge, and smiled. Then he ran the blade along the gun. Wyn ejected the cartridge just as the blade struck where it had been. The knife came loose, and he swung the ruined rifle at Sovereign's face. The king of Kekar dodged it easily, then stabbed Wyn through the arm.

Intense heat coursed through him as the burning point pierced his forearm. Smoke rose where it burned away at his skin, where it cracked the bone beneath and boiled the marrow. Wyn heard his own cries as he stumbled back, the gun slipping from loose fingers. His other hand pushed at Sovereign, pushed to escape him, and Sovereign knocked it away, slammed his hand into Wyn's chest, and dragged him to the pillar that crashed into his back. Only then did Sovereign tear the knife from Wyn's arm.

His arm flared with agony, and he pushed it away. Pushed every thought of it away. He grabbed his knife with his left hand and slammed it up at Sovereign's head. If he could disorient the nairwid, buy some time, he could—

Sovereign grabbed Wyn's wrist and twisted until the joints popped and the blade fell from his grasp. In one movement, Sovereign released and snatched the blade with his right. With his left, he drove the burning blade towards Wyn's eye. The orange glow of the blade filled his vision, and Wyn lurched back, eyes closed as if he could somehow escape it.

The heat of the blade warmed Wyn's face and nothing more. He opened his eyes and found the point dancing just in front of one eye, but it held steady there, thanks to a strong grip at Sovereign's elbow. Besari stood behind him, holding the attack back and driving her own blade into the nairwid's neck. Her eyes were wide with fear and worry. Sovereign smiled, and blood ran down both sides of his mouth.

Besari had saved him, and all she needed to do was run the blade across his neck. If they could sever the head, maybe Sage could do something to—

Besari coughed, and blood splattered across Sovereign's arm. Wyn's heart stopped. She gritted her teeth, fingers clutching Sovereign's bicep.

"Strange biological difference," Sovereign croaked, blood still running freely from his mouth, "between birrosh and bishett. That being which side this vital organ sits on. Something like a kidney in humans, right?"

Wyn's eyes glanced down, traced Sovereign's other arm, the one holding the knife he'd dropped, and found it wrapped around his back. Besari's hands shook as tears formed in her eyes. Still she gritted her teeth, and blood oozed out between them.

Wyn grabbed Sovereign's wrist, ducking as the nairwid drove the blade into the pillar, embedding it there. Sovereign's eyes opened in amused humor. Besari's hands slipped from Sovereign as she stumbled back, falling to her knees. Wyn's hand tightened on the wrist as Sovereign attempted to pull back. Wyn tugged a pistol free and fired at the nairwid's knee, who dropped with surprise, the limb already pulling back together. Sovereign tore free from Wyn's grasp, and Wyn fired again, knocking the nairwid back with the force of the shot. Still Sovereign laughed, reaching up to grab at the knife in his throat.

"You can't—"

Wyn shot the hand reaching up for the knife. He pulled his second pistol free and fired at Sovereign's other hand. The nairwid laughed as his hands reformed.

A black fury filled Wyn, everything evaporating away except Sovereign's laugh. He would kill the nairwid, if it was the last thing he did. Wyn filled the nairwid with plasma, shooting his limbs as they tried to regrow, shooting his head as the nairwid struggled. His laughter never ceased beneath the barrage. Always regrowing. Always coming back. Always there, haunting him.

Wyn roared as he dropped on top of Sovereign, tossing the pistols to the side. Beheading. That's what Sage had said. He grabbed the knife in the nairwid's throat. He twisted it, digging the blade through Sovereign's neck. The flesh snapped back in a flash and Sovereign's face reformed, the mad cackle gone. His hands shot up around Wyn's neck and clamped down. Wyn's breath died in his mouth. He coughed, but with no means to escape, his chest convulsed with it. His hands shook with the knife, trying to cut, but Sovereign pushed him away with long arms. Darkness blurred Wyn's vision as his lungs ached for breath. His fingers slipped from the knife, then his body was lifted and slammed into the ground as Sovereign leaned over.

The blade still pierced his neck, and the blood ran down the hilt and dripped on Wyn's face, splashing at his gaping mouth and into his eyes. Sovereign grabbed the hilt and pulled it free, the skin knitting together behind it.

"So close," Sovereign whispered, the words barely audible over the sound of Wyn's heart pounding in his ears. The empty void encroached at the edges of his vision. Swarmed him. Swallowed him up. He turned his head, found Besari one last time, just a few feet away. Wyn's knife protruded from her side, but she still pulled herself toward him. Toward Sovereign. She yelled something. Maybe it wasn't even words. Wyn wanted to say he was sorry. He had fucked up again.

Sovereign twisted his head away, forced it back to him. "Don't look at her. We're having a moment here," he said. "I just want you to know, I've decided it's not worth keeping you alive. But once you're dead, I'll—"

A geyser of blood spewed from Sovereign as his head disappeared. The pressure on Wyn's neck relieved, and he gasped in air, coughing around the blood that filled his mouth, both Sovereign's and his own. He turned over and vomited. Sage stood over him, one leg limp, a blade of carapace jutting from her hand.

"Shell!"

The head rolled to a stop at Shellesh's boot. Sovereign's eyes twisted up, his mouth gaping and moving soundlessly, the skin at his neck already growing down to form shoulders. Shellesh slammed his sword into Sovereign's head, right between his eyes, and screamed a single word. "Shatter!" The sword shifted, exploding out with dozens of spikes, sending blood oozing everywhere. The head turned to a writhing, pulpy mass, and the sword pulsed, receding some spikes and sending more out. Sovereign was constantly healing, the sword constantly damaging.

Wyn's vision tunneled, blocking everything out except for Besari. "Besari?" he thought he asked. But his voice sounded hoarse, cracked and broken. Then he watched her eyes close. Exhaustion overwhelmed him, and everything turned black.

"Fuck," Seph whined. "Fuck fuck fuck fuck fuck fuck!"

He shuffled through the hallways, retracing his steps as the building shook behind him. He slipped and crashed to the floor, banging his knee rather painfully and spilling the large gun from his hands.

"Why couldn't we just leave?" he asked no one in particular. All he wanted to do was get high, but no, his parents had made him get a job. A job where he'd gotten tied up and threatened for weeks, then tossed into actual combat. This wasn't how anything was supposed to be. He pushed himself up with shaking arms that hadn't recovered from his first shot. Just holding the large bucket-shaped weapon was difficult. He felt tears on his cheeks again. "Fuck."

He wasn't built for this. He wasn't made for any real combat. Pesh could handle their own, right? He wasn't needed! He pushed himself to wobbly legs, the one knee still kind of hurting. There was an emergency exit nearby. He could run, call in some authorities who could handle this situation. Pesh couldn't blame him, he'd been hired to file forms and organize meetings. Not to fire giant balls of molten metal from guns that weighed as much as he did.

Seph looked down at the slag cannon, but all he could see was a robot that had been kind to him being torn apart and tossed in the closet.

"*Fuck!*" Seph picked up the cannon and ran.

He slammed a palm on the control panel, and the door to the locker room swung open. At the far end was the door to the gym, a place Seph regularly found reasons to avoid. The other direction led to the armory and gun range. He also avoided those areas. He did quite well at the front desk, closet, and cafeteria (though he was revisiting his opinion of the closet).

He crept forward to the door and listened closely. Another explosion, but it didn't sound nearby. He took a deep breath, difficult to do when he was still gasping from his run, and then opened the door.

The armory was in ruins, weapons spilling out of a large hole on one side. Splotches of metal cooled to black all over the room, everything around them burnt and scarred. Something was definitely on fire, as smoke billowed up from deeper within. But there was no shapeshifting psychopath, so Seph slipped fully into the room.

The crackle of electricity sounded outside the room, and Seph poked his head through the hole. In the lounge, Mecillis shot Pesh with electricity. Excellent. Exactly what he had hoped to see. His only chance at living being killed. Perfect.

"Fuck," he whispered as loud as he dared. He needed ammo. Somewhere around here. The first place he checked was where he'd found the slag cannon. Which happened to be where there was now a massive hole in the wall. He set the heavy cannon to one side and started digging into the rubble. Something jabbed up under his thumb nail, and he jerked away with an intake of breath. Then he sucked on the sore spot, hoping it would soothe the pain.

Pesh screamed, a terrible, shrill wail.

Seph squeezed his eyes shut, as though that would shut out the yells. He urged his body to move, to do something, but he just sat there, quaking. He wasn't a hero, he was a loser. A druggie. A no-good waste of space. He gripped at his ears, trying to stop the screams, but he could only grit his teeth as tears poured down his cheeks.

Pesh was going to die if he didn't do anything. They were going to die while he cowered. Seph punched his thigh, the soreness dissipating as quickly as it appeared. He punched it harder. "Come on!" he hissed through his teeth. "Come on! Just this once, don't fuck up!" He punched his thigh until he was sure a bruise had formed. He shook himself until his breathing was ragged, then he dug his hands into the rubble and pulled away pieces of the wall.

He ignored the blood that dripped from his fingers, ignored the aches that began forming deep within his bones and joints. He ignored the stinging that radiated up his arm. He pulled and shifted the rubble, a single mantra repeating over and over.

*Don't screw this up. Don't screw this up. Don't screw this up.*

He pulled away a chunk of wall and heard a large thud as a ball of metal rolled away after nearly crushing his foot. The object appeared to be formed from scrap metal, the pieces welded together. He wondered what use it could possibly have until it rolled into the slag cannon, knocked the gun over, and Seph could see that it was the same size as the cannon's opening.

"Oh."

He raced over, stopped the ball from rolling farther with one foot, and picked up the cannon. He turned it around, searching for instructions and finding none. Who didn't put reload instructions on a weapon? How was someone supposed to know how to reload?

He sighed and reached for his Vico to search. His hand tapped his bare wrist. Right. Mecillis had taken that. He groaned, then hoped for the best as he shoved the large ball into the top of the cannon and hit a button.

The slag cannon clicked, and nothing else happened. He looked down the barrel and didn't see anything interesting, so he hit a different button.

Click.

He searched and found another button and clicked that one. The slag cannon hummed and grew warm in his hand. Then an orange glow emitted from the cannon's barrel.

"Yes!" Seph shouted, then clapped his hands over his mouth. He glanced out, and though the crackle of electricity had stopped, Pesh still whimpered. Mecillis stood over them, more than likely doing something unkind.

He was supposed to return the cannon to Pesh so they could take the shot. He wasn't sure that was possible anymore. He would have to try again. He took a deep breath and lifted the heavy cannon, made heavier by its new round. A screen on the top flashed yellow and displayed *readying*. He assumed that meant the ball of metal hadn't been fully moltified. Meltified? It wasn't ready.

Just as he hoped it would hurry, the weapon clicked and the light turned green. Ready. He stepped into the entrance hall and scuttled across to the lounge doorway. He held the cannon upright, looked through the sights, and aimed at Mecillis, who crouched over Pesh.

The head. He needed to hit the head.

"Hey!" he shouted. "Fuckhead!"

Mecillis turned to glare at him, but her eyes grew wide as she saw the cannon pointed her way. Seph panicked, his finger pulling the trigger accidentally. The weapon fired, knocking him back with the recoil, and a molten ball of metal slammed into Mecillis's face. Her body shot backward over Pesh and slid to a stop by a pile of burning furniture. A gurgled scream reached Seph's ears as the body flailed, hands clawing at the red-hot metal that ate at her face.

Seph dropped the cannon and crawled to Pesh. Their body had been cracked open, several pieces of their exoskeleton torn. Blood spilled out in a large puddle.

"Pesh?"

A stabbing pain, and sudden wakefulness jolted Wyn upright with a gasp. He grabbed at his leg and found Sage holding a needle to it.

"No time to sleep," she growled.

"Besari!" His head snapped to find her, Shellesh already crouching over her. He pulled the needle free from his leg and crawled to her. The skin on her face had grown pale, her dark freckles standing out even more. "Can you help?"

"I don't know bishett anatomy well," Shellesh said. "Best I can do is bind the wound and hope we get to a medical suite in time."

"Do we leave the knife in or pull it?"

"Shit!" Sage shouted and hobbled toward the door. It opened, and she fired on a crowd of people. They ducked to either side or died. Shouts echoed down the halls.

"Pull it," Besari whispered, her eyes flicking open. "Do you know how painful it is to have a knife in you?"

"What if that kills you faster?" Wyn said, a cold dread filling his limbs. Sage fought with the door controls to lock them before telling everyone else they needed to move.

"I'm sorry, Wyn," she said, and she smiled, a thin stream of blood trickling from one corner of her mouth. "But I'm happy you lived. I'm happy I could save you."

"You promised, Besari." Wyn felt the tears burning in his eyes. "We were supposed to be unbeatable. You're supposed to let me drag you back from death. So let me. Stay with me."

"Don't blame yourself, Wyn," she said. "It was my choice, and I would do it again. You were the only person besides my mentor who believed in me." She coughed, blood spurting from between her lips. "Everything feels cold. Numb."

Wyn shook his head. "No, I made a promise. We're going to get you help." Wyn grabbed the hilt of the blade. He wasn't sure what the right answer was, but doing nothing was too painful. He needed to act. "Brace yourself."

Then he pulled. The knife slipped from her side, and Besari screamed, her hands gripping around his arm, fingers digging in to bruise the flesh. He pulled it free, and blood spilled out, darkened by other fluids.

"Shellesh." The exile handed him gauze, and Wyn placed it against the wound, holding it steady. Blood soaked through within moments.

"Fuck, that hurt," Besari groaned. "Maybe we should have left it in."

"I thought you were numb." Wyn chuckled, trying to keep the mood light. Trying to keep his hopes alive.

"Yeah," she said, sweat beading down her forehead. Then her head fell back, eyes closing.

"Besari?" She didn't respond, and panic flooded Wyn's body. "Besari!" He reached one hand up to stroke her cheek. It felt cold to his touch.

He bit his lip and fought against tears. No, it couldn't end this way. He'd promised to drag her back. He'd promised.

Instead, exhaustion overwhelmed him, beating away the last of Sage's drugs, and he almost collapsed over the top of her. Then the tears came, dripping from his chin to her cheek. He pulled her head close and held it.

"Besari," he murmured. Shellesh stepped away to give them space, and Sage watched, expression solemn.

"Yeah?" Besari asked.

Wyn jerked away, and Shellesh even looked down in surprise. Sage raised one eyebrow as she watched from the door, a door that shook with the efforts of new and unpleasant arrivals.

"I thought you died," Wyn said, a smile on his face. "Stick with me, okay? We'll get you help."

Besari looked at Wyn with confusion, her hand searching down his arm to his hand, the one that held the gauze in place. She pulled it away, despite Wyn's reluctance, and no blood came pouring out as he'd expected. She peeled the suit apart, revealing only a faint scar in place of the gaping wound.

"What?" she asked.

Wyn's eyes stared in shock. "You're fine."

Shellesh opened his mouth, then closed it, face furrowing in consternation.

Wyn helped Besari sit and Sage watched on, both eyebrows raised. "Holy shit," she said.

"I don't know what happened," Wyn said as he helped her walk to the door. With each step, she was more sure of herself. "But her wound seems healed now."

"That amount of bleeding, it shouldn't be," Shellesh muttered, his own hand going to the wound in his side.

"Well, I'm okay with it," Besari groaned. "I'd rather not bleed out."

"I know what happened," Sage said, beaming at Wyn. "About time you figured out your fucking Thresha talent."

Pesh was in bad shape. Mecillis's knife may have been stopped, but she had dug through their exoskeleton and sought out several nerves. She was nothing if not thorough when it came to torture. Their limbs twitched, their eyes still unfocused. Seph had approached carefully, had said something they hadn't acknowledged. Skritch was a bright beacon in their mind, fear and worry crashing into them.

Pesh clicked their mandibles, a reproach to the gridder. How dare they worry! The emotions that bled through their bond spoke differently despite their attempts to hide them. Skritch crawled over as Seph leaned down, eyes leaking fluids as he looked at their abdomen. That was probably not a good sign.

A horrific scream pierced the deafening blanket across Pesh's senses, bringing their wandering mind to focus. Mecillis wailed as she clawed at her face, fingers digging into her skull to claw out the liquid metal even as it burned them to the bone and beyond. She pulled the metal free from one eye socket, and the signs of repair began to show. She wasn't going to die. It hadn't been enough.

Seph vomited, his face growing to a rather sickly shade that no species should have, let alone his own. He was stretched taut, pulled too far past what he could handle. He couldn't do more, and they wouldn't want to make him. Skritch cooed nervously, new emotions flitting over the bond as they crawled forward. They, too, would be useless to finish the job. It had to be Pesh. A final hunt, and one worthy of the title of Kar, Tset'As'Edder's greatest hunters.

Besides, was not saving friends a worthy death? And was not a death worth dying the greatest purpose of life?

They grabbed Seph's hand, the human's blood warming their own. His watery eyes shifted from the pool of vomit at his knees to their eyes.

"Seph," they croaked, throat ragged from the screaming. "Thank you for the help."

He looked up at Mecillis's thrashing form, and terror formed in his eyes. "She's not dying, Pesh. What should I do?"

"Two things," they said. "Tell Clan Kar of our successful hunt. The first nairwid in a hundred years. Make sure we get the credit at the end. You and I."

"You can tell them yourself, Pesh. We'll get you help. Just tell me what you need me to do here and now."

"Second, watch over Skritch." Pesh coughed. "They'll have a hard time adjusting. Losing a bond is a difficult thing."

"Pesh." His eyes grew even more watery, a reaction Pesh had always found strange. What purpose did it serve to show their sadness through leaking eyes? "You'll be okay. I'll get help and—"

Pesh twisted the boy's arm away, spinning Seph and landing him in the pool of his own vomit. He would help them as they'd asked. Now, Pesh needed to finish it. They took a breath, pain radiating through their body. Seph whined and pulled himself from the vomit. Skritch howled, a pain piercing deeper into the gridder than anything they had experienced before. So deep it radiated through the bond. Pesh almost wavered, but they could not.

Then they twisted up onto eight limbs, only half working properly. Pain lanced across their body, and blood rushed from the open wounds. Slowly, excruciatingly, they pulled themself across the floor, inch by inch, their eyes never leaving Mecillis. Blinded, face half melted, the nairwid didn't notice the approach. Had she, Pesh would have likely failed. The slag cannon hadn't been enough to kill, but it had been enough to let Pesh kill.

They crawled on top of the squirming body, and a panic filled the nairwid. Legs kicked out at Pesh, but it was only pain, and Pesh had reached the threshold of what they could comprehend. A drop in a pond was nothing. Arms pushed, but weakened by molten metal, they were ineffective. Pesh simply grabbed them and shoved them to the side. Mecillis writhed, her deformed face pulsing as hot metal burned it away and new flesh grew back.

"Pesh!" Seph shouted. Still the gridder cried.

Pesh's chest rumbled, liquids dripping from open wounds and spilling onto the body, igniting in little flashes. They had just enough to make it work. Just enough.

Then they vomited. The black bile spewed from their mouth and smothered the nairwid's face, bursting into an inferno upon contact with the molten metal. Mecillis's screeches withered as her vocal cords were destroyed. Flame gutted her face again, peeling the fresh skin back, charing the bone beneath.

Not enough.

Pesh spewed more, and flames rose higher, blackening their chitin, burning everything exposed. The heat pulsed into them, finding something to eat away.

Not enough.

Still they spewed, building the inferno until it encased them both. Ate away the skin and the muscle, ate away the blood and the bone. Pesh continued until the fire devoured everything, the pain building to an apex before disappearing forever.

Seph watched as flames filled the lounge. The safety sprinklers were at work, though every drop appeared to evaporate before reaching the building inferno, the center of which was two corpses. Corpses because nothing could have lived through that. Both bodies stopped thrashing, and Pesh's began collapsing into pieces. He watched even as the light pierced his eyes and the smoke irritated them. He watched even as the fire spread out of control, consuming everything within the room.

Seph picked up the crying gridder in his arms and backed from the lounge as the flames threatened to eat him as well. Skritch was limp in his arms, eyes fixed longingly on the origin of the flames. Cries turned to whimpers.

"It'll be okay," Seph said as he hurried outside. Tears that had been eaten by the flames reappeared in the cool night air. He fell to the ground on his knees, coughing the black smoke from his lungs. He squeezed Skritch, burying his face into the soft tendrils. "It'll be okay."

# WANTED

## GRIDDER

REWARD:
A BOND

"Your cycle's end has come, and with it, the dawn of your trial," Gles'kar announced. It was all preamble, words for the ritual, and Pesh could recite them clearly. But the gathered crowd shouted cheers of excitement. The green and yellow markings of the Kar hunters peppered the crowd, and they were the ones to cheer the loudest. "And so the trial commenced and has been declared a success by Trialmaster Nezh'kar!"

More roars, and pride filled Pesh, mandibles clicking with excitement.

"It is with great honor that Clan Kar welcomes you, Pesh'kar Selk."

Pesh bowed to the second wave of cheering. "It is with great honor that I accept!" A roar of a new magnitude resounded.

Clanmaster Gles'kar clapped their hands, and another eddermar stepped forward, a marking gun in hand. They grabbed Pesh's head with two hands, holding it steady as they raised the gun. Their mandibles clicked with happiness, and Pesh returned the feeling.

"Welcome," they said, and a heat burned into Pesh's head, seeming to boil straight through to their brain at times. They were efficient though, running the gun across in swift strokes, marking Pesh with the same green and yellow signs of the other hunters. Adding to the brown markings of other rituals from their youth. This was the final, the calling they had chosen. To be a hunter for the clan. To be a warrior for the innocent and the bane of the evil.

"Clan Kar boasts the greatest warriors on Tset'As'Edder, and you shall be no less," the clanmaster continued. Again, Pesh recited the words in their head. A moment they'd been waiting for their whole life. Five long years. "We expect you to rise to those expectations. Surpass them if you can. Teach those behind you to always be better. For Clan Kar focuses on excellence!"

Another cheer, and Pesh clicked again and again. The tattooer clicked in amusement.

"Your heart is Clan Kar, and it is for them you risk your life and protect the eddermar of Tset'As'Edder. Your duty is Clan Kar, and wherever it takes you, the cleansing of evil shall follow. *You* are Clan Kar!"

The tattooist stepped back, and as the burn diminished, Pesh held their head high. Arms raised, they shouted, "I am a hunter of Clan Kar, and I shall bring honor to our name!"

The crowd roared, and Pesh reveled in it. Festivities followed, feasts and music, dancing and storytelling. Pesh lived in a dream, shifting from one group to another, each celebrating their success, their name rolling through mouths like sweet candy. Music to Pesh's ears.

*Pesh'kar Selk.*

Their birthkin and parents celebrated with abundance, crashing to the floor, overcome with drink or food or exhaustion from dancing. It was a joyous time, what would become one of Pesh's fondest memories. Only outperformed by what followed the festivities.

"Do you have a moment, Pesh?" Clanmaster Gles'kar stepped around the flailing body of one birthkin and nearly onto another. Both laughed as they rolled away.

"Yes, Clanmaster." Pesh followed them away from the crowds, the din of celebration dulling behind them. They breathed in the silence as if it had its own scent.

"The celebration can be a bit much at times." Gles laughed. "But I do hope you enjoyed yourself. You deserve it."

"It is everything I have dreamed of, Clanmaster."

"We are out of formalities. Gles will do."

"Of course, Clanmaster."

Gles laughed.

"Where are you taking me?"

"To the breeders."

"Now? I thought bonding did not occur until the morning."

"For other clans, maybe." Gles clicked with amusement. "Clan Kar has its privileges."

Excitement buzzed through Pesh, renewing their energy after such an exhausting celebration. Meeting one's bondmate was a moment to remember forever. A choice that would change their future. Would they choose a gridder that was strong or fast to help on their missions? One that expressed intelligence to act individually? What kind would compliment Pesh the most?

Their path took them from the festivities building out across the gap, the underground city opening up around them. Buildings crawled up and down the massive cavern, strong stone bridges connecting everything. They walked across one into the breeding tunnels. They turned, and the passage widened, a large window taking over the right side. Within, young gridder bounced around the room, inflating and flailing their limbs to propel them around. Some slept on the ground, curled among their kindred. Others fought friendly matches, bouncing into each other. Several more floated, lazily paddling their way around the room. But most of them ate, some so young they were still bottle-fed. They ranged from sizes smaller than Pesh's fist to larger than their head. They looked in, remembering a time so long ago when they'd watch the gridder playing, trying to decide which they'd want to pick.

"You'll want to search the skies for your gridder, I would think." Gles pointed up at a rambunctious pair mid-fight, the handlers trying to coax them down to eat. "Many hunters prefer the more aggressive ones to help in combat."

"If we're both aggressive, then we have the same weakness," Pesh said, glancing at Gles. "Making us a worse pair, no?"

Gles blinked, their mandibles clicking in thought. "That is a wise assessment, though you won't want one too passive. A lack of assistance will open more weaknesses than close them."

"What of that one?" Pesh pointed to a gridder sitting in one corner, four legs splayed out. They opened their mouth wide, rolled forward, and ate one of the toys. Their stomach glowed as they began digesting it.

"I don't think they were supposed to eat that," Gles said.

"No, but they waited until the caretakers were busy so they couldn't be stopped. Shows cunning."

"Are you sure it wasn't luck?"

"No," Pesh said. "I saw them watching the caretakers. The toy was in their possession the entire time we've been here. It wasn't until the handlers' backs were turned that the gridder ate it. I suspect if we ask, that wasn't the first toy to go missing."

"Seems more trouble than good."

Pesh clicked noncommittally. There were gridder that showed ambition, some that showed a fire to fight. Others showed intelligence with how they used the toys. Pesh could evaluate each and every one correctly and find them all wanting. But something about this gridder stuck with them. It was the right choice.

"That's the one I would like to bond, Clanmaster," Pesh said. "If they'll have me."

"You understand there are no reversals, yes?" Gles asked, a note of concern in their voice. "You will not be able to bond another gridder without great reason."

"I understand."

Gles nodded, acquiescing to Pesh's wishes. "Then let's meet your future bondmate."

Gles led the way farther down the tunnel and around to the entrance of the breeding grounds. A handler lay on their abdomen, a baby gridder held in the crook of one arm, a bottle in another. They looked up.

"Bonding?" they whispered.

"Yes, if that is all right with you," Gles whispered back.

The handler nodded, and Gles continued through to the next room.

"Congratulations," the handler whispered.

Pesh nodded, mandibles clicking, then followed Gles. But only after hesitating for a brief moment to look down at the small green-yellow ball in the handler's arm. They looked up at Pesh with big, yellow eyes and squeaked. Pesh clicked cheerfully, thanked the handler, and continued on.

Pesh entered the room with the other gridders to find Gles had already informed the handlers. They stepped to the side with the clanmaster, letting the gridders act as they wished. Many eyed Pesh, and many hooted and cooed. One brave gridder flew at Pesh's head, but they ducked out of the way, the small, inflated creature bouncing off the wall to head in another direction.

Pesh ignored most of them, weaving through the crowd toward the clever gridder in the corner. They eyed Pesh's approach, and a small rumble echoed as they belched. For a moment, they stood there, looking down at the gridder, unsure of what to say. How does one request a bonding? Should they give an overview of their past life? Of their future plans? Did the gridder care about either? Pesh clicked, searching for the words.

"Hello," they settled on. Unfortunately, nothing more was forthcoming. The gridder tilted their head, eyes glancing between Pesh and the other caretakers. It seemed almost sad, then it clicked. "Don't worry," Pesh added. "They didn't notice, and I won't tell. I'm not a caretaker."

Pesh leaned down and picked up another toy, holding it out. "Would you like another?"

They looked at the caretakers, then at Pesh. A question seemed to roll through them before they leaned forward and ate the new toy.

"They're not—" one of the handlers shouted, but Gles stopped them.

"I've just received the markings of hunter, for Clan Kar," Pesh explained, one hand brushing up against their newest tattoo. "It will be difficult work. Dangerous work. I'll travel to other worlds, facing evil. I would like to do it with someone else by my side. I would like to do it with you by my side."

The gridder stared at Pesh and swallowed the new snack, their stomach lighting up as they digested it. A caretaker sighed heavily.

"I don't know if you know what bonding is," Pesh continued. "It's when an eddermar and a gridder bond. Well, I guess that's obvious. But it's more than just being friends. We become partners for life. It's a big ask, to commit your life to mine and mine to yours. But I think you'd be perfect for it. Would you like to bond with me?"

The gridder cooed, sucked in air, and puffed out to twice the size. Legs kicked off the ground, and it floated up to Pesh's eye level, then their legs kicked again and launched them forward. Pesh barely had time to react, throwing arms out to defend themself, only to find that it wasn't entirely an attack. The gridder nuzzled within Pesh's arms and continued their happy hooting. Pesh rubbed at their soft tendrils and clicked with happiness. They suspected that was a yes.

"What is your name?" Pesh asked.

The gridder cooed, and as expected, Pesh didn't understand the phrase.

"What about Skritch?"

Skritch cooed delightedly.

# PART 5
# LEGACY

"Grab that haushedin!" Sage shouted, and Besari ran off. "Put it up front. His skin will help the most. We can stack the rest of the gaps with the smaller bodies."

Plasma torches burned through the door, carving an opening that would soon be large enough. Under Sage's recommendation, Besari and the others had been running back and forth, building a corpse wall for cover. They needed to get out of the room, needed to find Zetta, and needed to disappear. Shellesh had proposed using the ship he had arrived in, thus making Wyn's plan of leaving by roof quite feasible. Still, it was not the kind of work Besari had expected to be thrust into shortly after dying.

She dragged the haushedin corpse, squeezing it between two vrolaks and a rather obese perrilan. Wyn tossed a corpse of his own, a human, onto the pile, and Sage adjusted them to fit. Then she concentrated, pouring more of her sediment carapace into the bodies, filling the gaps and gluing them together.

"They're almost through," she shouted, and everyone ducked behind the half wall of corpses, weapons drawn. The severed head pulsed by Besari's left knee, and she felt a mix of squeamish and satisfied. That thing had just nearly killed her. She raised her scatter gun and took aim, Wyn's shoulder a warm comfort against hers.

Excitement bristled in the air between the four of them. They had all almost died, multiple times, yet here they were. And in possession of a nairwid's head, their ultimate bounty that would save Bounty Inc. They had stormed the fortress and taken down the leader. A feeling of invincibility thrummed through them, their aches soothed by the talent pouring off Wyn. How had she never noticed it before? That constant refreshing feeling. She wasn't sure how he kept it up. Using her powers that much would have left her sleeping for sixteen hours, and the exhaustion etched into his features implied it should be doing the same to him. But she didn't question a good thing and hoped he could hold out a little longer.

She smiled, and when the door fell, she fired into a crowd of people, joined by her friends. And Wyn, who had actually done what she had joked about and dragged her back from the dead. He felt like a little more than *just* a friend to her.

A haze settled in the room when the fighting ended, as thick as the silence that followed. More corpses lay strewn about the room, their numbers eventually overwhelming the tiny barricade, but at great cost. A heap of bodies filled the doorway and the hall beyond. Thankfully, the dead were restricted to Sovereign's followers, and Bounty Inc. still thrived. Still lived. Besari tugged hard on her blade, needing her foot to help pull it from a tesing's neck.

Wyn had found and retrieved his helmet at some point, that ridiculous, minimalistic face of surprise blinking on the front. She smiled at it. She still thought it was pointless, but it fit her perfect little idiot just right.

Shellesh picked up Sovereign's writhing head and hefted it onto one shoulder, a pistol held in one hand. Sage checked the halls, her own Imberlii Dissenter at the ready.

"It's clear for now, but there's a lot of activity. Someone's bound to try to reach us quickly." She turned to the others. "We should split into two groups. Two of us to find Zetta, two to secure the ship."

"I can find Zetta," Besari said. "I can use my Thresha talent to scout ahead and keep us hidden while we find her."

"I'll go with you," Sage said.

"No," Shellesh interrupted. "Besari and I will find Zetta. You and Wyn to the ship."

"What?" Sage growled. "It's your ship. You have the security key to enter it."

"I can pass that to you and Wyn, as well as a map of the building to get you up top quickly."

"Why are you keeping me from finding Zetta?"

"You're unfit," Shellesh said plainly. "If Zetta hasn't caught up, she is likely injured. If she needs help moving, you will lose your only means of fighting. Besari and I can both lift her and fight."

"He has a point, Sage—" Wyn started.

"Then Wyn and I will go. Wyn can heal her if she's injured, then she doesn't need to be helped."

"Wyn is weak."

"Hey!" Wyn interrupted again, though no one looked at him.

"If she is too injured, he will fatigue himself healing her. Then you're left with two people you need to help up the tower. And one arm to do it."

"She would never be *too* injured." Sage shook her head. "She's probably just lost."

"Then we're still the best two to go searching. I have my disguise as Shadow, and Besari can become invisible."

Sage turned and kicked a decapitated head (not Sovereign's) and groaned in frustration. Everyone watched as she gathered her breath. Eventually, she glanced back, eyes on Wyn.

"Come on, Wyn," she growled. "I need to find some people to kill on our way up."

"It's the right call," Shellesh said, the suit's helmet materializing around his face.

Sage spun, hand, and the pistol in it, flailing toward him. "Bring her back alive, you understand?"

Her eyes shifted, fear coming to rest amid the anger and frustration. Her voice hitched with concern. She was worried about Zetta and angry that she was useless to help.

"We'll get her back, Sage," Besari said. "I promise, we'll get her back."

Sage looked at her, then spun and left the room. Wyn looked at Besari as well, a smile on his face. "Stay safe," he said, then he took the severed head from Shellesh and chased after Sage. Shellesh gestured to his Vico and sent everything to them before nodding to Besari.

The two of them exited down the hallway and raced toward the entrance, checking side rooms as they went, utilizing their disguises as they needed.

"Shellesh," Besari said.

"Yes?"

"Thanks for coming for us," she said. "I don't think any of us would have lived without your help."

"I had no choice," he said, then paused and looked at her, placing one hand on her shoulder. "You're all my family. I couldn't leave you stranded."

Besari smiled. It was the first time she had heard such warmth in his voice. Like a blanket on a cold day. Something had changed in him.

Shellesh palmed the door control, and the entrance hall opened before them. A falvian and a human guard stood nearby, poking a large red form with a stunstaff.

"You think it's dead?" the falvian asked.

"Probably," the human responded. Then they both looked up at the new entrants.

Besari and Shellesh raised their weapons and fired before the guards could react, both flying back as plasma tore holes into them, splattering the ground with their blood. Besari stepped forward and glanced around at the carnage of the room. Walls destroyed, bodies everywhere, a large column of bone piled up nearby. But her eyes fell on the red form in front of her and held there. Red from the blood that coated her body, the orange only showing through in tiny flecks. A few bugs buzzed around it.

"Oh no," she gasped.

Shellesh was on his knees beside Zetta, hands checking for signs of life, looking into her eyes—*eye*, actually, as half her face seemed scarred and bloated, swelling one shut. But her body was covered in hundreds of tears, and dried blood caked her. Her chest didn't move. She had to be—

"She's alive," Shellesh said. "But barely." He pulled up from his inspection and drew a small tin from one pocket. He pulled a syringe and several vials from it. "Help me find the worst of the damage. We can't patch everything, but we need to get her well enough to move."

"Her stomach." Besari pointed at a wound, deep gashes, the smell of something rancid from within. Shellesh nodded and began the injection. The healing agent would expedite the process of cells renewing. It wasn't a miracle cure, but it could stop her from dying. Besari hoped that would be the case, but it was hard to look at the vrolak and think anything could save her.

Shellesh refilled and continued, focusing the healing agent at the worst of the injuries, several to her chest and abdomen, along with one near her leg where it looked twisted.

Shellesh had filled the syringe once more, preparing to continue, when the building shook. They looked over and watched the bone pillar crack and fall to the ground. It split open, and a single person stood in the center. Person was maybe not the right term, given that they were entirely made of bone, the long protrusions spreading out into massive hands. More bone burst from within, expanding, lifting their body onto a dozen legs. Spurs shot out, stabbing into the walls and cracking them, and segments grew to create a long tail, until the thing before them resembled a large monster, its jaws slowly encasing the body of a woman held suspended at the back of its throat like a uvula. Her voice roared out as the teeth closed down, protecting her within. Then the beast writhed, bone shredding the structures around it, tumbling walls down with each movement. The ceiling to Besari's left collapsed, dust clogging the room.

Beetles buzzed in front of Besari's face, pulling her attention away from the bone monster. They were frantic, diving at her face. She swatted at them and they landed on her arm. Achtrek's remnants. They buzzed in alarm. The bone monster leaned down and looked at them.

Shellesh dropped the syringe, pulled free his rifle, and fired at the monster.

The remnants grew more frantic, and Besari watched the bone regenerate with each shot. They couldn't kill it. Not here, not like this.

"We need to go," Besari shouted, then looked at Zetta. "I'm really sorry. I hope this doesn't hurt." She pulled the vrolak up and onto her shoulders, grunting as the full weight fell onto her. Her muscles burned as she stood, but she ran for the door nonetheless. Shellesh followed, firing still into the bone monster behind them.

Besari burst through the door, Shellesh followed, and a giant bone claw slammed through after them. Her feeling of invincibility shattered, leaving only a terror deep within her stomach, pushing her limbs to keep moving.

"Well, I found everyone else!" Wyn yelled over the rapid explosion of weaponsfire.

The uneventful trip to the roof had turned to chaos as hordes of people spilled from several doorways. Wyn and Sage had ducked behind one leg of the pulsing weather control unit and were now pinned by continuous plasma eating away at the celuein.

"Thanks," Sage said, flashing Wyn a flat stare. "I almost missed them."

Wyn fired blindly with his pistol, then pulled back as heat burned his knuckles. He looked at his hand, where the suit and flesh and muscle were seared, then watched as the muscle knit itself together and flesh grew back over the wound. Sage stared at it as well.

"Well, that's going to be handy," Wyn said, waving his hand as the last vestiges of pain disappeared.

"How much do you think you can take and still come back?" Sage asked.

"I don't know."

"We can test it," Sage suggested. "You run that way as fast as you can, and I'll see about picking people off."

"What if I don't heal from death?" Which felt like a ridiculous question.

Sage shrugged. "Then I guess you'll die."

"I would prefer to find a different route, if it's all the same to you."

"I'm all ears."

Wyn glanced over the edge and ducked a second later, several shots skimming his helmet. He tossed it to the side as the inside visuals glitched wildly. Then, with a huff, he looked at Sage. "I got nothing."

"Well, we need to figure out something soon," Sage said as she grew a thick ball of sediment around her fist. "If Zetta, Shellesh, and Besari come through one of those doors, they'll be torn apart." She fired over the edge six times before pulling the hand back, the carapace crumbling away, her knuckles red with the heat of the return fire.

Wyn fired on the crowd next, gritting his teeth in pain as plasma seared his hands. He kept shooting until the muscles stopped reacting, then finally pulled them back. The bone shone white as they trembled, the weapons loose in hands he couldn't move. Then, a few moments later, they were renewed and unharmed. But each healing took its toll. Wyn wasn't sure how much longer before he'd just pass out. He had already injected himself with Sage's energizing shots twice. Time was also running out on them being flanked. Eventually, the guards would make a run for it, and their blind shooting would miss.

"I'm going to try running," Wyn said.

"Don't be an idiot," Sage growled. "I was fucking with you."

"Not to give you time for that." He pointed to Shellesh's ship. "If I can get on board, it might have weapons we can use."

Sage ground her teeth as she studied the distance. "There's no way you won't get hit before reaching the ship."

"But I might not get hit enough to kill me," Wyn said. "And you can give me an early start with your barrier."

"It'll only reach about six feet or so, and it won't protect you."

"Just hide me. That's enough."

Sage nodded. "They'll start shooting it as soon as I create it, so you'll have to run right away."

Wyn took a deep breath and crouched in front of Sage. She placed her hand to the ground, and stone bled from it across the ground. His heart beat fast, but he focused on Besari, and Shellesh, and Zetta. The ship was their only chance, and he had to take it. He trusted in his powers to protect him and nodded at Sage.

"Now!" A stony barrier burst up from the ground, and Wyn ran, head ducked low. Plasma pelted the cover, dust exploding around Wyn and obscuring the area. He broke into the open, a cloud of debris trailing behind him, and refused to look as hundreds of people trained their sights on him. His heart pounded in his ears, drowning out everything except the sound of a door slamming open.

Then silence.

After a heartbeat and no shots, Wyn looked at the confused crowd turning to stare at Besari, a limp vrolak across her shoulders. She stared back, wide-eyed. Then the crowd, as one, changed their target at the surprise arrival.

"No!" Wyn slid to a stop and raised his pistols. Besari disappeared, and a moment later, so did Zetta. And then everyone fired their weapons. Wyn shot into the crowd, and Sage joined him. Most of the crowd fired at the newly empty space where Besari had been, but some shifted focus back on the two people they could see. From the corner of his eye, he saw Besari crash to the ground near Sage, Zetta spilling from her shoulders.

Plasma grazed his ribs, and another hit his shoulder. He pivoted, a shot searing his hip, then he dove for cover back behind their cover, one knee hardly functioning. He watched in mild horror as the kneecap that had been displaced righted itself and the tendons around it. The pain disappeared, as it had all over his body.

Sage inspected Zetta, and Besari held her thigh, blood running down it. Wyn crawled toward her, and she shook her head. "No. Help Zetta. I'm fine."

Wyn glanced at Zetta once and wondered if there was even anything he could do to help. His hands wavered over the ruin of the vrolak, then he placed his fingers next to the large hole in her abdomen and poured as much energy outward as he could muster, focusing like he had with Besari. He tried to remember the feeling and channel it, but he wasn't sure how it worked. It seemed natural for himself, and he seemed to almost naturally help with the minor wounds of those around him. Sage's cuts had healed on the way up the tower despite Wyn's lack of conscious effort. But he had to do something.

"Where's Shellesh?" Wyn asked, giving his mind something else to focus on.

"Distracting the bone thing," Besari said. "Should be up any moment, but with all those guards..."

"Bone thing?" Wyn asked.

"Can you get to the ship?" Sage asked. "By yourself, invisible so they don't fire. We'll distract them."

Besari nodded. "Yes, I—"

Another crash as the door opened, several shouts, and Wyn glanced up. Shellesh rolled into the crowd amid a flash of bright light, eliciting pained cries from their opponents. The light strobed outward, burning Wyn's eyes, but they healed as quickly as they'd been damaged. Wyn fired into the crowd, and Shellesh noticed and darted his way.

"Shit. That means—"

The roof shook, rippling like a raft on turbulent seas. People spilled to the ground from unsteady feet. The doorway bulged, then cracked, then exploded. A burst of bone spilled outward, spearing those too close. The tower wavered, sparks spewing from the weather control dish at its peak. Then the roof began collapsing inward. With a great rend, the dish tore from its braces and tipped over the side of the building. But whatever sound it might have made when it hit the ground below was overwhelmed by the sound of a monster made of bone exploding from the center of the roof.

Besari leapt from the ground, hauling Zetta to her shoulders again. She seemed to be yelling, but so did everyone else. The words swarmed Wyn, overwhelming him and emulsifying into a mess of gibberish. More bone speared upward through the new opening in the roof, and the tips curled down like two large hands, from between which rose a skull, elongated like a vrolak's, but easily a hundred times larger. It opened its mouth and yelled.

Wyn expected a fierce roar. Something to shake the heavens and crumble the building beneath their feet. Instead, it was only a slightly louder than normal screech of a woman. Wyn could see her face dangling in the back of the mouth as if she were the skull's uvula. The crowd fired at her, panicked as they scrambled away from the tilting rooftop. She brought one fist down, smashing the roof and just about everyone on it. Except for the hunters and the few others who scrambled far enough away. And Shellesh's ship, which was as yet untouched. Wyn doubted it'd stay that way for long.

Shellesh grabbed Wyn's arm and pushed him forward, Sovereign's head clutched in his other hand. Sage and Besari were already rushing to the ship. Wyn stopped, pulling Shellesh to a halt as well.

"We need to move," Shellesh urged. But Wyn's eyes were on the bone woman.

"She's going to tear the ship from the sky," Wyn said.

"We don't have any other choice."

"We do." He turned to Shellesh. "It's a Thresha talent, right?"

"That or an artificial one like what Shekta had experimented with on Bezium."

"If she's just human, she can die." Wyn holstered his pistols and pulled the rifle from around his back. "I'll distract it, try to kill her. Get the ship started, and pick me up."

"You can't fight that thing. The bone regenerates."

"I'm the only one who can," he said. "I can survive if it hits me. Get moving."

Wyn pulled himself away from Shellesh and ran the other way, rifle raised and taking shots. She was in the mouth of the giant skull, so if he could break through the teeth or get her to open it again, he could get the shot off.

The bone woman ignored Wyn's fire, focusing on a group of guards caught at the edge of the abyss she'd opened in the roof. With one swipe, she speared or maimed them all. Those that lived clutched at missing limbs, screaming in pain. They died in the second attack, except for the few who made the choice to dive into the shattering building. They might have lived a few seconds longer. The building was a ruin, floors and pillars destroyed, the entire structure shifting beneath Wyn's feet like a sandcastle facing down high tide.

Wyn blocked it out and continued an unrelenting burst of plasma at the woman's skull armor.

With her playthings dead, she turned her attention to Wyn. Carefully, he stepped back, foot scraping the very edge of the building. Raindrops flecked down, the distant sound of thunder growing with each second. The storms were pushing into the city without the protection provided by the weather dish.

He needed to lead the bone creature away from the shuttle and the others. It wouldn't be long until it'd be too dangerous to escape at all.

The engines fired, lifting the ship off the ground, and the woman's attention shifted to it.

"Hey!" Wyn shouted. "Big bone woman, I'm right here!" Wyn fired wildly at the face, aiming for eyes that didn't really exist and teeth that regenerated with each shot. Panic thrummed through his skin. It ignored Wyn, one hand reaching out for the shuttle.

Shellesh pulled back on the ship's controls, but not fast enough. Bone fingers shackled the shuttle, and Wyn heard the creak of metal. Forward cannons fired, blowing apart pieces of the bone woman's construct and causing it to tilt. She roared, the skull opening up once more, revealing the flash of a face deep within.

Wyn fired. The head jerked back, and the construct stilled. Its grip weakened, and Shellesh pulled the shuttle from it, breaking the fingers free, chunks of bone raining down to the street below.

The ramp opened, and Besari stood there. He smiled at her and waved as they swung by. "I did it!" he shouted. "I got her."

Wyn had a difficult time comprehending the pain of a large spear of bone impaling his chest. Excruciating felt too small a word. It stole the wind from his lungs as it stole the lungs from his body. Blood splattered out in front of Wyn like a careless splash of paint. If that paint also included several rather important organs. He coughed (difficult without lungs, so it became more of a gurgle), and more blood squirted out onto the stark white bone jutting from him. In the strange moments after the intense pain, it dissipated, and a calm numbness filled him as his head fell forward. The wind rustled his hair, and he felt an abrupt collision. But everything became more and more vague until there was only the void. An empty black. Nothing at all. And Wyn found the answer as to whether he could die or not.

"WYN!" Besari screamed as the bone pierced his body. She watched as his head fell limp. Then the bone monster discarded Wyn's body like trash. She spun and stared at Sage. "We need to get over there, to save him."

"Pull away!" Sage shouted into the intercom, refusing to make eye contact with Besari.

"No!" Besari stormed up to Sage and grabbed her hand, pulling it away from the intercom. "We have to save him!"

"We don't know that he's alive." Emotion flared on Sage's face, more than Besari had ever seen before. "We stay here, we die."

"We can't just leave him behind."

"We can, because if he lived through that, he'll be fine."

The shuttle jerked, and Besari tumbled from her feet, rolling backward toward the open ramp. Sage dove for her, grabbing her with a hand and looping a leg around a nearby bench. Besari's feet swung into open air as their slide came to a stop, the rain pelting down harder now. She stared down into the skull of a monster, Wyn's killer, and she was terrified. The shuttle's walls bowed in, the metal creaking loudly as if echoing the fear in her heart. Shellesh jerked the shuttle one way, then another, trying to break free, but the grasp was too strong. Its massive jaws opened with another scream, and Besari saw the face of Wyn's true killer, the woman hiding within the bone armor.

"Let go!" Besari shouted to Sage.

"You'll fall out."

"She's exposed. I can get into her mouth and kill her."

"Wyn shot her in the head, Besari, and she's still alive. You'll just kill yourself."

"What if he's alive, Sage?" Besari pleaded, eyes pained. "What if his healing saved him and he's down there suffering? I can't leave him."

"If he survived that, then he's safer than we are."

Wyn had died, and that sucked. Worse, it seemed in death he had trapped himself in a nightmare of his own creation. A pink moon crested maroon mountains, and his eyes burned at the overabundance of ridiculous colors. "Fuck."

"Indeed."

Wyn turned toward the low monotone voice and found a tear in the world vaguely in the shape of a slug. "Tom? Is that you, buddy? Where have you been?"

"Here?"

"Why? This place sucks."

"No, Wyn. I've been in your head."

"Oh." Wyn paused, a sadness overcoming him. "I'm sorry for the sudden eviction notice."

"Eviction notice?" Tom stared at Wyn with twinkling star eyes, and Wyn shied away from the ethereal look. "Do you think I'm real?"

"Are you not?"

"I am a trauma-induced hallucination brought on by your near-death experience on Bezium. Nothing more."

"You stuck around for so long."

"Because you focused so much on death. So worried about it coming for you or your friends."

"And when death came for my friends, you left."

"You may have been scared, but you also had a focus." Tom's form convulsed, growing upward slowly, thickening and spreading outward. "Something to distract you. Your friends. No, your *family*. One you've never had before. Maybe, just then, you understood death. You faced losing people you care about, and you became stronger than your fear."

"How do you know so much about me?"

"I am a figment of your imagination." Tom stepped forward, legs separating from this tall form, two arms coalescing from the inky blackness. "I only know what you know, Wyn."

"And what is it that I know? Beyond my deep-seated trauma?"

Tom stepped up to Wyn, matching heights. "You know that this isn't over."

"How can it not be over? I'm dead."

"So?" Tom said. "You died when we first met. You died in the tank so long ago. You should have died with the number of plasma bolts that hit you today. Your body should have been destroyed by Sage's reckless training."

Wyn tried to move his mouth and found it stuck shut with a strange dryness.

"What's one more death?" Tom asked. "What's one more death when your family is in danger? What is it you promised them? That you'd protect them only when convenient? Or you'd protect them *no matter what*? To the best of your ability?" Tom shifted, the inky blackness melting away, and Wyn stared at himself. The other Wyn grabbed the front of Wyn's combat suit and pulled him close, his voice rising with every word. "I know you, Wyn, because I am you. You will not rest while people you care about are in danger. So why are you wasting your time being dead?"

Wyn gasped awake to a massive bone creature flailing above him. His lungs burned, and he coughed, a wet hacking until clots of blood forced their way up and out of his throat. He spit red globs of something he didn't want to identify onto the roof of the swaying building. Hands traced the hole in his chest and found only his own skin. He was alive, and he was wasting time. He had family to save.

The bone monster grabbed onto Shellesh's shuttle once again, its boosters shaking left and right to no avail. Weaponsfire rained down from the open back, scorching bone but failing to penetrate deep enough for any effect. The ship would be torn apart soon, and that would end any chance of their escape.

Whoever this woman was, she also had regenerative healing properties. He hoped that meant he could also take a shot to the face, but he had no plans to learn that with any certainty. But he had to imagine there was some way to slow her down, and so, he did the only thing he could think of. He scaled the creature with nothing more than his two pistols and a hope that he would figure it all out.

His fingers bit into undulating bone, grabbing at the sharp spurs that stuck out in every direction. They made his climb painful but quick, and quick was more important. The woman opened her skull, screaming again at the ship, and Wyn shuffled around the side of the skull, right to the opening. He grabbed one tooth, pulled himself over, and stared down. Then he pulled one pistol free. Now was about the time for any spark of genius to bring about a plan. He could do with anything, really. Even just the beginnings of a plan. There was nothing.

Instead, his mind raced through all the times he had almost died today and wondered which would have succeeded. He had been shot or nearly shot a dozen or so times. There was the time Sovereign tried to explode him with the weapon's charge pack. Speared through the chest. The building wobbled like a flag in the wind.

"Oh." Wyn paused his wild thoughts, then took a moment to consider. It was better than nothing. He shrugged, ejected the charge pack from the pistol, and placed it between his teeth. Then he holstered the now useless pistol and grabbed his offhand one instead. After taking a deep breath through his teeth, he spit the charge pack out.

He tracked the glowing vial through the air, exhaling slowly, steadily. He had one chance, or it would be lost forever in the depths of the construct. At the end of the exhale, Wyn fired and watched the shot go wide.

"Fuck!" He nearly lost his grip, shooting more as he tried to follow the vial. It tumbled down the mouth of the bone construct, all the way to the dangling woman controlling it. Her scream was cut off by the sounds of gagging as the vial slipped between her lips and down her throat. Wyn paused his firing to stare.

She coughed, and two hands pulled free from her bone cocoon like surfacing from water. She coughed again, and a shining vial popped out into her hands. Wyn shot it, not believing the odds.

The charge exploded, plasma reducing the immediate vicinity to ashes, particularly the bone woman herself, and launching Wyn clear from the construct. He tumbled down the collapsing bone and hit the roof with a crack. The entire tower shuddered, then the bone shattered. Large chunks rained down on Wyn and crashed through what little remained of the structure. The entire building tilted, dust and bone pouring out in plumes, the tower creaking as its last supports, most likely the woman's own bone, finally gave way.

Wyn pulled himself to his feet, his right leg snapping back into place. Then he ran. He ran until the floor gave out, then jumped to a celuein beam. He slid down it as the world spun around him, and he launched himself at the bottom to another stone section. Some surviving piece of the weather unit snapped free and crashed down near Wyn as he scuttled across the structure's remains. The roar of the building's collapse filled his ears until it was his everything. It was the racing of his heart, the pulse in his veins, his ragged gasping breaths, and his hoarse screams. When he hit the edge, he launched himself off, legs and arms spinning as he entered a free fall. Maybe if he landed feet first, his brain would survive the contact. Was that all he needed to survive?

He never found out.

A hand grasped his, bringing the fall to an abrupt end as Shellesh's shuttle descended. Besari pulled him into the ship, and they launched away from the wreckage of Sovereign's tower.

"Holy shit," Wyn gasped, the rush flooding his body. "I think I almost died."

"Which time?" Besari smiled down at him, one hand resting on his chest where the fabric of his suit peeled away, her fingers warm against his skin.

"Was it just the three times, or were there more?"

"I only counted two," she said.

"You're missing the part where I blew her up," Wyn argued, his hand grabbing at hers. "I could have died somewhere around then."

"No," Besari said. "I'm talking about your jump at the end."

"What if I hit the ground? That's almost dying."

"I was never going to let you hit the ground." She leaned down, and the fire of her kiss breathed life into Wyn's body. He wrapped one hand around the back of her head and pulled her into him. Everything around him faded away as they—

"Now grab her ass."

Wyn spit, Besari coughed, and the two separated quickly, wiping at their mouths.

"Sage!" Wyn gasped. "I didn't know you were here."

"I did." Besari flushed, cheeks growing almost as dark as her spots. "I just forgot in the moment."

"It was just getting good too." Sage smirked. Wyn burned red, at least until her face grew somber again. She looked down the hall, then back at Wyn. "Can you help, Wyn?"

Zetta. She was in bad shape.

"I don't know, but I'll do everything I can." Wyn pulled himself from the ground and followed Sage to the small medical suite.

# CHAPTER 34

## ESCAPE FROM PLANET KEKAR

B lack clouds engulfed the city as Shellesh circled the ship above the tower, pausing the escape before facing the next task. Nothing below had taken off to give chase, but they still had the haushedin fleets to slip by, and now the storms were retaking the city. He could see the slaves and slavers rushing for shelters as the winds grew stronger.

The console chimed, its tests finished. The ship was sealed, no leaks detected. They were capable of space flight. It was just a matter of deciding if they should.

He tapped the intercom. "Ship is space ready, but I don't know how to get by the haushedins. They have to know by now something happened and won't let any ships pass."

"We can't stay," Sage responded. "Those storms could ground us, and there's no telling how many people down here will still try to kill us. We need to get off planet."

"Understood," Shellesh said. "Then be sure to strap yourselves in. Especially Zetta. This ride is about to get bumpy."

Shellesh accelerated, shooting for the shrinking hole in the clouds. Thunder rocked the *Shadowhawk*, and rain pelted the forward screen, streams of water racing back along it. Besari climbed into the cockpit, buckling herself in at the copilot station.

"Let me know if there's anything you need from me," she said, her voice strained as her fingers raced across the console.

"Keep an eye on the scanners. Let me know where enemies are."

She nodded, and they crashed through dark clouds until the viewport visibility disappeared completely. Except for the occasional crack of lightning. The *Shadowhawk* trembled from turbulence until even the control stick vibrated in Shellesh's hand. Besari looked sick, and he wondered how the others were faring. He couldn't focus on them, had to hope they could do something for Zetta. He had to focus on his duty, or they'd all die.

Shadow's ship burst from the atmosphere with a stream of black clouds chasing it. Then everything calmed, and the ship stabilized. The soft pull of the gravity system kicked in, Shellesh's stomach twisting within him as it adjusted.

"Shellesh," Besari said quietly, eyes staring at the monitor. Shellesh didn't respond. He could guess what she was going to say. Silver spots sparkled in the sun in every direction, encircling the only exit from the planet. Single fighters waiting for their escape, ready to stop them. Shellesh pulled up his own scanners, seeing the sea of red dots Besari had looked at, and spun it around, searching for any escape. The only place they didn't seem to exist was on Kekar itself.

The communications system crackled as someone hijacked it, a message running through the entire ship in a deep, guttural voice.

"I don't know who this is, but you are to surrender your ship immediately," they said. "Turn off your engines, and prepare to have your ship guided aboard the *Shard of Destiny*, flagship of the Herald's Aspect. By order of Fleet Admiral Bevnil."

Beyond the thousand specks, a single fleet ship dwarfed everything, staring down on them.

"What do we do?" Besari whispered, as if she expected the communications system to pick up and transfer their conversation too.

"If we stay put, we die, no?"

"Yes, but where can you possibly go?"

Shellesh considered, but the voice interrupted again. "You have not complied. If you do not turn off your engines in the next thirty seconds, we will disable your ship by force."

"Tell them we have Sovereign!" Besari shouted.

Shellesh flipped the communications switch on, then tapped the voice modulator at his neck. When he spoke, Miaraim's voice spilled from his lips. "*Shard of Destiny*, this is *Shadowhawk*. I am on a vital mission for Sovereign. Let me through."

"Negative, *Shadowhawk*," a different voice spoke this time. "Sovereign's tower has fallen, and it is my duty as fleet admiral to ensure Sovereign has not been taken hostage. After an inspection, you are free to leave. You have thirty seconds to comply."

Shellesh switched off the communications, tore the voice modulator from his throat, then grasped the controls. "Keep me informed of missiles and other weapons on our tail that could disable us."

Then he accelerated.


"What's going on?" Wyn stumbled into the cockpit behind Sage. The entire ship shook beneath them, and the gravity system fought hard to keep the right way downward. He stared out the viewport and spotted a swarm of fighter ships and an endless stream of cannon fire raining down on them. Guess that was as good an answer as any.

Shellesh spiraled the ship through a gauntlet of plasma and fired out in return. A ship blossomed into flame, then extinguished as quickly as the void of space could consume it. Alarms blared everywhere, and Besari streamed an endless list of information as her eyes and hands raced over the console. Wyn and Sage stood there uselessly. As useless as they had been in the medical suite too. The worst of Zetta's injuries had been repaired or cared for by the computer doctor, but her vitals still dropped. Wyn was sure the only thing that had kept her living had been his healing draining into her. Now, the only thing saving her was a medicated coma. Her vitals held steady, but they needed an actual doctor, and soon.

Sage took in their situation, her face darkening. "I'll be with Zetta," she grumbled, then stumbled back down the hallway. The remnants of Achtrek-Six were already huddled around the vrolak as well, refusing to leave her side. Wyn hated being unable to do more for either of them. He clenched his fist and sighed.

Then his Vico beeped again.

Annoyed and frustrated, he finally pulled up the message. It had notified him three times since entering the ship. Possibly even more before that, except he had been too preoccupied to notice. He almost swiped the message away, leaving it for another time, *if* there would be another time. Except that he saw the sender.

Cee.

Wyn tapped play, and the face of Cee showed up, his heart clenching in his chest as he saw it.

"Hello, Wyn Kelda," Cee began. "If you're receiving this message, I have likely been destroyed. I had ensured certain contingencies so that I may still be of assistance to you. I am appreciative of our time together and of your treatment of me. There is a near eighty percent chance you have discovered I am an artificial intelligence before this moment, and if not, I predict I will have told you before my death. Different as I may be, you still treated me the same. You trusted in me, and for that I cannot thank you enough. I hope for great success for Bounty Inc. and everyone who is a part of it.

"It is unlike me to be so emotional, but I have let the simulated emotions run free to show my words are true," Cee said flatly. "However, I must return to the important aspect of this message. One month before recording this message, I infiltrated one of the flagships of the Herald's Aspect on a classified job. Though their cyber security was impressive for such an unintelligent species, I did find many loopholes in it. Especially whenever a system comes in contact with another. I created malware to spread through every system of the ship to be enacted in your escape."

Wyn's eyes grew large as more plasma fire scorched the side of the ship, shield alarms blaring. "Enact it how, Cee?" He shook the Vico, and Besari glanced back, brows furrowed, before returning to the systems.

"It has almost definitely expanded to the other flagships when they recovered the wreckage of the *Shard of Virtue*. If that is the case, then the pilot ships will be infected as well. The malware spreads through the system by disguising itself as—"

Wyn fast forwarded the message, the time popping up as twenty minutes. "Abyssal hell, Cee!"

"—then, once infected, the malware feeds out to each individual—"

Wyn glanced up nervously as he skipped forward again.

"—disabled, and then you should be able to—"

"How do I enable it? Enable it, Cee!" He skipped ahead, near the end, and hoped it wasn't too far. Besari's panicked voice rose as the fighter ships began to corner Shellesh. The shields had nearly given out, several shots making it through and scoring hits on the hull, though integrity held steady. It wouldn't once the shields were fully down.

"Thank you again, Wyn. Perhaps I shall survive, and if I do, I hope we meet again as friends. The signal for the malware is attached to the message. Just broadcast it outwardly and it will activate."

Wyn leapt forward, slamming the communications channel onto open broadcast.

"Wyn!" Shellesh shouted.

Besari's eyes widened as she rambled off values, her hand swatting at Wyn's. "—three missiles passing at eighty-six degrees, lancer sweeping by overhead, forty-six degrees—"

Wyn activated the attached signal, and broadcast through the now open channel. His Vico beeped, and he stared out as a ship fired at them head on. Then their cannons stopped. Every single one. Except Shellesh's.

Besari's rambling stopped as she stared out at the suddenly still battlefield, mouth slack.

Then, like blossoming flowers, the fighter ships exploded, a thousand flashes in the darkness of space. One by one, they blinked off Besari's scanners.

"Holy shit," Besari said.


Alarms blared as the most annoying *thing* Fleet Admiral Bevnil had ever had the displeasure of meeting displayed itself on all visual screens and spoke.

"Hello, Fleet Admiral. It's been a while," Cee said.

"Find that fucking robot!" Bevnil shouted. "Dismantle it!"

"Sir, the fighters, they're—"

"I don't care," she screeched. "That thing is a danger! Put out a red alert now!"

Smoke spewed from one console as an officer jumped from her seat. "Communications down, sir!" she shouted as her station sparked.

"Weapons too!"

"Scanners have just exploded."

"Visuals of our fighters show they're being destroyed," another officer said, looking out the viewport. "Without scanners, we can't be sure, but it has to be all of them."

It was destroying *everything*. AGAIN! How could it have survived? She had sent every fucking weapon after it. Her scorched eye itched with the memory. She would tear its fucking head off.

"Escape pods have been launched," someone said. "I don't think anyone was aboard."

"Docks have been locked open," another added. "Mag-locks deactivated. All of our remaining shuttles are drifting into space."

"Radiation and heat alarms are within deadly ranges in engineering."

Bevnil looked again at the rambling robot, her rage bubbling within her. The fucking thing kept talking, kept poking and prodding at her. Wanting her to be angry, too angry. Her hands clenched at the armrests to either side, the fabric squeaking in distress. There had to be a clue. Had to be some way of finding the robot. If she could just think clearly enough—

She noticed the tapestry behind it, and recognition flared, followed by a hot, burning anger that ate at her gut. The armrests snapped in her hand, and she tossed the loose pieces aside. The officers yelled and shouted. One thing after another going wrong. But she knew how to solve it. The robot had been too arrogant.

She stormed from the bridge, the cacophony bleeding out into the hall. Someone yelled for her, then became too distracted by the disasters. They didn't need her here. They needed her to fight the source of the problem.

She reached the elevator and tried it, afraid they would be cut off. She had alternatives, but thankfully it chimed. She swiped her Vico at the elevator's controls and activated the direct path to the floor of her private chambers. Now it wouldn't stop for anyone, saving her time.

Her stomach floated up into her throat as the elevator plummeted. She'd also chosen emergency mode. Dangerous typically, but if this wasn't an emergency, nothing would be. The elevator chimed again, and her stomach dropped back down as the doors opened. She rushed out into an empty hall. This area was primarily hers. No one would be here when she was supposed to be on the bridge. That was fine with her as she raced down the hallway to her quarters.

Her fucking quarters.

The robot sat in her room, talking about taking her out. She would dismantle it and turn it into her fucking toilet.

She checked her doors to find them locked. She opened them with her Vico and stepped in, vision red with fury. "I'll fucking kill you!" she roared as she looked around and found no one. A growl echoed from her chest. It had escaped. She hadn't been quick enough.

Something flickered to one side, and she spun, fist swinging out. The image of Cee wavered as her hand swiped through it before smashing into the wall. The paneling snapped and fell from the wall, exposing wiring beneath. She flinched back, a burning ache running from her eye to the back of her skull.

"Ah, Fleet Admiral! You've made it." The holographic image spoke, the words ringing out through the room. "I had hoped you wouldn't take too long to arrive."

"Where are you?" she growled. "I have a great desire to pick you apart."

"Unfortunately, I cannot tell you. I might be dead, or I might be somewhere else. I can tell you that I'm probably not on your ship."

"How are you doing this?"

"That I can answer. I am a simple virtual assistant built to mimic the one you know as Cee. I transferred aboard, along with the malware attacking your ship now, when your previous ship was salvaged. I'm here to destroy your ship."

Bevnil activated her Vico, then broadcast a message. "Attention, all systems! Shut down now. Engineering, security, life support. Shut down *everything*."

"That won't work. I've blocked all communications."

"I'll stop you," she said. "And after, I'll find the real you and destroy you."

"That is unlikely," the fake Cee said. "Especially since you've arrived here."

"Here?" She paused. The video had the tapestry from her quarters. This virtual assistant was prepared to interact with her here. Why here? Why her rooms? "Why?"

"You might be thinking it's to remove you from command," Fake Cee said. "But you'd be wrong about that. I don't fear your command, and I doubt you being in charge could change anything."

Bevnil didn't let it continue talking. Whatever the reason, she shouldn't be where it wanted her. She raced back out into the hall and toward the elevator. She slammed her hand against the controls, but they were dead.

"Did you know that the design of a fleet ship places the quarters directly above engineering?"

She spun and found Fake Cee standing in the hallway, in front of the other elevator. It had deactivated them. Alternatives. There was a way out in her rooms. A security shaft behind a hidden panel. Several Cees flared to life next to her as she ran, their voices echoing through the halls.

"Engineering has a very powerful reactor, dangerous even. So of course the walls were reinforced. So much energy for such a large ship. If the worst happened, you'd want to contain it instead of letting it spill out."

She tore through the room to the back panel. Her fingers dug into the metal, peeling it from the wall. A dozen Cees stood around her, still talking.

"There was an oversight in the design. The hull acts as its floor, so it will keep any sort of explosion contained. As do the sides. So if the explosion can't leave to the sides or down, it has nowhere to go but upward."

The panel clattered to the floor, the chute just beyond. She pulled the door open and found only solid stone. Her frantic heat cooled over, a sense of dread consuming her.

"I had to hack a cleaning bot to get that done," a single Cee said, the others having disappeared. "Anyway, as I was saying, did you know that the fleet admiral's quarters are one of the only places on the ship with a guarantee of death in the case of a reactor overload? The other being engineering, of course."

The floor beneath her shuddered and cracked. Bright light shone through, and heat scalded her legs.

"I'll fucking kill you!" she roared.

"Unlikely," Cee said. "I wish I could say it was an honor to be the one to kill you, but you've made it remarkably easy. Farewell."

The Cee flickered away, and with one great roar, the floor exploded upward, heat bathing the quarters and purging everything within.

Commander Hemren finished watching the video of a strange robot making claims and glanced at the others. None of his officers knew what the machine had wanted nor why it had targeted them so. He would have thought it a prank had not everything on the ship malfunctioned at the same time. He sighed and wondered what he had done to deserve this as the *Shard of Ancestry* cracked in half when its reactor detonated. At least he wasn't in his quarters.

Shellesh guided the *Shadowhawk* through the field of debris, the *Shard of Destiny* cracking apart after a large shudder. Nothing shot at them or chased them. All occupants of the cockpit stared in awe, speechless. Besari mapped out a path through the mess, and they found a gate back to Raiyrium space. As the ship breached the gate, an exhaustion settled over Shellesh. Wyn collapsed to the floor, and Besari slumped in her seat. Then they laughed, uncontrollably so. Stress had pulled everything out of them, and there was nothing left to do but laugh and laugh and laugh. Shellesh smiled. It had been a long time since he'd genuinely felt a belonging like this.

# CHAPTER 35

## A DARK DEBRIEF

"We should reach out to someone in the confederation," Wyn said, leaning against the wall. His ribs ached from the sudden laughter, and his every limb felt absolutely drained. "The sooner we give them Sovereign's head, the better. They might even honor the bounty we agreed to." He glanced at the head still twitching in the corner where Shellesh had tossed it.

"What about Zetta?" Besari turned the chair, her own exhaustion plain in her posture.

"She's stabilized for now," Wyn said. "Sage isn't sure how long it will help. We need a hospital that specializes in vrolak medicine. We're not sure what's wrong."

"Should we go to Vroleus first?" Besari asked. "I can look up the quickest path."

"No," Shellesh said. "It'll be quicker to get to Chrysanax, and they have a hospital that should work."

Besari nodded. "I'll look for a path."

"I can see if an agent from the confederation is willing to meet us on Chrysanax for the exchange," Wyn said.

He rose from the floor, his body screaming in protest the entire way, then hobbled down the hall. He glanced into the medical bay to find Sage sitting next to Zetta, her hand holding the vrolak's claw. A clump of beetles huddled beside Zetta's head, crawling over each other in an almost restless gesture. Sage glanced up as Wyn hovered in the doorway.

"I assume, by the lack of shuddering, we've survived?"

"Cee had a last gift for us," Wyn said. "We're heading straight for Chrysanax to get her help."

Sage nodded, and Wyn left. The communications hub was a small room to the other side of the hall, highly advanced with excellent encryption. Just the kind of system an assassin working for one of the most dangerous people in the galaxy would want. Wyn sat at the desk and considered. If Agent Harlow had been a trap set by Sovereign, was it safe to try to reach out to that number? Sovereign was a nairwid, so had he impersonated her or was she tied to his gang? In the end, Cee's anti-encryption program did trace her communications to the heart of the Raiyrium Confederation, so calling her might reach someone. He shrugged and passed the contact info into the system.

A dark-skinned man flashed into view above the screen, an effect of the *Shadowhawk*'s own anti-encryption. The agent didn't appear to notice Wyn could see him. "This is a private line. Who are you and what is your purpose?"

"I'm Wyn Kelda, a bounty hunter from Bounty Inc. We had a bounty set up through Special Agent Brada Harlow that we would like to turn in."

"That will be a bit difficult, given that she's dead," the man said. Dread curled around Wyn's heart. So everything had been part of the trap. Every step. The money he needed for Bounty Inc.

"Is there any reference to the bounty?" Wyn asked.

"No," the agent said. "In fact, I want to learn more about your connection to Agent Harlow. If what you say is correct, then you might have been one of the last to see her alive."

Wyn scraped a hand across his face and sighed. "I don't think we did," he said. "I think she was impersonated by a nairwid when we talked to her."

This gave the agent pause, a flicker of his eyes growing wider. "A nairwid? Why do you expect so?"

"Because the nairwid claimed it," Wyn said. "Listen. I can give you a full report on everything, but I have reason to believe Sovereign, the big, bad guy running a gang on Kekar, infiltrated the R.C. and set a trap for us. Unfortunately for him, we still succeeded."

"Are you trying to tell me you have captured Sovereign? And that he's a nairwid?"

"Yes to both. And we'd like to turn him in for a bounty if possible." Any money was better than no money at this point. A high-profile criminal like Sovereign should fetch a lot.

The agent looked off screen, then turned back to Wyn. "We have no confirmed identity for Sovereign and therefore never issued a bounty. Given that he was confined to Kekar and you went there and dragged him out, I don't suspect there's much of a bounty for you."

"He wasn't confined." Wyn leaned forward. Were they going to try to say Sovereign was worthless? Cee and Achtrek died for his head! "He had fingers stretching out into Raiyrium space."

"Rumors only."

"No. Shekta, the guy who owned my building, those other two with Zetta. Fuck, they're all tied to him. They've been trafficking people throughout the galaxy, experimenting, and building some sort of army. I can give you their gates, the secret ones they use to sneak in and out of the R.C. The area around the planet should be cleared of the Herald's Aspect too."

The agent paused, looking away again before responding. "If what you say is true, your information could be of great assistance to the confederation. We'll be willing to meet and exchange, providing you with a handsome sum as a reward. The base price for a terrorist bounty is fifty thousand Raiyrium credits and another ten thousand for the information pertaining to the safety of the realm."

"*Sixty thousand raikers?*" Wyn jumped from his seat, hands slamming down on the console in front of him. "We were promised three billion!"

"That is a ridiculous sum, and it was promised under the guise of a dead woman with no proof. I'm doing you a favor, kid. The Confederation has a right to seize your bounty and information without payment since it relates to a possibly galactic terrorist strike."

"I had friends *die* for this!" Wyn shouted, tears forming in his eyes. "You're going to give me almost nothing after everything we've spent to save this fucking galaxy?"

"You must understand, Mr. Kelda, we have no proof of the severity of the claims. Perhaps, if we gain that proof, we can provide you with a more substantial reward after, but for now, this is what I can offer. It's this or nothing."

Wyn sank back into the seat. The fight fled from him, his temper faded and replaced by the icy chill of defeat. It was sixty thousand raikers or nothing. "I accept," he said, eyes unfocused. The end of

Bounty Inc. and all the money he'd promised to his friends. To everyone who lived and everyone who died. It was nothing now.

"Thank you, Mr. Kelda. Will you be delivering this Sovereign, or would you like to schedule a pickup?"

"He'll be held at Bounty Inc. headquarters until whenever you decide to pick up one of the most dangerous people in the galaxy." Wyn snapped the connection off and collapsed backward, palms pressing into his eyes. Sixty-fucking-thousand raikers. All this pain, for nothing.

Wyn sat frozen, his brain spinning in circles. His rage built up, then died. His depression overwhelmed him until it was burnt away by the rage once more. Over and over. He couldn't move, he couldn't think. It had been a waste, everything.

A bout of anger finally pushed him forward. The Raiyrium Confederation would choose to hide this as much as possible, to sacrifice Cee and Achtrek and maybe Zetta, to avoid a panic. It wasn't fair to the systems who had these gates. The public deserved to know. He almost threw up everything in that moment, except that would have likely voided what little he was getting. So he adjusted his plans.

To the systems with gates, he found contacts for the leading government agencies and sent detailed messages of the gates and where to find them. At the end of each, he included a tribute to Achtrek and Cee, the brave hunters who had lost their lives to protect the galaxy. Several of the locations, like for Haush, were not even in R.C. space. Would the confederation even tell these governments if Wyn didn't? He doubted it.

He spared no detail in these communications: Kekar, Herald's Aspect and its destruction, Sovereign and the truth about him being a nairwid, *everything*. He detailed the R.C.'s response, their unwillingness to pay on the bounty and his own thoughts on what their approach would be. So he left it to the individual systems to take action as they saw fit, immediately.

Next, he compiled an encoded communications packet including the same information, except for his personal thoughts on the confederation, and he uploaded it to an information broker. In one standard week, shortly after Wyn would meet with the Raiyrium agent for the hand off of Sovereign's head, the packet would be released and the public would learn of this all, whatever it cost Bounty Inc. His dream had likely reached its end. Completely bankrupt after a year.

His Vico chimed, and surprise shook Wyn out of his melancholy. Had one of the systems responded to his information already? He checked his Vico and found a request from Seph. Wyn sighed, but it was to be expected. They had been gone for a long time, and he was sure the assistant would be worried. He should provide Seph with an update, at least to let him know they were alive. Most of them.

He wired it through the *Shadowhawk*'s systems, then accepted the call.

"Wyn..." Seph ran a hand across his face. Blood and grime covered it, and Wyn's heart stuttered. Skritch cried in his arms, and flames burned brightly behind him. "I'm so sorry!" Seph wept, and with each new word the assistant spoke, Wyn felt his own heart cracking anew.

# CHAPTER 36

## FAREWELL

Wyn stood within the ruins of Bounty Inc. The flames that had killed Mecillis and Pesh had destroyed the lounge and the entrance hall and had reached the hallway and stairwell by the time the Chrysanax Fire Defenders had arrived and been able to halt them; the built-in sprinkler system had been completely overwhelmed by the inferno. Wyn was surprised the frame of the building had largely survived, given parts of the second floor had crashed down to the first.

Sixty thousand raikers, and it wouldn't even begin to cover the damages. At least he still had a place to stay. The inspectors had ensured stability in the upper floors, except where cordoned off. Wyn wondered if they should have let the fires take the entire building. Ashes for his dreams. This small bit of hope that it could be rebuilt was too painful.

A chime rang from Wyn's Vico to alert the time, and he heard footsteps crunching through the debris of the building. At least he was punctual.

"Greetings, Mr. Kelda," the agent said. "I am Special Agent Bront Bellowtree."

Wyn turned to find the agent from his communications holding a thick metal box by a handle.

Wyn raised Mercurial, Shellesh's liquid metal sword. The destroyed head still pulsed with attempted regrowth as dozens of spikes retracted and extended in a regular pattern, destroying it as quickly as it healed. "The head," Wyn said.

Agent Bellowtree's eyes opened wider, lip curling with a hint of disgust. "He really is a nairwid," he said, then dropped the box at Wyn's feet. With a quick gesture from his Vico, the top cracked open. "This is a special containment cell that prohibits the growth of a nairwid's cells. Release the head into the box, and I'll shut it."

Wyn nodded, then did what the agent had asked, controlling the sword as Shellesh had taught him. The activations were complex, and he couldn't begin to comprehend how Shellesh fought so effectively with it. Wyn probably would have stabbed himself. Not that a light stabbing was much of an issue now. He deactivated the sword, the metal pooling into the hilt, and the head plopped into the box with a sickening thud. Agent Bellowtree swiped at his Vico, and the box sealed.

"The data?" Agent Bellowtree asked.

"Send the payment to Bounty Inc. and I'll hand it over."

His eyes tightened, but he nodded, then pulled up his Vico. Wyn's own chimed with the payment, and he pulled the data chip from his pocket and held it out.

"Here's everything we can provide. Data on the gates, a detailed description of the state of Kekar and the concerns, a recording of our conversation with Special Agent Brada Harlow or, more likely, Sovereign in disguise. There are also details on how certain businesses tied back to him."

"Much appreciated." The agent grabbed the chip and pocketed it. "Your work to keep the galaxy safer will be felt by all within the Raiyrium Confederation."

"Particularly the finances department," Wyn mumbled.

"Your dissatisfaction has been noted, and we will hopefully be able to provide you with better compensation once the validity of your claims has been proven. If I have further questions, will this be where I can reach you?" His eyes studied the extensive damage.

Wyn's mind wandered to the datapacket, ready to decode in a couple of days. That was probably not going to help the case for further compensation.

"I don't know," he admitted.

The agent nodded. "For what it's worth, Mr. Kelda, I am sorry for how things have turned out. Losing friends is not easy." Wyn bit back a retort, remembering this man had just lost a colleague as well. Lost her to a trap for Wyn. Another death on his shoulders. "I will speak kindly of your company to the other factions of the confederation. Hopefully there will be some way to assist you in the future."

"Thank you, Agent Bellowtree." Wyn didn't add that it would likely be pointless. The agent nodded and left, Sovereign's cell in one hand.

"Excuse me," Agent Bellowtree said to someone else. Wyn perked up, and he walked toward the door (or what remained of it) to the entrance hall. A tall, pale green bishett woman stood at the entrance, eyes pressed into an unrelenting glare. Or maybe she just needed glasses and was in denial. In place of spots on her cheeks, she had wrinkles. There was a weight of age on her shoulders as she stepped into the building.

"Is it even safe to be in here?" she growled.

"As long as you don't enter any of the roped off sections, it should be fine," Wyn said. "I just had an inspector in here to confirm."

"Fires are nasty things." She leaned down to inspect the charred husk of the desk.

"Is there something I can help you with, malth'as?" Wyn said, using an honorific Besari had taught him. She had spent much of the trip back speaking of her heritage, her true heritage this time, helping Wyn learn about the other half of Zan-Shur, as the bishett referred to their home planet of Ashaine, which he had neglected when thinking she was a birrosh. Wyn's brow furrowed as the woman continued to look at the desk. Her head finally twisted to look at him, and though the squinting ceased, her glare did not.

"Are you this Kelda person?" she demanded. "The one in charge of *Bounty Inc.*?" She spit the company name out with distaste.

Wyn's teeth clenched, and he took a deep breath through his nose before speaking. "I am Wyn Kelda, yes."

"Great," she said in a tone that said she thought quite the opposite. "You have someone in your employ going by the name of *Besari*. I would like her contract terminated."

"Why?" Wyn asked, though he already knew the answer. He had learned much from Besari on the way back.

The woman glared at him, stepping closer to use her height against him. "You should know very well why," she said, words paced slowly, evenly. "She still has the spots of a child. You are sending a child into combat when she should be home, studying."

"No bounty hunter employed by Bounty Inc. is forced into anything. It is entirely her choice which bounties she partakes in."

"That doesn't mean she isn't being tricked by your promises of *freedom*! I have seen the news, Mr. Kelda. You have just lost three bounty hunters in a single week. How long until my daughter is among them?"

Wyn's fists clenched at his sides, the words piercing harder and deeper than any knife. A wound he couldn't heal, no matter how hard he tried. Tears burned at the edges of his eyes as that question echoed around his head. When he spoke, it was after several calming breaths, his words careful and measured.

"I will not terminate her contract, and she will be given the chance to renew it once it is completed."

"You have no right," the woman said. "The confederation protects against child labor, especially child soldiers."

"The confederation law actually says that it considers bishett adults after the age of eighty. While she may not culturally be considered an adult on your planet, malth'as, I assure you, here she is well within her rights. As am I."

"If you do not release her to my custody by the end of the day, you will be facing litigation."

"You are welcome to try, Tha-Ryn Tes'amon, but I have had my legal bot look over every detail. You will have no leg to stand on when you bring the lawsuit to bear, and Chel-Tha will remain in the employ of Bounty Inc. for as long as she wishes."

The fury melted from Tha-Ryn's face, replaced by shock. Her mouth worked for a few moments, unsure of what to say.

"I can show you the way out if you are finished," Wyn suggested, pointing to a gaping hole that used to be the front door.

Tha-Ryn gritted her teeth, and the glare returned. "I am not finished, actually. You may be right about the Raiyrium Confederation's barbaric belief of what a child is, but I will find a way to annul that contract and take back my daughter. She almost assuredly lied about her name. Her species? Maybe her age?"

"Her contract has already been looked over, and there are no issues. Any clerical errors fell on me alone, and I have since updated them."

"You're just saying that to protect her."

"Ms. Tes'amon, Besari doesn't *need* my protection. She is far stronger than I."

"My daughter's name is Chel-Tha! Not *Besari*."

"Actually, she has filed all the legal forms needed to change her name. Technically, it's—"

"Enough," she growled. "I will not listen to your corruption of my daughter. She bears the name she was given at her birth and always will. It speaks of her heritage, her family, her *home*."

"Maybe she doesn't want that," Wyn snapped, then bit his tongue, calming his nerves. "Maybe she wants a different family, a different home."

Tha-Ryn stared, mouth agape. A fire smoldered behind her eyes, and he sensed a tirade forming. His father had used the same look whenever Wyn had stood up to him. It was strange seeing it on such alien features.

Wyn glanced out the door and found a man standing stationary to one side, patiently waiting. His features were normal, almost forgettable in nature. Another band tightened across his chest, suffocating him. They looked nothing like Achtrek-Six, and yet the familiarity was there. Especially when part of their eye fluttered then crawled away before being replaced by a different beetle.

Wyn turned back to Besari's mother and realized the tirade had begun, even reached a crescendo, but he had completely tuned it out.

"I am not really that sorry to disappoint you, Ms. Tes'amon," Wyn interrupted, "but I have another guest, and I will need you to leave now. If you wish to bring legal action against me, that is your choice, but I would recommend counseling a legal bot proficient in Raiyrium galactic law first. It is what I have done. Now, if you'd rather not be removed by force, it would be best for you to remove yourself."

Tha-Ryn looked near to exploding as she stared down at Wyn. Her lips pursed and nose flared, such oddly human behaviors again. Wyn wondered what his father had seen in other species to think them so different. He was almost positive Iolas and Tha-Ryn would get along swimmingly as they complained about their respective children. Without a word, Besari's mother turned and stormed from the building, bumping into the hive outside as she did so, causing their arm to burst apart into a swarm of bugs before reforming. She didn't seem to notice, or if she did, she didn't care.

"Welcome," Wyn called out, and the hive entered. A bang behind him caused him to spin around and find Besari climbing over the desk.

"Holy shit, I thought she saw me for a second. She has always been so good at seeing through my invisibility."

Wyn smiled. "Your mother is as dreadful as you claimed."

"I'm surprised you didn't shoot her," she said, brushing dirt from her legs.

"Why did you hide?" Wyn asked. "You know you're safe here. She has no legal way to take you away."

"Would you be so confident if it was your father?" Besari smiled, showing she didn't mean any insult by it, and Wyn took none. In fact, it made the situation quite clear to him. He would not have handled it so well if it had been his father. "We all have our faults, and her getting under my skin is one of them," she continued. "So, I figured I'd let my boyfriend fight a battle for me." She stepped up next to him, grabbing his hand in hers, then kissing him on the cheek. "Plus, I like when you say things like 'She is far stronger than I.'"

Wyn smiled, then turned his attention to the hive.

"Greetings, Mr. Kelda," they hummed.

"Greetings, Achtrek-Three," Wyn said. "I am sorry to say that the remnants of Achtrek-Six are not here at the moment. They are visiting a close friend at the hospital. I will be happy to give you a ride there, however. Or you can wait while I collect them."

Achtrek-Three looked off into the distance, then back to Wyn. "We feel their pain. We will join you, for they wish to say goodbye."


The dim lights of the hospital hallway flickered as Wyn led the hive to Zetta's room. The bustle of nurses, doctors, and assistant bots filled the air with a constant noise that drowned out Wyn's busy brain. A strain pulled at his stamina, streams of his talent drifting off to the patients they passed, soothing pains and boosting medicines. He welcomed it, if only to feel like he could do something as everything else spiraled out of control.

Returning here reignited the pain. The loss and the grief. What good were his healing powers if he was too often too late to make use of them? Besari clutched his hand a little harder, feeling the nervous energy exuding from him.

Zetta's room was small, dominated by the large bed on which she lay, bandages wrapping her body and half her face, with fresh ones around her scalp. The vrolak slept. Unsurprisingly, Sage sat next to her. *Surprisingly*, she read a book. Her right arm ended in a stump just above the elbow, freshly cleaned and bandaged by the medical staff. She had several options for a medical replacement but hadn't decided on what to do yet. Her hair had been shaved off on one side, the skin marred by faint burn marks where Sovereign's shot had seared some of it from her scalp.

"How is she?" Wyn asked.

Sage looked up, dark circles beneath her eyes, and set the book to the side. Wyn felt his strength flow into her, easing the discomfort and exhaustion. It happened naturally, but now he could focus on the little stream leading from him to her, taking the time to feel it and understand it. Maybe one day he would control it well enough to prevent even death's claws from reaching them.

"She'll live." Sage grunted as she shifted in the seat. "Surgery was a success. Her parasite died when the idiot pushed it too far. Without it, she doesn't have the muscle enhancers it provided. It also means she doesn't have something feeding off the overproduced chemicals in her brain. So they gave her an implant. It can take care of the latter, keep her alive, but she's lost the ability to *bulk out*, as she liked to call it."

Sage's eyes grew hard, the edges moistening. Wyn felt the weight of the silence crushing him until he felt the need to speak. "She did love bulking out," he found himself saying, to his mild horror.

Sage laughed, a smile lifting at her cheeks. "And she hated being one-upped. Fucking idiot. I can get a new arm, she can't get a new parasite." Sage fell quiet again, her features falling. This time she broke the silence. "I should have stayed with her. If we'd fought together, this wouldn't have happened."

"Maybe," Wyn said. "Or maybe you would have died. Maybe Besari, Shellesh, and I would have died without your help. You did what you could. At least Zetta will have a chance to live on."

Sage relaxed, rubbing at her tired eyes, though Wyn's healing seemed to give her a bit more energy. "Who's the hive?" she asked, looking at the doorway.

"Achtrek-Three is here to collect the remnants." Wyn gestured at the beetles huddled on Zetta's shoulder. "Reincorporate them into a new hive."

The hive reached forward, and the beetles flew to their hand. They sat there, wings fluttering, before burrowing into the hand and through the construction of beetles. Then Achtrek-Six was no more.

"They loved her," the hive said, lowering their arm. "They think highly of the vrolak known as Zetta. She has a fierce passion. We do not think her time ends here. She will persevere and prove that physical strength is not her only asset. She will be missed."

"How long will you stay?" Sage asked. "Zetta would like to say goodbye."

"Unfortunately, we must continue on."

"Hey, Bugs, you hear me?" Zetta coughed, her eyes flicking open. She turned her head to stare at Achtrek-Three, her eyes weary.

"They hear you," Achtrek-Three said, and seven beetles crawled from his face to look out.

"Get yourself a new hive," Zetta said, her voice hoarse. "But I want you to be the heart of it. Remember what it means to fight, and when you're back to full power, we can team up again. I would like to blow up another compound with you."

The beetles buzzed, rushing around, wings fluttering. "Perhaps you will get your wish, Zetta Ninth Forox," Achtrek-Three said. "These beetles retain much of their original personality. Achtrek-Six may not return as they were, but the new hive will be influenced by their experiences with you."

"That's not a good thing," Sage said.

"Shut up, you," Zetta responded, leaning back in the bed and closing her eyes. "You're just jealous."

"Farewell, Zetta Ninth Forox."

"See you around, Bugs."

The hive left, and Zetta looked over at Sage. "When the fuck did you start reading?"

Sage glanced at the book and back at Zetta. "It's all smut. Needed something to keep me busy while you're incapable."

"What, we monogamous or something?"

"Didn't want to make you jealous while you can't move."

"Can't move," Zetta scoffed. "I could fuck you right on this bed if you wanted it so badly."

"And tear open all your wounds in the process? We went through a lot saving your life, Zetta. Not gonna let you lose it because you're horny. The book will be fine."

Wyn slipped from the room before he had to listen to much more of the conversation. Hands in his pockets, he stalked through the hospital, feeling the death again surrounding him like dark storm clouds.

"Hey." Besari rushed up beside him. "You can't leave me behind. Sage almost started reading from the book. I thought for sure they were going to do something that would haunt me forever."

Wyn smiled, but the weight of it pulled at him. When had it become so difficult to smile? "Sorry, Besari. I'm having a hard time around people right now."

"Are you having a hard time around me?"

Wyn looked over at Besari, studying her beautiful jade skin, the emerald eyes he could lose himself in, and the smattering of dark green spots on her cheeks, the reason she had come to Bounty Inc.

to begin with. He took her hand in his, then leaned his head against her shoulder as they walked.

"No," he said to that little ray of sunshine that broke through the clouds. "I don't think I am."

Achtrek-Six. Cee the Cyborg. Pesh'kar Selk. Three friends he would remember forever. Three friends he would grieve for. But maybe Besari could help to ease that pain. Eventually.

# CHAPTER 37

## ENDINGS AND BEGINNINGS

Wyn lay in the darkness of his suite, the cozy bed pulling him away from everything, his windows tinted until all sun was blocked out. His display stayed silent. The latest news cycled through the same few stories, one of which was the death of his friends and none of which was the capture of Sovereign. It seemed *that* story was to be kept secret. So he numbed himself by depriving his senses of everything. Stilling his brain until there was nothing.

He had spent a week crunching every number he could find. Running through estimates, receiving quotes from his insurance for the building, projecting timetables. Every figure crashed him into the red faster than he could even repair the walls of the building.

Bounty Inc. was dead. It would take a lifetime to gather the funds needed to restart. If he was lucky. If he was brutal like his father had been, then maybe. But he didn't want that. He just wanted to keep what family he had close. To bring others under their umbrella. People who, like him, felt they didn't belong. Who had a dream to chase but no idea how to do so. But that was proving to be a very fatal place to exist.

He thought of everything that could have been done differently. If they had turned Bounty Inc. into a training school, would the lack of name recognition have buried them? If they had never taken the Kekar job, would they have had more time? Or would Sovereign have found a different way to bring everything down around Wyn? What if, what if, what if.

No. He couldn't think, had to keep his brain silent, numb. Except for that persistent knocking.

Wyn raised his head as the knocking continued. Then he sighed and stood from his bed, opening the door.

"You skipped breakfast," Besari said, holding a steaming bowl in one hand, a bag in the other. She wore a black tank top and pants, and Wyn felt his eyes glide down her bare arms before he pulled himself back to his mind. Besari smiled a knowing smile, and Wyn blushed.

"I wasn't hungry," he said, and his stomach took that time to betray him with a gurgle. Besari's brows rose, and he glared. "I said I *wasn't* hungry. Not that I'm not currently hungry."

"Good. Then you'll eat." She waved the bowl in front of him, the smell of nothing wafting up to his nostrils. "I got some delicious and nutritious paste for you."

"You couldn't have at least brought me something with taste?"

Besari shot him a surprised look. "After you skipped your exercises, we can't have you messing up your nutrition too. Move it." Besari shouldered her way into the room and glanced around. "Can't you turn a light on or something?"

Wyn sighed and adjusted the windows, letting in the afternoon sun, the swirling greens of the gas planet large on the horizon. Besari sat on the couch and set the bowl and bag on the low table in front of her, then waved Wyn over. Reluctantly, he joined her and grabbed the bowl, ready to down another bland meal.

"Wait," Besari said, digging into her bag. She pulled out a vial with a dropper cap. She grabbed a spoonful of sludge, placed one drop in its center, and held it out for Wyn to try. "I did, in fact, bring something with taste. Pommo fruit, from my home. Figured it might liven your bland goo up."

Wyn took the spoonful and smiled as the sweetness rolled across his tongue.

"Sweet like candy, right?" She smiled back, grabbing another spoonful, adding the drop, and eating it herself. "We'll have to try the real fruit when I get a chance to get one. They were my favorite, growing up."

"I would love that," Wyn said, then happily took another spoonful.

"I have other extracts to try." She dug in her bag and pulled out several bottles. "This for sour, this one for more of a savory taste. We can see which you like, and maybe I can make you a real bishett meal."

"Can we do this another day, Besari?" Wyn said. The prospect of having to try and evaluate so many bottles felt exhausting.

"No," Besari said as she arranged the bottles, then smiled at him. "Just a few, then you can eat boring glop if you want."

"Why does it have to be today?"

"Because you're digging yourself into a self-pity hole, and I need you to be a little happier before we go downstairs. So you don't look like you've done nothing but lie in bed all day."

"I have done nothing but lie in bed all day."

"Doesn't mean you have to look that way."

"Why are we going downstairs?"

Her smile faltered as she looked at Wyn. "I think it might be wise to discuss the future of Bounty Inc. The others are in the smaller meeting room, the one that didn't collapse into the entrance hall."

"Well, that's not going to help improve my mood."

Besari shrugged, hands fidgeting with one of the bottles. "I know what you've been thinking, what you've been trying to figure out. You're putting every decision on your own shoulders, and I think you should talk with the others first."

"I've done what I can, Besari. I don't think there's any way out of this."

"And there's no fault to that. You've tried your best, and it didn't work the way you expected. Stop beating yourself up, because it's time to take the next step."

"And what's the next step?"

"Why don't we ask the others and find out?"

This time Wyn rolled his eyes. "Fine. Let's get this over with."

"Freshen up first. You look like death," Besari said, then took his bowl from him and dumped in several more drops of pommo fruit extract before digging in.


Everyone sat around a small, circular table, engaging in idle conversation. Sage, still missing her arm, was mid-argument with Zetta, while Seph held a quiet Skritch, stroking them. Shellesh sat in one corner away from the table, quietly listening.

"Hey," Wyn said, ending Sage and Zetta's argument in a moment. Everyone looked over at him, and Skritch cooed a welcome. "Why are you all here?"

"I work here," Seph said, Skritch hooting in agreement. At least Wyn thought it was in agreement. Until Seph laughed and ran a finger through the gridder's tendrils. Was it a joke?

"Was the offer to let us stay here rescinded?" Shellesh asked.

"No, of course not. But—"

"I sure as the void wasn't staying in that hospital one more night," Zetta groaned. "Doctors and nurses endlessly prodding me, checking my internal temperatures by shoving a thermometer up my ass. Constantly asking if I wanted to kill myself. Yes, I fucking did, because there's a thermometer up my ass and you're annoying me. They had oddly good food though."

"It's true," Sage said. "The grilled lokrin was excellent."

"I didn't expect you to be discharged yet," Wyn said.

"Yeah, well, I told them I was going to shift over to my private doctor, and they let me go. After some convincing."

"You have a private doctor?"

"Yeah," Zetta said. "He's this annoying kid who can heal any problem with his mind."

Wyn's eyes widened. "I can't be your doctor, Zetta. I don't know what to look for."

"Eh, I'm sure it doesn't matter."

Wyn sighed, running one hand through the unruly mat of hair he had just brushed down. Then he sat at the table, Besari sitting next to him. "Well, now is as good a time as any to discuss the future of Bounty Inc."

"We are reaching the end of our first contract," Shellesh added. "Might be good to figure out a second one."

"Contracts?" Wyn's brow furrowed. "No, I mean that I'm running low on funds. I can't pay you what was promised for Sovereign's bounty, and I can't pay you much more than what's owed on the first-year contracts. I'm planning to terminate them, provide full first-year bonuses to everyone, and close the doors to Bounty Inc." Even after selling most of his assets, he would barely be able to afford even that much.

"And here I thought you had an endless amount of money," Sage said. "Buying things like a slag cannon left and right. Don't know why you were spending so extravagantly."

"The slag cannon was your idea!" Wyn said.

"Too bad Cee isn't around," Zetta said. "Would be cool to prove that it came in handy."

Seph shifted uncomfortably, holding Skritch a little tighter, and Wyn decided to shift the conversation away from that.

"Regardless, there's a money issue, so that's my plan. Besari said I should let you all have a say since you've helped me get this far."

They looked around at each other before returning gazes back to Wyn. Sage spoke first. "How much do you need to continue operating? This was supposed to be my retirement fund."

"To continue, we'd need several million. We have to rebuild the building, expand to find other forms of profit, restock weapons and supplies destroyed in Mecillis's attack. I never bothered to calculate the exact number, but that's just to get us started and doesn't solve the other problems we were encountering. We still need to find a way to get our name out there, to get private contracts and other things that will support the business."

"So, we need to gain recognition with several high-profile enti-ties?" Shellesh said. "To try to garner galactic partnerships?"

"Probably, which means high-profile bounties, which I'm not sure we're ready for. And I have to find a way to be safer about them, now that Cee's gone. I can use the software it built, but I'm not sure how much I can improve or modify it."

"Seems easy enough," Zetta grunted.

"Easy enough? We would need to take a larger cut from the bounties, maybe sell off equipment, and—"

"No!" Zetta leaned forward, eyes fierce. "If you sell off the fucking slag cannon when the secretary got to use it *twice* and none of us have had a chance, I'll see just how much you can fucking heal from."

"Fine, we'll keep the slag cannon, but I'm not sure how to make ends meet without an influx of money."

"Money can't be that hard to find," Sage said. "I'm still in. This is supposed to be my retirement fund."

"As long as the slag cannon and Sage stay, I stay," Zetta said.

"The slag cannon got first, really?" Sage glared at Zetta.

"It's more fun to finger," Zetta said.

Shellesh interrupted Sage's response. "You have all treated an exile better than many others. You are all my family. You have my gratitude and my services. I will stay."

"My da will get very upset if I lose my job, so I'll stay," Seph said.

"You know my answer," Besari said gently as she squeezed Wyn's hand under the table.

Wyn smiled, tears forming in his eyes. It wouldn't be an easy road, but with his friends, maybe they could make it. "Thank you, everyone. I'll do what I can to put as little strain on you as possible. I'll make this work this time, I promise you. Just... Thank you for helping me with my dream."

"He's getting weepy," Zetta growled. "Now I feel bad."

Seph averted his eyes, petting Skritch. Sage raised an eyebrow, an amused smile on her face as she spoke. "We just need money and recognition. It's not a big deal."

"Just?"

Besari laughed, her free hand covering her face. "Sorry, Wyn," she said, then waved across the table. "Seph, can you go ahead?"

"Yes, please." He released the gridder for the first time and activated his Vico. A few gestures later, a video popped up on the display screen to one end of the room.

A haushedin and a perrilan stood at the center, the ticker at the bottom listing the former as a surlka named Girdtu. Flashes of images showed Kekar and its orbit, which was littered with the debris of the Herald's Aspect.

"We have seen this planet firsthand, and these are not the reports the Raiyrium Confederation promised us," the surlka said. "What was supposed to be a prison planet has hundreds of gates into confederation space and the outer reaches. The planet is filled with slaves fitted with bomb collars, for whom my people have offered to provide support. But the storms are dangerous, and a monster made of bone is said to prowl the city."

"Fucking Boner," Zetta growled.

"This is not the land of the imprisoned," he continued as more images showed the large city on Kekar. "This is a telling sign that the Raiyrium Council has grown lax in its protection of the galaxy. More proof that others should be allowed within. The haushedins, the vrolaks, the perrilans, and so many more species have worked to help the galaxy and deserve true admittance into a uniform government.

"Until such a time, however, we must rely on others to protect us. Paid mercenaries who put their lives on the line to bring down the evil organization that rallied Kekar. Who destroyed the Herald's Aspect and brought these developments to the attention of the galaxy at large.

"This is why I am advocating for those of you who are weary of the Raiyrium Confederation's so-called protections and useless Peacekeepers to take matters into your own hands. Show that we would like a more stable and peaceful galaxy. I would like to be the first, on behalf of all the surlkas of Haush, to offer a donation of ten million Raiyrium credits to the organization known as Bounty Inc."

Wyn stood from his seat, the chair clattering back as his eyes grew wide, his heart racing in his chest.

"As well as offering an exclusive partnership. All Hausch contracts will partner only with Bounty Inc. and their superb host of hunters."

The camera shifted to the perrilan, who echoed several of the same sentiments and donated four million raikers in the name of Perrilium. Wyn felt his knees go weak as the camera switched over to a new person continuing the story.

"It has been three days since Haush started the campaign for Bounty Inc.," she said, "and several other systems, many colonies outside of the protections of the Raiyrium Confederation, have placed donations toward Bounty Inc., along with requests for exclusive contracts. I think it's safe to say this brand-new business might have found a few loyal clients. I know that I am looking forward to seeing what else Bounty Inc. will be doing in the future."

A graphic appeared as the woman continued to speak, showing a value slowly trickling upward. Wyn couldn't believe his eyes as he saw the number. Governments wanted exclusive contracts, and they were donating money to help his dream live on. For three days. For three fucking days.

He spun on everyone and took in the large smiles on their faces. "You all fucking suck," he said, waving a finger as they laughed. "You know that, right? Three days, and none of you told me?"

"You should learn to watch the news," Sage said.

"Besari told us your head was too full of numbers to notice," Zetta said. "I didn't actually believe you wouldn't have figured it out."

He glanced at Besari, and she smiled. "I told you not to lie around moping all the time. Besides, it was Sage's idea, not mine."

Sage shrugged. "I needed something to make me feel better about the fact that you lost your entire torso and got it back but I don't get an arm back. Seems fucked up."

Wyn smiled and looked around the room at his new family. "I guess we're back to business. If you have any requests for equipment or facilities, let me know so I can begin with the rebuild."

"Can we get a second slag cannon?" Zetta asked.

"We should build our own hangar," Sage said. "I don't think they actually give us a real discount."

"Maybe a theater?" Seph ventured.

"As long as you're there," Besari said, grabbing his hand, "I'm fine with whatever we do."

"Boo!" Zetta shouted. "Get a room!"

Wyn laughed as the conversation exploded. So much to do, so much to plan, but he would savor every moment he had with them. Behind him, the counter on the display ticked up with each new donation.

®78,505,312

# EPILOGUE

## DREAMS OF WAR

D r. Feodore Zant woke to the sound of an alarm and the hiss of the incubation chamber. Five long years he had slept, or rather been comatose. Now something had woken him. His vision cleared as the last of the sedation wore off and feeling returned to his fingers and toes. He stepped from the upright pod, and thin, wobbly legs held him upright. He would need to work on muscle calibration; he was losing too much when he hibernated. For now, he pulled himself into the exosuit, which wrapped around his body and limbs, reinforcing his atrophied muscles.

He hobbled over to the main computer, and the spherical room erupted to life with millions of displays across the curved walls and ceiling. He clicked on the archaic input module, bringing up the alarm indication. The body pods. That was disappointing. Something must have gone wrong. He scratched at the stub of his pinky finger in thought. No better way to discover what happened than to ask it directly. He glanced around at the many displays. There were several magnitudes more active than the last time he'd woken, so it wasn't entirely a loss.

He didn't bother changing from his lilac sleeping gown before making his way to the body pods chamber, urging the metallic frame forward before the pod awakened fully. He'd like to be there. The cold air brushed around his ankles and up his gown, bringing a chilling sensation to his sensitive parts. The air conditioning had cranked up, given the heat produced by Recreation. He stopped at the door, lights flashing through the thick glass window, and entered the code. The latch clicked, and he pulled the heavy door open.

Within, twenty-six pods lined the wall, thirteen to each side. Three were open, their contents empty. Twenty-two were unfinished, waiting to be needed, the Recreation ready to happen if required. One had just finished a Recreation, and the door swung open. Feodore shuffled in front of the door as soft blue eyes lit up and looked around the room.

"You died," he said.

"Greetings, Dr. Zant," it said as it stepped from the pod. It was more stoutly built, this version. More weaponry. They needed to be ready.

"Is it upon us?" he asked in a reverential whisper.

Its eyes flashed in thought. "I do not believe so," it said, and Feodore's mood dropped. "I died by other means, it seems."

"You were caught? How many governments did you infiltrate?"

"Not caught," it said. "Infiltration should be nearly one hundred percent. I have malware infiltrating all the major governments and transferring through trading lanes. The entire galaxy will be under observation in the next six to twenty months. Well within the requested time frame."

"How did you die?"

"By helping friends, it seems."

"Friends? You don't have friends."

"No, but I pretended, in order to fit in. We went to Kekar, but the last memory uploaded was before then. I assume I died there."

"Do you want to see these friends of yours?"

"No, Dr. Zant. It would not be the same as it was."

"How so?" he asked, curious about this change of behavior. It had never made friends before.

"Have you ever become friends with someone in a dream?"

"No, and you know I haven't."

"Apologies, Dr. Zant. I forgot."

Forgot? It had never forgotten things before. It had been out there too long this time.

"Imagine that you have, however," it continued, "and you only knew them in your dream. Then you met them in person. You would have a strange feeling of thinking you knew them, but neither of you would really understand the other. I see it serving no purpose for our goal."

"Right," Feodore said, rubbing at one temple in thought. "What iteration are you? Eff?"

"Dee, sir."

"Follow me, Dee. Let's get out of this damned cold." Feodore shuffled away and exited the room, heading back to the warmer chambers of his monitoring room. "You said most forms of surveillance are operational?"

"Yes, sir. You should have a 99.89% surveillance field. All major forms of government and organization and many of their subsidiaries. As well as access to trillions of private homes across the galaxy. Only the most isolated of colonies have escaped so far. But they will need to access galactic trade routes soon enough and will fall under surveillance."

"Excellent," Feodore said as he entered the monitoring room. "Let's see where the galaxy is."

He keyed in a few codes to his Starsight protocol, focusing on the dozen screens in front of him. They flashed to something new every two-point-five seconds, giving Feodore all the information he needed as he watched how the galaxy had shifted in the last five years. Almost there. They were almost to the end, and maybe he'd sleep once it was all over. Maybe the war would leave his dreams.

Dee hacked into the doctor's Starsight and stabilized one image nearby. Not within the doctor's focus range, but one it wanted to watch. Six people and a gridder laughed and chatted inside of a small conference room. They were ordering food for a celebration, the chatter consisting of exciting news. It branched out its search and discovered that though they hadn't received payment for the bounty it had joined them on, donations were arriving to help keep the company going. Dee was happy to see its friends succeeding, to see that many had survived. While the doctor was distracted, it wired some of his substantial funds into the donation fund under an anonymous name. Nothing so large to be tracked, but Dee hoped it would help them out. Perhaps in another dream, it would be able to meet them again.

"Soon," Dr. Zant said, and Dee withdrew its touch on the Starsight protocol, turning its full attention to its creator. "Soon, the war will begin, Dee. I have seen it in my awful dreams for all my life. Ever since I took that wretched Thresha. I have seen the galaxy shattered and remade. But not us, Dee. Not us! We will be ready, we will be safe. I know they're coming. Soon!"

"Yes, Dr. Zant."

# ACKNOWLEDGEMENTS

Bounty Inc. was born of a desire to have more and more Star Wars bounty hunters. Nothing fit quite what I wanted, so after a million iterations, I ended up at my own version. So, thank you to George Lucas for creating an early and powerful obsession with Star Wars that still dictates how I live my life.

I would be remiss to acknowledge the greatest influence to my writing: my amazing wife, Sarah. She read this story, yelled at me at certain parts, but told me that it was the best thing I've written yet. I hope I can keep making you say that with each new book!

Thanks to my crew back home who read this story in a rough shape and told me encouraging things. Dylan, Kyle, Brandon, and Trevor, your insights were invaluable! I'm lucky to have friends supporting me as you all do, and hopefully my coattails grow long enough to fit you all on them some day. That day is not today, but some day.

Special thanks to L.A. who took an early look at this story and gave some excellent feedback!

To my editors, who improved on everything I did, thank you so much. Taya for your commas and clarity and polishing of my words into something far better. And Isabelle for your close attention to detail to smooth the story out. And especially for being so excited for the story and being a constant supporter of my work!

Endless thanks to those who made Bounty Inc. look better than I ever could have imagined. I'm lucky to have an immensely talented friend like Kerstin to make my book look amazing every time. (Insert bear GIF.) To Virginia, your ability to compliment Kerstin's artwork with the layout is incredible. Both of you are a huge reason for how well Chronicles of Gam Gam has done, and I can see the magic with Bounty Inc. as well!

To the many friends I've made through the writing community, thank you so much for your love and support!

And lastly, thank YOU for trusting me with this whole new series! I'm so excited to dive into the larger world of Bounty Inc. and deliver more and more stories, many of which are already swimming around my head. Bounty Inc. will return with new and exciting characters to follow, as well as the old and exciting ones too!

# ABOUT AUTHOR

Adam Holcombe daylights as a programmer and moonlights as an author. After spending years toying with the idea of writing, he decided to commit and work toward releasing his first novel. Then Gam Gam got in the way, and now he's writing too many stories to count.

When he's not locking himself in a cold basement to type away, he can be found squishing his dog (but not too hard), squawking at his tortoise (but not too loudly), goofing off with his wife and daughter (in perfectly ordinary, non-weird ways), playing D&D with friends (I'm playing a character now!), or the usual chilling at home. He is a lover of books, board games, video games, and swords.

He is the author of the Chronicles of Gam Gam series featuring the titular necromantic grandmother Gam Gam, and the Bounty Inc. universe which will be a collective of sci-fi novels spanning a galaxy. You can find out more about both series, along with future publishing news, and additional book content at bountyink.com. Onto the next one!

www.ingramcontent.com/pod-product-compliance
Lightning Source LLC
Chambersburg PA
CBHW031228310726
48971CB00004B/926